ABOUT THE AUTHOR

John Harvey is the author of the richly praised sequence of ten Charlie Resnick novels, the first of which, *Lonely Hearts*, was named by *The Times* as one of the '100 Best Crime Novels of the Century'. In 2004 William Heinemann published *Flesh and Blood*, the first novel featuring retired Detective Inspector Frank Elder.

He is also a poet, dramatist and occasional broadcaster.

Find out more about John Harvey by visiting his website at:
www.mellotone.co.uk

Cutting Edge

Cold Light

John Harvey

arrow books

This edition published in the United Kingdom in 2005
by Arrow Books

Arrow Books
The Random House Group Limited
20 Vauxhall Bridge Road, London SW1V 2SA

Random House Australia (Pty) Limited
20 Alfred Street, Milsons Point, Sydney
New South Wales 2061, Australia

Random House New Zealand Limited
18 Poland Road, Glenfield
Auckland 10, New Zealand

Random House (Pty) Limited
Endulini, 5a Jubilee Road, Parktown 2193, South Africa

The Random House Group Limited Reg. No. 954009

www.randomhouse.co.uk

A CIP catalogue record for this book
is available from the British Library

Papers used by Random House are natural, recyclable
products made from wood grown in sustainable forests.
The manufacturing processes conform to the environmental
regulations of the country of origin

ISBN 0 09 190743 8

Printed and bound in Great Britain by
Cox & Wyman Ltd, Reading, Berkshire

Cutting Edge

John Harvey

arrow books

One

The first time she had taken off her clothes for him, he had told her she was perfect: not meaning to, not able to stop the word escaping. Perfect. He had met her at a dance two months before and now he pictured her not far from the hospital, occasionally glancing at her watch as she drank a second glass of wine, waiting.

Perfect.

'You look more dead than alive.' The words snapped him back to where he was, the staff nurse facing him, one hand pulling at her uniform where it had bunched above her belt.

'Thanks,' Fletcher said.

Sarah Leonard smiled. 'The new admission . . .' she began.

Fletcher blinked, willing himself to concentrate. He had slept three hours out of the last twenty-four, eleven from the past seventy-two and he thought he might be delirious.

'Probably a stroke,' Sarah was saying. 'Neighbour alerted the police. He'd been on his kitchen floor for two days.'

'How old?'

'Seventy?'

'I'll clerk him in the morning.'

'He's going to need fluids. You'll have to put in a Venflon tonight.'

'You could do that yourself.'

'You know as well as I do it's against policy.'

Fletcher smiled. 'I won't tell.'

1

She gave him the smile back a little with her eyes. Somewhere along the ward, a patient was breaking one hacking cough upon the back of another. Nearby, a youth with stitches latticed across his face was silently crying. Calls of 'Nurse!' rose and fell like a litany.

'Very well, staff,' said Fletcher with mock solemnity.

'Thank you, doctor.' She waited for him to move then fell into step beside him.

The patient lived alone on the twelfth floor of a tower block and it had taken two ambulance men and one police officer to get him down the stairs after the lift had jammed. Now he lay on his back beneath blankets, his face grey, legs and ankles swollen. He had to weigh close to seventeen stone.

Fletcher slapped the inside of the man's forearm with the back of his own fingers, searching for a vein. It wasn't only the excessive fat that was a problem: there were hypothermia, shock.

'He's peripherally shut down,' Fletcher said, turning over the arm.

Sarah nodded, watching the needle, waiting to apply the necessary pressure higher up.

'I'll try the back of the hand,' Fletcher said.

He opened his eyes wide and then narrowed them, focusing down. The point of the needle punctured the edge of the vein and passed through.

'Shit!'

He steadied himself and prepared to try again. Behind them, the screaming that had started several minutes ago showed no signs of stopping.

'Can you manage?' Sarah asked.

'Does it look like it?'

Quickly, she applied a tourniquet and left him to it. Fletcher succeeded in finding the vein this time, but was slow in releasing the tourniquet and blood jumped back before he could close off the end of the cylinder. A fine spray speckled his hands and the front of his white jacket and now a puddle was seeping through the top blanket.

He passed Sarah on her way back to the bed. 'A thousand ml of natural saline over twenty-four hours,' he said, not breaking his stride.

'Where are you going?' Sarah asked over her shoulder. 'Off duty.'

She picked up the bloodied needle from where he had let it fall beside the patient's arm and, shaking her head, deposited it in the *sharps* disposal. The blankets were slowly staining a deeper red and would need changing. Without seeming hurried, Sarah finished setting up the drip.

Fletcher bent low over the sink and splashed cold water up into his face. In the mirror he looked like someone who habitually spent long hours underground. He knew that if he didn't shave, his stubble would score Karen's skin raw but it seemed more important to get there before she grew tired of waiting. He would phone as he left the hospital and tell her that he was on his way.

He cupped his hands beneath the tap a final time, combed his fingers through his tangle of dark hair and pulled on a padded blue anorak over his doctor's coat.

For a change the telephone near the exit wasn't already in use, but in Karen's shared house nobody was picking up and answering. After a dozen rings he gave up and hurried up the stairs towards the upper level, fitting the headphones from his Walkman over his ears as he climbed. He pushed through the first set of double doors on to the pedestrian bridge as the duet from the final act of *Manon* was beginning. The bridge arched over the ring road midway between the underpass and the flyover, linking the hospital with the university and the residential areas that closed around it.

Fletcher immediately identified the familiar smell of

3

rubber that rose from the floor, although the personal stereo, turned up high, kept out the squeak of his shoes as he walked. The air was always stale, the warmth trapped in at either end, no matter the outside temperature.

He walked unsteadily, hands jammed down into his pockets, weaving slightly like someone the worse for drink. The lights of cars moving fast down hill, south from the city, blistered through the wired glass. Here and there, the sides had been flyposted, advertising social events, political meetings, a pram race along the canal.

Fletcher sang along with the music, suddenly energetic and off-key. If things worked out with Karen, he'd get tickets for Opera North next month and bribe himself a couple of evenings off. If things worked out ... Unobserved, the door giving access to the steps up from the street swung open at his back.

Fifteen yards from the far side and he had still not heard the accelerated tread of soft-soled shoes in his wake. Strange that he was thinking, not of Karen, but of Staff Nurse Sarah Leonard's half-smiling, half-accusing eyes, when finally he realized he was not alone. A quick reflection glimpsed in the glass door before him and Fletcher turned his head in time for the downward sweep of the blade, illuminated in a fast curve of orange light.

The blow sent him stumbling backwards, losing his footing as he cannoned against the centre of the doors and pitched forward, thinking before the belated sear of pain that he had been punched, not cut. The headphones had fallen from his face and Massenet poured tinnily out. Fletcher raised an open hand to ward off his attacker and the blade sank deep into his palm before swerving clear.

Somehow he got to his feet and began to run. A foot tripped him and his temple smacked against the wired glass, cracking it across. He kicked out, swung into a crouch and blundered through the first pair of doors, within his reach the exit, the steps, the street. His legs went from

4

under him and the side of his face hit the floor with a slap. Through the muffled sound of traffic, he could hear his attacker breathing hard. Not wanting to, he forced himself to turn his head. Through blood he saw black sweater, balaclava, black gloves. Movement. Fletcher screamed and on his hands and knees he tried to crawl away. The blade cut into his thigh and began to slice towards the knee.

Karen Archer upended the empty bottle into the waste bin in the corner of her room and fingered the portable TV set off. By the time she had got downstairs to the phone, whoever had been calling had rung off. It could have been Tim, wanting to tell her he was on his way, apologizing yet again for being delayed.

'Go out with a houseman,' one of her medical student friends had said, 'and that's what you get.'

'What?'

'Not a lot.' Laugh. Except that it wasn't.

The last time Tim Fletcher had been round he had been fast asleep within ten minutes; she had pulled off the rest of his clothes, tucked the duvet round and sat cross-legged beside him, wearing two extra sweaters and reading Eliot. He hadn't been a lot of fun either.

Karen took a pack of cigarettes from the back of her underwear drawer, failed to find a box of matches and put the pack back again. She didn't need one. If that had been Tim on the phone, he might be on his way.

She pulled on her ankle-length suede boots and took down from behind the door the camel coat her aunt had thoughtfully found in an Oxfam shop in Richmond. Pocketing her keys, she headed down the stairs, automatically stepping over the one with the missing tread. If she walked in the direction of the bridge, more than likely she would meet him.

Two

'Another, Charlie?'

'Better not.' Resnick shook his head. 'Time I was making a move.'

'Right. Right.' Frank Delaney nodded understandingly, reached over the bar and poured a fresh Guinness into the detective inspector's glass.

'Some of us start earlier than others,' Resnick said. The clock to the left of the small stage showed the wrong side of midnight.

'Sure you do,' Delaney winked. 'Sure you do. And after tomorrow I needn't be getting up at all.' He raised his own glass towards Resnick's face and smiled. 'A toast, Charlie. Early retirement.'

The glasses clinked and both men drank, Resnick sparingly.

'How long is it for you, Charlie?'

'Retirement?'

'Can't be long now.'

'Long enough.'

It lay ahead of him like some unwelcome sea, something to be swum through every morning, no matter the weather; the same aimless movements, made simply to be doing something, an illusion: either that or you trod water until one day you drowned.

'Tomorrow morning,' Frank Delaney said, 'eleven o'clock. I shall be in the bank in my best suit, shaking hands. Someone will give me a fountain pen with a 24-carat gold nib and not so many minutes later I'll be walking out of there with a cheque for a million pounds. Not bad, eh, Charlie, for an ignorant son of a bitch like me? Left school at fourteen with the arse hanging out of his trousers. Not bad.'

Resnick sipped at his Guinness and glanced around the room. When Frank Delaney had bought the place – what? Ten years back? More? – it had been little more than four walls and space on the floor for the drunks to fall safely. Frank had brought in carpets and couch seats with dark upholstery, chandeliers and a mishmash of mostly fake Victoriana. At the weekends, he'd instituted Old Time Music Hall and with a little persuasion would get up at the mike himself and lead the patrons through choruses of 'You Made Me Love You', 'Who's Sorry Now?'

In the week the doors were opened to other things: country and western, poetry and jazz. By this week's end the developers would be tearing out the inside, stripping it all away. Another office block in the making.

'We've had some good nights here, Charlie.'

Resnick nodded. 'We have.'

On that stage he had heard some of the best music of his life: David Murray, Stan Tracey – on a cold March evening, Red Rodney, who'd played trumpet with Charlie Parker when little more than a kid, had brought tears of pleasure to Resnick's eyes and goose pimples to his skin.

'Have I told you what folk said when I bought this place, Charlie?'

Only a dozen times.

'They said I'd go bust within a six-month. Bankrupt.'

Delaney laughed and opened another bottle of Newcastle Brown. 'I've shown 'em. Eh?'

Resnick covered his own glass with his hand and stood up. 'No regrets, then, Frank?'

Delaney gave him a long look across the rim of his glass. 'A million pound? From nothing, more or less. What have I got to be regretful about?' He got to his feet and shook

Resnick's hand. 'Anything else, that's sentimentality. Won't even pay the rent.'

Resnick walked through the partly-darkened room towards the door. Sliding back the bolt, turning the heavy key, he let himself out on to the street. Fletcher Gate. Directly across from him a youth wearing baggy jeans and with his shirt sleeves rolled high was vomiting chicken biriani against the brick of the car-park wall. A black and white cab rose up the hill from the station and Resnick thought about hailing it, but realized he was in no great hurry to get home after all.

'Hey, you!' the youth opposite called out at him belligerently. 'Hey, you!'

Resnick slotted his hands into his overcoat pockets and crossed the road at a steep angle, head slightly bowed.

When Resnick had first been a beat copper, walking these streets in uniform, himself and Ben Riley, the winos, the down-and-outs, the homeless had looked away as they passed. A scattering of old men who sat around their bottles of cider, VP wine. Now there were kids who hung around the soup kitchens, the shelters, young enough to have been Resnick's own. And these thrust out a hand, looked you in the eye.

Eighteen to twenty-six. Smack in the trap. Too many reasons for not living at home, too few jobs, precious little from the state: now they shared Slab Square with the pigeons, sprawled or hunched before the pillars of the Council House, the ornate mosaic of the city's coat of arms, the pair of polished limousines waiting to carry civic dignitaries to this important function or that.

The more you descended Goose Gate, the less prestigious the shops became. Two sets of lights and you were in the wholesale market, broken crates and discarded dark blue tissue, and beyond that Sneinton, where gentrification

8

was still a word best left to crosswords. Fourteen Across: A process of changing the character of the inner-city.

Before the first of those traffic lights the pavement broadened out and Resnick slowed his step. There were a dozen or more people between the telephone kiosk and the entrance to Aloysius House. Two were in the kiosk itself, keeping warm with the aid of a quarter-bottle of navy rum. *This is a dry house* read the sign by the entrance. A middle-aged man, wearing the upper half of a grey pin-striped suit and with dark trousers that gaped over pale flanks, leaned back against the wall as he drained a can of Special Brew, shaking the last drops into his mouth.

'Locked out?' Resnick asked the nearest of the men.

'Fuck you!' the man replied.

Resnick moved closer to the door, brushing against a couple who declined to step aside.

'Wondered how long it'd be before they sent for you,' one of them said accusingly.

Resnick's head turned instinctively from the cheap alcohol on his breath.

'Sodding copper!' he explained to his companion.

The second man stared at Resnick, cleared his throat and spat on to the pavement, close between Resnick's shoes.

'Need a bloody sight more than you to sort this out,' called someone. 'Bastard's in there with a bastard axe!'

Resnick knocked on the glass of the hostel door. There were two men in the small lobby, one of them sitting on the floor. Resnick took out his warrant card and held it against the glass, motioning for them to let him in.

Inside the dimly lit main room, bodies shifted and snored in the darkness. Here and there Resnick saw the dim glow of a cigarette. From one of the chairs, knees tucked into his chest, someone cried out in a dream.

The woman who had charge of the night shift came towards Resnick from the foot of the stairs. She was wearing a cream-coloured sweater over dark sweatpants,

Resnick couldn't be certain of the colour in that light. Her hair had been pulled up at the sides and sat a little awkwardly, secured by a pair of broad combs, white plastic. She was in her late twenties, early thirties and her name was Jean, Joan, Jeanie, something close. He had been introduced to her once at Central Station, he couldn't remember exactly when.

'Inspector Resnick?'

He nodded.

'Jane Wesley.'

That was it. He thought she was about to offer him her hand, but she thought better of it. She was a well-built woman, tall, five nine or ten, and she had the nervousness in her voice pretty much under control.

'I didn't send for you.'

'I was passing. Quite a crowd you've got outside.'

'They're all waiting to see what happens before they come back in.'

'What is going to happen?'

She glanced towards the stairs. 'That depends.'

'On what?'

When she grinned, the dimples at the edges of her mouth made her seem much younger, more carefree; the way she was before she got into social sciences and Christianity. 'On what he does with the meat axe,' Jane said.

'What seems to be his plan?'

'The last I heard, he was threatening to chop his foot off.'

'Unless?'

'Unless I stayed on this side of the door.'

'Which is what you've done?'

'So far.'

'Sounds reasonable.'

Jane frowned; the dimples were a long time gone. 'He's not on his own. There are two others in with him.'

'Friends?'

She shook her head. 'Not as far as I know.'

'Has he threatened to harm them?'

'Not yet.'

Resnick looked at his watch. It was a quarter to one. 'Why didn't you call the station?'

'I was about to. I think. With the best will in the world, every time somebody steps in here in uniform, we lose somebody else's trust.'

'Better than their foot,' Resnick suggested.

'Yes.'

'Besides, I'm not in uniform.'

'You don't need to be.'

'Will you shut up,' bellowed a voice from the corner, 'and let me get some sleep!'

Resnick went towards the stairs. 'Which room?' he asked.

'Straight ahead,' Jane answered. 'The reading room.'

Resnick depressed the switch for the landing light, but it remained stubbornly off. He knocked on the door and waited: nothing. Knocking again, he identified himself. No response. If there were three people inside and all three of them still alive, they were exhibiting more than usual control. It occurred to him that the excitement might have exhausted them to the point where they had all fallen asleep.

He tried the handle and it turned.

'All right,' he called. 'I'm coming in.'

'No!' The muffled voice stretched the word into two syllables.

'Stand well back,' Resnick warned.

'Open that door and I'll use this fucking thing! Don't think I'm fucking kidding!'

Resnick went in fast. Several piles of books had been strewn across the floor, mostly discarded paperback westerns and old copies of *Reader's Digest* donated by well-wishers. More books, dog-eared, sat on shelves to one side: Leon Uris, Wilbur Smith. Of the three people inside the room, however, none was showing the least interest in reading.

One man, his feet bare within open leather sandals, sat on the floor, a soiled grey blanket with red stitching at the hem, covering his head and shoulders. Another, eyes closed and aimed at the ceiling, sat on a straightbacked chair, hand inside his open fly, thoughtfully masturbating.

The third, narrow-cheeked, grey-haired and bespectacled, stood clutching a butcher's cleaver threateningly above one foot, from which, as if in preparation, he had pulled off both shoe and sock.

For some moments he didn't look up at Resnick and then he did.

'Just heard a kid who thought he'd rediscovered bebop singlehanded,' Resnick said. The man's eyes flickered. 'Bit like hearing somebody fluent in a language they don't understand.'

The eyes flickered again but aside from that the man didn't move.

'Time was,' Resnick said, 'you'd have blown him off the stand.'

'Aye, I daresay.'

'How about the cleaver?' Resnick asked, one cautious step closer.

The grey-haired man looked at the blunted blade, then at his foot. 'Charlie, I think I'll fucking do it this time. I think I will.'

Three

'She's a lovely woman, that.'

'Jane?'

'Lovely.'

They were in a cab skirting the Lace Market, passing Ritzy's on their right. The purple sign still shone above the door, although by now it was all locked up and the last dancers had made their way home. My place or yours? Resnick had been there on a few early, bachelor Saturday nights when it had been, simply, the Palais, and there were still couples quickstepping their way between the jivers. He remembered the women standing alone and sad-eyed at the end of the evening; men who prowled with something close to desperation, anxious to pull someone on to the floor before the last number faded.

'How old d'you think she is, Charlie? Tell me that.'

'Around thirty.'

'Too young for me, then, d'you think?'

Resnick looked at Ed Silver, leaning half against the window, half against the cab's worn upholstery. His grey hair straggled thinly across his scalp and bunched in snagged folds around his ears, like the wool of an old sheep; one lens of his glasses was cracked and the frames bent where they had been trodden on and twisted not quite straight. His eyes were hooded and watery and refused to focus.

'No,' Resnick said. 'Not a bit of it.'

Ed Silver eased himself further back and smiled.

13

When Resnick had talked Silver into handing him the butcher's cleaver and walking peacefully downstairs, Jane Wesley had been grateful and surprised.

'You know him, don't you?' she asked, spooning instant coffee into chipped mugs.

Resnick nodded.

'But before you went in there? There's no way you could have known who he was.'

Resnick shook his head, gestured no to milk.

'I don't know if I can let him stay. I mean, here, tonight.'

'He can come home with me.'

Her eyes widened; they were pale blue and seemed the wrong colour for her face. 'Are you sure?'

Resnick sighed. 'Just for a bit. While he sorts himself out.' It wasn't as if he didn't see the dangers.

Jane Wesley sipped at her coffee thoughtfully. 'That might take longer than you think.'

'Well,' said Resnick, 'maybe he's worth a little time.' He glanced over to where Silver was sitting in the near dark, fingering the air as if he could turn it into music. 'Runner up in the *Melody Maker* poll three years running. Alto sax.'

Resnick put down his mug of coffee, almost untouched, and turned away.

'When was that?' said Jane Wesley to his back.

The cab pulled over by a stone wall, a black gate that was in need of fresh paint. Lights showed from one of the upstairs rooms and through the stained glass above the front door, an exercise to deter burglars. Resnick leaned down to the cab window and gave the young Asian driver a five-pound note, waiting for the change. The radio was turned low, an almost endless stream of what the Radio Trent DJ would probably call smooth late-night listening for night-owls.

Ed Silver was steadying himself against the wall, while a

14

large black cat arched its back and fixed him with slanted, yellow eyes.

'This yours?' Silver asked.

'The house or the cat?'

'Either.'

'Both.'

'Huh.' Silver stood away from the wall and offered a hand towards the cat, who hissed and spat.

'Dizzy!' said Resnick reproachfully, opening the gate.

'There's one thing I can't stomach,' Ed Silver mumbled, following him along the twist of slabbed path, 'it's cats.'

Great! said Resnick to himself, turning the key in the lock.

Dizzy slid between his legs and raced for the kitchen. Miles came down the stairs from where he had doubtless been sleeping on Resnick's bed and purred hopefully. Bud, skinny and timid, backed away at the sight of a stranger, until only the white smudge beside his nose could be seen in the furthest corner of the hall.

'Christ, Charlie! You've got three of the little buggers!'

'Four,' Resnick corrected. Somewhere, paw blissfully blindfolding his eyes, Pepper would be curled inside something, anything, sleeping.

'If I'd known that, I'd never have left the cleaver.'

He made up a bed in the room at the top of the house. It smelt damp, but no worse, Resnick was sure, than his guest had become used to. Even so, he fetched up a small electric fan heater and set it working in one corner. By the time he got back downstairs, Silver had swung his legs up on to the sofa in the living room and seemed sound asleep. Resnick went back and found a blanket, draping it over him, smelling the rancid, sickly-sweet smell of his clothing. Urine and rough red wine. Carefully, Resnick removed Silver's glasses and set them down on the carpet, where

Miles sniffed at them curiously to see if somehow they might be food.

By now it was past two and Resnick was wondering whether he would get any sleep himself at all. In the kitchen he ground coffee beans, shiny and dark, doled out food into the cats' four coloured bowls, examined the contents of the fridge for the makings of a sandwich.

The last time he had seen Ed Silver he had not long been wearing his sergeant's stripes. Uniform to CID then back to uniform again: forging a career, following a plan. Silver had been guesting at a short-lived club near the top of Carlton Hill, so far out of the city that few people had found it. When Ed Silver had walked in, instrument cases under both arms, he'd looked around and scowled and called the place a morgue.

The first tune he'd tapped in a tempo that had the house drummer and bassist staring at each other, mouths open. Silver had manoeuvred his alto through the changes of 'I've Got Rhythm' at breakneck speed, but when he realized the locals were capable of keeping up, he'd let his shoulders sag a little, relaxed and enjoyed himself.

Chatting to Resnick afterwards, rolling cubes of ice around inside a tall glass of ginger ale, he'd talked of his first recording contract in seven years, a tour, later that year, of Sweden and Norway.

'See,' he'd said, stretching out both hands. 'No shakes.'

Then he'd laughed and set the glass on the back of one hand and after a few seconds the ice cubes ceased to chink against the inside.

'See!' he'd boasted. 'What'd I tell you?'

Resnick heard nothing more of him for over a year. There was a paragraph in one of the magazines, suggesting that he'd recorded in Oslo with Warne Marsh, but he never saw the album reviewed, or any announcement of its release. What he did read, near the foot of page two on a slow Saturday in the *Guardian,* was that Ed Silver had fallen face first from the stage at the Nuffield Theatre, Southampton, suffering concussion and a nose broken in two places.

Someone had done a good job on the nose, Resnick thought, finishing his sandwich, looking over at Ed Silver, fast out on his sofa. It looked to be the part of his face in the best shape.

He went quietly to the stereo and set Art Pepper on the turntable. Midway through 'Straight Life', he thought he saw Ed Silver's sleeping face twist into a smile. As the tune ended, Silver suddenly pushed himself up on to one arm and, eyes still closed tight, said, 'Charlie? Didn't you used to have a wife?' Without waiting for an answer, he lowered himself back down and resumed his sleep.

Four

Karen Archer found Tim Fletcher at around the time Resnick was beginning his walk down through the Lace Market towards Aloysius House. That is, she found something sprawled across the top of the metal steps which led up from the university grounds to the pedestrian walkway; something dark, wedged half-in, half-out of the first set of doors. An old bundle of discarded clothing, bin-liners stuffed with rubbish and dumped. It wasn't until she was almost at the head of the steps that she realized what was lying there was a person and at first she took it to be a drunk. What told her otherwise was the tubing of a stethoscope protruding from beneath it.

Karen held herself steady against the railing, staring down at the surface of the ring road, rainbowed lightly with petrol. The chipped metal was cold against the palms of her hands, cold on her forehead when she lowered her face against it. When the worst of her panic had passed, when her breathing had finally steadied, only then did she go back to the body. Get closer. Possibly three minutes, four.

She held the door open with her hip and dragged, then pulled, Fletcher inside. No part of him seemed to be moving, other than what she moved for him. As best she could, Karen turned him on to his back and lowered her face until it was close to his; her fingers fidgeted at his wrists, searching for a pulse. She tried not to look at his wounds, along which dark knots of blood had begun to coagulate.

18

'Tim!' She shouted his name as if the force of the cry might waken him. 'Tim!'

With a soft swoosh an articulated lorry moved beneath the bridge, its lights catching Karen's face as she stood. Fletcher's Walkman lay close by the inner door and, irrationally, she stooped to make sure it was in the *off* position, the battery not wasting.

She hurried through to the hospital, willing her legs to run but getting no response, the squeak, squeak of her trainers on the hard, grooved rubber following her across. She didn't know whether she was leaving Tim Fletcher alive or dead.

It took several moments for Karen to make clear what had happened, but from there all was quiet speed and efficiency. If the casualty officer who spoke to Karen was surprised, he did nothing to betray it. All she saw of Tim were blankets, a stretcher being wheeled between curtains. All she heard were the same quiet voices. Transfusion. Consciousness. Surgery. They sat her in a corner and gave her, eventually, tea, sweet and not quite warm, in a ribbed and coloured plastic cup.

'Is he all right?'

'Try not to worry.'

'Will he be all right?'

Unhurried footsteps, walking away.

'God!' Tim Fletcher had exclaimed, that first time in her room. 'God!' Staring at her face, her breasts. 'You're perfect!'

'Miss?'

Karen's fingers tightened around the cup, glancing up. The police officer had gingery hair and a face that reminded her of her younger brother; he held his helmet against his knee, tapping it lightly, arhythmically, against the blue of his uniform.

'I was wondering,' he said, 'if you might answer a few questions?'

Karen's chest tightened beneath her purple jumper and she began to cry.

The officer glanced around, embarrassed.

'Miss . . .'

The crying wasn't going to stop. He squatted down in front of her, took the cup from her hands and rested it on the floor beside his helmet. In the three months he'd been on the force, Paul Houghton had stepped between four youths squaring up with bottles after closing; he had lifted a panicking three-year-old from a second-floor window and out on to a ladder; close to the end of one shift, he'd followed screams and curses to an alley back of a pub and found a middle-aged man on all fours, the dart that his girlfriend had hurled at his face still embedded, an inch below the eye. In each case, he'd acted, never really stopped to think. Now he didn't know what to do.

'It's okay,' he said, uncertain, reaching out to pat her hand. She grabbed hold of his fingers and squeezed them hard.

'Maybe you'd like another cup of tea?' he suggested.

When she shook her head, Karen's breath caught and the tears became sobs. Inconsolable. Bubbles appeared at both nostrils and, with his free hand, Paul Houghton fished into his pocket and found a tissue, already matted with use.

'Here,' he said, dabbing gingerly.

Heads were turned, staring.

'Rotten bugger!' a woman shouted. 'Leave the girl alone.'

'Stick 'em in a uniform,' commented another, 'and they think they can do as they bloody like!'

'I'm sorry,' breathed Karen, using the soiled tissue to wipe round her eyes, finally to blow her nose.

'S'all right.'

He wasn't like her brother, Karen thought, looking at

him through blurred lashes, he was younger. She felt sorry for him then, beyond the mere platitude, meaning it.

Karen handed him back his scrappy tissue and he stuffed it out of sight, standing. The backs of his legs ached and he wanted to rub them, but didn't. He took his notebook from his breast pocket.

'I shall have to ask you some questions,' he said, blushing.

Resnick had finally got to bed at four and found himself unable to sleep. Miles and Bud were a weight at the bottom of the covers and Ed Silver's broken snoring filtered up from the floor below, nudging him where he didn't want to go.

Didn't you used to have a wife, Charlie?

No cats then and every penny counted. DC's pay. Elaine had kept the house well, having been the one to see it first, boxed advert in the paper, *must be viewed to be appreciated.* Walking him round from room to room, hand in his or beneath the arm, guiding. *That fireplace, Charlie. Look. Isn't it wonderful?* The mortgage had stretched them fine, his salary and hers; evenings of repapering and painting; front and back garden some nights till dark. *Just as well I'm working, Charlie. Without that, I don't know where we'd be.*

Back in Lenton, Resnick's answer, unspoken, St Anne's or Sneinton, a two-bedroom terraced with a bricked-in yard and a front lawn you could clip in fifteen minutes with a pair of shears.

Time a-plenty for moving, he might have said. When we need the room.

All that early interest in real estate, it prepared Elaine for the man she was to go off with, eventually, when the tacky weeks of subterfuge were at an end. That Tuesday afternoon when Resnick had driven through Woodthorpe, not his usual route at all, cutting down from Mapperley

21

Plains, he had seen the dark blue Volvo first, parked with its near-side wheels on the kerb, close to the For Sale sign at the gate. A man in a three-piece suit, not tall, keys in hand, walking towards it. And a pace behind him, buttoning up the tailored jacket that she wore for work, Elaine. Still smiling.

How many other empty properties she had visited with her lover, how many evenings she had passed in his Volvo, discreetly parked, Resnick had not wanted to know. Later, all out in the open, in court, nothing left to lose, Elaine had made sure that he did.

Knowing hadn't meant that he understood. Not exactly, not quite. The mystery of living with someone for so long and never really knowing them, little more than how they like their tea, the wrist on which they wore a watch, which angle they prefer to lie in bed.

Not long ago there had been three letters: the first two close together, the third after a gap of several months. There had been no mistaking the writing and by the time the last arrived, curiosity had got the better of him. He had read the first sentences quickly, the first communication from Elaine in almost ten years; glanced at the end, where she had written, *Love*. After tearing it, he had taken it into the kitchen and burned it.

Ed Silver had stopped snoring; the cats were curled into each other and still. Without meaning to, Resnick slept.

'How'd it go at the hospital, Ginge? Waste of time?'

Paul Houghton fidgeted with a collar that was always too tight. 'Not exactly, sarge.'

'Let's be having it, then.'

Only a brief way into Houghton's verbal report, the sergeant interrupted him, picked up the phone and dialled the uniformed inspector on night duty.

'If you've a minute, sir, you might care to come through . . . Right, sir. Yes.'

He set the receiver down and looked across at Paul Houghton with a half-grin. 'Making a bit of a habit of this, aren't you? Darts, sharp implements.'

Houghton shrugged. 'Suppose so, sarge.'

'Girl as found him, all right, was she?'

'Upset, sarge, naturally, but . . .'

'No, I mean was she *all right*?'

He could feel the red rising up his neck. 'I didn't really . . .'

'Held her hand, did you? You know, make her feel better.'

Paul Houghton was blushing so strongly that the backs of his eyes had begun to water.

Five

Season of mists and bollocking fruitfulness! Okay, it meant, with any luck, he'd be back in the First XV, a few jugs after the match, but that apart, what was it? Grey mornings when your car wouldn't start on account of the tossing damp and alternate Saturdays when, instead of playing a proper game, you were on overtime babysitting a bunch of pissed-up morons with shit for brains and arseholes where their mouths were supposed to be. Christ! Mark Divine thought, if there was one thing that summed autumn up for him, that was it. Hanging around the railway station waiting for some excursion special so you could crocodile a mob from Manchester or Liverpool or Chelsea (they were the worst, Chelsea, the ones for whom he saved his real loathing, no doubt about it) across the river to trade insults and worse with the Forest fans massed at the Trent End.

That was autumn, not the poncey crap Yeats or Keats or whoever reckoned it to be. And he'd seen that other soft bastard, not Keats or Yeats, six foot under the pair of them, dead from the neck down now as well as up, not them but Quentin, that bloody teacher, the one who had them all learning that gobbledegook, standing up and reading it out. Clearly, clearly, what are you mumbling into your boots for? That's it, Mark, you read it for us. Good and strong. Wonderful, Divine! Smirking at his own stupid joke, rest of the kids sniggering and making faces, bending their hands at him like he was some kind of poofter. As if it wasn't hard enough, going through school with a name like

Divine, without some clever-clever bastard taking the piss out of him in front of everyone.

Still, he'd seen him, Quentin, just the other week, standing in line at the post office, waiting to get his old-age pension most likely, poor old sod with one leg locked like he had bad arthritis and dandruff spread over the back of his jacket as though someone had been at his scalp with a cheese grater. Given Divine a lot of satisfaction that had, thinking about him shuffling off home to read some crap about getting old, dying.

It still brought a smile to his face now, signalling right going round Canning Circus, weather forecast on the radio, five to seven driving into the station for the early shift.

Divine spun the wheel hard, loosening his grip as it swung back, straightening before turning again, left this time, across the pavement and into the car park. One good thing about coming in at this time, always plenty of room. He grabbed his jacket from the rear seat and locked the car door. The only good thing, just about. The night's files to sort through, prisoners in and out, messages to be arranged into two sets, national and local, all of that so that the DI didn't stand there with his mouth gaping open when he took the briefing at eight.

Like as not there'd been the usual rash of burglaries in the small hours and that would account for the best part of his day, his responsibility, trying to have patience with some stupid cow who left the kitchen window open to let the air circulate and didn't reckon on her new video and CD player being put back into circulation at the same time.

And – pushing open the door past the custody sergeant's office, the corridor leading to the cells – on top of all that, he had to make the sodding tea!

Not this particular morning.

'I've mashed already.'

Bloody hell! What was he doing here? Hadn't noticed his car downstairs. Resnick sitting at one of the desks in the middle of the CID room, not even in his own office, chair pushed back on two legs and reading the paper. He wasn't supposed to be here for half an hour yet.

'You can pour us a mug if you like. Milk, not too much, no sugar. Couple of juicy break-ins waiting for you, by the look of it. Just carry on as if I wasn't here.'

Resnick turned another page of the *Independent*, dreading the obituaries these days, always another film star you'd lusted over in your youth, another musician you'd heard and now would never get to see. DC Divine walked past him, draped his jacket over the back of his chair and turned the corner to where the teapot was waiting.

Well short of nine the CID briefing was over and Resnick was back in his office, a partitioned rectangle with rotas pinned behind the desk and filing cabinets alongside. A number of the other officers were at their desks, finishing up paperwork before setting off. Mark Divine was already out knocking on doors, ringing bells, examining broken catches, faulty locks, standing straight-faced as homeowners practised on him the exaggerated claims they would foist on their insurance companies by first-class post. Diptak Patel, thermos flask, telephoto lens, Milky Ways and binoculars, was behind the wheel of a stationary Fiesta, watching a clothing warehouse on the Glaisdale Park Industrial Estate. His highlighted copy of Benyon's *A Tale of Failure: Race and Policing* was in the glove compartment for when this, the third successive day of obs, became too boring.

Lynn Kellogg, hair cut newly short and sporting a certain amount of shine from a henna rinse, was allowing Karen Archer an extra half-hour's rest before calling to ask questions about last night. Kevin Naylor stood at the back of the lift making its way up to the ward where Tim Fletcher was now a patient; the last time he'd been in the hospital had been when Debbie had been giving birth and if he were silent enough, he could still hear her voice as she screamed for Entonox, an epidural, anything to stop the pain.

Resnick's DS, Graham Millington, knocked on his door before leaving for a liaison meeting with officers from the West Midlands. A spate of organized thefts of cigarettes and liquor, lorries hijacked or broken into at service areas where they had been parked, had spread from the West Midlands to the East and back again.

'If this takes as long as it might, sir, OK if I nip straight home? Wife's got her Spanish class, starting tonight.'

'Thought it was Russian, Graham?' said Resnick, looking up.

'New term, sir. Thought she'd have a go at something different.'

Resnick nodded. 'Right. Ring in if that's what you're going to do. You can fill me in in the morning.'

He watched through the glass of the door as Graham Millington automatically adjusted his tie and gave a quick downward tug at the front of his jacket. If he wasn't necessarily going to be the brightest over at Walsall, at least he could be the best pressed. Cleanliness and godliness: a drawer full of perfectly folded shirts and seven pairs of well-buffed shoes set you right on the road to heaven. Millington's father had worked all his life for Horne Brothers and at weekends been a lay preacher for the Wesleyan Methodists.

Resnick checked his watch and collected his files. If he failed to knock on the superintendent's door by a minute short of nine Jack Skelton would count him as late.

'Charlie. Maurice.'

Skelton nodded at Resnick and the uniformed inspector in charge, Maurice Wainwright, recently down from Rotherham and still with a little coal dust behind the ears.

'Have a seat.'

While Wainwright was making his report, Resnick kept

his attention on the superintendent's face. Since Skelton's daughter had run wild not so many months back, shoplifting, truanting, acquiring a taste for Ecstasy, the lines around his eyes had bitten tighter, the eyes themselves more ready to flinch. A man who no longer knew where the next blow was coming from. Resnick had wanted to talk to him about it, allow the senior man the chance to unburden himself, if that were what he wanted. But Jack Skelton kept offers of help and friendship at a careful arm's length; his response to the rupture of a life that had seemed so symmetrical was to withdraw further, redraw the parameters so that they seemed even more precise, more perfect.

'How's the house-hunting coming along, Maurice?' Skelton asked, the inspector's report over.

'Couple of possibles, sir. Wife's coming down for a look at weekend.'

Skelton pressed together the tips of his spread fingers. 'Sort it soon, Maurice. Down here with you, that's where they should be.'

Wainwright glanced across at Resnick. 'Yes, sir,' he said.

'So, Charlie,' said Skelton, replacing one sheet of paper square on his blotter with another. 'This business at the hospital, doesn't look like your ordinary mugging?'

'Had nigh on fifty pounds on him, small wallet in his back pocket. One of those personal stereos. Credit cards. None of it taken.'

'Lads out for a spot of bother, then, drunk. Lord knows they need little enough reason, nowadays. Wrong place at the wrong time, wrong face, that's enough.'

'Possible, sir. You do get them using the bridge on the way back from the city. Anyone who'd tried a couple of clubs after the pubs'd chucked out and found themselves turned away, they might have ended up there around that time.'

'No reports?'

28

'Nothing obvious, sir. I'm getting it double-checked.'

'We know there was more than one assailant?' asked Wainwright.

Skelton shook his head. 'We know nothing. Except that he was badly cut, lost a lot of blood. Blow or blows to the head. More than one looks the most likely, either that or someone pretty strong and fit.'

'And presumably not pissed out of his socks,' Wainwright said.

'Someone with a reason, then, Charlie,' said Skelton. 'Motivation other than robbery, if we can leave that aside.' The superintendent uncapped his fountain pen, made a quick, neat notation and screwed the top back into place.

'Hopefully we'll be able to talk to the victim this morning, sir. Any luck, he'll be able to tell us something. And we're having a word with the girl who found him.'

'Chance, was that?'

'Girlfriend, sir. On her way to meet him, apparently.'

'Funny time of night.'

'Funny hours.'

'Worse than ours,' said Wainwright.

'It would be useful if we found the weapon,' said Skelton. 'Attack like that, especially not premeditated, likely to have thrown it.'

'Maurice has sent a couple of men out,' said Resnick, with a nod of acknowledgement in Wainwright's direction. 'Pretty wide verges either side of the bridge, front of the hospital to one side and all that warren of university buildings on the other. A lot to search.'

Skelton relaxed his frown sufficiently to sigh. 'As you say, Charlie, the poor bugger on the receiving end, he's our best hope.'

A more superstitious man than Resnick would have been crossing his fingers; touching wood.

Since being carried into the hospital in the middle of the

previous night, Tim Fletcher had encountered a considerable amount of hospital practice from the receiving end. After some cutting away of clothing, preliminary cleaning of the worst affected areas – right leg, left arm, face and neck, both hands – pressure bandages had been applied in an attempt to staunch further bleeding. A drip had been set up to replace the lost blood with plasma expanders. Those were the essential emergency procedures: the ones which kept him alive.

The casualty officer injected lignocaine into the wounds before beginning the careful, laborious process of stitching them up. Outside, in the corridor, sitting in wheelchairs, chairs, slumped over crutches or girlfriends' shoulders, stretched across the floor, the procession of those waiting for surgery grew. Traffic accidents, disco brawls, teenage bravado, domestic misunderstandings. The casualty officer, conscious of this, took his time nevertheless. As a fellow doctor, Tim Fletcher merited his best attentions – and trained professionals were not so thick upon the ground their potential could be easily wasted. The officer took especial care with Fletcher's hands.

After crossmatching his blood, the plasma was followed up by two units of packed cells. Fletcher, who seemed to have been shifting uneasily in and out of consciousness for hours, was given injections of intramuscular pethidine to help control his pain.

When Kevin Naylor stepped, somewhat self-consciously, on to the ward, Fletcher was lying in a side room, a single bed with its attendant drip attached to the back of his arm. One sleeve of the pyjama jacket he had been given had been cut to allow for bandages, which also swathed his hands and partially masked his face. When Naylor leaned over him, one of Tim Fletcher's eyelids twitched sharply, as if in response to something dreamed or remembered.

'Are you a relative?'

The nurse looked West Indian, though her accent was

local enough, Midlands born and bred. Her hat was pinned none too securely to thickly curled hair and the blue of her uniform lent a gleam to her skin.

'Relative, are you?'

Naylor realized that he hadn't answered. 'Kevin Naylor,' he said. 'CID.'

'Sister know you're here?'

Naylor shook his head. 'I phoned from the station, make sure it was okay to come. Not sure who I spoke to.'

The nurse moved alongside him, glancing down. 'I don't know how much sense you'll get out of him, sedated to the eyeballs. Still, he'll have to be woken soon for his obs. Every half hour.'

Turning back, she saw a smile crossing Naylor's face. 'What're you laughing at?'

'Obs.'

'Observation. What about it?'

'We call it that as well.'

'Same thing, is it then?'

'Similar.'

The nurse grinned: 'If you want to know your temperature, ask a policeman.'

Naylor looked back towards the bed; maybe he'd be better leaving, trying again later.

'I'll let sister know you're here,' the nurse said, heading back on to the main ward.

Tim Fletcher had been aware of various bodies around him during the preceding eight hours; pale faces, white or blue uniforms. Voices that were hushed to hide their urgency. In the midst of it all a single shout, sharp and clear. At one point he had been certain that Sarah Leonard had been standing there in her staff nurse's uniform, smiling down at him, telling him to rest, be assured it would be all right. But when he had tried to speak her name she had disappeared. And Karen. He had not seen Karen, awake or sleeping.

31

This time there was a young man, twenty-three or -four, wearing a pale blue shirt, a dark check jacket, dark blue tie. Brown hair that didn't seem to be obeying any rules. Doctor? No, he didn't think he was a doctor.

'Detective Constable Naylor,' said the man, younger than Fletcher himself though not looking it – except now, except today. 'I'd like to ask you some questions.'

Fletcher would have loved to have answers. The why and the who of it. Especially the who. All he knew for certain, it had been sudden, unexpected; he had been frightened, hurt. He remembered a black sweater, gloves, a balaclava that covered all of the head save for the eyes and mouth.

'What colour?'

'Black.'

'The eyes?'

'Balaclava.'

'And the eyes?'

Fletcher thought about it, tried to formulate a picture. Identikit, isn't that what they call them? 'Blue,' he said, almost as much a question as an answer.

'You're not sure?'

Fletcher shook his head; just a little. It hurt.

'It could be important.'

'Blue.'

'For certain?'

'No.'

'But . . .'

'As far as I know, as far as I can remember . . . blue.'

'Dr Fletcher,' said the nurse, 'if I can just put this under your arm?'

Naylor watched as the nurse slid the thermometer into the pit of Fletcher's bandaged arm and wrapped a cuff about the other, inflating it prior to checking his blood pressure.

'Go ahead,' she said to Naylor. 'Don't mind me.'

'The weapon,' Naylor asked, glancing at his notebook, 'did you see what it was?'

'I felt it,' Fletcher answered.

The nurse continued to pump up the rubber balloon, inflating the cuff.

'Then you didn't see it?' Naylor persisted.

Downward sweep of the blade, illuminated in a fast curve of orange light.

'Not clearly.'

'Was it a knife?'

'It could have been.'

'An open blade?'

Flinching, Fletcher nodded.

'Can you remember how long?'

'No, I . . . No, I can't be certain.'

'This long?' Naylor held his Biro before Fletcher's face, tight between the tip of his middle finger and the ball of his thumb.

'Blood pressure's fine.'

Fletcher closed his eyes.

The nurse eased the thermometer out from beneath his arm and held it against the light. 'Well?' she said, glancing down towards Naylor with a half-grin.

'Well, what?'

'Temperature, what d'you think?'

'Look,' said Naylor, a touch of exasperation.

'Thirty-seven point eight.'

'Smaller,' said Fletcher weakly, opening his eyes.

'You're doing fine,' the nurse said, touching his shoulder lightly, almost a squeeze. 'Soon be up and about. Dancing.' She looked at Naylor. 'The doctor here, he's a great dancer.'

'It was smaller,' Fletcher said again, an effort to breathe now, an effort to talk. 'Smaller. Like a scalpel.'

Six

Lynnie love, I know your job keeps you awful busy, but it do seem such a long time since your dad and me seen you. Try and come home, even if it's just for a couple of days. That'd mean a lot to your dad specially. I worry about him, Lynnie, I do. More and more into himself he's getting. Depressed. Sometimes it's all I can do to get him to talk, sit down to his supper. Make an effort, there's a love.

Her mother's words jostled inside Lynn Kellogg's head as she crossed University Boulevard, dark green of the rhododendron bushes at her back. Ahead of her was the brighter green of the Science Park, technology disguised as an oversized child's toy. Lynn had a friend she'd gone through school with, bright, but not much more intelligent than Lynn herself. 'My God! You can't be serious? The police? Whatever d'you want to throw your life away like that for?' The friend had gone to Cambridge Poly, got interested in computers, now she was earning thirty thousand a year plus, living with a zoologist in a converted windmill outside Ely.

Thrown her life away, is that what Lynn had done? She didn't think so, glad most of the time that she was in the job, enjoying it, something more worthwhile maybe than writing software programmes to record the fertility and sexing of Rhode Island Reds. What did it matter, what other people thought? The neighbours in her block of housing association flats, who only spoke to her if someone had been tampering with their locks, trying to break into their parked car. Patients in the surgery, where Lynn was waiting for her check-up and a new supply of pills; nudging one another, staring, know what she is, don't you? The way most men she spoke to in a bar or pub would evaporate at the mention of what she did, as if by magic.

Lynnie, no! You aren't serious?

The job.

She checked the address in her notebook and looked up at the front of the house. Mid-terraced, the one to its right was a prime example of seventies stone-cladding, that to the left sported a shiny new door, complete with brass knocker and mail box.

Twenty-seven.

Two curtains had been draped unevenly across the downstairs window, probably held up by pins. Among the half-dozen bottles clustered on the step was one ripe with yellowing, crusted milk. At least, thought Lynn, she didn't live like this.

The girl who finally came to the door was a couple of inches taller than herself, even in woolly socks. She had near-black hair to her shoulders, unbrushed so that it made a ragged frame around the almost perfect oval of her face. She was slender in tapered black jeans, with a good figure that two jumpers – purple and green – failed to disguise. Her eyes were raw from lack of sleep or tears or both. Looking like that, she'd get the sympathy vote as well.

'Karen Archer?'

The girl nodded, stepping back to let Lynn enter. She scarcely glanced at Lynn's warrant card, motioning her past the hall table with its telephone almost hidden beneath free papers, free offers, handouts from Chinese restaurants and taxi firms. A succession of tenants had etched numbers on to the wallpaper in a rising arc, some of them scored heavily through.

'Mind the fourth step,' Karen warned, following Lynn closely.

There was a poster stuck to the door of Karen's room, two lovers kissing in a city street.

'Go on in,' Karen said.

It had originally been a back bedroom, a view from the square of window down over a succession of back yards, old outhouses, an alley pushing narrowly in between. Cats and rusted prams and washing lines.

The interior was a mixture of arranged and untidy: neatly stacked books alongside music cassettes, each labelled in a clear, strong hand; earrings hanging from cotton threads, red, yellow, blue; on the bed a duvet bundled to one side, as though Karen had been lying beneath it when Lynn had rung the bell: tights in many colours dangling down from the mantelpiece and the top of the opened wardrobe door, drying.

'Sit down.'

The choice was between the bed and a black canvas chair with pale wooden arms and Lynn took the latter.

The room smelled of cigarette smoke and good perfume.

'Would you like some coffee?'

There were five used mugs, one on the scarred table, three close together on the floor beside the bed, the last standing on the chest of drawers, in front of a mirror with photographs jutting at all angles from its frame. 'No, thanks,' Lynn said with a quick smile. She was wondering which of the men in the photos was Fletcher.

'What d'you want to know?' Karen said.

They went through the worst first, the discovery of the houseman on the bridge, the fears that he might die, be already dead; then their arrangements for that evening, the phone call which might have been from Fletcher yet might as easily not.

'You haven't known him all that long then?'

Karen shook her head. 'Two months.' She lifted her head to see that Lynn was still looking at her, encouraging her to continue. 'I went to this Medics Ball, I don't know.'

She gestured vaguely with her hand, the one not holding a cigarette. 'I'd been going around with these medical students, I don't know how that started really, except most of the people on my course are a bunch of deadheads. Either that or posers of the first order.'

'Your course?'

'English. Drama subsid. If he didn't die before the Second World War, he didn't exist. That's English anyway. Drama's not so bad.'

'Are they all men, then, the people you study?'

'Sorry?'

'Writers. You said, he.'

Karen stared at her. What the fuck? A feminist policewoman? 'Figure of speech,' she said.

Lynn Kellogg nodded. 'The medical students you mentioned, were they male?'

'Mostly. To be honest, I think women are pretty boring, don't you?'

'No,' said Lynn. 'No, I don't.'

She could see the shifting look in Karen Archer's distressed eyes, the word forming silently behind them – dyke!

'Anyway,' asked Karen, 'what does it matter?'

Lynn sidestepped the question. 'Before you began going out with Dr Fletcher, you did have another boyfriend?'

'Yes.'

'One or several?'

'What's that got to do with you?'

'I mean, this relationship, the earlier one, was it serious?'

Karen dropped the end of her cigarette into a quarter-inch of cold coffee. 'I suppose so.'

'And the man?'

'What about him?'

'Was he serious?'

'Ian?' Karen laughed. 'Only things he gets serious about are anatomy and *Blackadder*.'

'Is he over here?' Lynn went to the mirror, Karen almost grudgingly following. 'One of these?'

'There.'

Karen pointed to a figure in a skimpy swimming costume, lots of body hair, posing at the edge of a pool with a champagne bottle in one hand and a pint glass in the other. There were three other pictures: Ian in a formal dinner jacket but wearing a red nose; Ian flourishing a stethoscope; Ian as Mr Universe.

Wow! thought Lynn. What a guy!

'He looks a lot of fun,' she said. 'Why did you stop going out with him?'

'Is that any of your business?'

'No.'

Karen shrugged and wandered over to the kettle, shaking it to make certain there was enough water before switching it on. 'Sure you don't want one?' she asked, opening the jar of Maxwell House.

'Thanks, no,' said Lynn. 'What's Ian's last name?'

'Carew.'

'And he's still a student here?'

'A medical student, yes. He's in his second year.'

'But you haven't seen him?'

'Not since I started seeing Tim.'

'Not at all?'

'I don't know. Once, maybe.'

'How did he feel about you and Dr Fletcher? I mean . . .'

Karen was laughing, shaking her head, reaching for another cigarette, all at the same time. 'I know what you *mean*. Poor old Ian was so heartbroken at being chucked, he couldn't cope. Especially when the other man was a qualified doctor and he was only a student. So he waited for him one night and tried to kill him: jealousy and revenge.'

The kettle had begun to boil and Karen did nothing to

switch it off. Lynn reached down past her and flicked up the switch, removing the plug safely, the way her mother had taught her.

'It's the sort of thing you see on a bad film on television,' Karen said, 'late at night.'

'Yes,' said Lynn. 'Isn't it?'

She turned back towards the mirror. Right across the top were the pictures of the man she assumed to be Fletcher. Young, young for a doctor, Polaroids that had been taken there, in that room, those strange reflections from the flash sparkling at the centre of his eyes. Bottom left was a strip from a photo booth, one they had sat in together, goofy faces, weird expressions, only in the last were they serious, kissing.

'Have you been to see him?'

'No. I phoned. They said this afternoon.' She glanced at her watch. 'After two.' She spooned milk substitute into the mug of coffee and went back to the bed, stirring carefully. 'I'm a bit frightened to see him, I suppose. After what's happened to him.' She sipped, then drank. 'What he'll look like.'

Does it matter? thought Lynn. And then, of course it does.

'You didn't notice anybody?' she asked. 'Walking to meet him. Hanging around by the bridge.'

'No one. Traffic. No one walking. Not that I saw.'

'You're sure?'

'Sure.'

'This Ian,' Lynn said, nodding over towards the photographs as she stood, 'someone will most likely talk to him.'

'That's ridiculous.'

'Maybe. But I expect it will be done.' Lynn hesitated at the door. 'If you do think of anything that might be important, give me a call.' She placed a card on the corner of the pillow. 'Thank you for your time, I'll see myself out.'

39

Karen stood up but made no move towards the door.

Lynn hurried down the stairs, remembering which step to beware, wondering why she had felt so hostile, offered the girl so little support. What combination had it been, she wondered, walking briskly up the street, that had made her withhold her sympathy? Why had she felt jealous and superior, the feelings hand in hand?

Seven

Mid-morning. Graham Millington was sitting in a smoke-wreathed room in Walsall, watching a DI write names and dates on a white board, using his coloured markers with a definite flourish. A detective sergeant stuck flags into a map of the Midlands at appropriate points and offered commentary in a flat Black Country accent. What was it the wife wanted me to pick up from the shops, Millington was thinking, mushrooms or aubergines? Millington had never been quite clear what it was you did with an aubergine. He copied information down into his notebook, glanced about him. Nine out of eleven smoking away as if their lives depended upon it. He tried to remember what he had heard on the radio earlier that week, research some Americans had been doing into passive inhalation of nicotine. God, he thought, if this goes on beyond twelve that's likely as not another six months off my lifetime ... or was it six minutes?

Patel pushed his tongue up against the back of his teeth, trying to ease away the last remnants of Milky Way. You could sit for just so long watching cream-coloured breeze-block without going into a trance. Meditation. Hadn't he been toying for ages with the idea of taking it up? He could hear them in the canteen if ever they found out. Yeah, great, Diptak, what comes next? Swallowing fire? Sleeping on nails? Except that they never called him Diptak. Or much else. To his face, anyway. He picked up his camera as two men in blue overalls came out of the nearest building and almost immediately set it down again. The men settled themselves up against the wall, facing what sun there was, unpacked their sandwiches, unscrewed their flasks. Patel wondered how long he could go before opening the empty orange juice container under the seat to take a pee.

'I think they must have got in through here.'

'Yes,' murmured Divine, 'most likely.'

He stood at the window of what estate agents liked to call a utility room, looking out over a quarter-acre of lawns, fruit bushes, shrubs with unpronounceable Latin names and flowers fading down into wooden barrels. Beyond that, on a lower level, was a full-sized tennis court, complete with green wire surround and floodlights. He wondered where they kept the swimming pool. Probably down in the basement, along with the steam room and the jacuzzi.

'You will do your best to catch them?'

Daft cow, standing there in some sort of silk dressing-gown, rings down her fingers enough to open a branch of Ratners and a bit of tangerine cloth round her head like she's thinking about joining a very select order of nuns.

'Yes,' said Divine, choking back the word 'madam'. 'We'll do what we can. You'll let us have a full list of what's missing, of course?'

The doorbell chimed four bars of Andrew Lloyd Webber.

'Excuse me,' she turned smoothly away, 'that must be the cleaning woman.'

Oh, yes, thought Divine, coming in the front door too, must have had good references. He was glad he'd forgotten to wipe his feet on the way in.

Lynn saw Kevin Naylor sitting on his own at the far side of the canteen and wasn't sure whether to go and sit with him or not. Up until recently she would have had no hesitation, but lately Kevin had been short with her, abrupt and eager to keep his distance. She knew there were problems at home with Debbie, with the baby. There had been an evening when they might have talked about it, Kevin and herself, almost had. Tired, he had come back to her flat for coffee, but instead of talking he had fallen asleep. Waking, he had only hurried away, half-guilty. Lynn recalled from that evening her hand momentarily against Kevin's upper arm. What had that been about? And asking him back – coffee? Come back for coffee? She thought about Karen Archer saying that to Fletcher after the Medics Ball, that or something like it. What had he understood by that?

There had been a film they'd shown on the TV, a year or so before, between the adverts. A young woman moving around her flat, making sure the bedroom door was open, clear view of the bed; the camera on the man's face then, suggesting what he was thinking, condoms, AIDS, wouldn't you like to stay the night? Was that what Kevin had been afraid of? She doubted it. She took her cup of tea and pulled out the chair opposite him. If he didn't want to talk to her, he could get up and move away.

'How did it go at the hospital?' she asked.

'It's your wife, sir,' called someone as Resnick left his office.

'What?'

'Your wife.' A young DC leaned back from his desk, holding a receiver aloft.

'Don't be so bloody daft!'

Resnick shouldered his way through the door and hurried down the stairs. He was already late for his appointment with the DCI. He wondered whether Ed Silver had woken and, if so, if he were still in the house. Remembering his remark about the cleaver, Resnick felt a twinge of apprehension on behalf of his cats. No, he thought, stepping out on to the street, if he tries anything funny Dizzy'll soon sort him out.

Ignoring his car, Resnick crossed in front of the traffic at an ungainly trot and set off downhill past the new Malaysian restaurant, raincoat flapping awkwardly around him.

'Kevin,' said Lynn, unable to lift the testiness from her voice.

'What?'

'We've been sitting here for almost twenty minutes and you've either said nothing or gone on about some nurse you reckon fancied you.'

'So?'

'So I thought we were supposed to be comparing notes, seeing if we're any closer to understanding why that doctor was attacked.'

'Funny. I thought we were having a tea break. Bit of relaxation. Besides, I never asked you to sit here.'

'Maybe you'd prefer me back in uniform – just a different kind.'

'Maybe I would.'

When she stood up, Lynn scraped her chair back loudly enough for several others to turn around. 'If you're thinking of going over the side,' she said, 'I should keep it to yourself.'

'What's the matter, Lynn?' said Naylor. 'Jealous?'

'You bastard!'

She pushed her way between the close-set tables, the backs of jutting chairs, her normally ruddy cheeks redder still.

'What's up?' said Mark Divine, all mouth and mock concern. 'Getting your period?'

Lynn Kellogg rocked back on her heels, swivelling to face him. Divine standing there with his tray balanced over one arm, the rest of the canteen watching.

44

'Yes,' she said, 'matter of fact, I am.'

Once before, in the CID room, she'd struck out at him, smack across the face, marks from her fingers that hadn't soon faded. She moved a half pace towards him now and his arm went up instinctively for protection. There was a large glass of milk on the tray, a cream cake, pie and chips.

Lynn reached out and took a chip. 'Thanks, Mark. Nice of you to be so concerned.'

The roar from the rest of the canteen cowboys was still loud around Divine as he found a seat, echoes of it following Lynn all the way back along the corridor.

'Espresso?'

'Large.'

Resnick looked at the girl as she turned away. Short hair like bleached gold at the tips, mud at the roots. Two silver rings in her left ear and a fake diamond stud at the side of her nose. He hadn't seen her before and he wasn't too surprised. Mario would take on a girl, teach her to work the machine and then she'd leave.

'Thanks,' he said as she set down the small cup and saucer, brown and white. He gave her one pound thirty and she looked surprised. 'Half's for the next one,' Resnick explained.

'Tomorrow?'

'Ten minutes.'

There had been a period of almost six weeks when the stall had closed down and Resnick had felt bereft. Usually, when he went to the indoor market near the Central police station and shopped at either of the Polish delicatessens, or bought fresh vegetables, fish, he would stop off at the Italian coffee stall for two espressos. Sometimes – the luxury of half an hour to kill, more than usual to read the paper in – he would have three and spend the rest of the day tasting them, strong and bitter, at the back of his throat. Then, suddenly, no warning: it was closed.

Resnick had asked around. He was, after all, a detective. There were rumours of grand changes, expansion, everything from toasted ham and cheese to microwaved lasagne. One morning, local paper under one arm, half a pound of pickled gherkins, soused herring and a dark rye with caraway in a carrier bag, it was open again, Mario himself behind the counter. There were new covers on the stools, fresh red and green paint on the counter, the cappuccino machine had been moved from one side to the other. Everything else seemed the same. Resnick had greeted Mario like a long-lost brother, a material witness he had never thought would show up at the trial.

'Coffee? Wonderful coffee!' sang Mario, as though he had never seen Resnick before. 'Best coffee you can buy!'

'What's happened?' Resnick asked. 'What's been happening?'

'The wife,' Mario said, 'she had a baby.' Explaining nothing.

Then, as now, Resnick drank one espresso and slid his cup back across the counter for another.

Across from him a mother and daughter, similar hair styles, identical expressions, listened to Mario declaring undying love to the pair of them and were pleased. A serious young man who had strolled in from the Poly refolded his *Guardian* as he spooned chocolatey froth from the top of his cappuccino. No more than eighteen, a woman prised the dummy from her three-year-old's mouth so that he could drink his banana milk shake. Along to Resnick's right, a man with check cap and a hump glanced around before slipping his false teeth into his handkerchief, the better to deal with his sausage roll.

'Inspector.'

'Ms Olds.' Resnick recognized the voice and didn't turn his head. He waited until Suzanne Olds had climbed on to the stool alongside him, careful to smooth down the skirt of her light grey suit, the hem settling several inches short of the knee. She lifted a small leather bag into her lap and snapped it open; its matching satchel, containing court notes and papers, rested by her feet.

'Ah!' cried Mario. '*Bellissima!*'

'Stuff it, Mario!' she said, enunciating beautifully. 'Or I'll have this man arrest you for sexual harassment.'

Resnick walked through the Centre with her, a tall woman in her mid-thirties, slender, an inch or two under six foot. Standing on the escalator, passing between the Early Learning Centre and Thornton's Chocolates, Suzanne Olds made him feel shabby, she made him feel good. She was talking about a case she was in the middle of defending, three black youths who had been stopped by a police car on the edge of the Forest, two in the morning. Illegal substances, backchat, a charge of resisting arrest.

'Why do it?' she asked, buses pulling away behind her, turning right into Trinity Square. 'When there are real crimes to be solved.'

'Hospital doctor attacked!' called the paper seller. 'Slasher at large!'

'Enjoy your say in court,' Resnick said, already moving.

'Next time the coffee's on me,' she called after him, but Resnick failed to hear her, her voice drowned in the sound of traffic as he hurried away, fists punched deep into his pockets.

Eight

'Ah, Tom.'

'Tim.'

'How're we today? Feeling better?'

'A little.'

'Good. That's the spirit.'

Tim Fletcher felt like shit. He winced trying to lever himself up in the bed; with one arm covered in bandages and the other attached to a drip it wasn't easy.

The consultant stood near the end of the bed, white coat open over a pair of ox blood brogues, beige trousers, a grey tailored shirt with a white collar and silk tie in red and navy diagonal stripes. His face was full around the jaw, more than a little flushed below pouched eyes; the pupils themselves were unclouded and alert. He took the file containing Fletcher's notes from one of the junior doctors, gave it a peripheral glance and handed it back.

'If you cut us, do we not bleed?' Laughing, the consultant took hold of Fletcher's toes through the blanket and gave them an encouraging shake. 'Gave the lie to that one, eh, Tom? Those buggers who think we're made of stone.'

He lifted his head for the approval which his entourage duly gave.

'Well,' he said, 'young chap like you, should heal quickly. Soon be ready for a spot of physio . . . Physio, yes, sister?'

'Yes, Mr Salt.'

'Soon have you back on your feet again.'

'Arsehole!' murmured Fletcher, as soon as the consultant and his party were out of earshot. And don't tell me, he thought, that I'm ever going to end up like that, parading around at the head of some royal procession.

He leaned back against the pillows and let his head fall sideways and that was when he saw Karen, hovering uncertainly, brown paper bags of pears and grapes clasped against her waist, a dozen roses, red and white, resting lightly against her perfect breasts.

Resnick opened the door and went in. A woman with greying hair and a pair of red-framed glasses looked away from her desk, fingers continuing to peck at the keyboard of her computer.

'Any chance of seeing Mr Salt?'

His secretary looked doubtful.

'It's to do with Fletcher, the houseman . . .'

'Such a dreadful business.'

'I understand Mr Salt was responsible?'

She blinked behind her lenses, wide, oval frames.

'He took charge himself,' Resnick said.

'Mr Salt went straight into theatre the instant he heard, insisted. One of our own.' She looked down at the warrant card Resnick was holding open. 'He's finishing his rounds.'

'Should I wait or go and find him?'

For a moment, the secretary glanced at the green monitor of the display unit. 'He sees his private patients in the afternoon.'

Resnick slipped his card back into his pocket. 'I'll go and see him now – before I have to pay for the privilege.'

Bernard Salt stood inside Sister Minton's office, hands behind his back, feet apart in the at ease position, giving a lie to the way he was feeling. He could feel the sweat dampening today's collar at the back of his neck, insinuating itself into the hair beneath his arms and at his crotch. He hoped to God she couldn't smell it. The last thing he wanted was for her to realize he was rattled, even a little frightened.

Helen Minton was aware of her own breathing; forcing herself to sit back in her chair, she closed her eyes. 'How many more times are we going to have to go through this?' she asked.

There was a single knock at the door and both started, but neither spoke; other than that, neither of them moved until Helen Minton opened her eyes and Salt was looking at his watch.

Two knocks at the door, followed close by two more.

'Come in,' Helen Minton said.

The first thing Resnick noticed was the rawness at the corner of her eyes; the second was the relief on the consultant's face.

'Sorry to interrupt,' Resnick said, introducing himself. 'I wondered' – looking at Salt – 'if I could have a word about Tim Fletcher?'

'Of course, inspector.' And then, 'Helen, would it be all right if we made use of your office? I shouldn't think we'll be many minutes.'

The sister held Salt's gaze until the consultant had to look away. Then she picked up the diary from the desk, the sheets on which she had been working out the next ward rota, and left them to it.

Bernard Salt closed the door lightly behind her. 'Now, inspector . . .' he began, moving across to sit in the sister's chair.

Bernard Salt, Resnick came away thinking, was a powerful man with powerfully held views; it had come as no surprise to learn that he had played rugby as a young man, swum butterfly and breast stroke; now golf three times a week and occasionally allowed himself to be badgered into an evening of bridge. More importantly, Resnick had gained a keener understanding of the wounds Tim Fletcher had sustained.

Those to the face were untidy but superficial; in time their scars would lend him a more interesting appearance than he might otherwise have grown into. The cuts to his upper arm had drawn a good deal of blood, but were less serious than the injuries to his hand. What interested Resnick, however, had been the consultant's description of the damage that had been done to the houseman's leg.

The blade had entered high in the thigh, having been driven with some considerable force into the gluteus maximus and subsequently drawn sharply through the remaining gluteal muscles and from there into the hamstring muscles at the back of the thigh; here pressure seemed to have been reapplied before the blade was forced through the gastrocnemius, running the length of the calf between ankle and knee.

Without the use of those muscles, Fletcher would be unable to flex either knee or ankle joints; unless they repaired themselves healthily, he would experience, at best, difficulty in walking or otherwise using the damaged leg.

'At worst?' Resnick had asked.

Salt had simply stared back at him without expression.

'The wounds to the leg, then?' Resnick had said. 'Quite a different nature to the rest?'

'More serious,' Salt had agreed. 'Potentially.'

'More deliberate?'

Salt had swivelled in the sister's chair, shaken his head and allowed a smile at the corners of his mouth. 'I cannot speculate.'

'But they could suggest an attacker who knew what he was about?'

'Possibly.'

'One with a knowledge of anatomy, physiology?'

'A member of the St John Ambulance Brigade, inspector? Anyone, I should have thought, with basic knowledge of how the body works.'

'And without wishing you to speculate, Mr Salt . . .'

'Please, inspector.'

'You wouldn't have formed any opinion as to the kind of weapon that was used in the attack?'

'Fine.' The same smile narrow at the edges of the consultant's full mouth. 'Sharp. Other than that, no, I'm afraid not.'

Resnick had thanked him and left the room, taking with him one further piece of knowledge that Tim Fletcher had yet to learn: the injuries to the tendons of his hand were unlikely to heal completely; the chances of him furthering his career in surgery or some similarly deft area of medicine were slight.

Fletcher was sleeping, Karen Archer's hand trapped beneath his bandaged arm. The roses beside the bed were already beginning to wilt. Resnick couldn't tell if the girl were bored or tired, sitting motionless in the centrally heated air. He wondered why Lynn Kellogg had felt about her as she did, the antagonism evident even in her verbal report. Half a mind to go over and talk to her, Resnick turned away instead, back into the main ward, reasoning that Fletcher needed all the rest he could get.

He sidestepped the drugs trolley and nearly bumped into a student nurse wearing a uniform that resembled a large J-Cloth with poppers and a belt. Just before the door he turned and there was the sister, looking at him from the nurses' station in the middle of the ward. Resnick hesitated, wondering if there were something she wanted to say to him, but she glanced away.

Resnick ignored the lift and took the stairs, no lover of hospitals. There was a queue of cars at the entrance to the multi-storey car park as he drove out. If whoever attacked Tim Fletcher had found his victim by more than chance, if he had sought him out . . . He? Resnick took the exit from the roundabout that would take him along Derby Road, back to the station. He was thinking about the medical student who had been Karen Archer's previous boyfriend: somebody with motivation to cause hurt, maim. Knowledge. The long trajectory from hip to knee and beyond. Resnick shuddered, realized that his own hand was touching his leg, as if to make sure it was still sound. He had to brake hard so as not to run the light by the Three Wheatsheaves, swerving into the left lane around a Metro which had belatedly signalled its intention to go right.

Ian Carew.

He would find out where he was living, pay a visit. Because something seemed obvious, that didn't have to mean it was wrong.

Nine

'Debbie!'

Kevin Naylor pushed the front door to, slipped his keys into his coat pocket and listened. Only the hum of the freezer from the kitchen. Faint, the sound of early evening television from next door. Walls of new estates like these, you need never feel you were all alone. Perfect for the first-time buyer, one point off your mortgage for the first year, wait until you'd painted, roses in the garden, turf for the lawn, something more than money invested before they hit you with the full rate, fifteen and a half and rising. A couple across the crescent, one kid and another on the way, they'd had their place repossessed last month, moved in with her parents, Jesus!

'Debbie?'

There were dishes in the bowl, more stacked haphazardly alongside the sink. In a red plastic bucket, tea towels soaking in bleach. Kevin flipped down the top of the rubbish bin and then lifted it away; the wrapping from packets of biscuits lying there, thin coils of coloured Cellophane pushed down between torn cardboard, treacle tart, deep-dish apple pie. He knew that if he checked in the freezer the tubs of supermarket ice-cream would be close to empty.

The neighbour switched channels and began to watch the evening news.

The baby's room was neat, neater than the rest; creams and talc on the table near the window, a carton of disposable nappies with its top bent back. A mobile of brightly coloured planets that Lynn had bought at the baby's birth dangled above the empty cot, suns and moons and stars.

'Where's the baby?'

Debbie was a shape beneath the striped duvet, fingers of one hand showing, her wrist, a wedding ring. Light brown hair lifelessly spread upon the pillow. Kevin sat on the edge of the bed and she flinched; her hand, clenching, disappeared.

'Deb?'

'What?'

'Where's the baby?'

'Who cares?'

He grabbed at her, grabbed at the quilt, pulling at it hard, tugging it from her hands; she pushed her hands down between her knees, curling in upon herself, eyes closed tight.

'Debbie!'

Kneeling on the bed, Kevin struggled to turn her over and she kicked out, flailing her arms until he had backed away, allowing her to seize the duvet again and pull it against her, sitting at the centre of the bed, eyes, for the first time, open. She loathed him. He could see it, read it in those eyes. Loathed him.

'Where is she?'

'At my mother's.'

Kevin Naylor sighed and looked away.

'Is that wrong? Is it? Well? What's wrong with that, Kevin? What's so terrible about that?'

He got up and crossed the room, opening drawers, closing them.

'Well?'

'What's wrong,' he said, facing her, fighting to keep his voice calm, 'is that's where she was this morning, yesterday, the day before.'

'So?'

Kevin made a sound somewhere between a snort and a harsh, humourless laugh.

'She is my mother, Kevin. She is the baby's grandmother. It's only natural . . .'

'That she should look after her all the time?'

'It isn't all the time.'

'Good as.'

'She's helping . . .'

'Helping!'

'Kevin, please! I get tired. You know I get tired. I can't help it. I . . .'

He stood at the end of the bed, staring down at her in disgust, waiting for the tears to start. There. 'If I want to see my own child,' he said, 'I have to make a phone call, make sure she isn't sleeping, get back into the car and drive halfway across the fucking city!'

He slammed the door so that it shook against its hinges. Switched on the radio so that he couldn't hear the sound of her sobbing. On either side of them, television sets were turned up in direct retaliation. At least, Kevin thought, when their kids cry I can sodding hear them.

There were tins of baked beans in the cupboard, packets of soup, chicken and leek, chicken and asparagus, plain chicken; four or five slices of white bread inside the wrapper but outside the bread bin. Eggs. Always too many of those. He could send out for a pizza, drive off for a take-away, curry or Chinese.

On the radio someone was pontificating about mad cow disease, the effects it might have on children, force-fed beefburgers for school dinners. Kevin switched it off and instantly he could hear Debbie, bawling. He switched back on, changed stations. Del Shannon. Gem-AM. Poor sod who shot himself. Well . . .

There was one can of lager left in the back of the fridge and he opened it, tossing the ring pull on to the side and taking the can into the living room. If Debbie's mother were there, she'd be tut-tutting, Kevin, you're not going to drink that without a glass, surely? But she wasn't there, was she? Back in her own little semi in Basford, caravan outside the front window and his bloody kid asleep in her spare room.

He scooped the remote control from beside the armchair and pressed Channel Three. Might as well have the whole street watching together, synchronized bloody viewing. Nothing on he wanted till the football at half past ten, bit of boxing.

Thinking of going over the side, Lynn had said in the canteen. Maybe, he thought, over the side and never coming back.

When Tim Fletcher woke he saw the roses and then he saw Sarah Leonard and he knew something wasn't right. She was standing at an angle to the bed; her staff nurse's uniform had been exchanged for a long, beige cotton coat, broad belt loosely tied and high epaulettes. Maybe she was still wearing the uniform underneath, but he didn't think so.

'Karen . . .' he said.

'She went a long time ago.'

Fletcher nodded.

'Girls her age,' Sarah said, 'they get restless. Haven't the patience.'

She was, Fletcher thought, what, all of twenty-seven herself, twenty-eight.

'I just popped in,' she said, 'to see how you were getting on.'

'How am I?'

She smiled. 'You're the doctor.'

He glanced down at his pillows. 'You couldn't . . .'

'Prop you up a bit? I expect so.'

She leaned him forward against her shoulder as she plumped and patted the pillows, the inside of his arm

57

pressing against her breast. 'Overtime, this.' Her face was close and he could feel her breath. Sarah leaned him back into the pillows and stood back.

'Thanks.'

'There's nothing else you want?'

Fully awake now, the pain was back in his leg, not sharp the way he might have imagined, but dull, persistent, throbbing. A nerve twitched suddenly in his hand and he winced, twice, biting down into his bottom lip. At least there was still a nerve there to twitch. 'No,' he said. 'I'm fine.'

She raised her head. 'I'll look in tomorrow.' She was almost out of earshot when his voice brought her back.

'You off home now?'

'Soon.'

'Walking?'

'Yes.'

'Be careful.'

Resnick arrived home to find the front door open on the latch and Miles pressing his nose against it while Pepper nervously kept watch. His immediate thought was that the house had been burgled, but a quick check proved this not to be so. Bud was lying on the top step of the stairs, ready for flight. Dizzy and Ed Silver were neither of them to be seen, off about their business, hard into the night.

Ed's note was propped against the edge of the frying pan, *Out for a quick one, back soon.* He had washed the plate but not the knife and fork, rinsed out his cup and left the tea stewing dark and cold inside the pot. Three tea bags. The bacon and the sausage he had found in Resnick's fridge, the oven chips he would have had to fetch from the grocer's on the main road. Also, the half-bottle of cheap Greek brandy, empty between the cats' bowls.

Resnick picked up Bud and nuzzled him, conscious of the animal's ribs like something made from a kit, balsa wood and glue. He dropped his coat over the back of a chair and, carrying the cat with him, pulled an Ellington album from the shelf. 'Jack the Bear', 'Take the A Train', 'Ko-Ko'. His friend, Ben Riley, twelve years in the job before he left for America, had sent him a card from New York. *Charlie – Finally got to take the 'A' train. Head-to-toe graffiti, inside and out, and anyone white gets off below 110th Street. Stay home. Stick to the music.* Ben, he'd stayed there: Resnick hadn't heard from him in more than two years, four.

Ed Silver had scorned the Czech Budweiser and Resnick opened a bottle and slowly drank it as he sliced a small onion carefully into rounds and overlapped them along two slices of dark rye bread. He covered these with Polish ham, then cut slivers of Jarlsberg cheese. Backtracking to the fridge, he found one solitary pickled cucumber, set rounds of this on the ham, then added the cheese.

The grill was gathering heat when he stood the sandwiches, open-faced, beneath it and finished the first beer, rolling his hand across his stomach as he reached for another.

When the cheese was brown and bubbling, he forked some coleslaw on to a plate, used a slice to lift up the sandwiches and set them down next to the coleslaw, balanced two jars of mustard, Dijon and mixed grain, on the rim, pushed his index finger down into the neck of the Budweiser bottle and headed back for the living room.

Ben Webster was just beginning his solo on 'Cotton Tail', rolling that phrase over the rhythm section, springy and strong from Blanton's bass, round and round and rich, like rolling it round a barrel of treacle. Just when it seemed to have become stuck, sharp little phrases from the brass digging it out, and then the saxophone lifting itself with more and more urgency, up, up and into the next chorus.

Resnick wondered what it must be like, being able to do anything with such force, such grace. Would he see Ed

Silver that evening or the next and in what state? You spent half a lifetime striving to reach a point of perfection and then one night, one day, for no reason that any onlooker could see, you opened your fingers and watched as it all slipped away.

In their two-bedroom, two-storey house, Debbie Naylor had fallen back to sleep, mouth open, lightly snoring. Kevin still sat in the chair before the television, watching, soundlessly, as two boxers moved around the square ring, feinting, parrying, never quite connecting.

Tim Fletcher lay on his back, awake in the half-light, counting stitches, trying to sleep.

Like a metronome, the even click of Sarah Leonard's low heels, along the pavement leading from the bridge.

Ten

Debbie Naylor stood looking down at her sleeping husband, alone save for the blue hum of the TV. The first time she had seen him, a friend had pointed him out, standing at the edge of half-a-dozen men at the bar, neither quite one of them nor alone. It hadn't been until he was driving her home, oh, three weeks later, home where she still lived with her parents, Basford, that he had told her what he did.

'You're kidding.'

'No. Why?'

'You just are.'

She had learned, some of it soon enough, the rest later. After the lunchtime meetings, Sunday afternoons with her family, Kevin embarrassed, wanting to leave; after the jokes from her friends at the office, the wedding with all of Kevin's friends, tall and shorthaired and already three-parts drunk, lining up to kiss her open-mouthed; not above, some of them, trying to cop a feel through the brocade of her wedding dress. Posing for the photographer, one of the bridesmaids had jumped in front of them, slipped a pair of handcuffs over their wrists.

After the honeymoon, the collision of late nights and early mornings; evenings with dinner in the oven and drying out, dreading the phone call that would, almost inevitably, come. Just a quick half. Wind down. With the lads. You know how it is.

She knew.

When Kevin had been accepted for CID it got better and

then it got worse. Put your foot down, her mother had said, else he'll walk all over you.

Better, Debbie had thought, than walking out.

She stood there, gazing down at him, asleep in the chair, looking little different at three and twenty than he had at nineteen. She couldn't believe that after all that had happened in the past four years, he was still the same. When she was so different.

'I'm sorry,' she said softly. 'I'm sorry.'

Kevin didn't hear her. She wanted to go down, carefully, to her knees and feel the side of her face against the warmth of his neck. Instead she left the room, pulling the door to but not closing it, not wanting to disturb him.

Alone, Kevin stirred and, waking, heard the soft thunk of the freezer door; Debbie, he thought, sneaking out for another pigging midnight feast.

The cats heard the phone moments before Resnick himself, jumping down from the bed and scuttling towards the bedroom door. Resnick blinked and groaned, lifting the receiver at only the second attempt.

'Yes?' he said, scarcely recognizing his own voice. 'What is it?'

He listened for less than a minute then set down the receiver. He had sat up for too long, hoping that Ed Silver might return, chasing the Budweiser with shots of vodka brought back by a friend from Cracow, the real thing. Setting his feet to the floor gingerly, he pushed himself up and padded to the kitchen. Miles and Bud had beaten him to it and were sniffing at their empty bowls expectantly. Pepper, who had taken to sleeping in an old plastic colander, yawned a greeting and reclosed his eyes, forgetting to put the red tip of his tongue back inside his mouth.

Knowing he was unlikely to get back to sleep, Resnick made coffee, drank half and put the remainder into a flask which he carried out to the car. Overhead lights shone a dull orange along the empty street. He went straight across the lights at the Forest, keeping the cemetery to his right. One last prostitute lingered against the wall near the next junction, shifting her weight from one foot to the other, face pale in the glow of her last cigarette.

When he began driving Resnick hadn't known for certain where he was going, but now he did.

Large blocks of brick and glass, by day the hospital didn't have enough character to be ugly. By night, most of its lights extinguished, some of them burning here and there, it was more inviting, mysterious. Resnick went slowly around the one-way system and parked fifty yards short of the medical school entrance.

A few swallows of black coffee and he took a torch from the compartment alongside the dash, locked the car and started to walk towards the bridge. It was a good hour later than the time Fletcher had been attacked, the flow of traffic was sporadic, there was no one else on foot. A short avenue of bushes and trees separated the hospital from the road. He flicked the torch on and shone it up the metal spiral before beginning to climb. Whoever had followed the houseman had either come directly after him from the hospital, or taken this route up from the road. This way, Resnick reasoned, pausing as his head came level with the glass above. Less likely to create suspicion, loitering about; easier to wait for your victim, pick him out.

The door at the top could have been locked, likely would have been if someone had not removed the bolt. Wonder, thought Resnick, exactly when that was done.

He pushed the door open and stepped through, turning left so that the hospital lay behind him, the bridge stretching out ahead. The occasional vehicle now, headlights sliding down the glass panels as they sped along the ring road, north or south. Resnick stood quite still, listening to the muted thrum of engines, concentrating on the double doors at the far end, the bridge spanning six lanes of highway, those doors a long way off.

Do people feel unhappy only during office hours? Black print on white paper, Blu-tacked to the wired glass. *Phone NITELINE 7 p. m. to 8 a.m.* Resnick tried to imagine being trapped in there, terrified, desperate to escape. He began to walk, slowly, towards the other side, the smell of rubber clearer with every step.

Whoever had seen Fletcher, followed him, what had determined his choice? Being there, now, the middle of the night, Resnick found it difficult to believe in a chance attack. Whoever had stalked the exhausted houseman almost the length of the bridge had done so for a reason. Resnick needed to believe it had been personal. He hesitated for a moment, staring down. He had to believe that, cling to it, knowing that if it were not true, there was somebody still out there, somewhere in the city, who had wreaked terrible havoc on Tim Fletcher's body for reasons that only a psychologist might ever understand. And who might do the same again.

City Life, read the poster facing Resnick as he went through the double doors. A bicycle had been left chained to the railings on the broad platform, two-thirds of the way down the steps. The air that touched Resnick's hands and face was surprisingly cold, driving up from the flyover. Something caught his attention, low by the wall of the first building and he brought up the torch.

It was only boxes, crammed with computer printouts: metallurgy, something close. Resnick switched off the torch and stood there, feeling the adrenalin in his body. Seek and you shall find. He crossed back over the ring road, stepping easily over the metal safety barriers at the centre.

Sitting in the car, he dribbled the last of the coffee into the plastic cup. There had been no mistaking his ex-wife's voice on the phone, nor, in those few not-quite-coherent sentences, the mixture of resentment and pleading he had thought forgotten.

Eleven

He had the kind of profile that could have been selling aftershave; thick hair, naturally curly and dark, a hunk wearing a black vest and loose-fitting sweatpants with a draw-string waist. He was wearing a pair of running shoes that had cost him close to eighty pounds, but that didn't mean he was running. He had walked down the street and now he stood outside Number 27 and rang the bell. When nothing seemed to happen, he hit the door with the flat of his hand, enough to make it shake. Pushing back the letter flap, Ian Carew called Karen's name.

A couple of minutes and he saw her through the couple of inches of door: salmon socks, double-knit and large and folding loosely back down her calves; hem of a white T-shirt bouncing as she came down the stairs, enough to give him a glimpse of expensive underwear, beige lace and broderie anglaise. There was a large Snoopy in relief on the front of the shirt. Carew let the flap snap into place and stood back.

Not far.

'What . . . ?'

He stepped in without speaking, anger in his face, forcing her back along the threadbare carpet at the other side of the mat.

She looked at him and shook her head and for a moment he thought she was going to bite down into her lower lip, like a child. Her hair was tied back in a loose pony tail and there was sleep in the corner of her eyes.

A woman walked past on the opposite side of the street,

Asian, wearing a purple and gold sari and pushing a pram, twins. Karen didn't think she'd ever noticed Asian twins before.

Carew moved forward, blocking her view.

'Good at it, aren't you?'

'I don't understand.'

'Natural. Comes natural. Something mummy fed you along with the milk.'

'Now you're being stupid.'

'And don't do that!' His hand was on her face before she could move, fingers squeezing against the sides of her jaw, forcing her mouth slightly open so that she could no longer bite the soft flesh inside her lip.

'Lying,' he said. 'That's what you're good at. Lying. "No, Ian, there isn't anything wrong. I'm not seeing anybody else, of course I'm not seeing anybody else." Weeks until I found out.'

Karen turned her head aside, laughed dismissively. 'Is that what this is all about?'

'What do you think?'

'Tim.'

'Gets himself mugged and you send the police round after me.'

'Oh, Ian.'

'Oh, Ian, what?'

She didn't want this conversation, didn't want this to be happening. She might have guessed that cow of a police-woman would put two and two together and come up with the wrong answer. Probably she should have warned him, but she hadn't. Now he was there in the house, angry, and she didn't think she could make him leave against his will, not by herself. She didn't think there was anybody else in the house.

'Look,' Karen said, 'let me get dressed. It won't take a minute.'

Carew didn't move.

Shrugging, she turned and went back upstairs, conscious that he was following her, looking at her legs.

'Mind the . . .'

'I remember.'

The room was much as he'd remembered it as well, clutter and last night's cigarette smoke. It had almost been enough to put him off her, the way, after a meal, after the cinema, after sex, she would automatically light up. Cheap. Expensive to look at but cheap underneath. He watched as she pulled on a pair of faded blue jeans and exchanged her socks for a pair of sports shoes, white with a pink trim.

She picked up the kettle. 'Tea?'

'When did I ever drink tea in the mornings?'

Karen spooned instant coffee into mugs, relieved that he seemed to have calmed down, feeling safer now that he was almost friendly, wanting to keep him that way, only not too much. Carew watched her as the water boiled, lounging with one of his bare elbows against the wall, posing.

'I should be really pissed off with you,' he said, as she spooned sugar into her own mug, ready.

'You mean you're not?'

'I ought to be.' Not leaning any more now, standing close as she lifted the kettle, almost touching her, touching her. 'Desperate without you, that what you reckoned? Thought of someone else in there with you, in bed, picture of it driving me insane?' His knee was resting against the back of her thigh, knuckles sliding gently up and down her arm.

Karen moved away, turning back towards him at arm's length, offering him the coffee.

'Thanks,' smiling through the faintest shimmer of steam.

Smug bastard! Karen thought. 'It was the police who asked me about you,' she said. 'I didn't mention your name.'

'I have been thinking about you, you know.'

68

'I doubt it.'

'It's true.'

'It's because you're here. If you weren't here, you'd be thinking about running, getting drunk, lectures, somebody else.'

'Well,' he said, reaching for her, hands up under the sleeves of her T-shirt, alternately pushing and stroking, someone who read an article on massage once but became distracted midway through the third paragraph. 'Well, I'm here now.'

Somebody along the street shouted at a dog, a cat or a child and slammed their back door so forcefully that Karen's window, despite folds of yellowing newspaper, rattled in its frame.

'Look,' said Karen, pushing his hands away, moving across the narrow room, picking up things and putting them down, trying to seem businesslike, 'I'm sorry about the police. Really. But now I've got to go. I'm already late for a lecture.'

'What?'

Hand on hip, she looked at him. Unmade, the bed was between them, a tatty stuffed animal poking out from beneath the rumpled duvet.

'What lecture?'

'It doesn't matter.'

'Then don't go.'

'I mean it doesn't matter to you, what does it matter, what bloody lecture I have to go to?'

'Hey, Karen. Calm down.' Oh, God! Trying the smile, giving his teeth their best shot. Don't bother! She opened the door to the room and left it open, wide to the stairs.

He didn't move.

Neither of them moved.

Karen prayed for the communal phone to ring, someone to come to the door, postman, milkman, double-glazing salesman, anyone, one of her fellow-tenants to return. She considered leaving him there and taking off down the stairs, but knew he would come after her and catch her, haul her back before throwing her down on the bed. It had happened like that several times before but then it had been different, she had enjoyed it, they'd been going together.

'What I can't understand,' Carew said, 'is why you'd prefer someone like that anyway.'

'Someone like what?' Karen said, knowing as soon as the words were out of her mouth that she shouldn't.

'Oh, you know . . .' He gestured with his hands. 'Small.'

Karen shook her head. 'You don't know the first thing about him.'

'I've seen him in the hospital. Scurrying around with those headphones on, like whatever, the white mouse, white rabbit.' He started around the bed. 'What's he listening to all the time anyway? Special little tapes you make for him?' He patted the duvet, patted the mattress, caught hold of the toy animal and tossed it to the floor. 'Little fantasies. Used to be good at those, I remember. Train carriage fantasy. Swimming pool fantasy.' Close again, voice low in his throat and that look in his eyes: she knew that look. 'Burglar fantasies.'

Karen turned and ran, swung herself round by the banister rail and jumped the first four steps, stumbled the rest. He caught hold of her before she reached the bottom, hip thrust into her side, a hand fast in her hair.

'All right, Karen,' he said, 'just like the old days. Like it used to be.'

'Someone with something against him, this Fletcher? That what you think, Charlie? Someone with a grudge?'

Resnick nodded.

'Professional or personal?'

'I don't know, sir.'

'But if you had to guess.'

'Fletcher's at the bottom of the heap. Starting out. I

shouldn't have thought he'd have stepped on the wrong toes, become involved in rivalries ... not enough to warrant this.'

'Personal, then?'

Again, Resnick nodded.

'This ...' Skelton glanced at the notes before him. '... Carew.'

'Claims to have been at the Irish Centre ...'

'Doesn't sound Irish.'

'He's not, sir. Claims he was there till one-thirty, quarter to two. Back home quarter past. Straight off to sleep.'

'Fletcher was attacked when?'

'Went off duty a few minutes after two. Staff nurse in charge of the ward where Fletcher was working is pretty certain of that. Quick trip to the Gents, find his coat, he'd be on the bridge in five minutes, ten at the outside. Anxious to get away, see his girlfriend.'

'That time of the morning?'

'Promised to wait up for him. Fletcher'd been talking to the staff nurse about it, earlier.'

'And the girlfriend, she found him?'

'Yes, sir.'

'How old?'

'Nineteen.'

Skelton's eyes flicked in the direction of the framed photographs, his daughter Kate. 'Carew alibied for the time he was at this ...'

'Irish Centre.'

'That's it.'

'Went on his own, left the same way. Claims to have seen several people there he knows.'

'Checked out?'

'Doesn't know all of them by name, not surname, anyway. We've spoken to two of the rest.'

'And?'

'One, another medical student, thinks he may have seen

71

Carew there, but he isn't positive. Place gets packed after eleven-thirty, twelve, and it isn't what you'd call well lit. The other one, however, postgraduate student in psychology, she's definite. Didn't see him all evening.'

There was a knock at the superintendent's door, discreet, and Skelton ignored it.

'You bringing him in?' Skelton asked.

'Thought we should give it a little time, finish checking him out,' said Resnick. 'Haul him in too soon, we might end up having to let him go.'

'No chance he's going to do a runner?'

Resnick shook his head. 'Naylor's down there, keeping an eye. Anything out of the usual, he'll stop him.'

Skelton inclined his head upwards, pressed the tips of his fingers together, outsides of the index fingers resting against the centre of his upper lip. There was a time, Resnick remembered, when the super used to have a neat little moustache.

'Keep me informed, Charlie.'

'Yes, sir.'

When Resnick was almost at the door, Skelton spoke again. 'Your eyes, Charlie, looking tired. Should try for a few early nights.' Resnick turned and looked at him. 'Single man your age, shouldn't be too difficult.'

Resnick liked to let Lynn Kellogg drive: it enabled him to set aside any charges of being hierarchical or chauvinist in one fell swoop and besides, it gave him time to think. Ian Carew was living with three other medical students in a house in Lenton, easy walking distance from the medical school, the hospital, the bridge. Naylor was sitting in a Ford Fiesta just around the corner from the Boulevard, there at the end of a short street of Victorian houses, the last on the right being Carew's. Lynn pulled up in front of him and Naylor got out of his car and walked towards theirs. He looked about as happy as he usually did, these days.

'Went out almost two hours ago, sir. Not been back since.'

Resnick glared.

'Had his running gear on, I thought, you know, just off for a jog. Couldn't exactly start chasing after him, sir. Not like this. Besides, I thought he'd be back in a bit. Shower and that. Sir.'

'Perhaps he's gone for a long run, sir,' suggested Lynn.

'Half-marathon, you mean?'

'Possible, sir.'

Resnick looked across at her. 'Any other ideas?'

After a moment, she said, 'Yes, sir. I might have.'

Resnick nodded. 'Good.' To Naylor he said, 'Hang on here, in case he comes back.'

Naylor was climbing forlornly back into the Fiesta as Lynn Kellogg was signalling left, filtering into the stream of traffic heading south along the Boulevard.

Carew had finally fallen asleep and Karen had lain underneath him, pinioned by his heavy leg, an arm, settling herself, moving as slowly as she could across the mattress; the last thing she wanted to do was to wake him. She was just sliding her arm free when the doorbell rang. Carew stirred and she pulled herself clear and hurried from the room, closing the door behind her, but not locking it.

There were two people at the door, man and a woman, and she wondered if they were Jehovah's Witnesses, travelling in pairs; then she recognized the policewoman from the previous day.

'Detective Inspector Resnick,' said the man, showing her his card.

'Hello, Karen,' said Lynn, no mistaking the way she was staring at her, at her face.

Karen touched high on her left cheek and winced; she couldn't see the bruising, only imagine it. Her mouth was swollen and now that she thought about it, she realized it felt numb. The Snoopy T-shirt was torn at one shoulder.

'Can we come in?' Lynn asked, Karen moving back from the door to allow them, Lynn going in first, Resnick, tall, bulky, careful to keep well behind her.

The door to Karen's room opened and closed and all three of them turned to face the stairs. Carew had pulled on his sweatpants and stood there barefooted, not quite focusing, someone who has just woken from a deep sleep.

'This is Ian,' Karen said, pointing, pointing him out to Lynn in particular. 'This is Ian Carew.'

Twelve

They made a disparate couple, sitting there, mid-morning, in the front of Resnick's car, not looking at each other, looking out. Resnick's jacket had become hunched up at the collar when he sat, the knot of his tie had gradually twisted as the day had worn on and the top button of his once-white shirt was either missing or undone. Alongside him, Ian Carew was showing good posture, smooth shoulders highlighted against the broad black straps of his vest. For minutes at a time, his expression wouldn't change. It was only his fingers that fidgeted slightly, smoothing the grey material of his sweatpants, toying with the slack string bow at the waist, nails pushing hard at the soft skin inside the first digits of each hand.

Resnick made himself wait, the watch on his left wrist just visible below his frayed cuff. Just because Carew had chosen not to go running, didn't mean he shouldn't sweat.

It was Lynn Kellogg who made the tea, straight in the mug, lifting the bag clear with a spoon before setting the mug into Karen's hands. Karen was sitting on the very edge of the bed, dangerously close to overbalancing. Lynn made tea for herself and sat carefully alongside her.

'If you want to talk about it,' Lynn said.

Karen brought the mug to her mouth but didn't drink.

'What happened,' Lynn continued.

The numbness in Karen's bottom lip caused her to misjudge and hot tea splashed on her bare leg, the white

75

and black rug. Lynn reached over and steadied the girl's hands with her own.

'Tell me,' she said, before letting go.

Instead Karen began to cry and Lynn took the tea away from her, resting it on the floor, holding her then, Karen's face warm on Lynn's white blouse, sleek black hair caught across the corners of Lynn's mouth.

'It's all right,' Lynn whispered. 'It's all right,' down into her hair, Karen's sobs growing and part of Lynn thinking how strange, to be sitting there on that strange bed, holding that hurt and beautiful girl.

'It's all right.'

Karen stopped crying almost as abruptly as she had begun. She wiped the hair from her face, careful round her cheekbone where the bruising was beginning to deepen, change colour.

'He didn't do it,' Karen said. 'He couldn't.'

'Didn't do what?'

'Tim. The other night. He wouldn't do that.'

'That's not what I'm concerned about,' Lynn said. 'Not now.'

Karen reached towards the mug of tea but changed her mind. Head up again, close to Lynn, less than a foot away, she bit down gently into her swollen lip.

'You've got to tell me what happened,' Lynn said.

Karen shook her head.

'Your face – how did that happen?'

'It doesn't matter.'

'It does. He hit you. Carew, he hit you, didn't he?'

'He didn't mean it.'

Lynn looked at where the flawless skin was hardening yellow, shading into purple: the cut mouth. 'Are you saying all that was an accident?'

'He didn't mean to hurt me.'

'No?' said Lynn. 'What did he mean to do?'

76

A few occasions, when Resnick had been young enough to think there were things you did because you should, because they would do you good, he had been to orchestral concerts, the Philharmonia, the Hallé. The Albert Hall it had been then, dodgy acoustics and a balcony that ran round three sides, red seats in fading plush that played havoc with your knees, a listed organ only heard by the Methodists on Sundays. It had taken him four or five visits and a little more self-confidence to admit that once the overture was over and the second movement of the concerto was underway, he was bored. Shitless. The ones who thought they understood jazz were the worst: Gershwin, Milhaud, Dvořák – that dreadful *From the New World*, its ponderous rhythms and emasculation of black gospel.

He had been reminded, on those rare, early visits, of Friday evenings when he was a kid, Sunday afternoons. TV off – Had they had a television then? He wasn't sure – radio on. 'For God's sake,' his father would say, 'sit still and stop the endless fidgeting.' George Melachrino, Semprini: old ones, new ones, loved ones, neglected ones. His mother, who sang around the house each and every day, old songs from her own country, hers and his father's, songs she had herself learned as a child, needed no warnings. In this, it seemed now to Resnick, as in all other things, she sensed what his father required of her and obeyed. She never sang in his presence. Listening to the radio or gramophone, she would darn socks and stockings, rarely speak. It was his father who switched on the set, controlled the volume, lowered the needle into place. Black shellacked 78s. *The Warsaw Concerto*, *Cornish Rhapsody*, Tchaikovsky's Piano Concerto No. 1, only the first movement. His father would tilt his head towards the ceiling, close his eyes. During *The Warsaw Concerto* his mother would cry, stifling the tears with her embroidered handkerchief, lest she be dismissed from the room.

To Resnick, all three pieces sounded alike; his mind would dovetail between football and sex, Notts County and Denise Crampton's knickers. 'What is the matter with you?' his father would demand. 'All that stupid wriggling.' His fellow patrons had shot him similar looks on those evenings when he had tried in vain to find a more comfortable position for his legs and struggled to be more sympathetic to composers who thought that jazz was something you could play from written scores with banks of musicians, the whole enterprise weighed down by such seriousness of purpose that it suffered from elephantiasis of the spirit.

Older, a man, though younger than now, his thoughts had skittered and soared and settled, finally, on those perennial mysteries, soccer and sex: when County got around to scoring would the earth move?

Sitting there in that side road beside Ian Carew, he thought about Ed Silver, slumped somewhere over an empty bottle of cider or wine, about where Carew had been between one forty-five and two-fifteen two nights ago; he wondered what his wife might have said into the telephone had he allowed her the time.

'Are you charging me?' Carew asked.

Resnick turned to face him. 'What with?'

'He had sex with you, didn't he?'

'What?'

'Did he have sex with you? Ian? Carew?'

'So what if he did?'

'Intercourse?'

'Yes.'

'This morning?'

'Yes.'

'Did you want him to?'

'Look, what difference . . . ?

'Did you want him to have sex, make love to you?'

78

'What?'

'Did you want it to happen?'

'No.'

'Did you tell him that?'

'That I didn't want him?'

'Yes.'

'Yes.'

'What did he say?'

'He laughed.'

'That was all?'

'He said he didn't believe me.'

'And?'

'Said I was dying for it.'

'And?'

'And he hit me.'

'He forced you.'

'He grabbed me on the stairs . . .'

'On the stairs?'

'I was trying to run away, I don't know, into the street. He caught hold of me and dragged me back here and dumped me on the bed.'

'You were still struggling?'

'I was screaming. I kicked him. As hard as I could, I kicked him.'

'What did he do?'

'Hit me again.'

'And then?'

'He had sex with me.'

'He forced you.'

'Yes.'

'He raped you.'

She started to cry again, soundlessly this time, her body still and not shaking; Lynn leaned over to comfort her but Karen shook her away. After several moments, Lynn stood up and went to the window. A large cat, pale ginger, sat perched on a fence post, catching the autumn sun where it fell between the houses.

She knelt in front of Karen and held her hand, both her hands. She said, 'You'll have to come to the station, see a doctor.'

Karen's eyelids, violet-veined, trembled. 'Have to?'

'Please,' Lynn said. 'Please.'

'You've got an alibi,' Resnick was saying, 'like a string vest.'

'I don't need an alibi,' said Carew. What the hell did he think he was doing, bastard, breathing garlic all over him!

'That's good to hear, if a little inaccurate.'

'And if you intend to keep me here any longer, I insist on seeing a solicitor.' Pompous now, Resnick thought. Practising his bedside manner. Breeding coming out of him under stress. Likely he was Hampshire or Surrey; looks like those, he didn't come from Bolsover.

'D'you know any solicitors?'

'My family does.'

'I'll bet they do.'

Carew sneered. 'What's that supposed to mean?'

'Probably not a lot.'

The sneer grew into a snort and Resnick's irrational impulse to punch Carew in the mouth was frustrated by Lynn Kellogg's tap at the car window. Resnick wound it down, responding to Lynn's expression by getting out on to the pavement. Behind her, the door to the house was open. Here and there, up and down the street, neighbours were beginning to take an interest.

Resnick listened and when he glanced round at the car, Carew had shifted over in his seat and was checking his hair in the rearview mirror. Resnick radioed for Naylor to collect Lynn and the girl, take them to the station. 'I'll go on ahead,' he said. 'With him. Make sure they're ready for you.'

Lynn was staring at Ian Carew, who had resumed his former position and was staring straight ahead. A woman came out of one of the houses opposite, dyed hair, man's overcoat open over shirt and jeans. Carew's eyes followed her automatically, mouth ready to smile.

'How's the girl?' Resnick asked.

Lynn shook her head. 'As good as can be expected. Better, probably.'

Resnick nodded and climbed back into the car.

'What now?' said Carew, midway between bored and angry.

Without answering, Resnick fired the engine, slipped the car into gear, executed a three-point turn and headed back towards the centre of the city.

Thirteen

Ever since the problems with his daughter had come to a particularly nasty head, Skelton had abandoned his early morning runs. Now he ran most lunchtimes instead. In the mornings he would try and spend time with Kate, toying with a slice of toast as, absent-mindedly, she spooned her way through a morass of Weetabix and Shreddies, warm milk soaking in until what was left resembled Trent sludge. Skelton asked about her school work, teachers, school friends, anything but what he wanted most to know – where had she been the evening before, who had she been with? He sat and listened to her halting, half-hearted replies, scraping Flora across his toast and wondering how much she drank, if she were back on drugs? Sixteen and a half: what were the chances that she was still a virgin?

Skelton was on his way out of the station as Resnick drew up, opening the door so that Carew could get out. Two men in running gear and Resnick between them with trousers that were too loose above the ankles, too tight at the hips, a jacket on which he could do up one button with ease but rarely two. Moments like this could induce paranoia: the certainty that at some point of each day, at some time within the twenty-four hours, everyone else goes running, jogs, works out, lifts weights. Everyone.

'Charlie.' Skelton beckoned him to one side. 'This Carew?'

'Yes, sir.'

'You've not charged him?'

'Here of his own volition, sir. Happy to answer any questions that might help us with our inquiries.'

Skelton glanced over at Carew. 'Happy?'

Resnick shook his head. 'Cocky enough.'

'Don't blow it, Charlie. Technicalities.'

Resnick changed position, shifting so that more of his back was towards Carew. 'Just might be something else, sir. Went to the girl's place this morning, pushed his way in, could be he raped her.'

Skelton's face was stone.

'Lynn's with the girl now, she's agreed to be examined. Take it from there.'

'Ex-boyfriend, isn't he?'

Resnick nodded.

'Difficult. Cases like that. Difficult to prove.'

Resnick turned towards Carew, motioned for him to go up the steps to the station.

'I'll not be gone long,' said Skelton, moving around on the spot, warming up. 'Make it a short one today.'

Oh, good, thought Resnick, following Carew towards the doors, just a quick four miles. Must remember when I get back tonight, fit in a few push-ups while I'm waiting for the omelette to cook.

A youth with gelled green hair and a gold ring through his left nostril was sitting opposite the inquiry window, dribbling blood and snot into his hands. At the window a middle-aged man in a suit, navy blue pinstripe, was explaining to the officer on duty exactly where he had left his car, exactly why he'd been stupid enough to leave his briefcase on the back seat. Inside the next set of doors, a uniformed constable was squatting down beside a girl of nine or ten, trying to get her to spell out her address.

The custody sergeant was in a heated argument with one of the detainees about the exact dimensions of the man's cell and whether or not they contravened the Geneva

Convention. Somebody was crying. Somebody else was singing the *Red Flag*. Not, Resnick assumed, someone on the Force. 'You wouldn't fucking believe it,' Mark Divine was saying on his way downstairs. 'The whole place covered in brown sauce. Not just the kitchen, the living room, everywhere. Before they'd left they'd emptied half-a-dozen tins of baked beans into the bath.' The young DC he was with didn't know whether to be sceptical or impressed. 'Packet soup in one of them things you sit on.'

'The toilet?' suggested the DC.

'No! One of those women things with taps on.'

'A bidet,' said Resnick, going past.

'Probably. Yes, sir. Thanks.'

'Up there,' Resnick said to Carew, pointing ahead.

'What the fuck they want one of those for?' Divine said to the DC as they left. 'Not as if they haven't got a bath.'

'We can talk in here,' said Resnick, showing Carew into his office and offering him a chair. 'Tea? Coffee?'

Carew shook his head. 'I hope this isn't going to take long.'

'Shouldn't think so,' said Resnick. 'If you hang on, I'll organize some tea for myself.'

He closed the door on Carew and moved out of sight, picking up the nearest unused phone and dialling the number of the woman officer detailed to deal with cases of reported rape.

Maureen Madden had passed her sergeant's exam almost a year to the day before she got her stripes. Twenty-nine and married, wanting to have a baby, not exactly eager for it, but suspecting, half-knowing that the further she turned past thirty, the more pressing that need would become. Let me get my promotion, she'd kept telling her husband, get a year in the job behind me, then we'll see. They kept offering her things she didn't want – traffic, community liaison. Then the rape suite. Women's things. Soft issues.

The times she'd arrived at a pub, fight going down, bottles flying, you hang on here, her male colleagues had said, no sense you going in there, you wait outside.

As if she were afraid. As if she couldn't handle herself.

She had gone in on her own once, up on the Alfreton Road, just short of closing, case of having to. Bloke had come out on his hands and knees, most of one ear left behind inside. She'd stepped in between three of these fellers squaring up, two on to one, broken pint glasses in their hands. If she'd been a man they'd have set on her, the lot of them, she was certain. As it was, they'd grinned like great kids, there'd been a lot of backslapping and some language, and they'd helped the injured man look for his ear while Maureen had radioed for an ambulance.

She knew she'd been lucky.

Until the night she'd run across to the Asian shop, been watching a video with her husband and got this sudden craving for custard. Tinned custard. Two youths had grabbed her from behind and had her on the floor in seconds, right there on the pavement. Not yet ten-thirty. She'd struggled and fought, kicked and screamed, still they'd torn her tights, kicked her face, left, one of them, a bruise the size of a fist below her breast. One white, one black, Maureen had been unable to identify them, they had never been caught.

All right, Maureen had said, I'll run the rape suite. All right.

'Hello,' she said to Karen when Lynn Kellogg brought her in. 'I'm Maureen. Maureen Madden. You must be Karen. Come over here and have a seat. The doctor won't be long.'

'I can leave any time I choose?' Carew asked, seeking confirmation.

'Absolutely,' Resnick said.

'Get up and walk out of your office?'

Resnick nodded.

'Right out of the station and no one will lift a finger to try and stop me?'

'Not a finger.'

'Right,' Carew said, making no attempt to move.

'Now,' said the doctor, adjusting her glasses, 'just one more swab and we're through.'

'I'd have thought,' Resnick said, 'that might be a bit of an understatement, pretty pissed off. Dropping you like that.'

Carew shrugged well-rounded shoulders. 'Happens, doesn't it?'

'Does it?'

'Don't tell me it's never happened to you.'

Resnick leaned sideways a little in his chair, made no reply.

'Happily married then, are we?' grinned Carew.

Cocky little shit! thought Resnick. Getting more sure of himself by the minute. 'Not any more,' he said. 'As it happens.'

'Then you must know what I mean,' Carew said. 'Unless it was you that left her.'

What is it about you, Carew, Resnick thought, makes me want to behave the way all those kids selling *Socialist Worker* outside Marks imagine I behave all the time?

'What did you want to do to him?' Carew asked, reading Resnick's silence correctly.

Resnick saw him, Elaine's estate agent, walking away from that empty house where he and Elaine had just made love, the suit, the Volvo and the keys. 'Hit him,' Resnick said.

'And did you?'

'No.'

'Not ever?'

'Never.'

Carew smiled. 'I bet you wish you had.'

Resnick smiled back. 'Satisfying, is it?'

Ian Carew's smile faltered.

Resnick leaned his weight in the opposite direction. His stomach made a low, groaning noise and he remembered he had had nothing for lunch.

'And Karen?'

'What about her?'

'You must have felt like hitting her. Lying. Seeing this man behind your back.'

Carew shook his head. 'I don't think you understand, inspector.'

'What's that?'

'I don't hit women.'

Maureen Madden was sitting to one side of Karen, Lynn Kellogg to the other. Both women were looking at her and Karen was looking at the pattern in the carpet, noticing a scattering of small burn marks. Cigarettes, she thought. She had that minute stubbed one out herself in the ashtray; now she lit another, waited till the first swathes of light grey smoke were rising to the ceiling. 'I'm not going to press charges,' she said.

Lynn and Maureen Madden exchanged glances over her head.

'We'll help you,' Maureen said gently. 'Every step of the way.'

'I'm sure,' Karen said.

'What's worrying you?' Maureen asked. 'Is it the court, giving evidence?'

Karen shook her head.

'Ian,' suggested Lynn, 'are you frightened he might come after you?'

'I'm not frightened.'

'Then what is it?'

Smoke veiled the brightness of her eyes. 'It's over. It's happened. That's an end to it.'

'No,' Lynn said too sharply, a warning look from Maureen.

'You agreed to come in,' Maureen reminded her.

'I was upset. I wasn't thinking.'

'Look at your face,' said Lynn.

'It's not only your face,' said Maureen. 'Remember what he did.'

'Oh,' said Karen, turning for the first time towards her, 'you don't have to worry about that. I was the one it happened to.'

'Then stop it happening again.'

'How do I do that?'

'Help us put him away.'

Karen lowered her eyes, shook her head.

'If he gets away with this . . .' Lynn began.

'Then don't let him.'

'Without you, without your evidence,' said Maureen, 'we wouldn't stand a chance. It probably wouldn't even come to court.'

'He'll get off scot-free,' Lynn said. 'He can do it again.'

'Think of other women,' said Maureen.

Karen squashed her cigarette into the ashtray as she got to her feet. 'You! You think of other bloody women. It's your job, not mine.' She reached past the two police officers for her coat. The corners of her eyes were red and blurred with tears.

Lynn moved towards the door, as if to prevent Karen leaving, but Maureen Madden shook her head. 'If you'll wait a few minutes,' Maureen said, 'I'll arrange for you to be driven back.'

'It doesn't matter.'

'I'll take you back,' said Lynn.

'I'll walk.'

Thanks, Lynn thought. Thanks for that. Thanks a whole lot! She opened the door and stood aside.

Resnick had the phone in his hand at the first ring. He listened and set the receiver back down, standing up. 'Excuse me a minute,' he said to Carew. 'Something's come up.'

'I'll go,' Carew said, beginning to stand himself.

'No,' said Resnick. 'Wait. Five minutes, that's all I'll be. At most.'

Ian Carew waited until Resnick had left the office before sitting back down. Patel was sitting near one of the windows in the CID room, typing up his report. 'If he tries to leave,' Resnick said, nodding his head back towards his office door, 'stall him.'

'I'll try, sir.'

'Do better than that.' He glanced down at what Patel was typing, trying to read it upside down. 'Anywhere with the clothing thing?'

'No, sir.'

Resnick hurried from the room. Lynn Kellogg and Maureen Madden were already in the superintendent's office and the expressions on all of their faces told Resnick what he didn't want to know.

'No chance she'll change her mind?' asked Resnick.

'She might,' said Lynn. 'A couple of hours later she'll have changed it back again.'

'How about the other business?' asked Skelton. 'It is the more serious charge.' He carried on, intercepting Maureen Madden's fierce look and ignoring it. 'GBH at least, attempted murder.'

'More serious than rape, sir?' said Maureen regardless.

'No time to ride the hobby horse,' said Skelton sharply. 'I treat rape every bit as seriously as you do.'

'Really, sir?'

'Well, Charlie?' Skelton said.

'Possible motivation, sir. Dodgy alibi. Now we know he's capable of violence. But, no, nothing to link him in directly. Not as yet.'

'So we let him go.'

'Sir,' said Lynn, cheeks flushed, 'he beat up that girl and raped her.'

'Who says? I mean, according to which account?'

'The medical evidence . . .' Maureen Madden began.

'Intercourse had taken place, cuts and bruising to the face and body – without the girl's sworn word, what does that prove? No worse than what goes on between couples all over the city every Saturday night. Consenting adults. What's to prevent him getting up and saying, well, it was how she liked it? Hard and rough.'

'Jesus!' Maureen Madden breathed quietly.

Lynn Kellogg stared at the floor.

'We can warn him,' Skelton continued. 'Even though she won't press charges, we can officially warn him, let him know that warning will be registered, documented. On that matter, that's all we can do and it will be done. For the rest – watch and wait.'

There was only the flat click of the wall clock, the sounds of four people breathing. Outside, along the corridor, officers and clerical staff walking, talking, getting about their business. The greedy persistence of telephones, like starlings.

'All right, Lynn?' Skelton said. 'Maureen?'

'Yes, sir.' Overlapping, subdued.

'All right, Charlie?'

'Yes, sir.'

Resnick's office was empty. Anxiety hovered around Patel's dark eyes. 'He walked out, sir. Insisted upon leaving. He said he had the right. I didn't think I could try and prevent him.'

'Don't worry,' Resnick said. 'Dig out Naylor and go and

pick him up again. No charge, no caution, get him back here just the same.'

'Yes, sir.'

Resnick's stomach gave another empty lurch. Time enough to cross to the island at the middle of the circus, have them make up a couple of sandwiches, smoked ham and Emmental, breast of turkey with wholegrain mustard, pickled cucumber and mayonnaise. He would have a quiet word with Lynn on his way out, perhaps she'd like to be present while he was giving Carew a good bollocking.

Fourteen

When Karl Dougherty had told his mother he was going to be a nurse, she had pointed through the kitchen window at the way the chrysanthemums were leaning over and blamed the rain. When he had told his father, the look in the older man's eyes had made it clear he thought his son was telling him he was gay. Not that Dougherty would have called it that: nancy boy, shirt-lifter, plain old-fashioned poof – those were the expressions that would have come to mind.

'You can't,' his mother had said after the third time of telling.

'Why ever not?'

Karl watched as she placed six pounds of oranges on the Formica work top and began to slice them with a knife. The copper jam-pot she had bought at auction was waiting on the stove. Soon the kitchen would be studded with glass jars, scrubbed and recycled, labelled in her almost indecipherable hand. Quite frequently at breakfast one of the family had spooned gooseberry chutney on to their toast by mistake.

'Why can't I?'

'Because you've got a degree.' His mother had looked at him as if that were the most obvious reason in the world and she couldn't understand why he hadn't thought of it for himself.

He had shown her the letter, accepting him for a place at the Derbyshire Royal Infirmary as a student nurse.

'There you are,' she said. 'You're not a student. You're

a BA, a good upper second. They've got it wrong.' She smiled up from the last of the oranges. 'There's been a mistake.'

Karl had found his father in the cellar, planing a length of beech. 'We can't support you,' his father said. 'Not again. We've been through all that.'

'I shall be paid,' Karl explained. 'Not very much, but a wage.'

'And living? Where will you live?'

Karl looked at the woodworking tools, arranged on and around the shelves in neat order, each wiped and cleaned after use. 'There's a place in the nurses' home. If I want it.'

'Good.'

When Karl was at the steps, his father said, 'I never wanted you to go to that bloody university in the first place, you know.'

'I know.'

'Waste of bloody time and money.'

'Maybe.'

'And you know one thing – this'll do for your mother. She'll not begin to understand.'

A few nights later, Karl had been in his room to the rear of the upstairs, writing a letter. His father had come in with a half-bottle of Scotch and two glasses, tumblers that had been given away with so many gallons of petrol.

'Here,' sitting on the bottom of Karl's bed and handing him one of the glasses, pouring a generous measure into them both. He had seen his father drink bottled beer on Sunday afternoons, port and the occasional sherry at Christmas; he had never known him to drink whisky.

They sat there for close on three-quarters of an hour, drinking, never speaking. Finally, his father tipped what remained into Karl's glass and stood up to leave.

'Was there something you wanted to say to me?' his father asked.

Karl shook his head. 'I don't think so.'

'I thought there might have been something you wanted to tell me.'

'No.'

The incident was never referred to again by either of them, but for some time, whenever they met, Karl's father would avoid looking him in the eye.

There was scarcely a week went by during Karl's training, he didn't consider throwing it in. Neither was there a week when something took place – usually an interchange with one of the patients – which didn't confirm for him the rightness of his decision. For the first time since he could remember, his life had a purpose: he felt he was of use.

'This is my son, Karl,' his mother said, introducing him to friends when he made an unannounced visit home. 'He's training to be a doctor.'

'A nurse,' Karl corrected her.

She smiled at her guests. 'There's been a mistake.'

The evening after Karl received notification that he had qualified, he called his father and arranged to meet him for a drink. They went to a pub on the old road from Eastwood to Nottingham and sat with halves of bitter while youths in leather jackets played darts and Elvis on the juke box. 'You think I'm gay, don't you?' Karl asked. 'Homosexual.'

His father sucked in air and closed his eyes as if a heavy foot had been pressed down on his chest.

'Well, I'm not. I just don't like women very much. I mean, only as friends. Okay?'

When his father opened his eyes, Karl reached out a hand towards him and his father pulled his own hand, sharply, away.

After his registration, Karl did a couple of years of general nursing before specializing; he worked on a genito-urinary ward for three years, not bothering to tell either of his parents the day-to-day focus for his skills. He spent two years nursing in the States, Boston and San Francisco, well paid and, he felt, under-used. Patients paying for their private rooms thought it was okay to summon him to fetch their newspaper from across the room, reposition the TV set away from the sun. Before he could do as much as issue an aspirin or clip a toenail, he had to call a doctor and obtain permission.

Back in Britain, he clung to his short haircut and the habit of wearing coloured T-shirts under lightweight suits, at least until the weather beat him down. For months there was a touch of a transatlantic accent to his speech and he wore a watch on either wrist, one of them set to West Coast time. After two years of general surgical work, he was appointed senior staff nurse, with the expectation of being promoted to charge nurse within the next eighteen months.

Karl Dougherty had been a qualified nurse for nine years; aside from Christmas and his mother's birthday, he had not visited his parents more than half-a-dozen times in the last four. Soon after returning from the States, he had breezed in wearing an off-white suit, a short-sleeved green T-shirt with a breast pocket and yellow shoes. He had a box of Thornton's special assortment in one hand, a vast bouquet of flowers in his arms.

'Oh, no,' his mother had exclaimed. 'There's been a mistake.'

'Hello, Karl,' one of the patients called. 'How was your night off?'

'About as exciting as yours.'

'Hi, Karl,' said a nurse, swinging the bedpan she was carrying out of his path.

'Is that accidental,' said Karl, 'or are you just not pleased to see me?'

Karl liked to get on to the ward a little early, have a sniff round before handover, things he might notice and want to ask questions about that might otherwise go unremarked.

'Where's sister?' he asked.

A student nurse glanced up from the care plan she was adding to and pointed her Biro towards the closed door. 'Hasn't shown herself for the best part of an hour.'

Oh, God! thought Karl, moving on, in there wrestling with the menopause again!

He turned into the side ward and found Sarah Leonard sitting on Tim Fletcher's bed, holding his hand.

'This isn't what you think,' Sarah said.

'You mean you're not taking his pulse.'

'Absolutely not. This is therapy.'

Karl raised an eyebrow.

'Comfort and consolation,' Sarah smiled. 'Tim's feeling forlorn today. His girlfriend failed to pay him a visit.'

'There's a singularly ugly man with halitosis and very little bowel control, back down the ward; he hasn't had a visitor in three weeks. Perhaps you'd like to hold his hand as well.'

Sarah Leonard poked out her tongue and got to her feet. 'I'd better go, before Karl here asserts his authority.' She gave Fletcher a smile, Karl a toss of her head and hurried away.

'Impressive!'

Tim Fletcher nodded agreement.

'How are you feeling?' Karl asked. 'Apart from horny.'

'Sore.'

'No more than that?'

Fletcher shrugged. 'I'm okay.'

'You don't want anything for the pain?'

'Thanks. I'll be all right.'

Karl patted his leg. 'I'll check with you later.'

Helen Minton came out of her office just ahead of Karl as he walked back down the ward, making a slight nod of acknowledgement in his direction and nothing more. Karl didn't think it was that she felt threatened by him, not that alone. She spent her days on duty as if everything around her might explode or evaporate unless she held it together by sheer force of will.

Poor woman! Karl thought. He had stumbled across her late one evening, standing with Bernard Salt beside the consultant's BMW. Whatever they had been talking about, Karl didn't think it was hospital business.

'Sister,' he said breezily, catching her up. 'Another fifteen minutes and you'll be finished. A free woman.'

The look she gave him was not brimming with gratitude.

Naylor and Patel had found Ian Carew sitting in the small yard at the back of his rented house, drinking pineapple juice and reading about ventricular tumours. For several moments, it seemed as if he might tell the two plain-clothes men to go and play with themselves; he might even have been tempted to take a swing at them, Naylor in particular. But then he grunted something about being left in peace, something else about people who could have been making better use of time and resources, grabbed an Aran sweater and followed them along the narrow alley at the side of the house.

'I don't have to put up with this,' Carew said as soon as he was in Resnick's office. 'This is harassment.'

Resnick was careful to keep his hands down by his sides. 'Coming from someone who not so many hours ago beat up a young woman in her own home and . . .'

'That's a lie!'

'. . . and forced her to have sex with him . . .'

'You've got no right . . .'

'. . . that comes over as a bit rich.'

'You can't *say* that.'

'What?'

Carew looked at the inspector, standing behind his desk, at Lynn Kellogg, in a white blouse and a mid-length pleated skirt standing off to his right. 'I want a solicitor,' Carew said. 'Now. Before I say another word.'

'You don't have to say anything,' Resnick said. 'And you don't need a solicitor. Just listen.'

Carew opened his mouth to say something more but thought better of it.

'In accordance with Home Office instructions,' said Resnick, 'I am issuing you with a warning about your future behaviour, in so far as it concerns Karen Archer. Although, up to the present, she has declined to press charges, there is little doubt from what she has alleged, backed up by medical examination of her injuries, that you have been guilty of an assault upon her person.'

'What assault?'

'Shut it!'

'What . . . ?'

'Shut it and listen!'

Carew retreated the half-step he had taken towards Resnick's desk.

'That girl,' said Resnick, 'was elbowed in the face, she was punched in the mouth, she was struck in the body. You're a big man, you're strong and my guess is you're used to having your own way.'

'That's bullshit!'

Resnick was around the desk more quickly than either Lynn or Carew would have given him credit. He didn't stop until his chest was all but touching Carew's, face almost as close as it could be.

'We've got photographs of her injuries, Polaroids of the bruises and they're going on file. Your file. I hope for your sake I never have to refer to them again. Stay away from her, that's my advice. A wide berth. She doesn't want anything to do with you. That's over. Leave it.'

Resnick moved his head aside, rapidly swung it back, so that Carew blinked. 'Word you've got to learn: no. Doesn't mean, yes. Doesn't mean, maybe. Girlfriend, wife, whatever. No means no. Understand it any other way and you're for it.'

Resnick stepped back: not far. He stared at Carew for ten seconds more. 'Now get out,' he said quietly.

Carew had to walk around Resnick to get to the door, which he left open behind him, anxious to leave the building as fast as he could. Lynn Kellogg wanted to go over to her inspector and say well done, she wanted to give him a hug; she settled for offering him a cup of tea.

Before Resnick could accept or decline, his phone rang. 'Yes?'

'Someone down here asking for you, sir,' said the officer on duty. And then, before Resnick could ask further, 'Think it's personal, sir. Should I . . . ?'

'I'll be down,' said Resnick. 'The tea,' he said to Lynn. 'Some other time.'

All the way down the stairs, Resnick's insides danced themselves into a knot. He knew what he would see, when he pushed his way through into reception: Elaine standing there, that distraught expression on her face, impatient, *who do you think you are, keeping me waiting* – what was it? – *ten years?*

'Charlie!'

Ed Silver was sitting with his back to the wall, meagre grey hair resting below a poster asking for information about a thirteen-year-old girl, last seen in Louth three months ago. Something matted and dark clung to the front of his jacket.

'Charlie,' he repeated, rising unsteadily to his feet. 'Lost my glasses. Didn't know where you were.'

Resnick looked at his watch. 'Half an hour,' he said. 'Three-quarters at most. I'll take you home.'

Fifteen

'N'cha got no real food, Charlie?'

'Such as?'

'You know, bangers, bacon, nice pork chop.'

Resnick shook his head. 'I can fix you a sandwich.'

Ed Silver made a face and tried the refrigerator again, unable to believe his bad luck.

'How about an omelette?'

'All right,' Silver said grudgingly, and Resnick began to chop an onion up small, half a red pepper, a handful of French beans he'd braised a few days before in butter and garlic.

'Vegetarian now, are you?'

Another shake of the head. 'Just can't bring myself to buy meat. Not red meat. Not often. I think it's the smell.'

'That beer you got in there,' Silver asked, pointing back at the fridge. 'You keeping it for something special?'

Resnick opened his last two bottles of Czech Budweiser and lifted glasses down from the shelf. 'No,' Silver said, reaching across. 'Have mine as it comes. Won't do to get too used to creature comforts; never know when you might pitch me out on me arse.'

He wandered off into the living room and several minutes later, as the butter was beginning to bubble up round the edges of the pan, Resnick heard a few bars of off-centre piano and then, instantly recognizable, the sound of a trumpet, burnished, like brown paper crackling; the soloist stepping into the tune with short, soft steps, deceptive. Clifford Brown. The notes lengthening, sharp blue smoke, rising. The *Memorial* album. Resnick doubted if he had pulled the record from the shelf in eighteen months, yet he could picture its cover.

> *a photograph of a playground, a trumpet*
> *lying on a swing, over there*
> *the slides, the splintery line*
> *of benches, chaotic segments of*
> *chain link fence, hazy*
> *apartment buildings beyond.*
> *Perfect.*

He continued to listen, tilting the pan so that the egg mixture rolled round the curved sides and down, forking in the onion, seconds later the pepper and the beans. He left it on the flame long enough to cut slices of bread, dark rye, gave the pan a shake and folded the omelette in two. Before Brownie had finished 'Lover Come Back to Me', it would be ready.

'They're all dying, Charlie.'

'Who?'

'Every bugger!'

Resnick handed him a plate, set his own down on a copy of *Police Review*, went back for forks and black pepper, started the LP again at the first track.

'Know how old he was when he copped it?' Ed asked.

'Twenty-six?'

'Five. Twenty-five.'

Less than half your age, Ed, Resnick thought, and you're still going – in a manner of speaking.

'Nineteen,' Silver said, 'he was in a car crash nearly finished him. Almost a year in hospital. Enough to kill you in itself, way some of those butchers wade in when they've got you strapped down. Anyway . . .' He pushed a piece of omelette on to a corner of the bread and lifted it to his mouth. '. . . got over that, started playing again, made it big and *wham*! Another sodding road accident. Dead.'

'Mm,' said Resnick.

'Twenty-five.'

'Yes.'

'Poor bastard!'

'Amen.'

'Stockholm Sweetnin' ' became ' 'Scuse These Blues'. Resnick took the plates into the kitchen and dumped them in the sink. He thought the last thing he should do was let Ed Silver catch sight of his bottle of Lemon Grass vodka, but the last stray gleams of light were striking the room at just the right angle and, whatever the risks, it seemed the proper thing to do.

'Cheers,' said Resnick.

'To Brownie,' said Ed Silver.

'God bless.'

They drank a little and then they drank a little more. There was a moment when Ed Silver's wispy grey hair and scarred scalp were outlined against deep orange light. Resnick looked at Silver's knuckles, cracked and swollen, and wondered when those hands had last held a saxophone; he wanted to ask him if he thought he might ever play again. Of course, he didn't. They drank a little more. Dizzy sneaked out of the half-dark and lay across Silver's lap, sniffing from time to time at whatever was matted thick on his jacket.

'They're all dead, Charlie.'

'Who?'

'Clifford, Sandy, Pete, Lawrence, Vernon, Marshall, Tom. All the fucking Browns. Gone.'

Muted, but jaunty, Clifford Brown was playing 'Theme of No Repeat'.

There had to be better places to spend the evening, Millington was thinking, than a lay-by close to Burton-on-Trent. Heavy lorries yammering cross-country between Derby and West Bromwich, bits of lads in tuned-up Fiestas driving as if they were on Donnington race track. Three nights before, a truck loaded with cartons of Embassy, packets of twenty, had pulled in here so that the driver could rest. He had been hoping for a cup of tea, something warm to eat, but the man who ran the stall had closed early and gone home. The driver had stood by the field edge to take a leak and someone had hit him from behind with a wrench and taken his keys. When he came to, surprise, surprise, the truck was gone.

It had been found early the following morning, abandoned and empty, close to the motorway. The police also discovered the driver to have two previous convictions for theft and one, when he was a youngster, for TDA. Which didn't mean that he had whacked himself round the head, nor agreed beforehand that somebody else should do it, but it did mean officers were keeping a keen eye on who he contacted and watching for tell-tale signs of unsuspected wealth, anything from a spanking new fifty-one centimetre flat-screen TV with a Nicam stereo decoder to a holiday for two in Tencrife.

Either of which Millington would have been pleased to receive. He stopped trying to figure out exactly what the couple in the car behind were up to by careful use of his rear-view mirror and got out to stretch his legs. The tea stall was actually an old caravan now devoid of wheels and painted all over in a bizarre tartan. Its proprietor was a Glaswegian with one glass eye and a five-inch scar down his cheek along which you could clearly see the stitch marks. Millington reckoned he'd been sewn up on a back-parlour table with a domestic needle and thread and a bottle of Glenlivet for anaesthetic.

'Tea, is it?'

Millington fished in his trouser pocket for the money.

'How about a steak and kidney pie? Keep away the cold. If you don't fancy eating it, you can always set it under your feet, like one of they old stone jobbies your grannie used to have.'

'That the best you can offer?' Millington asked.

'I've a hot dog or two in here somewhere,' the man said, lifting the lid from a metal pan and swishing away with a pair of tongs. 'Maybe a burger?'

'Yes.'

'A burger?'

'Yes.'

'You're certain?'

'Great salesman, aren't you?'

'Onions or without?'

'Onions,' Millington said. 'With.'

He tipped sugar into his tea and stirred it with a spoon that was attached to the counter by a length of chain. Three motor bikes throttled down and swung in off the road, stopping between the caravan and Millington's car. One of the riders was skinny and tall, totally bald beneath his helmet when he took it off; his companions were over-weight and stocky, one of them sporting a belly that hung over his studded belt like a pregnancy about to come to term. All three wore boots and leathers and were old enough to have seen *Easy Rider* and *The Wild One* when they were first released. The girls riding with them were none of them more than seventeen, pale, pretty faces, sharp features drawn sharper by hours staring into the wind.

They ignored Millington and joked with the Scot behind the counter, old friends. Millington took his burger, added some watered-down ketchup and walked back towards his car to eat it. The couple parked behind him had forsaken the front seat for the back. The burger was grey and greasy, pitted with white gristle; two bites and Millington tossed it into the surrounding dark. He thought about his wife, sitting on the settee with her legs curled beneath her skirt, chuckling over Mary Wesley. 'I don't know how she can even think about sex at her age,' she'd said, 'never mind write about it.' Millington had grunted non-committally and waited for her to change the subject: he knew that thinking about it was never the problem.

'Debbie?'

Kevin Naylor lay facing his wife's back, early night for once, both of them hoping against hope the baby would sleep right through.

'Deb?'

He touched the nape of her neck, above the collar of her nightdress, and felt her flinch.

'Debbie.'

'What?'

'We can't carry on like this.'

Not for the first time, Karl Dougherty was wondering why there were only fifteen minutes in which to hand over to the night staff; never enough, especially when they'd had two unexpected admissions, which had been the case tonight. The administrators who closed wards for financial reasons didn't seem to understand there were others who failed to respond to budgetary shortfalls: the sick and the dying.

'Now then,' Karl said to one of the nurses as she stood waiting for the lift, 'off home to a cold bed and an improving book, I hope.'

'Oh, yes!' she grinned. 'And the rest!'

As Karl walked towards the main road and the buses, he caught sight of Sarah Leonard in her beige coat ahead of him. Hurrying, he drew level with her at the entrance to the subway.

'Catching the bus?'

Sarah smiled and shook her head. 'Walking clears my head. Besides, by the time you've waited, you could be indoors with your feet up.'

'Well, I'd walk with you, only I promised to meet a friend in town for a drink.'

They came up from the subway at the far side of the street, side by side. 'Think of me,' Sarah said, 'settling down to a good-night bowl of cornflakes.'

Karl laughed. 'I'll be having mine later, don't you worry. Only with me it's Shredded Wheat. I keep thinking if I eat three at a time, it'll make a man of me.'

Sarah raised a hand as she started to walk. 'So much for advertising,' she said.

Karl was still at the bus stop, five minutes later, when Ian Carew drove past. Approaching the railway bridge short of Lenton Recreation Ground, he slowed down, the better to look at the tall woman he was passing, stepping out briskly in a long raincoat, definitely someone who knew where she was going. Even so, Carew thought, no harm in pulling over, offering a lift.

Graham Millington had read the *Mail* from cover to cover, back to front and front to back. All that was left was to try it upside down. The couple behind had come to a similar conclusion twenty minutes earlier, wiped two circles of steam from the windows and driven off to their respective spouses. Talking to the Scot in the caravan and trying to get some useful information had been like searching for the sea on Southport beach.

'Sod this for a game of soldiers,' Millington said to no one. 'I'm off home.'

Kevin and Debbie Naylor lay back to back, their bodies close but not quite touching, each assuming the other was asleep. Very soon, the baby would wake and start crying.

Karl Dougherty came up the stairs from Manhattan's and looked to see if there was a cab on the rank near the Victorian Hotel. Never when you want one, he thought, when you don't they're all over you like crabs. He crossed the street towards Trinity Square, thinking of cutting through towards the centre, pick one up there. Seeing that the light outside the Gents was still on, he realized that he needed to go again. Never mind it hadn't been more than ten minutes. Anything above two lagers and it went through him like a tap.

Ah! He stood at the centre of a deserted line of urinals and unfastened his fly. Better off if he'd said no to his appointment, hurried home like Sarah Leonard and got stuck into some cereal, lots of sugar, warm milk.

He fumbled with his buttons, thinking how inconvenient it was that zips had gone out of fashion. Laughing at his own joke, he failed to hear the bolt on the closet door behind him sliding back.

Sixteen

There must be some people, Resnick thought, for whom a telephone ringing in the middle of the night doesn't spell bad news. There he was, ear to the receiver, the clock across the room stranded between three and four. 'Yes,' he said, tucking in his shirt. 'Yes,' fastening his belt. 'Yes,' reaching for his shoes. 'I'll be there.'

Sheets of white paper, smeared with ketchup or curry sauce, littered the pavements; crushed cartons still holding cold gravy, mushy peas. Patel was standing on the street corner, concern on his face clear in the overhead lighting; he took his hands from his raincoat pockets as Resnick approached. One police car was parked outside the entrance to the toilets, another around by the fast-food pasta place, facing up the slope of Trinity Square. A uniformed officer stood at a kind of attention, doing his best not to look tired or bored.

'I wasn't sure, sir, if I should call you or not.'

Resnick nodded. 'Let's see.'

Patel and a DC from Central had been forming the token CID presence, overnight. The first report had only mentioned a male, white, late twenties to early thirties; it hadn't been till later that his profession had been referred to. When Resnick walked into the Gents, Patel behind him, DI Cossall was already there, taking a leak at the end urinal. Between them, the scene of crime team had finished dusting for prints and were firing off a few more Polaroids for posterity.

Across the floor, the thick chalk mark showed where the

body had fallen; rather, the position it had finally crawled into. One chalk toe damp at the foot of the urinal, a hand reaching towards the closet door, it looked less like the outline of a body than abstract art.

'Your young DC, there,' Cossall nodded towards Patel, 'could've let you get a few more hours' beauty sleep.'

Resnick was looking at the chalk lines on the floor. 'He *is* from the hospital?'

'So it appears.'

'Attacked with a knife, some kind of blade?'

'Yes.'

'Then Patel here did right. Anything less he'd have got a bollocking.'

Cossall pointed downwards. 'Pretty much like this sorry bastard, then. Sounds as if whoever went for him, tried to chop his balls off.'

A quick shudder ran through Resnick and, despite himself, he cupped one hand towards his legs, like a footballer lining up against a free kick. 'Let's get outside,' he said. 'The stink in here's getting up my nose.'

Cossall and Resnick were more or less contemporaries; their movements between uniform and CID ran parallel, the dates of their promotions approximately matched. Cossall had transferred outside the local force at one point, but nine months as a detective sergeant in Norfolk had been more than enough. 'The only place,' he'd once confided in Resnick over a drink, 'where the stories on the wall in the blokes' bog are about shagging sheep.'

'Trouble was,' Cossall was saying now, 'he lay there so long. Lost so much blood. Looks as if youths were coming in and out, stepping round him to take a piss. Likely thought he'd passed out, drunk.'

'What about the blood?'

'Figured he'd fallen, smacked his head, if they noticed at

all. It's a wonder some bugger didn't throw up over him into the bargain.'

'Where is he now?' Resnick asked.

Cossall shook his head. 'Somewhere between intensive care and the morgue, I should reckon.'

'And family?' Resnick said. 'They've been informed?'

'Ah,' said Cossall, looking away towards the light flashing intermittently from the roof of the nearest police car, 'I knew there was something.'

Resnick turned right alongside the Fletcher Gate car park and came to a halt outside the Lace Market Theatre. He switched off his headlights and let the engine idle. The only situation in which he was glad he'd never had children was this: the only part of the job he hated to do alone. Not so long back, he remembered, it had been Rachel he had woken with a phone call in the middle of the night. Come with me. A skilled social worker, she had been the perfect choice. There's a woman I have to talk to, I need your help. A woman, already crippled with pain, who had to be told her daughter was dead. Of course, he hadn't only wanted Rachel there for her expertise – when to speak, when to be silent, the right word, the touch at the proper time – however unconsciously he had been drawing her into his life. Sucking her in. So deep that before it was over she had nearly been killed herself.

Rachel.

The scrape of a shoe against the uneven pavement made Resnick turn. A woman stepping forward out of the shadow, collar of her dark raincoat eased up, hair that framed her pale face short and dark. Resnick reached across and unlocked the near side door.

'Sorry to haul you out,' Resnick said.

'S'all right, sir,' said Lynn Kellogg, 'I've done the same to you before now.'

Resnick switched back to main beam, slid the car into gear. 'I'll fill you in on the way,' he said.

Wollaton was the place that time forgot. An inner-city suburb of bungalows and crescents and neat detached houses with crazy paving and front gardens fit for gnomes. A light shone in the porch of the Dougherty house, dull orange. Resnick pressed the bell a second time and stepped back. Another light appeared, filtered through the curtains of the upstairs front. Cautious footsteps on the stairs.

'Who is it?'

'Detective Inspector Resnick. CID.'

Through the square of frosted glass set into the door, Resnick could see a figure, shoulders hunched, hesitating.

'It's the police, Mr Dougherty,' Resnick said, not wanting to raise his voice too loud and wake the neighbours. Wanting it to be over: done.

The figure came forward; there was a slow sliding back of bolts, top and bottom, a latch pushed up, a key being turned: finally, the door was inched back on a chain.

Resnick identified himself, holding his warrant card towards the edge of the door and stepping to one side so that Dougherty could see him.

'This is Detective Constable Kellogg,' Resnick said, pointing behind him. 'If we could come in.'

'Can't it wait? What's so important that it can't wait?'

'Your son,' Resnick said. 'It's about your son.'

'Karl?'

'Yes, Karl.'

The door was pushed closed, but only to free the chain. Dougherty stood in tartan slippers on a mat that said *Welcome* in dark tufts of bristle. His ankles were bony beneath the hem of striped pyjama trousers, the skin marbled with broken blue veins. The belt of his dark green dressing-gown had been tied in a tight bow. His hair tufted up at angles from the sides of his head.

111

'What about Karl?' he asked. 'What's happened to him?'

But the expression in his eyes showed that he already knew.

Not exactly, of course. That came a little later, in the small living room, the only light from a standard lamp in one corner, the three of them sitting on furniture that had been built to last and had done exactly that.

All the while Resnick had been speaking, Dougherty's eyes had flickered from the cocktail cabinet to the light oak table, from the empty vase they had brought back from Holland fifteen years ago to the small framed photographs on the mantelpiece above the variflame gas fire.

In the silence that followed, Dougherty's eyes were still. His fingers plucked at the ends of his green wool belt. Resnick wondered how much, how clearly he'd understood.

'Would you like us to take you to the hospital?' Resnick asked. 'You and your wife?'

'My wife . . .' Dougherty began, alarmed.

'We could take you,' Resnick repeated. 'To see Karl.'

'My wife can't go,' Dougherty said.

'She is here?' Resnick asked.

'I told you, upstairs. She can't go, she mustn't know, she can't . . .'

'She'll have to be told, Mr Dougherty,' Resnick said.

'No.'

'Would you like me to speak to her?' Lynn offered.

'She can't know.'

'What?' said Pauline Dougherty from the doorway. 'What is it, William? Who are these people? I woke up and you weren't there. That was when I heard voices. Your voice, William. I thought it was Karl. You know, one of his little visits. To surprise us.'

'What visits?' said Dougherty, staring at her.

'You know, his little . . .'

'He doesn't make visits,' getting to his feet. 'One year's end to the next, he scarcely comes near us.'

'He does, William. Oh, he does. You forget.'

William Dougherty closed his eyes and his wife stood close in front of him, recently permed hair held tight in a net, a dressing-gown of quilted pink and fluffy pink slippers without heels.

'William,' she said and he opened his eyes.

'Karl's dead,' Dougherty said.

'No,' Resnick said quickly, half out of his chair.

'He's dead,' Dougherty repeated.

'No,' said Resnick quietly. 'Mr Dougherty, that isn't what I said.'

'There you are,' Pauline Dougherty turned her head towards the inspector and then back towards her husband, reaching for his hand. 'There you are,' almost beaming. 'You see, there's been a mistake.'

The sky was lightening and the milk-float was only two streets away. Lynn Kellogg had spoken to Pauline Dougherty's sister in Harrogate, who would catch the first train down via York. One of the neighbours would be across to sit with her within the half hour, and meanwhile Lynn herself sat in the kitchen holding Mrs Dougherty's hands, watching the birds land for a moment on the cotoneaster bush and then fly off again. Going to the hospital meant acknowledging the truth of what had happened and Pauline Dougherty was not ready for that yet; Lynn wondered if she ever would be.

Meanwhile Resnick phoned the hospital, the station, the hospital once more. A uniformed officer came to take William Dougherty to see his son. Karl was in surgery and fighting for his life, struggling, unknowingly, to prove his father wrong.

Resnick and Lynn Kellogg went to the café near the

Dunkirk flyover and ate sausage baps with HP sauce and drank strong, sweet tea. Looking out through the steamed-over window at the blur of early morning traffic, neither of them said a word.

Seventeen

By eight that morning, Karl Dougherty was under constant observation in intensive care. He had come round for several minutes close to six o'clock; again, an hour later. His father had been sitting at the foot of his bed, but if Karl recognized him, he gave no sign. The cuts and lacerations to his face and forearms had been straightforwardly treated; wounds to his lower chest and abdomen had been more severe and required more careful surgery. Hard as he tried, the surgeon had been unable to save one of Karl's testicles.

Resnick drove Lynn Kellogg back to her flat, easing into the flow of early morning traffic. The first report on Radio Trent spoke of a man attacked in the city centre, detained in hospital in a serious condition. 'Think he'll pull through, sir?' Lynn asked. Resnick didn't know: just that if he didn't, if the incident changed to one of murder, a whole different set of procedures would fall into place. Fletcher, he was thinking, swinging left past the Broad Marsh, Fletcher and Dougherty – how much of that was coincidence? He shifted across to the centre of the road, indicating right; braked beside the Lace Market Theatre, back where they had started not so many hours earlier. 'Cup of tea, sir?' Lynn asked, car door open. 'Thanks,' said Resnick, shaking his head, 'any more, folk'll think I've got problems with the prostate.' He watched her walk from sight before reversing away. A few more like her in the Force wouldn't do any harm at all.

William Dougherty got up from his son's bed, told the nurse he'd be right back, took the lift to the ground floor and stood for several minutes, outside the main entrance, smoking a cigarette. It tasted old, stale, God knows how long it had been in his coat pocket, months. Ever since Pauline had taken to complaining if he smoked in the house, he had been cutting back. One in the garden on a Sunday, trimming back the hedges, straightening up the lawn. When they had first moved to Wollaton, Karl had been little more than a baby. Barely able to keep his feet as he followed his father around. 'Pay ball! Pay ball! Pay ball!' 'William, be careful of the flowers!' Dougherty put out the cigarette with forefinger and thumb and blew on the tip before dropping the nub end back in his pocket. Waste not, want not. Waste. *I never wanted you to go to university in the first place, you know. Waste of bloody time and money.* Now he looked like a robot, lying there, unreal. Something from science fiction, an astronaut. For a while that's what he'd wanted to be. Dan Dare. Thunderbirds. Something like that. Now he'd be lucky to be anything. Machines controlled the flow of his blood, the air from his lungs. Not that Dougherty understood, not exactly, but there was no avoiding the apparatus, the tubes, wires, digits on the faces of all those machines. Nurses who smiled at him deftly before reading off the figures like mechanics, noting them down. Not dead, the police inspector had said, not dead. What did he know? What was this? Instead of going back inside the hospital, he started walking away.

Resnick was not altogether surprised to see Reg Cossall queueing up for a second breakfast in the canteen, his sergeant, Derek Fenby, alongside him.

'What's up, Reg?' Resnick said. 'Don't they feed you enough down there?'

Cossall poked a finger into Resnick's stomach. 'Not as well as they do up here.'

'DCI,' Fenby said, his voice a natural growl, 'wanted us to report to your super.'

Cossall winked. 'Politics, Charlie. Argue till he's blue in the face, Jack Skelton, keep both cases up here. While since you lot had anything tasty.'

'Happy for you to handle this one,' said Fenby. 'Eh, boss?'

'Late-night emasculation,' said Cossall with a cock-eyed grin. 'Not our style.'

'Handy for some, though,' said Fenby, 'saves on the vasectomy.'

Jesus, thought Resnick, they're enjoying this. Keeping their knees clenched and thinking there but for the grace of God . . .

'Hey up!' said Cossall loudly at the woman behind the counter. 'Call that thing a sausage? I've seen better between our dog's legs.'

Jack Skelton's suit jacket was on its hanger behind his office door and all was right with the world. For now. The notebook and blotter on his desk were the regulation inch and a quarter apart, his fountain pens facing magnetic north. Only the photograph of Kate as a young girl had disappeared from its frame, replaced by another, a family group in which the background was unclear, the faces were blurred.

'What do you think, Charlie? Pull Patel off this jeans business? Be light-handed otherwise.'

'He'd be pleased, no mistaking that.'

'Let's have him out to the hospital then. Need someone with a bit of tact.'

'I was wondering about Graham Millington . . .'

Skelton was quick to shake his head. 'Put in a lot of work on those hijacks already. Be good to see a result. And it doesn't hurt us any, let them see over there we're not poor cousins.' He smoothed his hand across his upper lip,

117

stroking the moustache that was no longer there. 'Reg Cossall'd be happy to lend us Fenby.'

'I'll bet he would.'

'Nothing wrong with Fenby, Charlie. Good old-fashioned copper.'

'Exactly.'

'Just the job for something like this, lots of double-checking, knocking on doors. Wind him up and let him go.'

Resnick stood up and shuffled a few paces back towards the door, not quite certain he was through.

'Long day already, Charlie,' Skelton said, midway through dialling. 'Once you've got them going, get yourself home. Snatch an hour.' The superintendent's face slumped into a frown. 'This is going to get a sight worse before it gets better.'

When William Dougherty finally arrived home his shoes were damp and flecked with mud, but he had no clear sense of where he had been walking or for how long.

One of the neighbours sat in the kitchen, brooding over a pot of tea, too long mashed to be drinkable. Seeing Dougherty, she looked away and then, with a slow shake of her head, pointed towards the rear window.

Pauline was standing close to a pink rose bush, most of its petals blown. Her dressing-gown had become unfastened at the front and there was nothing on her feet.

'She won't come in,' the neighbour said. 'I asked her, but she won't.'

Dougherty nodded and let himself out through the side door. The sounds of birdsong seemed unnaturally loud, calls and responses laid over the dull hum of traffic.

'Pauline.'

Turning at the familiar voice, she smiled. 'William, the roses, we have to be careful . . .'

She forgot what it was they had to be careful about.

Gently, Dougherty took the watering can from her hand

and set it on the path before leading her back towards the house.

Without his helmet, the constable who escorted Sarah Leonard up to CID was scarcely the taller. He led her through the main door, knocked on the window to Resnick's office and left her. Glancing up, Resnick saw a woman with dark hair, lightly curled, a strong nose and a full mouth, dark eyes that fixed upon him and didn't let him go. For the first time in some little while, he thought of Rachel, shaking the thought free as he got to his feet and beckoned her to enter.

'Inspector?'

Resnick held out his hand. 'Have a seat.'

'Sarah Leonard,' she said. 'I work at the hospital.'

'You're a doctor?'

'I'm a nurse. Staff nurse.'

'And you work with Karl?'

Sarah nodded.

Resnick relaxed back into his chair, allowing his shoulders to slump just a little.

'We finished at the same time yesterday, nine o'clock, more or less. We went through the subway together. Karl doesn't live all that far from me, sometimes we walk part of the way together – last night he was catching the bus into the city. Said he was meeting someone for a drink.'

There was sweat forming lightly in the palms of Resnick's hands.

'Did he say who?' Resnick asked.

Sarah shook her head. 'Just a friend.'

'Nothing more?'

A slight tightening of the mouth and she shook her head again.

'You don't know if this friend was female? Male?'

The merest hesitations before Sarah said no.

'How about where they were meeting?'

'No, but . . .'

But, echoed Resnick inwardly. But . . .

'I know Karl used to go to this place near the Victoria Centre . . .'

'A pub?'

'More of . . . I don't know . . . not a wine bar exactly . . . a club.'

'Have you been there?'

'Once, yes, I think it was Karl's birthday. We . . .'

'Downstairs, is it? Underground?'

She nodded emphatically. 'Yes.'

'Manhattan's.'

'Yes.'

Resnick wiped his hands along his trouser legs. 'And you think that's where he was off to last night? Nine o'clock?'

'Nearer a quarter past.'

'But there?'

'I don't know. I think so. Yes. I looked back before the turn in the road and he was still standing there, the bus stop.' She leaned forward across Resnick's desk. 'If it was there, that Karl was going . . . It's close to where they found him, isn't it?'

'Yes,' said Resnick slowly. 'Yes, it is.'

Sarah stared at him hard. 'Whoever it was. Did this. He wants locking away.'

For several moments Resnick didn't say anything. And then he found a smile and thanked her for coming in so promptly. 'One of the officers will take your statement,' he said, escorting her through the door.

Rachel, he thought, would never have talked of locking the person who did this away; she would have spoken of safety, providing help and care. He remembered the consultant giving his description of Tim Fletcher's wounds, the sight of Dougherty, unconscious in his own blood. He didn't know who needed caring for the most.

Eighteen

'Borrowed one of your shirts, Charlie. Hope you don't mind.'

Ed Silver had dragged a stool close to the stove and was spreading peanut butter on the nub end of a rye loaf. Several tea bags oozed orangey-brown from where they had been dumped on a corner of the chopping board. Silver had also found a pair of Resnick's older grey trousers while rummaging through his wardrobe and wore those now, held at the waist by a red-and-grey striped tie. Resnick wasn't sure whether the socks were his or not. Without doubt the cat was. Dizzy, stalker of the night and the least susceptible to human advances, had found in Ed Silver a fellow spirit.

All these years, Resnick thought, and he'd misjudged him. Poor, blackhearted Dizzy. Not a football fan at all, a lager lout – in his soul Dizzy was something more serious, more tragic, an artist, an alcoholic *manqué*.

'Nearly out of this,' Silver said, tapping the peanut-butter jar with the blade of the knife.

Resnick was more worried about his vodka.

'You had a phone call,' Silver said, chewing earnestly.

'Message?'

'Said she'd ring back.'

'She?'

'Don't know how you do it, Charlie,' Ed Silver cackled. 'Pulling birds at your age.'

Resnick glanced at his watch. There wasn't time, but he wanted to shower. The smell of stale urine still clung to him, the memory of the wavering chalk line that had marked Dougherty's body. The expression on Pauline Dougherty's face, smiling: *You see, there's been a mistake*. Parents like that, those situations, the ones whose children had been buried high on cold ground or laid waste between the brick ginnels of blackened cities, what did they ever understand? What beyond the numbness and after the pain?

He dropped his clothing on the bathroom floor and switched the shower to full. Eyes closed, needle jets of water washed his body. Resnick turned up the temperature, turned his face towards the stream.

Patel sat outside intensive care, staring at his shoes. Better, at least, than surveillance outside another anonymous warehouse or factory, cold on the trail of 36 gross pairs of wide-fitting mislabelled jeans. Here one of the domestics would push a cup of tea into his hands, a biscuit; from time to time a nurse would slip him a sidelong smile.

Through a double set of glass-panelled doors he could see the apparatus around Dougherty's bed, observe, as if through water, the ritual observations of blood pressure, temperature, vital signs. The watchers watched.

Two doctors passed quickly through, white coats flapping around well-cut dark trousers, talking in hushed, conspiratorial tones. Consultants, registrars, housemen – Patel knew the names, didn't know the difference. His father had wanted him to become a doctor, had preached long nights about it, the honour, the prestige. Eighteen hours in a corner shop his father worked, seven days a week, every day except Christmas, all to make things easier for his children, easier than they had been for him, arriving in England with little more than names written on the back of an envelope. Welcome to Bradford. See, Diptak, you will receive an education, your brothers also. You will be a professional man. I will be proud of you.

After his degree, Patel had applied to join the police and at first his father had been less than proud. His friends, some of them, had ostracized him, cut him dead. *Traitor!* The word had dogged his footsteps along the streets where he had grown up, assaulted him from the walls; one evening, serving in the family shop, his best friend had spat in his face. The vehemence of it had been unsuspected and the hurt clung to him still, worse by far than the racist jokes his fellow officers would repeat to his face without a second thought, the calls of 'Paki bastard!' he had to ignore most days of his life, most nights in the city.

'Excuse me.' Patel got to his feet as the two doctors walked back through the doors. 'Excuse me, but Mr Dougherty, is there any change?'

They looked at him as if he could only be there in error.

'Is there any change in his condition?' Patel asked.

'No,' one of the doctors said, walking away.

'What do you think?' said the other. 'A jar before squash or after?'

No hats or trainers read the notice taped to the door. *Sorry no jeans.* No hats, thought Resnick, pushing his way through, must be some kind of code.

A short staircase wound down to the centre, a curve of seats and small tables off to the left, the DJ's decks to the right, more steps led down to the main floor and the facing bar. Knees resting on a rubber pad, a blonde-haired woman was polishing away at the wooden dance floor.

A pair of lights shone dully from beneath the glass shelves at the back of the bar. Alongside the Labatt's and Grolsch in the cold cabinet, Resnick spotted some bottles of Czech Budweiser and his admiration rose several notches.

'Anyone around?' he asked.

'Too early,' said the woman on the dance floor, not bothering to turn around. 'Come back in an hour.'

123

'You're the only one here, then?'

'Didn't I tell you?' she said, with a touch of put-on weariness. 'Are you thick or what?'

Hands to her hips, she arched her back and swivelled her head. 'Oh, it's you,' she said. 'I didn't recognize your voice.'

'Hello, Rosie,' Resnick said.

The last time she had heard his voice had been in court, Resnick giving evidence against two of her sons, the pair of them arrested and charged with offences under Sections 47 and 38, causing aggravated bodily harm and using force to resist arrest. They'd be back out any time now, but probably not for long.

'How's the girl?' Resnick asked. Rosie's daughter had been born with a severe disability to the spine that had kept her shuffling in and out of hospital for years.

'What the hell do you care?' Rosie said.

A door to the side of the bar opened and she picked up her polishing cloth and went back to her work. 'We're not open yet,' said a man in a loose white shirt and a maroon bow tie, hair gelled upwards in short, fashionable spikes. 'Come back in . . .'

'I know,' Resnick said, 'an hour.' He pushed his warrant card along the bar.

'What can I do for you, inspector?' the man asked.

'Are you the owner?' Resnick asked. 'Manager?'

'Derek Griffin. I'm the manager.'

'Here last night?'

'Most of the time, why?'

Resnick looked over towards the nearest table. 'Let's sit down.'

Resnick leaned against the padded backrest; Griffin perched himself uneasily on a stool, reminding Resnick of a cockatoo from the aviary in the Arboretum, likely to fly off at any moment.

'Can I get you something, inspector?' Griffin asked, glancing towards the bar.

'How many staff here with you?'

'Last night?'

Resnick nodded.

'Three behind the bar, bouncer on the door. Four.'

'That all?'

'Unless you count the DJ.'

'Five, then.'

'All right, five.'

'Names and addresses.'

'Look, what's this about?'

'You don't know?'

'No. Should I?'

'A man was attacked.'

'In here?'

'Outside. Between eleven and one.'

'Whereabouts outside?'

'He's in critical condition.'

'Where did it happen?'

'Toilet across the street.'

Griffin relaxed a little on his stool. 'Not here then, is it. I mean, it's nothing to do with us. It didn't happen in here.'

'We think there's a good chance he'd been in just before, for a drink.'

'Somebody see him?'

'You tell me.' The photograph of Karl Dougherty had been supplied by his parents and photocopied. It had been taken five years earlier and showed a half-way good-looking young man smiling into a friend's camera. There were palm trees in the background and Karl was wearing a T-shirt and a pair of shorts that finished just above his knees. It was the most recent picture they had. Griffin lifted it towards his face, stared at it for several seconds and set it back down. 'No,' he said.

On the level above them, Rosic was polishing tables.

'No, you didn't see him last night, or no, you don't know him at all?'

'Either. Both.'

'You're sure?'

'Certain.'

'Don't tell him a thing,' Rosie said, 'it'll get twisted arse-uppards and used against you. Though you're lucky, you got me as a witness.'

'How many d'you reckon were in here yesterday?' Resnick asked. 'Give or take.'

'Three hundred, maybe more. Not all at one time, of course.'

'None of them wearing hats.'

'What?'

'Skip it.'

'This bloke,' Griffin said. 'What happened to him? I mean, exactly.'

Resnick told him briefly, not quite exactly. It was still enough to make Griffin cross his legs and for sweat marks to dampen his shirt. If his bow-tie could have drooped, probably it would.

'The staff on last night,' Resnick said. 'Any of them in today? Lunchtime?'

'Maura. None of the others.'

'Tonight?'

'All except one.'

'Better get me the list,' Resnick said. 'Mark on it when they're here, days and times. Home numbers if you know them. We'll need to talk to them as soon as we can.'

Griffin nodded and crossed towards the bar. 'The customers,' he said, turning back towards Resnick. 'You're not going to be in here, bothering them as well?'

'Oh, yes,' said Resnick. 'I should think so. But don't worry, anyone I send, I'll make sure they're properly dressed.'

Once or twice, when he'd been younger, fifteen, sixteen, Kevin Naylor had been beset by panic: once in the middle of a crowded street, another time in the Broad Marsh Centre, Saturday afternoon. Everyone hurrying around him, scurrying past, purposeful, busy, knowing exactly what they were looking for, where they were going. Naylor had stood where he was, quite still, scared, unable to move, and they had continued to stream past him, these people, not seeing him, not even knocking into him: as if he weren't there.

He had experienced much the same sensation at training college, a large role-play exercise, civil unrest, riot shields and batons. Other trainee officers in jeans and jumpers, pretending to be students, strikers, loving it. The chance to scream and yell and charge. So easy to pretend emotion, feign feelings, hate. Call slogans till you were red in the face.

Wearing protective clothing, engaged in strategic retreat, Naylor had become separated, targeted. Stranded amidst all that simulated anger, faces, limbs and bodies flying past. Shatter of glass on the tarmacked ground. Flash of flame. He had stood exactly as he was while the fire sought to claim him. Awake and asleep: immovable till they had dragged him clear.

There had been a session with a counsellor after that, talk of nervous failure, unsuitability; only the diligence of his written work had prevented him from being back-classed.

Nothing as dramatic had recurred since then. Out on the job, first in uniform and now plain clothes, in most situations you simply responded, did what it was clear you had to do. Only occasionally did events threaten to overwhelm him and the possibility of panic return; rarely for more than moments at a time. There had been a cup match at Forest with several thousand United supporters locked out; eighty or so youths racing down the Forest towards Hyson Green in the half-light; now.

Two sets of nurses were moving between shifts, handing over; shouts for assistance, trolleys, bells; screens pulled around one, then another; at the nurses' station the telephone that never seemed to stop ringing and never seemed to be answered. Underpinning all of this, Naylor was aware of the near-mute chatter from a dozen television screens, the same banalities being mouthed, adultery and another slice of cake between the commercial breaks.

He had to check with the sister that it was okay to begin interviewing staff on duty; Lynn Kellogg was waiting to see those going off as they left. Helen Minton took hold of him firmly by the elbow and propelled him towards her office. 'I know this is important,' she said, 'but I'd appreciate it if this takes as little time as possible. What we're doing is important too.'

Vainly waiting for the chance to question Dougherty, Patel had found a copy of yesterday's *Mail* and was stuck on 13 Across: Vital to sustain life (9). He was still struggling over it when Karl Dougherty's blood pressure sank to 90/40 and they decided that a further transfusion would not be enough. Chances are he was bleeding internally. Patel sat there and watched as they wheeled Dougherty towards the theatre for more surgery.

Lifeblood.

He filled in the squares and thought about the next clue.

Nineteen

No more than a couple of hundred yards to Central Station, Resnick slid the Manhattan's staff list across to Fenby, five names, all of them needing to be checked.

'This one,' Resnick said. 'Maura Tranter. She's working this lunch time. I'll nip back over, see her myself.'

Fenby nodded slowly, the same speed at which he did everything. A Lincolnshire man with thick hair and a ruddy complexion, Fenby had grown up boot-deep in mud, face to face with the easterlies that came scudding in off the North Sea and cut through the Wolds like a rusty scythe.

'Report direct to you, then?' Fenby said.

Sir, Resnick thought. 'Yes,' he said.

Divine, with the help of two uniforms, was checking out any taxi drivers using the rank near where the incident had occurred, staff who would have been working at the other clubs and pubs in the area, restaurants and car parks, the toilets themselves.

NURSE FIGHTS FOR LIFE was the headline in the local paper. *Victim of an apparently motiveless attack* . . . It could have been worse. The last thing Resnick wanted to read were panic stories about some Midlands Slasher, intent upon carving up the NHS more speedily than Kenneth Clarke.

He took the escalator up beside Miss Selfridge and entered the market via the meat and fish. No time for an espresso, he paused at the first of the Polish delicatessens and allowed himself a small treat, deciding between the three kinds of cheesecake always a problem.

'This business last night,' said the man running the stall, 'that's for you to sort out?'

Pointing at the middle tray, Resnick nodded.

'I'm surprised you've time even to think of eating.'

Resnick lifted the white paper bag from the glass counter and hurried between the flower stalls, heading for the far exit, the second escalator that would carry him down again, landing him close to the entrance to Manhattan's.

It was busy already, plenty of people with time to drink as well as eat, the money to make it possible. There was a spare stool towards the end of the bar and Resnick manoeuvred towards it and sat down. He was always surprised when he went into a place like this, especially in the middle of the day, how many men and women under thirty could afford, not simply to be there but to be in fashion, able to pay the rising cost of keeping up appearances.

Haves and have-nots: trouble with his job was, likely you spent so much time with the have-nots, it was easy to see them as the norm, be surprised when you found yourself surrounded by those for whom the system, supposedly, worked.

'What's that?' said the young woman behind the bar, pointing at the bag Resnick had set on the counter.

'Cheesecake,' said Resnick. 'Cherry topping.'

'Can't eat your own food in here.'

'I'm not eating it.'

'That's what I said.'

She had an open face, cheeks a hungry squirrel could have hoarded nuts in; her hair was in a lavish disarray it had taken ages to arrange. Her accent placed her east of Kimberley, but north of Ilkeston.

'Are you Maura?' Resnick asked.

'Tuesdays, Thursdays, Fridays, Sunday afternoons. The rest of the week I'm Leslie.'

Resnick thought it best not to inquire why. 'Maybe your manager told you to expect me?'

'You're not the detective?'

'Mondays, Tuesdays, Wednesdays, Thursdays, Fridays, Saturdays.'

'What happens Sundays?'

'I rest.'

When she smiled, Maura's cheeks puffed out still further, for all the world like Dizzy Gillespie playing trumpet. 'According to Derek, you're fat and fifty and dressed like something out of the ark.'

Sooner that, thought Resnick, than someone who looked as if he should be inside it. 'No wonder you didn't recognize me,' he said.

'Right, you're not so fat.'

'Thanks.'

'Not like some we get in here: half a hundredweight of cholesterol on feet.'

'Hey, Maura . . .' called somebody along the bar.

'I'm busy,' she called back.

'This is the man.' Resnick unfolded the photocopy of Karl Dougherty and turned it towards her.

'Four halves of lager, pint lager shandy, orange juice, pineapple, tomato juice with Worcester sauce and a Cinzano and lemonade – if you can tear yourself away.'

'What about you?' Maura was looking at Resnick, not the photograph. 'Fancy anything?'

'Budweiser. Thanks.'

'For Christ's sake, Maura . . . !'

She sighed and swore not quite below her breath.

'Is there a problem here?' Derek Griffin appeared at Resnick's shoulder sporting a different tie and a piqued expression.

'No problem,' Maura said brightly.

'No problem,' said Resnick.

'You do get paid to work here, you know,' said Griffin.

Maura raised an eyebrow theatrically. 'Just,' she said.

Griffin turned away. Maura set a bottle and an empty glass at Resnick's elbow, opened the bottle, tapped the picture of Dougherty with a false finger nail and said, 'I'll be back.'

'Now,' she said, moving along the bar, 'what was it? Four small lagers . . .'

Resnick retreated and found another seat amongst the other lunchtime drinkers: well-groomed young salespeople from River Island, grey men in lean grey suits from Jessops talking earnestly about the partnership, bank clerks of both sexes from Barclays and NatWest. Dougherty had been here not so many hours before, enjoying a drink like these, maybe laughing, maybe not. He glanced over at the toilet sign, midway along the side wall. Was there anything strange in leaving here and going straight into the public lavatory across the road? If he did go straight there, that is? And besides, Resnick could remember, with embarrassment now and not pleasure, evenings when negotiating a path home via every toilet in the city centre had still not been adequate to prevent him slipping into an alley, urinating against the wall.

'Hi!' Maura pulled over a stool and sat close beside him, orange lipstick on the rim of her glass like a kiss, on the filter tip of the cigarette she held in her other hand.

'Sure this is okay?' Resnick asked.

'Don't fret.'

'I don't want to get you into trouble.'

'That's what the last one said.' Laughing.

'No, I mean it.'

'So did he. So he said. But then they all do. Try it on, lie. You expect it. Funny thing was . . .' She angled her mouth away to release a small stream of smoke, eyes staying on him. '. . . he said he was one of your lot, a copper.'

'And he wasn't?'

'Milkman. Dale Farms. Hardly the same, is it?'

Resnick grinned.

''Bout the only thing that interested me, really. The policeman bit.' She leaned back and moved her head so that her hair shook. 'Got a thing about authority, you know?'

'Tell that to your boss.'

'Derek? No, I mean the real thing. Not some little tosser spends half his time trying to push you around and the rest round the back, jerking off in front of the mirror.' She drank some gin and tonic. 'You need something to push against, you know? Otherwise where's the fun. Anyway, this bloke, the milkman. I thought he might be it.' She laughed loudly enough to make several people break off their conversations and stare. 'Till I went back to his place and talked him into putting on his uniform.'

'Maura!' came the shout from the bar.

'All right, all right.' She finished her drink in a swallow and stood up, leaning down until her hair covered her face. 'Yes,' she said, tapping the picture of Dougherty, 'he was in here, last hour before closing. Him and another guy, comes in quite a bit. Peter, Paul, one of those names. Don't know if they were having a row or what, but they were getting loud, I remember that.'

'You didn't hear what they were saying?'

Maura shook her head.

'You think any of the other staff might have?'

She shrugged. 'Possible. Ask.'

'I will.'

'Maura!'

'Got to go.'

Resnick pushed himself up. 'Right. Thanks for your help.'

Maura started to move away, then stopped. 'The other feller. Paul, Peter. I think he must work round here. Comes in lunchtimes, three or four days a week.'

'You sure he's working?'

'He wears a suit.' She grinned. 'Wouldn't use it as a floorcloth myself, but to him it's a suit.'

'Anything else special about him? Except for bad taste?' Standing there, Resnick was conscious of the creases in his bagged trousers, the stain on his jacket lapel.

'Hair.'

'What about it?'

'Not a lot of it. For someone his age.'

'Maura!'

'All right!'

Resnick picked up the photocopy and the now sweaty bag, dark where the fat from the cheesecake had run through.

'Look in again some time,' Maura said. 'When it's not so busy.' A toss of the head and she was heading back towards the bar. Outside it had started to drizzle and a thin film of water was collecting across the grey pavements. Breaking into an awkward trot to avoid a double-decker turning up into the square, Resnick sensed the bottom of the bag begin to break. A vain grab failed to prevent the cheesecake from falling, squashed, into the gutter, leaving Resnick licking cherry topping from his fingers on the corner of the street.

Twenty

It had taken William Dougherty the best part of two hours to calm down his wife, stop the persistent tremble in her hands, persuade her to focus on his words. Pauline listened and nodded and said something William couldn't catch. Before he knew what she was doing, her hands were under the sink, fumbling for the scouring powder, cream cleanser and cloths. He watched while she lifted the hard plastic bowl from the sink and set it on the draining board, upside down; slowly she began to rub at the already spotless metal; painstakingly, she twisted a thin strip between the links of the chain that held the plug.

'Did you understand what I said?' he asked. 'Any of it?'

Her permed hair, not so much as a comb through since morning, sat lopsided, like an ill-fitting wig. 'Yes, William. Of course I did.'

As she went back to her cleaning, Dougherty left the house. Asking the neighbour across the way to call in again and sit with Pauline, he caught a bus to the hospital. Without entering the unit he could see Karl's bed was empty and his knees buckled beneath him. Had Patel still been waiting, likely he would have reached Dougherty in time to steady him before he fell. As it was, Patel had left a note of where he could be contacted and returned to the station and it was a good ten minutes before one of the porters found William Dougherty slumped against the wall.

Nurses helped him to his feet and sat him down with a hasty mug of tea.

'Now then, Mr Dougherty,' one of the nurses said as she took his pulse, 'we can't have this. We don't want the whole family in here, sure we don't.'

'Karl . . .'

'Oh, we just had to pop him back into theatre. Don't you fret now. He's in recovery, doing fine. He'll be back on the ward in a while and then you can see him. All right now? I'll leave you to finish your tea.'

He sat there, one hand to his head, staring at the floor, uncertain whether he should be more worried about his wife or son.

Kevin Naylor tried Debbie a third time and still there was no reply. Probably round at her mum's but he wasn't going to phone there, he'd be buggered if he was.

'Okay?' Lynn Kellogg was standing further along the corridor, near the doors, arms folded across her chest.

'Yes. Why shouldn't I be?'

'Thought you looked a bit worried, that's all.'

'I'm fine.' Heading past her, hoping she wouldn't follow.

'Kevin . . .'

Naylor stopped short, breathed in slowly, then turned to face her.

'It's not Debbie, is it?'

'It's nothing.'

'Only . . .'

'Do us a favour, Lynn.'

'Yes?'

Naylor jabbed a finger at her like a hammer, like nails. 'Go out and get a bloke of your own. Then you won't spend so much time fussing round me.'

She flinched like she'd been hit. Naylor glared and walked away and Lynn watched him – whatever it was between us, she thought, now it's gone. Just another man who didn't like what he was feeling: choke it down until you're not feeling anything at all. Her notebook was in the bag that hung from her shoulder, all of the staff she'd talked to had known Karl Dougherty, thought he was wonderful – efficient, funny, caring: an outstanding nurse. The impression she was left with was that none of them knew him at all.

She would go and talk to Tim Fletcher before leaving; see if there wasn't something he could add.

Fletcher was sitting in an easy chair beside his bed, learning Italian care of his Walkman, eyes gently closed as he repeated the phrases over and over: *'C'è una mappa con le cose da vedere?' 'C'è una mappa con le cose da vedere?' 'C'è...'* He broke off, aware of someone's presence.

'Sounds really impressive,' Lynn said.

Tim Fletcher smiled. 'It could *sound* like *La Traviata*, I'm afraid I still wouldn't understand it. Most of it, anyhow.'

Lynn introduced herself and sat on the edge of the bed. After several minutes' polite conversation about his injuries, she asked him if he'd heard about Karl Dougherty and then how well he'd known him.

'Hardly at all.'

'You haven't worked together, then? I mean, on the same ward or anything?'

Fletcher shook his head. 'Not for any length of time. Not that I recall.'

'Wouldn't you remember something like that?'

'The way it's organized, I'm attached to a consultant, Mr Salt as it happens. Now it's likely the bulk of his patients will be in one or two wards, but, especially with the bed situation the way it is, the others might be just about anywhere.' For several moments he stared at her, vaguely aware that beneath his bandages there was an irritation waiting to be scratched. 'You don't think there's a connection, something more than coincidence, what happened to the two of us?'

'Oh,' said Lynn, 'I really don't know. Except, well, it is a bit of a coincidence, isn't it? If that's what it is.'

Fletcher didn't want to talk about it, not any more. Bad enough being reminded of what had happened every time you tried to turn over in the bed, each faltering move you made under the physio's eye. In the waste of night, his senses recreated for him the hot smell of hard rubber from the bridge floor with uncanny accuracy.

'All these flowers,' Lynn said, seeking a polite note on which to leave, 'from Karen, I suppose?'

'Not all of them.'

'They're lovely.' She got up from the bed and moved in front of Fletcher's chair. 'How is she? Karen.'

'I don't know.'

'I thought . . .'

'I haven't seen her.'

'Oh?'

'She called, left a message with the sister. Bit off-colour.' He glanced round at the bedside cupboard. 'She sent a card, lots of cards. I'm sure she'll be in tomorrow.'

'Yes,' Lynn said, 'I'm sure.'

Last thing she was likely to do, Lynn thought as she walked back through the ward, show herself with her face looking like a relief map of somewhere Wainwright might have hiked. Probably she was hiding in her room, waiting for the bruising to subside. No reason to think it was any more than that. Taking the stairs instead of the lift, Lynn glanced at her watch. It wouldn't be far out of her way and if nothing else it would set her mind at rest.

For what was still the middle of the day, the street seemed unnaturally quiet. The rain had stopped, leaving grey cloud overhanging the sky like a warning. The bottle of unclaimed milk on the doorstep was a crusted yellow beyond cream. Lynn had lived in shared houses and understood the tendency never to see what didn't immediately concern you; once you started taking out the garbage, you were saddled with it until you left. Holding her breath as best she could, Lynn rang the bell, then knocked. Through the letter box she could see the same pile of unwanted mail on the low table, the telephone. She had feared it might prove a wasted journey and the silence inside the house told her she had been right. Oh, well . . .

As she was turning away, Lynn heard a door opening inside.

She knocked again and eventually a man appeared, blinking at the dull light. He was in his early twenties, wearing a V-neck sweater over jeans with horizontal tears across both knees. Several days' stubble on a blotchy face. A student or out of work, guessed Lynn, she found it difficult to tell the difference.

She told him who she was and showed him her warrant card, but he was already shambling back along the narrow hall.

'Karen Archer,' Lynn said, stepping inside. 'Is she . . . ?'

The man mumbled something she failed to catch and pointed upwards. Closing the front door behind her, Lynn climbed the stairs, almost forgetting the broken tread but not quite. The picture of kissing lovers had gone from the door to Karen's room and the catch that had once held a small padlock stood open. There was a sudden burst of music, loud from below, and the top half of her body jerked. *The door to the garden had not quite been open.* Almost two years now, still whenever she went through a door, uncertain of what she might find, the same images came silently slipping down. *Stray ends of cloud moved grey across the moon. A bicycle without a rear wheel leaned against the wall. Her toe touched against something and she bent to pick it up.* Mary Sheppard had taken her two children to her mother's and gone out to meet a man; invited him home. What? Coffee? Mary Sheppard: the first body Lynn had found. *Dark lines like ribbons drawn through her hair*. Come on, Lynn. She turned the handle and stepped inside.

Stripped: stripped and gone. The box mattress, slightly stained and sagging at its centre, the veneered dressing table were the only furniture left in the room. Screwed-up tissues, pale blue, yellow and pink, clustered near one corner. A single sock, purple and green shapes that had begun to run into one another, lay in the space between window and bed. Looking down over the back yards, Lynn saw short lines of washing, a baby asleep in a pram, geraniums; on the end of a square wooden post, a white and grey cat sat immobile, ears pricked. In one of the dressing-table drawers Lynn found an old receipt from the launderette, in another an empty box of tampons. Curling already at the ends, the Polaroid strip had fallen behind and, easing the dressing table from the wall, she lifted it out. Karen Archer and Tim Fletcher making funny faces with the photo-booth curtain as backdrop; no matter how distorted Karen tried to make her features, it was impossible to disguise her beauty. Or, now she looked at the photos closely, Fletcher's hopefulness. There was a print mark on the bottom picture, the one in which they kissed. Lynn opened her shoulder bag and, carefully, placed the strip inside her notebook.

Downstairs in the communal kitchen the young man who'd let Lynn in was pouring warm baked beans over cold mashed potato.

'When did she leave?'

'Who?'

'Karen.'

'Dunno.'

Lynn wanted to force his head under the cold tap, wake some life into him. 'Think.'

He struck the underside of the sauce bottle with the flat of his hand and a gout of tomato sauce flopped out, most of it on the plate. 'Might have been yesterday. Must've been. Supposed to give us notice, four weeks. Now we've got to go tarting round for someone else.'

Lynn's heart bled for him. 'Any idea where she's gone?'

He looked up at her disparagingly. 'Home to mummy.'

'She's giving up her course?'

He shrugged and stirred the beans and potato together.

'Have you got an address for her?' Lynn asked.

'Somewhere.'

It was all she could do to stop herself from pushing his face down into his plate. She contented herself by plucking the fork from his hand, waiting till she had his attention firmly on her face. 'Get it,' she said. 'Wherever it is, the address, get it now.'

He didn't like it but he did as he was told.

During all of this, Resnick had been doing more than his share of window-shopping: anywhere with male assistants wearing suits. In succession, he had feigned a passing interest in bicycles, fourteen-day trips to the Yugoslavian coast, all-in, a new sports jacket, a signet ring, a char-grilled burger with fries and a 90-Day Extra Savings account; he had considered the possibilities of walking boots, cricket bats, Filofaxes, framed posters of James Dean, Marilyn Monroe and Elvis Presley, separately or together; now he was standing between broad rolls of carpet, listening to a disquisition on the virtues (or otherwise) of underlay, when he noticed one of the salesmen leading a couple towards a central table to confirm the details of a sale.

As the salesman filled in the form, pausing at intervals to ask a question, once to laugh, several times to smile, Resnick watched him. Twenty-five or -six, but already thinning on top, hair combed from either side towards the centre of his head in a vain attempt at disguise. He was wearing a double-breasted light grey suit that would have fitted somebody perfectly, but not him. Resnick waited until the final handshakes, the nod of the head, promise of delivery, beginnings of an accompanying walk towards the door. Don't go all the way, don't waste time, there is commission to be earned.

'Excuse me,' Resnick said evenly, approaching from behind.

The salesman blinked as he turned, moving half a pace back so as to get Resnick properly in focus. Family man, not about to spend a fortune, with any luck a three-bedroom semi in need of recarpeting throughout.

'Yes, sir.' Cheerily.

'Peter . . .' tried Resnick.

'Paul, as it happens. I . . .'

'You know a Karl Dougherty, by any chance?'

Paul Groves shot a glance towards the door and instinctively Resnick moved across to cover any attempt to escape. But: 'Is it still raining?' Groves asked. 'Wondered if I'd need a coat.'

Twenty-one

Resnick watched Groves all the way back to the station, alongside him in the back of the summoned car, one of his elbows resting against the window, not staring, not making it too obvious. Just the fifteen feet across the pavement from the shop doorway to the kerb had been enough to destroy the loose thatch of Groves's hair, one side falling past his left ear, the other sticking out like a mistake, pale scalp exposed clearly between. Even so, he didn't look too disturbed, now and again glancing out, interested, as if being driven through a city he only remembered. Sure, his fingers tugged at the slack of his suit trousers once in a while and the collar beneath his blue-and-silver striped tie was getting a touch too tight, but underneath he seemed unconcerned. As if, at base, he knew nothing could really get to him; he was safe. Resnick wondered.

Outside the CID room he told Groves to hang on and put his head round the door, beckoning Patel from the desk where he was diligently making his way through his paperwork.

'News from the hospital?' he asked quietly, as they turned into the corridor.

'Back in intensive care. Apparently stable.'

Resnick nodded and directed Groves into the nearest interview room, with a view across the sloping car park towards four-storey houses where two-bedroom flats were still fetching in excess of a hundred thousand. He pointed to a chair and waited for Groves to sit down, taking the chair opposite for himself, leaving Patel room to make notes at the end of the table.

'I knew you'd want to talk to me,' Paul Groves said. 'After what happened.'

Resnick didn't respond, not directly. 'You're here of your own volition to make a statement and can leave at any time. You understand that?'

Groves nodded.

'Why don't you tell us about last night?'

Groves loosened his tie a little, then tightened it again, holding the knot between the thumb and first two fingers of his left hand while he pulled on the short end with his right. No matter how easily they come to water, Resnick thought, rare that they rush to drink.

'Karl and I had arranged to meet for a drink,' Groves began. 'Half nine and he was late, but then he always was.' Resnick noted the always but let it go. Questions later. 'I suppose it was nearly ten by the time he arrived. We stayed there till closing, talking, as much as you can over the music, two or three drinks, that's all. We're not what you'd call drinkers, either of us.'

He paused and looked at Resnick directly, the first time since he'd begun talking.

'That's Manhattan's. That's where we were. But I suppose you know that?'

'Go on,' Resnick said.

'There's not a lot more, really. Karl left a bit before me, not long. I went home. I assumed he'd done the same. Until this morning when I heard the news. Local. They didn't give many details at first, not even a name. Went through the back of my mind it might have been Karl, but why should it have been? I mean, really? Why would it?' His arms were resting on the edge of the table, several inches back from the wrist; the more he spoke, the more he gesticulated with his hands. Now they closed into fists and were still. 'Then they said who it was.'

It crossed Resnick's mind that Groves had been practising this, rehearsing the shifts in tone, the moves.

'I called the hospital,' Groves said, 'wouldn't say a lot over the phone, but they did tell me how he was.' A quick glance up. 'I was going in to see him, tonight, after work. I mean, I would have taken time off, only with Karl being like he is . . .'

'Like he is?'

'Not conscious, not really conscious and in intensive care. They said they might have to operate again . . .'

'They did.'

Now the response was real, concern jumping across his eyes.

'Whatever they did,' Resnick said, 'seems to have been successful. The last we heard he was resting. Not out of the wood, but . . .' Resnick spread his hands, suggesting, with luck, everything would turn out all right.

'Is this going to take much longer?' Groves asked.

'There's just a couple of things . . .'

'Yes?'

'You say Karl left first?'

'Yes.'

'Why was that?'

Groves looked at him sharply.

'You met for a drink, spend – what? – an hour together, more, normal thing, I would have thought, you'd have left at the same time.'

'Karl was worried about getting home.'

'Oh?'

'He was on an early. Next day, today.'

'Arrived late, left early.'

'Yes.'

'One of the penalties, going out with a nurse.'

'Sorry?' Just a touch sharper, arms away from the desk, but not still, stretching away from his sides.

'Same with the police. Shift work. Plays havoc with

145

your social life. Police and nurses. Earlies and lates.'
Resnick leaned his chair back on to its rear legs, relaxed.
'That's all there was to it, then? His leaving before you?'

'That's what I said.'

'Yes,' Resnick nodded. 'So you did.'

He smiled at Groves helpfully, waiting for more.
Revisions of revisions. Groves fidgeted, the tie, the table,
creases in his trousers, the tie again. 'I can't think of any
other reason.'

Resnick could: several. 'It's not true there was an
argument, then? No truth in that?'

'What argument?'

'I don't know, it's only a suggestion.'

'Whose suggestion?'

'Probably nothing to it.'

'That's right.'

'There's nothing to it?'

'No.'

'Karl and yourself, you didn't argue?'

'No.'

'No raised voices?'

'No.'

Resnick lowered the front legs of his chair carefully to
the floor. He leaned forward across the table and, instinctively, Paul Groves leaned back. Of the two, Resnick was
by far the bigger man. 'Like I said, it was pretty noisy, the
music. Quite a few dancing. Almost had to shout to make
ourselves heard.'

'I expect that's what it was, then.'

Groves shrugged.

'Not a row at all.'

Groves looked at him. 'What would we have to row
about?'

Resnick gave him another encouraging smile. 'You tell
me.'

Three shots out of four, Divine could get the paper into the waste bin without it touching the sides. Mind you, that was after twenty minutes of concerted practice. The boss was in the interview room, safely out of the way, everyone else God knows where, and he was writing up another report. A couple of hours of sitting in taxis down round the square, all very well for them to have those NO SMOKING stickers in the front, came out of the cabs smelling like an Indian restaurant. Anyway, there's this bloke comes prancing by in that purple sports gear they all seem to fancy just now, brand-new ghetto-blaster in one hand and an Adidas sports bag in the other. All Divine had done was go across and talk to him, by the numbers, warrant card, name and rank, station. 'I have reason to believe . . .' Now the guy was threatening official complaint, witnesses, racial harassment. In the court just the other week, some clever-bollocks of a barrister trying to make him look like a lifelong supporter of the National Front. 'Why did you stop the accused, constable? Had my client been white, would you have acted in the same way?' If the bastard had been white, he'd have been a sight less likely to be walking home at two in the morning with half an ounce of crack and his wallet thick with dirty tenners he'd just ponced off the girls he pimped for on Waverley Street.

Racial harassment, it choked him up. If they didn't want to get harassed, why didn't they clean up their act? Go straight, get a job. Instead it's sponging off the State one minute and calling it for every evil, repressive pigging thing the next. If harassing the buggers didn't make for an improvement in the crime statistics, it would stop soon enough. Not his fault if it was like shooting fish in a barrel. Asking for it and when they got it crying foul.

He cursed and screwed up another piece of paper, lobbing it through a high arc, into the bin in one.

Same with the bollocking IRA, they were another bunch of two-faced bastards. Over here, over in Europe, up to their armpits in Semtex and sub-machine-guns, blowing women and kids to kingdom-bloody-come, someone from the SAS sticks a gun up against their heads and pulls the trigger. Smack through the brain pan, that'll do nicely, thank you, they start squawking about illegal acts, overstepping the mark, operating outside the rule of law. What the fuck were they doing, if it wasn't operating outside the rule of law?

No.

Either they fuck off back to their own country, the lot of them, go back to growing potatoes or whatever it was they did over there, else give up running behind the skirts of some Human Rights Commission and accept the consequences.

Over here, looking for trouble, IRA or any other bloody terrorist, *whap!* Have them up against the wall fast and let the rest see what they're up against. That'd soon put a stop to it, no mistake.

And in the mean time, don't let anyone waste their breath telling him he was prejudiced. Not anyone. He swivelled in the chair, arm raised, going for something more fancy, in-off, side of the desk on to the wall, down into the bin, when the door opened and Patel came into the office.

'Bollocks!'

The ball of paper rebounded from the wall and skittered across the floor.

'Paul Groves,' Patel said, handing Divine a page from his notebook with the address, 'the boss says can you check him through records?'

'When I've got time.'

'I rather think he meant now.'

Divine waited until Patel had left the room. 'What's wrong with doing it yourself, Diptak? Too busy rimming the old man's arse to find the time?'

148

'You haven't any ideas yet then,' Paul Groves was saying, 'who might have done it?'

'Oh, yes,' Resnick said. 'We've always got ideas.'

He stood up and held out his hand. After only the slightest of hesitations, Grove shook it, looking Resnick in the eye, but likely, Resnick thought, having to force himself to do so. Knowing it was the right thing to do.

'There's nothing else, then?' Groves asked.

Resnick smiled. 'Not for the present.'

Patel opened the door.

'DC Patel will show you out.'

Divine didn't know what Resnick had expected him to come up with, maybe nothing, but the way Groves was shaping up he was ripe for something. Two and a bit years back, he'd been charged with gross indecency; that had been lowered to behaviour likely to harass, alarm or distress, before being dropped altogether. Nine months after that he had received a warning for remaining in a public lavatory longer than was reasonable for the purpose.

Not for his purpose, Divine said to himself, little bugger spends his lunch-hours out cottaging.

Resnick was standing just outside the CID room, chatting to one of the other DCs about soccer.

'If I were you, sir,' the DC was saying, 'I'd give County the elbow. Better off going up the Chesterfield and watching John Chedozie.'

'Maybe you're right.'

Divine came across and handed Resnick the details. 'Won't pay to turn your back on this one, sir,' said Divine. 'He's a bloody poof!'

Twenty-two

Calvin heard his father's footsteps overhead and leaned on to his left side, wondering if he was about to come downstairs. But the steps carried on towards the kitchen and Calvin relaxed and made himself comfortable again on the bed, drawing down hard on the spindly roll-up to keep it alight. Trouble with dope, especially stuff as good as that, the lingering sweetness of the smell; one move of his father's towards the stairs and Calvin would have been across to the door that opened out into the garden, wafting in air, spraying aftershave around like it was going out of style. 'One thing,' his father had said, 'and one thing only. You bring home girls, I don't want you bringing them down to your room. And I won't have you smoking dope. Not in this house.' Calvin had nodded, agreed, not pointing out to him that was two things. What did it matter? It was like school, you said yes and carried on doing what you liked. Calvin had reasons to remember school: endless afternoons of woodwork and skiving cross-country runs, and kids who'd yell at him across the playground: 'What's the matter with you, Calvin? Not got the balls to be a real nigger!' Real niggers were black. Calvin, son of a Bermudan father and a Nottinghamshire mother, was a shade of light coffee. 'Hey!' the black kids would shout. 'You ain't one of us!'

They were right. Calvin wasn't one of anybody.

Closing his eyes, resting his head back, he could see his room as clearly as if his eyes were still open. Three of the four walls were painted matt black, the fourth, the one with

150

the window, deep purple; the ceiling was dark blue, the colour of the night; when all of the lights were extinguished he could lie on his back and stare up at the formations of stars and planets he had stuck there, iridescent and sparkling. The cupboard and the chest he had painted in white-and-black diagonal stripes; a black metal trolley held his stereo tape deck, record deck, amp and tuner. The cover draped over the bed was shiny black, fake silk. He had bought it in the market with the money his father had given him the day he was accepted for City College. He hadn't given him anything the day he'd quit. Not even a good shouting. When that had happened there had been other things on his father's mind.

There were no pictures on the walls, no posters. Only, in white letters he'd cut out himself, high above his bed, the name: Calvin Ridgemount.

The tape came to an end and clicked off. Calvin stubbed the last quarter inch out into a tobacco tin and slid it beneath the bed. Any minute his father would call down, asking him if he wanted anything to eat. He slid off the bed and straightened the cover; one thing you couldn't say about his room, you couldn't say it wasn't neat.

One of the differences Calvin had noticed in his father since it had happened, his father had taken to cooking. All the while they'd been together, a family, the only times he'd as much as entered the kitchen had been to fetch a cold can of Red Stripe from the fridge. He hadn't even carried out the plates after eating, not since Calvin had been big enough to do the job for him, Calvin or Marjorie. Marjorie was Calvin's sister, four years younger. It had seemed a long time before she had been able to manage more than the water glasses, Calvin having to take the remainder on his own.

Now, twice a day, three times on a Sunday, his father would fetch proper meals to the table. Nothing fancy, experimental, but none of that ready-to-serve, chill-cooked, out of a packet, out of a carton, out of the tin. Today, from the smell of it, it was onions, fried almost to a crisp till the sweetness came and all but went; sausages, too, fat ones, speckled with herbs, Lincolnshire. Though Calvin had a friend worked nights in a factory in the city, swore they were made right there.

'Hungry?' his father asked.

'Not very.'

His father spooned chick-peas on to one side of a plate, two sausages, then thinking about it for a moment before adding a third.

'Dad.'

'Yes?'

'I said I wasn't hungry, right.'

'That doesn't usually stop you,' his father said, although all that home cooking barely showed and Calvin, in his T-shirt and jeans, was still lean as cured bacon.

His father lifted the frying pan over the plate and tipped out half the onions, giving the pan a helpful shake. Finally, a thick tomato sauce distilled from several pounds of ripe tomatoes and molasses.

'Here,' his father said, passing the plate across to the breakfast bar where they usually sat to eat. 'You might need this.' He took the small, straight-sided bottle of Tabasco sauce from the shelf and set it close to Calvin's plate. 'Give it a little spice.'

Then he went back to serving himself.

A perfectly good dining-table in the living room, a picture window that looked right down across the park, and nine times out of ten they had their meals in the kitchen. Sixteen years they hadn't been able to get his father in there, now it was the devil's own job to get him out.

'Good?' Calvin's father asked.

'Mm,' Calvin responded through a mouthful of sausage. 'Umnh.'

His father had taken up cooking, but he hadn't any time for recipes. Making social security and his small disability pension stretch to feed the two of them took a special kind of enterprise and effort. He would spend up to half of each day wandering around the local shops, take the bus down into the city or up to Arnold, picking up stuff and feeling it, never seeming to notice when shopkeepers or stallholders told him to keep his fingers to himself. Once or twice a week he would get up at five and go down to the wholesale market at Sneinton, there and back on that old bike of his, pedalling home in laborious low gear, towing a little wooden trailer behind him – little more than a vegetable crate with wheels – loaded full of potatoes, cabbages, whatever was cheap and in season.

'You know all the colleges have started back now?'

Calvin grunted.

'I thought you were going to get yourself enrolled again?'

'I am.'

'When?'

'When I know what course it is I want to do.'

'And when's that going to be?'

'I'm still going through the booklets, in't I, prospectuses?'

'A little late, ain't it?'

'Takes time, I don't want to make another mistake.'

'No danger of that.'

Calvin set down his knife and fork. 'What's that supposed to mean?'

'Never enrol, no chance you've got of dropping out.'

It wasn't worth arguing. Every so often his father would nag him about it, he would stall and before long the matter would be forgotten. They would get back to what now seemed to have become their lives. Meals together, a couple of beers of an evening watching old films his father would rent on video. *Operation Petticoat. That Touch of*

Mink. He could never understand how his father could watch such garbage, laugh at it. Still, it didn't matter. Around ten he would go down to his room and lie back on the bed, headphones on his head. David Lee Roth, Eddie Van Halen. Calvin knew what he was supposed to play was Soul II Soul, New Kids on the Block, Niggers with Attitude. Crap like that.

Mouth still full, he pushed his plate aside.

'You haven't finished.'

'I've had enough.'

The local paper came through the front door and the flap of the letter box snapped back with a crack. Calvin fetched it through into the kitchen, unfolding it to show the front page.

'Seen this,' he said, pointing at the headlines: NURSE'S GRIM FIGHT FOR LIFE.

His father nodded gently and slid the paper away. 'What you left, I'll put in the refrigerator. You might fancy it later.'

Fifteen minutes later, Calvin was ready. He'd pulled a sweater over his T-shirt, black running shoes on his feet. A canvas bag hung from his shoulder, rested snug against his hip.

His father was at the sink, finishing the washing up.

'Right,' Calvin said, opening the front door.

'Where're you off to?' his father asked.

'Out.'

Twenty-three

'Dicey business, Charlie. Can't say that I like it.'

Skelton was on the prowl. Desk to window, window to filing cabinet, filing cabinet to coffee-maker, though it didn't seem to occur to him to offer Resnick a cup. The superintendent was so wired up himself, Resnick wondered if he'd been taking his caffeine straight, mainlining it into a vein. Truth was, likely he hadn't done any serious exercise for a few hours, needed a five-mile run to steady his nerves.

He'd been like this after the trouble had flared up with Kate, either hyped up or flatter than a slow Sunday out in the suburbs of Bramcote, Burton Joyce. Resnick wondered again how things were with Skelton's daughter, A-levels pretty soon – was that what they still called them? – off to be a student somewhere probably. Then let Skelton try and keep tabs on her. Or maybe with the new morality they didn't waste their energies on sex and drugs and rock 'n' roll? Straight into pension schemes and overdrafts to afford Paul Smith suits; long evenings lusting after fax machines while they listened to Nigel Kennedy or the Eric Clapton back-catalogue re-released on CD. He'd been a fair guitarist once; Clapton not Kennedy.

'What are you thinking, Charlie?'

' "Crossroads", sir.'

'Not bringing that back, are they? Thought it was all this Australian stuff, *Neighbours* and the like.'

'No, sir. "Crossroads". It's a blues. Robert Johnson. Skip James. It's . . .'

'Relevant, Charlie?'

'No, sir. Not really.'

Skelton gave him a short, hard stare and resumed pacing his office carpet. As a superintendent you get thicker pile and a choice of colours, replacement every five years if you had the right connections. The way Skelton was going, that might be something else to talk to Paul Groves about.

'It's distracting,' Skelton said, behind Resnick now and making him turn in his chair. 'That's what worries me. Leading us away from what I think should be our main focus.'

'But if it's there . . .'

'What, Charlie? What exactly?'

'If Groves and Dougherty were involved . . .'

'Come on, Charlie. We don't know that.'

'Seems pretty incontrovertible Groves is gay, bisexual at least.'

'Where's your evidence about Dougherty?'

'Close to thirty interviews, people who've worked with him, some of them for quite a while. Had a drink with him, socialized. Not a great deal, but a little. Never once, any talk of a girlfriend. Woman. Not once.'

'That means he's gay?'

Resnick shrugged. What was Skelton getting so worked up about? 'It's an indication.'

'Of what? That he doesn't like women? That he doesn't like sex? Maybe he's a very private person. Maybe it's his hormones. If we all had our sexuality determined by our rate of intimacy, where would that leave us?' Skelton was back behind his desk, constructing cages with his fingers. 'Come to think of it, Charlie, last couple of police functions, you haven't brought anybody with you, the opposite sex. Not significant, is it?'

Resnick found himself wriggling a little more than was comfortable. Either Skelton was accusing him of being a long time in the closet or being innately prejudiced, he wasn't sure which. Perhaps it was both. Or simply a game? No. The only games he could imagine Skelton being interested in had strict rules, required the utmost concentration and alertness, were important to win and absolutely no fun at all. Fun, Resnick thought, wasn't a concept the superintendent believed in.

Poor Kate!

'I'm sure there was something going on between them,' Resnick said. 'Something to make Dougherty leave early, more than this shift business. I saw Groves's face when I suggested they might have been having a row.'

'Lovers' quarrel, Charlie?' said Skelton dismissively.

'Could have followed him out of the bar, across the street. One thing, if Dougherty knew who his attacker was, that would explain why he was able to get close, get in the first blow.'

'From behind, Charlie?'

The thought set up possibilities neither man was prepared fully to consider. Skelton slid back one of his desk drawers and took out a blue folder, some papers clipped neatly together.

'Home Office statistics. Rise in recorded sexual offences, five per cent to twenty-eight thousand in '89, since then more or less holding.' Skelton flipped over two pages. 'Research into that extra five per cent, thirteen hundred cases, between half and a third indecency charges against men. One town's public toilets. You can imagine what the gays had to say about that. You know.' Skelton turned to another sheet, a photo copy of a magazine article. ' "The prosecution and persecution of gay men," ' Skelton read.

'With respect, sir . . .'

'Let the media get wind of this,' Skelton said, 'they'll have a field day. Gays carving themselves up in lavatories. The so-called silent majority will want officers on observation, armed with everything from mirrors to video cameras and everyone to the left of the Co-op Labour Party will be

157

organizing demos and picketing police stations on behalf of their oppressed brothers.'

Resnick allowed a small silence to collect around them. Beyond it a car went by, all of its windows presumably down, loudspeakers blaring. From further along the corridor, not quite decipherable, the familiar cadence of swearing. Telephones, their urgencies overlapping.

'If he had motivation, sir. Groves. Opportunity.'

'Yes,' said Skelton, subdued now. 'I agree. We have to check it out. But, Charlie, low profile, low key, be careful who you use. And remember, if there is anything in it, where does that leave us with the attack on Fletcher? The hospital, Charlie, I still think that's where we'll find our answers.'

'Yes, sir,' Resnick said, getting to his feet.

'The wrong kind of publicity, Charlie,' Skelton said as Resnick reached the door, 'it can only get in the way.'

Patel was worrying over the information that had come back from the hospital, fussing with the computer, opening files, finding facts to cross-reference and concluding there were too few. If there was a clear link between Fletcher and Karl Dougherty he couldn't pin it down. Aside from the obvious; apart from the fact that they had survived. In Dougherty's case, just. His condition was still giving cause for concern.

Naylor and Lynn Kellogg were talking into telephones, opposite ends of the office.

'Nobody tramps the streets with a pram for eight hours,' Naylor was saying. 'Nobody in their right mind.'

'And when she made this application,' said Lynn Kellogg, 'did she say what she was going to do? . . . Mm, hm. Mm, hm . . . And did she say where?'

Resnick stood for a while behind Patel's desk, looking at the characters springing up on the green screen. Names, dates, times. It should all be checked against a list of patients Fletcher would have had dealings with, patients from Bernard Salt's list, but that list was slow in coming. The consultant's secretary had greeted Patel's request like an invitation to perform a particularly unsavoury sexual act.

If Skelton was right and the hospital was where they were going to get their answers, they would have to do better than this.

'I would go back there, sir,' Patel said. 'But with the best will in the world, I don't think it would make a lot of difference. She is a very determined lady.'

Resnick nodded. The sort that, generations back, would have travelled across the Sahara by camel without ever breaking sweat or needing to urinate behind the nearest pyramid; who held the Raj together in the face of disease, the caste system and the occasional difficulty in getting a fourth for bridge.

'If you might call her yourself, sir,' Patel suggested.

'I'll get the super to do it.'

'I don't know,' Naylor was saying. 'As soon as I can. What does it matter anyway, if you're not going to be there?'

'Thank you,' said Lynn. 'If she does get in touch, you'll let me know?'

Resnick watched as Naylor slammed down the phone and left the office with a speed that nearly left a startled DC, who happened to be coming through the door, minus an arm. Resnick looked questioningly towards Lynn Kellogg and slowly she shook her head. The number of times Resnick had seen it happen: young officers who think a kiddie is all they need to bring them and their young wives back together.

He headed for his office and Lynn followed him.

'Karen Archer, sir. I've checked with the university. Seems she saw the student counsellor and was advised to take some time off. Compassionate leave, sort of thing.

The department secretary assumed she'd gone home to her parents, but didn't know for sure. I've tried to contact them and can't get any response.'

'You're worried?'

'Just a feeling, sir.'

'She had obviously moved out, though. Signalled her intentions.'

'Yes.'

'It's not as if Carew's gone after her again, no suggestion of that?'

Lynn shook her head.

'The concern is, then, what? She might have harmed herself?'

'Something like that, sir. Rape. The way Maureen Madden explained it, at least if she'd agreed to press charges, that would have been acknowledging what happened and saying that it wasn't her fault. Not leaving her trying to suppress it or feeling guilty.'

'Her parents. Where do they live?'

'Devon, sir. Close to Lynmouth.'

'Put through a call to the local station. Ask them to contact the parents if they can.' He looked across at her, a stocky, earnest woman with worried, sympathetic eyes. 'Take it from there.'

'Yes, sir.'

Before Lynn had left his office, Resnick was getting himself put through to Skelton. The superintendent brought his rank and authority to bear on Bernard Salt's secretary, who promised she would have the necessary information available by the end of the day. Resnick thanked him and checked that he could pick it up himself. He had another call to make that would take him close.

A little after five, Resnick was standing in the back garden of the Doughertys' house in Wollaton, balancing a cup and saucer in his left hand. The sky was losing light and across a succession of privet hedges bungalows were falling into silhouette. Inside, in the kitchen, Pauline Dougherty was washing their best dinner service, the one that had been a wedding gift, for the second time.

'I'm sorry,' Resnick said to William Dougherty, who was standing to his left, staring at some non-existent blemish on the lawn, 'but there's something I have to ask you about Karl. Something personal.'

Twenty-four

'Helen, this is simply not the best time.'

'No?'

'No.'

'But then, Bernard, it never is.'

Bernard Salt put both hands briefly to his face, covering his mouth, tiredness; his eyes alone had any brightness left in them and even they were showing signs of strain. All the damned day in theatre and now this.

'Look,' he extended his hands towards her, palms up, fingers loosely spread; the way he approached relatives, persuasive, calming; the way he approached them when the prognosis was poor. Helen Minton knew: she had seen it in operation many times before. 'Look, Helen, here's what we'll do. Your diary, mine, we'll make a definite date for later in the week . . .'

Already she was shaking her head.

'Go somewhere pleasant, that restaurant out at Plumtree . . .'

'No, Bernard.'

'Give us a chance to talk properly . . .'

'Bernard, no.'

'Relax. Surely that's better than this?'

Helen Minton lifted her head and began to laugh.

'Look at us. You're tired, I'm tired. It's the end of the day.'

'Yes,' Helen said, still laughing. 'It's always the end of the day.'

He came close to taking her by the arm but thought better of it. 'Helen, please . . .'

The laughter continued, grew louder. Salt glanced anxiously towards the connecting door, the faint shadow of his secretary at her desk, the soft purr and click of the electric typewriter maintaining the same even tempo. The laughter rose and broke and was gone.

'Don't worry about her, Bernard. She'll think I'm just another hysterical, middle-aged woman for you to deal with. I'm sure she's used to them, trooping in and out of your office. The fact that this one's in uniform probably doesn't make a lot of difference. She'll never betray your confidence, expose you to anything as unsavoury as gossip.' Helen smiled without humour. 'She's probably in love with you herself.'

Salt shook his head. 'Now you are being stupid.'

'Of course,' she said, 'I always am, sooner or later. If I weren't, how could you dismiss me so easily. Ignore me as a fool.'

The consultant shook his head and sat down. 'I don't know what to do.'

'Yes, you do. It's simple. Give me an answer.'

He looked up at her and back at his desk. Slightly muffled, there was a knock at the outer office door. 'I can't,' he said.

They stayed as they were, Helen staring at Salt, at the fleshiness around his jaw, hating it, sickened by it, the sight of him; if he turned his head towards her now and said the right words, she would weep with gratitude and fall into his arms.

'Excuse me,' said the secretary apologetically, opening the door, 'but the inspector is here. To collect the patients' details. He wondered if you had a minute to spare.'

Without another word, Helen Minton hurried out, past the secretary, past Resnick, into the corridor.

'Of course,' said Salt wearily. 'Ask him to come in.'

The book shop was on the ground floor, close to the medical school entrance. Situated in the broad corridor outside was the telephone from which Tim Fletcher had tried to call Karen Archer the night he was attacked; around the corner and through the doors was the bridge where it had happened.

Ian Carew was wearing a sports jacket and underneath it a T-shirt with the slogan, *Medics have bigger balls.* Navy blue sweatpants and running shoes. In his hand, held against his side, were an A4 file and a textbook on anatomy and physiology. He watched Sarah Leonard walk into the corridor from the hospital and cross towards the bookshop and go inside. He gave her half a minute and went after her.

In amongst all of the professional sections there were a few general paperbacks, Booker runners-up and beach reading. Carew pretended to browse through these, watching Sarah all the while, the way the muscles of her calves tightened as she reached for something from an upper shelf.

Suddenly, she turned to face him, as if aware that he had been watching her and Carew had only two choices. He walked straight to her, finding his smile easily, glancing at the books in her hands.

'Teasdale *and* Rubinstein. Heavy duty, even for a staff nurse with ambitions.'

Sarah looked at him as if expecting him to move aside, allow her to get to the cash desk.

Carew didn't move. 'I recognized you,' he said. 'From the other night.' Pointedly looking at the engraved badge pinned above her breast. 'Sarah.'

'Yes,' she said. 'You were kerb crawling.'

Carew tut-tutted. 'I offered you a lift.'

'You tried to pick me up.'

'Yes,' he said. 'Yes, I did.'

'Why?' she asked, sensing immediately it was the wrong thing to say.

Because of your hair, Carew thought, the way you were walking, striding out. He didn't say those things; not yet. He wasn't so stupid or inept.

'Are you really getting both of those?' he asked, tapping the uppermost of the books.

'They're not for me. One of the doctors . . .'

'Don't tell me he's got you running errands.'

'He couldn't get here himself.'

'Too busy.' Just an edge of sarcasm.

'He was badly injured. A few nights ago.'

'Not Fletcher? Tim Fletcher?'

'Do you know him?'

Carew shook his head. 'I read about him. Poor guy.'

'Yes.'

'How's he coming along?' Carew asked. 'On the mend?'

Sarah nodded. 'Slowly, yes.'

Carew angled his head back a little and seemed to refocus on her face. Sarah knew that he was going to change tack, ask her to meet him after work, something of the sort. She was conscious of the roof of her mouth turning dry.

'Well,' Carew said, 'nice to bump into you.' Stepping away. 'Maybe I'll see you again some time.'

And he was on his way out of the shop, a thick head of hair, good, muscular body, something of a bounce to his walk. Perhaps, Sarah thought, I was being a bit harsh on him, maybe he isn't so bad after all.

There were days and far too many of them when the only time Bernard Salt felt free of pressure was when he was in theatre. Anaesthetized in front of him, a problem to be solved and he knew the surest, the safest way to solve it. Of course, there were surprises, emergencies even. But they were what kept it alive: and they were surmountable. Within the span of his knowledge, of his hands. He stood there and at his bidding instruments were put into his hands, sterile, sharp. If something was rotten you cut it out.

As to the rest of it . . .

Twenty-four years of a marriage that had decently laid itself to rest. A mixture of rapaciousness and boredom that had driven him to find a solace for which he no longer had the inclination or the need. Why couldn't she accept that? Let go. That eternal whining, you promised, you promised. Of course he had promised. Wasn't that what he was supposed to do? A married man. Senior consultant. Seven, eight years ago when it had started, he would have promised her anything. Had. Now he would promise her anything to leave him alone, only she no longer believed him. Not without words on paper, evidence, commitment. All the times you said what we might do if only you were free.

Well, now he was free and fully intending to stay that way.

She was waiting by his car again and he considered abandoning it, heading back to the hospital and calling a taxi, but she had seen him.

'Helen,' Salt said, resting his briefcase on the roof of his car, fingers in his jacket pocket circling around the keys, 'how long do you think you're going to keep this up?'

She had changed out of her uniform into a white blouse and navy cardigan, a calf-length pleated skirt and, unbelted at the waist, a camel coat. Her hands were small, tight fists. 'For as long as it takes,' she said.

'And if I say no,' Salt asked.

'That's easy,' Helen said. 'You know what I'll do then.'

He drew his breath. In the masked fluorescence of the car park, her skin looked sallow and old. 'All right,' he said, 'no. The answer's no. Once and for all, no.'

Helen Minton slid a half-step sideways and steadied herself against the side of the car. Her mouth opened and there was a sound, harsh and hissing, like stale air making

166

its escape. She almost slipped as she turned away, recovered, and walked quickly between the avenues of other cars. Salt hesitated, started after her without conviction, and when she was lost to sight behind the door leading to the lifts, he stopped.

He had done it: said it.

Only then, quite still, did he realize the extent to which his own breathing had accelerated. He made himself stand for a full minute before heading back towards his own car.

Fitting the keys in the lock, fumbling a little, his head suddenly came up, alert. A movement off to his right, behind him. Moving then stopping. Salt looked off along the line of roofs, shadows. His first thought had been that it was Helen, calmed down, back to make her peace, apologize. He could see nobody: no doors opened, engines fired.

'Hello?' Salt's voice was oddly uncertain, hollow.

Then there was somebody, someone he knew, a fellow consultant making his way with crisp steps towards his Rover, waving: 'Hello, Bernard. Communing with the old carbon monoxide?'

Salt let himself into the car and waited until the Rover had slid from its space, reversing out and following it towards the exit.

By the time Calvin Ridgemount got home it was late. He let himself in, dropping his sports bag at the top of the stairs before going into the kitchen. There were two cartons of milk in the fridge, one already opened, so he opened the other and drank the contents down in four long swallows. From the living room he could hear the sound of recorded voices and soundtrack music, his father's laughter.

Calvin smeared plum jam on two digestive biscuits and put them together, taking a bite as he went towards the back of the house.

His father was sitting back on the settee, one leg hooked

over the side, can of Red Stripe in his hand, laughing at something Barbra Streisand had just said to what's-his-name? The one whose daughter married the tennis player Calvin couldn't stand. It didn't matter. He had seen it before, the film, something really stupid about boxing. His father had fetched it from the corner shop, two videos for a pound if you brought them back next morning, but this was being shown live, on TV, now.

'Where've you been?' his father asked, still smiling at what he'd seen.

'I told you,' Calvin said. 'Out.'

'Where you going now?'

'To bed.'

In his room, Calvin tossed the bag towards the far wall, below the window. Without bothering to switch on the light, he slipped *Fair Warning* from its case and switched the cassette player on. Lying back on his bed, he stared up at the ceiling, eyes growing accustomed to the blackness, watching the stars come out, one by one.

Twenty-five

Time was, Resnick thought, you would have walked into Manhattan's in the happy hour, and said the joint was jumping. Of course, he didn't know that for a fact. Just another bit of America that had found its way into his life via a record label. Thirty-seven or -eight. Herman Autrey on trumpet, Gene Sedric on tenor. Fats Waller and his Rhythm. Resnick had an uncle, a tailor with thumbs like sheet metal and fingers like silk; instead of coming to England in the months before the outbreak of the war, he had shipped out with his family to the States. Half a dozen of them sleeping toe to tail in a tenement off Hester Street. After VJ Day, the uncle had uprooted himself again, more opportunities in a smaller pond. Time had proved him wrong.

But Resnick could remember, as a boy, climbing to the upper floor of the house in St Anne's and poring over the enormous pile of 78s, black and brittle in brown covers of paper or card printed over with slogans for Vocalion, HMV. Sitting there, cross-legged, on his own, he had read the labels with fascination, inventing stories about the owners of those names before ever hearing their music: Count, Duke, Fats, Willie the Lion, Kid and King.

When first he heard them played, his friends were beginning to listen to – what? – Tommy Steele, Bill Haley and the Comets. Resnick had sat in hushed silence with black tea and dry cake while his uncle handsewed buttonholes and hems and his cousin swayed her legs softly to the Ink Spots, the Mills Brothers, four voices and a guitar. After a while, his uncle would tap his thimble on the table and wink at Resnick and then they would listen to Mildred Bailey, Billie Holiday, Luis Russell's 'Call of the Freaks', Fats Waller and his Rhythm, 'The Joint is Jumpin' '.

'You came back,' Maura said, as Resnick tried to edge into a space at the bar.

Her hair seemed to be suspended around her head, a mixture of fine gauze and candy floss. Since Resnick had last seen her, its colour had shaded from auburn towards orange. She was wearing a halter top, bright flowers on a black background. Rings on her fingers, earrings that brushed against her shoulders as she turned.

She set a bottle and a glass down in front of him and inclined her head towards the far side of the room, past the console where a hip black DJ was playing something Resnick was relieved not to recognize.

'I know,' Resnick said. He had spotted Groves as he walked in, sitting at a table against the wall with a couple of friends, back towards the door.

'You're not going to arrest him? In here?'

'What for?'

When Maura shrugged, her engraved metal earrings jingled. 'I've never seen anyone arrested, only on television.'

'That's where it happens most.'

She went back to serving customers and Resnick poured his beer, drank enough to get the remainder of the bottle into the glass and stood away from the bar, between there and the steps, occasionally glimpsing Paul Groves's prematurely balding head through the mass of drinkers. When he had finished his drink and Groves had shown no sign of leaving, Resnick moved to him around the edge of the dance floor and tapped him on the shoulder.

'Sup up,' Resnick said.

Beneath the volume of the music, Groves might not have

heard the actual words, but he caught their meaning. One of the young men with him, a white shirt with rolled-back sleeves and a wide paisley tie, looked as if he might be about to tell Resnick to mind his own business, but Groves shook his head and said it was all right and then stood up, leaving his lager unfinished.

'I've been reading your file,' Resnick said. They were crossing on to the pedestrian street that would take them to the rear of the Council House, the old Boots building. Usual for the time of year, it couldn't make up its mind whether or not to rain.

'I thought you might,' said Groves. His hands were in his trouser pockets, flaps of his jacket bunching back along his arms.

They were passing McDonald's, across squares of pavement on which a street artist had lovingly copied a madonna and child.

'What you are,' Resnick said. 'It doesn't matter, not to me. It doesn't make any difference.'

'Then why . . . ?'

'Except in so far as it's relevant.'

'Is it?'

'That's what I want to know.'

'You want to know if Karl and I were involved.'

'Were you?'

'What difference would it make?'

'I'm not sure. But your relationship with him, it would be different.'

'If we were both queer.'

They went right towards the square, past the girls with skimpy dresses and anxious eyes waiting between the lions, the Goths and Skins and would-be bikers gathered around the wall above the fountains, and sat on a wet bench in front of half-a-dozen damp and hopeful pigeons.

'How long have you known him?' Resnick asked.

'A year. More or less a year.'

171

Having learned when to question, when to listen, Resnick waited.

'I met him at the cinema. Late afternoon. It was my day off and Karl, well I suppose Karl's, too, or he'd worked an early. It doesn't matter. There we were in the smallest screen, the two of us and an old woman who ate her sandwiches and then fell asleep.' He gave Resnick a quick glance. 'We weren't sitting together, not anything like that. About as far apart as you could get. Karl spoke to me on the way out, something about the film, I don't remember what. We got outside and we were walking in the same direction. "I'm going for a pizza," he said, and laughed. "It's a wonder you didn't hear my stomach grumbling all through the film. I had half a mind to go and ask that old dear for one of her sandwiches." I laughed and there we were, sitting in the Pizza Hut, drinking large Cokes and arguing over which of us could build the biggest salad.'

A line of young women wearing fancy dress was congaing their way across the opposite end of the square, shrieking and singing. Paul Groves slipped both hands beneath the lapels of his coat.

'After that we'd meet up, usually once a week, go to a film, have a pizza, or if Karl couldn't get off in time we'd just go for a drink. Once in a while, after one of us had got paid, we'd go out for a meal. Karl wanted to go to that Japanese place, down in Lenton. Raw fish and it cost an arm and a leg.'

Resnick was aware of cramp spreading down his right leg, but didn't budge, didn't want to distract Groves from what he was saying.

'I nearly got him to come on holiday once. Greece, one of the small islands. Keen as anything until it came to paying the deposit and signing the forms.' Groves's voice was little more than a whisper; the conga line had moved off towards the Dog and Bear, to be replaced by a gang of jostling youths in Forest shirts, chanting and clapping their hands. The first of the police dog vans was parked at the north-east corner of the square. 'I went round to his place a couple of times. He had all these photos on the walls from when he was in the States, posters, more books than any normal person would read in a lifetime. Made a great thing out of grilling these hamburgers and having California wine. He'd never come back to my place, not once. Made excuses till I stopped asking.'

Groves moved his hands until they were gripping his knees.

'I touched him one time and you'd have thought I'd stuck a knife right in his back.'

'For Christ's sake,' Mark Divine said. 'What's your hurry?'

Naylor hesitated long enough for Divine to order two more pints.

'Fucking Friday night,' Divine said, elbowing his way towards a space by the doorway to the Gents, calling back over his shoulder. 'That's what it is.'

He glowered at a couple of underage lads and they slunk off.

'Ring her, tell her you're on obs. What's she going to know?'

'I already did.'

'You told her that?'

'Told her I was in for a half.'

Divine shook his head in disgust. 'Fucking women. Think they own you.'

'It isn't like that,' Naylor said.

'No? Tell us what it is like then?'

Naylor swallowed some more beer. He could no more begin to explain to Divine what it was like than he could get Debbie to talk about what it was that was wrong.

'Get these down,' Divine said, 'and we'll move on.' He

pushed at Naylor's shoulder with his fist. 'Strike lucky before the night's out, eh?'

Naylor drank his best bitter and didn't say a thing.

Resnick remained where he was, despite the dampness seeping up into his thighs and back, long after he had watched Paul Groves cross the square and climb into one of the cabs at the rank, heading home to Mapperley Top. If Karl Dougherty had only wanted companionship, a friend outside his work, Groves had wanted more. Sex. Love. It was difficult to believe that Karl had been ignorant of Groves's inclinations, that the younger man – he couldn't think of any other way to put it – fancied him. So what had he been doing? Pat phrases fell, fully formed, into his mind: stringing him along, playing with fire, dicing with death.

How frustrated would Groves have to be before striking out? How provoked? Two interviews in, Resnick did not consider Paul Groves to be a naturally violent man.

He remembered a pensioner who, after years of caring for his bedridden wife, waiting on her hand and foot, had blinded her suddenly with boiling tea; a fifteen-year-old youth who had stabbed his stepfather forty-two times with a bread knife and then tried to sever his neck with the end of a spade. Neither of them naturally violent, just driven till, like piano wire drawn tight inside them, their anger and frustration had sprung and snapped.

He passed the lavatory where Karl Dougherty had been attacked and thought about Reg Cossall. Likely he had seen which way the wind was blowing and been pleased to have the lot dumped into Resnick's lap, glad to be shot of it.

He could remember Cossall, a young sergeant then, still in uniform, fulminating against the openness in which a urinal close to the station was used for homosexual assignations. Men would gather there, two or three at a time, quick glances over their shoulders as they approached along the pavement that bordered the cemetery. Sometimes their cars were parked below on Talbot Street, ready for a quick retreat or later meeting. Sometimes a passing PC would whistle his approach, lean in and flash a torch. Occasionally, on the request of an indignant customer, caught short on his way home and unsuspecting, policing would become more positive. Word on the grapevine would pass along and the practice would fall away until things had calmed down and it was safe to return.

From time to dangerous time, the citizens of outrage, primed by beer and armed with sticks and worse, would take the law into their own hands. Resnick had watched as Cossall hauled out one who had been wading through the toilet's dim interior with the blunted bayonet his father had brought back from Cyprus.

'Go on, youth,' Cossall had said, retaining the weapon. 'Off with you, sharpish.'

One of the men they had helped out had been bleeding profusely from superficial wounds; another had to be stretchered to the ambulance, a gash opened up down his side, three layers of clothing exposed through to his ribs.

'Serves the bastards right,' Cossall had said, spitting towards the gutter. 'Bugger legislation, castrate the lot of 'em!'

There had been a high anger in his eyes and, seeing it again, in memory, Resnick thought of Karl Dougherty in the steady hum of intensive care, the blows that had been inflicted, Cossall's face as he had stepped down from the urinal, zipping himself into place. Was that what he had been thinking then? Serve him right. Just another bumboy getting more than he'd bargained for. Teach him a lesson.

Resnick wondered what the lessons were, exactly who was teaching whom? Queer-bashing. Paki-bashing. They broke out in phases, ugly and suppurating, cocky kids in short hair with right on their side. Something to do of a Friday night: someone to hit. Midway up that first stretch of Mansfield Road, Resnick turned and looked back at the city: nobody was learning anything.

Twenty-six

The only sign of Ed Silver was the broken glass shining dully in the light from the top of the front door. Bottle glass. The cats, anxious and eager and, as usual, late being fed, brushed around him and he shooed them away. When he went inside they scurried to the kitchen, where Resnick forked food into their bowls before going back out with an old newspaper. He wrapped the larger pieces of glass thickly inside its pages and dropped them in the green council dustbin. Then he used a dustpan and brush to sweep up as much of the rest as he could, finally down on his hands and knees to find any fragments that might end up in the cats' paws.

The envelopes he carried in from the hall floor were dull and brown and he left them beside the kettle while he ground coffee and gave the cats their milk. Pepper was losing hair in clumps along his back again and he would have to make time to take him to the vet: forty-five minutes of staring out the owners of schnauzers and Alsatians, pretending not to be embarrassed by his cat's whimpering.

One of the letters was from the Polish Club, reminding him that his subscription was overdue and inviting him to the eightieth birthday celebrations of one of its stalwart members. Second-class mail, it had taken five days to reach him, as the crow flies no more than a mile. A note had been penned at angles to the page: *Please come, Charles. We would all love to see you. Marian.* Marian Witczak, who kept the Polish flag in her window and an atlas open at Eastern Europe as if it were the A–Z. Step outside on to the street and the taxi that draws up will take you to the heart of Warsaw, fifteen minutes.

Resnick poured coffee, wondering about people who so strenuously denied the present, constructed a fantasy from the past. How many nights did Marian fall asleep dreaming of mazurkas and ball gowns? How much alcohol did it take before Ed Silver saw himself stepping up again on to the stand at Ronnie Scott's, slipping the shield from the mouthpiece, hooking his sax on to its sling, beating in time with his heel and launching into 'Dexterity' without even a glance back at the band?

He sliced the sausage he found in the back of the fridge and planned to fry it with pieces of cooked potato, a bulb of garlic, dust in a little dill and thyme. Before that he wanted something with his coffee and mourned for his lost cherry cheesecake. What he did have was honey, black bread it wouldn't take more than a minute to toast. Take it through and get the weight off his feet, a little rest and then the cooking. He was listening to Miles Davis, the trumpeter's namesake stretched purring between crotch and knee, a mouthful of coffee still in the cup, feeling better than at any time that day. He knew the phone would ring before the tune finished and it did.

There was one youth, hair cut like a mistake, boogying around the middle of the floor, doing a haphazard strip to Madonna, almost down to his boxers already and the bouncers anxious at the edge of the six-deep circle cheering him on.

'Any minute now,' said Naylor.

'What?'

'Trouble.'

Divine laughed. 'Fucking Friday night! What d'you expect?'

The girls he'd been eyeing up were back again, three of

them, standing close to the spiral staircase, pretending not to notice.

'Right,' Divine said. 'We're on.'

'What?'

'There.'

'Where?'

'Over there. Hanging out for it.'

All that Naylor could see was a trio of young women, nothing to differentiate them from the others packing the club. Hundreds of them. Lots of make-up, sun tan, streaked and permed hair, short skirts or low tops or both.

'Look at the state of that!' Divine nudged him urgently. 'Not wearing much more than a sodding belt.'

At least the woman who'd wriggled by might take his mind off the ones he'd been endlessly on about, but no, there he was again, looking interested, looking cool, wait for it, wait for it, now the grin. One of the three said something to the others and all three of them laughed.

'There you are,' Divine said. 'Let's get over.'

Out on the floor the impromptu stripper was shimmying a pair of boxer shorts with a design like psychedelic crazy-paving lower and lower on his hips. Half the crowd were clapping their hands and bellowing the chorus from 'World in Motion', the rest chanting, 'Off! Off! Off!' and the bouncers were flexing their muscles like substitutes about to be thrown into the action.

'We ought to do something about that,' said Naylor.

'Did we, fuck!'

'See what I mean,' Naylor said, as the first of the bouncers tried to barge through the crowd and took an elbow to the face for his pains.

'That's what we ought to do something about.' Divine turned Naylor round physically, the three girls looking at them openly now, the tallest giving them a touch of open mouth, letting the lip gloss do the work.

Two of the bouncers had broken through the cheering

179

cordon and made a grab for the stripper, managing between them to pull his shorts the rest of the way to the floor. 'Leave it,' Divine hissed. 'Just leave it alone.' A counter-section of the crowd had deserted the World Cup anthem for a few desultory lines of 'Why Was He Born So Beautiful?', dragged by the occasion from ancestral memory. Naylor found himself in front of the girls, only the tall one bolding it out, her friends turned away in embarrassment, real or feigned. 'Right,' said Divine. 'What are you lot drinking?' One of the bouncers grabbed up the stripper's clothes and tossed them in the direction of the nearest exit, while another held him by the shoulders and nonchalantly kneed him in the naked groin.

'What's he threatening to chop off this time?' Resnick asked.

'So far,' said Jane Wesley, 'nothing. He got into an argument with one of the regulars about football and there was a fight. Your friend came out of it rather the worse.'

'Far as I know,' said Resnick, 'Ed doesn't know a thing about football.'

'Exactly.'

Resnick sighed. All around them there was the smell of damp clothing and Old Holborn; urine, yesterday's and today's. 'Where is he?' he asked.

'In the office. I wanted to send for an ambulance, but he wouldn't let me.'

'Does he know you called me?'

'No.'

Resnick looked at her sharply.

'I thought, if he's going to have a go at somebody, rather you than some unsuspecting ambulance driver.'

'Right,' said Resnick. 'Thanks.'

Ed Silver was sitting, not on the chair but on the floor behind it, both arms wrapped around his head, which was resting on his knees.

'Will you be okay?' Jane asked.

Resnick nodded and she closed the office door behind them.

'Bastard, Charlie.'

'Who?'

'It's a bastard.' Silver's voice was muffled and even when he slid his hands clear of his face still sounded as if it were being filtered through cotton wool. 'Broken my bloody nose.'

In amongst the dried and drying blood and the swelling, it was difficult to see exactly what the damage might be. 'Looks like a trip to casualty,' Resnick said, already dreading it, far and away enough of hospitals recently.

Silver was shaking his head, even though it hurt to do so, mumbling no.

'You can't stay here with a broken nose.'

'Why the sodding hell not?'

'It needs attention.'

'I'll give it attention.' Silver placed his fingers to either side of the nose and began to push.

'Jesus, no!'

'What?'

'Don't do that.'

'Go back outside, Charlie. If you're squeamish.'

Instead, Resnick closed his eyes; it wasn't the blood, more the self-inflicted pain. There was a lot of squeezing, a quick click like balsa wood splintering and a lot more blood.

'There,' announced Silver, 'that's done it.'

'What exactly?'

'If the bastard wasn't broken, it is now.'

Naylor might not have believed it if he hadn't seen it with his own eyes, but there was Divine, leaning over these four lads and talking low and purposeful, smiling all the while.

A couple of minutes and the lads got up and vacated their table, great view down over the dance floor.

'What did you say to them?' Naylor asked as they sat down.

Divine winked. 'You don't want to know.'

The girls were all chatty enough now, not that it mattered what they were saying, most of it lost beneath the music and the low roar that rose from the floor and hung beneath the ceiling like hot air.

Divine put his arm around the tall girl's shoulders and she made a show of shrugging it off; Divine winking then, across the table at Naylor, giving him the thumbs-up when he thought the girl wasn't looking, though, of course, she was, pursing her lips at him, just a touch of tongue between the lip gloss.

'Fancy your chances, don't you?'

'I fancy yours.'

The other girls, sisters it turned out, in on the bus from Kirkby-in-Ashfield, Lord knows how they were expecting to get back, did some more nudging and giggling and Naylor thought, not for the first time, Christ, they can't be more than sixteen, seventeen.

'Mandy's a beauty queen,' said one of them, looking at the tall girl, who adjusted her profile into what she assumed to be a regal manner.

'Kevin over there's middleweight champion of the world, aren't you, Kev? Stings like a butterfly and sucks like a bee.'

Naylor blushed, the girls snorted into their banana daiquiris.

'I am, actually,' Mandy said.

'Yeh?'

'Yes. Miss Amber Valley. Two years running, as a matter of fact.'

'And she was runner-up the year before that,' added one friend.

'And she got into the heats for Miss East Midlands at Skeggy.'

'I can't cope with all this,' Divine said, getting to his feet, adjusting the crotch of his trousers as he did so. 'I'm off for a slash.'

'Coarse, your friend, isn't he?' the nearest sister confided in Naylor.

'Hey, Kev,' called Divine, turning back towards the table. 'What d'you reckon? Shall I get the coloured, the ribbed, or just the plain?'

The car hadn't been outside Aloysius House much more than twenty minutes, long enough for someone to throw up over the nearside of the boot.

'I hope you're not going to blame us for that,' said Jane Wesley, walking with Ed Silver and Resnick from the door.

'Wouldn't think of it,' Resnick said.

When they had manoeuvred Silver into the front seat, she said, angling her head away from the road, 'If this happens again, are you sure you want me to call you?'

'No,' Resnick shrugged.

'Does that mean you don't want me to?'

'No.'

'That's what I like,' she smiled, 'clear, decisive decision-making.'

Resnick raised one hand, open, towards her and went around to the other side of the car. A few more nights like this and he'd give up the idea of sleep altogether.

'Lovely woman,' Ed Silver said. 'Lovely.'

'So you said.'

'I did?'

'Last time.'

Silver picked at a scab on his upper lip and a thin line of blood began to run towards his unshaven chin. 'Have I seen her before? That woman?'

'Not clearly,' Resnick said.

'Hey!' Silver exclaimed some moments later, the car turning right to pass the central Probation Office and the old Guildhall courts. 'Was that a joke? Not clearly. Was that a joke?'

'No,' said Resnick. 'I don't make jokes.'

'Take 'em, eh Charlie. Take 'em. Not like that feller tonight, the one as did this. All that happened was, let me tell you this, he was blathering on about football or something, England, you know. That Parker, he said, not so bad but he'd play a damn sight better if he weren't black. You see, d'you see? So I goes, being black, that's part of it, makes him as fucking good as he is. Charlie fucking Parker. And he hit me, not with his fist neither, with his knee. Don't know how he managed it, but that's what it was, his knee. Ignorant drunken bastard, he calls me, don't even know his right bloody name.'

Resnick glanced sideways as they stopped at the lights below the Broad Marsh. The swelling round Silver's nose was certainly not going down; instead it was spreading across his cheeks, up towards his eyes. 'I knew he didn't mean Charlie Parker, somebody else . . .'

'Paul,' Resnick said. 'Paul Parker.'

'It was a joke.'

'Yes.'

'Fucking joke.'

'Yes.'

Silver rested a hand forward against the windscreen, blinking as he tried to focus. 'Where we going?'

'Casualty.'

'I'm not . . .'

'Ed?'

'Eh?'

'Shut up.'

One of those old Motown songs and Divine was pressing

himself up against the former Miss Amber Valley, grateful that she was tall enough for him to wriggle his tongue in her ear without having to bend too low.

'How about it, then? Shall we go?'

'What d'you mean?'

'Come on. Ready?'

'No.'

'Come on.' A tug at her wrist.

'No.'

No attempt at dancing now. 'Why not?'

'I can't.'

'Don't worry about your mates, Kev'll look after them all right.'

'It's not that.'

'What is it, then?'

'My boyfriend . . .'

'Your sodding what?'

'Boyfriend. He's meeting me here, picking me up.'

Divine shook his head in disbelief.

'One of his pals was having his stag night.'

'Well, that's it, then, isn't it?' He moved in again, hands low at her back, fingers against the top of her buttocks pulling her back towards him, edge of her little panties clear to the touch. 'You'll not see him till morning.'

'What d'you mean?'

'If he's been out on the piss with his mates, he's not going to turn up here, is he, ready to drive you home.'

'He will.'

'Be too drunk to stand up, most likely, never mind drive.'

She pulled herself away from him and stood there pouting, lip gloss all but gone. Divine had a sudden vision of the evening ending in nothing and he hated it.

'All right, then,' he said, grabbing her arm at the elbow, 'if he's out there waiting for you, let's go find him.'

Protesting, Mandy was pushed and pulled towards the

185

exit, until finally, grudgingly she walked with him out through the entrance, past the dinner-jacketed bouncers and round into the car park.

'Where is he, then?'

'I don't know . . .'

'Exactly.'

Divine ran his hand up her back and fondled her neck beneath the permed hair. He kissed her shoulder, slid his other hand over her breast as he turned her towards him.

'If you didn't want this,' he said, 'you should have said so before. But then you might not have scored so many free drinks.'

'You offered,' she said. 'What was I supposed to do?'

'This,' Divine said.

He was kissing her, pushing his tongue into her mouth, doing his best to stop her wriggling and get a hand inside her dress at the same time, when someone tapped him hard on the shoulder.

The second time it happened Divine turned to give whoever it was a mouthful and got hit by Mandy's boyfriend, a fourteen-stone West Indian, who brought an eight-inch spanner smack down on to Divine's left eye.

Resnick wanted to drop Ed Silver off at the doors to casualty and leave him there, but he couldn't bring himself to do it. Almost the first things he saw, after steering Silver towards reception, were two familiar faces amongst those waiting for attention. 'Naylor,' Resnick said. 'Divine. What are you doing here?'

Twenty-seven

'Course, I'd heard the records, a few of them anyway, but I'll tell you, Charlie, first time I ever saw Bird and Dizzy live, I almost pissed myself.'

One of the other problems with drunks, Resnick was thinking, they never knew when it was time to go to sleep. The visit to casualty had been shorter than some, less painful than many; Ed Silver had emerged with a well-washed face, a slightly remodelled nose and good intentions. 'One thing, Charlie,' he had claimed, getting into Resnick's car, 'this has done it for me, I mean it. My drinking, from now on it's going to be seriously under control. So help me. And you can bear witness to that.' They hadn't been back at the house half an hour, before Silver was going through cupboards, searching at the back of shelves. 'Just a tot, Charlie. Nobody can be expected to give up totally, just like that. The body wouldn't stand for it.'

Resnick had found tins of frankfurters and Czechoslovakian sauerkraut, the nub ends of a loaf of black rye, pickled gherkins; he had opened the only bottle of wine he possessed, the cheapest dry white he had found in the Co-op, bought months ago to make a recipe he had since forgotten.

Nervous of all this unwonted night-time activity, Bud chased his tail from room to room, occasionally stopping to look perplexed, the White Rabbit in *Alice*, terrified that he was late but with no idea what for.

'The first of the Dial sessions, Charlie, the ones with Miles and Max Roach, you must have those, eh?'

So they sat through the night, listening to the Charlie Parker Quintet – 'The Hymn', 'Bird of Paradise', 'Dexterity' – while, around them, Resnick's neighbours slept on, dreaming straight dreams unthreatened by flattened fifths.

Ed Silver's first attempts to play jazz had been as a clarinettist with a revivalist band in Glasgow, doing his best to sound like Johnny Dodds in the twenties. The first thing that changed that was, down south for a rare date at the Hot Club of London, this skinny guy had come up to him and started talking, an accent that stretched across the Atlantic and back to Aldgate. A musician himself, he'd played with a number of USAF band personnel stationed here during the war, taken a job immediately afterwards, polite music for dancers on one of the liners travelling from Southampton to New York. It was in his East End flat that Silver heard his first bursts of Charlie Parker, records he'd made with Jay McShann's band; each time Parker soloed, the everyday was suddenly pierced by the sublime.

Next day, Silver had pawned his clarinet in exchange for an alto and talked his way into a band working the boats. Anything to get to the Apple, 52nd Street, the Three Deuces and the Royal Roost.

'This is the group,' Silver said now, listening, catching a piece of cucumber at the third attempt and slipping it into his mouth, 'I saw at the Deuces. Amazing. Every last dollar I had on me I spent seeing them, three nights in a row, each time it was hotter and better.

'Anyway . . .' A gulp at the wine now, wincing a little as he moved his mouth. '. . . there I am the next day, pretty late on, due on board ship at half-seven, taking my last look down Broadway and there's Bird, crossing the street ahead of me, sax case in his hand. First reaction, Charlie, I'll tell you, no, it's not him, can't be. Then it is and I'm hurrying after him, slapping him on the back, shaking his hand, telling him I've come all the way from England just to hear him, every solo he's played the last three nights has been a fucking inspiration.

'Bird looks at me a shade off and then he smiles. "Hey, man. Lend me fifty bucks." I would have given that man every stitch of clothing on my back if he'd asked for it, but right then I didn't have five bucks, never mind fifty. I can't think of another damn thing to say and all I can do, Charlie, I think of it to this day, is watch him walk away.

'By the time he got to the studio, just a couple of blocks down, he'd copped from somebody else. Story goes he shot up in the studio bogs before going right in and cutting this stuff.'

Ed Silver leaned back and closed his eyes as, unison theme over, Parker's alto sailed out, clean and clear, over the swish of Max Roach's cymbals.

' "Dexterity",' Ed Silver said.

'Story also goes,' said Resnick, 'he'd killed himself before he was forty. Heart, stomach, cirrhosis of the liver.'

Ed Silver didn't say a thing; continued to sit there, eyes closed, sipping now and then at the last of the white wine.

Saturday: Debbie Naylor sat in the living room, curtains still drawn, trying to get the baby to feed. Up on the first floor, she could hear Kevin retching, head over the lavatory bowl. Serve him right, she thought, though with little satisfaction, let him find out what that's like, at least.

'What d'you call this?' Graham Millington asked, staring down at his plate. His wife was eating wholemeal toast, drinking camomile tea, reading the women's page of the *Mail*. If she could persuade Graham to drop her off at Asda and collect her, there would be time to get her evening-class homework finished before the boys needed ferrying to that party in West Bridgford. 'This isn't what we normally have, is it?' Millington persisted.

189

'Extra bran,' she said, 'fifteen per cent more fruit and nuts. No added sugar or salt. Thought it would make a nice change.'

Graham Millington mumbled to himself and carried on chewing.

Lynn Kellogg sat in the parked car and poured coffee into the flask's white plastic cup. When she'd been little, six and seven and eight, Sunday afternoon drives with her parents, east to the sea, south to watch the horses canter on Newmarket common, there had been milk in Tupperware containers, sugar – lumps for the horses, granulated for themselves, spooned from a paper bag – a packet of ginger nuts and another – treat of treats! – of jaffa cakes. Sitting there, watching the still deserted street, she could remember the first taste of jam, the quick sweetness of it the moment the chocolate coating broke through.

'What time did she get in last night?' Skelton's wife asked, tightening the belt of her dressing-gown, turn and turn and pull, a double bow.

'I don't know.'

'Of course you know.'

Skelton shook his head. Take the kettle to the pot, not the pot to the kettle: amazing how our parents' precepts stuck with us, governed the trivia of our lives, amazing and terrible. 'It doesn't matter,' he said.

His wife opened the glass-fronted cupboard, took out saucers, bone-china cups, white with a tasteful floral design. 'If it doesn't matter, why spend half the night sitting up, the rest of it lying in bed not sleeping?'

Divine blinked into the bathroom mirror with his one good eye. The other was swollen, yellow, stitches like Biro marks, blue-black, across it. 'Shit!' He leaned over the toilet bowl to urinate, one arm resting against the wall;

when he cleared his throat and spat it was like dredging Trent Lock. He didn't know what had been worse, the initial blow, the embarrassment or Resnick's face. Well. The swelling would subside, the stitches would come out and there was the inspector still to face. 'Slag!' wincing as the sound reverberated around his head. 'Slag!' slamming the wall with the flat of his hand. 'Fucking see her again, I'll teach her a fucking lesson!'

Calvin Ridgemount woke to the smell of bacon frying and knew instantly which day it was. He cleaned his teeth and splashed cold water up into his face. Same black jeans but a new T-shirt, Stone Roses, he liked the shirt design better than he liked the band. Smack on time, as Calvin entered the kitchen, his father was breaking the first of the eggs against the edge of the pan.

'You goin' to see your mother today?'

'You know I am.'

'That's fine. Just a couple of things I'd like you to do for me first.'

'Sure,' said Calvin, picking up one of the slices of bread his father had already buttered, folding it in half and starting to eat. 'No problem.'

'I've got a note somewhere for your mother, too. You give it to her, see that she reads it.'

'Sure.'

The same thing every fortnight, the same note, more or less, same words on blue-lined paper bought in a pad from the shop down on the corner and written painstakingly with a pencil. Knowing what would happen to them at his mother's hands, Calvin no longer bothered to deliver them, tore them into tiny pieces and pushed them out of sight behind the seat on the bus instead.

Helen Minton had thought she might write the letters by hand, but had decided instead that typing them would be

191

better. She had a small Silver Reed, a portable she'd bought at Smith's, oh, so many years ago she couldn't remember. Typing was far from natural to her, far from fast. Not often did she get through a sentence without having to wind the paper up, dab on the Tippex, wind it back down. She had been up since well before light, curtains open just a crack, lamp by her elbow, the typewriter on the living-room table. Four envelopes were fanned across one another like cards, addressed and ready, stamped. The tea had long gone cold in its mug and formed a viscous, orange rim. *Dear Mrs Salt*, she wrote, and *now that you and Bernard are divorced you may not think this concerns you directly*, and *during the last eight years of your marriage . . .*

Dear Father, wrote Patel, another letter of appeasement and promises, what he was doing, how close he was to sitting his sergeant's exam.

Dear Mum, wrote Paul Groves, *I don't want you to be too upset, but I might not be able to get home next week, something's cropped up . . .*

Dear Helen, wrote Bernard Salt and immediately tore it up.

In the intensive care ward, Karl Dougherty opened his eyes when the nurse spoke to him and, for the first time since he had been admitted, knew exactly who and where he was.

Amanda Hooson, a second-year social sciences student at the university, sweated on the floor of her small room, no way of knowing that she was pushing herself through her morning exercises for the very last time.

Twenty-eight

'Are you following me?'

'Not at all.'

'So what are you doing here then?'

'Not following anyone, just sitting.'

'You just happen to be sitting.'

'Yes.'

'In a parked car.'

'Yes.'

'At the end of my street.'

'Your street?'

'You know what I mean.'

'The street where you live.' Lynn had a sudden flash of memory, one of her mother's few records, its cover torn and bent at the edges, stained with greasy fingerprints and ring-marked by mugs of tea, Rex Harrison and Julie Andrews, *My Fair Lady*.

'What's so funny?' Carew said, a vein above his right eye standing out through the sweat.

'Nothing.'

'Then what's that smirk doing on your face?'

The smirk disappeared.

'I suppose you're here for the view?' Carew said.

'How was your run?' Lynn asked.

'Fine.'

'A little over twenty minutes. What's that, two miles, three?'

'Four.'

'Really? That's pretty good.'

'What? You want to be my coach or something?'

'Depends what you need coaching in.'

He leaned low towards the car window, a few drops of sweat falling from his nose down on to the sill. 'What would you suggest?'

'Oh,' Lynn said. 'I don't know. I should imagine it's difficult teaching much to a man like you.'

He gave her a glare and turned his back, started to walk away. He was wearing shorts this morning, despite the fall in the temperature, brief and tight across his buttocks. The muscles at the backs of his legs were thick and taut and shone with the dull glow of sweat. The hair along his legs and arms was thick and dark.

'When did you last see Karen Archer?' Lynn called after him.

Carew stopped instantly and Lynn repeated her question.

He faced her slowly, began to walk back. Lynn read the expression on his face and thought for a minute he was going to reach in and try to drag her from the car. The moment passed. 'You know I'm not allowed to see her,' Carew said.

'Does that mean you haven't seen her?' Lynn said.

'Remember? I'm warned off.'

'Not everyone pays attention to warnings.'

'Perhaps I do.'

I doubt that, Lynn thought. 'So you haven't spoken to Karen since you were at the station? You haven't seen her, there's been no contact?'

'That's right.'

'Because she's missing.'

'Oh, well!' Carew threw out both arms like a bad stage tenor. 'That's it then. It's obviously me. That's what you're thinking, isn't it? Karen's hidden in a cupboard somewhere. Ian Carew. No other explanation.'

'Is there?'

'What?'

'Another explanation?'

'I should think so, hundreds of them. You just like this one.'

'Why should I do that?'

'Because it's easy. You don't have to think further than the end of your nose.' He made a gesture, maybe automatic, perhaps not, a tug at the front of his shorts. 'Because you resent me.'

Lynn bit her tongue, best to let it ride. 'Why did you say a cupboard?' she said.

'Did I?'

'Hidden in a cupboard somewhere, that's what you said.'

'The sweat's drying on me,' he said. 'I need to take a shower. It's getting cold.'

'A cupboard,' Lynn persisted.

'That's right,' Carew smiling, 'that's where I've dumped her. Inside a sack after I hacked her to pieces.' He leaned close and leered. 'Why don't you come in and look?'

Lynn stared at him, stone-faced.

'Come on, search. You do have a search warrant, don't you?'

Lynn turned the key in the ignition. 'If Karen gets in touch with you, please let us know. Ask her to contact the station, ask for me.'

Carew sneered two soundless words, unmistakable. Lynn made herself let out the clutch slowly, check the mirror, indicate. When she reached the main road and swung up past the hospital towards the station, she was still shaking.

It was raining again: a fine, sweeping drizzle that seeped, finally, into the bones, chilling you as only English rain could. On a makeshift stage at the centre of the old market square, the Burton Youth Band were playing a selection from the shows to a scattering of casual listeners and a few sodden relatives who had made the journey over on the band coach. Off to one side of the stage, in a row of their own, a boy and a girl, eleven or twelve and not in uniform like the rest, sat behind a single music stand, mouths moving as they counted the bars. Resnick watched them – the lad with spectacles and cow-licked hair, the girl thin-faced and skimpily dressed, legs purple-patched from rain and wind – nervously fingering the valves of their cornets as they waited to come in.

It was close to where Resnick was standing that Paul Groves had sat, staring off, and talked about his friendship with Karl Dougherty. *I touched him one time and you'd have thought I'd stuck a knife right in his back.* Once, while he and Elaine were still sharing the same house, truths spilling like stains everywhere between them, they had passed close together near the foot of the stairs and Resnick, unthinking, had reached to touch the soft skin inside her arm. He could picture now the hostility that had fired her eyes; the already instinctive recoiling.

The band hit the last note of 'Some Enchanted Evening' more or less together and Resnick clapped, startling a few dazed pigeons. An elderly lady wheeled her shopping trolley across in front of the stage and dropped a coin into the bass-drum case that was collecting puddles and contributions towards the band's winter tour of Germany and the conductor announced the final number. Time to go, Resnick thought, but he stayed on as the two beginners lifted their instruments towards their lips. The conductor waved a hand encouragingly in their direction, the wind lifted their sheet music from its stand and their chance was lost. Without hesitation, the boy retrieved it and Resnick watched the girl's pinched serious face as, biting the inside of her mouth, she struggled to find her place in time for the next chorus. Only when they had played their sixteen bars and sat back, did Resnick turn away, tears, daft sod, pricking at his eyes.

Carew had taken his time over showering and now he sat in his room with the gas fire turned high, just blue-and-white striped boxers and a lambswool V-neck, eating a second apple and glancing through the review section of *The Times*. So many sections, it was getting difficult to tell Saturdays from Sundays. At hand but unopened, a book on neurosurgery that needed returning to the library, notes for an essay that should have been submitted the week before and for which he had every intention of applying for a further extension.

He refolded the paper and dropped it to the floor, walked on bare feet to the window. The car was back again, square to the end of the street, he could see the dark-haired silhouette clearly enough but not the face. Well, fuck her! He pulled on faded jeans, clean from the launderette, replaced his sweater with a white shirt. His black leather jacket was hanging behind the door. The door at the side of the kitchen led past an outside toilet, now disused, across a small flagged yard to a narrow entry. Half-way along, Carew let himself through someone's rear gate and slipped through the side passage into the adjacent road.

He wondered if she'd still be sitting there when he got back, or whether her patience would have run out. On the whole, Carew thought with a smile, he preferred the former. Maybe then he would make a show of walking past, returning when she didn't even know he'd left, give her something to think about. Or simply go back in the way he'd come out, leaving her none the wiser. Either had its advantages.

And which one Carew chose, what would that depend on? Whim, mood, or how he got on where he was going?

Lynn Kellogg shifted her position behind the wheel yet

197

again, stretching her legs as best she could before beginning another set of exercises to keep the circulation flowing, raising and lowering first her toes, then all of the foot, circling and lifting, pressing down. Ankling, her former cyclist boyfriend had called it, one of the few techniques he could be relied upon to demonstrate successfully, those times she caught him flat on his back on their bed. She told herself not to check her watch but, of course, she did. She tried to clear her mind and concentrate, not wanting to think about the state of her bladder, how many more Sundays she could go without driving home to Norfolk, exactly what Resnick would say if ever she had to explain what she was doing.

Twenty-nine

Cheryl Falmer looked at her watch for the second time in as many minutes and walked across to the desk to check that it was correct. She had arranged to meet Amanda on court at four and there she was, changed and ready, twenty past four and no Amanda. She was beginning to feel stupid, standing in the sports-centre foyer in that skirt, pretending not to notice the rugby players staring at her legs as they came in from training.

'It is four o'clock?' she asked the woman at reception. 'Badminton. Booked in the name of Hooson.'

'That's right. Not turned up?'

'No.'

'Maybe she's forgotten.'

Cheryl moved away, shaking her head. Amanda wasn't the kind to forget. Not anything. Every week they'd been playing, through the last two terms of the previous year and carrying on in this. She knew that Amanda marked it down in the little diary she always carried. Green dot with a four alongside it: badminton. Blue dots for essays in. Yellow for tutorials, red for you know what. Unlike a lot of her group, Amanda was serious, organized; not a stick-in-the-mud, not po-faced like the few feminist-Leninists or whatever they were, always scowling from behind their hand-knitted sweaters and hand-rolled cigarettes; a little older, more mature, she had chosen social sciences with a purpose, not fallen into it as an easy option or an academic back door.

Even so: nearly twenty-five past and no sign.

If it had been squash, it would have been worth going on to the court by herself and thwacking the ball against the wall for half an hour. But the prospect of lofting shuttles high above the net, practising her serve, didn't appeal. She would go back into the changing room and get into her Simple Minds sweatshirt, her denim jacket and jeans. If she cut across between the practice pitches, it was easy enough to call by Amanda's hall of residence and find out what had happened, what had gone wrong.

Jazz Record Requests was just finishing as Resnick entered the house. Hearing the signature tune, he assumed that Ed Silver had switched the radio on and left it playing, hardly expected him still to be there. But he was at the kitchen table, so intent upon Resnick's battered copy of *The Horn* that he scarcely looked up. Miles, who had been spread the width of Silver's bony knees, leapt off at Resnick's approach and ran towards his bowl.

'Thought you couldn't stand cats,' Resnick said.

'I can't,' not looking round.

Resnick shrugged off his damp coat and leaned his plastic bag of shopping against the fridge. The other cats were there now, all save Dizzy, and Resnick ministered to them before grinding coffee for himself.

'Cup?' he asked Silver.

Silver didn't answer.

The legs of Resnick's trousers were wet through from the knees down, his brown leather shoes stained nearly black and he knew that when he took them off his socks would be ringed with dye and all but soaked through.

'This book,' Silver said, eyes not leaving the page, 'bloke who wrote it, wouldn't know a real musician if one jumped up and bit him in the arse.'

A novel about drugs and jazz in New York, Resnick remembered it as being romanticized but readable; at least it wasn't *Young Man with a Horn*.

'This, f'r'instance. Listen to this.'

But Resnick wasn't in the mood to be read to. He left Ed Silver competing with Radio Three and went into the bathroom. Clothes off and dumped in a corner he considered playing truth with the scales, but decided he wasn't up to that either. In his experience, grey days such as this only got greyer. One hand holding in his paunch, he stepped under the shower. Having failed to sell the house he would have to get the bathroom retiled, cream wallpaper beginning to darken and buckle where it was exposed to the water.

'Persistent, isn't she?'

Opening his eyes, Resnick realized that Silver was standing just beyond the open doorway, book by his side.

'Who?'

'I don't know, do I? Same one as called before, I s'pose.'

'You suppose?'

'Sounded the same to me.'

'What did you tell her?'

'Asked her if she wanted to meet me later, buy me a drink.'

Silver's silhouette was fading behind a shimmer of plastic and steam. 'What did she say?' Resnick asked.

'Unprintable.' He flapped the paperback against his leg. 'Even in crap like this.'

'Did she leave a name?'

'No.'

'Number?'

'Too busy hanging up.'

Resnick tilted his face towards the stream of water and soaped his belly, buttocks, beneath his arms. He thought Silver had walked away, but when Silver spoke again, the voice was as close.

'The other call, some bloke, he said for you to ring back. Soon as you could.'

'Great.'

'What?'

'Telling me when I got in.'

'Forgot.'

'Yes. Too engrossed in that appalling book.'

'No,' Silver said. ' 'S'not that bad.'

'This bloke,' Resnick said, 'any chance he left a name?'

'Skelton,' Silver said. 'Wrote the number down somewhere. Lessee.' He fumbled through his pockets. 'Know I got it here somewhere.'

But Resnick had already switched off the water and was stepping out of the shower, reaching for the towel; the number he knew by heart.

The hall of residence was built around a central courtyard, dark pointed brick and uniform windows, a path that wound down towards it through a meadow of grass from the university itself. Only the police vehicles parked off the inner ring road suggested anything less than ideal. Resnick nodded at one of the forensic officers who was leaving, followed the directions of the constable standing inside to keep any of the curious at bay.

'DI in shot,' grinned the scene-of-crime officer with the video camera. Resnick held his ground while the man zoomed in hard on the bed and then out. Stick a camcorder in their hands and suddenly they're Alfred Hitchcock.

'Sorry, sir,' said Resnick. 'Came as soon as I could.'

'Not to worry, Charlie.' Skelton dropped the pair of white cotton pants he was holding into a plastic envelope and left it to be labelled and sealed. 'Just about through.'

The room looked as if it had been in the eye of a storm. Bookshelves had been torn from the walls, books strewn over the ground. Bedclothes were almost anywhere but on the bed. Shoes, a sports bag, articles of clothing; a tube of toothpaste caught inside a trainer. A4 file paper bearing orderly writing in purple or green ink, diagrams designed to give comparative readings in levels of employment, take-up of housing benefit.

'Lucky the girl found her when she did,' Skelton said, crossing towards him. 'Even so, she lost one hell of a lot of blood.'

Resnick hadn't needed telling, evidence of it enough on the striped duvet, sheets of paper, a pillow; a splash of it like paint someone had flicked against the porcelain of the sink.

'This done after or before?' Resnick asked, still surveying the mess.

'During. She put up quite a fight.'

'Is she going to be okay?'

Skelton shook his head. 'Let's go outside.'

They stood in the courtyard, two middle-aged men in raincoats, Skelton still wearing his gloves, heads together, talking. From different parts of the building, a handful of students stared down at them through glass. Not long from now, Skelton was thinking, my Kate could be one of these. He did not allow himself to think she could have been the one they were discussing.

'How long,' Resnick was asking, 'between when it happened and she was found?'

'Not less than two hours, likely not more than three. She was due to play badminton, four o'clock. When she didn't show, her friend came looking for her.' Skelton glanced at Resnick and then off towards the middle distance, trees glimpsed against the horizon, dark against darkening clouds. 'She was found around half four. Last anyone had seen her before that, as far as we can tell, far as we've been able to check, about half twelve she walked up that path to the university.'

'No one saw her come back?'

'Apparently not.'

Resnick turned in the direction of the room. 'No matter how quick that all happened, somebody must have heard.'

Skelton shook his head.

'There must be – what? – sixty students living here. More.'

'Most of them home for the weekend. Those that weren't, out somewhere. Shopping in the city. Working in the library. Just out.'

'Any sign of the weapon?'

'Not so far.' Skelton stood looking out across the slope of meadow. 'If it's out there somewhere, we'll find it but it'll take time.'

'The wounds,' Resnick said, 'were they . . . ?'

'Not too similar to the hospital incidents, if that's what you're thinking. More random. Frenzied. Whatever she was cut with, my guess is that it was a heavier instrument altogether, a thicker blade.'

Or whoever attacked her was angrier, more frightened. *Frenzied* – the superintendent didn't throw words like that around carelessly. Resnick looked directly at Skelton and Skelton read the question in his eyes.

'I don't know, Charlie. From the visual evidence alone, it was impossible to tell. But only the upper half of her body was clothed.'

'She could have been dressing when whoever it was broke in.'

'Or while he was there.'

Both men knew the other alternative. Until she was well enough to give an account of what had happened, or there had been time to examine all the evidence more closely, reconstruct as best they could what had taken place, they would not know.

'God help me, Charlie,' Skelton said, 'I know nothing good can hope to come of this, but something's been nagging away at the back of my brain denying any connection with all that other business; this isn't another Tim Fletcher, another Karl Dougherty. Poor woman, at least she was a student and not a nurse.'

'Was, sir?'

Skelton lowered his head. 'Figure of speech, Charlie, slip of the tongue. Let's pray it's nothing more than that.'

Resnick nodded. Amen to that.

Patel was sitting in the common room opposite Cheryl Falmer, notebook on his lap. The curtains had been drawn part way across and no one had thought to switch on the lights. It had been made clear to her that she could make her statement later, when she was feeling stronger, after she had recovered from the shock. But if you waited for that, you might be waiting forever.

Patel had been patient, letting the words fall out in broken clusters, content to piece them into sentences, a picture, a sequence of events. First she had knocked on the door, knocked again and turned to go away and for no reason she could think of now she had gone back and tried the handle. She did this and then she did that. Yes, Amanda had been inside.

'Would you like me to get someone to take you home?' Patel asked, when the story was finally told.

Cheryl shook her head. 'I think I'd like to sit here for a little longer.'

'All right.' Patel nodded understanding and sat with her, waiting as the shadows claimed the room.

The faces had disappeared from the windows. Lights burned behind several, illuminating photographs of families and boyfriends, posters for Greenpeace. A few TV sets or radios had been switched on. Those students who were in residence either sat on their beds stunned or got ready to go out for the evening. Saturday night. The search for a weapon had been abandoned and would be resumed at first light. Resnick had no excuse for not returning to his car and as he did so he was intercepted by a constable who had just taken a message on his personal radio: Resnick

**knew from the officer's expression that Amanda Hooson
was dead.**

Thirty

He wanted Ed Silver still to be there, reading his borrowed book with rapt attention and complaining about every paragraph, every other word. It was a night for company, conversation, a little controlled drinking: it was not an evening Resnick wished to spend alone. There were cups and glasses, unwashed, in the sink; upstairs Resnick's wardrobe door stood open and he wondered which of his clothes would come home next morning stiff with puke and cold. He thought of all the people he might call on the off chance and the list did not amount to much. Graham Millington had said to him, a month or so back, you must come round again and have a meal, the wife was asking. But Millington was parked in some motorway service area, a lorry park off the A1, cold and getting colder, asking himself over and over if all he'd joined the Force for had been this.

By the morning a murder incident room would have been set up, more uniformed officers drafted in, civilians to access all information, checking it via the Holmes computer. The investigation into the hospital attacks would continue side by side; CID resources would be stretched and stretched again. The DCI would be breathing down Skelton's neck, wanting a result. All of that was tomorrow: tonight Resnick didn't trust his own company.

Never having removed his coat, he let himself out again and hesitated between his front door and the gate. He sat in his car for fifteen, twenty minutes, letting the blackness thicken around him. Once, he thought he heard the telephone, muted, from inside the house. When it was quiet he got back out of the car and Dizzy ran along the top of the wall towards his hand. Against the black sheen of his coat, Dizzy's eyes were alive and dangerous. This was his time. Where Resnick wanted to be was somewhere dull and safe. Known. Hands in his pockets, he set off towards the main road, past homes where the plates were being dried and stacked away, something good on the box at half-past eight, be quick, don't be late.

Please come, Charles, we would all love to see you.

Only a dull light seemed to be burning deep in the hallway, faded orange through the triptych of stained glass beside the heavy wooden door. Resnick tried the bell again and heard another door, within the house, being firmly closed. Footsteps, brighter light, turning of the lock: when Marian Witczak appeared, the first of several clocks began to chime from different rooms, none pitched or set the same.

'Charles.' Surprise and pleasure mixed in her voice.

'The invitation, I know I should have replied . . .'

'Charles! Really, you are going to come? How nice.' She reached forward and took his hands, leading him into the tiled hall. 'I hoped, of course, but never really expected . . .'

'I know. I've not been a good friend.'

'Always, you are so busy.'

Resnick nodded and offered up something of a smile. He was already beginning to wonder if he should have come. Marian had obviously spent time getting ready. She was wearing a tightly-waisted orange dress that fell away in loose pleats almost to her ankles; her collar bones stood gaunt below thin straps, a silver brooch like a spider above her breast. Lifted off her face and tightly coiled behind, her hair accentuated the hollowness beneath her cheekbones. Her flat, black shoes had silver buckles, large and square.

'I shall not be the only one pleased to see you,' Marian said. 'There is a feeling, perhaps you have deserted us.'

Resnick shook his head. 'Don't make me feel guilty, Marian. Besides, it's you I've come to see, not the whole damned community.' He saw her disapproving face and found a more convincing smile. 'You did say it was a party. I remember how you like to dance.'

Marian reached out again and patted his hand. 'Please come and wait for me. I shall not be long.'

Holding his arm, she led him along the wide, tiled hall into a room of oak and dried flowers that had scarcely changed since Resnick had first seen it, more than thirty years before. Marian left him for a moment then returned, pressing a small cut glass into his hand. It was sweet plum brandy and he sipped at it as he stood by the French windows, looking out. It wasn't simply that Marian, more or less his contemporary, made him unusually conscious of his age – stepping across this threshold was like stepping into another country. One which had little place in reality, least of all, perhaps, in Poland itself.

During the strikes, the demonstrations, the celebrations of democracy, Marian and her friends had watched in fascination every television picture, scanned newspaper after newspaper, each of them searching for a face they recognized, a street corner, a café. Resnick had never been there, where Marian Witczak still called home. Whenever he said the word, Resnick saw different pictures in his head, heard different voices, St Anne's rather than the Stare Miasto, not the Vistula but the Trent.

'See, Charles, I am ready.'

She stood in the doorway, a shawl of rich, black lace around her shoulders; small, white flowers pinned above her waist. She smelt of lilies of the valley. 'Of course, Charles,' she said, 'I am grateful that you are here. But let us face the truth: I have written you such notes before.

What brings you here is less to see me, more whatever it may be you wish to turn your back upon.'

She put Resnick's glass aside and offered him her gloved hand. 'Tonight,' she said, 'we will have a fine time. You see,' glancing down at the gleaming buckles, 'I have on my dancing shoes.'

At first Resnick sat near the back of the main room, nursing his beer while Marian moved from table to table, table to bar, greeting those she had not seen since last year or last week with grave enthusiasm. The younger men stared at Resnick sullenly, knowing who he was and what he did.

At the head of the main table, the guest of honour drank peppermint vodka on the quarter hour and chainsmoked small dark cigars pressed upon him by his eager sons-in-law, mindful of what might one day soon be theirs. His daughters brought out a cake, festooned with chocolate flakes and candles and icing in red-and-white horizontal stripes: the committee made him a presentation and in the middle of his speech of thanks, the old man lost interest and sat back down to light a fresh cigar.

Resnick and Marian waltzed and polkaed and once essayed a nifty quickstep, until Resnick's subliminally remembered fishtail came to grief amongst the swirl of small children that jigged about his legs.

After that they ate *pieroqi*, and when the treasurer tapped Resnick on the shoulder, he reached for his cheque-book without delay.

'You see, Charles, you should join us more often. Then you would not look, always, so sad.' She touched the backs of her fingers lightly to his face. 'Here it is a haven; here you may forget.'

The accordion player did a passable job on Chuck Berry's 'Johnny B Goode' and then led the band into an old Polish dance that had the men dropping alternately to right knee and left, lifting their partners off the ground and whirling them round.

Marian clapped along until her hands glowed.

Someone came and whispered in her ear and she blushed and agreed, excusing herself from Resnick to climb on to the stage and stand well behind the microphone. In a small, strong voice, to a lilting tune, she sang about a young girl who has been abandoned by her lover and still waits for him at the field edge, before a bank of trees.

> *When my hair turns white*
> *Will you remember*
> *that I was once young here?*
> *I'll keep faith forever*
> *till only death overtake me.*

There was a pause and then applause, those at the rear slapping the tables, stamping their feet. The band began a waltz and she stepped off the stage towards Resnick, hands outstretched. What else could he do? They made two circuits of the small floor to more applause, before others joined them and when the dance at last ended there was scarcely room to move.

'I sang that once when I was twelve,' Marian said. 'We were all here, my family, your family. My father lifted me up on to a chair to sing and when it was over, your mother pushed you forwards to give thanks. Do you remember?'

'Yes,' Resnick said, remembering nothing. Surely it had been another boy, not him at all?

As they walked back towards their table, Resnick was aware of people looking at them, weighing their futures in the balance.

'At least,' Marian smiled, seeing his embarrassment, 'they're not saying what a lovely couple we make.'

'Oh, but you do!'

The exclamation came from close behind and as both

211

Resnick and Marian turned, a woman lurched towards them, dark hair and wild eyes.

'You do, you really do.'

Startled moments before Resnick recognized his former wife, before he recognized Elaine: sunken cheeks and patched skin, fiercely hacked hair, eyes that glowed back at him as if from the centre of another face.

'Well,' Elaine said. 'Old times. Me and you and Marian. This place.' She was standing unsteadily, never quite still. If she stops waving her arms, Resnick thought, she might fall down. 'Pretty wonderful out there, the two of you, prancing about. The light fantastic. Ginger Rogers and Fred Astaire.'

She smiled lopsidedly, slipped and when Resnick reached out a hand to steady her, she flapped him away.

'Got to hand it to you, Marian,' she said. 'The way you've prised him out of his shell. More than I could usually manage.'

Marian's eyes focused on Resnick, distressed, appealing. Around them people were ceasing to drink or talk, no longer pretending not to be watching.

'One quick turn round the floor at the end of the evening,' Elaine was saying. 'If I was lucky.' She smiled conspiratorially at Marian. 'It gets like that towards the end. They lose interest. All of them. You'll see.'

Marian looked away but it didn't matter: the words weren't really for her, and Resnick and Elaine both knew it.

'Elaine,' Resnick said. 'Please.'

'*Please*, Charlie? Is that pretty-please, or is it the other kind?'

Resnick sighed and looked towards the floor.

'Don't look so hangdog, Charlie. It's just girl talk. Marian and I having a nice little chat . . .'

'Elaine,' Resnick said.

'Yes?'

'This isn't the place.'

'Oh, but it is. You're here. She's here . . .'

'No.'

'Charlie, you're not embarrassed? Don't tell me you're embarrassed? Not after watching Marian singing about a late lamented lover. Some people might have thought that was a bit of a spectacle, Marian pretending to be a sweet little virgin, but there you were, Charlie, clapping along with the rest of them.'

Tears of shame in her eyes, Marian pushed her way towards the exit. Resnick started after her, stopped, turned back.

'Difficult, isn't it?' Elaine said. 'Which way for that famous bleeding heart to jump? Your lover or your wife?'

'She's not . . .'

'Your lover? I daresay. And I'm not your wife.'

The band had stopped playing. There were hardly any other voices to be heard.

'But you know all about that,' Elaine said, backing towards the dance floor, looking all around. 'Charlie's tragic divorce. You were at the wedding, some of you. Remember? Whom no man shall put asunder. Except you, Charlie. Not so much put asunder as shut out. And you know the reason? I expect you all know the reason, but just in case . . .'

'Elaine . . .'

'Just in case you don't . . .'

'Elaine . . .'

'The reason was I didn't want to have babies . . .'

'Elaine, for God's sake!'

'Pretty little babies to make him tall and proud . . .'

Resnick slid his face slowly down into his hands.

'. . . and call him Da-da.'

Resnick didn't move. Blood was pumping fiercely inside his head, against his ears and he didn't move.

'What's the matter, Charlie?' Elaine said. 'Too near the truth?'

He lowered his hands, opened his eyes and looked at her, anger thick in his face.

'You'd rather everyone thought you chucked me out because you caught me on the mattress of someone else's bed, fucking another man. They'd understand that, not, but not . . . No, Charlie, let me finish. Don't pull me! Don't touch me! Let me finish telling them what kind of a caring, compassionate man you really are. Let me tell them about the letters, Charlie. All the letters I sent you, the ones you never answered. All the times I rang up in pain and you hung up without a word.'

He wanted to strike her, hit her, wanted to smother her mouth, shelter from the taunt of her words and eyes. Her words broke over him as he turned and walked away.

'Stay and tell them about all that, Charlie. How you helped me with everything I've been going through. How you fucking helped . . .'

The sudden rush of cold air rocked him on his feet; a lorry climbing the hill missed a gear and he jumped. A black and white cab turned up from the city with its roof light shining and Resnick flagged it down, bundling himself into the warm upholstery of the back.

'Where to?' the driver asked.

'Anywhere,' Resnick said. 'Just drive.'

Thirty-one

'Shit!' Calvin exclaimed, stepping barefooted into the splashes that his father had left around the toilet bowl. 'Grown man, might have thought he'd've learned to piss straight!' He finished his own business, dabbed at the soles of his feet with a towel, tore off some sheets of paper and wiped up the floor. Might as well do the rest while I'm at it. Calvin used more paper around the rim and just a little way down into the bowl, dumped it inside and flushed. Now rinse your hands under the tap. Last thing he wanted to do, catch some kind of disease, end up in hospital: last place he wanted to be. Let those doctors get their hands on you and you never knew where it was going to end.

His father was in the kitchen, drinking black tea with lemon – his Sunday favourite – and reading his way through the *News of the World*. What was the matter with *Sunday Sport*, that's what Calvin wanted to know? Women with 62-inch chests and three-headed babies, something truly gross to get the day on its way.

'You ready to eat?' his father asked, scarcely looking up.

'Just about.'

'Pancakes?'

'Why not?'

Every week the same little ritual. The batter was already mixed, buckwheat flour and plain, a nub of lard that his father would wipe round the inside of the pan, barely greasing it over before cooking each one. Sugar. Lemons. Strawberry jam. Calvin checked to see if there was any juice in the fridge, but was out of luck. He flicked on the

215

kettle and reached for the huge caterer's tin of Nescafé his father had found on one of his foraging trips. Special offers, past-the-sale-date bargains, he would cycle half-way across the city to save fifty pence.

'You got in late last night,' his father said, refolding the paper.

'So?'

'Nothing. Simply a remark.'

'Yeh, well,' Calvin said, stirring hard to prevent the powder from collecting on the top of his mug, 'keep them to yourself, right?'

His father hummed a few bars of some old song Calvin vaguely recognized and lit the gas beneath the pan. 'How was your mother?'

Calvin shrugged, hunched over his drink, thin-backed in black. 'Same.'

'Sister?'

'Same.'

'Damn it, boy!'

'What?'

A rare anger flared briefly in Ridgemount's eyes and then it was gone. Shaking his head, he turned back to the stove, tilting the pan this way and that before pouring in the first of the batter. Calvin read the soccer reports. His father shook the pan to make sure the pancake wasn't sticking, tossed it through a lazy somersault and set it back down on the gas for a final minute.

'Your mother and me, we were together a long time. I just want to know how she is.' He slid the pancake, speckled brown, on to Calvin's plate. 'That so difficult to understand?'

'Yes.'

His father shook his head slowly and looked away.

'She left you. Walked out. Now she's living with some other bloke, won't hear your name mentioned in the house. Minute I walk into it, he sods off down the garden into his

216

shed or takes their pathetic dog for a walk. No, I don't understand.'

'She had her reasons.'

'Yeh, didn't she just!'

'Calvin . . .'

'Yeh?'

But his father was back at the stove, the next pancake soon on its way. 'Marjorie,' he said, eyes on what he was doing, 'she asked about me, didn't she? Asked about her daddy?'

'Yes,' Calvin said, through a mouthful of breakfast, 'course she did. I told her you were fine.'

'You say I was missing her?'

'That, too.'

'Good, good. Now here,' lifting the pan, 'you get ready for this one. I'll make mine next.'

Marjorie had asked about him, Calvin was thinking, just found time to stick her head round the door and squeeze the words out. Looking like she'd just spent more getting her hair done than Calvin had to spend in a week. Two weeks. 'How's school?' Calvin had said, but she was already lost to sight. 'She has such a lot of friends now,' his mother had said. 'Nice young people.' Calvin had watched a film with his father once, about a girl whose skin had been light enough for her to pass as white. Nice young black people, he wanted to ask his mother, or now you're stuck out here in Burton Joyce isn't there any such thing?

He squeezed some lemon juice, sprinkled sugar. 'How is your dad?' she had asked. 'Still having his attacks?'

'What attacks?'

'Oh, you know, nightmares. Whatever you want to call them?'

'No,' Calvin had said. 'No, he doesn't have them any more. He's fine.'

'Ready for another?' his father asked.

'In a minute. Do your own.'

How would he know the frequency of his father's screams, used as he was to falling asleep with the sounds of Aerosmith or Led Zeppelin throbbing in his ears, leaving the headphones in place all night long.

Certain that after his confrontation with Elaine he would never be able to sleep, Resnick had been fast off the moment his head had eventually hit the pillow. When he awoke it was to the rhythmic clawing of the cats and the rasp of an eager neighbour's hedge trimmer. His hair had been matted to his scalp by sweat and his sheets were a damp, cold tangle from which it was difficult to move.

He got ready as soon as possible, listening all the while for evidence that the previous night had not been a guilty dream. Now, more than before, when the telephone rang his first fear would be that it was Elaine. A taxi drawing up outside, ringing at the door – he didn't know when she would come, yet suspected that she would. Where had she gone at the end of that ghastly evening? Where in the city might she be staying? Questions that Resnick needed answering; answers he didn't want to know. He held his breath as he opened the front door, glanced along the street in both directions before letting himself into the car. Relax, Charlie, she won't skulk in shadows. Not now. She's spat all that out of her system, hawked the worst of the anger off her chest. Resnick slipped the engine into gear, indicated and pulled away. Now, he smiled ruefully, that she's broken the ice. Reaching the main road he turned right. We all know what waits beneath the ice, black, cold and seemingly unending.

He parked outside Marian's house and rang the bell.

Upstairs the curtains were forbiddingly drawn across; otherwise there was no sign of life. He could understand if today Marian had no inclination to speak to anyone, himself least of all. Still he tried again and waited. If she weren't inside, waiting for him to leave, she would be at

Mass. Resnick considered, but only for moments, waiting outside the Polish church for her to leave. All too easy to picture the scorn and curiosity on the faces of the congregation when they walked out of the incense and into the daylight, staring at him from their state of grace.

He got back into his car and set off towards the hospital. While there he would be able to buy some flowers, leave them on her doorstep with a note, *Dear Marian* ... Perhaps in another six months he would pick up the phone and she would answer, perhaps not. Now, thank God, there was police business to attend to.

Karl Dougherty was no longer in intensive care, back down on the same ward as Fletcher, though not the same bay. A nurse approached, smiling warily, about to shoo Resnick away until the start of proper visiting, but his warrant card and a returning smile won him access to the bedside and the expected warning. 'Don't stay too long now. He's still quite weak. Don't want to tire him out.'

Dougherty looked pale but pleased to have a visitor, sucking up pineapple juice through a bendy straw. 'I've been talking to a friend of yours,' Resnick said, the conventional queries and formalities over.

'Paul.'

Resnick nodded.

'Yes, he told me. Apparently he's your prime suspect.'

'I wouldn't call him that, exactly.'

Dougherty managed a grin. 'I'm sure you could do better. At least, I hope so. Wouldn't want to think that whoever did this was about to do it again.'

'I suggested to Paul you'd been having a row before you left Manhattan's. He didn't deny it.'

Dougherty was quiet. A domestic walked past, pushing a heavy, insulated trolley. Late breakfast, Resnick thought, before reasoning that it was early lunch.

'What were you arguing about?'

'The usual.'

'Which is?'

'Oh, you know, inspector. Who's the greatest psychologist, Jung or Freud? If you had three people in an air balloon, Mother Teresa, Bob Geldof and Princess Di, who would you throw out first and why?'

'Seriously,' Resnick said.

'Geldof,' said Dougherty. 'He's the worst singer.'

'No, I mean seriously.'

'Sex,' Dougherty said.

'When, where or how?'

Dougherty smiled and shook his head. 'If.'

'Paul was interested and you weren't, is that it?'

Dougherty nodded. 'Just about.'

'Why carry on seeing him?'

'Because I liked him, because ordinarily he's good company. Because he isn't a nurse. I was prepared to overlook the final five minutes of why won't you come back to my place, why can't I come to yours?'

'And that's what you were arguing about? That evening?'

'It was a routine Paul went through. We both expected it.'

'Then why leave early?'

'What?'

'Why leave early? You left early, left Paul there to finish his drink. If it was no different to the end of any other evening, why did you do that?'

'Paul,' Dougherty said after a moment, 'he was getting more and more insistent. Said that it was as if I was ashamed of him, he said I was using him, he said a lot of things. I didn't want to listen to it any more.'

'You walked out on him?'

'I suppose so. I suppose you could say that, yes.'

'That's the way he would have seen it?'

'He might.'

'He was angry with you already. Frustrated.'

'He didn't do this.' Dougherty glanced down and Resnick imagined the wounds beneath the blanket. 'He couldn't.'

'He could have followed you from the club, seen where you were going.'

'I didn't mean that. I mean, psychologically, he couldn't have done it.'

'Is that according to Freud or Jung?' Resnick asked.

Dougherty almost smiled. 'Both of them, probably.'

'Physically,' Resnick said, 'could Paul Groves have attacked you?'

'If he was worked up enough, I daresay he could have found the strength, but he could never have got that close to me without my hearing him, I'm certain of that.'

'You want to be certain. The last person in the world you want it to be is him.'

'Of course. But whoever it was, they came from directly behind me. From one of the lavatories, the stalls.'

'You heard them?'

Dougherty didn't answer straight off. 'I don't think so. Though sometimes when I'm running it all through, only sometimes, there's this faint half-remembered click, like the bolt of the door being pulled back.'

'And you saw?'

'As I said before, very little. A boot or maybe a shoe, black. Everything was black. Trousers . . .'

'Trousers, not jeans?'

'I think so, yes.'

'And size? Did you get some idea of that? How big? How tall?'

'Around my height. Strong, obviously. But I don't think he was, you know, I don't think he was a body builder or anything like that.'

Already the nurse was hovering at the end of the bed and Resnick could see that he was coming close to outstaying his welcome. 'Karl,' he said, getting to his feet, 'you rest now. Someone will be in to talk to you again.' He lowered his hand as if to pat the foot of the bed and Dougherty winced. 'Take care,' Resnick said. 'Get better.' He would walk along and have a word with Tim Fletcher while he was there, find out if any little memories had clicked into place in his brain.

The Yorkshire puddings had sat there in the gravy, staring back up at him like little brown diaphragms, but otherwise Sunday lunch hadn't been too bad. Now Naylor was sitting in the living room with his feet up, listening to James Hunt and Murray Walker disagreeing about who was in pole position for the World Championship. With a murder investigation about to get underway, he was going to need what little rest he could snatch. Not so often the baby slept through an hour without waking to tears and you didn't waste it.

Debbie came into the room but Naylor didn't look up.

'We ought to be going soon,' she said.

No response. Mansell made as if to overtake on the inside, but at the last moment chickened out.

'Kevin.'

God! The whine in that voice!

'Kevin!'

'Yes.'

'I said . . .'

'I heard you.'

'But you haven't moved.'

'That's because I'm not coming.'

'You're what?'

'You heard.'

'Mum's expecting us.'

I'll bet, thought Naylor. I can just see the corned beef sandwiches, turning up their edges in delight. He leaned further towards the screen and didn't say anything.

'You can't stay in all day, watching that.'

'Why not? Anyway, I shan't be staying in. I'm going out.'

'Where? Where if it's not . . . ?'

'If you must know, I'm going to see how Mark is.'

'That's right. You do.'

'I will. Don't you worry.'

'Sooner spend time with the likes of him than with your own family.'

'It's not my family, Debbie,' turning to face her now, splutter of engines from the set behind him, 'it's yours. She's your mother, you go and have tea with her. Get yourself bored stupid listening to her prattle on.'

The tears were there, but she was fighting them back. Naylor was looking at her and then he was looking at the flat, painted wood of the door. When he swung back to the screen, Mansell had accelerated into the straight and was going into the final lap in second place.

Thirty-two

Lynn Kellogg had drawn the early shift and the logs were on Resnick's desk and ready for his inspection a full fifteen minutes before he set foot in the station. Amongst the usual spate of break-ins that would require Lynn's attention was one in which some enterprising soul had squirted WD 40 through the letter-box to stun a pair of angry Rottweilers, picked the lock and walked away with several thousand pounds' worth of jewellery and furs and the dogs' studded collars as souvenirs. The distraught owner had woken to find the front door wide open and the animals wandering around the garden in a dazed state, unusually beatific expressions on their faces. The first phone call had been to the PDSA, the second to the police.

Graham Millington was in next, limping as a result of half the night cramped up in the rear of a hastily converted transit van, watching the lorry park off exit 29 through a hole the size of a new five-pence piece. He was experimentally jumping up and down in an attempt to get the circulation going when Resnick entered with a headache and a Brie and apricot sandwich he'd picked up at the deli across the road.

'Going into training, Graham?'

'Not exactly, sir,' said Millington, embarrassed, casting a sideways glance at Resnick's feet to see if he was wearing odd socks again.

Resnick went through to his office and nodded for Millington to follow. 'Good weekend?' he asked, making a space on the desk for his sandwich.

'Not bad, sir. Pretty good, really. The wife and I . . .'

Resnick skimmed through the night's reports, half an ear on his sergeant's domestic ramblings. What was it that made for a happy and lasting marriage, he caught himself asking? Perhaps it was a lack of imagination.

Lynn Kellogg brought in mugs of tea and cut the catalogue of grouting and trips to the garden centre mercifully short. After that lot, Resnick was thinking, it might come as a relief to be shut up in a van for six hours.

'These obs, Graham,' Resnick asked. 'Any luck?'

Millington shook his head. 'We were wasting our time up round Chesterfield, while they were in business outside Ashby-de-la-Zouche.'

Resnick spotted Naylor through the glass of the door and got to his feet, waving to get the DC's attention and losing a bright sliver of apricot jam to his shirt front in the process.

'Any sign of Divine?'

'Saw him yesterday, sir,' said Naylor. Sitting in Mark Divine's new studio apartment near the marina, watching a worn video of *9½ Weeks* while they worked their way through a six-pack of Carling Black Label.

'Coming in today?'

'No, sir. I don't think so. He's . . .'

'Wrong,' said Resnick. 'Wrong answer. Injured in the line of duty, one thing. Getting smacked for behaving like a yob with libido problems, that's another. Ring him now, tell him I expect to see him in thirty minutes. Here. Right?'

'Yes, sir.' Naylor went back into the main office, doing his best to figure out what a libido was; he thought that Divine had only had stitches above the eye.

Millington was midway through making a tortuous request to be relieved of working with the West Midlands Force, at least while there was so much heavy activity on his own patch, when Lynn Kellogg came back to the door. 'It's Ms Olds, sir. Wants to see you now.'

Wonderful! thought Resnick. 'Stall her,' he said. 'Try and interest her in the delights of the canteen.'

'I did, sir.'

'And?'

'She laughed in my face.'

Resnick sighed. 'All right. Five, no, ten minutes. Tell her it's the best I can do.'

Lynn nodded and withdrew.

Suzanne Olds tilted back her head and released a film of smoke from between perfectly made-up lips. When Resnick was using the perfumery floor of Jessops as a cut-through, making for the market, that was when he saw women the like of Ms Olds, perfectly groomed and hard as teak. He guessed one difference might be Suzanne Olds had the brains, too.

'Are you saying this is an official complaint?' Resnick asked.

Unnervingly, the solicitor smiled. 'Not yet.'

'Maybe we should wait till it is?'

She swivelled towards him in her seat. 'Police Complaints Authority, officers from an outside force, one of your own suspended. To say nothing of the possible accusations: victimization by a ranking officer, harassment, bias.'

'If, if Ian Carew was under surveillance, it was with no knowledge of mine.'

Suzanne Olds was enjoying this. 'In that case,' she preened, 'perhaps we should add incompetence to the list.'

'Jesus!' sighed Resnick.

'Yes?'

'It's a game to you, isn't it? Somewhere between Monopoly and Scruples.'

'There's nothing funny about a citizen having his civil rights . . .'

'Oh, come on!' Resnick on his feet now, turning away,

turning back. 'Don't give me Carew and civil rights in the same breath. It doesn't wash.'

'Somehow he's forfeited them? If that's what you're saying, I'd say it was a difficult argument to sustain.'

'Yes? Well, there's a girl out there who had her civil rights severely curtailed when your client beat her up and raped her.'

'Wait.'

'No.'

'Wait a minute.'

'Why?'

'My client, these alleged offences, has he been charged? Never mind brought to trial, found guilty, sentenced.'

'The only reason he hasn't, the girl withdrew the charges.'

'Maybe she changed her mind. In the light of day, decided she'd been rash, making accusations in anger. Who knows?'

'How about this? What happened to her was so appalling she couldn't face being dragged through it again, in front of witnesses, knowing that he would be there watching her.'

'Melodramatic, inspector.'

'Better than being smug.'

'And rude.'

Resnick made himself stand straight and still and with an effort brought his breathing back under control. 'I'm sorry,' he said.

'Apology accepted.'

'He was given an official warning,' Resnick said, 'as to his future behaviour.'

'Towards the girl?'

Resnick nodded.

'As far as your knowledge goes, has he seen her again?'

'No.'

'Has he made any attempt to?'

'I don't think so.'

'Then how is planting a police car at the end of his street to be construed? Exactly.'

'I've explained . . .'

'You know nothing about it.'

'Exactly.'

Suzanne Olds was smoothly to her feet. 'If I were in your shoes, inspector, I'd be at pains to find out. On this occasion I was able to persuade Mr Carew an informal approach might be best; if he's given any further cause for complaint, I suspect he won't be as charitable. Oh . . .' pausing at the door, a trace of warmth around the edges of her smile, '. . . and there's a smudge of jam, just there . . .' With one long, painted fingernail she traced a line down the silk of her blouse. '. . . the corner of your handkerchief and cold water, that should do the trick. Good day, inspector. I know my way out.'

'Where's Lynn Kellogg?' Resnick demanded, pushing angrily into the CID room.

'RSPCA,' said Naylor. 'PDSA. One of those.'

Divine sat at the furthest end of the room, one-half of his face like a battered pumpkin several days after Halloween.

'You!' Resnick said, jabbing his finger. 'My office. Now.'

Information about Amanda Hooson was being laboriously obtained, systematically annotated, organized. As an exercise it was less than cost-efficient, heavy on personnel, essential:

'Mandy,' said a student from her social-sciences group. 'God! She used to hate it when I called her that. Anyway, yeh, she was just, you know, pretty straight, together. All she wanted to do was get her 2.1 and get back out into the real world. Wasted too much of her life already, that's what she said. Mandy. God, I still can't take it in. Amanda.'

The lecturer tapped the bowl of his pipe and began scraping away at the interior with the blunt end of a penknife. 'She was rather more serious than a number of our students, that would have to be said. Older, you see, not old, but older. Here from choice, real choice, not like so many of them, arriving on the doorstep straight from school simply because they forgot to get off the bus.' After the dredging came the replenishing, the tamping down. 'Great shame, picked up a bit in her final year, might even have got a first.'

'Hot weather, oh yes, sit out on the grass across from PB, hoick her skirt up and sunbathe for hours, ginger-beer shandy and some book about the extended family in Mozambique, homelessness in the inner cities. Not like some of them, stagger about between the Beano and Viz and still end up with a headache. No, she was a serious girl, woman, I suppose you'd have to say. I liked her. Liked her a lot.'

'Amanda! You're kidding! I mean, I don't want to put her down, especially after what's happened, that's dreadful, it really is. But, I don't know, the idea of Amanda going out with any bloke, especially a student, well, if you'd have known her . . . I can't think of another way of putting it: stuck-up, that's what she was. No social life. Anything that wasn't on the syllabus, forget it!'

'Yes, I don't know who he was, don't know his name or anything, but yes, she was seeing somebody. I'm sure of it.'

'Amanda came to my seminars, sat there writing it all down, sometimes if I coughed I think she made a little notation in brackets. Good essays, of course. Solid. But discussion – never contributed a word. Not my idea of a good student, I'm afraid, but there you are. I could show you her grades, if you think that might be of any use.'

'Terrible, terrible, terrible. A tragedy. A tragic waste of a young life. Truly, truly terrible. Tragic. Um?'

'We went through this period, last year. Badminton, right? I was beating her time after time, 15–6, 15–7, 15–5. Found out that if I kept it high to her backhand, she just couldn't cope. Amanda came back after the holiday and wiped the floor with me. She'd found this guy, county player, talked him into teaching her, two hours a day for three weeks. Backhand smash, drive, backhand lob, she could do the lot. Not brilliantly. She was never what you'd call a natural. But she was like that with anything, anything she wanted, *really* wanted to do. Got down and worked at it, hard as she could. Little things, important things, it didn't matter. Amanda had these lists in the back of her diary and she'd tick them off one at a time until they were done. After that she'd start a new list. Goal-oriented, I think that's the term for it. Amanda would have known; if she didn't she'd have been off to the library to look it up.'

'This diary,' asked Patel, 'can you describe it?'

Cheryl pursed her lips and nodded. The shadows beneath her eyes were deep and dark from crying. 'Nothing special, not one of those – what-d'you-call-'em – Filofaxes, nothing like that. Sort of slim and black, leather, you know the kind? Student year, I think it was, September to September. Carried it with her all the time.'

'I see.'

'You haven't found it?'

'I don't think so. Not yet.' Patel smiled and when he did so, Cheryl thought, not for the first time, what a nice man he probably was; what a shame he was a policeman. 'I don't really know,' Patel said. 'I'll certainly check. Now . . .' turning a page of his note book, '. . . perhaps you can tell me something about her friends . . .'

It was Millington who, having temporarily talked himself

out of the hijack detail and finding himself with half an hour in the enquiry room, chanced to glance at a report form waiting to be accessed on to the computer. Amanda Hooson, twenty-six, previous education, West Notts College, previously employed for two years as an ODA at the Derbyshire Royal Infirmary and then back to the main hospital in the city.

'ODA?' Millington asked. 'What's one of them?'

'Search me.'

'Lord knows.'

'Wait up,' called one of the civilian operators, looking away from his screen, 'I don't know what the initials stand for exactly, but what it is, what they do, assist the anaesthetist, make sure the gear's all in working order, operations and the like. That's what it is. ODA. Yes. Saw one on television once ... *What's My Line?*'

Thirty-three

Lynn hadn't been able to work out if the woman was more worried about her floor-length musquash and her sable stole or the stupid dogs. She didn't know which might raise the woman up higher in her opinion and finally decided it was neither. How could you have respect for someone who drank Perrier out of cut glass and allowed her Rottweilers to crap on the kitchen floor rather than take them for a walk after dark? Nervous of getting mugged, she got burgled instead. 'It was stripped down to the original boards in here,' she'd said, pointing at the kitchen floor, 'but we had that taken up and new quarry tiles put down. So much easier. Scoop up and swab down, a matter of minutes.' Right, Lynn had thought, that and the money to pay someone to come in every morning, do it for you.

Five hundred yards away, Lynn knew there were families living in flats with rising damp, cockroaches, hot-water systems that broke down again before the repair van had reached the end of the street. 'It doesn't matter, Lynnie,' her mother had used to say, 'not where you live, it's how you live. My great-aunt brought up a family of five in two rooms with a tin bath you set down before the fire and an outside lavvie where the water froze across the bowl November to March. And you could walk into that place anytime, no warning, and not find a cup that wasn't washed up or a half-inch of dirt on or under anything.' Well, good for Great-aunt Queenie. Knew her place and kept it spotless. Huge bosoms and facial hair; a backside that made horses tremble. Lynn would have loved to see her weighing into the hardship officer at the DSS.

She swung left off the main road and turned quickly left again opposite the disused lido, bringing the car to a halt facing the university lake. Without thinking, she had been heading, not towards her own place, not back to the station, but to Ian Carew's. God's gift, that's what he thought he was. God's sodding gift! The way he'd come prancing past her while she was sitting behind the wheel, hours watching the short length of street, front of his house. Clever bastard, just to prove he could do it, show he didn't care. Sneaked out the back and gone off who knows where. A lot of people would have gone back in the same way, left her thinking he was inside all the while, a good boy, doing whatever good boys did. But, no, not in his nature. Cocky! Couldn't resist letting her see him, supercilious grin on his face and knowing she'd be looking at the way the material stretched tight across his behind. Much as Lynn hated to admit it, he had a great arse!

That wasn't what she was doing, was it? Fancying the man? Fantasizing about him? If she were, one picture of Karen Archer should do the trick.

Did you want him to have sex, make love to you?

The marks on Karen Archer's face, the eyes that could never once return your gaze.

He said he didn't believe me. Said I was dying for it.

The police in Devon had reported no sign of her; she still had not contacted her parents. What happened next? Posters in shopping centres and outside police stations up and down the country? An urgent message on Radio Four, between the weather forecast and the news? Or wait until a body turned up somewhere months from now? The wasteland south of Sneinton, along by the railway line. Wedged between the lock gates on the Trent Canal. Under a mulch of leaves and earth in the middle of Colwick Woods.

And now ... ?

Amanda Hooson had been murdered in the early hours of Saturday afternoon, exactly when Carew had apparently been out of the house she had been so uselessly watching. Common sense told Lynn that if he had had anything to do with that, the last thing he would have done was strut past and throw suspicion on himself. Not with Lynn sitting there, unwittingly providing him with an alibi.

Or would he? It depended just how clever, how cool he really was.

Lynn locked the car and walked towards the lake, not the crowds today of youngsters waiting to hire rowboat or canoe and get out on the lake; lads who splashed each other with oars, occasionally overturning their boats and falling in; couples who moored alongside the small island and made love in the undergrowth, feeding the condoms afterwards to unsuspecting ducks. A stroll around might clear her mind of this, at least, encourage her to think of other things: whatever was going on with Kevin and Debbie Naylor, whether they'd get through the year without divorce; if her mother could persuade her dad to talk to the doctor about his depression, and if ever he did what the doctor might say. There were days, Lynn thought, buying herself one of the last ice-creams of the year, when she wished she had more problems in her own life, save her worrying so much about those of others.

'I was wondering,' Resnick said, 'if you had five minutes? Couple of things you could help me with. Perhaps.'

'Five pairs of hands might be more useful.' Sarah Leonard brushed an arm across her forehead; a curl of dark hair had escaped beneath the front of her blue and white cap. Something about a woman, Resnick thought, almost as tall as yourself; the closeness of the mouth. If last time she had reminded him of Rachel, now there was no such misrecognition: he knew who she was and she was herself

'Let me change this catheter and I'll be with you,' Sarah said.

'Fine,' Resnick nodded, wincing a little at the thought.

'Don't worry, I'll wash my hands first.'

They went out into the corridor and stood at a window, looking down on to Derby Road. 'I don't know how you do it,' Resnick said.

'What? Catheters, colostomy bags, enemas, that sort of thing?'

'I suppose so. Partly, anyway.'

Sarah grinned. 'It isn't all piss and shit, you know. James Herriot without the friendly collie dog yapping encouragement round your feet. A lot of the time it's a good laugh.'

Resnick looked back at her, disbelieving.

'The other day,' Sarah said, 'this young lad on the ward. Asked one of the student nurses to fetch me over, something seriously troubling him. "Staff," he says, "I don't know what to do, I've got this erection and it won't go away. Can you help me do something about it?" ' Sarah laughed again, remembering.

'Dare I ask?' said Resnick.

'Took him along a bucket and told him to get on with it.'

'What I wanted to know . . .' Resnick began.

'Not you as well?' A knowing grin, sending him up just a little.

Resnick could see his own reflection in the glass, a mixture of embarrassment and pleasure. One day, he thought, if I should ever get to know you better . . . 'What I need,' Resnick said.

'Yes?'

'More in the nature of information.'

'Go ahead.'

'An ODA.'

'What about them?

'What do they do? That would be a start.'

235

'Operating Department Assistant. Attendant. Some hospitals, they call them Anaesthetist Technicians.'

'And that's their function, assisting the anaesthetist during an operation?'

'The main one, yes. Supervising the machines, making sure they're connected correctly so that the right mixture of oxygen and gases gets through to the patient. But they can do more than that, act as scrub nurse . . .'

'Scrub nurse?'

'Handles the instruments during the operation, passes them to the surgeon . . .'

'Scalpel.'

'Scalpel. Exactly. Whatever he's using. Hands them over, takes them back.'

'Responsible job.'

'And she doesn't spend the day dealing with faecal matter.'

'Amanda Hooson,' Resnick said. 'Don't suppose you knew her?'

Sarah shook her head. 'Should I?'

'Apparently she used to work here.'

'As an ODA?'

Resnick nodded.

'We've twelve theatres, fifteen to twenty ODAs. When was she here?'

'Left around two years ago.'

Sarah gave it a little thought. Below, traffic was driving into the hospital in a constipated stream. 'No, I'm sorry. Though there is something about the name.'

'How recently have you listened to the news?'

Sarah's shoulders slumped. 'Oh, God, it's her.'

'Afraid so.'

'At the university, the student who was murdered.'

'Yes.'

For a moment, she rested a hand on his upper arm, a grip strong enough for Resnick to be aware of each finger separately through his sleeve. 'I thought,' Sarah said, 'when I heard it, a woman attacked with a knife, whatever, stabbed, I thought it isn't, it can't be anything to do with us here, at the hospital. She's not a doctor, a nurse, she's a student.'

'I know,' Resnick said. 'That was what I thought, too.'

He knew he didn't want her to move away, not yet, but, of course, she did, the bounce and the snap that was there before quickly returned.

'We'll be talking to staff about security,' Resnick said. 'Officially, I mean. Leaflets, possibly, I don't know. In the meantime . . .'

Sarah grinned, broader than before. 'Be careful out there?'

'Sorry?'

'*Hill Street Blues*. The sergeant, at the end of roll call . . . you never saw that?'

Resnick shook his head.

'Shame. I think you'd have liked it.'

Resnick didn't think so. Police series, films, he liked his fantasies a little less close to home.

'Sarah . . .'

'Um?' She was at the end of the corridor, making a fool out of whoever thought the wearing of a uniform put her on a par with all the others. Eyes, Resnick thought: why is it always the eyes?

'Inspector?'

'Thanks,' Resnick said. 'Thanks for your help.'

Sarah pulled open the door. 'Whoever's doing this, catch them before they do it again.'

The way to prevent your take-away tipping over or getting thrown around the floor of the car, Lynn had discovered, was to slip the handles of the plastic bag they packed it in over the gear stick, then turn them twice, three times. One king prawn danshak with pilau rice home intact. She was

237

so concerned about getting it across the courtyard and into the flat before it got cold that she failed to notice the figure moving forward from the shadow until it was almost at her shoulder.

Lynn gasped and whirled around, bag ready as a weapon, poised to swing into her assailant's face.

'Whoa! Steady. I didn't mean to startle you.'

Lynn recognized the voice the same moment that she saw the face. 'God, sir! Don't do that.'

'I'm sorry,' Resnick said. 'I thought you'd have spotted the car.'

Lynn's breathing was less than steady. 'Other things on my mind.'

Resnick pointed to the white bag. 'Whatever you've got, think you could slip it into the oven on a low light, keep warm? By my reckoning, it's about time you and I went for a drink.'

Some pubs you ruined by making them over, rendering them new; others cried out for ruining before a dividing wall was pulled down or four generations of tobacco smoke was sandblasted from the walls. Sometimes the result was a freshened-up local with taramasalata or devilled prawns on the snack menu alongside cheese and onion cobs and pickled eggs. If you were lucky.

Resnick stood with one elbow on a convenient shelf and sipped at his Guinness, watching Lynn get down half a lager like it was water, which likely wasn't so far from the truth.

'I'm sorry,' she said, not quite bringing herself to look at him, unusual for her. 'I knew all the time I was sitting there it was stupid. Somehow, once it had started, especially after he'd come up to me, Carew, and done his macho bit . . . if I leave now, I thought, it's because he's intimidated me into doing so. And he'll know it.' She drained her glass. 'I wasn't going to let him do that, sir.'

Resnick didn't say anything until he'd fetched her another drink.

'You really think he's done something to Karen Archer? Something more?'

'I don't know, sir. I do think he's capable of it.'

Resnick glanced around. 'So are half the people in this bar, given the right circumstances. We don't stick officers outside their front doors at weekends, twelve-hour watch.'

Lynn looked towards the floor: black tights, sensible shoes.

'You've got good instincts,' Resnick said. 'A good copper. You've got a nose for it.'

Blood darkening the length of the landing until it stopped at the door to the small bedroom at the back of the house. The first time Lynn had interviewed William Doria in his office, something about him had prickled uneasily beneath the skin. At that time, there had been little enough reason for suspicion, a successful university academic, an expansive and loquacious man. Now, when there was more reason to regard a suspect with caution, why was Resnick holding her feelings up to question?

'Karen Archer,' he said. 'I wonder if that is where we should be looking?'

'You mean the new one, Hooson?'

'The timing could be right. We know he slipped out of the house, plenty of time for him to cut across the campus, meet Amanda, go back to her room.'

'Is there any reason for supposing he knew her?'

Resnick shook his head. 'She was seeing somebody, a man, we don't know who he was.'

'But Carew, isn't that too much of a coincidence?'

'Probably.'

'And besides, if I'm fool enough to be sitting there providing him with an alibi, why would he break it himself when he doesn't have to?'

Resnick gave her a quick grin. 'I don't know.'

'To say nothing of talking to a lawyer, making a complaint.'

A woman in Salvation Army uniform had come into the bar selling copies of the *War Cry* and Resnick reached towards his pocket. 'Maybe he likes drawing attention to himself, being at the centre of things, simple as that.' He gave the woman fifty pence and gestured that she should keep the paper. 'Unless he's being more devious, reckoning if he acts this way, it's going to take him out of the running.'

'Has it, sir?'

Resnick set down his half-finished glass. 'I don't want you getting into trouble on this, giving him cause to make his complaint official. And I don't want to be left feeling foolish again, not knowing what one of my team's up to.'

Lynn flushed, 'Sorry, sir.'

'On the other hand, I m not saying you're wrong. Let's keep him well in mind, see if something turns up that gives us reason for talking to him again.'

'Yes, sir.'

'Now, best get back to that curry before it's all dried out.'

Lynn smiled, close-mouthed. Resnick had one more swallow at his Guinness and followed her out of the pub.

He half-expected a letter from Elaine, a note; even his ex-wife herself, in the front garden of the house, waiting for what? Apologies? Reconciliation? Another burst of recrimination? Outside there was nothing, not even Dizzy, patrolling the night watch. On the living-room sofa, Ed Silver slept like a baby, wrapped in a blanket and still wearing a pair of Resnick's shoes that were several sizes too large.

Thirty-four

MURDER HUNT WIDENS

Police are stepping up their hunt for the sadistic killer
who viciously attacked pretty 26-year-old student,
Amanda Hooson, and left her for dead.

They have refused to confirm or deny that Amanda,
who was half-naked when her body was discovered,
had been sexually assaulted.

Police Superintendent Jack Skelton admitted yesterday that he fears a connection between this cruel
and senseless murder and recent attacks on hospital
personnel in the city.

Amanda, who had been studying for a Social
Sciences degree, had previously worked as an Anaesthetist Technician.

Superintendent Skelton is anxious to contact a man
whom they believe met Amanda for a drink at the
University bar only an hour before the slaying. They
are also urgently tracing her boyfriend, so far uniden-
tified, so that he can be eliminated from the enquiry.

Amanda's mother, 52-year-old Deirdre Hooson of
Amber Crescent, Belper, Derbyshire, said to our
reporter yesterday, 'Amanda was a quiet, thoughtful
girl. All she ever wanted was to help other people. I
still can't believe this has happened to her.' Mrs
Hooson continued tearfully, 'I keep expecting her to
come walking through the door.'

'Let's be clear on one thing,' Tom Parker said, 'no matter
what you may have heard or read with suggestions to the
contrary, none of the medical evidence points to a sexual
attack of any kind. That's not to say there might not have
been some kind of sexual motivation; you've all seen the

241

photographs.'

They were still pinned high along one wall of the room, curling already at the bottom corners. One glance was enough to remind the men sitting there of what they were engaged in and why. Aside from Resnick, the other DIs were Reg Cossall and Andy Hunt; the officer in charge of uniforms was Paddy Fitzgerald. Once this briefing was over, they would report back to their respective teams and set them on their way.

'We need something to break this open and quick,' the DCI continued. 'There's already panic talk out at the hospital, staff phoning in and crying off late shifts if they haven't got their own transport: the whole business will get worse before it gets better.'

'Surely, sir,' said Andy Hunt, 'the dead girl's connection with the hospital, tenuous at best?'

'That's what we're working to find out. Hopefully, by the end of today, we might have some answers. Meanwhile, we carry on exploring all the avenues we can.' The DCI stepped back, automatically buttoning his sports coat, unfastening it again as he sat down.

Jack Skelton got up and moved towards the A1 flip chart suspended from an easel alongside the desk. 'Should've been bloody Rommel,' Reg Cossall murmured.

'Wrong side, Reg,' whispered Paddy Fitzgerald.

'Huh,' Cossall snorted, 'bugger wouldn't have given a toss which side, long as he was running the show.'

Bernard Salt misjudged his turn, colliding with the end of the bed and banging his leg; he cursed beneath his breath and shot a fierce look at one of the nurses who was fighting hard to stifle a snigger. He'd been aware of them that morning, the way they were all looking at him, staring when they thought he wasn't noticing, openly some of them, curious, dismissive. Salt wondered what Helen had done. Pinned up a notice in the staff cafeteria? Called a meeting? All around him he could hear the tainted wriggle of tongues. The letter Helen had sent to his former wife, crammed with accusations and half-truths. The copy which had been delivered to the hospital by hand, together with a note: so reassuring after all these years to have my worst fears confirmed. I only hope the poor woman realizes how fortunate she is that you are letting her go too.

He looked at her now, Helen, fussing down the ward in her sister's uniform and it was beside belief that he had ever seen anything in her. A small-minded woman with a look of permanent disappointment in her eyes. Even then, when their affair had been at its height. Weekends in Harrogate and nights at the Post House near the Ml. Escorting Helen down to dinner when she was wearing that awful red dress, velvet, that looked as if she'd taken it down from the curtain rail and put it through the machine. Now he despised her. One look enough to turn his stomach, the sight of her thick calves sufficient to make him feel sick. There was a way of quenching her anger, but he knew that he could never take it. Not now.

He swept off the ward and stalked back to his office; damned secretary had been the worst, the look she'd given him, anyone would think it was her he'd been unfaithful to. A typed note waiting for him at the centre of his desk, cow asking for a transfer to another consultant, to be expedited as soon as possible.

Bitches the lot of them!

And there was that bloody inspector, loitering in the corridor like a shop steward from the TGWU. Man in his position ought at least to shine his shoes in the morning, see to it that, if he was going to wear a white shirt, it was decently ironed.

'All that guff you wanted,' Salt asked, showing Resnick through to his office, 'lead you anywhere?'

'Not yet,' Resnick said, relieving the consultant of the chance to keep him standing by sitting down.

'Some crackpot,' Salt said, settling behind his desk.

'Possibly.'

'Damned certainty. Lunatic with a bee in his bonnet. Been put out on the streets, most likely, instead of being kept locked up, safe where he belongs. Don't mind telling you, I think this government's come in for far too much stick, but health policy, mental care in the community . . . Saving pennies by wasting lives.'

'Amanda Hooson,' Resnick said.

'Worked here, ODA.'

'You knew her, then?'

'Yes, but not well. Consultant anaesthetists, registrar, that's who you should be asking.'

'Oh, we will,' Resnick said. 'We are.'

'Well, inspector, of course I'm anxious to help. But this is an especially busy day for me . . .'

Resnick was already on his feet. 'There's nothing out of the ordinary strikes a chord, nothing that would have involved Amanda Hooson with either Dougherty or Fletcher?'

'Not that I can think of. She could have had contact with Dougherty, of course, dealt with patients from the ward on which he worked. But only in the natural process of things.' He signalled with opened palms that Resnick's time was up.

'If anything does come to mind . . .'

'Of course.'

Resnick let himself out, past the secretary pecking away at her keyboard like a demented hen. One of the anaesthetists who'd worked with Amanda Hooson quite frequently had since retired, but Resnick had spoken to two of the others and their responses had been largely identical. Neither of them could think of anything about Amanda's work at the hospital that would have drawn attention to herself in any way; certainly there had been nothing about what she did or the way she did it which would have invited such violent wrath and anger.

Dougherty was still in bed, the number of tubes running into and out of him down to two. He smiled as Resnick sat down, then grimaced.

'What can you tell me,' Resnick said, 'about anaesthetic failure?'

'Simply as I can, it's this. Patient going into theatre, okay? They have an intravenous anaesthetic to start them off, but that's not going to last for more than the first few minutes. After that they're breathing in a mixture of oxygen and anaesthetic gases. What these do, they send the patient to sleep, numb all sense of pain, absolutely relax the muscles. Now occasionally, thank God not too often, but it happens, only the muscle relaxant works.'

Dougherty paused for a while, regaining his breath, allowing Resnick time for the implications to sink in.

'So,' Resnick said, something akin to nausea starting up at the pit of his stomach, 'the patient's lying there, unable to move, and all the while . . .'

'Exactly.'

'Jesus!'

'Uh-huh.'

'When this happens, they can feel everything?'

'Not necessarily, not always. Most times, probably not.'

'But sometimes?'

Dougherty nodded.

'During the actual operation?'

He nodded again. 'Right through it.'

'Not able to move.'

'Or scream.'

Resnick was thinking about what had happened to Amanda Hooson, to Fletcher, to Karl Dougherty himself.

'At least I could do that,' Dougherty said. He was smiling, but it wasn't at the memory.

'Not the sort of thing that gets broadcast about, is it?' Resnick said.

Dougherty winced and eased himself forward, encouraging Resnick to lean past him and push his pillows into shape. 'When I was in the States, just a twinge coming out of the anaesthetic was enough to bring down lawsuits like they were going out of style. Everyone from the head of the hospital to the relief cleaner. It's not like that over here, not yet, but with the spread of private medicine we'll be getting there.'

'You saying that's a bad thing?' Resnick asked. 'Compensation in cases like this.'

'Absolutely not. But it does make a naturally secretive profession even more so. You know what it's like trying to get a straight answer out of a consultant at the best of times.'

Resnick nodded and poured him some Ribena, pinched a handful of grapes and thanked him for his help. 'How about your parents?' he asked. 'How are they coping?'

For a moment Dougherty closed his eyes. 'My mother came in a couple of days ago. I was in a worse state than this, I don't know if she knew what was happening. I'm not even positive she knew who I was. I mean, she said my name, stuff like that, but twenty minutes after she'd arrived she was on her way again.' He smiled gently. 'My guess is, she thought it was all a big mistake.'

'And your father?'

'Doing pretty well considering. Comes in every day, sits for an hour, eats my grapes . . .' Resnick swallowed the last one guiltily, pips and all. '. . . doesn't say much, but then I suppose he never did.'

Resnick backed away from the end of the bed, raised a hand in farewell.

'How about Paul?' Dougherty asked. 'Is he still a suspect?'

'I don't think so.'

'If he doesn't know that already, it might help him a lot to be told. He's not finding any of this easy, either.'

'Okay,' said Resnick, 'you're right. I'll see that it gets done.' As he left the bay, sidestepping the tea trolley, his stomach gave a definite grumble. He wondered what the chances were of trying the new sandwich bar on Bridlesmith Gate before reporting back to Skelton.

Going into the hospital with a group of other medical students for one of their ward visits, a tasty little episiotomy to be viewed and mulled over, Ian Carew had spotted Resnick, recognized him from the rear and slowed his own pace, no wish to remind the inspector of his presence. That gormless little policewoman was one thing; Resnick, he guessed, was quite another.

Coincidence wasn't going to bring him so close to Sarah Leonard and, visit officially over and the students beginning to disperse, Carew took the lift up to the ward where he knew she worked. Through the end doors, he saw her, leaning across some old codger's bed and laughing; Carew only able to see the light in her eyes, dark opening of her mouth, not hear the sound. So simple to walk through, fall into step alongside her as she went back down the ward, pretty words in her ear. No. Not now, he told himself. Not now: wait for the time to be right.

Thirty-five

The senior Consultant Anaesthetist was a trim-looking man of medium build, a livid mark high on his left cheek, birthmark or burn. He greeted Jack Skelton as though he and the superintendent might long ago have been at school together, even shared the same dorm, eaten at the same refectory table, though, of course, they had not. The two men hadn't even leaned elbows against the same golf club bar, though, true to say, the consultant had done so with the Chief Constable. Yes, and the Chief Constable before that. Skelton was a runner not a golfer, a few rounds of pitch and putt on long-past family holidays the nearest he had ever come to a tight-fought eighteen holes then large gins and business at the nineteenth. His education had been grammar school, a good one at that, bringing the industrious middle classes the trappings of a public school – houses, prefects, an emphasis on keeping a straight bat while all around you are flashing across the line – without the expense. Or the kudos, automatic entry into the élite.

It would have been easy for the consultant to have patronized Skelton, so easy as to be automatic. Better, though, to rein that back, keep it under control; treat the man as a fellow professional, one who's risen to the top, an equal.

They shook hands and sat in comfortable chairs inclined towards the window; with only a slight effort it was possible to see the trees along the avenues of the university park, those around Wollaton Lake and the ornate turrets and chimneys of Wollaton House itself.

Skelton declined sherry, accepted the offer of coffee, which came in white china and with biscuits on the side. There was a preliminary feeling-out, during which the consultant let Skelton know how many of ficers he knew in the Force who were senior to the rank of superintendent. In total it didn't number many and the consultant knew nearly all of them.

Skelton had his best suit on and he felt scruffy; the fact that the man was so clearly making an effort to be pleasant and polite made it all the worse. He set down his cup and saucer and explained in terms as sharp and defined as the crease of the consultant's trousers what he needed to know and why.

'Anaesthetic failure,' the consultant said.

'Exactly.'

'You really believe, as a line of enquiry, this is . . . er . . . germane?'

'Amongst others, yes. Otherwise, I wouldn't dream of wasting your time.'

Don't patronize me, the consultant thought, taking his china cup towards the window and gazing out. To the left, just out of sight, was the bridge across the ring road where this wretched business had all started.

'What do you want to know?' he asked.

'Everything,' Skelton said. 'Everything that's relevant.'

The consultant drew a breath. 'What you must realize. First. The phenomenon we're talking about here is precisely that. Its occurrence is restricted to a tiny number of cases.'

Skelton waited.

'I wonder if you know how many operations are carried out each year in this country?'

The superintendent shook his head.

'Somewhere in excess of three million. So whatever incidents we're discussing, they have to be seen against that context.'

Skelton crossed his legs and waited some more.

'Recent research suggests – and like all research of this nature these results should not be considered conclusive – there may be some degree of anaesthetic failure in as few as one in every five hundred cases.'

It was very quiet in the room.

'As few?' Skelton said.

'Exactly.'

'But not exactly.'

'I'm sorry . . .'

'The figures, one in five hundred, you said they shouldn't be thought of as conclusive.'

The consultant nodded. 'They could be less.'

'They could be more.'

'In theory, yes, but . . .'

'But that's not a theory you would necessarily go along with.'

'That's correct.'

Time for Skelton to nibble a biscuit, recross his legs; for the consultant to check through his window that the trees were still there.

'As far as the patient is concerned,' Skelton said, 'some degree of anaesthetic failure means . . .'

'It means,' interrupting sharply, 'there is likely to be some small form of awareness . . .'

'Small form?'

'Some awareness of what is happening.'

'To the patient?'

'Yes, yes, of course. That's what we're talking about. For some reason, some mechanical failure, or mismanagement, or something unique to that particular patient, the nitrous oxide, the anaesthetic gases fail to function correctly.'

'The patient feels pain.'

'Yes, of course. The patient is being operated upon. The . . .'

'Cut open.'

'Generally, yes. The whole technique, the reason . . .'

'Then why doesn't he scream? He or she, whoever it is, as soon as the surgeon makes the first incision, why don't they scream?'

The consultant shook his head. 'They can't.'

'Why ever not?'

'Because, usually, although the anaesthetic is failing to have the desired effect, the other substance that is being breathed in, the muscle relaxant, is effective.'

'Effective?'

'Yes.'

'Please explain.'

'The patient's muscles are totally relaxed, any movement is impossible; there is no effect on either consciousness or the control of pain.'

There was a fly now, in the still room, somehow a fly, impossibly loud.

'All the patient can do, while the surgeon does his work, is lie there and give no sign.'

'Not actively, that is correct.'

'But there are signs?'

'Oh, yes. Generally. Arhythmia of the heart, a rise in blood pressure – the difficulty is that these same signs more commonly occur in association with other causes.'

'So there is nothing specific? Nothing that somebody around the patient might recognize as a sign of pain, a cry for help?'

'Sometimes,' the consultant said carefully, 'the patient may sweat and sometimes . . .'

'Yes?'

'Sometimes, although the eyes are taped shut, there may be tears.'

Thirty-six

Otis Redding, that's who the DJ was playing when Resnick went down the curved steps into Manhattan's. 'I've Been Loving You Too Long (To Stop Now)'. It hadn't been altogether true, what Elaine had accused him of that evening at the Polish Club. About having to drag him on to the floor, one dance before fumbling for the cloakroom ticket, fetching the coats. When they'd first been going out, going steady – only Elaine's grandmother had used the term 'courting' and then with the slyest of grins – there was a spell they'd be dancing – what? – every Friday night without fail. Once, at the second-string Palais that was now the MGM, the corner of Collin Street and Greyfriar, they'd walked in on some kind of Otis Redding tribute, some anniversary, and just about every number that was played or sung had some association with him. 'Sitting on the Dock of the Bay'. 'Mr Pitiful'. 'Fa-Fa-Fa-Fa-Fa-Fa-Fa (Sad Song)'. If they heard 'My Girl' once that night, they must have heard it a dozen times. Resnick scarcely moving, pushed up against Elaine and her arms round his neck, saying, 'See, just because it isn't jazz, doesn't mean it isn't any good.' Right there and then, Resnick would have listened to Alma Cogan, Clodagh Rogers, Des O'Connor, thought they were wonderful.

Maura was collecting glasses from the tables, her hair like orange whip. 'Hey!' she exclaimed. 'What're you doing here?'

'It's okay,' Resnick said, 'I'm not wearing a cap.'

'How about cheesecake?'

'I'm not wearing that either.'

Maura picked up another couple of glasses with her left hand and transferred them to the column she was balancing from the palm of her other hand all the way up to her shoulder. 'That bloke,' she said, nodding behind where Resnick was standing, 'he's over there.'

'Good,' said Resnick. 'Thanks.'

Paul Groves was sitting with a young Asian who was wearing a light-green polo shirt, bottle-green trousers and ankle-high trainers with the tongue out and the laces mostly undone. Groves was wearing the same suit, tie slacked down to half-mast.

Resnick pulled over a stool and sat opposite them and Groves introduced him to his friend, who had an accent that was Handsworth via Hyson Green.

'I was in to see Karl,' Resnick said.

Maura leaned between them and placed a bottle of Czech Budweiser and a frosted glass on the table.

'Thanks,' Resnick said.

'I'll put it on the manager's tab.' Winking, moving away.

'How was he?' Groves asked. 'Karl?'

'Seemed a lot better. Amazing, when you consider.'

Groves glanced at his friend, flicked ash towards the ashtray and missed. 'Did you see him?' he asked. 'When he was in there, after it had happened? Before they took him off in the ambulance.'

'No.'

Groves blinked away the smoke that was drifting up past his eyes. Two girls, couldn't have been more than sixteen, pushed past the back of his stool on their way to the ladies. 'Bleedin' cheek!' one said. 'All right, though, isn't he?' said the other. 'Well, wouldn't kick him out.' Giggling, they pushed into the crowd standing around in front of the DJ.

'I keep thinking about it,' Groves said. 'Trying to picture it. What he must have looked like.'

'Don't.'

'Lying there in all that . . .'

'Don't.'

'No. No, suppose it's stupid. Daft.'

'Want another?' his friend said, making the nail of his index finger ring against the rim of Groves's glass.

'Yeh, thanks.'

'You?' he asked, standing, looking over at Resnick.

Resnick laid a hand flat across the top of his glass. 'I'm fine. Thanks.'

There was an instrumental coming through the speakers, organ and sax, a churning, rolling blues and a few couples had started moving around the small dance floor.

'Firm I work for,' Groves said, looking not at Resnick but at his almost empty glass, 'got a vacancy. Northampton. I was thinking, you know, time I had a bit of a change. Might, like, take it.'

Resnick nodded.

'What d'you think? I mean . . .' Groves shrugged.

'New place,' Resnick said. 'Fresh start. Sometimes it's a good idea.'

'But as far as you're concerned?'

'Personally?'

'The police.'

'Oh. No. Let us know where you are if you like, but no, far as we're concerned, feel free.'

Groves relaxed on his stool, unfastened another button of his shirt. His friend was on his way back from the bar, carrying the drinks. 'Pursuing a new line of inquiries, then?' Groves half-smiled.

Resnick said he supposed that was true.

'I know.' Groves pulled out the newspaper from beneath his stool and folded it back at the front page. 'I was reading it in here.'

UNDER THE KNIFE

Resnick passed back the paper and stood up to go. 'What if he wants to go to Madisons?' asked one of the girls, coming back. 'Yeh, well,' said her friend, 'what if he doesn't?'

Resnick offered Groves his hand. 'If you go through with it, the move, I hope it works out for you.'

'Thanks.'

Resnick looked for Maura on his way out, wanting to wave goodbye, but she was intently talking at the bar, uncorking a bottle of Bulgarian red without taking her eyes off a man in a blue mohair blazer, short fair hair and a stud in one ear, more muscle across his shoulders than Resnick had in the whole of his body and roughly half Resnick's age.

There was nothing for it but to head home.

The smell of charred meat was strong, as though someone had decided to hold a barbecue there in the middle of the house. Smoke lingered close to the coving in the hallway and Ed Silver stood in front of Resnick's stove like the man who's discovered the wheel but can't immediately think what to do with it. 'Bastard thing!' Silver said, grudging admiration in his voice. He was wearing one of Resnick's light-blue shirts as an apron, sleeves knotted behind his back. Small darts of flame were sparking out from beneath the grill. 'Not be long, Charlie. Have it on the table in two shakes of a monkey's tit.' If the kitchen didn't burn down first.

Pepper's head lolled from the tin hat of the colander, half-asphyxiated, a cat in need of a gas mask.

Resnick went to take hold of the grill pan, but Silver stuck a bony elbow into his side. 'Relax, Charlie. S'under control.' Catching Resnick's breath, he turned to him disapprovingly. 'Bit early in the day to have been at the bottle?'

Whatever was simmering away in the various pans Silver had going on top of the stove was going to give new meaning to the words, well done. 'Right,' Resnick said through gritted teeth, 'I'll leave you to it. Everything you want's over there – salt, tomato sauce, fire extinguisher.'

He went upstairs to sluice his face, change his socks, work whatever had got lodged there out from his upper back teeth.

'What you've been missing, Charlie, someone to do this sort of thing for you. Make sure you've got a proper meal waiting for you when you get home. Never mind this sandwich, sandwich, sandwich. You must have a digestion like the M26 at rush hour.' It was always rush hour on the M26. Perhaps that was his point. 'Grazing, that's what it's called. Eating like that. Heard it on the wireless.' He gave Resnick a sharp, pecking look over his forkful of mashed potato. 'When I was with Jane.'

Let that one sink in.

'Jane?'

'You know. Wesley.'

'Wesley.'

'Yeh, that's her. I was helping her out.'

'At Aloysius House?'

'Yeh. Nothing, like – how would you say? – too specialized. Bit of cleaning, few things she wanted humping out the way . . .'

'No cooking?' Resnick had given up trying to cut what, in a former life, had been a lamb chop and was holding it between his fingers.

'Not yet, eh?' Silver winked. 'Got to ease into these things. Never does to go at it too hard. Full frontal, know how I mean?'

Resnick thought it was probably better that he didn't. He wondered if mushy peas had been Silver's original intention, or whether they'd simply happened along the way.

'Good, eh?' Silver said, pointing towards Resnick's plate with his knife.

'Distinctive.'

Silver beamed. 'S' what I said, Charlie. How it should be all the time. Job like you've got, can't be expected to cook for yourself. You need someone to do it for you.'

Was this how Ed Silver saw his future? Mornings doing good works for homeless alcoholics like himself; afternoons as Resnick's resident cook and butler.

No.

'She was here, Charlie. You know that?'

'Jane Wesley?'

'Elaine.'

Air clogged at the back of Resnick's throat.

'Earlier. Came to the door, didn't see as I could turn her away.'

'She came into the house?'

'Well, it did used to be half hers, Charlie. 'Sides, she looked terrible.'

'Ill?'

257

'Face like a bleached nappy. I had her sit down and made a pot of tea; slipped a drop of gin into it.' Whose had been the gin, Resnick wondered, Ed Silver's or Elaine's? 'We had quite a little chat.'

I'll bet you did!

'She's had a hell of a life, Charlie. Since she left you. One hell of a life.'

Resnick set down his knife and fork and pushed the plate aside.

'You've never finished! There's another chop waiting to be eaten. Apple pie in the oven, Mr Kipling, can't beat them. Winner every time. Charlie . . .'

'Let's be straight on this,' Resnick on his feet, back of his chair, staring down, 'it's fine for you to stay here, for a while, till either you get a room somewhere or decide to move on. But I don't want a nanny, I don't want a housekeeper, I don't want a cook and if I did, with the best will in the world, I don't think you'd get the job.' Silver sat there absolutely still, looking up at him. 'And I don't want a wife: especially the same one I had before.'

'Some people,' Ed Silver said a few minutes later, trying to coax Bud on to his lap with a piece of fat, 'don't know the meaning of the word gratitude.'

When the cat only sniffed the meat but wouldn't come any closer, Silver popped it into his own mouth, got up, and carried the plates towards the sink to do the washing up.

Ben Franks had been in the Buttery, taking his mind off an overdue essay with several bottles of Newcastle Brown, a couple of games of pool and the last half hour bopping around to a retro post-punk band with reggae leanings called Scrape the Barrel. He saw a bunch of students he knew ahead of him and called after them, running in a shambling sort of fashion past the library to catch up.

Four of them, three lads and a girl, they'd been across to the Showcase to see a film about a legless Vietnam vet who dies in a traffic accident and is reincarnated as a kung-fu Buddhist priest who's vowed to eliminate the Colombian drug lords. Chuck Norris, the girl said, was better than you'd have given him credit for. Especially playing the entire ninety-four minutes on his knees.

Somehow, heading down the grassed slope towards the hall of residence, all five became involved in a re-enactment of the plot, with the result that Franks finished up twisting his ankle and having to be supported the rest of the way home. Down on the level, they decided he could manage to hobble by himself and after a few steps his ankle went again under him, he pantomimed a dying fall and came down with a clatter amongst the dustbins. Groaning theatrically and allowing himself to be hauled to his feet, Ben Franks's hand brushed against something and he called for them to stop.

He picked it up and turned in the direction of the overhead light; he blew on it a couple of times, brushed away a persistent beetle and opened it up. There in his hand, Amanda Hooson's diary.

Thirty-seven

The slimline diary with the black imitation-leather binding and trim, metal corners at its four edges, lay on Skelton's desk, the sunlight shafting in from a cloudless sky, Indian summer. In a neat hand on the prelim pages, Amanda Hooson had written her name and both addresses, university and home, together with their respective phone numbers. Beneath she had put her passport number, current account number, national insurance number; the telephone numbers of her bank, doctor, dentist; the internal numbers for the Social Sciences Department and the Health Centre. Columns requesting dress size, hat size, shoe size had been left blank. At the foot of the right-hand page, she had filled in the name and address of her next of kin, to be informed in case of accident or emergency. There was an organ donor card sellotaped inside the back cover, but the necessity for a police post-mortem would have prevented it being used.

'Well?' Skelton said, early in the day but down to shirt sleeves already; things were going to get hotter as this day wore on.

Resnick and Paddy Fitzgerald were side by side, close against Skelton's desk. Resnick was wearing a green-hued tweed jacket with sagging pockets and frayed cotton at the cuff of its left arm. Fitzgerald was sweating through the dark blue of his uniform, little to do with the temperature or the unlooked-for sunlight.

'Well?'

Paddy Fitzgerald glanced, stiff-necked, at Resnick and Resnick looked away.

'I've had them in, sir, every man jack of 'em. Gave them a right bollocking.'

'If you'd done that sooner,' Skelton said, 'might have had some effect.'

'Yes, sir.'

'How many days searching that area?'

Fitzgerald blinked.

'Days?'

'Three, sir.'

'Officers?'

'Sir?'

'How many officers?'

'Twelve. All told, sir. Not, I mean, obviously not all at the same time, same shift . . .' Words withered away under Skelton's unflinching glare.

'I'm sorry, sir,' Fitzgerald said.

'You're . . . ?'

'Sorry, sir. I don't know how they . . . I don't understand how it wasn't spotted.'

'Maybe it was only put there last night,' Resnick suggested. 'Maybe whoever took it, kept it until yesterday, decided to get rid of it.' He shrugged. 'Always possible.' Even to himself, he didn't sound very convincing.

'Seen the state of it, Charlie?'

'Yes, sir.'

'Read it? The relevant pages?'

'Yes, sir.'

'You, Paddy?'

Fitzgerald nodded. The ripe scent of sweat was permeating the room and if things continued this way there was liable to be a puddle in front of Skelton's desk, not necessarily perspiration.

'What if,' the superintendent said, measuring every word, 'what if our laddie had sharpened up his blade, found

261

another victim, some young nurse say, walking home alone, what if there was another body on our hands? What would you think then?'

Fitzgerald stuttered. 'I don't know, sir.'

'It only takes five minutes,' Skelton said. 'Ten at most. You gave him seventy-two hours.'

The sun was strong on the right side of the superintendent's face, highlighting the fine strands of hair above his ear, making the skin at the curve of the ear gleam.

'It would be nice to think,' Skelton said, that when your men go back over the ground this morning, any weapon that might be lying around underneath the odd dustbin might be found before it takes another half-cut student to do their job for them.'

'Yes, sir.'

Skelton nodded and looked down towards the desk, allowing Fitzgerald the grace to leave the room. After another moment, Skelton picked up the diary and leafed through it, all the colour-coded dots beneath or alongside dates, the times of tutorials and seminars, notes of books to return to the library or pulses to buy from Hizicki or Oroborus, her father's birthday. When he found the right week, he angled the page across the desk so that they could both read what was written in the column for Saturday: *Buttery. 1pm. Ian.*

Resnick pushed the door to the CID room open wide enough to call round it. 'Mark, Kevin. Job for you.'

Carew had found a light cotton sweater, pearl grey, and he wore it now, draped across his shoulders, a deep purple singlet underneath, white running shorts with stripes in two shades of green and a high vent at the sides. Reactolite Polaroids with silvered frames. On each wrist a purple and green sweatband. He didn't want her to think he wasn't taking this seriously.

He rocked forward, legs straight out, and flicked an ant from the toe of his left shoe. Brand new LA Gear, he'd made a trip specially into the city to buy them that morning. What was the point of having parents who were prepared to supplement your grant if you didn't take full advantage?

'You didn't just happen to be here?' Sarah Leonard said.

'Uh-uh,' grinning that cocky grin of his, 'I was waiting for you.'

'How did you know I'd be here.'

'Easy. I checked your ward rota.'

'You checked . . .'

'Lying around on the sister's desk.' Carew touched the side of his sunglasses, but didn't take them off. 'It's hardly confidential. Surely?'

'I'm early.'

'I know.' All right for some, Sarah thought, bit of sun and they're lazing around, taking it easy; here he was, didn't care if he had to wait over an hour, just as long as he got a little more tanned. But instead Carew said, 'You're often early.'

'Am I?'

'More often than not.'

'You'd know, would you?'

He did take off his glasses then and smiled. Conceited bastard! Flashing those blue eyes, Sarah thought. Why are the good-looking ones always so conceited? Or gay?

'You sound as though you've been watching me.'

'I have.'

Something prickled at the root of her scalp, along the backs of the arms and legs: not the attraction, not the heat. Though they were part of it.

'Why?'

'Oh, come on!'

'No, why are you watching me?'

'Now? Take a look at yourself.'

Sarah was wearing a loose dress which buttoned up the

back, deck shoes, no tights. Sometimes she wore a slip with the dress and today, seeing the weather, she hadn't, so there she was now, wishing that she had. Her hair wanted cutting, she had no makeup save for a touch above her eyes, a smudge of blue; she knew exactly what she looked like.

'I don't mean why are you watching me now, I mean why before? Why the interest in my hours, when I come in and out? What?'

'You know,' Carew said, treating her to a lazy smile.

'So tell me.'

'Why?'

'If I already know, tell me again.'

'What's the point?'

'Maybe I'm wrong. I want to know if I'm right.'

'It's simple. I've already told you. I think you're attractive. I want to go out with you. I fancy you, all right?'

Sarah turned to walk away.

'Wait!' He was on his feet in a second, rolling back on his buttocks then springing up, jumping in front of her just as the unmarked car swung round from the main entrance and Resnick, seated in the back, leaned forward between Naylor and Divine, pointing, and said, 'There he is.'

'What?' Sarah said, Carew not looking at her now, somewhere else beyond her shoulder, something that changed his expression to one of concern, almost alarm.

When Sarah turned her head, the car had slewed up on to the grass, two of its doors already open, front and back, two men in the process of getting out. She didn't recognize the first, a tall man with a large plaster on one side of his face, but there was no mistaking the second.

'What's happening?' she asked.

Carew didn't reply. For a moment, she thought he was going to turn and run, saw his body tense and then relax, the moment passed now. By the time the officers were in front of him, each a little to one side, he was almost relaxed.

'Detective Inspector Resnick, this is Detective Constable Divine.' Sarah watched the faces, impassive, saw the warrant cards in their hands. Resnick reached out a hand, not quickly, and placed it firmly on Carew's right arm, midway above the elbow. 'We are arresting you in connection with the murder of Amanda Hooson. You do not have to say anything unless you wish to do so, but what you say may be given in evidence.'

Carew glanced at Sarah, much of the colour gone from her face; he looked at Resnick's fingers, quite tight around his arm. 'Made up your mind, hadn't you?' Carew said. 'Couldn't get me for one thing, you were going to get me for something else.'

Resnick withdrew his arm and the three men walked in close formation towards the waiting car. The last image Sarah had of Ian Carew was his face swivelled round toward the rear window, searching for her, smiling.

Thirty-eight

'Don't suppose either of you saw the match last night?' Carew said from the back. They were turning left into Gregory Street, passing the houses the health authority had built for doctors, but the doctors hadn't wanted to live in them. 'Highlights,' Carew said.

Nobody answered.

Carew was looking at the side of Divine's face; someone had fetched him one hell of a whack.

'What happened?' Carew asked. 'Your eye.'

Divine stared out through the opposite window.

'I suppose,' Carew said, 'they don't all come as quietly as me.'

'You call this quiet?' Divine said. 'Haven't shut your mouth since you got in the car.'

'It's called being sociable,' Carew said.

'It's called being a pain in the neck, that's what it's called.'

'It's . . .'

Resnick laid his arm along the top of the front seat. 'Sociable is what you do on day trips to Skegness,' he said. 'You'll get all the time you want to talk later.'

'I . . .'

'Save your breath.'

'We wouldn't make a detour via my place?' Carew said to the back of Resnick's head. 'Pick up some other clothes?' He was beginning to think that running shorts weren't going to be the most serviceable form of clothing.

266

'You have the right,' the custody sergeant said, 'to inform a relative or close friend that you are being detained.' Carew wasn't looking at him directly, but off to one side. Resnick and Divine were behind him, ten feet apart. All four men were standing. 'You have the right,' the custody sergeant said, 'to consult a solicitor.' He handed Carew a typewritten notice conveying the same information. 'Is that understood?' the custody sergeant asked.

Carew nodded and set the notice back upon the desk.

'You also have the right to examine the Code of Practice for the Detention, Treatment and Questioning of Persons by Police Officers, should you wish.'

'I want a solicitor,' Carew said.

'You wish to inform anyone else that you are here?'

'I want to inform my solicitor.'

'Nobody else?'

'How many times,' Carew said, 'do I have to tell you?'

The sergeant's eyes met Resnick's for just a moment then flicked back to Ian Carew's face. 'Twice, I think, will be enough.'

The first thing Suzanne Olds did when she walked into the police cell was to turn right around again and walk out. 'What the hell's going on in there?' she asked. Resnick and the custody sergeant were waiting by the sergeant's desk; the constable who'd escorted the solicitor to the cell wavered uncertainly in her wake. 'Well?'

Resnick and the sergeant exchanged questioning glances. 'You tell us,' the sergeant said.

'I didn't know,' Suzanne Olds said, 'you went in for this kind of thing. I'm surprised you didn't order him to strip and have done with it.'

'I don't quite follow . . .'

'He's in there in shorts. A skimpy pair of shorts and whatever the temperature might be outside, it's pretty damned cold in there.'

'He has a blanket,' the sergeant observed.

'In Northern Ireland,' Suzanne Olds said, 'it gets called sensory deprivation.'

'Really? Here we just call it sitting around in shorts.'

'I presume you're intending to question him like that as well?'

'I hadn't thought about it,' Resnick said. 'Not as an issue.'

'You don't think it might put my client at a disadvantage?'

'As I recall,' said the sergeant, 'he's got a good, strong pair of legs.'

'Has he complained?' asked Resnick.

'He will.'

'I'm sure of it.' The beginnings of a smile around the corners of Resnick's mouth.

'Did he ask you for some other clothing?'

'No,' the sergeant said.

'Yes,' Resnick said. 'When we were bringing him in. I didn't think he was very serious about it.'

'Perhaps you should have thought differently?'

'If your client would like to provide us with a key and permission to enter his property, I'll send someone round straight away. Whatever clothes he wants.'

'And a chance for you to search from top to bottom.'

'Difficult sometimes, putting your hands on the right pair of trousers.'

Suzanne Olds turned to the sergeant. 'Why don't you find something suitable he can wear? Something other than a blanket. I'll wait with my client while you see what you can do.'

Outside, the sun seemed to have exhausted itself early and given up. An articulated lorry carrying an assortment of toilet-roll holders, towel rails, toothbrush racks and toilet seats had been in collision with a blue five-hundredweight van at the south-eastern corner of Canning Circus. The van had run the lights off Derby Road and gone smack into the side of the lorry, which had been crossing lanes on the opposite diagonal, the driver having taken a wrong turning in his search for Texas Homecare. A 67-year-old woman, listening to Postman Pat as she drove, anything to keep her grandson in the back from yelling on and on about his lost marble, had swerved to avoid the rear of the lorry, done so successfully, but then swivelled round in alarm as she heard her grandson fall forward from his seat. Not looking where she was going, she had driven into a brand-new caravan setting out on its first trip to enjoy the autumn in Mablethorpe. Now traffic was backed up as far as you could see on all six roads leading into the circus, and those officers who weren't involved with sorting out the chaos were standing at the first-floor windows getting a lot of laughs out of the efforts of those who were. They were making bets, back and forth: first traffic warden to be verbally abused, first driver to get arrested, first punch to get thrown.

'To be clear,' Resnick said, 'Saturday lunchtime. You went into the university, to the Buttery, the bar, to meet someone for a drink?'

'I told you.'

'Someone you didn't know?'

'Of course I knew them. If I didn't know them, how could I expect to meet them?'

Resnick opened his hands and examined them, palms up against the edge of the desk. 'Tell me.'

Carew breathed deeply. 'I didn't know her name.'

Resnick's gaze came up slowly from the palms of his hands to Ian Carew's face. There was some sign of sweat at the temples and he was finding it difficult to look anyone in the room in the eye for more than seconds at a time. He was beginning to be uncomfortable, but he wasn't uncomfortable enough. A shame the uniform trousers the custody sergeant had found for him hadn't been tighter still, biting into the crotch.

'I bumped into her a couple of days before, in the video shop. She said she was a student, well, most people living round here, they are, one sort or another . . .'

'Which sort was she?'

'Sorry?'

'Student. Which sort of . . . ?'

'English.'

'Was English or she was doing English?'

'Both. Except it's called reading English.'

Sitting beyond the end of the desk, Divine looked up sharply. How the fuck else would you do English if it wasn't by reading it? Stupid tosser!

'Have you remembered her name?' Resnick asked.

'I told you . . .'

'Oh, yes. You never knew her name.'

'It didn't matter. It was no big deal. All I said was, if you're not doing anything Saturday lunchtime, why don't you meet me at the Buttery? We'll have a drink. You can tell me what you thought of *Wall Street*.'

'Where?' Divine said.

'It's a film,' said Carew disparagingly. 'A video. We were in a video shop.' Pronouncing each word as if addressing someone who was hard of hearing or short of understanding.

Five minutes, Divine thought, that's all I want with you. Five minutes. Alone. Later.

Feisty, thought Resnick, senses he's getting pushed back on his heels and fighting back. All right, let's see if we can't get him to overstep it. 'Did you meet her?'

'She wasn't there.'

'Wasn't that surprising?'

'I don't see why.'

'Oh? Surely you expected her to come? You had asked her, wasn't that enough?'

Carew bit back the word, *Usually*, looked across at Suzanne Olds instead. Sitting there with her notepad on her knee, spiky notes made with a gold-tipped fountain pen, skirt slipping back along her thigh, good legs. Maybe later, when this was over . . .

'Are you saying,' Resnick persisted, 'you went to the bar specially to meet someone whose name you didn't know, who you'd only seen once before for five minutes and who you didn't think anyway was necessarily going to turn up?'

'Yes.'

'You must have wanted to see her badly, then? Wanted to see her a lot.'

'I didn't give a toss.'

'You didn't . . . ?'

'One way or the other, I didn't care. I was going anyway.'

'For a drink?'

'That's right.'

'Pretty much a habit, was it? Saturday lunchtimes? To the bar for a drink?'

'No, not really. Not often. Better things to do.'

'Not this Saturday? The one in question?'

'That's right.'

'Besides, there was this girl to meet.'

'Yes.'

'The one without a name.'

'She wasn't without, I just . . .'

'The one you didn't really care if she turned up or not.'

'Yes!'

'So, to meet this person you scarcely knew and weren't even bothered about seeing, to do this, you went to the trouble of climbing out through the rear of the house where you were living and trespassed across someone else's property? Is that correct?'

'I've told you . . .'

'What have you told us?'

271

'Play it back, for God's sake! I've told you I went out that way because there was one of your lot out the front keeping watch.'

'Detective Constable Kellogg. And you didn't want her to see you leave the house.'

'Right.'

'Why?'

'What?'

'If what you had in mind was as innocent, as casual as you've said, why didn't you simply come out of your front door like anyone else?'

'Anyone else doesn't have a bloody policewoman parked outside the door!'

'Did that annoy you?'

'You know damned well it annoyed me. You know damned well I complained.'

'It made you angry?'

'You bet it made me angry.'

'So when you went out the back, letting DC Kellogg believe you were still inside the house, that was in the way of putting one over on her?'

'Yes, if you like.'

'Teaching her a lesson.'

'Yes.'

'Bit of a habit with you, isn't it? Teaching women a lesson.'

Suzanne Olds was fast to her feet. 'Inspector,' she said, 'I want to talk to my client, please. Privately. Now.'

Out on the circus, the lorry driver and the owner of the blue van had got into an altercation about lane and blame. One of the more maternal of the traffic wardens had offered to look after the little boy while his grandmother made her statement and the boy had taken a bite out of her calf. When the AA man with a tow truck tried to attach the crane to the rear of the van, its owner backed off from his argument

272

with the driver of the lorry to ask him politely what in fuck's name he thought he was doing. The AA man said if he needed to ask that there must be a six-inch square vacuum in the centre of his head where his brain was supposed to be. The van owner punched him in the face, whereupon he was promptly arrested by Ginger Houghton, who had been standing less than six feet away, watching. The crane was set in place, the back of the van swung round a shade too quickly so that the doors swung open and cartons of cigarettes began to tumble out.

'Any idea where your DS is?' Houghton asked from the door of the CID room.

'Sorry,' answered Patel from the midst of a half-ream of computer print-out.

'Only when you see him, tell him we've got a vanload of fags he might be interested in, bloke in the cells he might want to talk to.'

The sun might have packed it in for the day, that didn't mean it was getting any cooler. It was muggy instead. Suzanne Olds had removed her suit jacket and the cotton of her blouse was sticking to her; anywhere else, any other time she might have slipped into the ladies and removed her tights, but not now, not today.

'The name wasn't Amanda?' Resnick asked.

'No.'

'You're sure?'

'How can I be? I don't know what it was. That's the point.'

'Then it could have been?'

'Yes. I suppose so. It could have been anything.'

'Amanda Hooson.'

Carew scraped his chair until it was at right angles to the desk.

'Do I have to answer that?' he said, looking at Suzanne Olds.

'You already have.'

'Right.' Carew looked back towards Resnick. 'Right?'

Resnick nodded at Divine and Divine slid a 10" × 8" from inside a paper wallet and set it centre table. 'No,' Carew said, barely looking. 'That's not her.'

'Not?'

'The girl I was meeting. That's not her.'

'One o'clock.'

'What about it?'

'Saturday. The Buttery. One o'clock.'

'What?'

'You were meeting her?'

Carew was half out of his seat, eyes fixed on Suzanne Olds who shook her head and slowly he sat back down.

'Amanda,' Resnick said again.

'Inspector,' said Suzanne Olds, closing her notebook, fastening her fountain pen. The watch on her wrist was gold and told the phases of the moon. 'My client has been questioned now for a little over two hours. He's entitled to refreshment, a break.'

'Amanda Hooson,' said Resnick flatly.

'No,' said Carew, 'I don't know her. No. No. No. No.'

Resnick glanced at Divine, who reached into the wallet and removed a slim black book inside a plastic wallet and handed it to Resnick, who unfastened the wallet and lifted out the diary and opened it at the page marked by a thin strip of light brown thread and, placing it on the desk in front of Carew and pointing, read: *Buttery. 1 pm. Ian.*'

'I insist,' Suzanne Olds said, still pointing at her watch, standing now alongside her client's chair. 'I really must insist.'

'You know how many men there must be at the university called Ian?' Carew asked. 'Never mind the medical school. Have you got any idea?'

'I wonder,' asked Resnick, feeling oddly relaxed now, 'how many of those Ians bothered to avoid police

274

surveillance on Saturday lunchtime in order to go for a drink?'

'Inspector!'

'I wonder how many of them, within the last ten days, have been given an official police warning after attacking and in all probability sexually assaulting a young woman?'

Thirty-nine

In the bad old days before PACE, Carew might have been questioned through the night; kept awake by interchanging pairs of detectives until he was too tired to know what he was saying, so exhausted that he would say anything if it meant he could get some sleep. In some places Resnick was pretty sure such things still went on. On Jack Skelton's patch, especially with someone as sharp as Suzanne Olds looking over his shoulder, Carew was assured his hours of undisturbed rest, usually to be taken during the night.

But, Christ, he was a difficult bastard to shake, impossible so far to break down and maybe that was because, beneath it all, there wasn't anything to break. He'd quizzed men who were belligerent before, and clever, men for whom the interview was a challenge, a situation where you dug in your heels and won at all costs. He still hadn't been able to disentangle two thoughts in his mind: Carew was guilty of something; but try as they might they were not going to prove that he was guilty of this.

And if he were, what about the others? Fletcher? Dougherty? Motivation? Opportunity? Resnick crossed the street. Inside the entrance to Aloysius House, Jane Wesley was standing up to a stubbly young drunk with odd shoes on his feet and the behind falling out of his trousers.

'Look,' Jane was saying, 'I'm sorry, but I've already told you. You can't come in here in that condition.'

'What fucking condition's that?'

'You've been drinking. This is a dry house.'

'Of course I've been drinking. What the fuck else should I have been doing?'

'While you've got that much alcohol inside you . . .'

'Are you saying I'm drunk? Is that what you're fucking saying? 'Cause if it is . . .'

Resnick tapped him on the shoulder and the man turned faster than he should have been able and aimed a head butt into Resnick's face. Instinct swung his face away, enough for the man's forehead to clash with the protective corner of bone at the corner of Resnick's right eye. The man stumbled back against the doorway, blood beginning to run from a cut above his nose.

'Oh, God!' Jane Wesley said, quietly, a reflex sigh.

'Who in fuck's name d'you think you are, pal?'

Resnick told him.

Contempt seared the man's face. 'What's it now then? Assaulting a police officer? Eh? Resisting arrest?'

Resnick said nothing, didn't move.

'Resisting fucking arrest, eh? That what you fancy?' He turned and smacked his head against the inside of the door jamb, trying for a second time when Jane shouted out and tried to push herself between him and the door and Resnick caught hold of him by the arms and swung him round.

'Hey!' called the man. 'Hey!' A light in his eyes. 'Don't you fucking manhandle me! Enough fucking damage already, you! This . . .' He went unsteadily back across the wide pavement, pointing towards the blood that was now running freely down his face. 'Fucking this! You see that? You see that? Fucking police, bastards, they never change. Never change. But I'll see you done for this, I'll see you lose your fucking job over this. Bastard!'

'Okay, Charlie. Why don't you step inside, out the way while I get this sorted?' Ed Silver by Resnick's side, looking shaved and close to sober in a jacket Resnick was sure he recognized.

The two men looked at one another, a small crowd on the

pavement becoming less small every moment, the drunken accusations pouring on and on.

'Go on, Charlie.'

Resnick nodded and went through the small square entrance and into the main room, the same smell of damp clothing and urine and cheap tobacco, the same as it always was.

'Will he be all right?'

'Ed? Yes,' Jane smiled, relieved. 'You don't have to worry about him.'

'What will he do?'

'To calm him down? Oh, I don't know, give him a lecture, give him a hug, send him off down the road with a couple of quid to get another drink. I don't know.'

They stopped outside the door to Jane's office. 'You came to see how he was getting on, I suppose? Checking up on him. He said you would.'

'That makes it sound awful. I suppose I just . . .'

'Feel a sense of responsibility, I understand.'

'Maybe that's wrong.'

She shook her head, smiling with her eyes. 'It's not wrong. Not at all. If a few more people did . . .' The sentence remained unfinished, the smile disappeared from her eyes. 'It's not that type of world any more, is it?'

'No,' agreed Resnick. 'Though I'm not too sure it ever was.'

For a moment neither of them spoke.

Resnick nodded towards the door. 'Has he really stopped drinking?'

Jane shook her head. 'No. But he's cut down. He's getting it under control.'

'So what's going to happen here? I mean, is he going to work here, stay here? Are you actually employing him?'

'I think it's more Ed employing us,' Jane laughed. 'I think he's decided we're the therapy he needs. Situations such as the one you walked into, they're not infrequent. I

278

like to think that I can talk to these men, I can, I have done, but Ed, well, let's say, those that won't listen to me, they listen to him.'

'I'm glad. I only hope it works out.'

'Oh, you learn not to be too optimistic, but I think there's a chance.' She smiled again. 'As long as he stops trying to get his hand up my skirt whenever I walk upstairs.'

'You could try going up backwards.'

'Not the best logistical advice, inspector, if you think about it. No, the thing to do, I'll have to go back to wearing jeans.'

The baby was crying. Jim Davidson was telling jokes about Arthur Scargill and AIDS and Asians, and the baby was crying. Kevin had gone up and picked her up, petted her, patted her, changed her, set her back down. There was a lasagne drying out in the oven, pieces of the foil it had come packed in still sticking to the tomato sauce. Debbie was still wearing the dressing-gown she had been wearing when he'd left for work that morning. The baby was crying.

Kevin Naylor slammed shut the oven door and reached for his coat.

'You're not going out again?'

'No,' Kevin said. 'I was never here.'

The echo of the front-door slam was still reverberating in his head as he unlocked the car.

What I'll do, Resnick was thinking, make something to eat, coffee; half of the evening still ahead of him, he could play Lester Young and Basie, with Billie Holiday, Lester with the Kansas City Seven, the Kansas City Six, maybe the Aladdin Sessions, Jazz at the Philharmonic, 'This Year's Kisses' in '56 with Teddy Wilson, so slow that to listen to it was to feel the loss, the pain.

'Charlie.'

He turned sharply, the sound of her voice shuttling him through twenty years and back again, before she stepped from the shadows of the house they had lived in together: Elaine.

'The other evening,' Elaine said. They were standing stranded in the hall, not knowing where to go or why. 'When I was here with that friend of yours . . .'

'Ed Silver.'

'Yes.' The light from the stairs was making her face more gaunt than ever. 'Strange. Somehow I never thought I'd stand in this house again.'

'Neither did I.'

'You kicked me out, Charlie.'

'You went. He had the bloody Volvo outside with the engine running and you went.'

'And if I'd changed my mind? Said I'm sorry, Charlie, please forgive me, let's start all over again, would that have made any difference?'

'Probably not.'

'Don't forgive easily, do you, Charlie?'

He was breathing through his mouth, seeing her and not seeing her, under water, through glass. 'I suppose not,' he said.

'All those things I wrote to you . . .'

'I didn't read them.'

She stared at him.

'I didn't read them, tore them up, burned them, whatever.' He was staring at the floor, carpet close to threadbare from use, he could remember the day she'd met him off shift, driven him to Hopewells to look, pay the deposit, arrange delivery.

'What it took,' Elaine said, 'writing to you like that, forcing it all on to paper.'

'I'm sorry.'

'I was in hospital, Charlie.'

He turned his head aside.

'The valium wasn't working, it never did, not really. I went back to the doctor and he made an appointment for me at the hospital and they admitted me the next day. Once a week we'd sit in this room, all of us, and talk, but mostly there wasn't anyone to talk to, not anyone who was sane enough to listen, and besides there were the drugs and there were, oh, Charlie, there were other kinds of treatment, and because I needed to talk to someone about it I wrote to you.'

Now he was having trouble breathing at all, even through his mouth, though his mouth was still open and he knew the crying wasn't going to help either of them, hadn't then and it wouldn't now.

'Charlie,' she said, 'go and put the kettle on, for God's sake make us something to drink.'

There was a box of PG Tips that Ed Silver must have brought into the house and Resnick dropped three bags into the large pot, poured on water and together they waited in silence. After a while, Elaine left the room and when he found her again she was in the living room, leafing through last night's paper.

'It's you, isn't it? This girl who was murdered. That's what you're working on.'

He pushed a clearing on the table and put down the tea. 'Yes. One of the things.'

Elaine nodded. 'I used to sit here, when we were first married, worried sick over what might be happening to you out there, frightened that something would happen, that you wouldn't come back.' The mug of tea was in her hand, less than steady. 'Then later, when it had all changed, I used to sit here hoping you wouldn't come back at all.' She looked up at him. 'Does that shock you?'

'No,' sitting down. 'No.'

'I wished you dead, Charlie.'

'Yes.'

'So I could escape out of here and live happily ever after.'

'Yes.'

'You know, he had offices all over the Midlands, a house in Sutton Coldfield, a place in Wales with tennis courts and a swimming pool and I don't think he waited more than a couple of months after I'd moved in with him before he started screwing one of his secretaries. At the wedding reception I caught him in the bathroom with one of the bridesmaids. Last little fling, he said, and winked.'

'You should have left him then.'

'I'd only just left you. And, I suppose, part of me thought, all right, two can play at that game.' She glanced about her. 'I'd been dying here, Charlie, this house. I wanted something else.' She sipped at the strong tea. 'We screwed around for years, foursomes a few times, hard to believe, eh, Charlie, all those years with you when I wanted the lights out?'

Resnick sat there mesmerized by her face, this woman whose features were only half-recognizable, talking about a life he could only imagine.

'I was careless and I got pregnant. He wasn't interested, called me a daft cow, a stupid bitch, anyway, he needn't have worried. I took on all this fluid, problems with my blood pressure. Finally they got me into hospital just in time. The baby died and they told me I was lucky to be alive.

'No more babies. That's what they said: no more babies.

'Suddenly, the one thing more important than all the rest, now he knew I couldn't have one, he wanted a child, a son, an heir. God, Charlie, he turned into you. Except that he hit me. He drank more than usual, more than before, and he started hitting me. Places where it wouldn't be seen, wouldn't easily be noticed. Here, the lower back, the kidneys. My breasts. I backed his Volvo into the pool and I left him, sued for divorce. One after another his friends, the friends we'd had together, more ways than one some of them, they went up into the witness box and lied to their hind teeth. His barrister tore me apart and I was lucky to leave the court with the clothes I stood up in.'

She looked at Resnick and smiled ruefully.

'That was when I should have come back to you, Charlie. If I was going to do it at all. Instead of waiting till I became like this.'

'Elaine . . .'

'No.'

'Elaine . . .'

She placed her finger firmly on his lips.

'Don't, Charlie. Whatever you say now, by the morning you'll regret it.'

He would have been able, at that moment, to have taken her in his arms and forgiven her what little there was to forgive, maybe even forgiven himself. He could have foraged amongst the albums he never played and found *Otis Blue* and set it on the turntable and stood with his arms around her and said, 'Let's dance.'

Elaine stood up. 'If the phone's still where it used to be, I'm going to call a taxi.'

Resnick shook his head. 'No need. I'll drop you.'

'Charlie, you don't want to know where I'm going.'

At the front door, he said, 'Take care.'

'I'll try,' she said. And, 'Maybe I'll drop you a line some time.'

'Do.'

Elaine smiled. 'You can always tear it up.'

Forty

'Helen!'

Bernard Salt was wearing his white coat over shirt sleeves and a pair of tan cavalry twills that he'd bought from Dunn's more than ten years back and were still going strong. His tie was the one with little pigs on it his elder daughter had given him one Father's Day as a joke. That morning he'd slid it from the rack and knotted it swiftly, left the house before he realized and now he was stuck with it, no intention of appearing on duty without a tie. Besides, look at it this way, with half the hospital privy to his private life, half of those despising him as a heartless chauvinist, the remainder thinking, himself and Helen Minton, there wasn't much to choose between them, well, it was a gesture. Let them think he didn't care. If they were brainless enough to take the word of a neurotic woman, superficial judgements, well and good. He'd pig it out.

And with this other business, checks in and out, escorts and taxis home, extra security cameras, the staff whose job it was actually watching the screens instead of playing Find the Ball and reading the *Sun* – there were other things to preoccupy the hospital mind.

'Helen!'

This time she half-cocked her head, the slightest acknowledgement, before disappearing into her office and closing the door.

Salt opened it again and left it open, standing just inside.

Witnesses, no more meeting in car parks, fumbling behind closed doors. Fine!

'What do you want, Bernard?' Somehow she'd found time to have her hair re-permed and it was more like wire wool than ever. She stood ramrod straight, staring at him, this woman who had once teased from him a tenderness he had been almost frightened to realize he possessed.

'Very little, except to say how much I welcome what you've done. You were right, I have a freedom from personal responsibilities such as I haven't experienced in thirty years. Now that you have acted as you have, there is no way in which you can threaten that again. I didn't want you, Helen, I haven't wanted you for a long time. I don't love you and if I ever did, the way you have behaved is guaranteed to make me forget it.'

There was a slight tightening of the muscles in Helen's face, nothing more.

'Thank you,' Bernard Salt said.

Helen said nothing. A nurse came towards the open door, hesitated, went away again.

'I was chatting with the Senior Nursing Officer over coffee; I shouldn't be surprised if the hospital doesn't offer you early retirement, obvious stress, neuroses, maybe you could carry on doing a little part-time work . . . at a more junior level.'

Helen willed herself not to move until he had gone, from her office, from the ward. She willed herself not to cry. Tears enough already and what good had they done her? From the side drawer of her desk, she took the photocopy of the theatre report book and folded it carefully in half and then in half again before placing it in an envelope and sealing the envelope down. Better than crying.

'How long, inspector, are you intending to detain my client?'

'For as long as it takes?'

Suzanne Olds gave a quick little shake of the head. 'You don't have that long.'

'I'm sure the superintendent will authorize an extension of custody. In the circumstances.'

'The circumstances being that, aside from the girl's diary, you haven't been able to come up with a single piece of evidence that places my client in any relationship with the victim.' She used a small gold lighter to light a cigarette. 'Getting on for eighteen hours of frantic searching for what? A fingerprint? A sudden reluctant witness?'

'We can apply to the magistrate . . .'

'An application we would have every chance of successfully contesting.'

Resnick shrugged and wearily smiled. 'You'll do what you have to do.'

'And so will you.' She shifted the balance of the bag slung over her arm. 'The trouble is, you want to find him guilty for all the wrong reasons. You don't like him, do you? Not one little bit.'

Resnick looked back at her. 'Do you?'

Calvin didn't know what had got into his father lately. Dinner last night had been those little beef patties from the butcher down on the High Street, the one he'd sworn never to use again on account of some racist jibe he thought he'd overheard. Patties and tomatoes out of a tin, swimming around in all that pale red juice. Calvin hated that.

Breakfast today had been toast, toast and toast. The jar of beyond-the-sell-by-date honey had had a fungus growing over it a quarter-inch thick. And just as Calvin had been on the point of sweetening his tea with a couple of spoonfuls of that sugar substitute his father had bought by the twenty-eight-pound bag, he happened to look across at the paper and there the people who made the stuff, NutraSweet, were being accused of falsifying their research and pushing a product that could cause headaches, nausea, dizziness, blurred vision, depression, loss of memory, mood swings and swelling of the bodily extremities. Calvin let go of the spoon and sipped the tea as it was. He knew there wasn't a granule of real sugar in the house and though he knew some people liked to use honey to sweeten what they were drinking, he wasn't about to take a risk with that gunk.

Jesus! The tea had tasted terrible.

And Calvin never quite believed what he read in the papers anyway. He spooned in the NutraSweet and started to flip through, looking to see when Guns and Roses were appearing in the city, one thing they couldn't lie about, announcements, and he noticed that one of the pages had been torn away. The front one. He'd found the ad he was looking for and there was *Cancelled* printed all the way across it. Refunds available on receipt of the original tickets. Even when they didn't lie, newspapers, what they were full of was bad news.

His father had come back in from doing something to his bike, the chain slipping, something like that, and Calvin had asked him when they were going to get some decent jam again, out-of-date Oxford marmalade there was never anything wrong with that, what was he going to do with twenty-eight pounds of poisonous artificial sweetener, where was the rest of the paper?

His dad had mumbled something and rinsed his hands under the tap, wiped them on a tea towel and gone back outside to get them all oily again.

Calvin had found the missing front page in the bin under the sink, tea leaves and what hadn't been eaten of the tinned tomatoes wrapped inside it. Stained with a sort of dark orange, he'd read the headline: NEW HOSPITAL ALERT, the first few lines about somebody being arrested in the grounds, helping the police with their enquiries.

One of Calvin's friends had helped the police with their enquiries. He'd been off work for six weeks and lost his job, bruises consistent with falling down a flight of steps his parents had been told. Bruises consistent with being called a black bastard and out on his own with a holdall at one in the morning, that was more like it.

Calvin had pushed the paper back down into the bin and headed off to his room. He was fast running out of dope and just a quick hit listening to some music, that would set him up for the day, get out on the streets and score some more.

Skelton and Resnick were in the corridor, trying to ignore the phones that were ringing everywhere, footsteps, the rise and fall of voices. Graham Millington passed between them with a murmured *excuse me*, a man in a sense of dazed elation: twelve dozen cartons of cigarettes traceable to two different robberies and at that moment the magistrate was issuing a warrant to search a lock-up in Bulwell.

'Forensic have checked every print in the girl's room,' Skelton was saying. 'Nothing that doesn't come from the girl herself.'

'Still hoping for something from the university, sir. Someone must have seen them together.'

'If they were.'

'Apart, then. Carew admits he was there; the girl's diary suggests she was. We've got two officers sitting there in the bar interviewing people and so far no definite sighting of either of them. Might have been her, might have been him, all of that.'

'Ms Olds has been wearing out the carpet to my door, Charlie.'

'Mine, too, sir.'

'We need a break on this and soon.'

'Yes, sir.'

It was Lynn Kellogg who remembered something the nurse, Sarah Leonard, had said while being interviewed. The first time he spoke to me, Sarah had said, meaning Carew, I was walking home and he pulled over in his car, asked if I wanted a lift. One of those sports jobs, I can't tell one from another. Lynn could see the car clearly in her mind's eye, parked higher up the street and on the opposite side of the road from the house where Carew lived. She had thought nothing of it.

She needed written authorization and with Resnick back in the interview room she went straight to Skelton and got it within minutes, neat and precise and with his blessing. Her heart seemed to be alternately pumping faster and hardly functioning at all when she drew up alongside Carew's car and got out. There were a couple of medical textbooks on the back seat, a towel and an empty Diet Lilt can on the floor; as far as she could see only maps and some old Mars Bar wrappings at the front. The boot was locked and it took her an age to find a key that would fit. Squash racquet, tennis racquet, a pair of sports shoes, a can of Duckhams Multigrade, a sweatband, a Ruccanor sports bag with a white sports shirt stuffed down through the top. Lynn gingerly removed the shirt and slid the zip back.

Beneath a jock strap and a single white sock with blue and red bands at the top, a slim metal rod, silvered, five to six inches long.

'Tea?'

Ian Carew nodded and reached up for the styrofoam cup that Divine was offering him. Instead of letting go immediately, Divine held on and their fingers briefly overlapped, their eyes locked.

'What's this?' Resnick slapped the implement against the table hard, not waiting for Divine to return to his seat.

Despite herself, Suzanne Olds jumped in her seat.

Hot tea splashed over Carew's fingers.

'What – oh, Jesus!'

'Hardly an answer.'

'Where did you find that?'

'You tell us.'

Carew shook his head, did his little trick of pretending to

get up, settling back down. Trick or nervous habit, Resnick couldn't be sure. 'I don't believe this,' Carew said to Suzanne Olds.

Suzanne Olds was the only person in the room who, at that moment, didn't know what the object lying on the table was.

'It's a scalpel holder,' Resnick said. 'If I'm correct.'

Carew shifted his weight on the chair and folded his arms. He'd been offered the chance to shave after several broken hours trying to sleep in the cell, while somebody through the wall alternated between throwing up and blaspheming. He pushed his fingers into the corners of his eyes, then pushed up on the skin around the eyebrows, he was buggered if they were going to get him to say something he didn't want to say. Couple of smart-arse policemen, think they're so bloody clever!

'Carew?'

'It's a scalpel holder, so what?'

'You recognize it? I mean, this one in particular?'

'No, inspector, I do not. A bit like the police, see one, you've seen the lot.'

'Ian,' said Suzanne Olds, warning tone, warning look.

Oh, please, Divine was thinking, please give me just one chance. 'And you've no idea where we found it?' Resnick persevered. 'This particular one.'

'Well,' Carew leaning forward now, a little adrenalin jolting through him, take the high ground, 'the only point of asking me is if one of your minions found it somewhere in the house. Maybe even in my clothes. So, yes, all right. It was in the house.'

Resnick shook his head. 'The car.'

For a moment, Carew seemed genuinely bemused. 'The car? My car? What on earth was it doing in the car?'

'You tell us,' Divine said, easy on the menace.

'Oh,' Carew said. 'Right. The car.'

Resnick and Divine exchanged glances. Suzanne Olds

uncrossed her legs, turned the page of her notebook; after holding out all this time, there wasn't a confession coming?

'I nicked it,' Carew said.

'Say again?'

'The scalpel holder. Saw it lying around. At the hospital. I thought, right, that might come in handy, slipped it in my pocket. I think then, yes, that's what it was, I was driving up to Cripps for a game of squash. Dumped it in the bottom of my sports bag.'

'When was this?'

Carew shrugged. 'Oh, whenever we were in theatres, couple of weeks back now, must have been.'

'It's been in your possession all that time?'

Again a shrug. 'I suppose so, yes.'

'Thieve stuff from the hospital often, do you?' Divine asked.

'No.'

'Just scalpels?'

'Scalpel holders.'

'Easy to get the blades though, is it?'

Carew actually smiled. 'Easy enough.'

'You haven't told us why you bothered to take this implement,' Resnick said, 'and then, according to your version, leave it at the bottom of your sports bag for two weeks. That is what you're claiming?'

'Look, I saw it lying around. No use to anyone else. I thought it might come in handy. Then forgot about it.' He looked over at Suzanne Olds for support. 'Nothing sinister about that, surely?'

'Come in handy for what?' Resnick asked.

Carew shook his head and made a sound of mock exasperation. 'Oh, come on! I wouldn't have thought that was too difficult to work out, even for you. What am I?'

A jumped-up little prick, Divine thought.

'A medical student,' Carew continued. 'One day I might

291

decide to specialize in surgery. In fact, I think I shall.' He held Resnick's gaze. 'I suppose I thought it would come in handy for practising.'

'On what?'

Carew laughed in his face. 'What's the matter, inspector? On whom, isn't that what you mean? Although it would probably be on who if you actually said it. No, I could fit some blades and try it out on all kinds of things. Rabbit from the lab. Frog. Carve the Sunday bloody chicken with it, if you like.'

'Carve a body,' said Resnick.

'What about the anatomical skeleton you must have found in my room?' Carew asked. 'Maybe that was the one. Carved her up, boiled down the flesh and tied it up in neat little parcels, swilled away the blood, painted the ribs and spine that funny sort of flesh colour when I'd finished scraping away any last fragments of tissue. I expect this was what I used for that, too. Slice them up one minute, clean them up the next. All in a studious medic's work.'

'Ian,' Suzanne Olds was standing close to the door, about to pull it open. 'A break. A break, inspector.'

'Fuck breaks,' said Carew. 'I've had it with this. Old bloody scalpels, it's pathetic. The same name as mine in some girl's book. If that's all there is, all the so-called evidence there is, I'm walking out and not coming back.'

'You can't do that,' Suzanne Olds told him. 'You're still under arrest.'

'How much longer for?' Carew asked her.

Suzanne Olds looked at her watch. 'Between four and five hours, unless the inspector approaches a magistrate and requests an extension.'

'He needs evidence for that, does he? The magistrate has to hear the evidence and be convinced by it?'

'Yes.'

'Well, then,' Carew said, 'in that case we're laughing.'

Forty-one

The page had been photocopied from an operating theatre record dated 17 April, three years earlier. Cholecystectomy. Time operation began: 11.42 a.m. Time operation finished: 13.17 p.m. Surgeon's name. Assistant surgeon's name. Anaesthetist. Scrub nurse. Circulating nurse. Nature of operation. There were others noted on the same page, but Patel was in little doubt this was the one he should be concerned with. Whatever the exact reason the sister had handed him the envelope containing the copy, he was certain it had to do with this particular operation.

Cholecystectomy: he'd have to look that up.

Bernard Salt's signature at the end of the page; dashed off in no time at all, pitched between a scrawl and a flourish.

'Who usually fills in the record book?' Patel had asked, polite and always eager to learn. 'Yes, after an operation.'

The answer was the circulating nurse and this particular one was still at the hospital, that day, that moment in the recovery ward, a broad-boned woman with skin like raw washing left too long in the wind.

'Oh yes,' she said, Midlands accent, uncertain. 'Yes, that was me. You see, my handwriting, I'm afraid it's not the best.'

'And this operation, a long time ago, I know, but I was wondering . . . perhaps there is something you remember?'

The look in her eyes told Patel that there was.

'I don't know,' she said, casting her eyes about her

already, concerned that she might be overheard. 'We were asked, you see, not to talk about it.'

'Of course,' said Patel reassuringly. 'I understand. But this is a police enquiry.'

'Into this?'

'No. Oh, no. Of course not. But we think, well there is a possibility, there might be some connection.'

The nurse sucked in her lower lip, distorting her face.

'If it might help to put a stop to what's going on, you'd want us to know, wouldn't you. I mean, you'd want to help put a stop to all this, these attacks?'

'But this was three years ago. More than that even. I can't see . . .'

'Trust me,' Patel said. 'If it isn't relevant, nobody need ever know we've ever talked about it. I can promise you that.'

She sighed and he could see that she had made up her mind. 'The patient . . . he was on his way out of the theatre, being wheeled, you know, here to recovery, and I could see that he was crying, really crying, and I stopped, you know, the trolley and went to touch him, just on the shoulder, to touch him and he screamed. Screamed and screamed and screamed. Ever such a fuss and palaver we had calming him down. And then he told us – well, you don't know, do you? – but what he said was, right through the operation, he knew everything that was going on. He'd been able to feel the whole thing.'

Once, back in Bradford, Patel's paternal grandfather had been taken suddenly ill and rushed to hospital. Even as the old man lay there in the middle of a ward of strangers, palpably dying, it had been all but impossible to extract information from the doctors. Don't worry. No need for anxiety. The best thing you can do is not get upset. Nothing more than an exploratory operation. Tests. Examination.

Before the results had come through, his grandfather had been dead.

Trying to get information here had been little better: men and women, but mostly men, so used to obscuring the truth that it was second nature. Any question either ignored as by rote or weighed in the balance against any possible slur or taint of redress. Such records as existed were incomplete for the police's purposes and jealously guarded. So they had gone off digging, never sure of what they were searching for, another member of staff with a professional or private grudge or family with grounds for retribution? One veil prised away only for another to fall into place.

Excited by Helen Minton's gesture, Patel drove far too fast to the enquiry room and bullied his way on to the computer. Less than half an hour later he was knocking on the superintendent's door.

Carew had shifted gears: the bursts of belligerence, the bravado were gone and now he was playing for time, a straight bat, content to sit there and give the same answers, short as possible, again and again and again. More than one eye on the clock.

'I was wondering, sir . . . ?' Lynn Kellogg on her way across the CID room the moment Resnick appeared.

Resnick looked at her forlornly and shook his head.

'But the scalpel . . .'

'No way we can tie it in, nothing that puts him with the girl that lunchtime, any other time, nothing at all.'

'We've got his name in her diary, surely . . . ?'

'Eighth most popular name, A and B group parents, kind of statistic Amanda Hooson would have loved. Medical school, university, probably full of them.'

'If it is somebody else, he must know who he is, why hasn't he come forward?'

Resnick shrugged. 'Who knows? But Naylor did come

295

up with a student, positive he saw Carew sitting in the corner of the Buttery, watching the pool. Says he was on his own.'

Lynn Kellogg closed her eyes.

'His solicitor said it, I don't like him. Neither do you. Sort that gets under your skin, blurs your judgement.'

'Karen Archer, sir, you have questioned him about her as well?'

'He swears not to have set eyes on her after he received his warning. Hasn't heard from her, no idea where she is.'

'I don't believe him.'

'Isn't it what I just said? You don't want to believe him.'

'I don't think, where women are concerned, he's the kind of man that ever gives up, lets go.'

'I hope you're wrong,' Resnick said. 'I hope to God you're wrong. Meantime . . .'

'We're releasing him.'

'Maybe soon,' Resnick said. 'Not yet.'

Salt had screamed at the scrub nurse in theatre, fumbling with a clamp instead of slapping it down into his hand and the poor bugger on the table into a bleed that had his kidneys bobbing around like a coxless pair catching a crab. Of course, he'd apologized to her afterwards, no excuse for snapping like that and she'd said, no, it had been her fault, her fault entirely, but it had been her eyes that had told the truth.

Interesting, the way they were polarizing, attitudes towards him inside the hospital. Well, not interesting at all, really, take that back, more what you'd expect. Most of the nurses, female ones, the secretarial staff, social workers, their sympathies were with Helen, the other woman, used and then abused. Whereas the men – some of them it was nudge, nudge, wink, wink, sly old goose keeping a bit going on the side and pretty much getting away with it; others who'd found themselves on the receiving end of

Helen's tongue, they thought he was well shot of her. All brimstone and spare the treacle.

There was a message on his desk – he'd swear his secretary's handwriting had become more crabbed since this had come out into the open – would he please get in touch with a Superintendent Skelton as soon as possible?

Soon as he felt up to it: later.

Right now what he needed was a brisk walk, fresh air. He knew some surgeons who kept a silver flask topped up with one form of spirits or another, a quick tipple between jobs to keep the hands steady. Or so they claimed. One of his former colleagues, now gone to meet the great consultant in the sky, hadn't been above grabbing the mask when no one was looking and having a furtive go at the ether. Nine operations a day, that man, matter of routine. Of course, it had killed him. Heart. Four years short of fifty. Wife had remarried within six months, junior surgeon. New blood. Probably something going on there beforehand as well. Truth were known, they were all at it. Most of them. Human nature. What was that play? Restoration. Damn. English teacher had them read it at school. One that got the sack. *Way of the World*, that was it. True enough.

Bernard Salt stopped at the slip road to the car park and for only the second or third time since it had happened, he was thinking about the incident that evening after talking to Helen. A sound like a footstep, a movement, definitely a movement, and close, close to him. But then someone he knew had come along and after that, nothing. Which was in all probability what it had been.

Except . . .

That houseman, Fletcher, then Dougherty, it hadn't seemed anything that concerned him, that might impinge on his life, touch him at all. And then that young girl, the one who'd been an ODA. He had never wanted to admit to himself that there might be a connection.

Then he turned back towards the hospital and saw the

two men standing close to the entrance, neither of them men that he recognized as such, but the way they stood and waited, you didn't need to know their name.

'Superintendent Skelton,' said the taller man, showing his card. 'This is Detective Constable Patel. We appreciate that you have a busy schedule, but we were wondering if you could find time to talk to us. It may not take very long.'

Salt made a brief nodding motion, almost imperceptible. 'I have a cholecystectomy scheduled, which I should imagine, barring complications, will take an hour to an hour and a half. After that . . .'

'Will be fine,' said Skelton. 'There are other matters we can be checking into while we're here.'

Salt didn't ask what these might be; some of them he thought he might guess.

'Cholecystectomy,' said Patel, 'an operation to remove the gall-bladder, is that right?'

'Yes,' said Salt, 'it is. Absolutely.'

'What did you get your degree in?' Skelton asked as they were walking into the hospital.

'Mechanical engineering, sir,' Patel said, holding the door to let the superintendent step through.

'Rightly or wrongly,' Bernard Salt was saying, 'the impulse is always to calm the patient down, give something to deal with the residue of the pain, basically ensure as little agitation as possible. Last thing you want them to do, dwell upon what happened. Difficult enough to forget, I should have thought, without willingly reliving it all the time. No, you can apologize, you can try to explain.'

'Smooth it over,' suggested Skelton.

'Absolutely.'

They were in the consultant's office, Skelton and Salt facing one another from the two comfortable chairs, Patel off to one side on a straight-backed chair with a leather seat. Among the questions he wanted to ask, why wait until someone else gave us this information, why not come forward with it yourself? The sister who did point them in this direction, what were her motives? Another of a different kind, what was Skelton's degree in? But he remembered somebody saying, the superintendent was not a graduate at all. When Skelton had entered the Force, relatively few recruits had been graduates; even fewer had been Asian, black.

'There is always, I suppose,' Skelton was saying, 'the danger of legal action in cases such as this?'

Salt tapped his fingers together, brought his heavy head forward once.

'And so to do anything which might seem to be accepting liability . . .'

'Quite.'

Skelton let his glance stray towards the window. After the brave showing of sunshine, today's skies had reverted to an all over anonymous grey. 'I believe there was an instance, four years ago. An . . . er . . . laparotomy, if I have the term correctly.'

'An exploratory examination of the abdomen,' said Patel.

Salt glared at him with something close to hatred.

'The patient claimed to have been awake throughout the operation,' Skelton continued. 'Damages were sought from the health authority, who settled out of court for an undisclosed sum. You were the surgeon in charge of that operation.'

'The patient,' Patel said, less than comfortable with both of the older men staring at him, 'was in a ward on which Karl Dougherty was working as a nurse.'

Salt shook his head. 'I can only take your word for that.'

'It is true,' said Patel. 'Dougherty himself remembers the incident and, as far as we have been able, we have checked the records.'

'I'm sure you have,' said Salt, a tone neither quite accusation nor patronization. 'And I am sure you have discovered that in November of last year, during an appendicectomy, the anaesthetic was found not to be functioning correctly and the operation was abandoned.'

Skelton looked across at Patel and Patel, who had come across no such information, nodded wisely.

'Only a few months before the operation to remove the gall-bladder,' Skelton said, 'there was considerable adverse publicity around a woman who claimed to have been conscious while giving birth by Caesarian section.'

'Certain newspapers,' Salt said, 'I am sure sold a great many extra copies.'

'Not only were the health authority sued, but also the surgeon in charge and the anaesthetist. I think that is correct?

'In the light of that,' Skelton went on, 'it's reasonable to imagine the authority, the hospital managers, would be very loath to attract similar publicity so soon again. Quite apart from the financial loss, what might seem to the general public like a falling away of professional standards, that would be something to be avoided at all costs.'

'Not at all costs, superintendent. There is no sense of anything having been covered up. And as for this hospital, I can assure you that, cheek by jowl, our record in these cases compares very favourably with others of a similar size.'

'I'm sure it does.'

'The number of operations that are carried out . . .'

'Please' – Skelton spread his hands – 'Mr Salt, even if such issues were my concern, you would not have to convince me that what you say is true.'

Salt cleared his throat and stretched out his legs, drawing them back up again towards his chair.

Skelton glanced over at Patel and nodded.

'The operation to remove Mr Ridgemount's gall-bladder, sir, the anaesthetist was Alan Imrie and his assistant was Amanda Hooson.'

'Correct.'

'At the time of the operation, Tim Fletcher was attached to you as a junior houseman?'

'I believe . . . I should need to check to be . . . Yes, yes. I suppose it's possible.'

'The surgical ward in which Mr Ridgemount was a patient, Karl Dougherty was a staff nurse on that ward.'

'He may have been. I'm sure you know that better than I.'

'Dougherty, Fletcher, Hooson – after the last of these, at least, why didn't you come forward?' Skelton asked.

'I had never drawn the connection you are suggesting.'

'Never?'

'Superintendent, Dougherty may have been one of the nurses who cared for Mr Ridgemount. During his time at the hospital, so would a good many others. And as for Fletcher, I can't imagine that his contact would have been more than peripheral.'

'So you never thought it might be relevant – what happened to Ridgemount?'

'What he alleges happened.'

Skelton looked at the consultant keenly. 'He made it up?'

'An operation, superintendent, it's a traumatic thing. It has been known for patients to hallucinate, for their imaginations to distort what actually happened under the anaesthetic.'

'And you're saying that's what happened in Ridgemount's case?'

'I'm saying it's a possibility.'

'It's also a possibility that he was telling the truth.'

'Yes.'

'Ridgemount,' said Patel, 'he was threatening legal action also.'

Bernard Salt nodded. 'At one time.'

'Against yourself, the senior anaesthetist and the health authority?'

'So I believe.'

'You've no idea, sir,' asked Patel, 'why the action was dropped?'

'None. Although, my supposition at the time was that whoever had been advising him didn't consider his case strong enough to take to court. Either that, or he changed his own mind about what actually happened.' Salt made a point of looking at his watch. 'Gentlemen,' he said, rising to his feet, 'I am in danger of being late for theatre.'

'The anaesthetist in charge that day,' Patel said as they were passing through the door, 'Imrie, wasn't he also involved in the Caesarian section? The case that was settled out of court?'

'I believe he was.'

'If we wanted to speak to him?' Patel said. 'He no longer appears to be on the staff of the hospital.'

'Eight months after the Ridgemount operation,' replied Salt, turning in the corridor to face the two policemen, 'when legal action was still threatened, Alan Imrie committed suicide.'

Instead of going directly to the operating theatre, Bernard Salt went to Helen Minton's ward, where she was just finishing hand-over.

'I assume this is more of your dried-up spite. Dragging this wretched Ridgemount affair back into the open.'

Helen Minton arched her back and stood her ground. 'I thought telling people of your inadequacies as a man was not enough. I thought they should understand how far the same inability to face the truth or to accept your responsibilities is present in your professional life as well.'

While this confrontation was taking place, a zoology student named Ian Bean, fresh back from a field trip to Robin Hood's Bay, walked into Skelton's station and asked to speak to whoever was in charge of the Amanda Hooson murder enquiry.

Less than an hour later, Ian Carew was released from police custody without charge, thirty-two hours after he had been arrested.

Forty-two

'Whatever you do or don't do,' Ridgemount said to his son, 'don't be forgetting the split peas. One thing I don't want, come back out of breath from pedalling up that hill, find the peas have gone to mush, bottom of the pan burned out. Am I understood?'

'Umh,' grunted Calvin, headphones pushed tight inside his ears. 'Um, umh, umf.' What he liked about those old bands like Black Sabbath, when they hit a rhythm it stayed hit.

'Calvin!'

Calvin's eyes widened and he swayed out of his father's reach. Headphones were going to be removed, he'd do it himself.

'You hear what I said?'

'Split peas, watch 'em. Satisfied?' Sound squeaked from the headphones that dangled from one hand.

'Listening to that garbage the whole time, turned up loud as it can go, be deaf this side of twenty-one.'

'Better than being a fool.'

Calvin started down the stairs to his room, his father standing by the front door, pointing his finger. 'Take care, boy. Just you take care.' Whether he was still going on about the peas, or meant Calvin's mouth, Calvin didn't know.

'Whatever else we've done on this one,' Skelton said, 'we've not exactly covered ourselves in glory. The Assistant Chief's already had the Senior Consultant

Anaesthetist on the phone talking about undermining public confidence, asking where the virtue is in unnecessarily tarnishing professional reputations, causing additional distress to the relatives of the dead.'

'Imrie?'

Skelton nodded.

'Not much concern about the poor bloody patient in all that lot.'

'Closing ranks, Charlie. We know about that as well as anyone. A copper stands accused, one of the public brings a complaint, nine cases out of ten, what's the first thing we do? Get the waggons round and form a circle. Keep the buggers out. Doctors, they're no worse than any others.'

'Maybe, sir.'

'All I'm saying, Charlie, if we are close to something, let's not screw it up. Take care. Just take care.'

'Right,' Resnick said. 'Kid gloves.'

David McCarthy had promised Resnick fifteen minutes, no more, a meeting in the brasserie on High Pavement, across from St Mary's Church. Around the corner, in Commerce Square, the first of the old Victorian lace factories was in the hands of the developers and would soon be architect-designed studio apartments, luxury condominiums, a gymnasium, a pool, a sauna.

Resnick had met McCarthy once before and recognized him as he came in, a slightly hunted look, briefcase in one hand, portable telephone in the other. He was finishing a call as he came through the door.

'So,' McCarthy said, carrying his glass of Aqua Libra over to the corner Resnick had staked out, 'why the renewed interest in this old chestnut?'

Briefly, Resnick told him.

McCarthy leaned back and folded his arms across his chest. Cuff links, Resnick thought, noticing the solicitor's

305

pale blue shirt, thought they were a thing of the past. Like those daft suspenders for men's socks.

'You're not, of course, asking for anything that might be considered privileged information?'

'What I want to know,' Resnick said, 'why was the action dropped?'

'Client's wishes.'

'Not your recommendation?'

'Absolutely not. We had every chance of building up a good case.'

'If anything, then, you'd have been encouraging him to stay with it?'

'Financially, it would have served his interests best.'

'But not in other ways?'

McCarthy took a drink, glanced at his phone as if it were about to ring. 'A similar situation to cases of rape, balance out the distress a client is put through reliving the experience in court against the potential gains. Here's a man, held down, physically violated and powerless to do anything about it at the time. How much does he want to talk about it, describe it, have what he believes to be true attacked, even ridiculed? No, he decided enough was enough.'

'Nothing to do, then, with Alan Imrie's death?'

'Imrie?'

'The anaesthetist.'

McCarthy pursed his lips. 'I'd forgotten.'

'You can't remember Ridgemount talking about it at the time?'

'No,' the solicitor replied after some moments' thought, 'he would have been aware of it, I'm pretty sure of that. But, no, I can't recall him mentioning it. As far as I know, it didn't affect his decision.'

Resnick nodded. McCarthy sampled the well-publicized delights of Aqua Libra. Libra, Resnick thought, anything but what it was. 'The other personnel involved in the operation,' he said, 'even though they weren't named in the suit, you'd have determined who they were?'

'Right down to whoever pushed the trolley in and out.'

'You'd have told your client the names?'

McCarthy fidgeted with the mechanism of his briefcase's double lock. Some people used the first digits of their phone number as the combination, others their wife's birthday.

'I can't see why I should. No, I don't think so.'

'Not if he'd asked? Straight out.'

'I don't know.' His telephone rang and he picked it up almost before the sound could register, listened, nodded a couple of times and told the caller he would ring right back. 'I really don't recall his having done so.'

'The names though, they would have been around, committed to paper? It couldn't have been out of the question for him to get a look at them without you realizing. At some point he would have had the chance to write them down, make a photocopy even. What I mean is, he could have known who they were, as you say, even the porter wheeling the trolley.'

'Yes,' said McCarthy. 'That's right. That's reasonable to assume.'

His portable telephone rang and Resnick got to his feet.

'You don't have to rush off,' McCarthy said, one hand over the mouthpiece. 'I'm okay for another few minutes.'

'Enjoy them,' Resnick said. 'Do the concise crossword. Dismantle the phone.' He touched McCarthy lightly on the shoulder in passing. 'Thanks for your help.'

Great thing about the way the house was so high up, built near the crest of a hill, even his own room below stairs, there was no way in which he was overlooked. Except from the garden and who was likely to be standing out there in the garden? His father, maybe, but his father was off somewhere, hopefully getting back into being a fetcher and carrier, bringing home something good for their dinner.

Calvin stretched back on the bed, rearranging the pillows a little, get them really comfortable. This new stuff he'd got, Jamaican, the kid who'd sold it to him had said, but Calvin knew enough to know that didn't mean a thing. It was good, though. Good stuff. Good shit. So good, in fact, he thought he would have another joint. Sometimes, lying there, instead of smoking, he would masturbate, thinking, maybe about the woman who worked in the ice cream van in the park. Sitting inside surrounded by all those Cool Kings and Juicy Fruits and Raspberry Torpedoes. Got the radio tuned to the pirate reggae station. White overalls: he was certain she didn't have anything more than some skimpy kind of stuff underneath. Often, in the park, he would choose a spot where he could see her clearly, sprawl there listening to his music, watching what she did. Never once, she paid him any heed, gave any sign she knew he was even there. But Calvin knew enough to know different.

The tape in the stereo came to an end and Calvin swore and then realized he had his Walkman next to the bed. All he needed now was another tape from his bag and a light and hey! What was that Robert Plant thing? 'Stairway to Heaven'.

Pretty soon, eyes closed, singing along at the top of his voice to Twisted Sister, himself and Dee Snider duetting, except that Calvin kept forgetting the words, getting them wrong, especially in the verses, getting it right for the chorus. Eyes shut tight. Take another hit, that's it, hold it there and suck it down. Arms spread wide. Sing, you crazy bastard, sing! Calvin didn't hear the first tentative taps at the window, only when Divine's fist banged against the frame did Calvin sit up with a jolt and see the man's cock-eyed face grinning in.

Whatever condition he was in, Calvin knew enough to

understand this wasn't the window cleaner, come knocking for payment.

Panicked, he jerked the headphones clear and threw them across the room, pinched out the joint with his fingers and pushed it from sight. Perhaps no one would notice, figure he was resting there enjoying Bensons King Size? Another of them rattling at the back door now, that fool with a plaster the size of a fist stuck to his face, still grinning like he'd woke up and suddenly it was Christmas.

Calvin wafted the air on his way down the room. Quicker to respond, he could have bolted up the stairs and out into the street, made off on foot, but what the hell, what did he have to run for anyhow? Englishman's home was his castle, right?

The underside of a boot struck the door, low by the jamb, and it shook.

'Hey!' Calvin yelled. 'Hey!'

He unlocked and they came in, forcing him back out of the way, not exactly pushing him, never using their hands, the one with the plaster making straight for the bed, easing the last inch and a half of his joint out into the light.

'Home grown?'

'Old Holborn,' Calvin said. 'Cheaper to roll your own.'

'Sure. And I'm Mike Tyson.'

Shit! thought Calvin. You're not even the right colour.

The other one was flashing his card. 'Detective Constable Naylor. This is Detective Constable Divine.'

Divine grinned some more. He was having a good time. The inside of the kid's room smelled like some of the parties he used to go to when he was nineteen, twenty. Wherever he was getting his stuff, it was bloody good.

Naylor had spotted the sports bag on the floor and was making a beeline for it.

'Man,' Calvin said, 'you got a warrant to come busting in here?'

'We didn't bust in,' Divine said. 'You let us in.'

'That or stand there and watch the door kicked in.'

'You didn't invite us on to the property?' said Naylor.

'Damn right!'

'That's okay, because we've got a warrant.'

'Like fuck you do!' said Calvin and wished he hadn't because the bigger of the two looked as if he might be about to belt him one.

Kevin Naylor took the warrant from his pocket and held it in front of Calvin's face.

'What you expect to find anyway?' Calvin asked.

Naylor and Divine were exchanging glances over the bag, lying on the floor between them.

'That's my stuff,' Calvin said. He could hear the whine sneaking into his voice and hated it but there wasn't anything he could do about it. 'That's my personal stuff.'

'Show us,' Divine said.

'Huh?'

'All you have to do,' said Naylor, 'unzip the top, pick it up and turn it out on the bed.'

Calvin didn't see where he had a lot of choice.

He held the bag over the bed and they all watched the contents tumble out. Old rolled-up copies of *Kerrang!*, maybe ten spare sets of batteries for his Walkman, EverReady Gold Seal LR6, must have been twenty to thirty cassettes, most of them pristine, Cellophane-wrapped, stickers still in place, HMV, Virgin, Our Price.

'Kid's a collector,' Divine said.

'Yes,' said Naylor, 'bet he's got the receipts too.'

Two of the T-shirts that now lay on the bed were also in their original wrapping, several others that he'd pulled and worn for a few hours and then rejected. A red-backed exercise book in which Calvin had copied the lyrics of his favourite songs, one day, he'd figured he'd start to write his own. All he wanted was the inspiration. A little more time.

'Shake it,' Divine said.

'Hmm?' Calvin looked back at him blankly.

310

'The bag. Shake it some more.'

This time it came rolling out of the corner where Calvin had desperately been trying to hold on to it with his thumb. Naylor lifted up the plastic bag, the kind Debbie used to buy in Tesco to keep his sandwiches fresh. He sniffed at the contents and passed it across to Divine, whose attention had been drawn to the bundle of tapes.

'Whatever,' he asked, perplexed, holding up a copy of John Denver's Greatest Hits, 'are you doing with this?'

'That shit,' said Calvin. 'I don't play that shit. I just sell it again.'

'Right,' said Divine, now holding the bag of marijuana, 'to buy shit like this.'

'Hey,' said Kevin Naylor, moving towards the door, looking upwards. 'Does anybody else smell burning?'

Ridgemount had smelt it too, even before he'd eased himself off the saddle and wheeled his bike over the pavement, trailer behind it full with potatoes, onions, ten pounds of bruised Bramleys that he was going to simmer down into apple sauce. Honest to God, Ridgemount thought, I knew it. I just knew it. One thing I asked that boy to do, one thing and he can't even do that. He was sliding the key into the front door lock when Patel came up behind him and spoke his name.

'I don't want to buy anything from you,' Ridgemount said, 'I don't want anything on credit and right now I can't stop to discuss the Bible, because my nose tells me there's a small emergency going on in my house. Now if you'll excuse me.'

But Patel showed him his warrant card instead.

'I'm sorry,' Ridgemount said, 'I have to deal with this first.'

He pushed the door open and left it wide. A man he didn't recognize was standing half-way up the stairs, Calvin two steps from the bottom with another man right behind him, a hand on Calvin's arm. Ridgemount stepped across the hall and into the kitchen; the windows were thick with steam and clouds of it had collected over the ceiling and were beginning slowly to descend the walls. He took a tea towel from its hook and bunched it in his hand, turned out the gas and lifted the pan from the stove. What had been a pound and a half of split peas was now a blackened mass crusted across the pan. Between the stove and the sink, the bottom of the saucepan fell out but the peas clung on, welded to the sides.

'Mr Ridgemount,' said Resnick, who had walked over from his car and followed Patel into the house, 'Detective Inspector Resnick. I'd appreciate it if you'd come with these officers to the police station. There are some questions we'd like to ask you.'

'Dad?' said Calvin from the hallway.

'These questions,' Ridgemount said. 'What are they about?'

'Oh,' Resnick said, 'I think you know.'

Ridgemount looked past Resnick to where Calvin was standing, Divine and Naylor at either side of him, Naylor still holding his arm.

'Let my son go,' Ridgemount said.

Resnick looked questioningly towards Naylor. 'Possession of an illegal substance, sir. Namely, marijuana. Possession of stolen goods.'

'Sweet Jesus!' Ridgemount breathed.

Resnick nodded towards Patel, who went forward and reached his hand towards Ridgemount's shoulder.

'*Nooo*!' Ridgemount screamed and backed clumsily against the stove, cleaving the space between Patel and himself with his fist. 'No! Don't touch me! Don't touch me!'

Patel moved in again but now there was a knife in Ridgemount's hand, a kitchen knife, tears and fear glistening in his eyes.

312

'Steady!' called Resnick

Behind him, Calvin struggled to be free. 'He won't . . . You can't . . . He won't let you touch him. Not at all. He can't.'

Resnick nodded, understanding.

'Let the boy go,' he said and Naylor, querying the order with his eyes, did exactly that. 'Now, Mr Ridgemount,' said Resnick, moving round Patel, slowly extending one hand, fingers spread. 'Please let me have the knife. You have my word, we won't touch you. Give me the knife and all you have to do is walk to the car and wait with one of the officers. We do have a warrant to search these premises and we'll see that's finished as speedily and with as little disturbance as possible. After we've searched the house, you'll be driven to the station.'

'And Calvin?'

'He'll come with us also. He can ride in the same vehicle as you if you wish.'

Ridgemount reversed the paring knife and placed the handle, carefully, in Resnick's hand.

Forty-three

The postcard was from the island of Mykonos and off
beyond the low, white buildings what Lynn presumed to be
the Aegean was a dark stain like an ink blot in the
monochrome copy on her desk. She imagined how blue it
would be and Karen Archer stepping down to it through
sand, even this far on in the year, to swim. We thought you
would like to see this, Karen's parents had said in their
covering letter, we hope it sets your mind to rest.

> Sorry to have been out of touch for so long but felt
> I just had to get away. Thank God for Thomas
> Cook and Access!! Think of me in the sun, pigging
> out on ouzo and olives!!! I'll phone the minute I'm
> back in England. Take care and try not to worry.
> I'm fine!
>   Heaps of love, Karen XXXXXXXXXXXX

Well, good for you, Lynn thought. Be nice, wouldn't it,
if everyone in your position could go swanning off to
Greece and pretend it had all been a bad dream. She sat for
a moment, resting her head down into her hands. What's
the matter with you? Did you really want her to be a body
somewhere, just so that you could have another victim,
something to trace back to Ian Carew's hand?

'Everything that's said in this room,' Resnick explained,
'everything you say, will be recorded on this machine,
afterwards the tapes will be sealed and signed to show that
they're a true record.'

Ridgemount nodded to show that he understood.

'What I'd like you to do is say what happened in your own words, exactly as you want. If there's anything that doesn't seem clear, I might interrupt to ask a question, but other than that all I want to do is listen. All right?'

Ridgemount nodded: all right.

Carew hadn't been certain whether to go up to her when she was with other people or wait again until she was alone. He hadn't known whether to wear something not exactly formal but a little less sporty. Suggest that this was serious, not play. Touch and then go. Finally he settled on a faded denim shirt, white slacks, moccasins. Wallet buttoned down in his back pocket in case she said, 'Terrific! Let's go for a drink, celebrate!' Later they could get something to eat, that new place up from the Council House, all white tablecloths and single-stem flowers, Sonny's, he'd been wanting to go there.

In the event, she didn't say a thing. Stood there, staring at him as if not really able to believe it was him. The others that were with her, three of them, nurses, uncertain what to do, whether to walk on or stay, staring from Sarah to Carew and back again. Beneath her long, open coat she was still in her uniform, belted tight at the waist, dark sheen of her hair: perfect.

'Surprise, surprise!' Carew said.

'See you tomorrow, Sarah,' called one of the others, continuing on her way.

'Fine,' Sarah said. 'Bye.'

Then they were alone in the middle of the broad corridor, doors off. Paintings by local primary children on the walls. 'I thought you were in jail,' Sarah said.

Carew smiled. 'I was. It was a mistake.'

'There must have been something. They must have arrested you for something.'

'Is that what you think?'

'Well, yes.'

A doctor, stethoscope around his neck, came into the corridor and walked towards them. He had a squash ball in his hand and he was squeezing it rhythmically, pressing it hard into his palm.

'Well there was something,' Carew said. 'They seemed to think I'd murdered someone. A woman.'

Scarcely missing a beat, the doctor turned through one of the doors and disappeared from sight.

Sarah Leonard was staring at him, unable to work him out. 'And now they've changed their mind,' she said.

Carew smiled. 'The wrong Ian. You see, they found her diary, the woman's, and there was a name there, Ian. They thought it was me.'

'Why would they do that?'

'I don't know. But it was a mistake. The real Ian turned up, the one from the diary and, well, here I am.'

'What for?'

'Um?'

'What for? Why are you here? I don't understand.'

The smile shifted from the mouth to the eyes. 'I thought, you know, we had some unfinished business.'

Sarah waited.

'When we were talking, before, if I remember rightly, we'd just got to the point.'

'Of what?'

'Finalizing the arrangements. Where we were going to go, where we were going to meet. Italian or Chinese. You know the kind of thing.'

'I may do. But what makes you think I'd ever agree to going out with you? Especially now.'

'Exactly my point.'

'What?'

'Especially now. It's not every day the police decide you didn't murder somebody after all. We have to go and celebrate.'

Sarah shook her head. An elderly woman was manoeuvring the length of the corridor on a Zimmer frame, pausing every fifteen feet or so to draw breath.

'We've got to,' Carew said.

'You're the one. It's nothing to do with me. You celebrate.' She began to walk towards him, veering left to go past. As she drew level he caught hold of her hand.

'It's no fun on your own.'

'Tough!'

'I mean it.'

'So do I.'

One of the side doors opened and she pulled herself clear. A porter backed out a trolley bearing a sheet and blankets, nothing else. He was chewing gum and whistling 'When You're Smiling'; recognizing Sarah he winked and grinned and switched the gum from one side of his mouth to the other, all without quite losing the tune.

'Just one drink,' Carew pleaded. 'Half an hour. On your way home.'

'No.'

'But . . .'

'No. How's it spelt?'

Carew hung his lower lip, made a good pass at crossing his legs standing up and stared at her as if she'd asked him to explain the theory of relativity. 'Er,' he stuttered. 'Um . . . er, um . . . the first letter, miss, it's not an M?'

'No.' Willing herself not to find his little-boy act funny, just absurd. Pathetic.

'N? It's an N, isn't it? N for no.'

Unable to stop herself smiling, Sarah nodded. 'Yes.'

'Yes?' Carew was suddenly no longer the timid boy, moving confidently towards her. 'You did say yes.' He'd been saving his best smile for last, the one that never let him down. 'Half an hour,' he said. 'An hour at most.'

'I was lying there,' Ridgemount said, 'I was lying there

317

with my eyes taped over shut and I couldn't move. They had this tube, see, this tube clamped over my mouth. Taking the air down to my lungs. And they've been saying, before, you know, they give me this shot, put me under, she was saying, this girl, not much more than a girl, just a few seconds and you won't feel a thing. Not till you're back in recovery and it's all over.

'Well, I went spark out all right. Next thing I know, I seem to come to and there I am thinking it's just like sleeping, nights you go to bed and you're so tired you can't as much as remember your head hitting the pillow but the next second you're waking up and it's eight hours or more later. So I'm there thinking, okay what did she say this place was, recovery? All right, I'm in recovery, except my mouth is still covered and my eyes are still taped over and I reason I'm still in the operating room, must be going to wheel me out any minute.

'They don't wheel me out. Nobody's about to wheel me out.

'Even though I've got this tape across my eyes, somehow I can see these bright lights right there above me and it's like, you know when you've been looking up at the sun and you close your eyes and for a while you can see this hot blur, like it's printed on the inside of your eye, that's what it's like. Not only that, I can hear voices. Not too clear what they're saying, not clear at all, so I try and say something, speak to them, what's going on? Only there's no way I can say anything, not a word. I try to move, can't move a muscle. Just stretched out there and I realize, shit, they haven't done this operation, taken out this damn gall-bladder, haven't even started yet. My head's panicking and my body can't move and I can't shout or scream and all I can see is the blur of those lights and I'm thinking, no, it can't be going to happen, no, it can't be going to happen, no, it can't and then it does.

'It's like wire being pulled clear through me. Thin wire.

Only it's hot. It's a piece of red-hot wire and I swear I can hear the flesh tear when he pulls it through. And all I can do is pray for it to stop. Pray to die. 'Cause I know it won't stop ever. Won't stop till it's done.'

Carew was drinking his second single malt, savouring it, the look he gave the stupid little cow behind the bar when she asked him if he wanted ice in it should have made her pee her pants. Where was the point in drinking the good stuff like this, only to water it down with frozen algae out of the Severn-Trent?

'D'you ever come in here?' He looked round at the wide room, stuffed red chairs and shiny black-top tables, like something off a P. & O. cruise ship.

Sarah Leonard shook her head. It was only after he made a fuss about ordering bitter lemon – what kind of a celebratory drink was that? – that she'd relented and had a dry white wine and now she was regretting it.

'We should have gone somewhere a bit livelier. More style.' He leaned forward across the table exactly as she knew he would. 'We still could.'

'Oh, no.'

'Come on. Let's go dancing, for heaven's sake. When was the last time you went dancing? Venus. New York, New York. God, we could even go to the Irish.' He reached for her hand and she pulled it away. 'How about it?'

The wine tasted sour and old, as if the box it had been squeezed out of had been mouldering in a cellar somewhere for years.

'Why don't you ever give up?'

'It's not in my nature,' Carew smiled, 'to accept defeat.'

Sarah put down her glass and stood up.

'Where are you going?'

She pointed towards the door alongside the bar. 'Ladies.'

Carew nodded. 'Sarah,' he called when she was half-way across the room. Swivelling her body, she stopped to look back at him. 'Don't go slipping out the back way now, will you?' And he laughed.

'You could tell from their faces, the way they were all over me, fussing with this, fussing with that, you could tell they knew something had gone wrong. But they never said, never said a thing to me and I couldn't . . . at first, when they pulled the tube away from my mouth, all the time I'd been wanting to shout out and scream and cry and when I could do it I couldn't get a sound to come out.

'Later, yes. Then I would scream and call them barbarians and butchers and they would come running and slide this needle into my arm. Keep me quiet. Take away the pain. That's what they say, make you feel comfortable, take away the pain. It's too late, I say, it's too late for that. And they slide the needle home.'

'What's that?' Sarah asked, pointing at the glass.

'Bitter lemon.'

'And?'

'Ice.'

'And?'

'Gin.'

She picked it up and carried it over to the bar. 'There was a misunderstanding,' she said. 'I didn't want this.'

'I'm sorry,' said the girl behind the counter. 'You can't have your money back.'

'Fine.'

Sarah gave Carew a quick look, see how he was taking that, and headed for the door. A picture in denim, that was how he saw himself. Mr Irresistible. She wondered when a woman had last turned him down and what had happened to her when she had. She had thought he might jump up and come after her, flash another of those practised-in-the-bathroom-mirror smiles, but Carew continued to sit where he was, drinking his malt whisky, looking cool.

A quarter of a mile on, she was less angry about it already, just another bloke trying it on, this one, maybe, a touch more persistent than the rest. Approaching the road that led down towards the old Raleigh factory, Sarah's face opened to a smile. Had he really imagined she was going to go off with him, dancing, dressed like that? The badge on her uniform that spelled out her name and rank. Ridiculous.

And suddenly there he was in front of her, posing at the corner of the side street, having to struggle to control his breathing and pretend he hadn't had to sprint fast to double around that block and get ahead of her in time.

'Now what?' Sarah said, angry again.

'Easy. I walk with you to your door, say good night, turn right around and go home. End of evening. Okay?'

'No.'

Ian Carew didn't say anything; he didn't even smile. He just looked.

Sarah began to walk and he danced into step alongside her, not attempting to talk, simply walking. All right, Sarah thought, five minutes, another five streets and it will be over.

'When I got home from the hospital I could still feel the pain. I didn't go to bed at night, I wouldn't lie down, as soon as I did I'd be waiting for it again, waiting for it to start. The cutting. The wire. I slept sitting up, wherever I was and even then, though I wasn't lying down, I would scream.

'At first my wife, she would come to me and try to calm me down but if she went to touch me I screamed all the more. I couldn't ever bear to have anyone touch me.

'My Marjorie . . . she was little then, she says to her mother, why does daddy shout at me like that, why won't he let me near him, why does he hate me?

'In the end they couldn't take it any more and they left me and Calvin he stayed. No matter what that boy does, I'll always love him for that. He stayed by me when nobody else would.'

Sarah's house was in a short terrace that backed on to a playing field. She had bought it when prices in the city had been lower than almost anywhere aside from Belfast, which was just as well because on her salary it had been all she could afford. She stood with her back to her front door, hands in her coat pockets, fingers of one tight about some loose change, the others round her keys.

'Right,' Sarah said.

'What?'

'Good night.'

The smile was back. 'Good night.'

Sarah didn't budge. 'Let me see you walk away.'

'Just one thing . . .'

'No.'

'Just . . .'

'No!'

'Tim Fletcher, I wanted to ask . . .'

'What about him?'

'You were getting pretty friendly with him, running errands and all that . . .'

'Errands?'

'You were buying books for him, remember?'

'The condition he was in at the time, he wasn't exactly in a position to do that for himself.'

'That's what I wanted to know. How is he? His mobility? I mean, is he ever going to regain that?'

'He's made a lot of progress, yes.'

'I'm sure he has,' said Carew, 'but no matter how hard he tries, however much you do for him, he's never going to get it back fully. Is he?'

Sarah Leonard watching him, Carew was off down the street, not exactly hurrying but gradually lengthening his stride, stepping out, showing his paces.

Forty-four

'Where's Calvin?'

Resnick looked up from changing the tape. 'He's being questioned by detectives.'

'About me?'

'Not directly, no.'

'I want to see him.'

'Afterwards.'

'After what?'

Resnick pressed record and pause simultaneously. 'I think what you were about to tell us was to do with the legal action, why you didn't proceed.'

Sarah Leonard's blue uniform hung down from the handle of the bathroom door, ball-point pens poking from the breast pockets, one side weighed down by a stethoscope, a notebook, her watch still pinned to the front, beneath her badge.

Sarah knelt in the bath, running the water from the mixer shower over her face and hair. She was thinking about Tim Fletcher, how easy he was to talk to, how she might have found him attractive if only he were a little taller. God! Sarah laughed up into the spray of water. If only for Ian Carew's body, Tim Fletcher's personality, his mind. She closed her eyes tight and brought the shower rose closer to her face.

'You can't tell me that man did what he did through anything other than guilt. It had already happened when he

323

was in charge of those machines one time before. And he'd been proved guilty for it. Why else pay all that money out of court? He knew, Imrie, he knew that was his responsibility, same as what happened to me, and he couldn't live with it no better than I could. Except he didn't actually know the pain, he didn't feel the pain, he just knew he caused it and that's why he swallowed all them pills and then took a razor to his wrists on account he didn't want to take any more chances. Risk something going wrong, not when it was his own life he was dealing with. No.'

Ridgemount dampened his bottom lip with his tongue; Resnick signalled to Patel, who poured some more water and left it within reach of Ridgemount's right hand.

'I thought that was some kind of sign. I thought that meant that man had accepted all the blame to himself and now it was going to be over. Except the dreams never left me and I could never get back to sleeping normal like anyone else and all that did leave me was my wife and my little girl. So I knew . . .' looking at Resnick, searching his face, 'I knew that wasn't the end of it. I knew there had to be something more.

'See, it would have been better if they had killed me, there on that operating table, if they had killed me dead, 'cause what I was, what I had become, that was worse than being dead. But God had left me alive and I had to find a way of dealing with that and I knew I couldn't turn round and do what that man had done and take my own life, not after God had sent me through that fire and brought me out on the other side.

'I thought, they are all at fault. What they got to do is accept their blame.

'And I waited and meantime the pains in my head got worse and still they done nothing, so little by little I took it on myself to find out where they were, what they were doing, and they were all, most of them, carrying right on like before as if nothing had ever took place. And I kept watching them, them who'd been in there with me during my operation, I watched them and I waited for something to tell me what I could do that might finally ease my pain.

'Me and Calvin, we lived our life best we could and all the while I was waiting for some kind of sign.'

Sarah watched the pan, waiting until the boiling milk had bubbled almost to the rim before whisking it off the gas and pouring it into the mug, spooning in three heaped teaspoonfuls of hot chocolate and stirring hard. On the way over to the sink she licked the pieces of dark chocolate away from the spoon before dropping it into the bowl. She collected her book and carried book and chocolate up towards the bedroom. She was just settling into bed, wondering if she might get to the end of her chapter before falling asleep when she heard the glass break.

Her first thought, as she sat up in bed, it was someone on the way home from the pub, kids coming out of the Marcus Garvey Centre; once before a neighbour across the street had a brick thrown through her window, some people's idea of fun.

But this had not been at the front, the sound had come from the back.

Sarah stood at the door to the bedroom, eased the door open and held her breath. Nothing moved below: no light save that from the street which filtered through the front room curtains and the pebbled glass above the front door.

Still she waited.

It need not have been her house at all, it could as easily have been next door. It could have been someone throwing stones from the field. If it had been a burglar, it was possible she had already frightened him off; or he could be down there, waiting. For what? Part of her wanted to turn round and get back into bed, pull the covers up over her head. Whatever she had downstairs that was worth taking, let him take it. Not for the first time, she cursed herself for not having a phone point put in the bedroom. Even so, surely that's what she should do, go downstairs and telephone the police.

'What they all still had' – sweat was beading along Ridgemount's lip, running into the corners of his eyes and making them sting – 'was their liberty to do as they chose, have affairs with other women, other men, go off and study, anything they liked and I was trapped by what had happened to me and what had happened to me was their fault.

'So I watched that nurse, the way he would come on laughing and joking all the time with the other nurses and patients, always letting on like there was never a care in the world. No, you're fine, nothing's going to happen to you. Nothing's going to go wrong, you take my word for it, you trust me, this operation's going to be the best thing ever happened to you, put another ten years on your active life.

'And that young woman, the one whose job it was to make sure that anaesthetic machine's working right, she's up to the university making out she's so smart and clever, going to get herself a degree and everything, thinks she's so wonderful, couldn't see the machine going wrong.

'All of them, what I wanted, what I was waiting for, a way to take their liberty away without taking a life, 'cause the taking of a life, that's wrong. That don't help anything.'

'How about Amanda Hooson?' Resnick asked. 'What about her life?'

'Now that,' Ridgemount said, looking straight at him, 'that was never meant to happen. I never knew anyone could struggle so. That was a mistake.'

'Sarah!'

The second she heard the voice, she knew whose it was and she rocked sideways against the door, a single low breath expelled from her mouth.

'Shall I come up to you or are you coming down to me?'

He was leaning against the wall between the front door and the foot of the stairs. In the faint light she could see only his face at all clearly and as she got closer she saw that he was no longer wearing the same clothes as before, but black jeans and a black cotton sweater. Hands in his pockets as he leaned there, nonchalant.

'You see,' he smiled, 'I said it wasn't over.'

'What? What isn't over? What?'

He came towards her and she backed up the stairs, four or five treads, before thinking this is the last thing I have to do, show him I'm afraid. So she went back down, didn't stop until she was face to face with him, more of a sneer than a smile at the corner of his mouth, she could see that now.

'What do you want?'

Before she could react, he grabbed the front of her dressing-gown and pulled hard, throwing her off balance, hard into him. She pushed herself clear, one hand clawing for his face, but he only laughed and pulled again twice with the hand that had never let go and her dressing-gown was wide open, the shirt that she wore in bed with its buttons torn away.

'What I want,' Carew grinned, 'the same as you.'

Sarah kicked out with her bare leg, fast but not quite fast enough, her shin catching him high inside the thigh, and as he hopped back she aimed her elbow at his face, felt it strike something and barged past him towards the front room and the phone.

He caught her below the waist and flung her round, the knuckles at the back of one hand grazed against the iron of the fireplace and her head and shoulder thumped against the side of the easy chair. He jerked her again and lost his grip and she fell heavily on the base of her spine and cried out with the sharpness of the pain.

'Now,' Carew said, not unpleasantly, 'why don't we stop all this silly pretending?'

'When exactly was it,' Resnick asked, 'that you realized what you had to do?'

Ridgemount's gaze lifted from the table. 'When I read it in the paper, what had been done to that young doctor, the way they described how he'd been cut, with a scalpel, cut about the legs so's likely he'd never walk again. That's when I knew. Joseph, I said to myself, that's what you have to do.'

Resnick's pulse was beginning to race. He had to be sure. 'This young doctor, what was his name?'

Ridgemount looked surprised. 'Fletcher. Tim Fletcher.'

'You weren't responsible for that attack?'

Ridgemount glanced over towards Patel, shook his head. 'Haven't I been telling you?'

'Wait,' said Resnick, on his feet, keeping his voice as calm as he was able, 'with Mr Ridgemount. Let him continue with his statement. I'll send someone else along.'

He closed the door firmly and then began to run towards the CID room.

'Now isn't this better,' Carew was saying, 'instead of all that fighting? And over what?'

He was lying next to her, part on top of her, one leg and the weight of his chest pinning her down, pressing her back against the front of the settee. The roughness of the cheap carpet was rubbing against her leg, against her hip, and her other leg was going numb. Carew was playing with her breast, pausing every now and then to kiss her mouth, the side of her face, to slide his tongue inside her ear.

'And just wait,' he smiled, 'it'll get a good deal better.' He lowered his mouth to her face and licked a line from below her ear around towards her chin. 'That's what I could never understand about Karen. Silly little cow!

Didn't know a good thing when she felt one. Dumping me for Fletcher. Pathetic!' Carew slid his tongue inside Sarah's ear and slowly out again. 'Still,' he grinned, 'soon cut him down to size.'

The two cars cornered too quickly, almost colliding with one another as they swung into Carew's street. A third was pulling up in the road at the rear, not wanting to get caught out the same way a second time. Divine hammered hard at the door and when a sleepy medical student opened it warily, he barged him aside and went in, Naylor close behind.

Sitting in the second car next to Lynn Kellogg, Resnick thought, he isn't going to be there, eating a take-away and watching television, it isn't going to be that easy.

'When we picked Carew up,' Resnick said, 'he was chatting up one of the nurses, Sarah Leonard . . .'

'You think he might be out with her?'

'I don't think we should wait around on the off chance they come wandering back, hand in hand. Get through to the station, see if her address is on file. If not, check with the hospital. Don't let them give you no for an answer.'

Resnick got out of the car and walked along the pavement to where Divine and Naylor were now standing.

Carew readjusted his weight, used his knees to ease Sarah's legs further apart.

'Aah,' he breathed, closing his eyes. 'This is going to be beautiful.' Opening them again, face so close to hers, 'Don't you think?'

'Yes,' Sarah said.

Ian Carew smiled and sank himself down.

Sarah braced the fingers of both hands against his forehead, found his eyes with her thumbs and pressed as hard as she could. Carew screamed and arched back and she continued to squeeze her thumbs into the sockets, rocking him off balance without slackening her grip and managing, almost, to roll him over, till he punched her in the stomach and she couldn't prevent one of her hands from jerking away and then the other. He screamed at her and this time she hooked her thumbs into the corners of his mouth and pulled. Carew swung up and knocked her clear, forcing her away with his legs; stumbling to his feet then, jeans around his thighs, unable to keep his hands from rubbing at his eyes.

Sarah pushed at him hard, stiff-armed, and as he fell backwards she raced for the door. She had the top bolt back and was working on the second, the one that always stuck, when Carew staggered into the hall. For a moment she froze, thinking he was going to come for her, but instead he went in the other direction, towards the scullery where he had broken in; a wave of relief swept through her and she ran back into the front room for the phone.

He hadn't gone away: he had gone to the kitchen for a knife.

His words came with difficulty, jagged spaces in between.

'You bitch . . . fucking stupid . . . bitch . . . I'm going to . . . kill you for that.'

Sarah screamed.

She grabbed at a cushion and held it out in front of herself as Carew closed in with the knife. She continued to scream, loud enough to be heard in the street.

Resnick charged the front door with his shoulder and very little happened. He and Lynn barged it together and it shifted against its hinges but wasn't about to give. Resnick lifted the green dustbin from the front yard and yelled a warning just before putting it through the glass of the front window.

The screaming stopped.

Lynn Kellogg was in the room first, in and racing towards the back of the house, following Carew. 'Lynn!'

Resnick called. 'Let him go!' He knew Divine and Naylor were out there somewhere, covering the back alley. To his right, Sarah Leonard swayed and Resnick moved swiftly to her, fearing she might fall. 'Are you all right?' he asked, sensing the emptiness of the words as he spoke them. Sarah nodded once and shivered as she pulled the cushion close against herself and hugged it tight. Resnick picked up the phone to call for a doctor, the ambulance.

As he ran, Carew clawed at the jeans that were slipping back down his legs. He couldn't properly see where he was going and he was rocking from side to side, scraping himself against the chain-link fence, grazing his leg against the brickwork of the wall.

Lynn saw the discarded pram in time and hurdled over it, cursing herself for being so unfit, aware that by rights Divine and Naylor were waiting to pick Carew up but knowing how much she wanted him herself.

Thirty yards ahead of her, Carew's toe caught the edge of a sodden mattress and he lost his footing and that was all she needed. When she took hold of him, one arm in a choke hold round his neck, her free hand tightening on his right wrist, Carew still had the kitchen knife gripped tight. Lynn shifted her balance so that one of her knees was pressing hard into the small of Carew's back and then, as she would say later in her report, she applied the necessary pressure to the prisoner's arm to make him drop the weapon he was carrying.

The flicker of light came from Divine's torch as he and Naylor hurried towards her.

'Are you sure you're okay?'

'Yes. Yes. Thank you. I'll be fine.'

Resnick stood over her, hesitating. The sound of the ambulance siren could be heard as it approached along the main road heading into the city.

Sarah Leonard had refastened her dressing-gown and sat

331

the cushion in her lap; she had only looked at Resnick once in the past few moments. She looked up again now as Kevin Naylor came into the room from the rear of the house. 'We've got him, sir. Lynn got him. And a knife. He's on his way back to the station.'

'Good work.'

Sarah started to shake then, cry tears of relief. Resnick knelt alongside her and held her until the ambulance arrived and the paramedics helped her away.

'Make sure nothing gets moved till forensic are through. Just in case we can't prove what he did to Fletcher, I want to make this one stick.'

'The woman, sir. No danger she won't, like, give evidence?'

'No danger at all.'

Resnick unbolted the front door and let himself out on to the street as the ambulance pulled clear. In the space before the next police vehicles arrived it was quiet. Neighbours had retreated back into their own lives, the *News at Ten*. Above the upward slope of houses he could see the amber light that hung over the centre of the city. He thought about Ridgemount about to spend his first night in a police cell and the things he'd felt driven to do to find peace. He thought about Sarah Leonard, the next time she was in her house alone, the response to every unfamiliar sound, each opening of the door. And somewhere, in some small hotel or rented room, Elaine. He left the car where it was and began to walk, hands in his pockets, wanting something to clear the air, wanting rain.

Cold Light

John Harvey

arrow books

Although this novel is set in a real city, it is a work of fiction and its events and characters exist only on its pages and in the author's imagination.

One

She slid out from beneath Gary's sleeping body and
eased herself to the edge of the bed. Always the same,
the way he would turn towards her each night, arm
and the heft of his thigh heavily upon her. Weighing
her down. Since they'd been moved here it was worse.
He couldn't sleep without her. Holding her breath,
Michelle waited for the thin squeak of the bedframe
to still. Cracked lino cold at her feet. Gary sighed and
when she looked round she could see his face, young
in the faint light, open-mouthed. She saw the way one
hand gripped the sheet, the knot of skin above his eyes
and was thankful she knew nothing of his dreams.

Slipping one of Gary's sweaters over her T-shirt, a
pair of his socks on to her feet, she left the room.

The children had a bedroom of their own along the
narrow landing, but these past weeks it had been too
cold. Ice overlapping on the insides of the windows
and their breath pigeoning the air. Get an oil stove in
there, neighbours had said, keep it low. But Michelle
knew of two house fires less than half a mile from here
since winter had set in, ladders reaching up too late
and never close enough, kiddies trapped upstairs and
overcome by fumes.

Now they banked up the living-room fire with slack,
made sure the guard borrowed from her parents' home
was fixed in place. Natalie's cot they lifted into the
middle of the room once the TV had been switched

off and Karl's bed was the settee, curled beneath a nest of coats and blankets, thumb in mouth and dead to the world.

Downstairs, Michelle smiled at the baby, who had wriggled round again until her head was pressed against the bottom corner of the cot, one leg poked through the bars. Raising both hands to her mouth, Michelle warmed them before touching her daughter's tiny foot and easing it back, carefully, out of the cold. Both of them would need changing when they woke. She was reminded that it was her bladder that had woken her and she braced herself for the bathroom, the old scullery that had been converted and badly, quarry tiles laid on bare earth and made uneven by the frost.

She rubbed a circle from the inside of the window and the dark looked back at her. No more than two or three blurred lights pale along the street. If she were lucky, she might yet sit with yesterday's paper and a pot of tea, a little stolen time before the children woke to crying and she heard Gary's feet upon the stairs.

Resnick had been awake since four. So attuned to disruption, he had been blinking back sleep and reaching towards the telephone before, it seemed, he had heard its first ring. Kevin Naylor's voice was indistinct and oddly distant and Resnick, irritably, had to ask him to repeat everything twice.

'Sorry, sir, it's this mobile phone.'

All Resnick heard were particles of words, breaking up like starlings in the early morning air.

'Redial,' Resnick said, 'and try again.'

'Sorry, sir. Can't hear you.'

Resnick cursed and broke the connection himself and when Naylor rang back he could hear him perfectly. A taxi driver had been taking two youths from the city centre to an address in West Bridgford; as they neared Lady Bay Bridge, one of them had tapped on the window, asked the driver to pull over as his mate was feeling sick, like to throw up. When one young man got out of the car on to the pavement, the other went around to the driver's side and threatened him with an iron bar. Before the driver could pull away, the windscreen had been splintered in his face. The youths dragged him out of the cab and beat him around the head and body. He had been crawling across the centre of the road when a milk lorry turned on to the bridge and stopped. The youths had run off and the driver's takings had gone with them.

'The weapon?' Resnick asked.

'Tried to chuck it into the Trent, sir, but only landed in the mud.'

'And the driver?'

'Queen's. Accident and Emergency.'

'Who's with him?'

'Uniform patrol should be there now, sir. There's nobody . . .'

'Graham Millington . . .'

'Leave, sir. He and the wife, they were going away. In-laws, I . . .'

Resnick sighed; he should have remembered. 'Divine, then. But I want someone with him all the time. The cabbie. We don't know how many chances we'll get.'

'I could . . .'

'You stay where you are.' Resnick narrowed his eyes towards the bedside clock. 'Twenty minutes, I'll be there. And see no one gets their sticky fingers all over that cab.'

Absent-mindedly, he lifted away a cat that had

3

folded itself into his lap and set it back down on the bed. One of the others was over by the bedroom door, scratching its head against the heavy edge of wood. The last time something like this had happened, the weapon had been a baseball bat and the taxi driver had died. Quickly, he showered and dressed and went downstairs, grinding coffee for a cup he would only half drink before stepping out into the cold light of another day.

'Bloody hell!' Gary said. 'What sodding time is it?'

'It's late.'

'It's what?'

'It's past seven.'

'And you reckon that's late, do you?'

Michelle arched her back and shifted the baby's weight against her arm. She didn't think Natalie was taking any milk now, just suckling for the comfort of it. 'Depends how long you've been up,' she said.

Gary was leaning sideways inside the doorway, head stooped, still wearing the boxer shorts and County shirt he had slept in. 'I've been down since before six,' Michelle told him, though he hadn't asked.

Gary gave himself a scratch and walked past the end of the table where she was sitting. 'I suppose that's my fault, too,' he said, not quite loud enough for her to be certain.

'What?'

'You heard.'

'If I heard, why would I . . .?'

'You waking so early, I suppose it was my fault.'

'Don't be silly.'

'What's silly? Don't tell me I'm fucking silly. Everything else is my fault, why not that?'

'Gary . . .'

4

'What?'

Sitting between them, eating a mush of warm milk and cornflakes too big for his mouth, two-year-old Karl's eyes flicked from one to the other.

'Gary, no one's saying it's your fault. Not any of it.'

'No?'

'No.'

He tossed his head and glanced away. 'Wasn't what you said the other day.'

'Gary, I was angry. I lost my temper, right? Don't you ever lose your temper?'

She knew it was a stupid thing to say. She watched his fingers tighten around the curve of the kitchen chair.

'Gary ...'

Michelle stood carefully with the baby still at her breast and went to him. He turned from her and she rested the side of her face soft against his back, unkempt curl of her hair brushing the nape of his neck. The baby wriggled a little between them and Michelle shushed into the feathery down of her head.

The last job Gary had had, six months back, labouring on a building site, cash in hand at the end of the week, no questions asked, had ended when the firm went bankrupt. Gary had turned in one morning to find the whole place cordoned off, all the heavy machinery being repossessed. Before that it had been the night shift in a factory that manufactured plastic switches for the fitments on table lamps. Then there had been piece-work, Sellotaping free floppy discs to the covers of a short-lived computer software magazine. Three jobs in as many years. More than a lot of people they knew; more than most.

'Gary?'

'Mmm?'

But he knew. Michelle's free hand was stroking him through the striped cotton of his shirt, sliding up against the edges of his ribcage, along the flat of stomach just above the top of his shorts. She craned up to kiss him and his mouth was slightly sour from sleep. Behind them, Karl spun his spoon around the bowl too fast and it landed on the floor. Michelle lifted Natalie away from her breast as she turned and at once the baby screwed up her face and began to cry.

Mist rolled off the river in swathes. Hard against the kerb, its offside door wide open, the cab sat cordoned off with yellow tape. Bright in the headlights of Resnick's car, glass sparkled on the surface of the road like ice. Immediately beyond, the road narrowed to a single lane across the bridge and Resnick knew that within an hour the traffic would be building up into the city worse than ever: Christmas Eve, for many the last day of this working year.

The scene of crime team were dusting the outside of the taxi now, the interior would be more safely and thoroughly examined when the vehicle had been removed. Uniformed officers were sifting carefully through the frosted mud and sparse grass of the river-bank below, others checking the path which led back off the bridge towards the city. This was the direction in which the driver of the milk lorry had seen two men running, down the slope towards the all-night garage and the road that would take them – where? On towards Colwick and the Country Park, the race course, or left into Sneinton. Yet according to the message the driver had called into base and the entry he had made in his own log, the destination for this fare had been across the river. A ruse, or had they simply run off, unthinking, panicked by what they had done?

'Sir?'

Naylor stepped towards him, the usual hint of deference and apology in his voice. At first Resnick had found it grated on him, waited for it to change with use and time; now he simply accepted it, the way the man was. The reverse, perhaps, of Mark Divine's bullish eagerness. How had Lynn Kellogg described Divine? All mouth and trousers? Resnick's mouth widened, letting in a smile.

'The cabbie – they've moved him to Intensive Care.'

The smile faded: an all-too-familiar pattern falling into place.

'Mark wants to know, should he stick around or come back in?'

'He stays. As long as there's any chance he'll get some answers, he stays put.'

'Yes, sir,' said Naylor, hesitating. 'Only . . .'

'Well?'

'I know it's not . . . it's just, he seemed a bit het-up about getting stuck there all day. The shops, you see, they close early some of them and . . .'

'And he wants to be let off duty to do a bit of last-minute Christmas shopping?'

'It is for his mother,' Naylor said, not believing it for a moment.

'Tell him he'll be relieved in the usual way, as and when we can.'

'I'll say you're keeping it in mind, then.' Naylor grinned.

'If you like,' said Resnick. One of the scene of crime team was walking towards him; likely they were ready to winch the cab on to the waiting lorry and drive it away. The last thing Resnick wanted cluttering up his mind – thoughts of what Divine might be putting into someone's Christmas stocking.

Two

She'd been getting things for the kids for months now. Oh, nothing much, not a lot, not expensive. Just, you know, little things that had caught her fancy – a Dennis the Menace T-shirt for Karl, bright red on black, a toy dog for the baby, yellow, with blue stitching for its paws and nose, not too big, soft, something she could cuddle up to in her sleep. Michelle had joined the Christmas Club at the shop on the corner, opposite the old Co-op. Putting by a pound a week, not telling Gary, slipping in when she was on her own.

As long as there was something there for the children Christmas Day, enough to make it feel special. Not that either of them really knew, not yet, what it was all about. Too young to understand. They had been to the fair, though, the one in the Old Market Square; walked around the Christmas tree in its red tub outside the Council House, staring up at the coloured lights and the star at the top. A present from Norway or Sweden or somewhere, though no one seemed to know why.

Gary'd bought them a jumbo hot dog, running over with tomato sauce, onions crisped, some of them, till they were black and brittle. They'd sat on the wall behind the fountain, sharing it between them, Michelle blowing on a piece of sausage and chewing it a little before pushing it into the baby's mouth. All around them, other kids with parents, kids on their own in gangs. Pushchairs and prams. Arms and coats to tug at. 'Dad, can I have this?' 'Can I have a go on that?' 'Can't I? Can't I? Can I not? Oh, Mum! Dad!'

Michelle thought their Karl was like to carry on the same when he first saw the carousel, all the horses, brightly painted, prancing up and down. But she did his work for him, taking hold of Gary's hand to ask him softly, 'Do look at his face, you can see how much he wants to have a go.'

'You're all right,' said Gary. 'Just this once.'

They had stood back and waved at him, Michelle shaking the baby's hand as well, and Karl, for all his smiles, had never quite felt sure enough to loose his grasp of the saddle and wave back.

'Snowman,' said Gary later, pointing at the figure in front of the dodgems with its yellow hat and gloves. 'See the snowman, Karl?'

'Noman,' Karl had replied, excited. He had seen snowmen in his cartoons on TV.

'Snowman,' Gary laughed. 'Not noman, you daft pillock! Snowman.'

'Gary,' Michelle said, starting to laugh herself. 'Don't call him that.'

'Noman!' sang out Karl, jumping up and down. 'Noman! Noman! Noman!'

He lost his footing and went sprawling, bruising his face and grazing the fingers of the hand from which he'd earlier lost his glove. Not long after that they all caught the bus home.

Michelle looked up from what she was doing and listened; footsteps that might have been Gary's outside on the street. As they went on past, she slid her hands back into the soapy water, washing out a few clothes in the sink. Natalie she'd put down half-hour back and mercifully she'd stayed. Last time she'd checked, Karl was belly down in front of the TV lost in a programme about lions; at least he was quiet.

She lifted the clothes clear of the water while she emptied the bowl ready to rinse. She only hoped Gary would be pleased with what she'd got for him, a replica goalie's shirt, twenty-eight quid it'd set her back; they'd kept it on order for her at the County shop, twenty-eight pounds less one penny.

Well, it was only once a year after all.

The door stuck as she was taking the washing through to the back yard to peg out and when she nudged it with her hip the bottom half of the door came away from the frame.

'Michelle! Michelle! You there?'

'I'm out back.'

'You might've shut the door behind you. Like a bloody fridge in here.' He stopped short, staring at the twisted hinge.

'I'm sorry,' Michelle said. 'It wasn't my fault.'

Gary turned on his heel and a moment later she heard the front door open and slam shut. Upstairs in her cot, the baby woke up crying.

'Ion,' said Karl from the doorway. 'Ion!' And he made his tottering run towards her, hands stretched high like claws, growling loudly.

Mark Divine was three degrees short of pissed off. First they'd told him, sorry, he'd have to wait outside the Intensive Care unit, they'd be certain to let him know the minute Mr Raju regained consciousness. So he'd sat there, his bulk awkward on the low chair, legs at all angles, watching various other Rajus as they were shepherded in and out, whispering and wailing. The one time he wandered off in search of the WVS canteen and a decent cup of tea, one of the staff nurses came out looking for him.

'He's come to, then, has he?' Divine asked when finally she found him.

As well as the plastic cup of tea, which was threatening to burn a hole in his fingers, he was trying to balance two chocolate cupcakes and a lemon puff.

'Concerned about your sugar levels?' the staff nurse asked, raising an eyebrow in the direction of Divine's one-handed juggling.

'Not as I know of,' Divine said cockily.

'Well, perhaps you should be.'

One of the cupcakes fell to the floor and rolled underneath the nearest chair. 'Don't worry,' she said, 'the cleaners will find it. Why don't you put the rest of them down on the table over there and come through?'

'You mean now, like? This minute?'

'You do want to see him, don't you?'

'Yes, but . . .'

'Ask him some questions?'

'Yes.'

'Then I should do it before they take him down to theatre.'

Divine took a large bite from the lemon puff, risked burning his tongue on a swig of tea, and followed the staff nurse through the double set of doors towards the ward. Nice arse, he thought, wonder if they've got any mistletoe strung up in Intensive Care?

Resnick arrived back in his office after a brisk thirty minutes with the superintendent, to find a large parcel stuffed into his waste basket. Brown paper and string inside a pair of plastic bags. Around ten pounds, he thought, weighing it in his hands. One of the plastic bags contained quite a little puddle of blood. He hadn't realised Lynn Kellogg was due back in the office so soon.

The files detailing the night's events, messages and memoranda, the movement of prisoners in and out of police cells, still lay on his desk barely touched. Half-a-dozen men and one woman drunk and disorderly; Resnick recognised most of the names. Likely by now they'd been cautioned and pushed back out on to the streets. By noon most of them would be drunk again, winding themselves up for the night. After all, it was Christmas, wasn't it? Wasn't that what Christmas was about?

In the outer office two phones began ringing almost simultaneously and Resnick switched them from his mind.

Considering the possibilities – so many homes left empty, all those expensive presents ready-wrapped – the increase in burglaries was less than might have been expected. Even so, enough people would have returned from their firm's annual pre-cooked Christmas dinner, the ritual risqué jokes and innuendo, to find the golden goose had flown. All those expensive tokens of status and admiration liberated in under fifteen minutes by eager hands using a pair of the homeowner's socks as gloves.

The phones were still ringing. Resnick pushed open the door to his office, ready to shout an order, and realised there was no one there. A filing cabinet with the drawer not pushed fully back, mugs of tea staining deeper and deeper orange, typewriters and VDUs all unattended. Resnick picked up the nearest receiver, identified himself and asked the caller to hold while he dealt with the second. A postman had been cycling to work at the sorting office off Incinerator Road when a taxi had turned past him, heading for the bridge;

he'd got a pretty good sight of the two youths in the back. A woman on her way back from the garage shop with a packet of cigarettes and a carton of milk had nearly been knocked off her feet by two lads rushing past. Resnick made a note of their names and addresses, was still arranging for the postman to come into the station, when Lynn Kellogg came backwards through the door.

When she turned to face him she had two sandwiches in her hands, two cups of filter coffee, one of them black. Medium height, hair medium brown, red-faced, stocky, Detective Constable Lynn Kellogg, back from her parents' poultry farm in Norfolk, by way of the deli across the street.

'Mozzarella and tomato,' Lynn said, handing Resnick a brown paper bag already leaking French dressing. 'I thought you might not have eaten.'

'Thanks.' He prised the plastic lid from the coffee and drank. 'I thought you weren't due in till this afternoon?'

Lynn widened her eyes and moved to her desk.

'Things at home not so good?' Resnick asked.

Lynn shrugged. 'Not so bad.' She shook some loose pieces of lettuce from the paper bag and pushed them back inside her sandwich.

'I found the turkey,' Resnick said, nodding in the direction of his office.

'Good.' And then, suddenly grinning, 'It's a duck.'

'I was just wondering,' Divine said. He was on his way out of the ward, interview over, and he'd timed his move to perfection, coinciding with Staff Nurse Bruton's purposeful walk towards the drugs trolley. Lesley Bruton – tall, her height accentuated by the mass of dark hair untamed by her nurse's cap . . . it was there on her badge, printed out for all to see. 'Like I say, Lesley, I was wondering . . .'

'Yes?'

'What time you got finished? You know, came off shift.'

'I know what it means.'

'So?'

She gave him a look that would have scuppered a more sensitive man and lifted a clipboard from the side of the trolley.

'Look, it's not a chat-up, you know. No way.'

Amusement flirted across her eyes. 'Help you with your enquiries, can I? Something like that?'

What? Divine thought. Give me half the chance!

'No,' he said, 'not official . . .'

'I thought perhaps not.'

'See, what it is, I've got to stay here till he gets back on the ward. Raju. Could be – well, what? – hours.'

'Could be.'

'Thing is, there's this present I've got to get. You know, for tomorrow.'

'Special, is it?'

Divine nodded, looked sincere.

'Girlfriend?'

'Sort of.'

'Underwear, then?'

Divine treated her to his lop-sided grin; he was starting to sweat more than just a little.

'Black and sexy?'

'Could be. Why not?'

She looked at him, saying nothing. Waiting.

'There's this place,' Divine said. 'That arcade back of the Council House. Real posh.'

'I know it,' Lesley Bruton said. 'My boyfriend buys me stuff there all the time.'

15

Jesus! Divine thought. His eyes slithered down her uniform, wondering if she was wearing any of it now.

Lesley slid her hands along the rail of the trolley. 'And you'd like me to pop in there when I finish?' she said. 'Pick up something for you. For your girlfriend. A bra and pantie set. Maybe a camisole top. One of those teddies.'

'Yes,' said Divine, 'that sort of thing.' Wondering if a teddy was what he hoped it was, one of those all-in-one jobs like a swimsuit made out of lace.

'Maybe try them on for you while I'm there?'

'Why not?' Divine said, not quite able to believe his luck.

'Why not?' Lesley said, fixing him with her eyes. 'For you?'

'Well, I . . .'

For a moment, voice lowered, she leaned towards him. 'In your dreams,' she said. And without a second glance, she walked away.

Gary had been working on the door the best part of two hours, more, if you included the time it had taken him to walk up the street to his mate Brian's house and borrow a decent-sized screwdriver and a rasp. Michelle had finished a second lot of washing, fed Natalie, given Karl fish fingers and beans and made herself some toast. Gary had said he wasn't hungry. Her mum had asked her to take the kids round some time that afternoon so she could give them their presents and even though it meant carting the pushchair off and on two buses, Michelle thought she'd better make the effort. First thing in the morning, her parents would be off up the A1 to Darlington to have their Christmas dinner with Michelle's older sister, Marie, and her family. Three-bedroom semi, that's what they had. Picked it up dirt cheap after it was repossessed.

'Michelle!' Gary's voice from the back.

'Yes?'

'Lend us hand, will you?'

'Be there in a minute.'

'No, now.'

The kettle was coming to the boil, Natalie was getting into a right old grizzle, Karl was calling something from the front room and she couldn't tell what; she'd thought while the tea was mashing, she'd see if there was mincemeat enough left to make some more mince pies. Last she'd made were almost as good as you could buy in the shop.

'Michelle! You coming or what?'

Michelle sighed and pushed the teapot to one side. Through the open front-room door, she could see Karl painstakingly climbing on to the settee so he could roll back off.

'You be careful now,' she called at him on the way past. 'You'll only hurt yourself.'

'Here,' Gary said, pointing. 'Steady that for me there.'

'Where?'

'Jesus Christ, girl! There!'

Michelle pushed two fingers against the top of the hinge, her thumb against the bottom.

'Okay, now budge over, give me room to get the screwdriver to it.'

She could hear his breathing clearly, loud and slightly ragged beneath his shirt. He hated doing jobs like this.

'Right. Whatever you do, don't let go. Hold it firm. Push.'

There was a shout, sudden and loud, from inside the

house and she knew that Karl had fallen and hurt himself.

Gary sensed her move and stopped it. 'I'll be done in a minute. Hang on.'

'It's Karl, he . . .'

'I said bloody hang on!'

Gary gave a final turn and the screw splintered sideways through the wood of the frame, jerking the screwdriver from his hand. The hinge fell away from Michelle's fingers and the whole door slid sharply outwards, wrenching the bottom hinge away with it.

'Fuck!' Gary yelled. 'Sodding bastard fuck!'

'Gary!' Michelle called. 'Don't.'

From somewhere, blood seemed to be running between her fingers, collecting inside her hand.

Karl was standing close by the doorway, fists jammed against his eyes, mouth widening through a succession of screams.

'Fuck!' Gary swore again, kicking at the frame. 'And you,' he said, grabbing Karl by both arms and lifting him into the air. 'You want something to bloody cry about!' He dropped his son towards the floor and before he could land, had cracked his hand, hard as he could, back across Karl's face.

Three

'Crying out for it, she was.'

Meal time in the canteen and Divine, relieved from his duties at the hospital, was telling Kevin Naylor about his encounter with Staff Nurse Bruton over the drugs trolley. A year or so back, Naylor would have been impressed; now his expression was, to put it mildly, sceptical.

'No, she was. Straight up.'

'Told you, did she?' Naylor asked. 'I mean, you know, came right out and said it?'

Divine dipped one of his chips into the pool of brown sauce spreading across his plate. 'Don't need to *say*, do they? Know what's what, you can tell.' He pointed his fork across at Naylor, sprinkling the table with sauce. 'Lot of your problem, you and Debbie . . .'

'Debbie and I don't *have* a problem.'

'For now, maybe.'

'We don't have a problem.' Naylor's voice getting louder, attracting attention.

'All I'm saying,' Divine went on blithely, spearing another chip, 'all the evidence shows, you know bog all about bloody women.'

'Whereas you,' Lynn Kellogg leaned over from the next table, 'expert by now, aren't you, Mark?'

Sarcastic cow! Divine thought. 'Don't believe me,' he said, 'catch me in action, this do tonight. The man who made pulling an art form.'

19

'I can't wait!'

'No?' Divine forked up a piece of meat pie. 'Well, shame but you just might have to. I mean, I'd like to help out, but there's just so many others in line before you.'

Lynn pushed back her plate and stood up. 'What do I have to do to keep it that way? Wear a cross round my neck? Eat garlic?'

Divine gave her a swift appraisal. 'No need. Just keep looking the way you do.'

He leaned back and winked across at Naylor, as Lynn walked away, muffled laughter from some of the other officers flushing her face.

'You didn't need to say that,' Kevin Naylor said quietly.

'Nobody asked her to stick her nose in. Any road, it's no more'n true. I mean, would you fancy it? Be honest.'

Naylor looked back down at his plate and made no reply.

'That prick,' Lynn said to herself on the stairs, 'knows as much about women as the average five-year-old.' She remembered him picking a magazine off her desk once, attention drawn by blonde hair and bright red lips and the headline, *Shere Hite and the Clitoral Tendency.* Divine had thought they were a new pop group.

Gary James had been waiting close to two hours and there were still five people in front of him, two of them Pakis. Turn a place over to them and the next thing it'd be swarming, aunts and uncles, sisters and cousins, floor to ceiling like bugs. He'd seen it happen. Next to them, this couple lolling all over one another, tongues in each other's ears half the time, looked as though they should still be at school, not in the bloody Housing

Office. Tattoos all up their shoulders and necks, her with enough little rings in her nose to open a shop; bloke with his hair twisted round like some Rasta, though he was white as Gary himself. Down the row from Gary there was this West Indian woman the size of a sodding house herself, three kids clinging to her and another one on the way.

Jesus! Gary didn't have a watch and the clock on the waiting room wall had been at twenty-five past seven the past three times he'd been there.

'Hey, mate,' he said, tapping the nearest Paki on the shoulder, then pointing to his own wrist in case the bloke didn't understand. 'What time you got?'

'Very nearly a quarter to four,' the man said politely and smiled.

Don't smile at me, you smarmy bastard, Gary thought as he sat back down, save that for when you get in there. And then, Christ, that's nearly three hours, never mind two.

'Hey!' he shouted. 'Hey, you!' He pulled one of the metal-frame chairs out of line and pushing it hard towards the wall. 'Think I'm going to sit here all bloody day? I want to see somebody and I want to see them bloody now!'

'Sir,' the receptionist said. 'Sir, if you'll just go back to your seat, you'll be seen as soon as possible.' All the while her fingers moving towards the panic button underneath the counter top.

Resnick had gone to talk to Mavis Alderney himself. Mavis thankful for the chance to catch a fag out back from the laundry off Trent Boulevard where she worked.

It had been Mavis who had come close to being sent flying by two youths that morning. 'Arse over tip,' was

21

how she put it. 'Someone wants to get hold of the like of them and give them a good thrashing. Well, don't you think? Should've been done to 'em long time back. Then happen they'd not be the way they are now.'

Resnick had grunted something non-committal and pressed for her to be more specific with her descriptions. 'A pair of them tearaways, you know, them boots and jeans, no respect for anyone, not even themselves,' wasn't quite going to do it.

Now he was in the market, upstairs in the Victoria Centre, all the seats around the Italian coffee stall taken and having to stand to drink his espresso, listening to an animated discussion about why both the city's soccer teams were languishing near the bottom of their respective leagues.

'Ask me,' someone said, 'best thing could happen, bloody managers ship 'emselves either side of Trent, swop jobs.'

'Now you're talking rubbish, man.'

'Well, they couldn't do a lot worse.'

'No,' put in somebody else, 'I'll tell you what. Best present they could have, both clubs. Christmas morning, chairmen of directors gets 'em both, Cloughie and Warnock on the phone, wishes them a merry Christmas and tells them they're both sacked.'

'What? They'll not sack Cloughie, they'd never dare. They'd have a full-scale bloody riot on their hands.'

'Aye, maybe. But not as much as if they go down.'

Resnick smiled and reached between two of the men, setting his cup and saucer back on the counter. On his way out of the market he'd buy a little Polish sausage to go with his duck, a chunk of Gruyère and some Blue Stilton, a good slice of apple strudel and some sour cream to take the place of a Christmas pudding.

Down below, crowds were pushing their way from store to store and last-minute shoplifting was in full swing. Even more people than usual were gathered around the Emmett clock, holding up small children to see the fantastic metal animals revolve and laugh with wonder as streams of water splashed off its gilded petals as they opened. Again, again, again.

Suspended from the high ceiling, a Santa on a bright red sledge chased polypropylene reindeer through stale air.

Resnick was out on the street when he heard the first siren.

Nancy Phelan had emerged from her office at the sound of shouting, curious to know whoever it was making all that noise. Besides, she could do with a break from her present assignment, explaining to a couple with an eighteen-month-old kid that by leaving the damp basement room for which the girl's mother had been charging her a robbery of a rent, they had made themselves voluntarily homeless.

'Voluntarily sodding homeless,' the man kept saying. 'What in buggery is that?' Not loud, not even angry, simply swearing by rote.

What it bloody is, Nancy had thought, and not for the first time, was an almost meaningless form of words dreamed up by some official to get the housing authority off the hook.

That hadn't been what she'd said to her client; what she'd said was, 'Sir, I've already explained it to you several times.'

Several? Half a hundred.

Whatever disturbance was going on outside, it had to be more interesting than that. A little light relief.

Wrong.

Gary James – Nancy thought she recognised him, thought he might even be one of hers, though she could never have put a name to him – was standing pretty much in the middle of the corridor, both hands holding a chair above his head. The metal kind with the canvas seat and back. The receptionist, Penny, was cowering against one wall, bent forward, arms folded up in front of her face. He'd either hit her with the chair or was about to.

Howard, the security guard, was down at the far end of the corridor, squinting hopefully in their direction. Nancy knew for a fact he could scarcely see his own hand in front of his face without his glasses on.

'You!' Gary called over one shoulder.

'Me?'

'It's you I want to see.'

Oh, God, Nancy thought, it would be. Her second application to join a TEFAL course, train to teach English to polite, suited businessmen in Hong Kong or Japan, had just been turned down. This morning she'd been convinced – though it was difficult to tell – that one of her stick insects had died. And if that wasn't enough she was three days late.

Now this.

'You're the one me and Michelle saw before, right? About getting us out of that dump you moved us into.'

'I said I'd try, yes . . .'

'Look! I'm telling you. You'd better do more than fucking try. And you, just stay where you fucking are or I'll take this tart's head off her fucking shoulders.'

Penny flinched and stifled a scream and Howard retreated a few feet more than he had advanced.

'Do you have an appointment?' Nancy asked, keeping her voice as normal as possible.

Gary shot her another glance. 'What do you think?'

24

'Well, if you'll wait till I've finished with my present clients, which shouldn't take long, I'll be happy to review your situation.' Nancy, thinking all the while she was speaking that she'd picked up so much official gobbledegook, she sounded as if she'd learned English as a second language herself.

Gary swung the chair through a half-circle and brought it crash against the wall, close enough to Penny's head to make her hair curl.

'All right,' Nancy said. 'Why don't we talk now?'

'Yeh?' said Gary, panting just a little. 'What about Clint Eastwood down there?'

'Howard,' Nancy said. 'It's okay. I'll see Mister...' She looked at Gary hopefully.

'James.'

'I'll see Mr James in my office. There's no need to be concerned. But you might look after Penny here, see that she's all right.'

Gary was watching her, uncertain. This woman not much older than himself, if that, taking control, coping. She didn't seem frightened at all. Tall, Gary thought, five eight or nine, likely had something to do with it. Not bad looking, either. Standing there in her smart blue jacket and the pleated skirt, waiting for him to make his next move.

When he said nothing, Nancy turned to the couple she'd been interviewing, now agog outside her door, and explained to them this was something of an emergency and if they wouldn't mind waiting a while, she would talk to them again and see if they couldn't sort something out. From her purse she handed them some coins and suggested they try the drinks machine on the next floor.

'Please,' she said to Gary, holding open her office door. 'After you.'

A shade hesitantly, Gary lowered the chair to the floor and walked in. For the briefest of moments, Nancy hesitated; up to now she'd been working on instinct, training, defusing the situation without any special regard to herself. Only now did it strike her, the degree to which she was placing herself in danger. She made a quick face down the corridor that said, do something, and then stepped smartly after him, closing the door behind her.

Four

'Lock the door,' he said.

'What?'

'Lock the door.'

Nancy sweating a little now, wondering what she'd got herself into. 'It's against regulations . . .' she began, but she could see Gary, increasingly edgy, looking round the room for something to break. Something to break over her. Quietly, she slid open the small drawer to the right of her desk and took out the key.

No sooner had the door been locked and Nancy sat back down than the phone rang, once, twice, three times; looking at Gary for a sign that she should pick it up.

'Hello,' she said into the receiver. 'Nancy Phelan here.'

A pause, then: 'No, I'm fine.' Glancing across the desk to where Gary was still standing. 'We're fine. Yes, I'm sure. No. Bye.'

Deliberately, she set the receiver down and, as she did so, Gary bent towards the floor and pulled the wire from its socket above the skirting.

'Well,' Nancy said, 'why don't you sit down?'

But Gary was staring round her office, taking it all in. The postcards from foreign holidays she'd Blu-tacked to the filing cabinet, the ivy that needed repotting near the window, the overflowing in-tray, a colour photograph of her cousin's twins. In a clear plastic container with an air-tight lid, green leaves and pieces of thin twig. Gary picked it up and shook it.

'Don't!' Nancy cried, alarmed. Then, more quietly, 'I'd rather you didn't do that. There's something... there are stick insects in there. Two of them. I think.'

Gary held it up to his face and gave the container an experimental shake.

'They were a present,' Nancy said, uncertain why she felt the need to explain. 'A client.'

'I think they're dead,' Gary said.

Nancy thought he might be right.

The first response car had only arrived at the Housing Office moments before Resnick walked in, strudel, cheese and sausage in a plastic bag in his left hand. In the lobby, a young PC was talking to the security guard, another, slightly older, having problems using his two-way radio to call in. Not recognising either of them, Resnick produced his warrant card.

'PC Bailey,' said the officer with the radio. 'That there's Hennessey.'

Not, Resnick assumed, the one that used so effectively to police the Forest midfield. He listened to a quick run-down of the situation and moved towards the stairs.

'D'you not think we should wait for some support, sir?' Bailey asked.

'Let's see what we can do ourselves,' Resnick said. 'Whoever he's got in there might not thank us for hanging about.'

Most of those who had been queuing to be seen and a growing number from other floors had crowded into the corridor outside the locked door.

'Keep everybody back,' Resnick told Hennessey. 'In the waiting room with the door shut.'

'I spoke to Nancy on the phone just after they went in,' the receptionist said. 'She said she was all right.'

Resnick nodded. 'Can I talk to her?'

Penny shook her head. 'The line's gone dead.'

'The man,' Resnick asked, 'do we know his name?'

'James. Gary James.'

'And did he seem to be armed? Was he carrying any kind of weapon?'

'He tried to hit me with a chair.' At the thought of it, Penny's shoulders gave an involuntary shake.

'Gary James,' Resnick told Bailey, who was already entering the name in his notebook. 'Get him checked out, see if he's known.'

'And the back-up, sir?'

Resnick half-smiled. 'If there's any to spare.' Turning back to the receptionist, he asked, 'Has there been any shouting from inside? Signs of a disturbance?'

'I went up to the door, close as I dared,' Penny's voice, a little breathless, telling it. 'On and on about the state of the place where's he's living, that's all I could hear. How cold it was and damp and how it would be a miracle if his kids got through the winter without pneumonia. That was a while back, though. I haven't heard a dicky-bird since.'

'Someone must have another key to the room?'

'Oh, yes. The caretaker. For the cleaning staff, you see.'

'You've tried contacting him?'

'Oh, no. I'm sorry. With all the fuss, I didn't think. I can try for him now, though, to be honest, I'm not sure where he is this time of day. Somewhere with his boilers, I dare say.' She indicated the security guard, blinking behind his glasses. 'Howard might know.'

'All right, ask Howard for me if he can track him down.' Resnick held his carrier bag of provisions out towards her. 'And do me a favour, will you? Look after this.'

Taking the bag, Penny glanced inside. 'Would you like me to pop and put them in the fridge? We've got a fridge.'

Resnick shook his head. 'Your colleague, Nancy, what's her other name?'

'Phelan. Nancy Phelan.'

Resnick thanked her and walked towards the door.

'You know something,' Gary said. It was the first time he had spoken – either of them had spoken – in several minutes.

'What's that?' Nancy said.

'I know you.'

'Yes, you said. When you and your wife . . .'

'She's not my wife.'

'Well, whatever.'

'Me and Michelle, we're not married.'

'When you and Michelle came in before, you said that was when you saw me.'

'But that's not what I mean. Nothing to do with being here. This place. I mean I *know* you, from before.'

Nancy didn't think so.

'From school. We were at the same school. Don't you remember?'

'No.'

'Top Valley. You were two years above me. Yeh. You went around with – what's his name? – Brookie. Him and my brother, they was mates.'

Malcolm Brooks. Brookie. Watching him play pool in the pub, evenings, sipping a rum and coke and waiting for him to drive her home. He'd park his old man's Escort round the back of Tesco's till Nancy told him

30

how she'd catch it if she was in late again. She hadn't thought of Brookie in years.

'Nancy,' said Resnick's voice through the door. 'Nancy, are you all right in there?'

Gary reached across faster than she could judge and caught a hold of her hair. 'Tell him,' he snarled. 'Tell him it's okay.'

'Nancy, this is the police. Detective Inspector Resnick, CID.'

'Tell him,' Gary said, twisting her hair in his hand. 'Tell him he'd better sod off and leave us alone.'

'Hello? Inspector?' Her voice muffled, difficult to judge the tone. 'Listen, there's nothing for you to be concerned about. Really.'

Nancy angled her eyes towards Gary, wanting him to look at her. The way he had hold of her hair, tugging against the roots, it was all she could do not to cry.

'Are you sure?' Resnick asked, face all but resting on the cream paint of the door. Nothing solid about it at all, a couple of good whacks and it would be down. 'You sure everything's okay?' Listening hard, Resnick could only hear his own breathing. 'Nancy?'

She was staring into Gary's face, willing him to let her go.

'Nancy?' Resnick knocked on the centre of the door, not hard, even so it moved a little against the frame.

With a look and a sigh, Gary leaned away, loosening his grip on her hair. She read the look and it was that of someone realising they were deep into something from which there was no easy way out.

'We're talking,' Nancy said, raising her voice, never taking her eyes off Gary. 'About a problem Gary has with his housing. There was just a misunderstanding, that's all.'

'And Gary,' Resnick said. 'Let me hear your voice, will you? Just say something. Say hello. Anything.'

Gary said nothing.

Bailey beckoned Resnick back along the corridor. 'James, sir. Quite a tasty little record. Petty stuff as a juvenile. Supervision orders. Right now he's on probation. Aggravated assault. Actual bodily harm. Troops are on their way.'

'What it seems to me, Gary,' Nancy was saying, 'the sooner this is over, the less trouble for you.'

'Oh, yeh,' Gary said, lip curling. 'I can see you being worried about that – trouble for me.'

'Gary,' she said, 'I am. Really, I am.'

'Nancy,' Resnick said from outside, 'as long as everything's all right in there, do you think you could unlock the door?'

She was looking across at Gary; the sweat was beginning to stand out like pimples on his skin and his eyes refused to hold her gaze. Nancy had thought not to leave the key in the lock and now it lay at the end of the table between them, eighteen inches from her right hand. And his. She began to crab her fingers towards it and then stopped, reading his intention clearly.

'No,' Nancy said, voice raised but even, 'I don't think I can. Not right now.'

Bailey signalled that reinforcements had arrived outside the building; soon Resnick would hear their feet as they charged the stairs.

'Gary,' he said, 'this is your one and only chance. Come on out of your own free will before we have to come in and get you.'

'You see,' Nancy said, leaning her face towards him, pleading.

'I don't know,' Gary said, licking sweat from the soft hairs sprouting round his top lip. 'I don't fucking know.'

His voice was trembling and he reminded Nancy of the way her younger brother had looked caught stealing from their mother's purse, all of nine years old. Slowly, very slowly, so that he could see what she was doing, Nancy took the key between forefinger and thumb, stood, and walked the four paces to the door.

'Okay, Gary?' she asked, glancing round.

When she turned the key and pushed the door wide, they were inside in a flash: Bailey and Hennessey and two others, grabbing Gary as he tried to move, hands, arms, swinging him hard about and forcing him up against the wall, feet kicked wide, legs spread, arms yanked back and round, the cuffs as they went on biting at his wrists.

'Are you all right?' Resnick asked, touching Nancy lightly on the shoulder.

'I kept telling you, didn't I? I'm fine.' She stood aside, arms folded across her chest, her breathing going ragged now and seeking to control it, turning her head as Gary was hauled out into the corridor, no longer wanting to look into his face, see his expression as they bundled him away.

Five

'Things not so good at home', was that what Resnick had said? Lynn smiled grimly, changed down and indicated that she was taking the next left. Not so good could be measured by the way her mother had stood, tight-lipped and close to tears, still stirring the last of her Christmas puddings with only days to go. Other years, there would have been at least three of them, fat in their white basins, ready in the cupboard by the end of October.

'It's your dad, Lynnie,' all she had said.

Lynn had found him mooching between the hen houses, an unlit cigarette loose between his lips, fear in his eyes.

'Dad, whatever is it?'

The electrical equipment used to stun the birds before slaughter had malfunctioned and, at the height of the busiest season, forty-eight hours and several thousand pounds had been lost before it was set to rights. Worse for her father, before the fault was discovered, some hundred force-fed capons had been doused alive in scalding water, their throats slit, feathers plucked – he would wake at four, against all logic, reliving their screams. 'Come on, Dad,' Lynn had said, 'there's nothing you can do about it now.'

She should have known there was something more. On the morning she left, she found him in the kitchen at first light, hand round a mug of well-brewed tea.

'It's the doctor, Lynnie. He says I've to go to the hospital, see this consultant. Something here, in my gut.' He had stared at her along the table and Lynn had hurried from the room before he could see her cry.

It was a little after four in the afternoon and the dark was starting to close in. Still you could read, graffitied in two-foot-high letters on the Asian shop-keeper's wall, *Keep Christmas White – Fuck Off Home*. Lynn glanced at the street atlas again and readied herself for another three-point turn.

Michelle had not been home long. The buses had been overloaded with shoppers and those whose working day had finished in the lunchtime pub; sporadic bursts of carol singing, most often with the words changed to crude parody, drifted down from the upper deck. A ginger-haired man, still wearing his postman's uniform, sat with his legs out into the aisle, performing conjuring tricks with a deck of cards. As they were veering across the roundabout at the end of Gregory Boulevard, a businessman, wearing a grey pin-stripe suit and a red and white Christmas hat, had leaned wide from the platform of the bus and lost his lunch beneath the wheels of the oncoming traffic.

Natalie had fallen asleep, rocked by the vehicle's motion, and Karl had sat close, clinging to the sleeve of Michelle's coat, wrapped in the wonder of what was going on around him. When the postman leaned across and magicked a shiny ten-pence coin from behind Karl's left ear, the small boy squealed with delight.

'Whatever's happened to him, poor lamb?' Michelle's mother had asked, pointing to the swelling puffing out the side of Karl's face.

35

'He fell,' Michelle had said quickly. 'Always rushing at everything. You know what he's like.'

'Aye,' her mum had said. 'Bit of a madcap, like his dad.'

There were Christmas lights in some of the windows as they walked back up the street towards home; tiny red and blue bulbs glinting from plastic trees. A neighbour called out a greeting and Michelle felt a sudden rush of warmth run through her. Maybe this wasn't such a bad place after all. If they could just see off the winter, it really could be a new start.

She had called out opening the front door, expecting Gary to be back; the queue at the Housing must have been even longer than he'd thought. Quickly, she'd got the children changed, shipped Karl off in front of the TV with some bread and jam while she spooned rice and apple in and around the baby's mouth. Once fed, she'd put her down and tend to the fire, get it going before Gary returned, settle down to watch *Neighbours* with a fresh pot of tea.

The knock on the door was clipped and strong and though her first thought was that Gary had mislaid his key, it didn't sound like his knock at all.

'Michelle Paley?'

'Yes.'

'Detective Constable Lynn Kellogg. I'd like to talk to you a minute, if I could.'

Michelle took in the warrant card, the neat dark hair, the sureness of the stance, cheeks that showed red in the light spilling from the house.

Lynn glanced past Michelle into the room and saw the beginnings of a fire, a cartoon Dracula on the television, volume turned low. On a carpet that had seen better days, a mousey little kid with both legs in the air behind him, squinted round.

'You'll be letting in the cold,' Lynn said.

Michelle nodded and stood aside, closing the door behind Lynn as she walked in, pushing the folded square of rug back against it to keep out the draught.

Lynn unbuttoned her coat but made no move to take it off.

'What's happened?' Michelle said, sick to her stomach, fearing the worst. 'It's Gary, isn't it? Is it Gary? Is he all right? Tell me he's all right.'

'Why don't we sit down?' Lynn said.

Michelle swayed a little as she felt her legs starting to go.

'Nothing's happened to him,' Lynn said. 'You don't have to worry. Nothing like that.'

Michelle did sit, uneasily on to the sofa, reaching for the arm to steady herself down. 'He's in trouble, then,' she said.

'He's at the station,' Lynn said. 'Canning Circus. He was arrested earlier this afternoon.'

'Oh, God, what for?'

Lynn was conscious of the small boy, leaning back against the legs of the TV set, paying them all his attention. 'There was a disturbance, at the Housing Office...'

'A disturbance? What kind of...?'

'It seems he threatened the staff, physically. At one point he locked himself in a room with one of them and refused to let her out.'

Michelle's face had drained of what little colour it had.

'I don't know yet,' Lynn said, 'if he'll be held overnight. It's possible. We thought you ought to know.'

'Can I see him?'

37

'Later. I'll give you a number you can ring.'

Upstairs, the baby began crying and then, just as abruptly, stopped.

'Did he hit anyone?' Michelle asked.

'Apparently not. Not this time.'

'What d'you mean?'

'He's done it before, hasn't he? He's on probation.'

'That was ages ago, what happened.'

'A year.'

'But he's changed. Gary's changed.'

'Has he?'

Karl was rocking backwards and forwards as, on the screen above him, a fading football manager vouched for the splendours of British Gas.

'That's your little boy?' Lynn asked.

'Karl. Yes.'

'What happened to his face?'

Divine thanked the sister from Intensive Care and replaced the receiver: Mr Raju had returned from Recovery, was sleeping, sedated, his condition critical yet stable. It was unlikely he would be strong enough to speak with anyone until the morning.

'You've not changed your mind, then?' he said, as Naylor crossed the room behind him.

'About what?'

'Bringing Debbie along tonight.'

Naylor dropped two folders on to his desk: transcripts of interviews pertaining to the taxi driver's assault. Several thousand words and still no clear identification. Two youths in boots and jeans, much like many others. 'Why should I?' he said.

Divine's grin was broad as a dirty joke and about as subtle. 'Last chance for a bit of spare this side of the stuffing.'

'Forget it, Mark, why don't you?' Naylor flipped open the first file and began to read. It had taken all of his persuasion getting Debbie to agree to come with him. 'You don't want me there,' she'd said, 'getting in the way. You'll have a lot more fun on your own.' Times were, back when things were going wrong with their marriage, Naylor would have been the first to agree. Jumped at it, the chance for a night out on his own, with the lads. Now it was different; he felt it was different. 'All right,' he had told her, 'if you don't want to go, I'll stay home.' That had done the trick.

Now he looked at his watch, the workload on his desk; best give Debbie a quick call.

Lynn was sitting in Resnick's office, telling him about her visit. Earlier, Resnick had interviewed first Gary James and then Nancy Phelan, conversations in still, airless rooms with the tape machine ticking digitally across the long afternoon.

Gary had been alternately contrite and angry, constantly bringing things back to rotting wood and sagging doors and damp that ran down the insides of walls.

'You realise,' Resnick had said, 'behaving the way you did, it's not going to do your case any good.'

'No?' Gary had said. 'Then tell me what is.'

Unable to answer, Resnick had handed him over to the custody sergeant and now he sat sulking in one of the police cells.

Nancy Phelan was adamant that Gary had done nothing to really hurt her, she had never felt in any actual danger. It had simply got out of hand.

'Then he didn't strike you?' Resnick had asked.

'No.'

'Never as much as touched you?' A pause and then,

pressing her fingers to her scalp, 'I suppose he did grab my hair.'

'And you weren't frightened?'

'No, he was.'

Resnick thought about that as he listened to Lynn describing the marks on the boy's face, the swelling that had all but closed one eye, the bruise coming out strongly, yellow and purple and darkening.

'She said, the mother, that he'd fallen,' Resnick said.

Lynn nodded. 'Running out the back door. The door was actually off, I don't know, she and Gary, they were putting it back on when the boy came running. Went smack into it.'

'It's plausible, surely?'

'Yes.'

'But you don't believe her?'

Lynn crossed and recrossed her legs. 'In different circumstances, I might. But this Gary James, his record . . .'

'Nothing to suggest any violence towards the children.'

'Something must have got him in a state before he got to the Housing Office. Something more than simply having to wait.'

'Well . . .' Resnick got to his feet, walked round from behind his desk. Through the glass he could see Divine speaking into the telephone, Kevin Naylor painstakingly making notes, the pen in that awkward-seeming grip he used, as if it were an implement he was still struggling to control. . . . 'Best have a word with social services.' He checked his watch. 'If they've knocked off early for the day, you can try the emergency duty team.' Though not for long, he thought, rumour was that with the next wave of cuts they were to be axed.

Which would mean the likes of Karl waiting till past Boxing Day.

Lynn paused at the door. 'James, sir, are we keeping him in?'

Resnick made a face. 'Christmas. I'd not want to, not if it can be avoided.'

'But if the boy's at risk?'

'I know. Let's get someone round there, get him to a doctor, have him properly examined. Till then young Gary James can kick his heels.'

'Right.' Lynn stepped out into Divine's raucous laughter and the sound of an ambulance going past outside, another victim of the festivities on the way to Queen's. She paused near her desk and turned back towards the open door to Resnick's office. 'I don't suppose there's any good trying to talk to his probation officer? Might throw some light, one way or another.'

'You could always try,' Resnick said. His expression suggested she would probably be wasting her time. Relationships with the probation service were not the most trusting, either way; and this wasn't the most propitious of times.

'I'll check anyway,' Lynn said over her shoulder, 'see whose client he is.'

'Pam Van Allen.'

Lynn was looking at him.

'I gave Neil Park a call. Earlier.'

'But you've not spoken to her, sir, Van Allen?'

Resnick shook his head.

'You don't mind if I . . .'

'You go ahead.'

Back at his desk, for a moment Resnick closed his eyes; he could see her walking out of sight, Pam Van Allen, a meeting that had turned out badly, her hair glinting silver-grey against the light. 'Pressure, Charlie,'

41

her senior, Neil Park had said later. 'Male, high-ranking, used to telling people what to do and expecting them to do it. She resented it.' Resnick didn't think he would have any luck there. If Lynn could talk to her, so much the better. Even so, he found himself staring at the phone, part of him wanting to call.

'Sir,' Lynn knocked on his door and pushed it wide enough for her head to lean in. 'She's gone home for the day. For the holiday.'

'All right,' Resnick said, 'we'll hang on, see what social services have to say. Oh, and Lynn . . .'

'Yes?'

'This business at home – whatever it is – if you need to talk about it . . .'

For the first time in a while, she found something close to a smile. 'Thanks.'

Back across the CID room her phone once again was ringing. Someone was humming 'Silent Night'. From somewhere, Divine had acquired a paper hat, red and green, and he was wearing it as he read off an entry from the VDU, a sprig of mistletoe poking hopefully from his breast pocket.

Six

'So what was he like?' Nancy's flatmate, Dana, asked, her voice blurred beneath the rush and splatter of the shower.

'What was who like?'

'Your kidnapper, who else?'

Nancy pulled her head clear from the spray of water. Opaque, through the thick, flowered plastic of the curtain, she could see Dana on the loo, all but naked, taking a pee. Six months ago, when they had started sharing, Nancy would have been, well, not shocked, but certainly embarrassed. Neither would she have felt comfortable doing what she was doing now, turning off the shower and pulling back the curtain, stepping out on to the tiled floor to dry herself down.

'So?' Dana said, glancing up. 'Was he sexy or what?'

Nancy gave a wry smile. 'Hardly.' She remembered the patchy hair, faint around his mouth, the way he had perspired, the nervous jerkiness of his hands, hollow of his eyes. 'Besides, situations like that, sexiness doesn't come into it.'

'Doesn't it?' Dana said. Pulling off a length of toilet paper, she folded the sheets again and then again before dabbing between her legs. 'Somehow I thought it did.'

Nancy was vigorously towelling her hair. 'That's because you think it comes into everything.'

43

Dana laughed and sent water flushing round the bowl. 'What was he like then?' she said.

'A boy. A kid.'

'So?' Dana arched a camp eyebrow and laughed some more.

The time Nancy had come home unexpected and found her flatmate grappling with a seventeen-year-old on the living-room carpet had been, in more ways than one, a revelation. 'He's advanced for his age,' Dana had explained. 'Two A-levels already. Working hard for his Cambridge entrance.'

'I noticed,' Nancy had said. What she'd noticed were the marks on the youth's back as he'd pulled his Simple Minds T-shirt on over his head.

'Didn't I tell you,' Nancy said now, 'this Gary, we went to the same school?'

'No, really?'

'Yes, two years below me.'

'And that's his name? Gary?'

'Uh-hum.'

'And you remembered him?' Dana was standing slightly on tip-toe before the bathroom mirror, examining her breasts.

'Not at all.'

'Then he remembered you.'

Nancy wound the first towel around her head and reached for another. 'I used to go out with this boy, he was a friend of Gary's big brother.'

'You see, it all makes sense. There he was, Gary, adoring you from afar and you never as much as noticed him. The stuff that pimply wet dreams are made of.'

Nancy grimaced and laughed and pretended to throw up over the toilet bowl.

'You don't think this is a lump, do you? Look, here?'

Serious, Nancy stared at her friend's left breast.

'I don't know. I can't see any . . .'

'Feel.'

Nancy reached out a hand and Dana took it, guiding it to the right spot.

'Well?'

Pressing down with her fingertips, Nancy rolled the flesh across and back; there was something there, the smallest knot of muscle possibly, not a lump. 'No,' she said, 'I think you're fine. Nothing to worry about at all.'

'Of course not,' Dana smiled. Another of her friends, just thirty-five, was due in hospital for a mastectomy first thing in the new year.

'Can I borrow your hairdrier?' Nancy asked. 'Mine's on the blink.' And then at the bathroom door – 'This do tonight, we don't have to get too dressed up, do we?'

Dana's smile was genuine this time. 'Only to the nines.'

What might have helped, Nancy thought, on her way to the bedroom, if this afternoon had been more of a fright than actually it was, it might have done something to bring me on, get this blasted period of mine moving.

Martin Wrigglesworth no longer considered his working days in terms of good or bad; simply, they were gradations of the later – bad, less bad, badder, baddest. A classical education not entirely gone to waste. There were days, he thought, his all-but clapped-out Renault Five stalling at the Noel Street lights, when the whole of Forest Fields should be swept into care. Why stop there? Hyson Green. Radford. The lot. Wheel everyone over sixty into residential homes for the aged; whisk children under eleven into the welcoming arms of foster parents, twelve-to-seventeen-year-olds into youth custody. Anyone left could be swept on to a massive Workfare programme and work for their dole, performing useful services like cutting the grass on the Forest with nail clippers through the daylight hours. Those were the thoughts that got Martin through his less bad days.

At home in Nuthall at weekends, repainting the bathroom, waiting to collect the boys from swimming, helping his wife fold the washing in from the line, he tried to recall the exact moment, the feeling that had drawn him into social work, a good and honourable profession.

And what, Martin thought, turning into another narrow street in a warren of narrow streets, could he do? What honourable course might he take? Brutus would happily have fallen on his sword, of course, being an honourable man, but so far the mortgage and the pension plan and the irredeemable dream of renovating a dilapidated farmhouse in the South of France had kept any such thought firmly in Martin's scabbard.

'Martin,' his wife would say wearily over her marking, 'if it's making you feel so low, why don't you hand in your notice? Resign. You'll find something else.' With over three million out of work, he knew only too well what he would find. Instead of resigning he was resigned.

Number 37, he said to himself, checking the hastily scribbled note on the seat beside him. A row of two-storey, flat-fronted houses, front rooms opening out onto the street. Locking the car, he crossed the narrow, uneven pavement towards the chipped paint of the door. A late referral from a police officer fearful for the safety of a child: Lord knows what he would find on the other side. Not so long ago, here in the city, a young mother had dipped her two-year-old son's penis in hot tea and spun him round inside a spin-drier.

'Hello,' he said, as Michelle opened the front door. 'Ms Paley? Martin Wrigglesworth, Social Services . . .' Showing her his card. ' . . . I've called round about your son, er, Karl. I wonder if we might talk inside?'

'How do I look?'

Nancy was standing in the entrance to Dana's room in a silver crochet top, short black skirt, silver-grey tights with a pattern of raised silver dots, leather ankle boots with a slight heel. When Dana had asked her, back in mid-November, if she would like to go along to her firm's Christmas dinner and dance, it had seemed like a good idea. 'Terrific,' Dana enthused. 'You look terrific.'

'I feel ten feet tall.'

'Better than five feet wide like me.' Dana looked as if she had dived into her wardrobe head first and emerged swathed in colour, bright yellows, purple and green. Nancy was reminded of a parakeet with cleavage.

'No, seriously, I feel stupid.'

'You look wonderful. Every man in that room is going to take one look at you . . .'

'That's what I'm worried about.'

' . . . and be falling over themselves asking you to dance.'

Nancy was looking at herself in Dana's full-length mirror. 'I look like I'm auditioning for principal boy in *Aladdin*.'

'So, fine. You'll get the part.'

Nancy recrossed the room, trying to walk small.

She'd met one or two of them already, architects and such, they hadn't seemed too bad. More interesting than the people she worked with herself. 'Maybe this isn't such a good idea,' she said. 'Maybe I shouldn't go at all. They're your friends, people you work with, I shall hardly know a soul.'

'*You're* my friend. And besides, I've told them all about you . . .' Nancy placed one hand over her eyes. ' . . . and one more thing, there's no refund on the price of your ticket.'

'All right,' Nancy said, 'you talked me into it. I'm coming.'

Dana lifted her watch from the dressing table and held it closer to her face. 'Taxi's here in twenty minutes.'

'I thought we didn't have to be there till eight?'

'We're meeting first for a drink at Sarah Brown's.'

'Won't it be terribly crowded?'

'All the better. Rub shoulders with the rich and nearly famous.'

'All the same,' Martin Wrigglesworth was saying to Michelle, 'I think, just to be certain, I'd be happier if we could just pop him along to the doctor, let someone have a proper look at him.' From somewhere he dredged up a smile. 'Better safe than sorry.'

'You don't mean now?' Michelle asked. 'You want to take him to the doctor now?'

'Yes,' Martin said, clipping his biro into his top pocket. 'Now.'

The taxi arrived almost fifteen minutes early and the driver wanted to charge them waiting time, but Dana soon disabused him of that. Nancy had changed out of her black skirt into a pair of loose-fitting black trousers and then back into her skirt again. She had borrowed one of Dana's topcoats, bright red wool, a regular bull's delight.

'You've got your ticket?'

Nancy patted the sequinned bag she held in her lap.

'Condoms?' Dana laughed.

Nancy stuck out her tongue. 'It isn't going to be that kind of night.'

Dana, sitting back in the corner of the cab, smiling. 'You never know.'

Nancy did: what she had in her bag, ever hopeful, were three Lillets.

The cab swung out of the Park, into incoming traffic on Derby Road. They were approaching Canning Circus when Nancy suddenly leaned forward, asking the driver to stop.

'What's the matter?' Dana asked. 'What've you forgotten?'

'Nothing.' Nancy opened the nearside door. 'I'm just popping into the police station, that's all.'

'Whatever for?'

'It doesn't matter. You go on. I'll meet you at the hotel. Go straight there. Bye.'

Nancy pushed the cab door closed and stood a moment, watching the vehicle pull away, Dana's face, perplexed, staring back through the glass.

The officer on the duty desk had phoned Resnick's office to inform him he had a visitor, not quite able to keep the smirk out of his voice. It wasn't until Nancy Phelan walked in through the door to the deserted CID room that Resnick understood why.

'Inspector . . .'

'Yes?'

'I was here earlier today . . .'

'I remember.' Resnick smiled. 'Not dressed like that.'

Nancy gave a half-smile in return. She had unbuttoned the borrowed red coat walking up the stairs and now it hung loose from her shoulders. 'Christmas Eve, you know how it is. Everyone out on the town.'

While Kevin Naylor held the fort, Resnick had nipped home to feed the cats, brushed his best suit, ironed a white shirt, buffed his shoes, scraped a few fragments of pesto sauce from his tie. The one night of the year he tried to make an impression. 'I've got changed myself,' he said pleasantly.

'Sorry,' Nancy said, 'I hadn't noticed.'

'Yes, well . . . what exactly was it you . . .?'

'About this afternoon . . .'

'Yes?'

'Like I said, nothing really happened, to me I mean. It wasn't, you know, this big traumatic thing or anything.'

'But it's on your mind all the same.'

'Is it?'

Resnick shrugged large shoulders. 'You're here.'

'Yes, but that's not because of me. It's him.'

'Him?'

'James. Gary James.'

'What about him?'

Nancy fidgeted her feet on the office floor. 'I'm not sure. I suppose . . . All it was, I had this thought, like, when I was passing, literally, going past outside . . . I didn't want to think that he was cooped up in here, in some cell over Christmas because of me.'

The social worker had contacted Lynn Kellogg after the doctor had carried out his examination: Karl's injuries were not inconsistent with the explanation that his mother had given – he had run headlong into a heavy wooden door. Social Services would keep a watching brief and if there was any further cause for concern ... Gary James had been released a little over half an hour ago, warned as to his future behaviour and made to understand there was a possibility charges might still be brought.

'You don't have to worry,' Resnick said. 'We've let him go.'

Nancy's smile was a delight to behold. 'And that's the end of it?'

'Not necessarily.'

'But ...'

'There are other things, other issues involved.' Resnick moved towards the door and she followed him, the worn carpet muffling the clip of her heels.

'You won't be needing me again then? Testimony in court or anything?'

'I shouldn't think so. It's unlikely.'

Somehow, close in the doorway, she seemed taller, her face only inches from his own.

'Well, Merry Christmas, I suppose,' Nancy said, and for one absurd moment Resnick thought she was going to breach that distance between them with a kiss.

'Merry Christmas,' Resnick said, as she walked down the corridor. 'And tonight, have a good time.'

At the head of the stairs, Nancy raised her hand and waved. 'You too,' she said.

Resnick turned back towards his office, started putting out the lights.

Seven

How it worked was this: large-scale bookings were given a banqueting room of their own, smaller parties were encouraged to share. Either way the format was the same – long lines of tables on opposite sides of a central dance floor, a DJ in a cream suit waiting to slip Elvis' 'Blue Christmas' in between Abba and Rolf Harris doing terrible things to 'Stairway to Heaven'. Plates of food were bounced down in efficient relays; soup, egg mayonnaise, a blue ticket brought turkey, a pink, salmon; the fruit salad came with cream or without. Two bottles of wine every eight people, one red, one white; any further drinks you fetched yourself from the cellar bar. If that became too crowded, it was always possible to cross the courtyard into the main body of the hotel, pass between reception and the wide armchairs of the foyer and use the bar there.

'All right now!' the DJ over-pitched into his mike above the final scraping of plates and the rising tide of conversation. 'Who's gonna be the first ones on the floor?'

'What d'you say, Charlie,' Reg Cossall barked into Resnick's ear, 'we get ourselves out of here and get a real drink?'

'Later, maybe, Reg. Later.'

Cossall scraped back his chair, pushed himself to his feet. 'I'll be across the other side for a bit, if you change your mind. Then, likely, I'll head down the Bell.'

Times long past, Resnick had closed too many bars with Reg Cossall to forget the mornings after. He'd stick where he was for another half hour or so, long enough to show willing, then slip away and leave them to it. He could see Divine revving up already, on his feet a couple of tables down, trying to encourage one of the new WPCs on to the floor, offering to pull her Christmas cracker.

'Come feel the noize!' called the DJ, turning the volume up on Slade and letting the decibels bounce off the ceiling.

Jack Skelton was wearing a dinner jacket, a midnight-blue bow tie; he was standing against the side wall, deep in conversation with Helen Siddons, recently promoted DCI and using the city as a stepping stone on her fast track to the top. They made an elegant pair, standing there, Siddons in an ankle-length pale green gown.

From his seat, Resnick glanced around, concerned that Skelton's wife might be sitting in need of company. What he saw were Kevin Naylor and his wife Debbie, smiling into one another's eyes, holding hands. Second honeymoon, Resnick thought, and not before time. Like a lot of marriages in the force, this one seemed to have been disintegrating before his eyes. It was more than a sign of the times; even when families had seemed more stable and relationships didn't come with their own sell-by date, police divorce figures had been high. How many times had Reg Cossall bought the CID room cigars and signed his name in the registrar's book? Two? Three? And rumour had it he was trying for one more. Resnick sat back down. Either you were like Reg or you tried once and when that was over, shut the doors and threw away the key.

Which is it with you, Charlie?

He could see Skelton's wife Alice now, three rows down, tilting back her head as she finished her wine, reaching out to refill the glass, tapping a cigarette from the pack on the table before her, small gold lighter from her bag, the head tilting back again as she released a swathe of grey smoke, feathering past her eyes.

'Alice?' He stood alongside her, waiting for her to turn.

'Charlie. Well ... how nice. A social call?'

Resnick shrugged, suddenly uncomfortable. 'I saw you ...'

'On my own? A damsel in distress. Alone and palely loitering.'

There was a whoop from the dance floor, an attempt at a Michael Jackson going badly out of control, legs and arms akimbo.

'For heaven's sake sit down, Charlie. You're like a spare prick at a wedding.'

Resnick took the chair beside her, calculating how much she had likely drunk, how soon before leaving she'd got started. In all of their infrequent social meetings, stretching back ten years, he had never heard her raise her voice or swear.

'Send you over, did he, Charlie?'

Resnick shook his head.

'Keep an eye on me. Get me talking. Do me a favour, Charlie, keep her happy. Give her a bit of a spin, out on the floor.'

'Alice, I don't know – '

Her hand, the one not holding the glass, was on his knee. 'Come on, Charlie, don't play naive. We know what it's like, all boys together, doesn't matter how old. You cover my back, I'll cover yours. ' She drank and exchanged the glass for her cigarette. 'That's what it all comes down to, Charlie. In the end. The covering of backs.'

Smoke drifted slowly past Resnick's face. At the edge of his vision he could see Jack Skelton leaning lightly against the furthest wall, Helen Siddons turned towards him, both heads bowed in conversation. As Resnick watched, Skelton's hand moved towards his jacket pocket, inadvertently brushing the DCI's bare arm on its way.

'Aren't you drinking, Charlie?' Alice Skelton held the bottle towards him.

Resnick nodded back to where he'd been sitting. 'I've got one over there.'

'Abstemious, too. Abstemious and loyal. No wonder Jack's so keen to keep you where you are.' She emptied the bottle into her glass, little more than the dregs.

'I'll get you another . . .'

Her hand had moved from his leg but now, as he made to rise, it was back. Resnick was starting to sweat just a little; just as some would be clocking Skelton and Siddons, how many were noticing himself and Skelton's wife, putting the numbers together to see how well they fit?

'Alice . . .'

'What you have to see, she's not just fucking him, Charlie, she's fucking you too.'

'Alice, I'm sorry . . .' He was on his feet, but she still had hold of him, fingers pressing hard behind the knee. Squeezing past on the other side of the table, one of the civilian VDU operators laughing on his arm, Divine caught Resnick's eye and winked.

'What do you need to know, Charlie?' He had to

bend towards her to catch what she was saying above the noise; didn't want her raising her voice any further, shouting it out. 'Rules of evidence. How much proof d'you need? Catching them doing it, there in your bed?'

'I'm sorry, Alice, I've got to go.'

He prised away her hand and pushed his way between the backs and chairs, the laughter, all the huddled promises and thoughtless betrayals hatching on the night.

Lynn Kellogg was wearing a strapless dress, royal blue, and had done something to her hair Resnick had not noticed before. The man in the dress suit, between them at the crowded bar, was clearly taken. 'Let me get those.' Smiling, twenty-pound note in his hand. 'No, thanks. You're all right,' Lynn said, turning away. 'Later, then?' 'What?' 'Let me buy you a drink, later.' She shook her head and pushed through the crowd.

Resnick watched her go over to where Maureen Madden was standing, Maureen wearing a dark frock-coat and jeans, looking more like a country singer on the loose than the sergeant who supervised the rape suite. Reg Cossall was shouting at him from the far end of the bar and waving his empty glass.

'A pint of whatever he's drinking,' Resnick said to the white-coated barman, 'and a large Bells to go with it. Bottle of Czech Budweiser for me, if you've got it.'

He had. Resnick pushed his way along and listened for a while to Cossall laying down the law about the unemployment rate, young offenders, overpriced imported beer, Brian Clough, the social benefits of castration. Half a dozen younger officers stood around, drinking steadily, gleaning wisdom. Resnick remembered when he and Cossall had been like them, eager to ape their elders and betters; back when you had to be six foot to get on to the force and either it was draught Bass, draught Worthington or you didn't bother going back for more. Twenty years before.

When he'd heard enough, Resnick moved away and found Lynn Kellogg and Maureen Madden, sitting now on the stairs near the entrance to the lounge.

'Quite an admirer back there,' Resnick said to Lynn, nodding back towards the bar.

'Oh, that. He'd been drinking. You know what it's like.'

'I wish you'd stop doing that,' Maureen said.

'Doing what?'

'Putting yourself down. Assuming that for some man to fancy you he has to be half-pissed.'

'It's usually true.'

'Don't you think she looks great?' Maureen asked Resnick, craning her neck to look up at him.

'Very nice,' Resnick said.

Lynn felt herself starting to blush. 'Have you been out on the floor yet?' she asked, covering her embarrassment.

Resnick shook his head.

'He's waiting for you,' Maureen teased.

'More like waiting for them to turn the volume down,' Resnick said. 'Play a waltz.'

'Now that's not true,' Lynn said. 'My first year, you were out there bopping till everyone else dropped. "Be-bop-a-hula", stuff like that.'

Despite himself, Resnick smiled: something attractive about the idea of Gene Vincent in black leathers and a grass skirt, strumming away at an Hawaiian guitar.

'Well,' Maureen announced, setting her empty glass on the floor, 'I'm in the mood. What d'you say, Lynn?

57

Game? Before your admirer over there comes and asks you.'

The man in the dress suit, glass in hand, was sitting in one of the easy chairs in the lounge, making no pretence of not looking in their direction.

'Come on,' Lynn said, getting to her feet. 'Let's get out of here.' Maureen was already on her way. 'Coming with us?' Lynn asked.

'You go ahead,' Resnick said.

With a last look back, Lynn followed Maureen Madden towards the main door.

'Like watching 'em leave the nest, Charlie?' Reg Cossall said at Resnick's shoulder.

'How d'you mean?'

'You know, young ones, fledglings . . .'

'She's scarce a kid, Reg.'

'No matter.'

'Old enough to be . . .'

Cossall's hand squeezed down firm on Resnick's shoulder. 'You can be a literal bugger sometimes, Charlie. When it fits your purpose.' Cossall treated Resnick to his best philosophical stare. 'Kids. Families. Can't get 'em one way, we get 'em another. More's the bastard pity.'

He lit small cigar and cupped it in his hand. 'Not on for one in town, I suppose?'

'I don't think so.'

'Please yourself, then. You always bloody do.'

Resnick turned back to the bar and prepared to wait his chance to order a final beer.

Back in the Friar Tuck Room, things were throbbing towards some sort of climax. Whitney Houston, Rod Stewart, Chris De Burgh, the Drifters – hands clutched shiny buttocks that were not their own. Divine, tie forsaken, shirt all unbuttoned, was executing a limbo dance to 'Twist and Shout', sliding his legs beneath a line of brassière straps linked together. Off to the side of the room, Skelton and Helen Siddons scarcely seemed to have moved, the same urgent conversation, heads angled inwards; one strap of Helen's dress had slid from her shoulder. Lynn and Maureen Madden were dancing with a group of other women, laughing, clapping their hands in the air. Oblivious of the tempo, Kevin Naylor and Debbie were dancing cheek to cheek, bodies barely moving. Resnick couldn't see Alice Skelton anywhere and was grateful.

'Five minutes to Christmas,' the DJ announced. 'I want to see you all in a big circle, holding hands.'

Resnick slipped out through the door.

'Inspector?'

He glanced up and saw long legs, a sequinned silver bag, a smile.

'I didn't know we were partying in the same place,' Nancy Phelan said.

Resnick half-smiled. 'So it seems.'

'How's it been? Nancy asked. Resnick was aware of a car on the curve of the courtyard, waiting. 'You been having a good time?'

'Not bad, I suppose.'

'Well . . .' Smiling, she gestured outwards with open hands. 'Merry Christmas, once again. Happy New Year.'

'Happy New Year,' Resnick echoed, as Nancy walked out of his vision and, hands in pockets, he turned left and crossed the cobbled courtyard to the street.

Eight

For Christmas, Resnick had bought himself *The Complete Billie Holiday on Verve*, a new edition of Dizzy Gillespie's autobiography and *The Penguin Guide to Jazz on CD, LP and Cassette*. What he still had to acquire was a CD player.

But there he'd been, not so many days before, sauntering down from Canning Circus into town, sunshine, one of those clear blue winter skies, and glancing into the window of Arcade Records he had seen it. Amongst the Eric Clapton and the Elton John, a black box with the faintest picture of Billie on its front; ten CDs and a two-hundred-and-twenty-page book, seven hundred minutes of music, a numbered, limited edition, only sixteen thousand pressed worldwide.

Worldwide, Resnick had thought; only sixteen thousand worldwide. That didn't seem an awful lot of copies. And here was one, staring up at him, and a bargain offer to boot. He had his cheque book but not his cheque card. 'It's okay,' the owner had said, 'I think we can trust you.' And knocked another five pounds off the price.

Resnick had spent much of the morning, between readying the duck for the oven, peeling the potatoes, cleaning round the bath, looking at it. Holding it in his hand. *Billie Holiday on Verve.* There is a photograph of her in the booklet, New York City, 1956: a woman early to middle-age, no glamour, one hand on her hip, none too patiently waiting, a working woman, c'mon now, let's get this done. He closes his eyes and imagines her singing – 'Cheek to Cheek' with Ben Webster, wasn't that fifty-six? 'Do Nothing Till You Hear From Me.' 'We'll Be Together Again.' The number stamped on the back of Resnick's set is 10961.

So much easier to look again and again at the booklet, slide those discs from their brown card covers, admire the reproductions of album sleeves in their special envelope, easier to do all of this than take the few steps to the mantelpiece and the card that waits in its envelope, unopened. A post mark, smudged, that might say Devon; the unmistakable spikiness of his ex-wife's hand.

The duck was delicious, strongly flavoured, fatty yet not too fat. Certainly Dizzy had thought so, up on to the table with a spring before Resnick had noticed, enjoying his share of breast, a little leg, happy finally to be chased off down the garden, jaws tight around a wing.

Resnick sliced away the meat from where the black cat had eaten and shared it amongst the others, Miles rearing up on his hind legs, Bud pushing his head against Resnick's shins, Pepper patient by his bowl.

As well as those he had set to roast around the bird, Resnick had cooked potatoes separately and mashed them with some swede, sprinkled that with paprika, poured on sour cream. Sprouts he had blanched in boiling water before finishing in the frying pan with slices of salami, cut small. Polish sausage he had simmered in beer until it was swollen and done.

He had not long finished foraging for his second helping when Marian Witczak called him on the phone. 'Charles, how are you? I have been meaning all day to wish you a merry Christmas, but, I don't know, some-how it has all been so busy.'

Resnick pictured her, alone in the extravagant Victoriana of her house across the city, drinking Christmas toasts to long-departed Polish heroes, pale sherry in fragile crystal glasses; sitting down, perhaps, to play a little Chopin at the piano before taking some General's memoir or some book of old photographs down from the shelf.

'So, Charles, you must tell me, my presents, what did you think?'

They were still on the hall chest, neat in their snowy paper, white and red ribbon tied with bows.

'Marian, I'm sorry, thank you. Thank you very much.'

'You really like them?'

'Of course.'

'If only you knew how much time I spent deciding, well, I think you might be surprised. But the colours, the design, it had to be just right.'

Socks? Resnick thought. A tie?

'Even so, I have kept the receipt. Should you decide to take it back and exchange . . .'

'Marian, no. It's lovely.' A tie.

'And the other gift, Charles, what did you think of that?'

The other? He pictured a second package, square and flat, he had taken it for a card. But, no, Marian's card was in the living room, a starry night over Wenceslas Square.

'It was not too presumptuous, I trust.'

'We're old friends, Marian . . .'

'Exactly. This is what I tell myself.'

'You know me well enough . . .'

'So you will come?'

Come? Resnick swallowed most of a sigh. Come where?

'We will both wear, Charles, what would you say? Our dancing shoes.'

The conversation over, Resnick went through to the hall. Faced with the broad expanse of the chest's wooden lid, Bud had chosen Marian's presents to curl up on. The tie was silk, a swirl of soft colour, blue on blue. Inside the second package was his ticket to the Polish Club's New Year's Eve Dinner and Dance. What was it, this sudden desire of everyone to get him out on to the floor?

The same films were on the television, immovable as the Queen's Christmas Address. What he wanted was a good old-fashioned first division encounter, Southend and Grimsby, one of those. Where the long ball hoofed out of defence was deemed creative play and tackles thudded in so hard the TV set seemed to shake with the impact. What he got were daring prisoners-of-war, straw men, a sweep of hills on which, if only people would stop singing, you might hear edelweiss grow. Was it Exeter, the name smudged almost out of recognition? Exmoor? Exmouth? Resnick held up the envelope, angled against the light. Through it he saw, in veiled outline, something that might have been a coach with horses, reindeer with a sledge. *Let me tell them about the letters, Charlie. All the letters I sent you, the ones you never answered. All the times I rang up in pain and you hung up without a word.* With care, he set it back upon the shelf. *Tell them all about that, Charlie. How you helped me with everything I've been going through.*

He had not heard from Elaine for years, not since the divorce. And then they had started arriving, envelopes on which it was sometimes difficult to read his own address. Afraid of their contents he had shredded them into fragments, turned them to ash, pushed them deep to the back of the kitchen drawer. He had not wanted to know and it had taken Elaine to tell him, face to face, her voice strident and off-key, puncturing his seeming indifference with its accusations and its pain; later, in this house, this room, she had outlined with disturbing calmness her journey from miscarriage and desertion to the hospital ward, the treatments, the analyst's chair.

Resnick had felt sympathy for her then, love even, not the same but a different kind. Almost, he could have crossed the floor and held her in his arms. But guilt had numbed him. That and a sense of self-preservation too.

She had walked out of the house and he had not heard from her again.

Till now.

From the upstairs window he mourned the slow fading of the light.

Coffee, he ground fine and made strong, drank with a tumbler of whisky at its side. Sliding an Ellington album from its buckled sleeve, he set it to play. The notes on the incident at the Housing Office and Gary James' interview he had brought with him and he scanned them now, wondering again if it had been right to release him, let him return home. Injuries to a small boy consistent with what? Running smack into a door. Smack into his father's fist. One of the cats jumped into Resnick's lap, nudged his fingers with its nose, turned twice and settled, lay a paw across his eyes and fell asleep. Jimmy Blanton's bass was rocking the whole band. Exmouth or Exeter? A coach or a sledge?

Miles stared up at Resnick resentfully as he was set down on the floor. So easy, the act of sliding a finger behind the envelope's flap, tearing it open, shaking the contents down into your hand. It was a stagecoach, holly at its windows, snowflakes round its wheels; someone akin to Mr Pickwick beamed from the driver's seat and lifted his hat. *Forgive me, Charlie*? it said inside, and then, below, the words close to falling off the bottom of the card, *Merry Christmas, Elaine.*

No love, no kiss.

Forgive me.

He heard Alice Skelton's harsh whispers. *How much proof d'you need? Catching them doing it, there in your bed*?

It had been someone else's bed, an empty house, the duvet carefully replaced, pillows slightly overlapping, not quite so. When he had lifted the duvet aside and brought his face close to the centre of the sheet, there had been no denying it, the lingering warmth, the tang of recent, hurried sex. The smile upon Elaine's face when he had seen her leaving, minutes before. That smile. When Resnick brought his hand to his face, as he did now, and closed his eyes, he could taste, deep in the cracks between his fingers, that memory, salt like the sea.

Nine

Dana hadn't given much attention to the compliments being paid her at their Christmas Eve function. Not at first, anyway. The usual remarks about what she was wearing, her hair, her natural contours, the comparisons with Madonna. 'Someone's giving you *Sex* for Christmas, I'll bet.' 'Come on, Jeremy, you can see, she's already got it.' For some of them, some of the men she worked with, it came as naturally as breathing. Especially the married ones: all the things they no longer said to their wives. She didn't even think of it as sexual harassment. She didn't feel threatened, hardly ever embarrassed; it was constant, within the bounds of the generally acceptable, and even if it did become a little wearing, well, it was better than spending your time with a bunch of yobbos who were likely to break into 'Get your tits out for the lads!' at the first opportunity.

The other thing was, she did like to be noticed. And by men. It wasn't that she flaunted herself in front of them, but it did please her when they knew she was there. As she'd said to Nancy, if you're never allowed a little sexual repartee, if the flower didn't attract the bee – well, how was anything ever going to happen? And she had this certain feeling: too much repression was harmful. Tip-toe around each other pretending you've got blinkers on, not a word or a glance out of place and then, suddenly, there's this guy, can't control it any longer, hurling you down behind the colour photocopier, leaving his unrequited passion all over the floor. 'Mmm,' Nancy had said, uncertain, 'maybe there's something in between.'

Well, Dana had thought, when Andrew Clarke, hand just touching her elbow, had guided her out on to the floor, maybe there was.

Andrew was a senior partner, Victorian house in the Park, all the original architraves, things like that. Family car was a BMW, but Dana had noticed recently this little Toyota MR2 in his slot in the parking lot. Red, something to run around in now the days of public school fees were coming to an end. The most provocative remark he'd ever made to her in the office was about the air-conditioning. No, he was scrupulous, correct; she'd never even caught him looking at her as she walked away, admiring her backside.

'Not very good at this, you know. Even though my daughters try to teach me at family parties.'

There were so many crowded on to the small circle of polished floor, it didn't matter that Andrew Clarke's attempts to boogie resembled the final struggles of a man trapped in quicksand. In fact, there was something about the earnestness with which he went about it which Dana found almost endearing.

So, when the music switched to some old Stevie Wonder and he pulled her into some kind of smoochy waltz, she didn't object. Though she was surprised, after a while, to feel something remarkably close to an erection pushing against her thigh.

She was on the steps outside the cloakroom, after one o'clock, when she saw him again. He had on his Crombie overcoat, a little rucked up at the collar, and his car keys in his hand.

'Going home alone?'

It looked like it; Nancy, despite her earlier protestations, seemed to have found congenial company.

'Still in that place on Newcastle Drive, aren't you? On my way. Why not let me drop you off?'

The inside of the car smelt of leather polish and cologne. She was ready for the invitation to coffee when it came, had determined to say no, the exact tone rehearsed inside her head so as not to offend.

'Yes,' she said. 'A quick cup. All right.'

The family, of course, had headed north that morning, getting an early start. 'Little place off the Northumbrian coast. Had it for years. Nothing special.' Dana noticed a photograph of Andrew and his sons in front of what looked like a small castle, Andrew and the eldest boy with their shotguns, smiling as they held up dead birds.

'Still ...' pressing a large glass of brandy into her hands ' ... their not being here, affords us a bit of privacy. Chance to get to know one another better.'

When Dana limped out forty minutes later, her bra strap was round her neck, unfastened, her tights were torn, she had lost the heel from one of her shoes. Andrew's mood had switched from amorous to angry and back again and when finally she had slapped him hard, pushed him clear and told him to grow up, he had astonished her by bursting into tears.

Back in her own flat, Christmas Day was already two hours old and no sign of Nancy. Dana only hoped she was having a better time than herself. Quickly, she undressed and showered and made herself some camomile tea. Cross-legged on the floor in front of the TV set, she raised a cup to her reflection in the blank screen. 'Happy Christmas to you, too.'

At some point she must have woken cold and found

her way into her bed, but when she came round beneath the floral duvet at what felt like half-past six, she couldn't remember it. The digital clock on the floor read 11:07. The telephone was ringing. Dana stumbled towards the bathroom, rubbing the residue of make-up from around her eyes. On the way, she lifted the receiver from the body of the phone and set it down, unanswered. In the mirror she looked fifty years old.

Thirty minutes in the bathroom reduced that by all of five years. Great! Dana thought. Now I look like my mother just back from a fortnight on a health farm. She pulled on a T-shirt, sweater and old jeans. There were two mandarin orange yoghurts in the fridge and she ate them both, washing them down with some stale Evian. Well, Nancy, midday – must be having a pretty good time.

When she remembered the phone, a woman's recorded voice was instructing her to replace the hand set and redial. The moment she put the receiver back in place, it rang again.

'Hello?'

It was Nancy's mother, calling from Merseyside to wish her daughter a merry Christmas. From the background noises, the rest of the family were waiting to do the same.

'I'm sorry, Mrs Phelan, she's not here now.'

'But we thought she was spending Christmas Day with you. She said . . .'

'She is, she is. It's just . . .' It's just that she's not back yet from getting laid. 'She's popped out. A walk. You know, clear her head.'

'She's not ill?'

'Oh, no. No. Just last night, we went to this dinner-dance . . .'

There was a silence and then, indistinctly, the sound

69

of Mrs Phelan reporting back to the family. 'Be sure to tell Nancy I called,' she said when her voice came back on the line. 'I'll try again in a little while.'

Which she did several times over the next few hours. And on each occasion the questions were increasingly anxious, Dana's responses increasingly vague. When she was fast running out of excuses, Mr Phelan spoke to her himself. 'Enough of this pissing about, right? I want to know what's going on.'

Best as she could, Dana told him.

'Why on earth didn't you say that before?'

'I didn't want her mother to be upset.'

'The minute she drags herself back in,' Mr Phelan said, 'you tell her she's to call us, right?'

Right. At the far end of the line there was a sharp swerve of breath before the connection was broken.

Dana looked at the turkey taking up most of the refrigerator, the black plastic vegetable rack overloaded with several weeks' supply. She pulled a frozen broccoli lasagne, only two days past its use-by date, from the freezer and put it in the microwave. In the time it took to cook, she had looked at her watch, at the clock on the kitchen-diner wall half a dozen times. When Nancy's father next phoned, she had the directory open on her lap and was about to try the casualty department at Queen's.

'Is it like her?' Mr Phelan asked, no attempt to disguise the anxiety he was feeling. 'Not to let you know where she is?'

'I don't know.'

'You're living with her, girl.'

'Yes, but I mean ... Well, it's not as if there've been a lot of occasions ...'

'So being down there hasn't turned her into a tart,

70

her mother will be pleased. Now have I to get in the car and drive down there or what? Because it seems to me you're not treating this as seriously as you should.'

'I really don't think we have to worry, I'm sure she's fine.'

'Yes? That's what you'd want our Nancy thinking if you were the one not come home, is it?'

A pause. 'I was about to phone the hospital when you called,' Dana said.

'Good. And the police, I dare say.'

Ten

Christmas morning or no Christmas morning, Jack Skelton had been for his normal four-mile run, setting off while his wife was still apparently sleeping, returning, lightly bathed in sweat, to find her staring at him accusingly in the dressing-room mirror.

'Have fun last night, you two?' Kate asked disarmingly at breakfast.

Skelton pushed the back of the spoon down against his Shredded Wheat, breaking it into the bottom of his bowl; carefully, Alice poured tea into her cup.

'Like to have seen it,' Kate went on into the silence, 'the pair of you, dancing the light fantastic. Bet you were a regular Roy Rogers and Fred Astaire.'

'It's Ginger . . .' began Alice, sounding her exasperation.

'She knows,' Skelton said quietly.

'Then why doesn't she . . .?'

'Can't you tell when you're being wound up? It was a joke.'

'Funny sort of a joke.'

'Isn't that the usual kind?' Kate said, no disguising the malicious glint in her eye.

'Katie, that's enough,' Skelton said.

'Your trouble, young lady,' Alice said, 'you're altogether too smart behind the ears.'

'It's what comes of having such clever parents,' Kate replied.

Half out of her chair, Alice leaned sharply forwards, about to wipe the smile from her daughter's face with the back of her hand. Kate stared back at her, daring her to do exactly that. Alice picked up her cup and saucer and left the room.

With a slow shake of his head, Skelton sighed.

'Did you have a good time last night?' Kate asked, this time as though she might have cared.

'It was all right, I suppose.'

'But not great?'

Skelton almost smiled. 'Not great.'

'Neither was mine.'

'Your party?'

'All so boring and predictable. People getting drunk as fast as they were able, chucking up all over someone else's floor.'

'Tom there?'

Tom was Kate's latest, a student from the university, a bit of a high-flier; in Skelton's eyes a welcome change from the last love of her life, an unemployed goth who wore black from head to toe and claimed to be on quite good terms with the Devil.

'He was there for a bit.'

'You didn't have a row?'

Kate shook her head. 'He hates parties like that, says they're all a bunch of immature wankers.'

Skelton managed to stop himself reacting to her choice of word; besides, it sounded as if Tom had got it pretty right. 'Why on earth stay? Why not leave when he did?'

'Because he didn't ask me. And besides, they're my friends.'

The same friends, Skelton was thinking, you used to take E with at all-night raves.

'I hope you're not expecting,' Kate said, 'me to hang round here all day. I mean, just 'cause it's Christmas.'

The day wore on in silent attrition. The turkey was dry on the outside, overcooked, pink and tinged with blood close to the bone. Alice accomplished the moves from sherry to champagne to cherry brandy without breaking stride. Kate spent an hour in the bath, as long again on the phone, and then announced she was going out, not to wait up. As it was beginning to get dark Skelton appeared at the living-room door in his navy-blue track suit, new Asics running shoes.

'In training for something, Jack?' Alice asked, glancing up. 'Running away?'

Before the front door had closed, she was back with her Barbara Vine.

When Skelton returned almost an hour later, Alice was sitting with the lights out, feet up, settee pulled close to the fire. She was smoking a cigarette, a liqueur glass nearby on the floor.

'Why are you sitting in the dark?' Skelton asked.

'There was a call for you,' Alice said. 'From the station.' And as he crossed the room. 'Don't hurry. It wasn't from her.'

The pavement outside the police station was littered with broken glass. Crepe paper and tinsel hung, disconsolate, from nearby railings. In the waiting area, a young woman with half her ginger hair shaved to stubble and the remainder tightly plaited, was nursing a black mongrel dog bleeding from a badly cut ear.

'PDSA?' Skelton said to the officer on desk duty.

'Every day except Christmas, sir.'

When Skelton went close to the dog it barked and showed its teeth.

Upstairs in his office, door to the CID room open, Resnick was talking to a well-built woman Skelton took to be in her early to mid-thirties. Friend of the girl who'd gone missing, he assumed. Not a bad looker in a blousy sort of a way. At opposite sides of the room, Lynn Kellogg and Kevin Naylor were on the phones.

'When you've a minute, Charlie,' Skelton called from the doorway, 'all right?'

He was tipping ready-ground decaf into the gold filter of his new coffee machine when Resnick knocked and walked in.

'So, Charlie, where are we? Not throwing up panic signals too soon?'

Resnick waited until the superintendent had added the water, flipped the switch to on. New machine or no, he was thinking, it'll still be too weak to stand. When Skelton was back behind his desk, Resnick took a seat himself and relayed Dana Matthieson's concern over her flatmate, Nancy Phelan.

'That's not the same woman involved in that incident yesterday? Phelan?'

'At the Housing Office, yes.'

'Threatened, wasn't she?'

'In a manner of speaking.'

'The man responsible . . .'

'Gary James, sir.'

'We released him.'

'Last night, yes.'

'No suggestion he might have been involved?'

Resnick shook his head. 'Not as far as we know.'

'What happened at the Housing place, was it personal between them?'

'Not as far as we know.'

'We know damn all.'

'Very little, so far.'

Skelton crossed to the side of the room; the coffee had all but finished dripping through.

'Black, Charlie?'

'Thanks.' When the superintendent held up the glass pot of coffee, Resnick was alarmed: you could see right through it.

'You've got someone out having a word with him, James, all the same?'

'Not yet, sir.'

Skelton sat back down. 'Boyfriend?' he asked.

'No one special, not at the moment. Not according to her flatmate. She gave us some names, though. We've started checking them out.'

'Family?'

'We're in touch.'

Skelton squeezed the arms of his chair. He had never noticed before the way Alice's eyes followed him from that photograph on his desk; carefully, with forefinger and thumb, he angled her away until all she could see was the blackening brick of the city beyond the window. 'How long since anyone saw her last?'

'Nineteen hours, give or take.'

'Around midnight, then.'

'I think, sir,' Resnick said, reaching down to rest his coffee on the floor, 'the last person to see her, so far as we know, it was likely me.'

He had the superintendent's attention now, taking him through Nancy Phelan's unscheduled visit to the station, his chance meeting with her later in the hotel courtyard, the engine ticking over just beyond the edge of his vision, the car.

'Make? Number?'

Resnick shook his head. 'Saloon, four-door probably. Standard size and shape. Astra, something close.'

'Colour?'

76

'Black, possibly. Certainly dark. Dark blue. Maroon.'

'Damn it, Charlie, there's a lot of difference.'

'There wasn't a lot of light.'

'I know, and you had no reason to pay special attention.'

Which doesn't stop me, Resnick thought, from thinking that I should.

'We can't be certain, presumably, the car was waiting for her?'

'No.'

'You didn't see her get into it?'

'No.'

'So she could have been going back into the hotel?'

'It's possible, but from what she said . . . I'd guess she was about to leave.'

Skelton leaned back, locked his fingers behind his head.

'If the car, any car, had gone past me,' Resnick said, 'between there and the castle, I think I'd have noticed. But all he had to do was turn right instead of left, I'd never have seen him.'

'He?' Skelton said.

Elbows on his knees, Resnick brushed a hand across his forehead, closed his eyes.

Eleven

Dana Matthieson was sitting on the edge of a chair in Resnick's office, trying to concentrate while he double-checked the names of people who had been at the dinner, the connections between them, making sure it had all been noted down. The door to the outer office was open a couple of inches, enough to let the overlapping conversations, occasional bursts of anger or laughter slide through. It was difficult not to keep thinking about Nancy, where she might be.

'This name here,' Resnick said, 'Yvonne Warden . . .'

'Andrew's assistant. She'd have the list of invitations, everything would go through her.'

'And Andrew is?'

'Andrew Clarke. The senior partner.'

'He was there?'

Dana visualised Clarke's expression when he had asked if she wanted a lift home, did she want to pop in for coffee? The narrowing of those piggy eyes. How could she have been so naive? 'Oh, yes,' she said, 'he was there.'

Resnick wrote something on the sheet of paper. 'We should talk to him, certainly.'

'Yes,' Dana said. 'I think you should.' She was wondering if there were others in the office Clarke had tried it on with. Probably, she decided. Clarke and men like him. Carrying on as if sexual harassment was a headline they passed over in the morning paper, nothing to do with them. Men in authority and middle-age. She was looking at Resnick across his desk, tie twisted inside his shirt collar, worry lines pouched deep into his face. When she had been close to tears, earlier, blaming herself for persuading Nancy to go with her, he had been sympathetic, straightforward, done his best to assure her that her friend would turn up safe and well.

'Then why are we doing all this?' Dana had asked. 'Going to all this trouble?'

Resnick had smiled reassuringly with his eyes. 'A precaution. In case.'

Now he was standing, telling her there was nothing more. 'The minute you hear from her, you'll let us know?' Dana assured him that she would.

Resnick had spoken to Nancy's parents several times within the past hour; the mother alternately tearful and bravely matter-of-fact, her father ever closer to anger, frustrated that as yet there was no one for him to aim that anger at. Resnick spelt out all that they were doing, wanting them to feel involved, not wishing that anger to be directed at him. If Nancy's disappearance proved not to be voluntary, they were going to need the parents on their side.

'Shall you not be wanting a picture? Her mother's bound to have something recent . . .'

Resnick explained they were getting one from Dana, taken only a few weeks before. A detailed description had already been forwarded to all stations in the city, all officers on duty.

'And shall you put it, like, on tele? On the news?'

He had discussed this with Skelton, Skelton with the chief superintendent. They had decided not to go public for another twelve hours.

'I thought you were treating this as urgent? That's my bloody daughter . . .'

'Mr Phelan, we still think the most likely explanation is that Nancy decided at the last minute to spend Christmas Day with a friend.'

'Without letting anyone know?'

'It's possible.'

'Aye, and pigs might bloody fly!'

'Mr Phelan, we have to – '

'What you've got to do is get off your arse and bloody find her!'

'Mr – '

'Listen. Never mind your cock and bull theories. Whatever our Nancy took it into her head to do, Christmas Day she would have phoned her mother. And what about her friend, her as she lives with, she'd have got in touch, told her what she was up to, surely to God? I mean, how long's it take to make a phone call, after all?'

'The most likely assumption, the one we're working on, is that she met a man on Christmas Eve . . .'

'What man?'

'We don't know the answer to that yet. We're still – '

'What bloody man? Someone she knew or what?'

'Not necessarily.'

'Are you telling me my daughter's a whore?'

A hundred miles or more to the north-west, a telephone receiver was slammed against the wall. Better a whore and alive, Resnick thought, than virtuous and dead.

Naylor and Divine were working through the lists that Lynn had compiled: men that Nancy had dated, those that she'd danced with, spent significant time talking to on Christmas Eve. No way had Dana been able to swear either list was complete.

There had to be easier things to do, easier times.

Receiver cradled between chin and shoulder, Divine fumbled another extra-strong mint from its pack; finishing the call, he checked off another name on his list.

'Yes, sir,' Naylor was saying across the room, 'Phelan. P-H-E-L-A-N. Nancy. Yes, that's right.'

Deaf, Divine thought, or daft. Comatose. All those blokes having to haul themselves off the couch where they'd fallen asleep after a surfeit of mince pies and turkey. Divine hadn't surfaced till mid-afternoon himself, coming out of a bitter and Bacardi haze with a head like a rear tyre in need of a retread.

'Hello, love. Yes. Can I speak with Mr McAllister, please?'

Divine was at his desk against the rear wall, the wall where his *Sun* calendar used to hang before Lynn had lost her rag and torn it into little pieces. Pissed him off no end, that had. Kellogg getting into her hard-hat feminist routine every time her pre-menstrual cramps came visiting. Still, the one he'd bought for next year, *Page Three Lovelies*, that was already up in the bathroom at home: give himself a lift each time he stepped out of the shower.

'Hello, Mr McAllister? DC Divine here, CID.'

When Andrew Clarke's wife told him there was a police officer on the line wanting to speak with him, he had just got back from a long walk with the boys along an almost deserted beach. Gulls low over the water as the tide turned and began to roll back in. Haze of moon in the sky and the light almost gone. They had walked briskly, as briskly as one could on sand, well wrapped against the cold. Later there would be mulled wine, sandwiches, snooker, cards.

'Sure it's for me?' Clarke asked, unwinding his scarf, feeling the first signs of panic tickling his gut.

His wife had raised an eyebrow and turned back to the kitchen table.

'Hello,' Clarke said, picking up the extension in the hall, 'This is Andrew Clarke.'

At the other end of an imperfect line, Resnick identified himself and said there were a few questions concerning the Christmas Eve dinner-dance.

Oh, Christ, Clarke thought, I was right. The stupid bitch has only gone and made a complaint to the police.

'How can I help you, Detective Inspector?' he said.

'There was a young woman,' Resnick said, 'one of the guests...'

Oh God, thought Clarke, here it comes. In his mind he was erecting excuses, explanations, I'd been drinking too heavily, under severe stress at work, she led me on.

'... as far as we can tell she left at around midnight, possibly accepting a lift, and hasn't been seen since.'

'Dana,' Clarke said.

'Sorry.'

'The woman you're talking about, Dana Matthieson.'

'No. Not Dana. Her friend.'

'Friend?'

'Yes. Nancy Phelan.'

Resnick clearly heard the gear change in Andrew Clarke's breathing. 'You do know her then?' he asked.

'I'm afraid not, no. Dana, of course, she's been with us for quite a while. A good worker. Very good. Reliable, shows initiative...'

'Nancy Phelan,' Resnick said.

'No, not at all. That is, I may have met her. We

may have been introduced. I'm afraid I can't quite remember.'

'You don't remember dancing with her, for instance?'

Andrew Clarke laughed nervously, more of a bark. 'Not much of a dancer, Detective Inspector. Not my style.'

'Even so, Christmas. Special occasion. I should have thought, just to show willing . . .'

'I did dance, of course. Once or twice.'

'And that would be with Mrs Clarke?'

'My wife wasn't present, she . . .'

'With somebody else, then?'

'Of course. You don't think I'd make a fool of myself . . .'

'And this person you were dancing with, it couldn't have been Nancy?'

'No.'

'You're sure?'

'Haven't I said . . .'

'But if you're not certain you knew who she was, Nancy, isn't it possible she could have been . . .?'

'Inspector, I know the person I was dancing with.'

'And you wouldn't mind telling me, just for the . . .?'

'It was Dana Matthieson, as a matter of fact.'

'Dana.'

'Yes.'

'And at the end of the evening?'

'What do you mean?'

'As I said, to the best of our knowledge someone offered Nancy Phelan a lift in their car.'

'It wasn't me, Inspector.'

'You're sure of that?'

'Positive.'

Resnick let him have a moment of time; not too

long. 'Functions like that, Christmas Eve, it's easy to forget . . .'

'I assure you . . .'

'I mean, at first you *said* you hadn't danced, but then, when you thought about it, you remembered that you had.'

'Detective Inspector . . .'

'Mr Clarke, it's important that we compile as accurate a picture of what happened yesterday evening as possible. You realise the potential seriousness of the situation, I'm sure.'

Clarke shifted his stance so that his back was towards the kitchen door. 'As it happens I did give somebody a lift home . . .'

'I see.'

'Dana, actually.'

'Dana Matthieson.'

'Yes. She lives not so far away from me.'

'So must Nancy then.'

'I suppose so. I really don't know.'

'And you didn't see her when you drove Dana home?'

'No.'

'What happened exactly? I mean, did you just drop her off outside, did she invite you in, coffee maybe? What?'

The pause was too long. 'Outside,' Clarke said. 'I dropped her off outside.'

'And she'll confirm that? I mean, if necessary?'

'We didn't go directly there,' Clarke said, voice lowered, 'we stopped off at my place on the way.'

'For coffee,' Resnick said.

'A nightcap, yes.'

'And then you drove her home?'

'Not exactly, no.'

'Not exactly?'

'She decided to walk.'

'Wasn't that, well, a little odd? I mean, having accepted a lift from you in the first place.'

'Perhaps she wanted to clear her head.'

'Is that what she said?'

'I can't remember.'

'You can't recall what reason she gave for wanting to walk home after accepting a lift?'

'No.'

'So you had, in fact, no idea that she got home all right?'

'I assumed . . .'

'Of course. People do. But her friend, Nancy Phelan, seemingly didn't.'

'I told you, Inspector, I know nothing about that. Nothing about that at all. I may have noticed her once or twice in the course of the evening, talking with Dana. At least, I assume it was her. But later, no. I'm sorry. I wish I could be of more help.'

'When do you think you'll be back down here, sir? In the city.'

'We'd planned to stay here until after the New Year.'

'There are some addresses we still haven't been able to track down,' Resnick said. 'You've no objection if we ask your assistant for her help?'

'Yvonne? No, of course not. The firm will do anything it can.'

'And you, Mr Clarke? Yourself?'

'Of course, but I really don't see . . .'

'Thank you, Mr Clarke. Thanks for your time.'

When Andrew Clarke went back through the flagstoned kitchen, seeking out some fifteen-year-old malt, his wife remarked that for some reason he seemed to be sweating. She hoped he wasn't coming down with something, a cold.

Divine's back was aching, sitting in the same position too long, asking the same questions. Naylor had been out in search of a takeaway and returned empty handed, everywhere shut tight as an old maid's arse. Even the mints had run out.

'Oh, her with the dress and the legs,' a voice was saying at the other end of his phone. 'You kidding? Course I remember her. What about her?'

There was a moment when Dana arrived back at the flat when she was certain Nancy would be there. It lasted only as long as it took to push the front door closed behind her, slip the catch on the lock and feel the emptiness settle round her shoulders like a shroud.

Twelve

'Another cup of tea?'

'Say what?'

'Another cup of tea?'

Gary reached out and turned the TV down, unable to hear Michelle from the kitchen above the roar of pre-recorded laughter.

'Tea?'

By that time she was in the doorway, ski pants and sweater and even though the sweater hung loose he could see how she was getting her figure back after Natalie. See: he knew. Strands of hair hung loose across her face. Gary wanted to give her a look, the look towards the stairs, but he knew what she would say. Karl's this minute dropped off; the baby'll be awake soon anyway.

'Gary?'

So, all right, what was wrong with down here? Least, in front of what was left of the fire, they'd keep warm.

'C'm here,' he said.

'What for?'

But she knew the grin, the way it was meant to make her feel. 'I've got the kettle on,' she said.

'Then take it off.'

'Oh, Gary, I don't know.'

'Well, I do. Come on.' Winking. 'While it's hot.'

Pushing the hair out of her eyes, Michelle went back into the kitchen and switched the kettle off. She'd been so pleased when Gary had come home, late on Christmas Eve, relieved; she would have made love to him there and then, but all he'd wanted was to carry on about the bastard coppers, the bastard law, bastards at the Housing whose fault it all was anyway. Hadn't even wanted to see the kids. Ask after Karl. Take a look at his face.

She hadn't told Gary about that. Not any of it. The social worker, visit to the doctor, none of it. It would only make more trouble. He couldn't stand it, Gary couldn't, not ever, every Tom, Dick and Harry coming round from Social Services, barging into the place as though they owned it, telling him how to bring up his own kids.

'Get us a decent place,' that was what he'd said last time. 'Get us a decent place and then we'll bring 'em up decent, you see.'

But what if they don't, Michelle had wanted to ask? What if we have to stay here? What then?

'Michelle? You coming or what?'

When she got back into the room, he had switched off the television, turned out the light, pushed the settee closer to the fire. He was leaning back against the far end of it, legs stretched out, slightly parted. Those jeans on, no way she couldn't tell he was excited.

'Well?'

Forcing a smile on to her face, she started towards him; if only she could get the memory of him hitting Karl out of her mind, it might be all right.

He was kissing her, tongue pushing against her teeth, one hand reaching under her sweater when Lynn Kellogg knocked sharply on the door.

Lynn had talked to Dana earlier, back at the station, drinking tea and trying not to mind that the smoke from the other woman's cigarettes kept drifting into her face, irritating her eyes. What is she, Lynn thought? Six years older than me? Seven? One of those round faces, not unlike her own, in the right circumstances they were full of life; dark eyes with an energy, a glow. But sitting there, on and on about Nancy, the same details, facts, suspicions, what Dana had looked was heavy-featured, exhausted, her face flabby and pale.

'Isn't there a friend you could stay with?' Lynn had asked. 'Just for tonight. Rather than being on your own.'

But Dana had insisted, she had to be there, by the telephone when Nancy rang, by the door when she walked back in.

'You think she's all right, don't you?' Dana had said suddenly, clutching Lynn's arm. 'You do think she's all right?'

It wasn't yet twenty-four hours; there was still time for her to turn up unannounced, unharmed. A postcard. Phone call. I just had to get away, Sorry if you were worried. Chance came along and I took it. It happened all the time. People taking off on an impulse, a whim. Paris, London or Rome. Those weren't the incidents Lynn had to deal with, not closely, not often. The twenty-four hours would stretch to forty-eight and if there'd been no word from her by then, no sign . . . Well, there was still time.

Although the lights seemed to be out, she could hear voices inside; reversing her gloved hand, she knocked again.

'Yeh?' It was Gary who finally came to the door, still pushing one side of his shirt back down into his jeans. Behind him, Michelle had switched on the light.

Lynn showed Gary her warrant card and asked if she could come in.

'What's this about then?'

'It might be easier if we talked inside.'

'Easier for who?'

'Gary...' Michelle began.

'You keep out of this!'

In the centre of the room, involuntarily, Michelle flinched, a spasm of fear passing across her eyes.

Lynn set one foot on the scarred boards inside the door.

'Who said you...?'

'Gary...'

'I thought I told you...'

'Better we talk here,' Lynn said, 'than back down at the station. Surely?' Gary's head dipped and he stepped away. 'You'll not want to let too much cold in,' Lynn said. 'Night like this.' And she pushed the front door closed.

'I was going to make tea,' Michelle said.

'She'll not be here that long,' Gary said. 'This isn't going to take all night.'

'A cup of tea would be nice,' Lynn said. 'Thanks.' She smiled and Michelle headed off for the kitchen, glad to be out of there and leave the two of them alone.

Except that the settee had been moved, nothing seemed to have changed since Lynn was there the day before. The same squares of worn carpet, oddments of furniture that had come from *Family First*. Two or three Christmas streamers, held in place with pins. A few Christmas cards. Mould in the corners, damp on the walls. Despite what was left of the fire, it was cold enough for Lynn to think twice before taking off her gloves.

'Well?' Gary lit his cigarette, then dropped the spent match on the floor.

'Where were you last night?' Lynn asked.

'You know bloody well where I was last night.'

'After you were released.'

'Where the hell d'you think I was?'

'That's what I'm asking.'

'Here, of course. Where d'you think I was going to fucking go?'

In the doorway, Michelle bit her tongue; if only Gary didn't lose his temper all the time.

'So you were here all evening?'

'Yes.'

'From what time?'

'Listen, I want to know what all this's about.'

'From what time were you here?'

'From right after you bastards let me out!'

'Which would be when?' Lynn said. 'Eight? Half-past eight?'

'It was twenty to nine,' Michelle said. 'Almost exactly. I remember.'

Gary looked as though he was going to tell her to keep quiet, but he scowled instead.

'And you didn't go out again?'

'Isn't that what I just said?'

'Not exactly.'

'Well . . .' Coming towards her now, past the edge of the settee, right up close. ' . . . that's exactly what I'm saying now. I come in and I never went out. Not till this morning. Right?'

Lynn could smell his tobacco breath, warm on her face. Dinner. Beer.

'And Nancy Phelan?'

'Who?' But she could tell in his eyes that he knew.

'Nancy Phelan.'

'What about her?'

'You do know who I mean, then?'

'Course I know.'

'And did you see her?'

'When?'

'Yesterday.'

'You know bloody well . . .'

'Not at the Housing Office. Later.'

'When?'

'Any time.'

'No.'

'You didn't see Nancy at any other time?'

'No.'

'Not that evening? Later yesterday evening? Christmas Eve?'

'I told you, didn't I? I never went out.'

Michelle was hovering in the doorway. 'How d'you want your tea?' she asked.

'How d'you think she wants it? In a bastard cup.'

'I mean d'you want sugar?'

'One, thanks.'

Gary turned away disgusted. He's a kid, Lynn thought, younger than me. Stuck in this place with a wife and a couple of kids. Except she isn't even his wife. And what is he? Nineteen? Twenty? Twenty-one? Is it any wonder he needs to shout? And at me. If Divine had come round instead, she thought, Kevin Naylor, he wouldn't be carrying on like this. At least, not while they were here. The anger, he'd bottle it up for later.

She remembered the flinch of pain on Michelle's face. Karl's bruising.

Injuries consistent with the mother's story that he had run smack into a door.

'I'll give a hand with the tea,' Lynn said.

'No need,' said Gary, but he did nothing to stop her going into the kitchen.

Michelle poured in the milk first, UHT from a carton, then the tea. One tea bag, Lynn reckoned, for a large pot.

'How are the children?' Lynn asked.

'Sleeping, thank heavens. They got so excited earlier, you know, presents and everything.'

'And Karl?'

Michelle paused in sugaring their teas, spoon tilting in mid-air.

'How's Karl?'

'The doctor said . . .'

'I know what the doctor said.'

'Well, then. That's it, isn't it? He's fine.'

'He was hurt.'

'It was an accident. He . . .' Michelle's eyes flicked towards the door in response to a sudden noise: the television had been switched back on.

'The sugar,' Lynn said.

'What?'

'You're spilling the sugar.'

Lynn took the spoon from her hand and began to stir one of the mugs of weak tea.

'I never told him,' Michelle said in a rushed whisper. 'I never told him anything about it.'

'Never told me anything about what?' Gary said from the hallway, stepping into the room.

'Here,' Lynn said, handing him a mug. 'Your tea.'

'Never told me anything about what?' Ignoring her, staring at Michelle.

Michelle's hand went to her throat.

'When I was here yesterday . . .' Lynn began.

'I never knew you was here yesterday.'

93

'That's what Michelle meant,' Lynn said.

Gary was all but ignoring her now, intent upon Michelle. 'Why didn't you tell me?'

'I don't know. When you came home I was so pleased, I suppose I forgot.'

'How could you forget something like that? Bloody law . . .'

'It wasn't important,' Lynn said. 'I just dropped by, tell Michelle where you were.'

Gary had put his mug down and now he snatched at it, splashing hot tea across his hand. One taste and he had dashed it down the sink. 'What the hell d'you call that? Like bloody dishwater!'

'I'll make some fresh,' Michelle said, reaching for the kettle.

'Don't waste your time.'

Between his sullen shout and a fanfare of television sound, came a whimpering from upstairs.

'It's the baby,' Michelle said, setting the kettle back down.

'When isn't it?' Gary grumbled.

'Gary, that's not fair.'

Gary didn't care; he was on his way back into the living room, leaving Natalie to cry upstairs. Michelle looked at Lynn uncertainly.

'You go up,' Lynn said. 'I'll see to the tea.'

When Lynn came in from the kitchen, three mugs of fresh tea balanced on a breadboard she was using as a tray, Michelle was sitting in an easy chair with curved wooden arms, the baby restless against her breast. Gary was on the settee, pretending to watch the TV, sulking quietly.

Lynn drank her tea, chatting to Michelle about Natalie, keeping things as light as she could. She would have liked to have gone upstairs, taken a look at Karl, but sensed that if she asked Gary would object. Better to have another word with the social worker, let them do what they were trained to do.

When she got up to leave, Michelle went with her to the door, Gary grunting something from where he slouched that could have been goodbye.

Moving past Michelle at the door, Lynn said quietly, 'If you need someone to talk to, get in touch. Phone me. All right?'

Michelle stepped quickly back inside, shutting out the cold.

Later, as she lay curled away from Gary, listening to the suck and whine of his breathing, Michelle was unable to sleep, thinking about it. Not what Gary had said only minutes after Lynn had gone, about keeping things from him; not the ache in her ribs where he had punched her, low where it wouldn't be seen. Not those, but what he'd said when she'd asked him, the police-woman, if he'd gone out again that night, Christmas Eve. Why he'd lied.

Thirteen

'Kevin?'

  'Sshh!'

'What time is it?'

'Early. You go back to sleep.'

'The baby . . .'

'I gave her a drink and she went off again.'

Debbie rolled on to her side, face to the pillow. It was dark in the room, even the gap at the top of the curtains, where they refused to meet, offering no light.

'You're on an early.'

'Yes.' Dressed in all but his jacket, Kevin sat on the edge of the bed, close to her bare arm.

'I'm sorry, I forgot.'

Lightly stroking her shoulder, Kevin smiled. 'Doesn't matter.'

'You used to hate that.'

'What?'

Slowly lifting her face, a thin skein of spittle stretched from the pillow to the corner of her mouth until it snapped. 'When I used to forget your rota, which hours you were on.'

'I used to hate a lot of things.' Her mouth was damp and warm and musty from sleep. 'Love you,' he said.

'I know,' Debbie said. She brought her other arm around him, crook of her elbow tightening against his neck. One breast slipped free from the Snoopy T-shirt she wore in bed.

'I'll be late.'

'I know,' Debbie said.

She kissed him hard and let him go.

Pulling the front door shut and stepping out on to the street, the same, now familiar feeling closed cold around his stomach: how close he had come to losing this, all of it, letting it go.

Resnick had woken something short of four, finally got up at five. When he had opened the garden door to Dizzy, the black cat had entered with sprung step and hoisted tail as if there were nothing new in this. Below freezing outside, Dizzy's fur was sleek and tinged with frost.

Resnick warmed him milk in the pan, testing the temperature with his finger before pouring it into the dish. The cat's purrs filled the kitchen as it ate and Resnick sipped hot black coffee: a secret between them, no one else awake.

The first news of Nancy Phelan's disappearance would go out on the local news at six, would possibly rate a minor mention on the national network an hour later. Jack Skelton had called a meeting for nine. The evidence, such as it was, would be assembled, evaluated, broken down; assignments would be made, which interviews warranted following up, which gaps had still to be filled. Her father's pain and anger on the phone. Doing everything we can. He remembered the way Nancy had looked in the otherwise empty CID room, red coat unbuttoned and loose at her shoulders. Later that evening, the voice that had seemed to come from nowhere, silver of her smile, breath that had hung between them in the air.

*

97

'Very well, ladies and gents, let's come to order if you please.'

The new DCI wore his Wolverhampton Polytechnic education like a thin veneer; a supercilious smugness which his Black Country vowels disavowed. Recently promoted over the pair of them, Malcolm Grafton was ten years younger than either Resnick or Reg Cossall – as Reg never failed to remark.

'Jesus, Charlie! You don't think he wore those for his interview, do you?'

As Grafton had resumed his seat on the platform, one leg had crossed high over the other, revealing a sock that looked, as Reg Cossall remarked, as if it had been dipped in a late-night curry disaster then hung on the line to dry.

Resnick grunted and kept his own counsel; only a while back he had noticed he was wearing odd socks himself, dark blue and maroon. No wonder he hadn't pinned down the colour of the car waiting to drive Nancy Phelan away.

'For the present, we're looking at three areas for the possible abductor . . .' Jack Skelton was on his feet now, gesturing towards the boards to his right. ' . . . boy-friends, men friends, call them what you will, that's for starters; guests at the hotel on Christmas Eve – initially that's those at the same architects' do as her, but ulti-mately anyone and everyone who used the place that evening.' A groan from the assembled officers at this. 'And lastly, at the moment no more than an outside chance, this man, Gary James.'

Heads swivelled to where Skelton was now pointing and Gary's whippet face stared back at them, full-on, from between twin profiles, left and right.

'As most of you'll know,' Skelton continued, 'there was an incident at the Housing Office the same afternoon, James became violent, offered threats to various personnel, including the missing woman, Nancy Phelan, whom he kept a prisoner in her office for a time. The initial grudge he has against her seemed to stem from an argument over the housing allocated to James, his common-law wife and their two children. Whether, as a result of anything that happened yesterday, it's gone beyond that, we don't know.'

Skelton stepped back, seeking out Lynn Kellogg through the rising haze of tobacco smoke. 'Lynn, you saw him yesterday, I believe.'

Slightly self-conscious, buttoning then unbuttoning the front of her jacket, Lynn got to her feet.

'I spoke with James yesterday, sir. Claims he was home the later part of the evening and his wife, Michelle Paley, that is, she supports him in that.'

'You think he's telling the truth?'

'I've no reason not to think so.'

'But you're not convinced.'

A pause. 'No, sir.'

'The woman, Michelle, she'd lie to alibi him?'

Without hesitation, Lynn said, 'She'd be frightened not to.'

'Knocks her about, does he?'

'No direct evidence, sir. No obvious signs. But he's got a temper; flares up out of nothing. And there are the injuries to the little boy.'

'I understood we'd cleared that up?' Skelton was looking towards Resnick now. 'Clean bill of health.'

'According to the doctor,' Resnick said, half out of his chair, 'bruising and swelling tallied with the mother's story. Accidental injury.'

'But you think it could be something else?'

Resnick shrugged. 'Possible.'

'The situation's being watched?'

'Social Services, yes.'

Skelton nodded gravely, pressing the tips of his fingers tight together; Resnick lowered himself back into his seat.

Lynn was still on her feet.

'Yes?' Skelton said.

'I was wondering, sir, whether that was enough. The whole situation there, I don't know, it's like something waiting to explode.'

'We've heard, Social Services are keeping an eye . . .'

'Even so, overstretched the way they are . . .'

'And we're not?' There was more than a touch of anger in Skelton's voice.

'But if James is a strong suspect . . .'

'Is he? Is that what we're saying? He's really a viable suspect here?'

Lynn didn't answer; glanced across at Resnick for support. At the back of the room, Kevin Naylor shuffled his feet and looked embarrassed on her behalf.

'Are you saying it's possible,' Malcolm Grafton put in, 'that James could have been the driver of that car, waiting to whisk Nancy Phelan away?'

'We don't know that's what happened,' Resnick said.

'Best bet, Charlie. Your call.' Grafton leaned back and recrossed his legs, giving his socks another airing. 'Got to be where we're looking, surely? Not this sorry bugger. Knocking his wife and kids about, throwing chairs at women clerks, that's his mark.'

'That doesn't mean – ' Lynn began, colour leaping to her cheeks.

'Lynn . . .' Resnick was out of his seat, faster this time.

'You're not suggesting, sir,' Lynn said, gripping the chair in front of her hard, 'that domestic violence . . .'

'I think what the DCI means . . .'

'Thank you, Charlie, but I don't need an interpreter,' Grafton said.

'Just a decent pair of socks,' murmured Reg Cossall.

'Our concern here is finding Nancy Phelan, what happened to her,' Grafton continued. 'Anything else, it gets in the way.'

Slowly, Lynn sat back down.

''Bout chuffing time!' Divine said to no one in particular. 'Now we can get bloody on.'

Grafton allowed himself a quick smirk.

'Nevertheless,' Resnick said, 'man with a record of violence, currently on probation, already subjected the missing woman to an actual assault, we wouldn't be dropping him from our enquiries entirely. Would we?'

Grafton stared down at him through narrowed eyes.

'A watching brief, Charlie, your team.' Skelton was back on his feet, quick to intervene. 'Not priority, though; that's Nancy Phelan's boyfriends, they're down to you. Reg . . .'

'Here we bloody go!' stage-whispered Cossall.

' . . . the guests at the hotel, if you please. Malcolm's arranging for you to have some extra bodies.'

'Old ones he's done with, is that, then?'

'Sorry?'

'Nothing, sir. You're all right.'

As Skelton continued, Cossall leaned towards Resnick, talking behind the back of his hand. 'Ever occur to you, Charlie, if any one of us was going home to his little semi of an evening, carving up corpses and stuffing 'em into plastic bags, our Malcolm up there's your man?'

There had been fifty-seven guests at the dinner: Andrew Clarke's assistant had provided the names, almost all of the addresses. Times of departure would be ascertained and, where possible, double-checked; modes of transport, makes and types of car. When was the last time that evening they remembered seeing Nancy Phelan? Where had that been? Who had she been with?

Once that had been done, answers compared and tabulated, leads and questions followed up, the lists, still slowly being compiled, of the hotel's other clients would be waiting. Somewhere between three and four hundred in total – without casual callers at the bar.

Reg Cossall, extra bodies or no, was going to have his work cut out.

Resnick was in his office with Lynn Kellogg, Naylor and Divine, looking at the names Dana Matthieson had supplied of the four men Nancy had recently been involved with. Patrick McAllister. Eric Capaldi. James Guillery. Robin Hidden. Divine had already talked to McAllister on the phone and was due to call on him that afternoon. Naylor had made contact with Guillery's parents, who had informed him their son was on holiday in Italy, skiing, and wasn't expected back until after the New Year. Eric Capaldi's answerphone offered some blurry piano music and not a lot else. Robin Hidden had so far remained, well, hidden.

'It's not possible,' Kevin Naylor said, 'there's others? I mean, that her flatmate didn't know about?'

'As far as I know,' Dana had said. 'This's who she'd been seeing. The only ones she talked about, anyway.'

'You think there could have been someone else then? That she never mentioned.'

'It's always possible.'

'Was she secretive, though? Things like that?'

'Not specially. But, you know ... there's always

somebody, isn't there? Whatever reason, the one you won't talk about, not even to your best friend.'

Is there? Resnick had thought.

And then – yes, of course.

Now, prompted by Naylor's question, he thought of Andrew Clarke. Was that the kind of relationship Dana had been hinting at? Older, married, somebody where she worked?

'The receptionist from the Housing Office,' Resnick said.

'Penny Langridge,' Lynn read from her notes.

'Have a word with her, see if there was anything between Nancy Phelan and any of her colleagues, something she might not have wanted broadcast about.'

'Quick knee-trembler back of the typing pool,' Divine grinned. 'That the sort of thing?'

Lynn shot him a quick angry look. Any other time, Resnick thought, she would have had a sharp remark to go with it. But now part of her mind was on other things.

The minute Resnick was alone in his office the phone rang: it was Graham Millington calling from his in-laws in Taunton, just this minute heard about the missing girl on the news and wondering if they could use him back at the station.

Fourteen

Graham Millington had met his wife in the Ladies' lavatory of Creek Road Primary School, a little after eleven in the morning and caught short in the middle of a talk to forty-seven ten-year-olds. Millington, not his wife.

One thing he hated above all others, worse than charging into the ruck of a Friday night bar-room fight with glass flying, barging into the Trent End on a Saturday afternoon to collar the smart-arse bastard who's just felled the visiting goalie with a sharpened fifty-pence piece to the head, was standing in front of a class of kids in his best suit and behaviour, lecturing them on the dangers of solvent abuse and underage drinking. Knowing sneers on their scrubbed little faces.

And this particular morning, fielding the usual sporadic questions about aeroplane glue and which brands set to work fastest, he was overcome by a sharp sudden pain deep behind his scrotum, an urgent message that he needed to pee.

'I wonder...' he stammered to the deputy head-teacher, sitting at the corner table, filling out what suspiciously resembled a job application. 'Could you...?'

The nature of Millington's discomfort was clear for all to see.

'First right down the corridor, second left.'

Millington remembered it wrong, first right, first

left instead. He was just easing himself through his fly, looking wildly for the appropriate stall, when, with a swift whoosh of water, Madeleine Johnstone stepped out from the cubicle in her bottle-green Laura Ashley dress, pale green tights, sensible shoes.

'Sorry, I . . .'

'Here,' Madeleine said, pushing open the cubicle door, 'you'd better go in here.' And then, as he dived past her, slamming the door shut and fumbling the bolt across, 'I'll keep watch outside.'

Something wrong, she thought, out there in the corridor surrounded by all that project work on Third World hunger, a man of his age with problems of the prostate.

He had met her next in the Victoria Centre, Madeleine backing out of the Early Learning Centre, weighed down with plastic bags of presents for her sister with the twins, Millington whistling his way across to Thorntons, mind set on a quarter-pound of peppermint creams, maybe the odd Viennese Whirl.

'Sorry!' as he cannoned into her and a slew of carefully designed and educationally approved packages spilled around his feet.

He knew that she had recognised him by the way her eyes flickered downwards in the direction of his trousers, checking that he wasn't flashing at her in artificially reproduced daylight.

Millington picked up a package of brightly coloured balls (eighteen months to three years) and set it in her hand. She suggested tea and led him to the coffee bar in Next where he perched uncomfortably on a black leather stool and ate a teacake that tasted oddly of lemon.

'It's because they use the same board,' Madeleine explained, 'for making the salad and buttering those.'

The girl who served them was black and disdainful and her dark hair was curled like spun glass.

'She lovely, isn't she?' Madeleine said, following Millington's hopeless gaze.

Even Millington, perhaps not the most sensitive of men, understood this meant what about me? Look at me.

Madeleine was broad at the shoulders, narrow to the hips, good strong calves that suggested lots of school-girl hockey or netball or both. She had brown hair a few shades short of chestnut, a healthy down on her upper lip, eyes that were disconcertingly blue. A complexion like that, Millington wagered a week's wages she came from somewhere south, Sussex or Kent or further south-west, soft winds and cream.

Some detective, it had taken him till now to check the third finger of her left hand.

'They're not for me, if that's what you're thinking.' Madeleine glanced at the bags by her feet. 'My sister. Twins. It runs in the family.'

Something inside Millington shuddered.

'It's considered old-fashioned, nowadays, isn't it?' Madeleine said. 'For men to wear wedding rings.'

They hadn't been able to have children. Not so far. Not for want of trying. Whatever was in the family, the genes, the almost careless fecundity of her several sisters, it wasn't there for them. They had had therapy, tests, everything short of acupuncture, the thought of which had reduced Millington's eyes to tears. 'Graham, they don't put the needle there.' It hadn't mattered; acupuncture was out.

Madeleine applied for promotion and was rewarded; she embarked upon a never-ending series of self-improvement classes, everything from Chinese cuisine through European languages to British Visionary art and beyond. On the kitchen wall she kept a chart, colour-coded, on which she annotated the ages and birthdays of her nieces and nephews so that none would go uncelebrated, unremarked.

Christmas, in her parents' vast house in Taunton, had been a maelstrom of unrestrained young middle-class voices, each intent on clamouring its instant needs above the rest. Madeleine and her sisters had sat around the oak table that had once graced the refectory of a nearby abbey and laughed about old photographs, old jokes. And all around them, in and out and up and down, the children ran and ran, with only the occasional, 'Oh, Jeremy!', 'Oh, Tabetha! Now see what you've done!' to acknowledge they were there at all.

Millington had listened to her father's ideas on law and order and the breakdown of family, the lack of respect for authority and the failure of religion, the seemingly equivalent evils of the single-parent family and the admission of women priests into the Church. Even grace on Christmas Day had been accompanied by a sideswipe at leniency towards young offenders, before sinking the knife deep inside the bird.

'Are you all right?' Madeleine asked from time to time, passing him by chance.

'Me? Yes, of course. Fine.'

And then she had been off again, attention tugged away by some tousled three-year-old pulling at her sleeve. 'Oh, yes, Miranda, that's lovely! Let's go and show it to Granny, shall we?'

He had been seeking refuge in the bathroom when he had heard the news, trimming the ends of his moustache for want of something better to do. The small Roberts portable, dusted with talcum powder on the shelf, had been left on low. Hearing the city's name, he had turned the volume up. A young woman who had gone missing on Christmas Eve; the parents' concern; police investigations proceeding.

Millington had used the drawing-room phone. 'Graham, sir. Wondering if I could be any use.'

'How soon can you get here?' Resnick had said.

Millington grinning as he weaved his way between small children, opening doors, looking for his wife so he could tell her sorry, but there was no alternative, he was leaving.

Fifteen

'Made a real fool of myself, didn't I?' Lynn was sharing a cemetery bench with Resnick, one of the few places near the police station it was possible to find sanctuary. In front of them, the ground dipped away steeply, paths winding between Victorian tombstones raised in loving memory of Herbert or Edith or Mary Ellen, aged two years and three months, gone to a better place. In the middle distance, beyond Waverley Street, the green of the Arboretum shone dully in mid-winter sun.

Resnick finished chewing a mouthful of chicken salad sandwich. 'You said what you thought needed saying.'

'It wasn't the time,' Lynn said. 'And standing up to Grafton like that, it was stupid.'

'What he said wasn't over-bright.'

'But tactically . . .' Lynn shook her head. 'If I stopped to challenge every statement by a senior officer that was sexist or insensitive, how long d'you think I'd last in CID? Never mind promotion.'

Resnick crunched down into a pickled cucumber, head dipping forward in a vain attempt to prevent vinegar splashing across his shirt.

'What would really worry me,' Lynn went on, 'would be if it meant Gary James didn't get taken seriously. You know, just Lynn again, riding another of her hobby horses.'

Resnick grinned ruefully. 'People have been saying that about me for years.'

Lynn looked back at him. She didn't say and where's that got you, because she didn't have to. They both knew a younger, less experienced man had been promoted over him.

'You really fancy him for this, James? Nancy Phelan?'

'If not for that, then for something.'

'The kiddie.'

'Maybe.'

Resnick's stomach stirred uneasily. 'You've been back to Social Services?'

'Martin Wrigglesworth, yes. Well, I've tried. Left messages, but so far he's not come back to me. Off duty, bound to be.'

Getting to his feet, Resnick screwed the paper bag that had held his lunch into a ball, brushed crumbs from the front of his coat. 'Let's hope you don't have to wait till after the New Year.'

As they were walking back through the archway towards the broad sweep of road, Lynn prompted him about Gary James' probation officer. 'Pam Van Allen, I do think she'd be more likely to talk to you than me. You never know, she might throw some light.'

Without any great enthusiasm, Resnick nodded. 'I've got Nancy Phelan's parents in half an hour. After that, I'll see what I can do.'

The holiday traffic was light enough to allow them across all four lanes and on to the central island without breaking stride. A dusty Ford Prefect with its off-side door painted a different colour was just turning into the car park alongside the police station: Mr and Mrs Phelan had arrived early.

Harry Phelan's father and grandfather had worked on the Albert Dock before it became a home for shopping boutiques and an art gallery; Harry had grown up with every intention of following in their footsteps. But by the time he was ripe to leave school, the writing had been scrawled all too clearly on the wall and he had got himself apprenticed at Raleigh making cycles and moved to the East Midlands. Now that trade, too, was virtually dead and the family had moved back to its roots.

Harry was a tall man, strongly built, with failing sandy hair, a fair moustache and broad hands which sprouted reddish hair between the knuckles. His tie was knotted too tight and he tugged at it constantly, this way and that. His wife, Clarise, no more than a couple of inches above five foot, wide at the hip and big at the bust, was forever fidgeting with the black handbag that she held in her lap, always close to tears.

Resnick saw them with Jack Skelton, four seats pulled round in the superintendent's office, one of the uniformed PCs bringing a pot of tea from the canteen, Rich Tea biscuits overlapping on a small plate.

Increasingly agitated, Harry Phelan listened to the explanations of what steps had been taken, which directions the investigation was following. What he wanted to hear about were arrests, appeals, rewards, not computerised cross-checks, methodical questioning, the gradual elimination of people from the enquiry.

'Looks like,' he said finally, 'you're treating this about as serious as someone lost their second-best sodding coat!'

'Harry, don't,' said Clarise, fumbling a small square handkerchief from her bag.

'One of your lot, we'd see something different, no two ways about that.'

'Mr Phelan, I can only assure you . . .' Skelton began.

But Phelan was on his feet now, chair pushed back against the wall. 'And I can assure you . . .' jabbing a hand in the superintendent's direction, ' . . . if someone doesn't pull his finger out here, I'll raise such a bloody stink, you'll be back on the beat and lucky for it.'

'Harry,' begged Clarise, 'you'll not do any good.'

'No? What bloody will, then?' He pointed at Skelton again, swinging his arm wide to include Resnick also. 'Forty-eight hours, that's what they reckon, isn't it? Forty-eight hours. If you don't find them in that, likely they're sodding dead!'

'Oh, Harry!' Clarise Phelan covered her face with her hands and began, loudly, to cry.

Resnick was out of his chair, moving automatically to comfort her, when Harry Phelan set himself in his way. There was no avoiding the anger, bright in Phelan's eyes. For a moment Resnick held his stare; then slowly he backed away, sat back down.

'Come on,' Phelan said, taking hold of his wife's arm. 'We're only wasting our time here.'

'When are you going back?' Skelton asked, as they walked away.

'We're not going bloody anywhere. We're staying here till this is sorted.' He didn't add, one way or another.

'Is there an address, then,' Skelton asked, 'where we can contact you?'

Harry Phelan gave them the name of a small hotel on the Mansfield Road.

'You'll have to forgive him,' Clarise said through her tears. 'He's upset, that's what it is.'

Harry bustled her into the corridor, slamming the door shut behind them.

Skelton and Resnick sat for some little time, avoid-

112

ing each other's eye, saying nothing. Skelton tried a mouthful of tea, but it was cold. When Resnick moved, it was to look at his watch. 'Little under ten hours to go.'

Skelton raised an eyebrow.

'Till it's forty-eight,' Resnick said.

Divine and Naylor visited Patrick McAllister together. His address was in Old Lenton, a factory that once had made fruit machines and which since had been transformed into an apartment block for upwardly mobile singles and young couples passing through. McAllister was waiting for them at the head of the stairs, khaki chinos and artificially faded check shirt, deft handshake, blokes-together smile. Happy to invite them inside.

They asked him questions as they looked around.

Sure, McAllister said, he knew Nancy Phelan. Had done. Been out with her quite a few times, matter of fact. Clubbing, you know, pictures once or twice, evening or two in the pub. Nice girl, lively, spoke her mind. Liked that about her. Couldn't stand women who sat there all night, no more than half a dozen words to their name and two of those, please and thanks.

There were photographs on the wall in the small living room, McAllister with various young women; others clamped to the front of the fridge by magnetic fruit, raspberries, pineapples and bananas. Divine lifted one of those clear and took it towards the light.

'Here . . .'

'Don't mind, do you?'

McAllister shrugged and shook his head.

'Where's this, then?' Divine asked. McAllister was sitting outside a café, somewhere warm, white shirt

113

open over red trunks; alongside him, Nancy Phelan was smiling, holding a tall glass of something cool towards the camera. She was wearing a pale bikini top and tight shorts and she looked lithe and tanned. Divine could see why McAllister would have wanted to get involved.

'Majorca,' McAllister said.

'You went on holiday together?' Naylor asked.

'Where we met. June. She was there with that pal of hers.'

'Dana Matthieson?'

'That's her.'

'Holiday romance, then,' Naylor said.

'How it started, I suppose. Yes.'

'Love at first bite,' Divine said, slipping a corner of the photograph back beneath a plastic banana.

'Sorry?' McAllister said.

'Nothing.'

'How long did you carry on seeing her?' Naylor asked. 'Once you got home.'

'Couple of months, more or less.'

They were looking at him, waiting for more.

'You know,' he shrugged, managing to avoid looking at either of them, 'way it goes.'

'She dumped you,' Divine said.

'Like hell!'

'She didn't dump you.'

'No.'

'You dumped her.'

'Not exactly.'

'What exactly?' Divine was enjoying this.

Through one of the small windows, Naylor could see a man wheeling his bike beside a narrow strip of canal; an older man, almost certainly asleep, fishing.

'We just stopped seeing one another.' McAllister's

expression suggested they should understand, men of the world, it happened all the time.

'No reason?'

'Look . . .'

'Yes?'

'I don't see the point of all these . . .'

'Questions?'

'Yes. It's not as if . . .'

'What?'

McAllister seemed to be getting a little warm for the time of year, but then the room was small. The cuffs of his shirt were folded back just one turn. 'I saw it on the news. Christmas Eve, too, it's hard to believe. Girl like that.' He looked first at Naylor and then at Divine. 'I don't suppose you want – should have asked – cup of coffee? Tea?'

'What do you mean?' Naylor asked. 'A girl like that?'

McAllister took his time. 'You always think, don't you . . . I mean, it might not be fair, but what you think, well, maybe they weren't too bright, couldn't see what was coming . . . You know what I mean?'

'Who are we talking about?' Naylor said.

'These women you read about, getting themselves kidnapped, attacked, whatever. Agreeing to meet some bloke they don't know, stuff like that.' He flexed his shoulders, hands in pockets. 'Try getting Nancy to agree to something she didn't want to do, forget it.'

Divine glanced over at Kevin Naylor and grinned.

'Where were you on Christmas Eve?' Naylor asked, notebook at the ready.

'The Cookie Club.'

'You're sure?'

'Of course, I'm . . .'

'All evening?'

115

'From – oh, what? – ten-thirty, eleven.'

'And before?'

'Er, couple of drinks in the Baltimore Exchange, few more in Old Orleans, Christmas Eve, you know how it is. Fetched up at the Cookie, yes, not later than eleven. Eleven-thirty, the very outside.'

'And you stayed till?'

'One. One-fifteen. Walked home. There was a line waiting for a cab on the square, hundred, hundred and fifty deep.'

'You've got witnesses,' Divine asked.

'Witnesses?'

'Someone who'll back up your story, swear you were where you say.'

'Yes, I suppose so. I wasn't on my own, if that's what you mean. Yes, there were people, friends. Yes, of course.'

'You'll give us the names?' said Naylor. 'So we can check.'

McAllister's mouth was dry and his eyes were starting to sting; damn central heating. 'Look, I suppose you have to do this, but . . .'

'When did you last see her?' asked Divine, moving in.

'Nancy?' Wetting his lips with his tongue.

'Who else?'

'Six weeks ago? No more.'

'Date, was it?' Divine was close to him now, close enough to smell the heady mix of aftershave and sweat.

'Not exactly, no.'

Divine smiled with his eyes and the edges of his mouth and waited.

'A quick drink, that was all. The Baltimore.'

'You go there a lot.'

'It's near.'

Not to say overpriced, Divine thought. That's if you can get someone to serve you in the first place.

'I haven't seen her since,' McAllister said. 'You've got my word.'

'So what d'you reckon?' Naylor asked.

They were crossing the narrow street towards the car. In front of them was the Queen's Medical Centre and Divine had a quick memory of Lesley Bruton teasing him with her offer to model underwear. Over a day now and there'd been no fresh news of poor bloody Raju, still languishing in Intensive Care.

'Well?' Naylor was standing by the nearside door.

'No doubt about it,' Divine said. 'She dumped him.'

Sixteen

There were times, Resnick knew, what you didn't do was play Billie Holiday singing 'Our Love is Here to Stay'; when it was self-pitying, not to say foolish, to listen to her jaunty meander through 'They Can't Take That Away From Me' because it felt as if they already had. What was okay was Ben Webster wailing through 'Cottontail', the version with Oscar Peterson kicking out on the piano; Jimmy Witherspoon assuring the Monterey Jazz Festival 'Tain't Nobody's Business What I Do'. Or what he set to play now, Barney Kessel's 'to swing or not to swing' with its lower-case title and dictionary definitions on the cover. The tracks he liked best were up-tempo, carefree, Georgie Auld sitting in on tenor, 'Moten Swing', 'Indiana'.

Bud cradled along one arm, he went down the steps into the kitchen and began opening fresh tins of cat food, pouring milk, surveying the interior of the fridge for the sandwich he was going to make himself later. It was true, it appeared, Reg Cossall was intent upon getting his name in the registrar's book for the third time. The woman in question was the matron at an old people's home out past Long Eaton. Bright-faced and bonny, Resnick had met her twice and she had scarcely seemed to stop laughing. 'Getting set for your retirement then, Reg?' a foolhardy DC had suggested. Cossall had been all for castrating him with his reserve set of dentures.

As he ground coffee, Resnick tried to think what it was about Reg Cossall – sour, cynical and foul-mouthed – that made him such an attractive proposition. But then, Charlie, he thought, waiting for the water to come to the boil, it isn't as if you haven't had offers either.

Marian Witczak, waiting for him to step into her peculiar time-warp, careful not to broach the possibility herself, of course, relying on old friends at the Polish Club to do the hinting for her. And then there had been Claire Millinder, the estate agent engaged in the fruitless task of moving him out of this Victorian mausoleum into something compact and modern with a microwave oven and flush doors you could punch a hole through with your fist. 'What does it have to be with you, Charlie? True love?' The last he had heard, Claire had gone back to New Zealand; there had been a card from the Bay of Plenty where she and her fruit-farmer lover were raising kiwi fruit and babies.

There was a small moan of complaint from near his feet as Dizzy hustled in on Bud's bowl and Resnick scooped up the big cat by its belly and put him out in the garden.

Maybe it didn't have to be true love, after all; nor love of any kind.

He poured himself a small scotch, a bottle of fifteen-year-old Springbank single malt he'd won in the CID raffle, and took it, together with his black coffee, into the front room.

Pam Van Allen's number was in the phone book. Turning down the stereo, he dialled. What had it been? Certainly less than a year ago, walking into that wine bar opposite the snooker hall, their first and last meeting: alone at a table close against the wall, an open book and a glass of wine, perfectly self-contained. He knew that calling her now was a mistake, crass, stupid, but before he could break the connection, she had answered.

'Hello?' The tightness of her voice there in just that word.

'Oh, Pam Van Allen...?'

'Yes?'

'Charlie Resnick.'

'Who?'

'Detective Inspector...'

'What gives you the right to call me at home? And today? This is a public holiday.'

'I know and I'm sorry, but if it wasn't important...'

'Get to the point, Inspector.'

'Gary James, he's one of your clients, I believe...'

'And I'll be in my office tomorrow morning. As long as you're not trawling for information to which you have no right, you can contact me there.'

And the conversation was over. Resnick eyed the receiver as though it might have been some way responsible for Pam Van Allen's anger, then placed it carefully down. Not much of a whisky man, nevertheless he downed it in one. With a mock-cheery coda, Barney Kessel's 'Twelfth Street Rag' pranced to a close. In the room it was silent. Resnick stroked Pepper, knuckle of one finger behind its ear, until the cat began to purr.

He was back in the kitchen, shaving several-day-old Stilton on to a mixture of duck meat and tomato, when the phone rang.

'I'm sorry about that. You caught us in the middle of an almighty row.'

The 'us' resonated in Resnick's mind. 'That's okay,' he said.

'But then,' Pam Van Allen continued, 'it *is* Boxing Day.'

He thought if he could see her she might almost be smiling. 'Well, is it all right now, to talk, I mean? If you're in the middle of something . . .'

'It's fine. Seconds are out, I think. I'm in the bedroom. Getting my second wind.'

Resnick tried to picture it; tried not to.

'You wanted to say something about Gary James?'

'More ask something, really.'

'Ah-huh.'

'Share some information . . .'

'Share?'

'Of course.'

This time he heard her laugh. 'A little early for New Year's resolutions, isn't it, Inspector?'

'Charlie.'

'What?'

'It's my name.'

'Inspector comes more easily to the tongue.'

Sidestepping his best intentions, Resnick's mind hopped into the unseen bedroom. Was she really resting, pillows propped up behind her, legs stretching slimly before her? Jesus, Resnick thought! What is the matter with me?

'Share away,' Pam said.

He told her about the incident at the Housing Office, about Nancy Phelan's disappearance, Lynn's suspicions about the injuries to Karl's face.

There was silence at the other end of the line, Pam Van Allen thinking. 'You want to know what I think he's capable of?' she said eventually.

'I want to know anything that might be useful.'

After more consideration, Pam said: 'I've got time for him, Gary; he gives one kind of impression, but he's not as bad as you might think. It would have been easy for him to have left Michelle alone with those two kids, lots of men in his place would. It's not even as if they were married. But he's not like that, Gary. Not irresponsible. Not really. But the situation he's in, no work and not for lack of trying, precious little money, a house that either wants a small fortune spending on it or knocking down, it's no wonder he gets frustrated and that the frustration shows. And he has got a temper. He is physical. The education he had, it's all he can be.'

She gave Resnick time for that to sink in.

'So if you're asking me, could he have struck out at that lad of his, I'd have said he could; just like being kept sitting around at Housing could get him banging the odd chair about. None of it's premeditated though, and that's what I can't see. Gary bearing that kind of a grudge, planning something out, some kind of revenge, waiting to carry it out.'

Resnick thought a few moments more, weighing up what Pam Van Allen had said. 'Thanks, I appreciate that. I value your opinion. I'll pass it on to my DC.'

'Glad I could help.' There was another pause in which Resnick struggled for the right thing to say and he was sure she was about to say goodbye. Instead she said, 'Last time we spoke, you said something about a drink or something, after work.'

'Yes.'

'Well?'

'You said you'd get back to me. You were going to think about it.'

With a smile in her voice, she said, 'I lied.'

'I see.'

'But I'm thinking about it now.'

'And?'

'Can I call you? Next couple of days?'

'Of course.'

Muffled in the background, Resnick could hear another voice raised. 'Round two,' Pam Van Allen said, and for the second time that evening broke the connection.

Gary's pal from up the street had knocked before nine, on his way to the corner pub. 'Spent up,' Gary had said, but Brian pulled a twenty-pound note from his back pocket and flourished it with a whistle. 'Jammy bugger!' Gary had exclaimed. 'Where d'you get that?' 'Sharon's gran,' Brian grinned, 'sent it her for Christmas.' Michelle had almost said something, but she bit her tongue instead. No sense in risking an argument. Not another. 'Not be late,' Gary had said, and off they'd gone, wide-eyed and laughing, a couple of great kids.

As well he left when he did, really, because within fifteen minutes Karl started screaming from upstairs, some kind of nightmare, and Michelle had to go up and comfort him, take him a drink and sit with him awhile until he was ready to go back to sleep. It was cold in there, not as cold as the night before, but still Karl's legs were like ice under the covers and, too early to carry him downstairs for the night, she put him in their bed, hers and Gary's, and doubled the blankets round him. Natalie woke soon after and Michelle changed and fed her and sat with her down on the sofa, Natalie asleep against her breast while she watched a comedy show with Bobby Davro.

The clock said five to ten and despite what Gary had said she knew he wouldn't be back till chucking-out time. Gone. She made up her mind that by then she would have the children tucked up down here, the kettle on in case Gary fancied a last-minute cup of tea, and be ready herself for bed.

At least Gary didn't get riled up when he had a drink or two inside him, not the way it was with some. Didn't get randy, neither. She'd heard from Brian's wife about him stumbling home late, not able to get the key in his own front door, but still expecting her to do it with him the minute he got into the house. What Gary did was fall asleep. Get a bit cuddly first, he would, snuggling up to her back and mumbling away, nothing she could ever understand, and then after a while he'd roll on to his back, fast off. Sweet, he looked then, lying there with a sort of smile on his face, young, too, really young.

The news was on now, Michelle thinking she would get up and switch it over, switch off. But little Natalie's head was just so, her breath warm close against Michelle's skin. Missing since before Christmas, the newscaster said, and there was a photograph of her there, dark hair, down past her shoulders, the woman she and Gary had been to see together at the Housing, the one who, after a lot of prodding and pushing and form-filling, had found them the place they were now. Nancy Phelan.

Michelle was on her feet, pacing, the baby whimpering a little, upset at being disturbed. All of the questions that policewoman had been asking. Have you seen her? When have you seen her? At the Housing Office? Not later? Not later?

The news had moved on to another item, a tanker aground somewhere north of Scotland, but Michelle could still hear the newscaster's words: last seen late on Christmas Eve, shortly before midnight.

Gary standing up to her, the policewoman. 'I come in and I never went out. Not till morning. Right?'

Michelle's hands around the baby were clammy and cold.

'You didn't see Nancy at any other time?' the police-woman had asked.

'I told you, didn't I? I never went out.'

Michelle pressed her mouth softly against Natalie's head, hair that was light as feathers and faint. 'If you need someone to talk to, get in touch.'

Michelle's legs were beginning to shake.

Seventeen

Robin Hidden put through a call to the police station at ten-thirty-five on Boxing Day Night. He had been sinking a pint of Boddington's in a pub in Lancaster; earlier that day he had been climbing on the east side of the Lakes and then driven back, muscles pleasantly aching, to his friend Mark's place near the university to dump their boots and change their clothes. They were sitting in the small bar, in front of them plates that had once held pie and chips and gravy, now wiped clean with doorsteps of bread and butter. The beer was going down a treat, backs of their legs just beginning to stiffen. The television set had been on in the other bar, attached to a bracket high on the wall, and Mark had chanced to glance over his shoulder as the picture of Nancy flashed on to the screen.

'Hey! Isn't that . . .?'

By the time they had hobbled through into the main room, Robin fumbling with his glasses, the programme had moved on and scarcely anyone they asked had paid much attention to what had gone before.

'Christ knows, pal,' someone had said, 'but whatever it was, it weren't good, you can bank on that.'

'That lassie,' the barman said, pulling a pint, 'gone missing. Didn't know her, did you?'

Robin Hidden pulled a five-pound note from his trouser pocket and placed it on the counter. 'Ch-change please, as m-much as you can. For the phone.'

The constable who took the call wouldn't give a lot of detail, only the facts, such as they were known, simple and unadorned. He listened when Robin said that he had known Nancy, known her well, wrote down his name and asked a few questions of his own.

'When would it be convenient for you to come into the station, sir? I'm sure one of the officers dealing with the case would like to talk to you, face to face as it were, possibly make a statement.'

Robin's first reaction had been to drive back down there and then; but he'd had two pints of beer, as Mark pointed out; and driving all that way in his condition, he'd be lucky not to get cramp in his legs.

'You'll fall asleep at the wheel,' Mark said. 'What's to be gained from that? Far better to sleep now, set the alarm for half-five, get an early start.'

'Mid-morning,' Robin Hidden told the officer. 'I'll be there by mid-morning at the latest.'

'Very well, sir. I'll be sure to pass that on. Goodnight.'

Mark gave his friend's shoulder a sympathetic squeeze. Not that he wanted anything awful to have happened to Nancy, of course, but the way Robin had been mooning on about her all the time they were walking... Besides, they'd never really been suited, anyone who knew Robin could tell that.

James Guillery's parents had tried contacting their son in Aosta, but the hotel he was supposed to be staying at denied all knowledge of him; there had been a mix-up with the travel agency, over-booking. They were given two other numbers, one of which seemed to be permanently engaged, while dialling the other resulted in a high-pitched, unbroken tone which suggested it was unobtainable. The travel agency was closed and its answering machine swallowed the Guillerys' message half-way through.

'I don't know how he met her,' Mrs Guillery said. 'Nancy, that is. Wherever it was, he went out with her a few times . . .'

'More than a few,' Mr Guillery put in.

'Do you think so? Yes, well, I suppose it was. Though I don't think it was ever what I'd call serious.'

'He wasn't going to marry her, that's what she means,' Mr Guillery interpreted.

'No, what I mean, James seemed to like her well enough, that is, he spoke well of her, but, as I said, it never occurred to me they were what I'd call serious.'

'What she doesn't understand,' Mr Guillery confided, 'young people today, it's not the same. Not like it was even in our day. Young people today, they can be serious without being serious. If you see what I mean.'

Eric Capaldi's neighbours in Beeston Rylands knew very little about him, beyond the fact that he was an engineer for BBC Radio Nottingham. Or was it Radio Trent? He owned a sports car, not new, one of those little jobs, close to the ground; forever stretching an old blanket and a piece of tarpaulin on the street, he was, then crawling underneath the engine.

One person thought he might have recognised Nancy Phelan from her photo as someone he'd once seen Eric with, but he couldn't swear to it. How could he? Late evening it had been and the street lights down there, all very well for the council to be saving money, but when you could hardly see a hand in front of your face without there was a moon, that couldn't be right, could it?

The woman on the switchboard at Radio Nottingham confirmed that Mr Capaldi was on a fortnight's leave and she had no idea where he had gone. Yes, certainly, if it was important she would try to find out. Who was it calling?

Andrew Clarke kept a half-size snooker table in the room that was still called the breakfast room and he shut himself in there with a bottle of sherry and practised running through the balls on the table, all the reds and then the colours, right up to the black. Steadying each shot, remembering to bend low, eye along the cue, right hand firm.

'You don't think, Andrew,' his wife said when she found him there, 'you ought to go back down?'

'Whatever for?' The brown was a fraction too close to the cushion and he chipped it back next to the D.

'Well, you are sort of involved.'

'Nonsense.' Better shot now, let the cue ball spin back for the green.

'It was your affair . . .'

'Affair?'

'Your do, that she disappeared from.'

'That hardly makes me responsible.'

Audrey wished he would look at her when he spoke, not keep wandering round the blessed table all the time, squinting down at all those balls like a general poring over a battle plan. 'Besides,' she said, moving herself so that she was close to his eye line, 'isn't she your librarian's best friend or something?'

'Dana, mm. Live together, I believe. Flat-share, not you know . . .' He made his shot and the green rolled slowly towards the pocket and hovered there, close to the rim, refusing to drop out of sight.

'Not what, Andrew?'

With something of a sigh, he straightened and

reached for the chalk. 'I mean they're not – what-d'you-call-it? – gay.'

'Really? However would you know?'

'Surely you can tell?'

'I don't know. Can you? I shouldn't have thought it was that easy. Especially nowadays.'

'Likes the men, too much, Dana. You've met her, seen the way she dresses. Christmas Eve, for instance, more out of that frock or whatever it was than in.'

'Andrew, I don't think all lesbians have their hair cut short and wear motor-cycle suits.'

For a moment, he stared at her; he didn't think he had ever heard his wife say the word lesbian before.

'Anyway,' Audrey Clarke tasted the tip of her forefinger; she had been making tartlets with lemon cheese. 'It's just not like you, that's all. You're so anxious to be on top of things. As a rule.'

'Audrey, if I thought my presence would make the least difference, I should be there already. As it is, I'm on holiday and I intend to enjoy it. With you.'

There had been a time when Audrey Clarke had found that somewhat anxious smile of her husband's attractive, skin furrowing deep between his eyes; she supposed she must have.

'I'm popping out,' she said, 'stroll down by the sea.'

He watched her walk away, a middle-aged woman in a long tweed skirt, a barbour jacket and green wellington boots, a Liberty print scarf tied about her head. When she was well clear of the house, Andrew Clarke looked up Dana Matthieson's home number and dialled it from the hall.

The answerphone clicked on first and Andrew was lowering the receiver when Dana's voice broke through. 'Nancy? Nancy, is that you?'

'It's Andrew,' he said, more high-pitched than he

had intended. 'Andrew Clarke. I was just wondering how you were. I mean . . .'

But Dana had hung up and he was left talking to the air.

'Bastard!' she whispered softly to herself. 'Bastard!'

Dana was squatting by the low table where she had taken the call. She had been getting out of the bath when Andrew Clarke had phoned and she had two towels carelessly round her, water trickling on to the floor. Every time she looked in a mirror and saw her mascara smeared down her face again, she told herself she was through with crying, she had no more tears left. Shivering, she clasped her arms across her chest and rocked lightly heel to toe, forwards and back, crying again.

Eighteen

'So, Charlie, getting any closer, d'you think?' Skelton had both hands flat against the wall, arms straight, stretching his legs muscles till they were fully taut; last thing he wanted, running back up Derby Road, one of his hamstrings going.

Resnick shrugged. 'This lad Hidden's coming in today, all accounts he was the one went out with her most recent.'

'And the bloke Divine and Naylor checked out yesterday?' Skelton was lifting one leg with his hand, fingers around the toe of his running shoe, holding it so that the heel touched his buttock, right leg first and then the left.

'Got an alibi for all the relevant times. We're checking it out. But what I've heard, I don't fancy him, frankly.'

'The car, Charlie, that's the key.'

Resnick nodded: as if he needed reminding.

'You've not come up with anything more yourself? Not got a clearer picture?'

Stubborn as a stain, the dark blur clung to the edge of Resnick's vision, refusing to take on true colour or shape, its driver a notion of a person, nothing more.

'Someone offered her a lift, Charlie, no two ways. Like as not, someone she didn't know, met that evening, fancied her, danced with her a bit, like as not.

Whisked her off with his eye to the main chance. After that, who knows?'

With any luck, Cossall and his team would have pushed through their initial enquiries by the end of the day. Matching men and cars that had been present. After that, it would be a slow process of elimination. And time, they knew, was the one thing Nancy Phelan likely didn't have.

'There's a press conference at three,' Skelton said. 'Her parents'll be there, too. Not what I'd've wanted, but nothing I could do about it. So if you think Hidden's going to lead us anywhere, you'll let me know as soon as you can.'

'Right.'

Skelton turned away, jogged a few paces on the spot, lifting his knees, then set out along the pavement at a tidy pace, fumes from the incoming traffic dancing round his head.

Resnick knew it was Graham Millington in the Gents' as soon as he arrived at the door. From inside, the unmistakable sound of Millington whistling his merry way through the songs from the shows told him that his sergeant was back on duty.

' "Phantom of the Opera", Graham?'

' "Carousel", that,' Millington said, slightly offended. 'Wife and I went down to see it in London before Christmas. That Patricia Routledge – never've thought she'd have a voice like that, never.'

He shook himself a few more times, just to be sure, zipped up and stepped away. 'That song – what is it? – "You'll Never Walk Alone", scarce a dry eye in the house.'

'Fellow coming in this morning,' Resnick said,

'Nancy Phelan's boyfriend. Sit in with me on that, will you?'

'Right.' Checking in the mirror, Millington brushed a few flecks of white from the shoulders of his dark suit. Dandruff best not be coming back, he thought he'd seen the last of that. 'Right, I'll be there.'

And he sauntered off into the corridor, reinterpreting Rodgers and Hammerstein with an atonality that would have made Schoenberg proud.

Robin Hidden was late. Three sets of roadworks on the M6, a caravan overturned on the A1M. He was perspiring beneath his sweater and corduroy trousers when he made his way into the station, stammering when he announced his name. It was something that happened when he was feeling excited or stressed. Nancy had teased him about it, how the words he called out when they were making love came in spurts.

'Robin Hidden?'

Startled, he looked round to find a man with a roundish face and trim moustache, smart suit and neatly knotted tie. 'Detective Sergeant Millington.'

Robin didn't know if he were supposed to shake hands with him or not.

'If you'll just come with me.'

He followed the sergeant up two steeply winding flights of stairs and right along a corridor to an open door; behind this was an empty space, nothing that you could call a room, and beyond that another door.

'Through here, sir, if you please.'

This was more what he had been expecting, what he had seen on the television, the table, plain, pushed over towards the side wall, empty chairs on either side. What he'd been less sure of, the tape machine on a shelf at the rear, double recording decks, a six-pack of cassettes, cellophane-wrapped, waiting to be used.

'Mr Hidden, this is Detective Inspector Resnick.'

A large man coming towards him, holding out his hand; the grip was firm and quick and almost before it was broken, the inspector and his sergeant pulling out their chairs, sitting down. Waiting for him to follow suit.

'Should be some tea along, any minute now,' said Resnick, glancing back towards the door.

'Likely need something,' Millington added pleasantly. 'Long drive like that.'

'If you want to smoke . . .' Resnick said.

'Have to be your own, though,' Millington smiled. 'Getting my resolutions in ahead of the New Year.'

'It's all right, thanks,' Robin Hidden said. 'I don't.'

'Wise,' said Millington. 'Sensible.'

There was a knock on the door and a uniformed officer came in with three cups on a tray, spoons, several sachets of sugar.

'You heard about Nancy how?' Resnick asked.

'Television news, this pub in Lancaster . . .'

'You'd been walking?'

'Yes, I . . .'

'Alone, or . . .?'

Robin shook his head. 'With a friend.'

'Female or . . .?'

'Male. Mark. He's . . .'

'Oh, that doesn't matter,' said Millington, reaching for his tea. 'Not now.'

Robin tried to tear a corner of the sugar with his fingers and failed; when he used his teeth, half of the contents spilled down his arms and across the table.

'Not to worry,' Millington said. 'Good for the mice.'

Robin had no idea if he were joking or not.

135

'Nancy,' Resnick said, 'how was it you met her?' As if it were something he already knew but just couldn't call to mind.

'The marathon . . .'

'Local?'

'The Robin Hood one, yes.'

'You were both running?'

'N-no. Just me. Nancy was watching. Lenton Road, where it goes through the Park. I got cramp. Really bad. I had to stop and, well, lie down, massage my leg till it went off. N-Nancy was there, with her friend, where I dropped out.'

'You got to talking?'

'They asked me if I was okay, if I n-needed a hand.'

'And did you?'

'No, but she said, Nancy's friend said . . .'

'Is that Dana?'

'Y-yes. She said if ever I wanted someone to rub in Ralgex, she knew someone who'd be happy to oblige.'

'Meaning herself?'

'M-meaning Nancy.'

'Took her up on it, then?' Millington smiled. He was doing a lot of smiling today; glad to be back at work, away from Taunton, back in tandem with the boss, enjoying it. 'Kind of offer doesn't come every day. Not when you're already down to your shorts, I dare say.'

'I didn't take it seriously. Thought they were just joking, having me on, but before I got back in the race, Nancy said, "Here," and gave me her phone number. Corner of her Sunday paper.'

'Stick it down your athletic support?' Millington wondered. 'Keep warm.'

Robin shook his head. 'In my shoe.'

Millington smiled again and looked across at

Resnick, who was jotting odd words on a sheet of paper.

'Sh-shouldn't we . . .?' Robin said a moment later, glancing over his shoulder at the tape machine.

'Oh, no,' Millington said. 'I don't think so. Just background this. An informal chat.'

Why, then, Robin Hidden wondered, didn't it feel like that?

Dana had been thinking about Robin Hidden that afternoon, walking in Wollaton Park, making a series of slow circuits around the lake, scarf knotted high at her neck. His body aside – and it had seemed a good body, right from their first sight of him there had been no doubt about that – she could never see the attraction. He wasn't especially interesting, no more than run-of-the-mill, a medium-grade job with the Inland Revenue, something at Nottingham 2. Evenings out with Robin seemed to consist of a visit to the Showcase to watch *Howard's End*, then rhogon josh and a peshwari nan at the curry place on Derby Road. Better still, letting Nancy cook pork and mushroom stroganoff and eating it in front of the telly, Robin blinking behind his glasses at a programme about the disappearing llamas of Peru. The only time she had seen him really come to life had been when he was planning their weekend walking in the Malvern Hills, designed to get Nancy in shape, get her prepared for the mountains to come.

Yet Nancy had seemed happy with him, content anyway, more than with the others. Eric, who, when he wasn't whisking her round motor accessory shops on a Sunday to buy bits and pieces for his car, used to drag her off to the back rooms of pubs to listen to bands with names like Megabite Disaster. Or that weirdo Guillery, who wore combat boots and woollies his mum had knitted him and persuaded Nancy to go to horror movies, where they sat in the front row and ate popcorn. Once, according to Nancy, after they'd gone to bed together – a strange experience in itself, apparently, though she wouldn't go into detail – Guillery had insisted on reading her his favourite bits from something called 'Slugs' while he stroked her inner thigh with his big toe.

All of them, though, were preferable to that smart-arse McAllister they'd had the misfortune to meet when she and Nancy had both been under the influence of too much sun and Campari. She'd even fancied him herself, God help her! A Paul Smith T-snirt and a subscription to *GQ* – would have been a yuppie if he'd known what it meant. A brain the size of a mange-tout out of season and, though she'd never actually asked Nancy, most likely a dick to match.

A pair of Canada geese rose up from the far side of the lake, completed a lazy circle above the trees, and skidded back on to the icy water near where she stood. Hadn't she read somewhere that they'd stopped migrating and there were council workmen in some London park going out at dawn to shoot them? She couldn't recall if that were true or why it might be.

Nor why it was that Nancy, who was bright and certainly good-looking, anything but lacking in confidence, had so much trouble finding a man who was any kind of a match? By the time you got to her own age, you could start to say they had all been snapped up or they were gay; but Nancy, still in her twenties, seemed, nevertheless, to go from one near-disaster to another.

Maybe that was what had made Robin Hidden so appealing: the oddest thing about him was probably that he laced his hiking boots up the wrong way. Was that what Nancy had been doing? Cutting her losses and thinking of settling down? Babies and Wainwright's guide to the White Peak with Mr Dependable?

'Serious, then, Robin, is it? Between the two of you, you know?'

'I – I'm not sure I do.'

'Not just fooling around.'

'No.'

'True love, then?'

Robin Hidden blushed. There was half an inch of tea, cold, at the bottom of his cup and he drank it down. 'I love her, yes.'

'And does she love you?' Resnick asked.

'I don't know. I think so. But I don't know. I think she doesn't know herself.'

'You'd say you were close, though?'

'Oh, yes.'

'Close enough to spend holidays together, for instance?'

'Yes, I think so. C-certainly, yes. We went ...'

'Not Christmas Day, though?'

'Sorry?'

'You hadn't planned to spend it together, Christmas Day?'

'No, I was going to ... usually, I went to my parents', they live in Glossop, and Nancy, she wanted to keep D-Dana company. D-didn't want her to be on her own.'

'You went on from Glossop up to the Lakes, then?' Millington asked. 'Boxing Day?'

'Early. Yes.'

'And you drove up to your parents' when? Christmas Eve?'

'No.'

139

'Not Christmas Eve?'

Robin Hidden swallowed air. 'C-Christmas D-Day.'

'So you were here on Christmas Eve?' Resnick asked, leaning forward a little, not too much. 'In the city?'

'Yes.'

'Strange, isn't it,' Millington said, almost offhandedly, 'you didn't see one another, you and Nancy, Christmas Eve? Specially since you weren't going to be together Christmas Day. Close like you were.'

Sweat trickled into Robin's eyes and he wiped it away. 'I asked her,' he said.

'To see you Christmas Eve?'

'She said no.'

'Why was that?'

Robin wiped the palms of his hands along his trouser legs.

'Why did she say no, Robin?' Resnick asked again.

'We'd h-had this, well, not row exactly, discussion, I suppose you'd say, a couple of days before. She'd said, Nancy had said, let's go out to dinner, somewhere nice, special, my treat. It wasn't easy, getting a booking, you know what it's like, Christmas week, but we did, that place in Hockley, fish and vegetarian, it's called . . . it's called . . . stupid, I can't remember . . .'

'It doesn't matter,' Resnick said quietly, 'what it's called.'

'I suppose I was excited,' Robin said, 'you know, about us. I thought she'd made up her mind. Because she hadn't seemed certain, one time to the next, like I said before, what she felt, but I was sure, since she'd made such a thing out of going there, she was going to say she felt the same as me. I w-was p-p-positive. I said let's go out again, Christmas Eve, r-really celebrate. She said she was sorry but she realised she wasn't

140

being f-fair to me, leading me on; she didn't want to see me again, ever.'

Robin Hidden lowered his face into his hands and behind them he might have been crying. Reaching out, Resnick gave his arm a squeeze. Millington winked across at Resnick and got to his feet, signalling he was going to organise more tea.

Nineteen

Robin Hidden's car was parked close against the side wall, steeply angled across from the green metal post which had the security amera bolted near the top. He had bought it nine months before, the deposit borrowed from his parents when his father's redundancy money had finally come through. The remainder he was paying off over three years at a reasonable interest.

'A bit on the large size, isn't it, son,' his dad had asked, 'should have thought one of them compact jobs, two doors, Fiesta or a Nova, more the kind of thing for you. More economical, too.'

But Robin had fancied something comfortable for cruising along the motorway, weekends; throw your walking gear in the back and you were away. Friday nights, once the traffic had fallen off, setting out for Brecon Beacons, Dartmoor, Striding Edge. Travel back on Sunday with a minimum of stress. If a friend or two from the office fancied coming along, which occasionally they did, no problem, plenty of room.

After a little shopping around, he'd tracked this one down to a garage on Mapperley Top, one owner only, sales rep it was true, but one advantage of all that high mileage was it kept the price down within reason. 'No,' he had told his father, just this past couple of days, 'good investment, that. No doubt about it.'

Resnick and Millington saw it first on the monitor, black and white, picture vibrating a touch as the

142

camera shivered in the wind. From just outside the rear door of the station, the vantage point of the top step, they could see the way the dirt of its recent journey had risen in waves above the car's wheels, had been smeared by inefficient wipers across the windscreen in faint curves. The aerial, partly withdrawn, was bent over near the tip. A good car, though. Reliable. Robin Hidden's Vauxhall Cavalier, J registration, midnight blue.

They had left him alone in the interview room, door wide open. Just a few minutes, sir, if you wouldn't mind hanging on. The tea was strong and this time there were biscuits, digestives and a chipped lemon cream. He could walk out and down the stairs and be in the street in moments. There was nothing they could do to stop him. Surely. Here of his own volition. Anyone with information . . .

Footsteps approached along the corridor and, automatically, he sat straighter in his chair, brushed biscuit crumbs from his thighs. The steps carried on past.

'It's over then, is it?' his friend Mark had asked. 'You and Nancy?'

Oh, yes. It was over.

'So what are you telling me, Charlie? You've got a suspect or not?'

'Early days, sir.'

Skelton frowned. 'Try telling that to the girl's father.'

'Better than giving him false hope.'

Skelton sighed, turned towards the window, checked his watch. The car that was to drive him to the Central Station and the afternoon press conference would appear at any minute, up the hill from the city.

'You're saying about the Cavalier . . .?'

'It could be the one.'

'Could?'

'No way I can be sure. But the shape, the colour . . .'

'The registration?'

Resnick shook his head.

'Jesus, Charlie!' The superintendent moved round from behind his desk, shook a clean handkerchief from his pocket, cleared his nose, glanced quickly at the contents of the handkerchief before slipping it back. 'How about – a friend of the missing woman, providing useful background information?'

'Say that and it's like breathing murder suspect down the back of their necks. They'll have his picture on the front pages by tomorrow's first editions.'

Skelton sighed again. 'You're right. Better to say nothing. Let them think we're bumbling around, slow and steady, chasing our tails. Till we've got something more.'

Resnick nodded, headed for the door.

'Gut feeling, Charlie?'

'Ditching him the way she did, she hurt him more than he's letting show.'

'Enough to want to cause her harm?'

'Sometimes,' Resnick said, 'it's the only way people think they've got of making the pain stop.'

'I don't want to say it,' Mark had said. They were out on a ledge overhanging a valley swathed in mist. Mars bars and a thermos of coffee laced with scotch. Careful not to stop for too long and let the muscles seize up.

'Then don't,' Robin had said.

'You should never have got mixed up with her in the first place.'

'Mark, come on . . .'

'Well, she wasn't exactly your type.'

144

'Exactly.'

'Exactly what?'

'That was why, wasn't it. Because she wasn't some Ramblers Association groupie who couldn't see beyond the next youth hostelling weekend in the Wrekin. She wasn't like anyone I'd ever been with before and I'm not likely to find someone like that again.'

Mark tipped the flask high over the cup, shaking out every last drop. 'Girls like her, two a penny.'

The way Robin had looked at him then, rearing up, for all the world as if he might have thrust out an arm, sent his friend hurtling from the ledge.

'Hey!' Mark had shouted, swinging back, alarmed. 'Don't take it out on me. I'm not the one led you on and then said, thanks very much, goodbye. That was her. Remember? If you want to take out your anger on someone, take it out on her.'

And Robin had stood close to the edge, very close, staring down. 'I'm not angry with Nancy. What right have I got to be angry with her?'

'Mr Hidden?' Millington said. 'Robin?' He'd been so bound up in what he was thinking, remembering, he hadn't noticed the sergeant coming back into the room. 'There are just a few points we'd like to clarify,' Millington said. 'If you can spare us the time.'

Robin Hidden barely nodded, blinked and turned his chair back in towards the table. Millington closed the door and waited for Resnick to sit down before crossing to the tape machine.

'I thought this was the same as before? Just a few things, you said.'

'So it is,' Resnick said.

Millington took hold of the tab between forefinger and thumb and pulled, freeing the tape from its wrapping, did the same with a second, slotted them both into place. Twin decks.

'For your protection,' Resnick said. 'An accurate record of what you've said.'

'Is that what I need?' Robin asked. 'Protection?'

'This interview,' Millington began, sitting down, 'is being recorded on the twenty-seventh of December at . . .' Checking his watch, ' . . . eleven minutes past two. Present are Robin Hidden, Detective Inspector Resnick and Detective Sergeant Millington.'

'What we're interested in, Robin,' Resnick said, 'is where you were, late on Christmas Eve.'

It was a slow day in Fleet Street. No coded messages from the IRA to Samaritans' offices, giving details of bombs left outside army barracks or in shopping centres; no cabinet ministers with their fingers caught in the Treasury till or the knickers of women other than their wives; no photographs of starving children newsworthy enough after the Christmas overkill; no gays to bash, no foreigners to trash, no sex, no drugs, no rock 'n' roll.

So it wasn't only the local Midlands press who were there at the news conference, nor had the Nationals sent their stringers merely; these were the big boys, men and women with serious expense accounts and bylines, the real McCoy. Both Central TV and the BBC had their cameras loaded and ready, each had earmarked Skelton for seperate interviews later, one on one. A researcher from 'Crimewatch' was there with rubber-covered notebook and mobile phone.

Four papers, two dailies and two Sundays, were primed to speak with the Phelans afterwards, sound them out about an exclusive contract – 'Our Daughter

Nancy' – in the tragic eventuality that when she was found she was dead.

– 'So are you saying, Superintendent, that after all of this activity, the police have no leads at all? Either as to the whereabouts of the girl or the possible identity of her abductor?'

– 'Would you tell us, Mrs Phelan, just what you're feeling about your daughter's disappearance?'

– 'Mr Phelan, would you care to comment on the way in which the police investigation has been conducted so far?'

'So you went back out at around ten then, Robin?'

'Yes.'

'Nothing special in mind?'

'No.'

'No plan, no destination?'

'No.'

'And you were in the car?'

'Yes.'

'The Cavalier?'

'Yes.'

'And you just drove?'

'Yes.'

'Around the city?'

'Yes.'

'Round and round?'

'Y-yes.'

'You never stopped once?'

Robin Hidden nodded his head.

'Does that indicate yes or no?' Millington asked.

'Y-yes.'

'You stopped the car?' Resnick said.

'Once or tw-twice, yes.'

'Where was this?'

'I d-don't remember.'

'Try.'

The whirr of the tape machine faint in the background.

'Once by the square.'

'Which side of the square?'

'Outside Halfords.'

'Where else?'

'King Street.'

'What for?'

'S-sorry?'

'Why did you stop on King Street?'

'I was hungry, I wanted something to eat. A burger, cheeseburger. Chips, you know, fries.'

'Where from?'

'Burger King.'

'And you parked on King Street?'

'It was the nearest I could get.'

'Nancy,' Resnick said, 'you knew where she was spending Christmas Eve?'

'With Dana, yes. At this stupid dance.'

'But you knew where?'

'Where what?'

'Where it was being held,' Resnick said.

'This stupid dance,' Millington smiled.

'Robin, you knew where it was, the dinner-dance? Dana's firm's function, you knew where . . .?'

'Yes, of course . . .'

'Where Nancy was?'

'Yes.'

'And you drove round all that time – what? – two hours, give or take. Round and around the centre and you never went, never once went near where you knew she would be?'

Robin Hidden's body had half-turned in his chair

and he was staring at the floor; it looked as far off, as hazy and unclear as a valley viewed from some high place. 'If you want to take out your anger on someone,' Mark had said, 'take it out on her.'

'Not on the off-chance,' Millington said, leaning in a little closer, 'that you might bump into her?'

'Catch a glimpse?' Resnick said.

'All r-r-right, so what if I did? So what if I went by there, by the stupid bloody hotel, all those idiots dressed up like clowns, prancing about and flashing off their money, so what if I did?'

'You did go to the hotel then, Robin? That night?'

'Isn't that what I just said?'

'Did you drive past outside or did you turn into the courtyard, by the main doors?'

'The courtyard.'

'I'm sorry, could you say that more clearly.'

'The courtyard. I d-drove into the courtyard.'

'And parked?'

'Yes.'

'What time was this?'

'About . . . about . . . it must've been j-just before twelve.'

'And that was when you saw Nancy? When you were parked in the hotel courtyard a little before midnight on Christmas Eve?'

'Yes,' Robin said. 'That's right.' His voice seemed to come from a long way off.

Twenty

Dana had spent the first hour that morning sorting out her room, tidying away things she'd long forgotten existed. By the time that particular task was over she had filled four plastic bin bags with clothes, three of which would be passed on either to Oxfam or Cancer Research, the other – mostly things which were too worn, too soiled or simply beyond repair – she would put out for the bin men.

That done, she defrosted the freezer, cleaned the cooker – the surface, not the oven, she wasn't that much in need of distraction – wiped round the bath. She was on her knees, rubbing a Jif-laden J-cloth around the inside of the toilet bowl when she remembered a scene from a film she'd seen recently: a young woman – that actress, the one from 'Single White Female', not her, the other one – giving the inside of the lavatory bowl a shine with the blue T-shirt some man had left behind.

What she would have liked to have done with Andrew Clarke was push his head down till his nose reached the U-bend and hold him there while she flushed the chain.

What she might do, Dana thought, up on her feet with a new spring to her step, was sue the bastard for sexual harassment in the workplace. See what that did for his senior partnership, his place in the country, his snazzy little sports car.

She switched on the radio, a few minutes of Suede and she clicked it back off; fumbling through her tapes for Rod Stewart, she hesitated over Eric Clapton or Dire Straits, finally found what she was looking for inside the cassette box labelled Elton John. This was more like it. Old Rod. 'Maggie May'; 'Hot legs'. Forget the new haircut, remember the bum. Listlessly she flicked through the pages of *Vanity Fair*. One more thing, sort through the drawers of her dressing table, and then she'd get out to the shops, buy herself something she didn't really need in the sales.

Her mood lasted as long as finding one of Nancy's earrings jumbled amongst her own: it came back to her then like cold wind, chilling her where she stood; she didn't think she would ever see Nancy again.

Kevin Naylor had taken the call from the hospital, listened a moment, before holding out the receiver towards Divine. 'For you.'

'This is Staff Nurse Bruton, it's about Mr Raju.'

Poor sod's bought it, Divine thought.

'He's been making a good recovery, and he's certainly well enough now to be able to talk to you.'

'Well,' Divine said, 'the thing is, something big's come up here, this woman that's gone missing, and I really don't know . . .'

'He could have died,' Lesley Bruton said.

'Sorry?'

'Mr Raju, what those youths did to him, he could have died.'

'I know, I'm sorry and . . .'

'And it doesn't matter?'

'Look, I should have thought you'd have been pleased. I mean, this is a woman this has happened to and . . .'

'And this is only an Asian man.'

Oh, Christ, Divine thought, here we go.

'I'll tell him you're too busy, then, shall I?'

'No,' Divine said.

'Perhaps you could send somebody else?'

'No, it's okay . . .' Looking at his watch, ' . . . I could be there in forty minutes, give or take. How'd that be?'

'If he has a relapse,' Lesley Bruton said, 'I'll try to let you know.'

The queue just to get into Next was right across the pavement outside Yates's and curled, four-deep, around the corner and up Market Street as high as Guava Records. Warehouse was hip to hip with customers eager for the twenty-five to fifty per cent markdowns and Monsoon was crammed with well-bred women over thirty-five wearing what they'd bought at last year's sale.

Dana walked up past the futon shop into Hockley and considered treating herself to lunch in Sonny's; discretion sent her down Goose Gate to Browne's Wine Bar, a glass of dry house white and a chicken salad baguette. One glass became two and then three and from there it was a short, less than steady walk to the architects' office where she worked.

'Closed till January 3rd', read the card in neat black italic calligraphy taped to the centre of the door.

She had the keys in her bag.

For a while, she wandered from room to room, past the drawing boards and the intricately made models and into the library where she worked amidst carefully cross-catalogued collections of slides and plans.

She walked back to Andrew Clarke's office. Only gradually, sitting on the corner of his matt-black executive desk, toying with the lipstick she had bought that morning at Debenhams, did the idea form, in Moroccan Scarlet, in her mind.

For all that Raju was out of the woods, Divine thought, he still had one hell of a lot of British taxpayer's money hooked up to him, one way and another. It was all he could do to manoeuvre a place to park his chair amongst all those stands and tubes and dials.

But old Raju, now he was propped up and looking perky, he came up with the goods as far as descriptions were concerned. One of the youths, the one who had done all the talking, the one'd who tapped on his window for him to stop, he had a small scar, the shape of a half-moon, there, underneath his right eye. And fair hair. Very, very fair. Divine knew full well none of the other witnesses had said anything about fair hair.

'You're positive,' he said, 'about the hair?'

'Oh, yes. Indeed.'

More than likely, the bugger's still a bit delirious, Divine thought.

The second youth, the one who had hit him from behind, Raju was sure that he had several tattoos along his arms. Some kind of strange creature on one of them, a serpent maybe, something like that. Someone on a horse. A knight? Yes, he supposed that was right. And a Union Jack. No confusion about that. But left arm or right – no, sorry, he couldn't say.

'Age?' Divine asked.

'The age you would expect. Young men. Sixteen or seventeen.'

'No older?'

Raju shook his head and the movement made him draw a sharp breath. 'A year or two, perhaps. No more.'

Divine closed his notebook and eased back his chair.

'You will be able to catch them now?'

'Oh, yes. Now we're armed with this. Two shakes of a dog's tail.'

Leaning back against his pillows, Raju, smiling, closed his eyes.

Lesley Bruton was talking into the telephone at the nurses' station and Divine had to bide his time until she was through. 'Thanks a lot,' he said. 'Raju, there. Tipping me the wink.'

She looked back at him, saying nothing, waiting.

'Look,' Divine said, 'I was thinking. You wouldn't fancy coming out for a drink sometime?'

'This is,' Lesley Bruton said, 'some kind of a joke? Right?' And she brushed past Divine so close he had to step out of the way; it was three-fifteen and she had an enema to organise.

'Have you got a solicitor, Mr Hidden?' Graham Millington asked.

They were in the corridor outside the interview room. After his second session, Robin had been decidedly shaky and they had suggested he walk up and down for a bit, make sure the windows were open, get some fresh air. Voices rose and fell along the stairways at either end. Someone's personal radio flared to life, overloud. Behind doors, the muted clamour of telephones.

'No, why? I don't see . . .'

'It might be as well if you contacted one. If there isn't anyone you know personally, there's a list we can provide.'

Robin Hidden stared into the sergeant's face, the brown, unblinking eyes, curl of the mouth beneath a moustache so perfect it could have been a fake.

'I thought once I'd answered all of your questions, it would be all right for me to leave,' he said.

154

The mouth widened to a smile. 'Oh, no, I don't think so, Mr Hidden. Not quite yet. Not now.'

Twenty-one

The solicitor appointed to represent Robin Hidden was David Welch, a forty-nine-year-old bachelor with two small Jack Russells, which he left in the back of his BMW, with a request to the officer on the desk that they be let out to do their business after a couple of hours.

Welch was experienced but lazy; some years before he had realised that he lacked certain requisites for a really successful career. He lacked a wife, but clearly he wasn't gay; he was neither a Mason, nor a Rotarian, nor the possessor of the right stripe of school or college tie; not driven by burning ambition, he had never successfully cultivated the appearance of someone sure to succeed. Poor David, he didn't play bridge or poker; he didn't even play golf. He had looked around and understood the score. It would have been possible to move to another practice, another city, start again; he could have sought a new career – what he had settled for was an easy life.

'Your client's waiting, Mr Welch,' Millington said. 'Along the corridor, third on the left.'

'I suppose you've been allowing him all the proper breaks? Rest periods? A decent meal?'

'Cod and chips,' Millington said chirpily. 'Tea. Two slices of bread and butter. Turned down the syrup sponge and custard.' Millington patted his own stomach. 'Not want to be putting on weight, like as not.'

'I'd like a good half hour,' Welch said.

'All the time you want,' said Millington. They both knew it was a lie.

*
*

Divine was at his desk in the CID room, talking to a young woman who, two hours before, had had her handbag and two carriers of new purchases stolen from her in the middle of the city. Late lunchtime. Sandra Drexler had been walking through the underpass below Maid Marian Way, the one with the news kiosk at its centre, close to the Robin Hood Experience. Several families had been passing through at the time, children wearing Lincoln-green hats made from felt and waving bows and arrows in the air. Two youths in jeans and shirt sleeves had come running down the steps from the entrance nearest to St James Street, caught hold of Sandra Drexler's arms and swung her round in what had seemed, at first, like a drunken game. A couple of six-year-olds had pointed and laughed and their mother had shushed them on their way. But the youths had pushed Sandra hard against the tiled wall and torn the bags from her hands, her bag from her shoulder. They had gone running past the kiosk and along the tunnel towards Friar Lane and the castle, leaving Sandra on her knees, shocked and in tears, people walking wide to avoid her. Five minutes in which she had limped slowly towards the street, before an elderly woman had stopped to ask if she was all right.

'These tattoos,' Divine said, interrupting her account.

Sandra was in her second year of an Art and Design course at South Notts College. She took a sheet of A4

157

and a pencil and sketched them within minutes, the Union Jack, St George and the Dragon.

'Sixteen, seventeen, you say?'

'That's right.'

'And you're sure about the hair?'

'Yes, quite sure. Sort of washed-out sandy colour. Really fair.'

Divine thanked her for her trouble and gave her his second-best smile; if he weren't so full of himself and wearing that awful suit, Sandra thought, he might be almost good looking.

Resnick was weary. The muscles at the back of his neck were beginning to ache and he had drunk so much canteen tea it felt as if there was a coating of tannin furring his tongue. Across the table, Robin Hidden, with his solicitor's encouragement, had withdrawn into his shell. Saying as little as possible, giving nothing away.

'Robin,' Resnick said, 'don't you think we're making this more difficult than it has to be?'

Robin didn't respond; pointedly, David Welch looked at his watch.

Inside the machine, the twin tapes wound almost silently on.

At any moment, Resnick knew, Hidden was going to exercise his right to get up and go. Any solicitor other than Welch would surely have advised him to do so already.

'All right,' Graham Millington said, business-like, 'let's get it clear once and for all.'

'Is it necessary to go through this again?' Welch asked.

'You arrived at the hotel between half-eleven and a quarter to twelve,' Millington went on, ignoring him.

158

'Parked the car at the edge of the courtyard and took a quick look in the main bar, hung around for a while, no more than five, ten minutes, then got back in the car. You drove round the block a few times, came back to the hotel...'

'By then it must have been close to midnight,' Resnick said.

'Almost midnight,' Millington said.

'And that was when you saw Nancy.' Resnick looked at Robin Hidden squarely and Robin blinked and stammered yes.

'And she saw you?'

'No.'

'No?'

'I don't know.'

'She saw the car?'

'I d-don't know. How could I know?'

'You can't expect my client to speculate...'

'Nancy did know your car, though,' Resnick said, leaning back, softening his tone. 'She must have been in it a number of times? Associated it with you.'

'I suppose so, but...'

'Detective Inspector...'

'But on this occasion, either she didn't make the connection or if she did, chose to ignore it. Ignore you.'

Robin Hidden closed his eyes.

'And you did nothing? Stayed in the car and did nothing, no move to attract her attention, you didn't call her over, get out of the car, you didn't do anything – is that what you're saying?'

'Yes, I've told you. H-haven't I t-told you already?'

'Inspector...'

'All right, Robin, listen...' Reaching forward, Resnick, for a moment, rested his fingers on the back

159

of Robin Hidden's hand. 'Listen. I don't want to make a mistake here. You were upset about not seeing Nancy, upset at the way things were going, the way they seemed to be falling apart. You were out on your own, driving around, thinking about her. Is that right?'

Robin nodded. Resnick's hand was still close to his, close on the table's scarred surface. His voice was deep and quiet in the still room.

'You thought that if you could only talk to her, you might be able to sort things out, put them right.'

Robin looked at the table, the marks, his hand, how small his own fingers seemed, narrow and thin; his breathing was more agitated, louder.

'And when you went back to the hotel the second time, there she was. Walking across the courtyard towards you. On her own.' Resnick waited until Robin Hidden's eyes met his. 'You had to talk to her. That was why you were there? You did talk to her, didn't you? Nancy. Either you got out of the car or she came to you, but you did talk to her?'

'No.'

'Robin . . .'

'N-no.'

'Why ever not?'

Head in his hands, the words were indistinct and Millington would ask him to repeat them for clarification. 'Because I was frightened. Because I knew what sh-she'd say. She'd tell m-me she d-didn't ever w-want to see me any more. N-not ever. And I c-couldn't, I couldn't s-stand that. So I w-waited u-un-til she'd gone past and then I drove away.'

The tears came then without restraint and David Welch was on his feet to protest, but Resnick had already turned aside, Millington was looking at the ceiling, embarrassed, and for all intents and purposes the interview was over. Five thirty-seven p.m.

Twenty-two

'Struck lucky, then, Charlie. Took the old golden bol-
locks out of their case and give 'em a bit of a shine.'
Reg Cossall was leaning against the open door of
Resnick's office, leering his lop-sided grin.

Resnick came close to sighing; he'd like to think
Cossall was right.

'What? Boyfriend told to go walkies. The night
before Christmas. Jesus, Charlie, don't have to be much
of a wise man to work out that one.'

'Too easy, Reg.'

Cossall looked for somewhere on Resnick's desk to
stub out his cigarette; made do with the heel of his
shoe. 'Never too easy. Blokes like that. Make 'em
cough, bang 'em up, get yourself over the pub by opening time.' As a philosophy of police work it remained,
in Cossall's mind, undented by the fact that most pubs
now stayed open all day. It also depended, from time
to time, on not being phased by the exact truth.

'Still a way to go, Reg,' Resnick said.

Cossall tapped another Silk Cut from its pack. 'Least
you and Graham've got a live one to get your teeth
into. I'm still half way up the arse in computer print-
out and sodding cross-reference.' When his lighter
refused to work, he fumbled out a box of matches from
his jacket; the spent match he snapped between finger
and thumb and dropped back down into his pocket.
'Meeting up with Rose in the Borlace, likely go for a

bite later on,' he released grey-blue smoke through his nose, 'fancy joining us?'

Resnick shook his head. 'Thanks, Reg. Things to do.'

Cossall nodded. 'Some other time then.'

'Maybe.'

'Partial to you, you know, Rose is. Reckoned as how you've got a sense of humour. Told her she must be getting you mixed up with someone else.'

'G'night, Reg.'

Cossall laughed and walked away.

Was it too easy, Resnick thought? Too simple? He conjured up the look on Robin Hidden's face when the young man had talked about his last evening with Nancy, their last meal together, all those expectations dashed. The lie about seeing her outside the hotel. How much anger did it take? How much hurt? Pain like a vivid line, drawn through Robin Hidden's eyes. How many other lies?

'How d'you want to play it?' Skelton had asked. 'Hold him overnight? Keep pushing hard?'

Resnick's sense was that, for now, Hidden had been pushed as far as he could usefully go. Shocked by his own admission he had closed in on himself fast and even David Welch was on the ball enough to encourage him in his silence. So they had let him go home to the flat in West Bridgford, Musters Road, second floor of a detached house with a car port and an entryphone. Home to his microwave and his OS maps and his thoughts. 'We'll be wanting to talk to your client again,' Millington had smiled benevolently at the door.

Resnick stood up, rubbed the heels of both hands against his eyes. Through the window the shapes of the buildings were wrapped in purple light.

Lynn's flat was in a small housing association complex

in the Lace Market, balconies facing in on a partly cobbled courtyard. The rooms were large enough that she didn't fall over her own feet, not so big they encouraged her to own a lot of stuff. The floors she hoovered or mopped about once a week, the surfaces she dusted when there was a chance someone might call. A film of soft grey attached itself to her fingertip as she drew it along the tiled shelf above the gas fire. A gentleman caller, where had she heard that expression? She tried to blow the dust away but it stuck to her skin and she wiped it down the side of her skirt as she bent low, turning the circular switch alongside the fire to ignition. She remembered now, a film she had seen on television, *Glass* something, *The Glass Menagerie*, that was it. This young woman with a limp, not so young actually, that was part of it, surrounding herself with these little glass animals, waiting all the while for her gentleman caller to arrive at her door.

The radio was in the kitchen and Lynn switched it on before half-filling the kettle; a singer she failed to recognise was singing an Irish song. The voice was soft and warm and for no good reason it made her think of home. Swishing warm water around the inside of the pot then emptying it into the sink, she saw her mother, year on year, doing exactly the same. She clicked the radio off, dropped a single teabag into the pot. How long had it been, Lynn asked herself, since she had stopped waiting for gentlemen callers herself? Before the tea had time to brew, the telephone rang.

'I've been calling you all day,' her mother said.

'I've only this minute got in from work,' Lynn said, shorter-tempered than she'd intended.

'I tried the station once. The line was busy.'

'I'm not surprised. It's the holidays, we're more

164

understrength than usual. And you know there's a girl gone missing.'

Most often, any such remark would have brought forth from her mother a warning about being extra careful, bolting the door top and bottom, checking the window locks before going to bed; to her mother, any city bigger than Norwich was a place of constant danger, the worst she'd read about New York and New Orleans combined. But now there was nothing, a dull silence. Then, out in the courtyard, the sound, muffled, of a car starting up, misfiring. Lynn wondered if she could excuse herself a moment, pour the tea, bring it back to the phone.

'Lynnie, I think you should come home.'

'Mum . . .'

'I need you here.'

'I was there just a couple of days ago.'

'I'm at my wits' end.'

Lynn suppressed most of a sigh.

'It's your dad.'

'Oh, Mum . . .'

'You know he was going to the hospital . . .'

'That's tomorrow.'

'It was changed, the appointment was changed. They rang to tell him. He's been already. Yesterday.'

'And?'

In the hesitation she heard the worst, then heard it again in her mother's words. 'He's got to go back. Another test.' I don't want to know this, Lynn thought. 'To check, that's all it is, the doctor explained. Only to make sure that he hasn't got . . ., well, what they thought, you know, he'd got, he . . .'

'Mum.'

'They thought, all this trouble he was having, his

eating, going to the lavatory and that, it might be a growth, there, you know, in the, the bowel.'

'And it's not?'

'What?'

'It's not a growth, is that what they're saying? Or are they still not sure?'

'That's why he's got to go back.'

'So they're not sure?'

'Lynnie, I don't know what to do.'

'There's nothing you can do. Not until we know for sure.'

'Can't you come?'

'What do you mean? You mean now?'

'Lynnie, he won't sit, he won't eat, he won't as much as look me in the eye. At least if you were here . . .'

'Mum, I was there. Just days ago. He hardly spoke to me either.'

'You won't come then?'

'I don't see how I can.'

'He needs you, Lynnie. I need you.'

'Mum, I'm sorry, but it's a difficult time.'

'You think this is easy?'

'I didn't say that.'

'Your poor dad's not important enough, that's what you said.' She was close to tears, Lynn knew.

'You know that's not true,' Lynn said.

'Then go with him to the hospital.'

Lynn rested the top of the receiver against her forehead.

'Lynnie . . . ?'

'I'll see if I can. I promise. But you know what hospitals are like, that won't be for ages yet.'

'No, it's soon. The man your dad saw, the consultant, he said he wanted him in as soon as possible. The next few days.'

166

Then it is serious, Lynn thought. 'This consultant,' she said, 'you can't remember his name, I suppose?'

'It'll be written down somewhere, I don't know, I'll just see if I can find it if you'll . . .'

She heard her mother scrabbling about amongst all the scraps of paper that were kept by the phone. 'Mum, call me back, okay? When you've found it? All right. Talk to you in a minute. Bye.'

The skin along the tops of Lynn's arms was cold and her face was unusually drained of colour. The small medical primer she kept with her dictionary and handful of paperbacks almost fell open at the page she wanted: the alternative name for cancer of the bowel was colorectal cancer. Its highest incidence was in males in the sixty to seventy-nine age group. Fifty per cent of colorectal cancers are in the rectum. She let the book fall from her fingers to the floor. In the kitchen, she tipped away the remains of a carton of milk that smelled sour and struggled to open another without splashing too much over her hands. She put one spoonful of sugar in the mug and then another. Stirred. Two sips and she carried the mug back to the telephone.

When her mother rang back she was crying at the other end of the line.

Lynn let her sob a little and then asked her if she'd found the name. She got her to repeat it twice, spelling it out as she wrote it down.

'Is Dad there?' Lynn said.

'Yes.'

'Let me talk to him.'

'He's out in the sheds.'

'Call him in.'

There was a clunk as the phone was set awkwardly down; Lynn drank her tea and listened to the voices of youths in the street at the rear of the flat, raised half-heartedly in anger. One of her neighbours was listening to opera, a young man who wore black turtle-necks and ignored her when they passed on the stairs.

'I can't get him to come in,' her mother said.

'Did you tell him it was me?'

'Of course I did.'

Her upstairs neighbour was not only singing along, now he was stamping his feet in time with the chorus. 'I'm going to get in touch with this consultant,' Lynn said, 'see if I can find out when Dad's likely to be in. Then I'll see if I can get leave. Okay?'

She listened to her mother a few minutes more, reassuring her as much as she could. She tipped away what was left of her tea and poured herself a second cup. Turning on the hot tap in the bathroom, she sprinkled some herbal bubble bath into the stream of water. Only when she lowered herself into the steamy warmth did she begin to relax and the pictures she had begun to conjure up of her father begin to fade, at least for the time being, from her mind.

Twenty-three

Resnick had fed the cats, made himself coffee, squeezed half a lemon on to a piece of chicken he'd rubbed with garlic and set it under the grill. While that was cooking, he'd opened a bottle of Czech pilsner and drank half of it in the living room, reading an obituary of Bob Crosby. One of the 78s his uncle the tailor had prized had been 'Big Noise from Winnetka' by the Bobcats. Bob Haggart and Ray Bauduc, bass and drums and a lot of whistling. If Graham Millington ever came across it, the whole station would be in peril.

Back in the kitchen he turned the chicken and poured some of the juice back over it with a spoon. The last half of a beef tomato he cut into chunks and added to some wilting spinach and a piece of chicory on its last legs; these he tipped into a bowl and dressed with a trickle of raspberry vinegar and a teaspoon of tarragon mustard, a liberal splash of olive oil.

He ate at the kitchen table, feeding Bud with oddments of the chicken, washing it all down with the rest of the beer. There was something nagging at him, the impression he had got of Robin Hidden that afternoon, and the idea of a man attractive and lively enough for Nancy Phelan to take willingly to her bed – two sides of a puzzle that refused to come together.

He cut the last of the chicken into two and shared

them with the cat; licking his fingers, he went towards the phone.

'Hello, is that Dana Matthieson?' Hearing the voice, Resnick remembered a biggish woman, lots of hair, round faced. Not unlike Lynn, he supposed, but more so. Colourful clothes. 'Yes, this is Inspector Resnick. We talked . . . I was just wondering, if you're not too busy, if you could spare me a little of your time? Say, half an hour? . . . Yes, okay, thanks. Yes, I know where it is . . . Yes, bye.'

Dana had been ironing some several-days-old laundry until she had got bored and now blouses and cotton tops and brightly coloured trousers lay across the backs and arms of chairs and in a loose pile on the ironing board. The television was on with the sound at a whisper, a film with James Belushi, a great many car chases and at least one large dog. All five attempts at writing her letter of resignation to Andrew Clarke and Associates, Architects, had been torn in half and half again and were now spread, unfinished, over the glass-topped table.

She had been well into a bottle of Shingle Peak New Zealand Riesling when Resnick had phoned and there was just a glass left to offer him when the door bell rang. If it came to it, Dana thought, not that she could see why it should, she could always open another.

Resnick shook off his coat, exchanged a few pleasantries and took the offered seat. Dana's face was fuller than he had pictured it, swollen around the eyes, from drinking or crying he couldn't tell.

She held the bottle out towards him and he shook his head, so she emptied the contents into her own glass.

'There's no news,' she said, scarcely a question.

170

Resnick shook his head.

Dana poked at the hem of an orange top that was either half inside her belt or half out. 'I didn't think so or you would have said. On the phone.' She tilted the glass back and drank. 'Unless the news was bad.'

He looked up at her steadily.

'Oh, God,' Dana said, 'she's dead, isn't she? She's got to be.'

Resnick reacted in time to catch the glass as it fell from her fingers, what was left of the wine splashing across his sleeve. With his other arm he steadied her, fingers spread high behind her waist so that she fell heavily against him. Eyes closed, her face was close to his; he could feel her breath on his skin.

'That's not what I came here to say.'

'Isn't it?'

'No. No, it's not.'

Through the soft material of her clothing he could feel her breast against his chest, hip hard against his thigh.

'It's all right.'

She opened her eyes. 'Is it?'

He was more aware of her body than he wanted to be. 'Yes,' he said.

Just a simple movement, the way she raised her mouth towards his. A moment when something tried to warn him this was wrong. Her breath was warm and she tasted of wine. Their teeth clashed and then they didn't. He could scarcely believe the inside of her mouth was so soft. Gently, she took his bottom lip between her teeth.

Without Resnick knowing exactly how, they were on the floor beside the settee. The sleeve of his jacket, the cuff of his shirt were dark from the wine.

'I've ruined your clothes,' Dana said.

171

They managed to get his jacket half off; one at a time, she licked his fingers clean.

'I don't know your name,' she said. 'Your first name.'

He touched her breast and the nipple was so hard against the soft flesh of his finger that he gasped. Dana moved beneath him so that one of his legs was between her own. She took his face in her hands; she didn't think he could have kissed anyone in a long while.

'Charlie,' he said.

'What?' Her voice soft and loud, tip of her tongue flicking the lobe of his ear.

'My name. Charlie.'

Face pressed into the softness of his shoulder, she began to laugh.

'What?'

'I can't believe . . .'

'What?'

'I'm about to make love to a policeman called Charlie.'

He moved his leg and rolled away but she rolled with him and as she leaned over him her hair fell loose about her face and the laugh was now a smile.

'Charlie,' she said.

The look of shock was still there in his eyes.

Taking his hands again, she brought them to her breasts. 'Careful,' she said. 'Careful, Charlie. Take your time.'

'Charlie, are you all right?'

They were in Dana's big bed beneath a duvet cover awash with purple and orange flowers. The room smelled of pot pourri and sweat and sex and, faintly, Chanel No. 5. Dana had opened another bottle of wine and before bringing it back she had put music on the stereo; through the partly open door, Rod Stewart was

172

singing 'I Don't Want to Talk About It'; inside Resnick's head Ben Webster was playing 'Someone to Watch Over Me', 'Our Love is Here to Stay'.

'I'm fine,' he said. 'Just fine.' Aside from the obvious, he had no idea what was happening and for now he was happy to keep it that way.

'Quiet, though,' Dana said. He looked to see if she was smiling; she was.

'Hungry?' she asked.

'Probably.'

Kissing him on the side of the mouth, she pushed herself off the bed and took her time about leaving the room. It amazed him that she was so unselfconscious of her body; when he had needed to go to the bathroom, he had fished his boxer shorts from the bottom of the bed with his toes and pulled them back on.

Dana had taken off Resnick's watch because it was scratching her skin and now he lifted it from the bed-side table: eleven-seventeen. Cupping both hands behind his head he closed his eyes.

Without meaning to, he dozed.

When he came to, Dana was walking back into the room with a tray containing two cold turkey wings, one leg, several slices of white breast meat, a chunk of Blue Stilton, plastic pots of hummous and taramasalata two-thirds empty, a small bunch of grapes browning against their stems, one mug of coffee and another of orange and hibiscus tea.

'Budge up,' she grinned, settling the tray in the centre of the bed and then sliding in behind it. 'We haven't,' she said, 'a slice of bread or a biscuit in the place.'

Slowly, she slid her forefinger down into the pink taramasalata and brought it, laden, to his mouth.

'When you rang, asked to come round,' she said, 'is this what you had in mind?'

Resnick shook his head.

'Honestly?'

'Of course not.'

Dana sipped her tea. 'Why, of course?'

Resnick didn't know how he was supposed to respond, what to say. 'I just didn't ... I mean, I wouldn't ...'

'Wouldn't?'

'No.'

She arched an eyebrow. 'Clean in thought, word and deed, the policeman's code.'

'That isn't what I mean.'

'What you mean is, you didn't find me attractive.'

'No.'

'No, you didn't, or no, you did?'

'No, that isn't what I mean.'

'What is then?'

To give himself time, he tried the coffee; it was almost certainly instant, certainly too weak. 'I meant I knew you were an attractive woman, but I hadn't thought about you in this ... like this, I mean, sexually, and if I had I probably wouldn't have called up like that and invited myself round so as to ...'

'Why not?'

He put the mug back down. 'I don't know.'

'You're involved with somebody else?'

'No.'

'Then why not?'

Not knowing why this was so embarrassing, nonetheless he looked away. 'It wouldn't have seemed right.'

'Oh.'

'And besides ...'

'Yes?'

'I'd never have thought you'd be interested.'

'In sex?'

'In me.'

'Oh, Charlie,' touching the side of his face with her hand.

'What?'

'Don't you know you're an attractive man?'

'No,' he said. 'No, I don't.'

Smiling she let her hand slide around to the back of his neck as she leaned towards him for a kiss. 'Of course,' she said, 'that's one of the most attractive things about you.' And then, 'But you are pleased to be here?'

He didn't have to answer; she could see that he was.

'Before it's too late,' she said, 'why don't we just move this tray?'

She was stretching to set it on the floor when Resnick ran his hands down her back on to her buttocks, then, more slowly, out along her thighs. He heard her breathing change.

'Dana,' he said.

'Mmm?'

'Nothing.' He had just wanted to hear how it sounded when he spoke her name.

It was after one. The second mug of coffee had been stronger and black. The same Rod Stewart selection was playing, more quietly, in the next room. Resnick lay on his stomach, Dana with one leg and arm carelessly across him. This time she had been the one to fall asleep, but now she was sleepily awake.

'You know, I saw him once,' Resnick said.

'Who?'

'Rod Stewart. That's who it is, isn't it?'

'Mm.'

'Years ago. He was with the Steam Packet. Club down by the Trent. Almost couldn't get through the doors.'

'Not surprising.'

Resnick smiled over his shoulder. 'Could've counted on one hand, most likely, those who'd as much as heard of him then, never mind gone specially to see him. Long John Baldry, he was the one they were there for.'

Dana shook her head, she hadn't heard of him.

'Him and Julie Driscoll, they were the main singers with the band. Stewart came on first, did a few numbers at the start of the set. Skinny kid with a harmonica. Rod the Mod, that's what he was being called.'

'Good, though, was he?'

Resnick laughed. 'Terrible.'

'Now you're having me on.'

'No, I'm not. He was dreadful. Appalling.'

Dana's face went serious. 'You're not, are you, Charlie?'

'What?'

'Having me on? Messing me around?'

Resnick pushed himself around, sat up. 'I don't think so.'

'Cause I've had enough of that. One night stands.'

She had turned away from him, shoulder slumped forward, and although he could neither see nor hear, Resnick knew she was crying. He didn't know what to do; he left her alone and let her cry and then he moved close and kissed the top of her back, just below the dark line of her hair, and she turned into his arms.

' 'Oh God!' she said. 'It doesn't seem right. Doing this. Feeling this good. After what's happened to Nancy. You know what I mean?'

Her tears had smeared what little make-up remained on her face.

'We don't know,' Resnick said, 'what's happened to Nancy. Not for sure.'

Though in their hearts, they were certain, both of them, that they did.

'What time is it?' Dana said. In the darkness of the room, she could see that Resnick, between the end of the bed and the door, was fully dressed.

'A little after two.'

'And you're leaving?'

'I have to.'

She sat up in bed, the edge of the duvet covering one breast. 'Without telling me?'

'I didn't want to wake you.'

Dana stretched out an arm and Resnick sat on the side of the bed, holding her hand. She stitched her fingers between his.

'You never did tell me,' she said, 'why it was you wanted to see me.'

'I know. I thought maybe I should leave it to another time.'

'What was it, though?' She brought his hand to her face and rubbed his knuckles against her cheek.

'Robin Hidden . . .'

'What about him?'

'I wanted to ask you about him.'

Dana released his hand and leaned away. 'Surely you don't suspect Robin?'

Resnick didn't answer. She could see little more than the outline of his face; impossible to read the expression in his eyes, tell what he was thinking.

'You do, don't you?'

'You know what had happened between them?'

'Nancy had chucked him, yes. But that doesn't mean . . .'

177

'He saw her that evening, Christmas Eve...'

'He couldn't have.'

'He went to the hotel, looking for her, just before midnight.'

'And?'

Resnick didn't immediately reply; had said already more than probably he should.

'And?' Dana said again, touching his hand.

'Nothing. He saw her and drove away.'

'Without talking to her?'

Resnick shrugged. 'That's what he says.'

'But you don't believe him?'

'I don't know.'

'You think there was some kind of awful row, Robin lost his temper and...' Dana had raised her hands as she was talking and now let them fall to her sides.

'It's possible,' Resnick said.

Dana leaned towards him. 'You've spoken to Robin, though? Talked to him?'

'Yes.'

'And you still think he could do something like that? Hurt her? Harm her?'

'Like I said, it's possible. It's...'

'He wouldn't do that. He couldn't. He's just not the type. And besides, if you'd seen him with Nancy, you'd know. Whatever she thought of him, he really loved her.'

Exactly, Resnick thought. 'Sometimes,' he said, 'that's enough.'

'God!' Dana pulled at the duvet and moved away, swiftly to the far side of the bed. 'I suppose it's no surprise, doing what you do, you should be as cynical as you are.' Barefoot, she took a robe from where it was hanging on the open wardrobe door and slipped it around her.

'Cynical,' Resnick said, 'is that what it is? Loving somebody so much you lose all perspective.'

'Enough to want to hurt them? Or worse? That's not cynical, it's sick.'

'It's what happens,' said Resnick. 'Time and again. It's what I have to deal with.' He was talking to the open door.

Dana took a sachet of herbal tea from the packet and hung it over the edge of a freshly rinsed mug. When she pointed at the jar of Gold Blend, Resnick shook his head. 'I'll wait till I get home.'

'Suit yourself.' Sitting at the table, Dana toyed with a spoon, avoiding Resnick's eye.

Resnick was starting to feel more than uncomfortable; he wished he were no longer there, but couldn't quite bring himself to go. 'I didn't mean to upset you,' he said.

'I was already upset. What happened, it made me forget it for a while, that's all.'

On the narrow shelf, the kettle was coming noisily to the boil. She was still refusing to look at him and still he hovered near the doorway, reluctant to leave. 'Their relationship, Nancy and Robin, it was, well, as far as you know, it was sexual?'

Dana laughed, without humour, more a simple expelling of air than a laugh. 'Did I hear the usual groans and gasps through the wall? Why not? She's an attractive woman; Robin's athletic, a good body whatever else.'

'It was passionate, then, between them?'

She was staring at him now, open faced. 'Is that all the proof you need, Charlie? That someone's capable of passion? Is that enough to tip the scales?'

'I'll call you,' Resnick said, stepping back into the hallway.

If Dana heard him, jinking the sachet in and out of her tea, she gave no sign. Mindful of the hour, Resnick closed the door firmly yet quietly behind him.

Twenty-four

What little had been seen of the season of goodwill was soon lost in a fog of malevolence and discontent. Uniformed officers summoned to a night club in the city after receiving an emergency call claiming that a man had been knifed, walked into a blitz of bottles and bricks and one hastily assembled petrol bomb was rolled beneath their car. A firefighting team arriving to tackle a blaze in the upper storeys of a terraced house two streets away from Gary and Michelle, found themselves pelted with rubbish and abuse by a gang of white youths, one of their hoses split by an axe, the tyres of an engine slashed. The family living in the house, two of whom suffered broken limbs jumping to the ground while others, children between five years and eighteen months, suffered severe burns, were from Bangladesh.

At something short of five one morning, a young woman with a Glasgow accent stumbled into the police station at Canning Circus with blood running freely from a wound to the side of her head and one eye tightly closed. She and her boyfriend, a twenty-nine-year-old known to be a small-time dealer, had been smoking crack cocaine in an abandoned house near the Forest; she had drifted off and been woken by the sound of his fists pummelling her face. Medical examination in casualty revealed a fractured cheekbone and a detached retina in the eye.

The driver of the last bus from the Old Market Square to Bestwood Estate refused to accept the fare of a clearly drunken man who had been offering him verbal abuse and had a piece of masonry thrown at his windscreen, splintering it across. Another taxi driver was attacked, this time with a baseball bat.

A memo was passed round, offering overtime for officers willing to be drafted in to assist the Mansfield division in policing a concert by right-wing skinhead rock groups to be held in the old Palais de Dance. The event had been advertised in fascist magazines all over Europe and at least two coachloads were expected from Germany and Holland.

'Sounds like just the thing for our Mark,' Kevin Naylor remarked, passing the memo across the CID room.

'Knowing him,' Lynn said, 'he'll have his ticket already. Front row.'

Nancy Phelan's parents made a ritual of visiting the station twice, sometimes three times a day, demanding to speak with either Resnick or Skelton to find out what progress had been made. Between times, they turned up on one or other of the local radio programmes, wrote to the *Post*, the free papers, the nationals, petitioned the Lord Mayor and the city's M.P. Clarise Phelan took to standing in front of the stone columns of the Council House at one end of the Market Square with a placard bearing a blown-up photograph of Nancy and underneath, *My lovely daughter – missing and nobody cares.*

After forty-eight hours when the temperature had risen high enough for Resnick to discard both scarf and gloves, the weather bit back. It hit freezing and stayed. Trains were cancelled, buses curtailed; cars slid into slow, unstoppable collisions which blocked the roads for hours. Understaffed, close to overwhelmed, Skelton and Resnick struggled to delegate, prioritise, keep their feet from slipping under them.

Both of Nancy Phelan's missing boyfriends returned, shocked by what had happened, but unable to shed any light on how or why. James Guillery was stretchered off the plane at Luton Airport with a broken leg, victim not of the snow, but an accident involving the chairlift and a snapped bolt. Eric Capaldi had sped in his low-slung sports car to the outskirts of Copenhagen and back. His aim had been to interview, for a potential radio slot of his own, a fifty-two-year-old percussionist who had been a counter-culture star for fifteen minutes in the late sixties and was now composing minimalist religious music for trans-European radio. After the interview and most of a bottle of brandy and to Eric's abiding confusion, he had ended up in the percussionist's arms and then his bed.

Robin Hidden continued to maintain that he had driven away that night without speaking to Nancy Phelan and had finally issued a statement through his solicitor saying that, as far as that particular subject went, he had nothing more to say.

As David Welch, smiling for once, had expressed it, handing Graham Millington the envelope, 'Put up or shut up, you know what I mean?'

'Cocky so-and-so,' Millington thought. 'Well above himself.' But he and Resnick knew only too well Welch was right. Arrest Hidden as things stood and within twenty-four hours, thirty-six at most, he would be back out on the street again and what would have been gained?

What did happen, inevitably, was that Harry Phelan got wind of what was going on. A new-found friend of a friend, drinking late one night in his Mansfield Road hotel, had told him one place to find the crime reporter for the *Post* was in the Blue Bell of a lunchtime, swopping yarns and enjoying a peaceful couple of pints. Next day Harry went along and stood around and by the time he'd bought his round, had heard about the young man the police had been questioning.

'Where is the bastard?' Harry Phelan had yelled later, catching Skelton coming back from one of his runs to the station. 'Why haven't you bleedin' arrested him? Just wait till I get my hands on him, that's all. Just wait.'

Skelton calmed him down and invited him to his office, tried to explain. 'Mr Phelan, I assure you . . .'

'Don't insult me with that,' Harry Phelan said. 'Assure. Look at you. Out there friggin' about in that poncey gear, joggin', instead of saving my poor bleedin' kid! You – you couldn't assure me of shit!'

Meanwhile, Reg Cossall and his team had interviewed one hundred and thirty-nine men and forty-three women, thirty-seven of whom had a clear recollection of seeing Nancy on Christmas Eve. Five of the women had spoken to her, eight in all remembered what she had been wearing. Seven of the men had spoken to her, five had danced with her, two had asked her if they could give her a lift home. She had said no to them both. And both had gone home with someone else.

As police work went it was painstaking and thorough and it didn't seem to be going anywhere. 'Like farting down an open sewer,' Cossall said, disgusted. 'Not worth parting your bloody cheeks.'

By the time Resnick had arrived home after his night with Dana Matthieson, walking all the way across the

184

city, down beside the cemetery to the gates of the Arboretum, through towards the site of the old Victoria railway station and up past the Muslim temple on the Woodborough Road, he had convinced himself that it had all been a mistake. Enjoyable, yes, exciting even, but certainly a mistake. On both sides.

Naturally, he reasoned, after what had happened to her flatmate, Dana had been upset, disorientated, looking for comfort and distraction. As for himself – Jesus, Charlie, he said to the empty streets, how long is it since you went with a woman?

Is that what it had been, then? Only that? Going with a woman?

Suddenly chilled, he had pulled up his coat collar and shivered, remembering the warmth of Dana's body.

And of course, he hadn't done as he had said, he hadn't called. For the first couple of days, whenever the phone rang in his office or at home, he had lifted the receiver with the same strange mix of anxiety and anticipation. But it was never her. Easy to stop waiting for it to happen.

When, finally, three days later, Dana did call, Resnick was talking to Lynn Kellogg about her application for leave, a day accompanying her father to the outpatient department of the Norfolk and Norwich.

'An endoscopy,' Lynn said, the word unfamiliar on her tongue.

Resnick looked at her enquiringly.

'An internal examination. As far as I can tell they pass this thing, this endoscope up into his bowels.'

Resnick shuddered at the thought.

Lynn breathed uneasily. 'If they suspect cancer, most likely they'll take a biopsy.'

'And if it is,' Resnick asked, 'what kind of treatment...?'

'Surgery,' Lynn said. 'They cut it out.'

'I'm sorry,' Resnick said. There were tears, suddenly, at the corners of Lynn's eyes. 'Really sorry.' Part way round his desk towards her he stopped. He wanted to take her in his arms, reassure her with a hug.

'It's all right.' Lynn found a tissue and blew her nose, leaving Resnick stranded where he was. Thank God for the phone.

'Charlie?' said the voice at the other end of the line. 'Hello?'

'It's me, Dana.'

By then he knew.

'You didn't call.'

'No, I'm sorry. Things have been, well, hectic.' Without meaning to, he caught Lynn's eye.

'I've been thinking about you,' Dana said.

Resnick transferred the receiver from one hand to another, studied the floor.

'Do you want me to wait outside?' Lynn said.

Resnick shook his head.

'I've been thinking about your body,' Dana said.

Resnick found that hard to believe. He thought about his own body as little as he could and when he did it was usually with dismay.

'I want to see you, that's all,' Dana said. 'No big deal.'

'Look,' Lynn was almost at the door, 'I can come back later.'

'Is this a bad time?' Dana said. 'Is it difficult for you to talk?'

'No, it's fine,' Resnick said, waving Lynn back into the room.

'When can I see you?' Dana asked.

186

'Why don't we meet for a drink?' Resnick said, as much as anything to get her off the phone.

'Tomorrow?'

Resnick couldn't think. 'All right,' he said.

'Good. Eight o'clock?'

'Fine.'

'Why don't you come here? We can go on somewhere else if you want.'

'All right. See you then. Bye.' By the time he put down the phone he had started to sweat.

'First-footing,' Lynn said.

'What?'

'You know, tall stranger crosses the threshold with a lump of coal.'

'Oh, God!'

'Problem?'

Only that he'd forgotten it was New Year's Eve. And now Marian Witczak's voice came instantly back to him: 'We will both wear, Charles, what would you say? Our dancing shoes.'

'Double-booked?' Lynn asked.

'Something like that.'

'I'm sorry, I shouldn't be laughing.' She didn't seem to be laughing at all.

'This day's leave,' Resnick said, 'it'll be tight, but no question you must go. We'll cover somehow.'

'Thanks. And good luck.'

'What?'

'Tomorrow.'

Dana lit another cigarette, poured herself another drink. She had already had several, finding the courage to phone him when he hadn't phoned her. And at work. Probably she shouldn't have done that, probably that had been a mistake. Except he had said yes, hadn't

187

he? Agreed to come round for a drink. She smiled, raising her glass: he was worth a little seeking out, a little chasing after. She liked him, the memory of him: big, there was something, she thought, about a man who was big. And she laughed.

Twenty-five

Gary was sprawled across the settee wearing his County goalkeeper's shirt over the top of two pullovers in an attempt to keep warm. He was watching a programme about Indonesian cookery and Michelle couldn't for the life of her see why. The extent of Gary's cooking in the past few months had been opening a tin of beans and, five minutes later, slopping the contents, lukewarm, over burnt toast and then yelling at Karl because he wouldn't eat it. Beyond that, all Gary knew about cookery was 'What's for dinner?', 'Where's me tea?'

Michelle didn't say anything; knew well enough to let him be.

Brian's wife, Josie, had offered to take Karl down to the Forest along with her two and Michelle had leaped at the chance. Natalie had lain, alternately cooing and crying in her cot, some twenty minutes after feeding but now she was quiet. Michelle had wiped round the sink in the kitchen, taken the rubbish out to the bin; for once in his life, Gary had grunted no instead of yes to the offer of a cup of tea and she'd taken her own upstairs to have a sort out, tidy round.

There were balls of dust collecting at the corners of the stairs.

In the small room at the back, Natalie was sleeping with her thumb in her mouth and one leg poking through the bars of the cot; Michelle took the tiny foot in her hand and slipped it back beneath the covers. So cold! Gently, she touched her lips to the baby's cheek and that was warm, at least. Leaving the door ajar, she crossed to the other bedroom and shivered: it was like an icewell in there.

There were two pairs of tights hanging from the end of the bed, one of them laddered almost beyond repair. Gary seemed to have dumped bits and pieces of clothing everywhere, a shirt, pair of boxer shorts, one sock. From the state of the collar, the shirt could just about last out another day so she hung it back inside the chipboard wardrobe they had got from Family First. Gary's zip-up jacket, his favourite, stuffed down there on top of the shoes, getting all creased – Michelle bent down to pick it up and that was when the knife fell out.

She jumped and thought she must have cried out loud, but nothing happened; the baby didn't wake, Gary didn't call up from downstairs. The television commentary continued in a blur from which she was unable to distinguish the words.

The handle of the knife was rounded, wrapped around with tape; the blade, close to six inches long, curved out then in, tapering to a point. Near to the tip, a piece of the blade had broken away, as if it had been struck against something resisting and hard.

It lay against her one decent pair of heels, daring her to pick it up.

'You didn't see Nancy that evening? Later that evening? Christmas Eve?'

'I told you, didn't I? I never went out.'

Slowly, not wanting to, Michelle bent down towards the knife. Tried to imagine it being raised in anger in a man's hand.

''Chelle? Michelle?''

A second before the voice, she heard the board, loose along the landing, squeak. Breath caught hard in her mouth, she pulled the jacket back across the knife, pushed both with her foot further back inside, shut the wardrobe door.

'Here you are.' Smiling that way with his mouth, parted just a little, twisted down. 'Wondered where you were.'

She was certain, the way it was pumping, he must hear her heart.

'What's up?'

Afraid to speak, Michelle shook her head from side to side.

'That cooking,' he nodded back downstairs, 'all it is, chop everything up small, meat and that, stick it in a jar of peanut butter.' He winked. 'Reckon we could try that.'

Michelle had steadied her breathing enough to move away from the wardrobe door.

'Natalie sleeping is she?'

'I'll just see . . .'

Gary caught her arm as she went past. Something had got stuck in the fine straggle of hairs beside his lip.

'Wondered what you'd come up here for.'

'I was just tidying round. Those things . . .'

'Oh, yeh? Thought you might've had other ideas. You know . . .' His eyes grazed the bed. ' . . . Karl out the way for a change.'

'They'll be back . . .' Michelle began.

One hand reaching for the belt to her jeans, Gary laughed. 'Oh no, they won't.'

All the while they lay there, blessed by the squeak and roll of the wire mattress, Michelle thought about the knife. Gary above her, thrusting down, eyes clamped tight, mouth opening only to call her that name she hated, over and over, finally to cry out; through it all she could only see the swelling of the blade, feel its point.

When he had collapsed sideways, pulled away from her, face down into the sheet, she felt gingerly down there, certain amongst all that wetness there would be blood.

'Michelle?'

'Yes?'

'Be a sweetheart, make us a cup of tea.'

She was on her way downstairs, sweater and jeans, hair uncombed, when Josie arrived back with the kids.

'Jesus, girl! Look like you been pulled through a hedge backwards.' And, leaning close enough to whisper in her ear, 'Not been knocking you around again, has he?'

Michelle shook her head. 'Not the way you mean.'

Josie rolled her eyes. 'Oh, that! You know, when I was – what? – seventeen, eighteen, I used to reckon if I didn't have some bloke poking away at me every night the world was going to come to a sodding end. Now . . .' She shook her head and looked at Michelle knowingly. ' . . . most of the time I couldn't give a toss. 'Fact, far as Brian's concerned, sometimes that's all I will give.'

She was laughing so much now she had to grab hold of Michelle so as not to lose her balance. Josie. By Michelle's reckoning, she was all of twenty-one.

Twenty-six

Lynn woke slippery with sweat and it was too many moments before she realised she had been dreaming. The blanket she had pulled on to the duvet in the night to combat the cold was wound, tight like a rope, between her legs; the duvet itself had been thrown to the floor. T-shirt, knickers, socks, all were drenched. Coils of dark hair clung fast to her head.

In her dream she had been between the henhouses, walking in a nightgown she had never owned, long and stiff and white like something from *Rebecca* or *Jane Eyre*, when she had heard the sound.

As she ran, moonlight threw shadows against the packed earth, the worn boards of the henhouse walls. A cry, high and shrill, like the mating of feral cats: except it wasn't that. At first she thought the high, wooden door was locked, but as she threw her weight against it, she realised it was only jammed fast. Little by little it gave, then sprang suddenly backwards and she stumbled in.

Through the high, meshed windows the moon shone with a muted fall. Her father had climbed to the high conveyor and now he hung there, attached by the neck; his throat had been cut. Spurred by the silence, flies thrummed their wings, blue, and busied themselves in the dark and drying blood.

As Lynn fell fast against his legs, the body tore and tipped and spilled against her. His feet and hands were bony and cold and hard and when his eyes met hers they smiled.

She screamed herself awake. The sheet and pillow were soaked. Lynn stripped them from the bed and dropped them to the floor beside the blanket and her clothes. For several moments she stood with her head bent towards her knees, steadying her breath. It was twenty-five past three. Against all her judgement, what she wanted most of all was to phone home, make sure her father was all right. She pulled on her dressing gown and tied it tight, filled the kettle and switched it on, brought a towel from the bathroom and vigorously rubbed at her hair.

If anything had happened, her mother would have rung her. And she had worries enough already, without picking up the pieces of Lynn's dreams.

Lynn could remember her, inevitable apron smudged with flour, sitting on the side of the narrow bed Lynn had shared with a family of somewhat disabled dolls and a ragged panda, patting her hand and shushing, 'Just a dream, my petal. All it was, a silly old dream.'

Lynn had forgotten to buy any milk on the way home and so she drank half a cup of tea, black, before going back into the bathroom and standing under the shower. It was only then, hot water cascading from her head and shoulders, that she began to cry.

Worried about the lack of progress over Nancy Phelan, worried by the unfamiliar drawn expression he had noted on Lynn Kellogg's face, the dark shadows beneath her eyes, worried by his seemingly unresolvable predicament over New Year's Eve, Resnick had gone to bed convinced that he would never be able to sleep and had slept like the proverbial log. It had taken Dizzy's insistence to spin him awake, the cat's paws working rhythmically into his pillow with something close to desperation. It was a few minutes short of six o'clock, but Resnick felt as if he had overslept, head coddled in cotton wool.

Dizzy waited outside the bathroom while Resnick showered, sharpening his claws against the frame of the door. The other cats were in the kitchen, waiting to greet him, Pepper purring with anticipation from inside an old colander he had commandeered as his favoured sleeping quarters.

Coffee brewing, cat food distributed into coloured bowls Resnick concentrated on layering alternate slices of smoked ham and Jarlsberg on to half-toasted rye bread. He was adding a touch of Dijon mustard when Lynn phoned, saying she needed to talk.

'Something about Gary James?' Resnick asked.

'No, it's personal,' she said.

'All right,' Resnick said, 'give me half an hour.'

He pressed the pieces of toast together into a sandwich and cut them in two, poured the coffee, took both back upstairs to finish getting dressed. Before leaving the house, he called Millington at home.

'Graham, wasn't sure if I'd catch you.'

'Only just.' Millington had been sitting at the circular table in the kitchen, chewing his way through an assortment of bran and wheatgerm that was about as appealing as the floor of his old nan's budgie's cage.

'At your age, Graham,' his wife insisted, 'it doesn't pay to take chances. You have to keep your arteries open.' She'd been browsing through those leaflets she brought back from the well-woman clinic again, Millington had thought.

'Looks like I shall be a few minutes late,' Resnick said. 'Hold the fort for me, will you?'

Millington, of course, was only too pleased. Much of

his sergeant's life, Resnick suspected, was spent waiting for some unforeseen and appalling accident to befall his superiors. At which time, only he, Graham Millington, mind alert, shoes buffed and hair gleaming, would be ready to step into the breech. His moment of glory. What was it the dance director said to little Ruby Keeler in *42nd Street*? 'You're coming out of that dressing room a nobody, but you're coming back a star.'

The postman was at the end of the drive when Resnick left, sorting through a vast bundle of mail.

'Not all for me, I hope?' Resnick said, scarcely breaking his stride.

The postman shook his head. 'Just the usual. *Readers' Digest*, Halifax, the AA, and free garlic bread if you order one large or two medium pizzas.'

Resnick raised a hand in thanks. Exactly the kind of postal worker there should be more of, sifted through the junk mail for you so all you had to do was transfer it directly to the bin.

*

Lynn was waiting for him at the door, had heard his footsteps, heavy across the courtyard and turned up the flame under the Italian coffee pot she had recently bought. The coffee you put, ground, into a small perforated container which stood over cold water in the bottom section; light the gas and not so many minutes later the water had somehow pumped up and there was your coffee, strong and black and ready to pour. In truth, she doubted she'd used it more than a few times since buying it in the autumn. She hoped the coffee was strong enough; she hoped it didn't taste stewed.

'Good smell,' Resnick said as soon as he was inside.

'You want some toast? I'm going to have toast.'

'No, thanks,' looking for somewhere to put his coat, 'I've eaten already.' And then, 'All right, why not? Just one.'

'Here, give me that,' Lynn said, and hung his raincoat from one of the hooks just inside the door.

The radio was playing quietly in a corner of the room, not quite tuned. Trent-FM. 'Let me turn that off.'

'No, it's okay.'

She switched it off anyway and Resnick mooched around the room while she was in the small kitchen, reading the titles of the books on the shelf, glancing at an old copy of the *Mail*, the back page with the headline, *FOREST FOR THE DROP*? Among the photographs above the fireplace was one of a happy Lynn, chubby and smiling, in her father's arms. Five years old? The pictures of her former boyfriend, the cyclist, seemed to have peddled off into the dustbin.

'Butter or marge?'

'Sorry?'

'On the toast, butter or ...'

'Oh, butter.'

Resnick settled himself in the centre of the two-seater settee, Lynn at an angle on a chair.

'How's the coffee?'

'Fine.'

'Sure it's strong enough?'

'Why don't you tell me what's worrying you, what's happened?'

She told him about her dream. Neither spoke for a little while.

'You're bound to be frightened,' he eventually said. 'For yourself as well as for him. It's a difficult time.'

Lynn pulled her legs towards her chest, wrapped her

arms around her knees. 'If it is cancer,' Resnick said, 'what are his chances?'

'They won't really say.'

'And treatment? Chemotherapy?'

She shook her head. 'I don't think so.' She was focusing on a spot on the side wall, anything rather than look at him directly. 'They cut it out. As much as they can. He'll probably have to have a colostomy. That's a . . .'

'I know what it is.'

'I can't imagine . . . he'll never cope with that, he never will. He . . .'

'Better that than the other thing.'

'I don't even know if that's true.' Her knee banged against the chair as she got up. She wasn't going to cry in front of him, she wasn't. Fingers digging into the flesh of her hands, she stood by the small window, staring out.

'I remember,' Resnick went on, when my father went into hospital. Trouble with his breathing, his lungs. Half a dozen stairs and he sounded like one of those old engines, winding down. He went into the City for tests, treatment, a rest. They gave him, I don't know, some kind of antibiotics. Physiotherapy. I'd go in sometimes to visit, I might just have been over that way, you know, passing, and this woman would be there, white tunic and trousers, pleasant but serious, deadly serious. "Come on now, Mr Resnick, we have to teach you to breathe." "What does she think I've been doing, Charlie, these past sixty years if it's not breathing?" he used to say as soon as she'd gone.' He sighed. 'I suppose they did what they could, but he hadn't made anything easy. Even as a kid, I can scarcely picture him without a cigarette in his hand.' Resnick looked across at her. 'But they did what they could. Got him so he

198

was able to come out of hospital, come home for another few months.'

Lynn turned sharply. 'And you think it was worth it?'

'Yes, on balance I do.'

'Did he?'

Resnick hesitated. 'I think so. But truly, no, I don't know.'

'He didn't say?'

'Oh, he moaned. Complained. I won't lie to you, there were days when he said he wished they'd let him die; he wished he were dead.'

'And yet you can still say it was right? For him to go through all that discomfort, the pain, the . . . loss of dignity, all for what? A few extra months?'

Resnick drank some more coffee, giving himself time. 'There were things he was able to say, we were able to say to one another, I think they were important.'

'To you, yes?'

'Lynn, listen, you've got to realise, hard as it might be, this isn't just about him. About your dad. It's about you too. Your life. If he . . . if he dies, whenever he dies, one way or another you've got to find a way of living with that. And you will.'

She let herself cry now and he stood close to her, a hand on her shoulder and for a short while she rested her head sideways against his arm, so that her face lay on his wrist and hand.

'Thanks,' she said then and got to her feet and blew her nose and wiped her eyes and carried the empty cups and the plates back into the kitchen and rinsed them under the sink. 'We'd better be going,' she said. 'It's not as if there's nothing to do.'

Cossall was pacing the corridor, drawing heavily on his fifth or sixth cigarette of the morning. 'Charlie, in here. You've got to hear this.'

Resnick checked with Millington that everything was proceeding smoothly, then followed Cossall to the interview room, getting the details on the way.

Miriam Richards had been employed at the hotel on Christmas Eve, casual work as a waitress with which she augmented her student grant. On this particular evening she had been assigned to one of the larger banqueting rooms, shared for the occasion by the senior management of one of the larger department stores and an ad-hoc group of dentists, dental nurses and technicians. At a little after half past eleven, Miriam had been clearing away the last of the coffee cups when a man had slid his hand between her legs, pushing the black skirt she was forced to wear hard between her thighs. No way it was any kind of an accident. Miriam had swung round, told him to keep his hands to himself and slapped her right hand across his face. There was a cup and saucer in it at the time. The man screamed and landed with a jarring thump on his knees; amidst a lot of blood were the fragments of not one, but two broken teeth. Miriam thought there was poetic justice in this, until she found out the man worked not with fillings but furniture.

Of course, at first he denied as much as touching Miriam, never mind goosing her; all he would eventually admit as a possibility was that, being a little the worse for wear for drink, he had lost his footing getting up and reached out to steady himself.

'Bullshit!' Miriam declared resolutely, the term sounding somewhat at odds with her Cheshire accent. But she was doing American Studies and took the aculturation seriously.

When the member of the hotel's management team instructed her to apologise, she told him in no uncertain terms where to put his skirt and apron. She was on her way out of the hotel, irritable and prepared to walk back to her digs in Lenton, when she saw a car pull up beside a woman just in front of her. The driver shouted a name out of the window, jumped out when the woman didn't stop, ran after her and grabbed her arm.

Miriam had held back for a while, worried in case what had just happened to her was about to happen to someone else. But after a few minutes of raised voices, mostly his, a little arm tugging, the woman shrugged her shoulders and seemed to change her mind. Anyway, she walked around to the passenger side of the car and got in, the driver followed suit and they drove off, turning left down the hill.

'Descriptions?' Resnick asked.

Cossall grinned. 'Talk to her yourself.'

Miriam was wearing a blue denim jacket with a button reading *Spinsters on the Rampage* on one lapel, a larger one, *Hillary for President*, on the other. She wore a faded denim shirt and a yellow roll-neck under the jacket, black wool leggings and Doc Martens. She greeted Resnick with a wary half-grin.

'I'm sorry to ask you all this again . . .'

'S'okay.'

'But this woman, the one you saw get into the car, how old would you say she was?'

Miriam rolled her tongue and Resnick realised she was chewing gum. 'Could have been a couple of years older than me, not a lot more.'

'Early twenties, then?'

'Yes.'

'And she was wearing?'

Miriam glanced over at Cossall before she answered. 'Like I said, silvery top, matching tights, short black skirt; she had this red coat across her shoulders. Bit posey, I thought. Still . . .' She looked from Resnick to Cossall and back again. 'It's her, isn't it? The one who's missing. Jesus Christ, I could have done something, stopped it.'

'I doubt you could have done anything,' Resnick said. 'You waited to see what was going to happen, that's more than most people would have done. But she got into the car of her own accord. There was no reason for you to interfere.'

'But when I heard about it, on the news, back home, you know, over the holiday – I'm so stupid! – I never as much as thought.'

'It's okay, love,' Cossall said. 'Don't get so worked up.'

'Tell me,' Resnick said, 'about the car.'

'Four-door saloon, blue, dark blue. Course, if I'd had any sense, if I hadn't been so worked out about that wanker . . . that idiot at the hotel, I would have thought to write down the number, just, you know, in case. But it was J reg., I'm sure of that.'

'The make?'

'Can't say for certain. I could probably recognise it, though, if I had the chance.'

'Tell him about the driver,' Cossall said. 'What he looked like.'

Miriam described Robin Hidden – his height, slightly stooped posture, wiriness, spectacles – to a T. Everything except the stammer.

'Knew he was lying,' Millington said. 'Just bloody knew it.'

'Felt it in your water, Graham?' Cossall grinned.

They were back in Resnick's office, while Lynn Kellogg gave iriam a brief tour of the station, offered her a cup of tea, asked what exactly was American Studies.

'Let's do it carefully,' Resnick said. 'No slip ups now.'

'You'll want an identity parade,' Cossall said, one leg cocked over the corner of Resnick's desk. 'Best have a word with Paddy Fitzgerald, see if he can't fix that. Graham here could probably make sure young Hidden doesn't do a runner.'

Right, Millington thought, thanks a lot!

'At least that hasn't been handed over to a bunch of private cowboys yet. We catch 'em, get them into court and some half-assed security guard lets them go.'

'It'll take more time organising the cars,' Resnick said. Since the Police and Criminal Evidence Act, there had to be a minimum of twelve vehicles of a similar type presented to the witness.

Cossall nodded. 'Best get the car established though, hold off on pulling Hidden in for the ID; then if both come up positive, we can collar him while he's on the premises.'

Resnick nodded. 'Let's be about it.'

'Talked to Jolly Jack?' Cossall asked over his shoulder, heading for the door.

'Next thing,' Resnick said. And then, 'Graham, when you go out for Hidden, under wraps as much as you can. We're right here, this'll be enough of a circus as it is.'

Twenty-seven

Dana had gone to bed full of good intentions. The alarm set for seven-thirty, she was going to make an early start, get in a full day; attend to all of those things she claimed there was no time for due to her job. Well, now was her chance; she would get down to it first thing, shower, clear her head, make a list.

Idling through her wardrobe, she wondered about buying something special for tonight. Detective Inspector Charles Resnick, investigating officer, making a personal call at eight sharp. Charles. Charlie. Her hands ran down the sleeve of a silk shirt, apple green, smooth to the touch. Dana smiled, recalling how gentle he had been. A surprise. Lifting the shirt clear on its hanger, she thought about his hands against the softness of the material. Large hands. When she thought about it, now and since, it surprised her, the extent to which his initial clumsiness had disappeared. Yes, she thought, laying the shirt out on the bed. Apple green. Good. She would run the iron over it later, wear that.

In the shower she wondered if it had been right to phone him at work; not the best of times, either, from the way he had answered, a mixture of circumspect and abrupt. With some men, though, it was what you had to do. Make it clear that you were interested, what was what.

Slowly, savouring it, Dana soaped her shoulders, sides, what she could reach of her back; better to be positive, she thought, than yield the initiative from the start.

Miriam sat reading, alternating between *Light in August* and the *New Musical Express*; the earphones from her Walkman were leaking a little Chris Isaak into the CID room. At the other side of the desk, Lynn Kellogg struggled to catch up with the never-ending demands of paperwork; tried not to think about her father, just below the level of consciousness always waiting for the phone to ring, her mother's voice, 'Oh, Lynnie . . .'

Divine and Naylor returned, bullish, from the Meadows. Raju had looked at the sketches drawn by Sandra Drexler and confirmed they closely matched those he had seen on one of his attackers.

'Hey up,' Divine said none too quietly, pointing across the room at Miriam. 'What d'you reckon to that?'

Miriam let him know that she had heard; staring him down, she cranked up her Walkman and turned the page of the *NME*. Finish the singles reviews and then she'd get back to Faulkner. A seminar tomorrow about shifting points of view.

Lynn explained the process more assiduously than Miriam considered strictly necessary; but then, she told herself, quite a few of the people they had to deal with, the police, probably they weren't any too bright.

The vehicles had been arranged in two lines, facing, and Miriam was left to walk, taking her time, between. At one point she came close to giggling, feeling suddenly like the Queen, inspecting her loyal troops in some Godforsaken scrap of land. What a farce! The more that came to light, the more you realised that life amongst the Royals was a cross between *Northern Exposure* and *Twin Peaks*. Without a moment's hesitation she picked out the car. A midnight blue Vauxhall Cavalier.

Robin Hidden heard them draw up outside and almost before they had approached the house, realised who they were. Millington he recognised by name, the dapper suit, the smug smile when Robin opened the street door.

Two other officers waited behind him on the path, also plain clothes; the expression on one of them slightly mocking, as if faintly hopeful that he would panic, cut some kind of a dash, provide an excuse for a chase, a bit of action.

It was all little more than a formality, Millington explained. A witness to confirm you were where you said you were, the night your Nancy disappeared. Nothing to worry about, as long as you were telling the truth.

Harry Phelan was in the station entrance when the car arrived bringing Robin Hidden in. Two and two had rarely come together so fast to make four. Phelan managed to hold himself in check until Hidden was level with him, then launched himself forwards, landing a two-fisted blow to the back of the head, just behind the ear. Millington moved quickly, setting himself between the two of them, Phelan's boot deflecting off his shin and catching Robin Hidden's thigh as he fell.

Before he could do any more damage, Millington took a choke hold around Harry Phelan's neck and dragged him back towards the uniformed officer who had run round from behind the desk, handcuffs at the ready.

'Enough!' Millington shouted just in time. 'It's okay.'

Opportunely, Divine had chosen this moment to appear. He seized Harry Phelan's shirt with one hand, the other, bunched into a fist, raised above his face.

'Mark,' Millington said, 'Let it be.'

Divine stepped back and Phelan was swung round hard and pushed against the wall, feet kicked wide, arms stretched out straight behind, cuffs clicked tightly into place.

'Inside and book him,' Millington said, straightening his tie. 'And now we've done our job of protecting Mr Hidden here,' Millington smiled, 'let's escort him safely inside.'

Robin Hidden looked at the seven men standing still in a haphazard sort of a line. For some reason, he had expected to have come face to face, if not with carbon copies, then people who bore more than a passing resemblance to himself. But these – about the same height, certainly, none of them fat, roughly of similar age – in reality he looked nothing like them. He supposed that was part of the point.

'Like I said,' the officer in charge of the parade said, 'pick your own place in the line.'

Seven, Robin thought, that's the number most people choose all the time. He went over and stood between a man whose hair was more gingery than fair and another slightly taller than himself.

Number four.

'Spectacles on first, gentlemen, please.'

As Robin Hidden fumbled his glasses from their case, he observed, as if in some kind of joke, all of the other men taking out the pairs of glasses they had been given and putting them on.

Miriam took her time. Up and down the row twice as required, hesitating, asking if she might walk the line a third time. Silent as everyone waited, the officers, the solicitor watching her, the men staring straight ahead, blinking, some of them, behind unfamiliar glasses. Silent, save for the breath of the man she knew already she would choose. She had done since practically the first moment; but she was enjoying it, the drama of it, acting it out.

'Is the man you saw on the Christmas Eve present in the parade?' the investigating officer asked when, finally, she stood in front of him.

Nervous now, despite herself, Miriam nodded.

'And will you indicate, please, the number of that person?'

'N-number four,' Miriam said, stammering for perhaps the first time in her life.

Twenty-eight

The blinds in Skelton's office were drawn, closing out what was left of the winter light. Skelton's earlier conversation with the assistant chief had made him sweat. The afternoon editions of the *Post* had headlined Harry Phelan's arrest at the police station, featured a photograph of him angrily descending the steps to the street after being released. Another quotable diatribe about police incompetence, sloth. 'Only time they put themselves out nowadays, something political or if it's one of their own.'

'Questions being asked, Jack,' the assistant chief had said. 'What in God's name's going on on your patch? You used to run such a tight ship, everything battened down. Trouble with a reputation like yours, things start to get out of control, out of hand, people notice. They want to know the reasons why. Oh, and Jack, give my best to Alice, right?'

Resnick had noticed, this past week or so, that the photographs of Alice and Kate, so prominent and exact on Jack Skelton's desk in the past, had disappeared from sight. He was in Skelton's office now while Robin Hidden took his statutory break, getting the superintendent up to speed.

'Robin,' Resnick had said, his voice reasonable, soothing, 'no one's accusing you of lying, deliberately lying. We know this has been a difficult time for you,

209

emotionally. What was happening, the rejection, you were bound to be upset. After all, this was somebody you loved and who you thought had loved you. Any of us would find that hard to cope with, hard to handle. And there you'd been, driving round all evening, desperate to see her, going over all the things you wanted to say inside your head. And then, suddenly, there she was.'

Resnick had held his moment; waited until Robin Hidden was looking back into his eyes. 'Like I say, we'd any of us, situation like that, we'd find it hard to know how to react. Hard to remember, afterwards, exactly what we did or said.'

Hidden's head went down. It wasn't clear whether or not he was crying.

David Welch had leaned forward from the edge of his chair. 'I think my client . . .'

'Not now,' Millington had said quietly.

'My client . . .'

'Not,' repeated Millington, 'now.'

And not for one moment did Resnick allow his gaze to shift away, waiting for Robin Hidden's head to come back up, blinking at him through a gauze of tears. 'She t-told me,' he said, 'she thought I was being s-st-stupid, p-p-pathetic. She didn't want to talk to me. Not ever. S-she wished she'd never had anything to do with m-me, n-never seen me at all.'

Skelton was sitting bolt upright, fingertips touching, forearms resting on the edge of his desk. 'And the boy, how did he respond?'

'Admits to getting angry, losing his temper.'

'He did hit her?'

'Not hit exactly, no.'

'Semantics, Charlie?'

210

Resnick glanced at the floor; from somewhere a splash of brown, dark and drying, had earlier attached itself to the side of his left shoe. 'He says that he took a hold of her, both arms. I imagine he's got quite a grip. Shook her around a bit, trying to get her to change her mind. That's when she agreed to get into the car.'

Skelton sighed, swivelled his chair sideways, waited.

'They drove down towards the Castle, on into the Park. Stopped by the first roundabout on Lenton Road. What he wanted was to get her to talk about what was going on.' Resnick shifted on his seat, less than comfortable. 'What he wanted, of course, was for her to change her mind, agree to keep seeing him. Anything as long as she didn't carry on with what she was doing. Shutting him right out of her life.'

'I love you,' Robin said. Against her will, he was holding her hand.

Nancy looked through the side window of the car, up along the steadily sloping street, shadows from the gas lamps faint and blurred. Frost along the privet hedge. 'I'm sorry, Robin, but I don't love you.'

'A shame she couldn't have lied,' Skelton said.

'She pulled her hand away and he did nothing to stop her. Got out of the car and walked back down Lenton Road; turned off right, down towards the Boulevard.'

'And he just sat there?'

'Watching her in the mirror.'

'Nothing more?'

'Never saw her again.'

'He says.'

Resnick nodded.

Skelton was back on his feet, desk to wall, wall to window, window to desk, pacing it out. 'She's gone

211

without trace, Charlie. Good looking young woman. You know what it's like, cases like this. Spend more time than you can afford checking on sightings by every looney and short-sighted granny from Ilkeston to Arbroath. This time it's like a desert out there. No bugger's seen a thing.'

Back by his desk, Skelton picked up his fountain pen and unscrewed the cap, glanced at the nib, replaced the cap, put the pen back down. Resnick shuffled around on his seat, clasped and unclasped his hands.

'Nine times out of ten, Charlie, it's not some wandering nutter, spends his hours poring over true-life stories of serial killers like they're the lives of the saints. You know that as well as me. It's the husbands, boyfriends, the frustrated wives.'

The drawer to which the pictures of Alice had been consigned was close to Skelton's right hand.

'You're right to tread careful, Charlie, God knows. But let's not let him get the upper hand, think he can play with us as he likes, little here, little there. We've got him this far, Charlie, let's not let him slip away.'

Twenty-nine

Dana had spent the best part of the day shopping and had stopped off at the Potter's House for a coffee on her way home. Liza, her neighbour from the flat above, Liza of the pinched laugh and squeaky bed, was sitting at a table upstairs. She had been for a tan and wax session and was recovering with a pot of Earl Grey and a slice of coffee and walnut cake. A magistrate's clerk, Liza was filling in time before it was safe to go round to the house of the sixty-four-year-old chairman of the bench with whom she was having a furtive affair. When he had called on Liza once and Dana had opened the house door to him by mistake, she had thought he was collecting for Help the Aged. Now whenever the bed creaked over her head, Dana held her breath and waited for the call to emergency services, the sound of the ambulance siren approaching.

Dana persuaded Liza to order a fresh pot of tea and joined her in a relaxing gossip about winter cruises to warmer climes and the painful necessity of maintaining a neat bikini line. By the time they parted, Liza to visit her clandestine lover and Dana to lug her bags of shopping the remainder of the way back to Newcastle Drive, it was almost six o'clock.

Dana had opened her packages, put her new blouse carefully away, folded her new Next underwear inside the appropriate drawer, slipped the Sting CD on to the machine and started it playing. Poor old Sting, she wished he could stop worrying about the world and write another song like 'Every Breath You Take'.

The bottle of chardonnay she was saving for later safe in the fridge, she opened a Bulgarian country white she had bought at Safeway, fancying a little something to take the edge off the waiting. One mouthful made her realise that she should have something to eat as well. Tipping the contents of a carton of potato and watercress soup into a pan to heat through, she found the last of the Tesco muffins at the back of the freezer and sliced it in two ready to toast.

She ate the soup in the kitchen, thumbing through some old travel brochures; before she had finished her second glass of wine she had got as far in the quick crossword as three across, nine down and it was still well short of seven o'clock. Over an hour to go and that was if he arrived on time. In desperation, she phoned her mother, who, thank heavens, was out. Oh well, Dana thought, when all else fails, run a bath.

Undressed, she picked up the Joanna Trollope paperback a friend had given her for Christmas, the gift tag poking out so she could remember who to thank. The mirrors were already hazed in steam as, with a gasp of pleasure, Dana settled herself in. She read a chapter of the book, scarcely taking it in, dropped it over the side and closed her eyes. Charlie, she decided, was almost certainly a figment of her imagination. At least, the Charlie she had rolled around with, cuddled up to in her bed, the one who had stared at her with shocked and startled eyes the moment before he came.

It was half-past seven by the time she climbed out and began to dry herself. In the circle she had cleared with her towel in the glass, Dana caught herself wishing, not for the first time, that she could lose six or eight pounds.

When she tried it on with her new skirt that buttoned down the side, the apple green shirt looked exactly right. What it needed, of course, was a different pair of tights. Nancy had a pair, she remembered, dove grey, that would be perfect. Well, of course, had she been there she would have said go ahead.

She lifted Sting off the stereo, settled Dire Straits in his place and crossed to Nancy's room. When she opened the door, the silver crochet top that Nancy had been wearing Christmas Eve was on a hanger hooked outside the wardrobe door, the short black skirt had been folded neatly across the back of a chair, her silver-grey tights were draped over the wardrobe mirror and her leather boots were in the middle of the floor.

Cold clung to Dana's arms and neck like a second skin.

Thirty

There was a clean suit he'd found, charcoal grey with a narrow red stripe, still in its plastic cover from the cleaner's; a light blue shirt that didn't need too much ironing and missing only one button from its cuffs. Near the back of the drawer Resnick found the dark blue tie that Marian had given him in desperation for a similar function two years before. Maybe three. When Resnick held it under the light there were faint spatterings of what was probably bortsch, dried into the fabric, and he scraped at these, more or less successfully, with his thumb.

Already it was ten past eight and the cab he'd ordered for a quarter to still hadn't arrived: New Year's Eve. Bud was nudging round his feet and he bent to scoop the small cat into the air and carried it across the room, nuzzled against his cheek. The battered album cover on the table showed a smiling Thelonious Monk waving from the back of a San Francisco tram. Scratched and worn, the pianist was noodling his way through 'You Took the Words Right Out of My Heart'. Resnick remembered buying it on the way back from watching County lose a two goal lead in the last five minutes of a game; winter it had been, frost that had never left the railings and cups of Bovril at half-time, gripped tight to let the warmth seep into his hands. Sixty nine? Seventy? Resnick had taken it home and played it, both sides, beginning to end then through again, fascinated. Only the second or third Monk LP that he had owned.

He was about to call the cab company and complain when he heard the taxi draw up outside; he switched off the stereo, switched off the light, picked up his topcoat in the hall, patted his pocket for his keys. One foot into the chill night and the phone was calling him back.

'When?' he asked, interrupting abruptly. 'When was this?'

The duty officer told him what she knew.

'All right,' Resnick said, interrupting again. 'Make sure scene of crime have been alerted. Contact Graham Millington, tell him to meet me there. I'm on my way.'

Dana's first instinct, after phoning the police, had been to run. Get herself out of the flat, anywhere outside, lock the doors and wait. She had asked first for Resnick by name; being told that he was no longer there, she had explained as carefully as she could; no ordinary intrusion, no ordinary burglary. Fortunately, the officer she had spoken to had been sufficiently quick-witted to make the connections Dana left implicit.

'Please, whatever you do,' the officer had said, trying not to alarm Dana any more than she was already, 'don't touch anything.'

She felt foolish standing out in the hall, exposed in the street; after no more than a few minutes, she let herself back into the flat and tried not to keep staring at the clock. She had touched the wine bottle and her glass enough times already and, anyway, she didn't think the police would be interested in those; pouring herself a drink, for the first time in ages she found herself craving a cigarette. Her hand shook as she brought the glass to her mouth and wine tipped over wrist and fingers, darkened the sleeve of her apple green shirt.

'God,' she said to the walls, 'now I'm becoming a sloppy drunk.'

And all, she thought, well before my fortieth birthday. Reaching out to steady herself, she sat carefully down. Nancy was as many years short of thirty. Dana sighed: she had struggled to understand the implications of what had happened and then she had struggled not to. She put down the wine and looked at her watch.

There were two police cars there when Resnick arrived, successfully blocking his cab's progress along Newcastle Drive. He wasted no time telling them to repark, ordered the one whose lights were still flashing to turn them off. Millington had got there a few minutes before him and was standing close against the entrance to the flat, earnestly talking to the officer in charge of the scene of crime team. Leaving them to it, Resnick walked quickly past.

Dana was in the centre of the living room, standing, hands down by her sides. As soon as she saw Resnick she pitched against him and he caught her like he had before, only this time the circumstances were different; there were three plain-clothes men in the room readying cameras and other equipment, and all Resnick could do was hold her while she cried. Two of the men winked at one another and then they kept their eyes averted and got on with their job. The items of clothing that had reappeared would be photographed in place and then tagged and bagged for special attention, after which the rest of the flat would be dusted for prints, pored over for fibres, anything which didn't belong. Nancy's room and the door to the flat were prime targets, entrance and exit; however careful people tried to be, it was unusual to leave no trace. The problem would be making that trace count.

'Want me to give Lynn a ring?' Millington said at Resnick's shoulder, eyeing the way Dana was continuing to clutch hold of him. 'Bring her in to give a hand?'

'No need,' Resnick said. 'Not now. She's enough on her plate as it is.'

He spoke quietly to Dana, mouth close against her hair, and when she lifted her face towards him, he led her into the kitchen and helped her to sit down.

'Will you be okay for a minute? I ought to take a look.'

She fashioned a smile and nodded.

'I'll be right back,' Resnick said.

He left her there and joined Millington in the doorway to Nancy's room. From where it was still hanging outside the wardrobe, the silver top caught the flash from a camera and spun it back into Resnick's eyes.

'How's it been? You been having a good time?'

Long legs, a sequined silver bag, a smile.

'Well, Merry Christmas, once again. Happy New Year.'

Skirt, top, boots, tights. The skin along Resnick's arms burned cold. 'Any sign of a bag?' he asked.

'What kind?'

'So big.' He made a shape, the size of a hardback book, with his hands. 'Not everyday, fancy. Silver sequins on both sides.'

'Dress bag, then.'

'If that's what they're called.'

'Matching the top.'

'More or less, yes.'

The scene of crime officer shook his head. 'Not so far.'

Resnick asked Dana if she'd seen Nancy's bag and she said no. The flat would have to be searched anyway, wall to wall, floor to ceiling, and if it were anywhere it would be found.

'I'm going to get changed out of this,' Dana said, indicating the button-through skirt, the shiny green shirt. 'I feel stupid.'

'You look fine.'

'I'm going to change anyway.'

She came back out of the bedroom wearing blue jeans and a loose white sweater, blue canvas shoes on her feet. Her hair she'd tied back with a strip of patterned cloth.

'It couldn't have been Nancy, could it?' she asked. 'Brought them back herself?'

'It's not impossible.'

'Not likely.'

'No.'

'Then it was him.'

Resnick looked at her.

'Whoever she went off with. Whoever took her away. He was here in this flat.' Fear shivered, alive, across her eyes.

One of the scene of crime team came towards them and Resnick turned aside to speak to him.

'No sign of forced entry. Not anywhere. Most likely used a key.'

Resnick nodded. Nancy's key would have been in the missing bag.

'Why would he do this?' Dana asked, as the officer walked away. 'Why go to all this trouble? What's the point?'

'I don't know,' Resnick said. 'Not yet. Not for certain.'

'He's showing off, isn't he? Being clever. That's what

it is.' Dana folded her arms across her chest, fingers clenched tight. 'Bastard!'

Outside, officers were knocking on doors, ringing bells, beginning to talk to neighbours, those who were still home, asking if they had noticed anything unusual, seen anyone they hadn't recognised coming into the building, hanging about outside. Dana had been out of the flat from mid-morning until early evening; whoever had brought Nancy's things into the flat could have done so at any point during that time. Not so far short of eight hours.

Resnick was thinking again about Nancy's clothing, what had been returned. 'How about underwear,' he said. 'I don't suppose you've any idea what she might have been wearing?'

'You mean, exactly?'

'Yes.'

Dana shook her head. 'Not really.' She shrugged. 'Something nice.'

'When they're through in there, would you mind taking a look? Through the drawers. Wherever she kept things like that. You might just notice something, you never know.'

'Of course.'

'Is it okay,' Resnick asked, 'if I use your phone?'

'Go ahead.'

As he dialled the number he looked back to where Dana was now sitting on the arm of the settee, hands on her thighs, wide pale face close again to tears.

Alice Skelton had been waging a silent war of attrition throughout the evening, pointedly ignoring her husband in front of the two couples who were their guests. By the start of the main course, she was well on the way to being drunk and had taken to insulting him openly.

'Jack, here,' she proclaimed, passing the redcurrant jelly, 'was the man for whom the term anally retentive was invented.'

Skelton disappeared to fetch some more wine. His guests wished they could do the same.

When the phone rang a little while later, Skelton was on his feet before the second ring, praying it was for him.

'It's probably her,' Alice's taunt chased him from the room. 'The ice maiden. Wishing you a happy New Year.'

It wasn't; it was Resnick. Skelton listened for long enough then told Resnick to meet him at the station as soon as he could finish up where he was.

'Something urgent?' Alice mocked. 'Something they can't possibly handle without you?'

Skelton apologised to their guests and headed for the door.

'Give her my love,' Alice shouted after him. And quietly, into the aubergine parmigiana, 'The stuck-up bitch!'

'Is there anywhere you can stay?' Resnick asked. 'For tonight, at least.'

'You don't think he'll come back?'

'No. No reason to think so, none at all. If you were really worried we could leave a man outside. I just thought you'd feel more comfortable somewhere else, that was all.'

Dana was leaning forward slightly, looking into his eyes. 'I couldn't stay with you?'

Resnick glanced around the room to see if anyone had overheard. 'In the circumstances, best not.'

'All right,' Dana said. Clearly, it was not.

'Surely there's a friend you could go to?'

'If I did stay here,' Dana persisted, 'would you come back? Later?'

Resnick thought about Marian at the Polish Club, counting down the hours till midnight; thought about other things. 'I don't know,' he said. 'I couldn't promise. Probably not.'

Dana reached for the address book near to the phone. 'I'll find someone,' she said. 'You don't have to worry.'

'D'you want to let me have the number?' Resnick asked. 'Where you'll be.'

'There isn't a lot of point, is there?' Dana said.

He touched her arm, just below the sleeve of her sweater, and goosebumps rose to meet his fingers. 'I'm sorry,' he said, 'it's worked out like this.'

She was just smiling, grudging, wary, as Millington approached.

'Hang on here, Graham,' Resnick said. 'Make sure nothing gets missed. And see Miss Matthieson's taken wherever she wants to go. I'm off in to see the old man.'

He paused in the doorway and glanced back inside the flat, but Dana had already moved from sight, back into her room.

Thirty-one

The station was different at night, quieter yet more intense. The blood that had been splashed across the steps and the entrance hall was fresh blood, so bright beneath the overhead lights that it glowed. A sudden shout from the cells aside, voices were muted; footsteps along the corridors, up and down the stairs, were muffled. Only the telephones, sharp and demanding, retained their shrillness.

Skelton surprised Resnick by not being in his own office, but in the CID room, standing over by the far wall in front of the large map of the city. He was wearing a dark blazer and light-grey trousers instead of the normal suit. Unusually, the top button of his shirt had been unfastened above the knot of his tie. He didn't speak as Resnick walked in and when he did, instead of making a remark about what had happened, he said, 'Since you and Elaine were divorced, Charlie, d'you ever catch yourself wishing you'd married again?'

Taken aback, uncertain how to respond, Resnick went over to where the kettle stood on a tray, lifted it up to check there was enough water inside and switched it on at the wall.

Skelton was looking at him still, waiting for an answer.

'Sometimes,' Resnick finally said.

'I'll be honest,' Skelton said. 'Living the way you do,

224

on your own, I thought you were a miserable bugger. Night after night, going back to that place alone. Last thing I reckoned I'd want to be, living like that.'

'Tea?' Resnick said.

Skelton shook his head and Resnick dropped a single tea bag into the least stained of the mugs.

'You get used to it, I suppose,' Skelton said. 'Accommodate. Learn to appreciate the advantages. After a while, it must be difficult to live any other way.'

There were footsteps in the corridor outside and Resnick turned to watch Helen Siddons push open the door and walk in. Whichever occasion she had been called from had scarcely been informal. Her hair had been pinned up high and she was wearing a dress not unlike the one Resnick remembered from Christmas Eve, except this was blue, so pale it seemed almost all the colour had leaked out of it. Somewhere along the way she had changed into flat shoes and the raincoat round her shoulders could have been a man's.

'I asked Helen to join us,' Skelton said. 'Her experience might be useful here.'

What experience? Resnick caught himself thinking. 'Kettle just this second boiled,' he said. 'If you want some tea.'

'When Helen was on secondment to Bristol and Avon she was involved in that Susan Rogel business, you remember?'

Something about a woman whose car was found abandoned on the Mendip Hills, somewhere between Bath and Wells. No signs of a struggle, no note, nothing to explain the disappearance; if there had been foul play, no body had been found to substantiate it, no evidence either.

'I thought the suggestion was she'd taken off of her

225

own accord,' Resnick said. 'Wasn't there some kind of affair that had got out of hand?'

Helen Siddons drew a chair out from one of the desks and Skelton moved to help with her coat. 'She'd become involved with her husband's business partner,' Helen said. 'They ran an antiques business, branches all over the south west.' She took a cigarette from a case in her bag and Resnick half expected Skelton to lean over and offer her a light but he allowed her to do it for herself. 'Seems that the husband knew what was going on, had done for some while, but hadn't said anything as the business was in a pretty shaky state and he didn't want to rock the boat any more than it was already.' She arched back her long neck and released smoke towards the ceiling. Skelton was staring at her like a man transfixed. 'When it became clear they were going to go bust anyway, he gave his wife an ultimatum. Stop seeing him or I want a divorce. The wife, Susan, she would have been happy to jump the other way but faced with the possibility her lover backed off. Preferred to carry on sneaking around, didn't want to get married and make it all respectable, settle down.' It was the slightest of glances towards Skelton, probably no more than coincidental. 'All this had made Susan ill, she'd seen a doctor, was taking all kinds of pills for stress, depression, whatever. There's a suggestion, unproven, that she made at least one attempt on her own life. We do know that on more than one occasion she told a girl friend that she couldn't be doing with either man any more. She just wanted to get out.'

'So she staged this business with the car as a red herring and headed for Spain or wherever?' Resnick asked. 'That's the assumption?'

Helen tapped ash into the metal waste-bin near her

feet. 'A lot of the evidence pointed that way. There was a suitcase and clothes missing from home and her passport wasn't found. But I never believed it.'

'Why not?'

Behind blue-grey smoke, Helen Siddons smiled. 'Because of the ransom demand.'

If she hadn't had all of Resnick's interest before, she had it now. 'I don't remember anything about a ransom,' he said.

'We asked for a media blackout and got it.'

'And you think that's what's happening here?' Resnick asked. 'With Nancy Phelan? Ransom?'

Helen Siddons took her time. 'Of course,' she said. 'Don't you?'

Half an hour had passed. More. From somewhere Jack Skelton had magicked a half-bottle of Teacher's and they were drinking it from thick china mugs. Somehow the clock slipped past midnight without any of them noticing and no toasts were offered up. Ash sprinkled here and there down the pale blue of Helen Siddons' dress as she talked.

Painstakingly, she took them through the Rogel case, stage by stage. When the first ransom note had been delivered, pushed through the door of the missing woman's parents' house in the early hours of the morning, it had gone unnoticed for the best part of a day, the envelope pushed between a pile of old newspapers and unsolicited catalogues. When a follow-up phone call was made, at four o'clock that afternoon, Susan Rogel's mother had had no idea what it was referring to, took it as some kind of sick joke and hung up. By the time the second call came through, though, they'd found the note. It was asking for twenty thousand pounds in used notes.

Rogel's father was a retired army colonel, not someone to be toyed with. He made it clear they wouldn't as much as think of handing over a penny without proof. He also immediately contacted the police.

Nothing happened for three days.

On the fourth, the Rogels drove to the nearest supermarket to do their weekly shopping and when they returned, someone had jimmied open one of the small windows at the rear of the house. Naturally, they thought they'd been burgled, looked anxiously round but found nothing obviously missing. What they did find, folded neatly inside tissue paper in one of the drawers in the spare bedroom, the room that had been Susan's when she had lived at home, was one of her blouses, the one she had been wearing when she was last seen, filling her car with petrol at a garage on the Wells road.

The family wanted to pay the ransom, asked for time to find the money; they were given another three days. Instructions were given about leaving it in the courtyard of a pub high on the Mendips. All of this information was passed immediately to the police. On the morning the drop was to be made, the location was carefully staked out, it would have been difficult to be more discreet.

'What happened?' Resnick asked.

'Nothing. The money was left in a duffel bag by the outside toilet of the pub. No one came near it. Not many vehicles came over the tops that day and all that did were checked. Nobody suspicious.'

'He got scared then? What?'

'There was one final call to the Rogels the following day. Angry with them for trying to trick him, get him caught, going to the police. There was no attempt at contact after that.'

'And Susan Rogel?'

Helen Siddons was standing against the window, outlined against the white strips of blind. 'No sign. No word. If she did simply run off, if the ransom note was somebody's bluff, she's never resurfaced, never been back in touch with anyone in her previous life. Husband, lover, parents, not anyone.'

'And if it was real?'

Helen smoothed one hand down the leg of her dress. 'This was almost two years ago. If someone kidnapped her, it's difficult to believe she's alive now.'

'You double checked everyone in the area of the pub that day?' Skelton asked.

'Double, triple.' Helen shook her head. 'No way we could connect any of them with Susan Rogel or the way she disappeared.'

'How easy would it have been for this person to find out you and her parents were hand in glove?'

Helen Siddons lit another cigarette. 'I was the liaison officer. Any meetings we had were well out of the way, never the same location. Phone calls call box to call box, never to their house or the station. No mobile phones used because they're more susceptible to being tapped. If he found out, rather than guessed, that wasn't the weak link.'

'Have you any idea what was?'

She gave a quick shake of the head. 'No.'

'Near enough two years back,' Skelton said, looking at Resnick. 'Time to lay low, move maybe, try again.'

'Blouse aside,' Resnick said, 'there's not much says this case is the same.'

'Not yet, Charlie.'

'Wait till Nancy Phelan's parents get the morning post,' Helen said. 'Special delivery.'

'And if they don't?'

Helen blinked and looked away.

Skelton tipped the last of the bottle into the three mugs. 'So, Charlie, what d'you think? If this is a runner, where does that leave young Hidden in the scheme of things?'

'Between Dana Matthieson leaving the flat and our bringing Robin Hidden in for questioning, he had time and plenty to get round there and leave those clothes. And he knew the layout of the flat well, remember, in and out in no time.'

'I thought you had your doubts about Hidden for this,' Skelton said. 'That was the feeling you gave. Now you want to keep him tied in.'

'One way or another, he already is.'

Skelton looked thoughtful, sipped his scotch. 'Helen?' Skelton said.

'I think we should make good and sure,' she said, 'the minute anyone contacts the Phelans, we know about it. And by the time they do, we know how we're going to respond.'

'Charlie?' Skelton said.

'That only makes sense,' Resnick said. He was uncomfortable with the knowledge that he was bridling inside every time Helen Siddons said *we*, at the way she seemed to be edging herself more and more into the heart of things.

'I'll give you a lift then, Helen,' Skelton said, hopefully holding her coat.

Resnick knocked back the last half-inch of whisky, rinsed out the mug from which he had been drinking and wished them both good-night; whatever was going on there, as long as it didn't get in the way of the task in hand, it didn't have to concern him.

*

'Night, sir. Happy New Year, sir,' said the young constable at the desk.

Resnick nodded in reply and stepped out on to the street; it wasn't clear if someone had wiped the blood away or whether it had been trodden clean by a succession of passing feet. Above, the sky had cleared and there were stars, clustering close to the moon.

In little more than minutes he was standing at the far end of Newcastle Drive, hands in pockets, looking up at the blank windows to Dana's flat. If she had decided to stay, he hoped by now she would be safely asleep. For several long moments he allowed himself to recall the warmth of her body, generous beside him in her bed.

'If I did stay here, would you come back? Later?'

By the time he had crossed town, avoiding the raucous celebrations continuing in and around the fountains of the Old Market Square, and arrived at the Polish Club, almost the last of the cars was turning out of the car park, exhaust fumes heavy in the air. Those that remained belonged to the staff. There was a taxi idling at the far side of the street, but Resnick didn't linger to see who it was waiting for. He would call Marian tomorrow, make his apologies with a clear head.

Dizzy was sitting on the stone wall at the front of the house when Resnick arrived, stretching his legs and trotting along the top of the wall beside him, tail arched high in greeting.

Happy New Year.

Thirty-two

Michelle opened her eyes to see Karl staring down at her, his face close enough to hers for her to feel the faint warmth of his breath. How long he had been standing there she didn't know. Through the gap at the top of the curtains, the street light shone a muted orange. Karl started to speak but she shushed him and smiled and pressed her finger lightly against first his lips and then her own. As usual, Gary had fetched up close beside her in the bed and Michelle eased herself sideways, slipping out from beneath the weight of his arm and leg.

'I not sleep,' said Karl on the stairs. 'Cold.'

Michelle tousled the tangle of hair on his head and shooed him into the living room. Natalie had bunched herself sideways along the top of her cot. When Michelle reached under the covers to move her she was shocked by the child's coldness. Natalie stirred, whimpered, fell back to sleep.

'Come on,' she whispered to Karl, 'let's go and make the tea.'

Even with slippers and two pairs of socks, the damp seemed to seep up through the kitchen floor. While she watched, Karl took two slices from the packet of sliced bread and placed them on the grill to toast; once she had swilled almost boiling water around the pot and emptied it down the sink, he lifted two tea bags from the box and dropped them inside.

232

'Good boy,' Michelle said encouragingly.

''ood boy.'

'Soon be able to do all this by yourself. Bring me and Gary breakfast in bed.'

Karl looked uncertain. The swelling at the side of his face had mostly gone down and even the bruise was beginning to fade.

Michelle caught herself yawning and when she moved her hand to her mouth she realised she was nursing a headache. She and Gary had been to the pub last night, along with Brian and Josie. Where Brian got the money from to spend on drink she couldn't imagine, didn't want to know. Generous, though, she'd say that for him. Even if, when he'd had his fair share, he wasn't above pushing his leg against hers under the table, once or twice sliding his hand along her thigh. Michelle had mentioned it to Josie when they were on their own and Josie had just laughed. Brian having a bit of fun. Gary wouldn't laugh, not if he knew, she was certain of that. Gary saw him as much as put his little finger on her and he'd kill him for it.

She pulled out the grill pan just in time before the toast started burning. 'You're supposed to be watching that,' she said. 'What d'you want? Marmalade or some of that strawberry jam?'

Pam Van Allen was at work early, earlier than usual; only her senior's Escort was in the car park ahead of her, right on slogans occupying a goodly proportion of its rear window. Although no more than thirty yards from the entrance Pam wrapped her scarf around her neck before reaching to the rear seat for her briefcase and *Guardian*, and locking the car door. Chilly again this morning, but at least it was bright.

Neil Park was in his office, leafing through reports

on green and yellow paper, sipping at the first of many cups of Maxwell House. He called a greeting as Pam walked past reception and while she was making coffee for herself, he came out and joined her.

'Some offices,' Pam said, 'have a decent coffee machine. Real coffee.'

'But we have biscuits,' Neil said, offering her the tin. Inside were a couple of plain digestives, the wrong half of a coconut cream, a Rich Tea and a lot of crumbs.

'Good night last night?' Pam asked, opting for one of the digestives.

'Terrific, Mel and I fell asleep in front of the TV. Woke up and it was next year.'

Pam smiled. After failing to interest any of her friends in joining her in a search for something to eat, she had settled for a chicken and black-bean takeaway and the remains of a bottle of white wine. It had been the ideal opportunity for watching those programmes she'd taped about the lives of women between the wars. These were so depressing, she had found a documentary about the Sequoia National Park and watched it through twice.

'Who've you got today?' Neil asked. 'Anyone interesting?'

'Gary James, first thing.'

'Oh, well,' Neil said, wandering off with the last half of coconut cream, 'start as you mean to go on.'

Gary was close to fifteen minutes late, par for the course in his case, though less than desirable. Old Ethel Chadbond was out there already, spilling herself and her belongings across three seats in the waiting area and already imbuing everything with a healthy smell of methylated spirits and Lysol.

Pam restrained herself from looking too pointedly at her watch. 'Gary, take a seat.'

He slouched sideways, soccer shirt, jumper, jeans jacket, jeans. Gave her that look that said, so, what do we do now?

'That interview I arranged for you, at the training centre.' Pam picked up the sheet of notepaper as if it were relevant. 'You didn't go.'

'No.'

'You mind me asking why?'

On and on for a further fifteen minutes, Pam's questions, remarks, suggestions, all of them fielded with the same sullen indifference; part of a ritual both knew they had to go through. God! Pam thought, sliding open a drawer for something to do, coming close to slamming it shut, was this the first day of a new year? Another three hundred and sixty four days of this?

'Gary!'

'What?' He sat bolt upright, eyes wide open and she realised she had shouted, startling him.

'Nothing, I'm sorry. It's just . . .'

It's just you're getting your monthlies, Gary thought.

'It's just we seem to be going over the same ground, you know. Over and over.'

He breathed heavily and leaned back in his chair: what d'you expect me to do about that?

'The house,' Pam asked, 'have you made any more progress finding somewhere else?' She knew as soon as the words were out of her mouth it was the wrong thing to say.

'That poxy fucking place,' Gary said. 'Ought to be against the fucking law bringing up kids in there.'

'Gary . . .'

'You know how cold it was this morning when I got out of bed? D'you know? Put my hand on the baby's

235

face and I thought she was fucking dead! That's how cold it was.'

'Gary,' Pam said, 'I'm sorry, but I've told you before, that's not really my province. That's the Housing department's responsibility, it's not . . .'

He was on his feet so fast, the chair skittered backwards beneath him and collided with the wall. His fists were so close to her face, Pam let out an involuntary shriek and covered herself with her hands.

'You know what fucking happened when I went to the fucking Housing. You know about that, don't you? Eh? One of these bits of bloody paper'll've told you all about that.' With a sweep of his arms, he cleared everything from the desk: pens, paper, diary, telephone, paper-clips. Pam was on her feet, backing away, staring at him. There was a panic button underneath the ledge of her desk, but no way now could she reach it. 'You and that tart up at Housing, that dirty cow as used to spread her legs for my brother's mates every chance she got, you think you can shit on me like I'm nothing, don't you? Eh?' He walked on into the table and it jarred sideways off his thigh. 'Nice Gary, good Gary, here Gary, good dog, Gary.'

He snorted at her in his anger, took another step towards her before moving suddenly sideways to the door. 'You wouldn't treat one of your pets the way you treat 'Chelle an' me.' He wrenched at the handle and pulled the door wide open. Neil Park was standing anxiously outside, wondering whether he should intervene. 'None of you.'

Neil Park had to step back quickly to get out of Gary's way.

'You all right?' he said finally, walking into Pam's room.

'Terrific.'

'Here, let me give you a hand with this,' he said, taking hold of one end of the desk.

'Tell Ethel Chadbond I might need a few more minutes,' Pam said, when most things had been rescued from the floor.

'You want me to see her?'

'No, it's okay. Thanks.'

Once Neil had gone and she had closed the door, Pam sat for some little while thinking about the abrupt violence of Gary's anger, the nature of the remarks he'd made about Nancy Phelan, that tart, that dirty cow, wondering whether or not she should telephone Resnick, tell him about this latest outburst.

Thirty-three

Resnick had woken full of good intentions. He would write a note to Marian, apologising for last night, wishing her all the best for the New Year. On his way to work, drop in at the market and order some flowers, arrange for them to be delivered. Three attempts at the brief letter and when he'd almost got it right, a thick splodge of apricot jam slid between the cream cheese of his breakfast bagel and obliterated Marian's name and half the first sentence. Sitting at the coffee stall later, he changed his mind about the flowers; a bouquet, over-dramatic, open to misinterpretation. Besides — sipping his second espresso — flowers arranged in that way always made him think of his father's funeral. The coffin laden with them: and afterwards, laid out near the rose garden at the back of the crematorium. 'Don't let them do that to me, Charles. A priest and a requiem mass. A coffin for my ashes to wither away in.' At the end, when so many people come to God, his father had lost his faith. 'A bit of fertiliser, let me do that much good at least.'

Resnick walked away from the market with a heavy heart and indigestion. He would give Marian a quick call from the office, maybe later in the day. Or tomorrow.

Divine's fascist night out had been a shade disappointing. No major rucks, no riots, not even many arrests.

Most of the evening, bad music and easily shepherded bands of youths wearing BNP badges and off-the-peg Nazi regalia; the worst Divine had thrown at him, taunts and a half of warm lager. On the plus side, he had found himself cheek by jowl with a couple who answered the descriptions of Raju's and Sandra Drexler's attackers to a T: fair, sandyish hair, St. George and the Dragon tattoo.

Along with six or so other officers and a couple of dogs, Divine had stopped a dozen or so likely lads passing by outside the Town ground and ordered them back against the wall to be searched. Three blades, two lengths of chain, a piece of two-by-four with a nail protruding from it, one manky sock stuffed with sand, a handful of pills. Nothing spectacular.

The youth with the tattoo had been in the middle of the group, combat trousers and jeans jacket, mouthing off about police harassment. Divine had chanced to kick him in the back of the calf, pure accident. Instinctively, the youth had rounded on him, fist raised.

Bingo!

The noble St. George, lance at the ready, right before Divine's delighted eyes. Not enough to prove anything on its own. But when, at Divine's polite enquiry as to whether he'd taken any good taxi rides lately, the youth and his mate panicked and tried to do a runner, well, dead giveaway, wasn't it?

Shame was, in the ensuing scuffle, Divine didn't get to land as much as a solid punch. The lads, though, had spent a mournful night in Mansfield nick and were on their way down to the city that morning. Positive identification and they'd be up in front of the magistrate without a leg to stand on. Trouble was, instead of getting banged up, doing some real time, more than likely some soft sod on the bench would give them all of six months' community service, a supervision order, be good boys and talk politely once a week to your probation officer.

Made you wonder, sometimes, why you bothered.

Divine wished he'd given the little shits a good thumping while he'd had half a chance.

There were several reasons for liking Jallans at lunch-time, not least they did a chicken club sandwich which easily outstripped anywhere else in the city. Not only that, on a good day you might go from Miles Davis to Mose Allison to Billie Holiday, one CD after another slipping on to the player behind the bar. Resnick thought he was there before her, but no sooner had he picked out a table over by the far wall than he saw Pam Van Allen making her way between the tables from the other side of the room.

'Is this okay?' Resnick asked.

'Fine,' Pam said, pulling out a chair. 'Fine.'

'I didn't see you . . .'

'I was in the Ladies'.'

She was looking, Resnick thought, more than a little strained. Smart enough in her striped wool jacket and grey skirt, well-cut silver-grey hair, but the make-up she discreetly wore failed to lessen the tiredness, disguise the jumpiness around her eyes.

'I already ordered,' Resnick said, 'at the bar.'

'Me too.'

'You said you wanted to talk about Gary James,' Resnick said. 'You've seen him again?'

She held Resnick's gaze before answering. 'And how,' she said.

The waitress brought over Resnick's chicken club with salad and for Pam a jacket potato with prawns; Resnick asked her if she wanted anything to drink and she shook her head. He was drinking black filter coffee himself.

'That stunt he pulled at the Housing Office,' Pam said, spreading a little extra butter over her potato, 'he came close to doing the same with me.'

Resnick listened as she took him through what had happened, picking up half of his sandwich every now and then and trying not to let too much of the filling spill down his sleeves. 'And this anger,' Resnick said when she was through, 'd'you think it would disappear almost as suddenly as it came? Or was it the kind he'd cling on to?'

'Like a grudge, you mean?'

He nodded and she took his meaning, knew what he was thinking: the anger he felt towards Nancy Phelan, could he have held on to that for close to ten hours, harboured it long enough to go out and find her, let that anger out?

Pam took her time. A group of women from the Victoria Street branch of the Midland Bank, all wearing their uniform blouses under their coats, settled at the long table behind them. 'I don't know,' she said, 'I really don't know.'

Resnick had a refill of coffee and finished the demolition job on his sandwich; more than half of Pam's baked potato was still inside its jacket, but she had already pushed the plate away.

'You like that, don't you?' she said.

'The chicken club? It's . . .'

'Eating,' she smiled. 'Just eating. That's all.'

'I suppose,' Resnick said, mouth quarter-full, 'I suppose I do.'

She waited till he'd finished before fetching a book of matches from the counter and lighting a cigarette.

Resnick didn't know why, but he'd assumed she didn't smoke.

'Stress,' she said wryly, reading his thoughts. And then, 'Something's happened, hasn't it?'

'In the investigation?'

Blowing smoke down her nose, she gave a slight shake of the head. 'To you.'

'Has it? How?'

'Before, when we've met, spoken on the phone, whatever, you were always interested in me.'

Resnick was looking at the table, the few stray filaments of cress green upon the plate, not at her.

'Don't misunderstand me, not some great passion, but, well, like I say, interested.' She shrugged. 'Now overnight you're not.'

'Overnight?'

The smile was warmer and crinkled the lines either side of her mouth. 'I presume it was overnight.'

Resnick gave her a little of the smile back with his eyes.

'Congratulations. Who's the lucky woman? Anyone I'm likely to know?'

'I shouldn't think so, no.'

'And are you happy? Is it going well?'

Does it ever, Resnick thought, go well. He would have let it drop there, but Pam was looking at him, waiting for an answer. 'It isn't that kind of a thing, not . . . I mean, what you said made it sound like a proper relationship . . .'

'Improper would do.'

' . . . and I don't think it is that. At least, not yet.'

'Not ever?'

Aside from the not inconsiderable complication of Dana being closely involved in the case he was working on, Resnick could see a number of other obstacles.

Her flamboyance, her drinking – sex aside what could they hope to find in common?

'Probably not,' he said.

Pam Van Allen laughed: 'Spoken like a true man,' she said.

'Let me get this,' said Resnick, reaching for the bill. 'Or is that acting like a true man again?'

'Not nowadays,' Pam smiled.

'You realise,' Pam said, 'that if Gary finds out I went running straight to you and told you about this morning, I'll forfeit whatever small amount of trust I've built up?'

'Don't worry. There's no need for him to know.'

They were walking towards Holy Cross and the spot where Pam had parked her car. It was cold enough for them both to be wearing gloves.

'You're keeping an eye on him, though?'

'Not me personally,but yes. DC Kellogg, I don't know if you know her?'

Pam nodded. 'By reputation. Maureen Madden thinks a lot of her.'

'So do I.'

They were level with Pam's car. 'Good luck,' she said. 'With all of it.'

Resnick thanked her and walked away, off in the direction of Low Pavement. Key in the car door, Pam stood a while, watching him go. She hadn't been at all sure what she'd thought of him before, didn't think she liked him but now she thought probably she did; she could. Old-fashioned as it seemed, he was what you'd end up calling, for want of a better term, a nice man.

She opened up and slid behind the wheel.

Timing, she thought, somewhat ruefully: that's where it lay, in the timing.

Thirty-four

Helen Siddons had chosen her clothes with care. Alienating Nancy Phelan's parents further was the last thing she could afford. So nothing that might be considered expensive, nothing too stylish, but neither was she going to go marching in with shoulder pads and heels and a suit that shouted authority. She wore a mid-length skirt and jacket in neutral colours, a woollen scarf and flat shoes. Her hair was neat and orderly, make-up discreet to the point of non-existence. No perfume.

She sat with Harry and Clarise in the small lounge of their hotel, the three of them leaning awkwardly forward in worn red and gold armchairs. Clarise poured tea from a metal pot and offered round a plate of brittle biscuits. Helen, polite, deflected, as best she could, Harry Phelan's aggression, his assertion that the police were only going through the motions. The room was heavy with the scent of furniture polish and stale tobacco smoke. Helen declined Harry Phelan's grudging offer of a cigarette and lit one of her own. 'There's been a development,' she said.

If Resnick had been expecting a great deal from Forensic, he would have been disappointed. 'What we want here,' the lab man had said, 'is your average sicko. Can't wait to toss himself off over the lot. Give me that and a little time, I could let you have more than his blood group, I could give you his telephone number. As it is . . .'

The best he had been able to come up with was a grease mark high on the side of Nancy's silver top, close to the arm; some kind of oil mixed with human sweat. The sweat, of course, was most likely Nancy's own, but they didn't know that yet for a fact. They were doing more tests.

There had been no prints on the doors, none in Nancy's bedroom, none anywhere. Resnick stalked the corridors of the station, waiting for something to happen.

Dana had woken in the night more times than she cared to remember, alerted by every sound. The slamming of a car door in the street outside, creak of the bed overhead, each had her gripping the edge of the duvet, adrenalin flooding her veins. By the time she climbed into her morning bath, she felt a wreck.

She was drinking herbal tea, trying to concentrate on whatever they were saying on Radio Four, when the phone broke into her already jagged thoughts.

'It's Andrew,' Yvonne Warden said, 'he's found your little surprise package. I think signing it might have been a mistake.'

With all that had recently happened, Dana had managed to forget the tipsy message she had left for her boss on his office wall, lipsticked graffiti graphically testifying to his failed attempt at seduction.

'Oh, shit!' Dana said.

'Exactly.'

Dana was at a loss for what to say.

'I think you should give him an hour to climb down off the ceiling,' Yvonne said, 'then put in an appearance. I imagine he'll want a word with you by then.'

'I can guess which one it is.'

'Between ourselves,' Yvonne said, 'showing him up for what he is, it's not before time.'

'Christ,' Dana said, 'don't tell me he's had a go at you, too?'

'What time' Yvonne said, 'shall I say you'll be in? Ten? Ten-thirty?'

Dana sat for several minutes, staring at the phone. Then she pulled herself together, put on her good black trouser suit with a scarlet silk shirt, paid even more than usual attention to her hair and make-up, drank two strong cups of coffee, the second laced with brandy, and she was on her way.

'You're looking surprisingly good,' Yvonne Warden said admiringly. 'In the circumstances.'

'Don't,' Dana said, 'let the bastards grind you down.'

'He's expecting you,' Yvonne said.

Dana smiled and breezed on through.

There was a smell of fresh paint which grew appreciably stronger when Dana opened the door. Andrew Clarke was speaking to somebody on the phone, but as soon as Dana entered he lowered the receiver and rose to his feet. Behind him a workman in blue-grey overalls was repainting the rear wall where Dana had lipsticked her graphic version of her Christmas Eve struggle with her employer. The final picture, just visible through the first coat, had a distraught Andrew, sweat flying, running down the street after her, flies agape, penis swaying limply in the wind.

'I suppose you think this is funny?'

'Don't you?'

Behind them, the painter sniggered.

'Outside!' Clarke snapped.

'But I haven't . . .'

'Out. You can finish it later.'

247

The painter edged past Dana wearing the smuggest of grins and left them together.

'You realise you've left me no alternative other than dismissal,' Andrew Clarke said.

'Resignation?'

He coughed into the back of his hand. 'Very well, if that's what you want.'

'I was thinking of yours, not mine.'

'Then you're deluded.'

Dana smiled. 'Dismiss me and I'll bring charges of harassment and sexual assault. Be patient while I apply for another job, give me a good reference and a bonus, something equivalent to six months' salary, say, and I won't even post the letter I've got here in my bag addressed to your wife. Think about it, Andrew, think about exactly what Audrey might say and do. When you've made up your mind I'll be in the library. There's a new batch of slides that want cataloguing.'

Outside the door she winked at the workman. 'I think you can go back in now.'

The envelope had arrived second delivery, addressed to Superintendent Jack Skelton and marked personal. It had stayed downstairs until mid-afternoon, when the duty officer had sent it up to the superintendent's office, along with a bundle of papers and other mail. There it remained on the side of his desk until a little before five, when Skelton pulled it out from between two Home Office circulars, and gave it a preliminary shake. The flap had been secured with two staples before being Sellotaped round. Skelton cut the tape at the edges, then pulled the staples free; when he held the envelope over his desk, the cassette slipped down into his hand.

Thirty-five

A low hiss lasting several seconds, broken by two clicks, evenly spaced. A quarter-second's silence, almost imperceptible, before the voice.

Hello, this is me. Nancy. I have to tell you that I'm all right. I'm well and nothing... nothing bad has happened to me, so I don't want you to worry...

There is a slight fade as the voice disappears, the briefest of pauses during which the familiar background hiss can just be heard. The voice itself is pitched low but quite strong, perhaps surprisingly so; there is only a faint tremor at the end of certain words.

I am a prisoner, though, I'm not staying away because I want to but I don't... because I don't have any choice...

Most of the time I'm kept tied up, tied up and chained and I have... I have to squat down or lean against the wall or lie on the floor and I wish I could have more...

I am given water to wash with and a bucket to use as a toilet and I'm not hungry, there's food and water to drink and once a day I get a cup of tea and...

What I want to say to you is this – Mum, Dad,

whoever hears this – the person who's keeping me here, making me do this, you should believe what he says, do what he says. He's clever, yes, clever, and please, please, if you want to see me again, do whatever he says.

The click of the machine being switched off. Several seconds of constant hiss. The experts who listen to copies of the tape will disagree in their interpretation of the speaker's state of mind here, one placing her near to the end of her tether, another suggesting a resilience that goes unimpaired. What they agree upon is that Nancy is speaking under duress, that although she does not seem to be reading from something previously prepared, nonetheless she has been fairly carefully rehearsed. Considerable significance is found in the detailed description of her routine as a prisoner, her subservience to her captor, her enforced regression to an almost fully dependent child-like state.

The break in the sound is followed by another double click, similar to before. The man's voice is slightly distorted, slowed somehow in the process of recording, slurred. And the accent is regional, without being strongly so; enough, just, to blur the edges of received pronunciation. First attempts to place it centred on the north-west, not Manchester exactly but close, a touch softer and less well-defined. Somewhere, perhaps, to the south, towards the Welsh border. There seemed a strong possibility of one naturally absorbed mode of speech merging with another.

I do hope you will pay attention to that advice and listen to me carefully. Of course, I'm sure you will; I'm sure you are, right now, listening to me with such special care, playing my voice backwards and forwards and backwards again, shaking it upside down and inside out to see if you can shake me out.

But you can't.

Nancy, you see, she's right. About me, I mean. Oh, not that I'm clever, really clever, that's not me. I'm not one of those geniuses who go to Oxford at twelve and thirteen to get a degree in Mathematics, no, I wasn't even especially clever at school, but that's only because I was never given the right chance. Because no one, you see, ever listened to me, really listened to what I had to say.

And now you will.

Close to the microphone, a laugh. low and generous, drawing the listener in.

I'm sorry, it's just that I can see you now, excited, thinking, ah, he's given himself away, told us more than we should know. But, no. It isn't true and if it were it wouldn't really matter. I could tell you my date of birth, size of shoe, the colour of my eyes. Even Nancy could tell you the colour of my eyes. She could tell you that much. But it wouldn't matter. There still wouldn't be time.

So listen very carefully. Don't make any mistakes. Do as I say to the letter and Nancy can return, free and unharmed, to where she came from.

The day after you receive this tape you are to take two identical bags, each containing twenty-five thousand pounds, to two locations. The bags must be duffel bags, plain black, no markings, and the money must be in used notes, fifties and twenties only. The first location is the Little Chef at the intersection of the A15 and the A631 at Normanby. The second is the Little Chef on the A17 south of Boston. The bags are to be driven to the restaurants in unmarked cars, one driver and one passenger only, neither in uniform. The cars must both arrive at their destinations at a quarter to five in the evening. Park outside and leave the engine running while the passenger takes the bag into the Gents' toilet and leaves it on the floor beneath the hand drier. As soon as that has been done, that person must get straight back into the car and the car must drive off. There's no reason this should take any more than two minutes and if it does the deal's off. If there are any other police cars in the area, marked or unmarked, the deal is off. If the locations are visited earlier in the day for the purpose of setting up microphones or hidden cameras, the deal's off. Anything, any attempt to detain me and the agreement is null and void.

So, remember, nothing bad has to happen here and if it does it will be at your door, your fault – and I'm sure you don't want to live with that. Especially if it means somebody else is not.

The same low laugh, and then a click, louder than before. Silence. How he loves this, the experts will say, the psychologists, the precision of his orders, the control, like someone moving counters around a board. A man seizing the chance to laugh at others where previously others have laughed at him. About his apparent self-confidence there is a division, to one it is assumed, a delusion to be easily shattered, to another it is real – the confidence of someone in the process of constructing a world in which he is master, believing this more and more.

But this will come later.

Now, in the room where they have been listening – Skelton, Resnick, Helen Siddons, Millington – no one moves, speaks, swivels in their chair, cares, for several moments, to look anywhere other than at the floor. Nothing bad has to happen here and if it does it will be at your door, your fault. Finally, it is Millington who clears his throat, crosses and recrosses his legs; Helen Siddons who reaches inside her bag for cigarettes. Skelton and Resnick look one another in the eye: a quarter to five tomorrow. Give or take a few minutes, it is a quarter to five today.

Thirty-six

Through the slatted blinds of Resnick's office, the city folded in upon itself in pools of orange light softly washed by rain. He knew all too well the results of profiling in this type of crime, studies carried out initially by the FBI and confirmed here at the Institute of Psychiatry. Four basic types: those needing to compensate for their own feelings of sexual inadequacy; those who experience excitement and pleasure as a direct response to their victim's suffering; the assertive with a need to express more fully their sense of domination; those whose hostility is a reaction to deepseated anger.

He was also aware that a high proportion of sexually-motivated criminals, those who sought to exercise power over their victims, were also obsessed with the police. They read books and articles, followed cases, watched trials, collected anything and everything, from warrant cards to uniforms, they could lay their hands on. As far as Resnick knew, they were fully paid-up subscribers to *Police Review*.

He knew all that, the theory of it, and at that moment it was little help. Twenty-four hours. *It wouldn't really matter... There still wouldn't be time.* And they still had to make sure the voice on the tape was genuine, Nancy's voice.

Resnick turned away from the window towards the telephone.

As soon as she recognised his voice, Dana's face broke into a smile which as abruptly disappeared. 'I'm sorry to have to ask you this,' Resnick said, 'but if we can avoid it, we'd prefer not to inform her parents before we must.'

All assurances aside, Dana came into the CID room wearing the expression of someone asked to identify a body. She sat in Resnick's office, the tape player between them on the desk, and it was as if the two of them had scarcely met, never touched.

At the first sounds of Nancy's voice, a gasp tore from Dana's body and she began to shake. Resnick paused the tape so that she could regain control. He signalled through the glass and Naylor brought in a mug of tea which sat in front of her, ignored. When he played the tape again, she listened in silence, the tears falling slowly down her face.

'You're sure then?' Resnick asked.

'Aren't you?'

'It is her voice, there isn't any doubt?'

'No, for God's sake. No. What's the matter with you?'

'Do you want someone to drive you home?' Resnick said from the door.

'It's all right. I'll be fine.' And then, 'At least, she's still alive.'

'Yes. That's right.' But the pause before he spoke was too long to allow anything but cold comfort.

Helen Siddons was finishing off a takeaway chicken tandoori, chasing the rice around the foil container with a plastic fork. The ends of her fingers were stained orange-red from where she had used her hands. A bottle of mineral water was almost empty beside the ash tray. Helen had been on the phone to her old headquarters, ordering up the available paperwork relating to Susan Rogel. The copy of the ransom note had already been faxed. *Obey my instructions to the letter*. She could still remember the scorn on the faces of some of her so-called colleagues. Overstepped the mark on this one, hadn't she? Standing beside her car with the wind coming hard off the tops and nothing to show but cracked lips and cold and empty hands.

'You want it to be him, don't you?' Resnick spoke from the doorway. 'The same man.'

'I want him to be caught, whoever.'

'But if it turned out that way . . .'

'Then, yes. Great. But you don't have to worry, I'm not about to develop tunnel vision.'

'Am I worried?' Resnick said.

'I don't know you well enough to say. Perhaps you always act like this.'

'Which is?'

Helen made a small shrugging movement with her shoulders. 'Suspicious. Resentful. Almost hostile.'

'And that's what I'm being?'

'Where I'm concerned, yes.'

'I don't think so.'

Helen smiled. 'Naturally.' There was nothing warm about the smile.

'Those calls that were made to Susan Rogel's parents,' Resnick said. 'I don't suppose any of them were taped?'

Helen shook her head. 'There's someone coming in first thing. Loughborough University. Make a comparison between the Rogel note and the voice on the cassette. Vocabulary, phraseology, whatever.'

Resnick nodded. The lingering smell of chicken was making him realise he was hungry. Part of his mind was sorting through the contents of the food cupboard, the refrigerator: a snack at bedtime. 'See you in the morning, then. Early start.'

'I think I'll stay here,' she said. 'Catch an hour in the chair.'

Resnick said goodnight and walked towards the stairs. Outside, he noticed that Skelton's car was still backed up against the fence.

Thirty-seven

Lynn had decided to drive over the night before. She hadn't had too bad a day, a couple of burglaries to check out, both of them big places in the Park, carriage lamps bolted either side of the front door and enough personal jewellery in the main bedroom to take a dozen homeless off the streets full-time. One woman had been pleasant, matter-of-fact, had offered her tea and walnut cake and even made some nice remark about Lynn's hair. At the second house she had spoken to a man, a fleshy-faced barrister who smoked small cigars and made half-hearted attempts to look up Lynn's skirt when she crossed her legs. She could tell from the way he answered her questions about what was missing that the list which finally reached his insurance company was going to be fifty per cent speculation.

Oh, and she had called in to see Martin Wrigglesworth, caught him between clients and talked a little about Gary James and his latest outburst. Wrigglesworth had been guarded, looking anxiously over his shoulder like all social workers now, worried that if he intervened too soon and with too little cause, he was likely to end up on the wrong side of a public enquiry. 'But what about the kids?' Lynn had asked. Wrigglesworth had fidgeted with the stray hairs of his moustache: 'We've taken the boy to the doctor once and he's been cleared. We're going to need something more

258

before we can do that again.' How much more than a badly bruised two-year-old face did you need, Lynn had thought? 'You don't think you could find an excuse for dropping by, some time in the next few days?' Martin Wrigglesworth had said he would try. Lynn left, knowing that was the best she was going to get; hopeful still that what would happen was, Michelle Paley would use the number Lynn had left her, make her call.

Lynn had not really been hungry before she left, but neither did she want to break her journey. Unwilling to be more imaginative, she drove out to the McDonald's near the new Sainsbury's, not so new any longer, and sat in the window, looking out into the lights of the passing traffic and trying not to think too hard about the fillet of fish she was eating. Twenty-nine per cent fresh fish, the advertisements boasted. What was the rest?

She had been aware of a new excitement in the Nancy Phelan business back at the station, out on the fringe of it though, not yet party to what was going on. They'd found a body, someone had said, in the canal by Beeston Lock. She hadn't heard anything to corroborate that. Kevin Naylor had been tying up his paperwork in the CID room and she had asked him. 'There's been contact from the bloke who took her, some kind of ransom note, that's all I know.' She had been at her desk when Dana Matthieson had left Resnick's office, pasty-faced and close to crying; something about the way she had looked back at Resnick from the door, as if, Lynn had caught herself thinking, there might be something more between them. Well, biting down into the batter of her fillet of fish, so what if there was? What business was it of hers? Five minutes later, she was on the road.

For a moment, as she turned off the road and her headlights swept across the pebble-dashed exterior, Lynn thought the house was in darkness. But there was a light burning in the kitchen and her mother threw open the back door and smothered Lynn in her arms.

'How is he?' Lynn asked as she released herself.

'Oh, Lynnie, it's just awful.'

Her father was in the room at the front of the house, the one that was kept for occasional Sunday teas and special occasions; the last time Lynn could recall seeing her father in there was after her Auntie Cissie's funeral, awkward in his red hands and black suit, anxious to be away from the polite grieving and the sausage rolls, back amongst his hens.

Now he was sitting, stiff and straight, on a hard mahogany chair, the seat of which he had padded with two cushions.

'Dad, why don't you rest on the settee?'

His eyes looked at her from grey channels of pain. 'You know,' he said, wincing a little as he turned towards her, 'they buggers won't let me have as much as a glass of milk.'

He had been on a semi-solid diet for two days, this last day allowed only clear fluids, nothing more. Lynn sat on the arm of the settee and reached for his hand. The purgative the doctor had given seemed to have sucked all the life out of him. When she bent to brush her lips against his cheek, it was sallow and cold.

'What's going to happen to your mother?' he said.

'What d'you mean, happen to her? Nothing's going to happen to her.'

'After I'm gone.'

'Oh, Dad, for heaven's sake. It's only an examination, a precaution. You'll be fine, you see.'

The veins on the back of his hand were like maps.

'Dad.' She took one of the hands and held it against her mouth and his fingers smelled of waste and decay. 'What's going to happen,' he said, 'to your mother?'

The hospital was close to the city centre and from a distance seemed to have been made from sections of Lego by an unimaginative child. The interior was low-ceilinged and lit by strip-lighting from overhead. Staff walked briskly along corridors, while visitors stopped to peer at the neatly engraved directions, white and green. They shared the lift with an elderly woman sleeping on a trolley, tubes running from a pair of portable drips into her wrist. The porter whistled 'Mr Tambourine Man' and smiled at Lynn with his eyes.

The nurse would have made two of Lynn and left room to spare. She called Lynn's father pet and told him she'd look after him, promised him a nice cup of tea when it was over. 'If you'd like to have a word with Mr Rodgers about the endoscopy,' she said to Lynn.

There were flowers on the desk and a wooden bowl, polished and stained to bring out the natural grain. The abdominal registrar wore a white coat and suit trousers and tennis shoes on his feet; he had octagonal rimless glasses and an accent that had never shaken seven years of public school. He greeted Lynn with a firm handshake and a glance at his watch. 'Please,' he said, 'sit down.'

Lynn opted to stand.

'What we're about to do,' the registrar said, 'is take a little look inside your father's colon. We do this by means of a fibreoptic tube, an endoscope, which is passed along the bowel.' Lynn felt her stomach clenching at the thought. 'As procedures go, it can be a trifle uncomfortable, but it need not necessarily be painful.

So much depends upon your father's attitude. And yours.'

'He's terrified,' Lynn said.

'Ah.'

'He's convinced he's dying.'

'Then it's up to you to convince him this is not so. Be strong for him.'

'If you do find something,' Lynn asked, 'what happens next?'

Another glance towards the watch. 'If we do come across what appears to be a growth, then we may decide to take a biopsy, have a closer look. After that we'll know more.'

'And if it's cancer?'

'Then we'll treat it.'

He was wearing a white overall that tied at the back, sedated but awake.

'Don't fret,' the nurse said, 'I'll hold his hand all the way through it.' She laughed. 'There's a TV screen in there, he can watch what's happening if he wants.'

Lynn thought it was unlikely: her father wouldn't even sit with her mum and watch 'Blockbusters'. She went downstairs and sat in the WRVS canteen, chatting about the weather with a middle-aged volunteer who assured her that the jam tarts were home made. Lynn bought two, cherry and apricot, and a cup of tea. The walls were decorated with paintings done by the children from the local First School, bright as hope and full of life. The pastry might have been home made, but the fillings were out of a tin. She was wondering, if anything did happen to her father, how they would ever manage. Accumulating all the reasons why, whatever happened, she shouldn't apply for a transfer, return home.

'Your father's fine,' the registrar said, back in his office. 'Complaining a little of the discomfort, but otherwise, absolutely fine. A character.'

Lynn gulped down air: it was going to be all right.

'There is a blockage, however. A small growth.'

'But . . .'

'We've taken a biopsy while we had the chance.'

'You said . . .'

'One definite thing in his favour, if it does turn out to be cancerous, it is pretty high up in the bowel. Easier, once we've snipped out the offending part to join the rest together and leave things functioning pretty much as normal.' He looked at Lynn to see if she were following. 'No call for a colostomy, you see.'

All the way home, her father stared through the window at the edges of buildings blending with the gathering darkness, memories of fields. Several times Lynn spoke but got no answer, secretly pleased, not wanting to discuss what sat heavy between them, waiting to be discussed. The car radio drifted through talk of the recession and ethnic cleansing and the rise of the German Right. Lynn switched it off and stared along the tracks her lights made in the lightly falling rain.

Her mother had made a meal, cold ham and salad, halves of boiled egg, each with a teaspoon of mayonnaise on top, thick slices of white bread and butter. Tea.

'Stay the night, love.'

'Sorry, Mum, I can't. Early call.'

At the door she held her father close till she was sure of the beat of his heart.

Rain fell more heavily, bouncing back from the black

shine of tarmac, swishing across her windscreen in a wave whenever another vehicle sailed past and suddenly she was crying. From nowhere, tears ransacked her face and she began to shake. Clutching the wheel, she leaned forward, peering out. A lorry swung out behind her and as it passed the slipstream dragged her wide. Her mirror blazed with the glare of headlights and a car horn screamed. Blinded, Lynn struggled to regain her lane as the wind gusted into her broadside. Mouth open, sobbing hard, she felt the car begin to skid and when her foot tried to find the brake it slid away. With a jarring thump, the nearside struck something solid and cannoned forward, Lynn's seatbelt saving her from the windscreen but not the steering wheel, blood and tears now stinging her eyes.

Thirty-eight

One of the good things about Blue Stilton, Resnick was thinking, ripe enough it had a flavour that would survive no matter the company. This particular piece, the last of a chunk he had brought back from the market the other side of Christmas, he mashed down into a slice of dark rye bread before layering it with narrow strips of sun-dried tomato, half a dozen circles of pepper salami, a piece of ham, a handful of black olives cut into halves; a second slice of bread he rubbed with garlic before buttering and setting it on top. There were tomatoes in the salad box, a nub of cucumber, several ailing radishes, the last of an iceberg lettuce which he shredded with a knife. Somehow he'd allowed his stock of Czech Budweiser to run out, but near the back of the fridge he knew was a Worthington's White Shield in its new-shaped bottle. In fact, there were two.

Of course, he had still not bought the CD player and the Billie Holiday box set sat on the living-room mantelpiece gathering dust, an expensive rebuke. Resnick placed his sandwich on the table near his chair, watchful that one of the more adventurous cats, Dizzy or Miles, didn't jump up and start nibbling round the edges. He pulled one of his favourites, the Clifford Brown Memorial album, from the crowded shelf and slipped it from its battered sleeve. Music playing, he poured his beer, careful not to let the sediment slip down into the glass. Half of the sandwich he lifted towards his mouth with both hands, catching the oil from the sun-dried tomatoes on his tongue.

The Penguin Guide to Jazz was proving good reading, fine for dipping into, interesting as much for who was left out as who was included. Branford, Ellis and Wynton Marsalis, but not Delfeayo. Endless sections devoted to European avant-gardists who recorded hard-to-get cassettes in Scandinavia, but no room for Tim Whitehead, whose quartet Resnick had seen recently in Birmingham, nor the altoist Ed Silver, so much a part of the early British bop scene and Resnick's friend.

Resnick set down the book and reached for his glass.

A couple of years back, he had talked Ed Silver out of severing his own foot from his body with an axe, taken him into his home and kept him company long into a succession of nights. Resnick listening to Silver's reminiscences about gigs he had played, recordings he had made, promoters and agents who had cheated him out of what was rightly his. The day, speechless, he came face to face with Charlie Parker in New York; the night he almost sat in with Coltrane. All the while easing him off the booze, encouraging him to regain a grip on his life.

As suddenly as he had materialised, Ed had disappeared. Eight months later, a card from London: *Charlie, back in the Smoke. Somehow they don't want me at the Jazz Café, but I've got this little gig at the Brahms & Liszt in Covent Garden, Friday nights. Come down and give a listen. Ed.* Somehow, Resnick had never been down.

By the time he walked into the kitchen for his second White Shield, Resnick's mind had been reclaimed by other things: Harry and Clarise Phelan, awake in bed in their hotel, waiting to hear if their daughter were still alive; Lynn, driving back from Norfolk after taking her father to the hospital, alone in the night with what news?

Michelle was half way down the stairs when she heard Gary outside. At least, she presumed it was Gary. All she could make out at first were voices raised in anger, muffled and harsh. She hugged the baby to her and Natalie whimpered; lowering her face into the fine wispy hair, Michelle shushed her and hurried towards her cot. She was sure it was Gary now. Brian, too. What on earth was going on? Gary and Brian, best mates for years.

She was tucking Natalie's blanket around her when Gary lurched through the door.

'Gary, I wondered what was . . .'

At the sight of the blood, she stopped. A line of it, bright, like a Christmas streamer on the side of Gary's face.

'Gary, what's . . .?'

With the back of his arm, he pushed her away.

'Gary, you're bleeding.'

'Think I don't fucking know that?'

At the sound of their raised voices, Karl rolled over in his makeshift bed on the settee, Natalie began to cry. Michelle followed Gary to the bathroom and stood in the doorway, watching.

'Bastard!' Gary said, as he looked in the mirror. 'Bastard!' wincing as he touched his cheek.

'Gary, let me. . .'

With a snarl, he slammed the door in her face.

She lay in bed, listening to the sound of the rain, clipping off the loose slates on the roof; the sound of her own breathing. Outside on the landing, where the water was coming through, it dripped in rhythm into a plastic pail. Natalie had gone off again and Karl, thank God, had never really woken. After he'd finished in the bathroom, she'd heard Gary banging around in the kitchen, presumably making a cup of tea. She thought he might switch on the tele, curl up next to Karl and fall asleep: until she heard his footsteps on the stairs.

'Michelle?'

Soft thump of his jeans on the threadbare square of carpet, lighter fall of his sweater and shirt.

''Chelle?'

His hand on her shoulder was cold and she jumped.

'I'm sorry. I am, you know.'

Face against her back, his fingers reached round and found her breast.

'Shouldn't 've lost my temper, not with you. Weren't nothing to do with you.'

Michelle rolled away, freeing herself from his hand. 'What happened then? Tell me.'

'It wasn't nothing. Really. Just me and Brian, messing around.'

'It didn't sound like you was messing around. And this . . .' He flinched as she stretched towards him, but allowed her to touch the place just below the hairline where he had been cut.

'We was just foolin' about, that's all. Got a bit silly. You know what Brian's like after a few pints.'

Again Michelle stopped herself from asking, whereabouts is he getting all this money?

'Still,' Gary said, 'over now, eh? What'd my mum say? Spilt milk.' He lifted his hand back to Michelle's breast, shocking her with his gentleness, stroking her lightly until, through the thin cotton of the T-shirt, he felt her nipple harden against his thumb.

Thirty-nine

How long someone had been tapping on the window, Lynn didn't know. Opening her eyes, she groaned, gritted her teeth and looked out. The car had come to rest close against a farm fence, the nearside wing buckled by a concrete post. Gloved, the hand knocked again. Oh, shit! thought Lynn. My head hurts! In the rearview mirror, she could see the sidelights of the car that had pulled in behind her, faint through the blur of rain. A man's face now, bending close to the glass, words she could read without hearing: 'Are you all right? Is there anything I can do to help?'

Traffic continued to swish by, unconcerned.

She turned the key in the ignition and the engine sputtered momentarily and died.

He looked to be in his forties, clean-shaven, hair plastered dark to his head by the rain. The shoulders and arms of his jacket were soaked through and Lynn wondered how long he had been standing there, anxious to help. She wound the window down a few inches, enough to be able to talk.

'I saw you come off the road, ahead of me. Wanted to make sure you were all right.'

'Thanks. I think I'm fine.'

The right side of her mouth was numb and when she touched the tip of her tongue to her lip she could tell it was swollen. Wiping away steam from the mirror,

269

she could see a swelling over her left eye, already the size of a small egg and growing.

'You were lucky.'

'Yes, thanks.'

Lynn knew she should get out and look at the car, examine the extent of the damage. Even supposing she did get the engine to start, it might not be possible for her to drive away. The man, standing there, kept her where she was.

'You haven't got a phone in your car?'

'Afraid not.'

Neither, in this car, did she.

'Look,' Lynn said, winding down the window a little further. 'It was good of you to stop, but, really, I'll be all right now.'

He smiled and began to back slowly away. Lynn took a deep breath and got out into the rain. The rear of the car seemed to have collided with a pile of gravel as it left the road, then spun forward into the gate. Somewhere, out in the semi-dark, were the shapes of cattle, hedges converging. Lynn pulled up her collar and squatted near the front wheel. The metal of the wing had been forced back sharp against the tyre and the tyre was flat. The headlight was a tangle of silvered metal and broken glass. Maybe she could pull the metal out and change the wheel, but even then she doubted if she'd get far.

'Why don't you let me give you a lift?' He had come back and was standing back beyond her left shoulder, looking on. The wind had relented a little but not much. 'Just as far as the nearest garage.'

Lynn shook her head; she wasn't about to compound one stupidity with another.

'There's one six or seven miles down the road. I think it's open twenty-four hours.'

Lynn looked directly at his face, forcing herself to make judgements. In the circumstances, she thought, what else was she going to do? Walk and risk getting sideswiped by a passing car? Stick out her thumb and hope for the best?

'All right,' she said. 'Just as far as the garage. Thanks.'

Rain brushing his face, he smiled. 'Fine.'

Lynn retrieved her handbag, locked the offside door, and, hurrying to the man's car, got into the back seat.

'Michael,' he said over his shoulder. 'Michael Best. My friends call me Pat.'

Lynn smiled, more of a grimace than a smile. 'Lynn Kellogg, it was good of you to stop. Really.'

'Brownie points up there, I suspect,' smiling back at her, nodding towards the roof of the car. 'Few good ones to set against the bad.'

Clicking on the indicator, he waited until there was a clear gap before swinging out into the traffic, not wishing to take unnecessary chances now.

The signs were not good. Michael turned into the fore-court and parked behind the pumps, but the main lights inside the adjoining building stubbornly refused to come on. Only the safety light burned, illuminating faintly the usual collection of motoring maps and engine oils, packaged food and confectionery, on sale audio cassettes by forgotten groups and a special offer in troll dolls with purple hair.

'I'm sorry,' Michael said. 'I could have sworn this place stayed open all night.'

'Not to worry,' Lynn said. 'It's not your fault.'

'I travel this road quite a lot, though. I should know.'

'Me, too. I had half an idea you were right.'

'Perhaps it closes at twelve?'

'Perhaps.'

Lynn felt a little stupid now, sitting in the back the way she had. There was this man, perfectly nice, out of his way to help her, and there she was sitting in the back like Lady Muck.

'So what . . .?'

'What . . .?'

Their words collided and simultaneously they laughed.

'Had I best run you back to your car, then?' Michael asked.

'Looks like it.'

'Unless . . .'

'Unless what?'

'Unless you're heading for Derby.'

'Nottingham?'

'Fine.'

Lynn leaned back in her seat. 'Thanks,' she said.

It was warm in the car, cocooned from the cold and rain. For a time, Michael chatted about this and that, his words half lost in the swish of other wheels, the rhythmic beat of the wipers arcing their way across the windscreen. Ten years ago he had left a steady job, started a small business of his own, following a trend; two years back it had gone bust, nothing spectacular about that. Now he was picking himself up, starting from scratch: working for a stationery suppliers, there in the East Midlands, East Anglia, glorified rep. He laughed. 'If you're ever in the market for a gross of manilla envelopes or a few hundred metres of bubble wrap, I'm your man.'

As they reached the outskirts of the city, sliding between pools of orange light, the rain eased, the wind dropped. Life shone, dull, through the upstairs nets of suburban villas as they approached the Trent.

'Whereabouts?' Michael asked. They were slowing past the cricket ground, the last customers leaving the fast-food places opposite with kebabs or cod and chips.

'Anywhere in the centre's fine.'

'The square?'

'You could drop me off in Hockley. The bottom of Goose Gate, somewhere round there.'

'Sure.'

Shifting left through the lanes as they went down the dip past the bowling alley, he drew into the kerb below Aloysius House. A small group of men stood close against the wall, a bottle of cider passing back and forth between them.

'Thanks,' Lynn said, as Michael pulled on the handbrake. 'You've been really great.'

'It was nothing.'

'If it weren't for you, I'd still be out there now, probably. Condemned to spend a night on the A52.'

'Oh, well . . .'

Lynn shifted across the seat to get out. 'Goodnight.'

'I don't suppose . . .'

She looked at him.

'No, it's all right.'

'What?'

'It's late, I know, but I don't suppose you'd have time for a cup of coffee or something? What d'you say?'

Lynn's hand was on the door and the door was opening and she knew the last thing she wanted to do, right then, was walk up that street and turn the four corners that would take her to her flat, walk inside and see her reflection in the mirror staring back.

'Okay,' she said. 'But it'll have to be quick.'

The all-night café was near the site of the old indoor

market, opposite what had once been the bus station and was now a car park and The World of Leather. The only other customers were taxi drivers, a couple, who from the look of their clothes were on their way to Michael Isaac's night club up the street, and a woman in a plaid coat who sang softly to herself as she made patterns on the table with the sugar.

They ordered coffee and Michael a sausage cob, which, when it arrived, made Lynn look so envious, he broke off a healthy piece and insisted she eat it.

'I'm in the police,' she said. The first cups of coffee had been finished for some time and they were starting on their second.

He showed little in the way of surprise. 'What branch? I mean, what kind of thing?' His eyes were smiling; in truth, they had rarely stopped smiling the past half hour. 'You have a uniform or what?'

'God!' she said and laughed.

'What?'

'Why is it that's always the first thing men ask?'

'Is it?'

'Usually, yes.'

'Well, do you?'

Lynn shook her head. 'I'm a detective. Plain clothes.'

'Is that so?' He looked impressed. 'And what do you detect?'

'Anything. Everything.'

'Even murder?'

'Yes,' she said. 'Even murder.'

The couple across from them were laughing, well-bred voices as out of place as good china; the girl was wearing a long button-through skirt in what might have been silk and it lay open along most of her thigh. From time to time, carelessly, the young man stroked her with his hand. They were probably nineteen.

274

'What's the matter?' Michael said.

Lynn realised she had started crying. 'It's nothing,' she said, unable to stop. A couple of the cabbies were looking round.

'It'll be the accident,' Michael said. 'Delayed reaction. You know, the shock.'

Lynn sniffed and shook her head. 'I was crying when it happened. That's what did it.'

'But why,' said Michael, leaning forward. 'Why were you crying then? What was it all about?'

She told him: everything. Her father; fears: everything. In the middle of it he reached across and took her hand. 'I'm sorry,' he said, when she'd finished. 'Really, truly sorry.'

Lynn released her hand, ferreted in her bag for a half-dry tissue and gave her nose a good blow.

'Shall I not walk you home?' he said, out there on the street.

'No, it's all right.'

'I'd feel happier.'

'Michael . . .'

'Young woman such as yourself, doesn't do to be walking home alone at this hour . . . Heavens, is that the time?'

'You see.' Lynn laughing, despite herself. Tears gone.

'Come on,' he said, taking her arm. 'Show me the way.'

She slipped free of his hand, but let him walk with her nonetheless, up past the Palais and into Broad Street and the new Broadway cinema, where she kept meaning to go without quite making it.

'*The Vanishing*,' Michael said, looking at the posters. 'Did you ever see that?'

Lynn shook her head. 'No.'

'It's a fine film,' he said.

At the entrance to the courtyard, she turned and stopped. 'This is it.'

'You live here?'

'Courtesy of the Housing Association, yes.'

Slowly, he reached for her hand. God, how I hate this part of it, Lynn thought. Deftly, she moved towards him, kissed him on the cheek. 'Goodnight. And thanks.'

'Will I see you again?' he called after her, voice echoing a little between the walls.

She turned her head for a moment towards him but didn't answer and Michael didn't mind: he knew he would.

Forty

The assistant chief constable's last words to Skelton: 'However else this little lot turns out, Jack, keep track of the bloody money.'

'Enough here,' Graham Millington had said thoughtfully, weighing one of the duffel bags in his hand, 'to keep the Drug Squad in crack till next year.'

Skelton's instructions had been clear, hands strictly off, keep your distance, no diving in: watch and wait, the name of the game. As he came down the stairs after the briefing, the strain on his face clearly showed.

'If this bastard's tossing us around, Charlie,' Reg Cossall said, 'jolly Jack there's going to be scraping the shit off his boots for weeks.'

Resnick and Millington had charge of the A17 team, Helen Siddons and Cossall were north on the A631. 'Big chance, eh, Charlie,' Cossall had laughed, 'me and Siddons, parked off for a few hours, chance to find out what the old man's getting his Y-fronts in a state about. Taking precautions, mind.' He winked, and pulled a leather glove from his side pocket. 'Not be wanting to catch frostbite.'

Two officers had been installed in each Little Chef since the previous night; cameras with infra-red film and the kind of zoom lenses normally used for spying on Royals were trained on both parking lots and entrances. The pairs elected to make delivery sat with the ransom behind them on the rear seat, joking about how they were going to pull a switch themselves, take off for a month to the Caribbean, the Costa del Sol. Intercept vehicles, radio linked, were stationed at intervals along all major routes leading away from the restaurants. Once their quarry showed, he would be followed in an inter-changing pattern until finally he went to ground. All in all, resources from three forces were involved.

Watch and wait: the clock ticked down.

Divine sat on a packing case in the storage area, feet on a carton of oven-ready chips. Four in the afternoon, but he was eating his second Early Starter of the day. In between, he'd tried the gammon steak, the plaice and a special helping of those hash browns that went with the American Style breakfast, just four with a couple of eggs. All in all, he thought the Early Starter was best.

'Ought to get something down you while you can,' he called across to Naylor, who was over by the small rear window, peering out. 'Not every day it comes free.'

'Soon won't be able to see a thing out here,' Naylor said. 'Not a bloody thing.'

'D'you hear what I said?' Divine asked, biting down into a sausage.

'Another half hour and he could come from those trees over there, right across this field, and none of us would see a thing.'

'Jesus!' Divine exclaimed. 'Might as well talk to your chuffing self.'

Naylor came over and took a piece of bacon off the plate.

'Get your own!'

Naylor shook his head. 'Like my bacon crispier than that.'

'Yeh? I can see Debbie fancying everything well done, eh?'

Naylor gave him a warning look, shut it!

Divine wasn't so easily dissuaded. 'Gloria, though, out there waiting tables, got her eye on you. Play your cards right, you could be away there. Quickie down behind the griddle.'

The store-room door swung open and Gloria came in, a big woman from King's Lynn whose white uniform needed extra safety pins to keep it in place. 'Feet off there,' she snapped, looking at the oven chips. 'People got to eat those.'

'Kevin here was just letting on,' Divine said, 'how he could really fancy you.'

'That's nice,' Gloria said, treating Naylor to a smile. 'I always like the quiet type, they're the ones that take you by surprise. Not like some.' Delicately, her chubby fingers lifted Divine's remaining sausage from his plate. 'All that talk and then they're about as good for you as this poor thing. Look at it. First cousin to a chipolata.'

Resnick checked his watch; less than five minutes since he'd looked last. All the while sitting there, hoping he wouldn't be proved right. Susan Rogel over again. Another wild-goose chase, another woman unaccounted for. Cold sleep in a shallow grave. Beside him, Millington unscrewed the top of his second thermos and held it towards him. Resnick nodded and waited while Millington half-filled the plastic cup.

Straitened circumstances, he thought it might taste better than the first time. 'Wife not back into dandelion coffee, is she, Graham?'

'Gilding, sir.'

'Come again.'

'Gilding. You know, old furniture and the like. Restoration. Sent off for details of this course, Bury St. Edmunds way. Two hundred quid for the weekend. Eighty-five for the video. Daylight robbery, I told her, but, no, Graham, it's the cost of all that gold leaf, she says . . .'

Controlling a grimace, Resnick sipped the coffee and continued to stare through the windscreen, letting his sergeant's chatter fade inconsequentially into the background. He couldn't quite rid his mind of the image of Dana, pale faced, listening to the replay of the tape. *Nothing . . . nothing bad has happened to me, so I don't want you to worry . . .* Dana, listening to her friend's voice, fears strung along the edges of her imagination. This woman, who to Resnick had been so lively, irrepressible, slumped in the chair with all the life drawn out of her. If he had no longer felt any connection between them, it was because Dana no longer had anything with which to connect. Well, partly that. Ever since that first astonishing, joyful evening, Resnick had been aware of the shutters coming down, drawn by his own hands.

'Look!' Millington said suddenly, interrupting his own conversation.

But Resnick was already looking. The green Orion had passed the Little Chef sign once, reappeared from the opposite direction less than two minutes later, and was now approaching it again.

'He's slowing right down,' Millington said. 'Go on, you bugger, turn in, turn in.'

They watched as the vehicle followed the white arrow painted on the car-park surface, drove forward fifteen feet towards the entrance, stopped, took a left

280

lock and slowly reversed into the broad space between a green 2CV and a reconditioned Post Office van.

Through the binoculars, Resnick could see the driver's face behind the wheel, white, clean-shaven, middle-aged: alone.

'Time, Graham?'

'Four forty-two.'

Having parked the car, the man was making no attempt to move.

'Want me to check out the licence plate?' Millington asked.

'Not yet. For all we know he's got a short-wave radio scanning the police channels. Wait till he's out of the car. And then alert Divine and Naylor first.'

Millington looked at his watch. 'Four forty-four.'

Resnick nodded. 'Here comes the delivery car, right on time.'

'This is it, then. What he's waiting for.'

'Maybe. Maybe he's just tired, taking a nap.'

'With both eyes open?'

The unmarked police car moved across the forecourt and drew to a halt as close to the main door as it could get. Resnick wiped away the first dampening of sweat. Headlights burned low against the field fence and the red tail lights blinked. The detective on the passenger side slid clear, leaned back across the seat and lifted the black duffel bag clear.

'All right,' Millington said, 'pay some bloody attention.'

Detective and duffel bag disappeared from sight.

'What's he doing?' Millington asked.

'Nothing.'

'Come on, you bastard. Move.'

Four forty-seven and the plain-clothes man reappeared, went briskly around the back of the car and resumed his seat; without rushing, the car drew away.

'I don't believe it,' Millington said. 'He's not going to do a thing.'

'Yes, he is.'

Resnick held his breath as the door to the Orion opened and the driver set his feet on the tar-covered surface. 'Radio, Graham.'

But Millington was already giving the signal to Mark Divine.

'Right!' Divine said in the store room and was on his way. Out in the main body of the restaurant, he took his time, saw the man coming towards him through the double set of glass doors. At the cash desk, he hesitated, picked up a roll of extra strong mints and placed the money in the cashier's hand. The man had to break step to get round him, Divine apologising, stepping into his path by mistake, apologising again and heading for the door.

'Smoking or non-smoking, sir?' the cashier asked.

'I'm just off to the Gents' first,' the man said. 'But either's fine.'

'Orion's licensed to a Patrick Reverdy,' Millington said in the car, 'address in Cheadle.'

'Long way from home,' Resnick said, glasses focused on the restaurant door.

When the man emerged from the toilet, he was still rubbing his hands together after using the drier. Naylor was now sitting in the smoking section near the door, stirring sugar into his coffee. He watched as the man told the waitress he was expecting a friend and accepted a double seat towards the rear window. While he was waiting, he ordered a toasted tea cake and a cup of tea. Home-going traffic built up steadily on the road outside. Resnick talked briefly to Skelton, keeping him informed; at the other location, Siddons and Cossall were drawing a blank.

Another ten minutes, teacake consumed, the man checked the time, picked up his bill and walked between the tables towards the cashier; paying his bill, he left a fifty-pence tip on the counter, turned towards the exit, changed his mind and turned back again towards the toilets. Naylor's stomach muscles knotted tight.

'He's staying too long,' said Millington, staring at his watch.

'Maybe he's being careful,' Resnick replied.

When the man stepped back into the restaurant with the duffel bag in his hand, Naylor's breath stopped. Nonchalant as you like with it, little swing with the right hand. 'May be nothing,' the man said to the cashier, 'but someone seems to have left this in the Gents'. Thought you might want to keep it safe out here. All this talk of bombs, someone might panic, stuff it down the loo.' He was holding the bag out towards the cashier, but so far she had made no move to take it. 'Don't worry,' he said, 'I stuck it against my ear and had a good listen. Nothing ticks.'

Divine detained the man before he drove away and while Resnick checked back with Skelton, keeping him up to scratch, Millington came over and had a word. Nothing serious, no reason to get alarmed. The man's driving licence showed his name to be Reverdy; he'd driven there to spend an hour with a woman he'd met at last year's Open University summer school. 'Lives in Spalding, but can't always get away. Married, you see.'

'And you drove all the way from Cheadle?' Millington said.

'I know,' Reverdy said. 'The things you do for love.'

In her car, parked at the far side of the garage on the
A631, Helen Siddons set down the receiver and sighed,
grim-faced. 'Okay, that's it. Let's head back. It's over.'

'Just so's the day's not a complete blow-out,' Cossall
mumbled, 'I suppose a quick fuck's out of the
question?'

If she heard him, Helen Siddons gave no sign.

Forty-one

Skelton was waiting for Resnick inside the double doors, falling into place alongside him on the stairs; no early run this morning, exhaustion in the superintendent's movements, the veins that showed red in his eyes. Twice he had tried contacting Helen Siddons but her phone had been disconnected; sleepless he had lain beside the cold rebuke of Alice's back.

'About the only thing that's bloody clear, Charlie, one way or another, the bill for this one's going to be firmly nailed to my door.'

Resnick shook his head. 'I don't see what else we could have done. As long as there's still a chance the girl's alive, we had to play along.'

At the landing, Skelton turned aside, shoulders slumped. 'Half an hour, we'll review where we are.'

But within half an hour both local radio stations had played extracts from the second tape on the air. It had been delivered by hand, a messenger with a motor cycle helmet and scarf wound about the lower part of his face, no chance of recognising who it was. Someone in the news room had given the tape a cursory listen, switching off after several minutes when it became apparent what they'd got. After phone calls to department heads, solicitors, copies were made and sent to the police; one question asked – the assertion that an earlier tape had been received, demanding a ransom, was that true? The police spokesperson would neither confirm nor deny. That was enough.

Radio Nottingham put the item at the top of its scheduled news; Trent interrupted its programming with a special bulletin. Each newscaster gave a brief introduction covering Nancy Phelan's disappearance and the lack of subsequent success in tracking her down before referring to an apparently unsuccessful attempt by the police, yesterday, to apprehend a man who claimed to have kidnapped Nancy and who had made a ransom demand. The extracts from the tape which followed were remarkably similar.

The instructions given to the police were clear and precise, as were the warnings. Unfortunately for everyone concerned, these were not heeded. It was simple, you see, all they had to do, these people, was follow what I told them and then my promise could have been kept and Nancy Phelan could have been reunited with her family and friends, safe and sound. But now . . .

I hope you're listening to this, Jack, I hope you're listening carefully, you and those advising you. Remember what I told you, Jack, if anything bad happens it's going to be your fault, your fault, Jack, not mine. I hope you can cope with that, that responsibility.

Lynn had called Kevin Naylor early and arranged for him to give her a lift. Hedged in between the traffic on Upper Parliament Street, she recounted her mishap with the car.

'Sounds as if it could've been a sight worse.'

'Say that again.'

'Not dead yet then?'

Lynn touched the side of her head. 'Just a little sore.'

Kevin grinned. 'No, I mean chivalry.'

'Oh. No, I suppose not.'

'Seeing him again?'

She was looking through the window at the knot of people waiting to cross at the lights near the underpass, a man with a florescent orange coat sweeping up rubbish outside the Café Royal. 'I shouldn't think so.' She had no idea how strongly she believed that, nor whether she wanted it to be true.

They were drawing level with the Co-op when the news item came on the radio and Kevin reached for the switch, turning up the volume so they could hear the voice on the tape.

Robin Hidden had hardly left his flat for days. Phone calls from his office, enquiring about his absence, had gone unanswered. Mail lay downstairs beside the Thomson's directories and the bundle of newspapers someone had once tied up with string and left, intending to take them to the recycling bin. Robin ate tinned tomatoes, cheese, muesli with powdered milk; he left the television picture on all the while, volume down, the radio just below the level of normal conversation. He did crosswords, ironed and re-ironed his shirts, scraped every vestige of mud from his boots, pored over maps. Offa's Dyke. The Lyke Wake Walk. Wainwright's guides to the Fells and Lakes. The Cleveland Way.

He was writing the same letter to Mark, again and again, so important to get it right. Explain. Mark was his best friend, his only friend, and he had to make him understand why Nancy had been so important to him, the ways in which she had changed his life.

That morning he had been up since shortly before six, cold out and dark. Frost on the blackened trees and thick on the roofs of cars. He drank tea absentmindedly, struggling with draft after draft, his thoughts like a tangle of wool which spooled along the page for sentence after sentence, seemingly clear, before becoming snagged impossibly down. Nancy, now and then, then and now, over and over, again and again. The only woman who, for however brief a time, had allowed him to be as he was, accepted him as a man. Who had loved him. She had loved him. Another sheet of paper was screwed up and thrown aside to join the others scattered round the floor.

Dear Mark,
  I hope you don't mind . . .

At the first mention of Nancy's name, the pen rolled free from Robin's hand. The broadcaster's words, the voice on the tape, blurred in his mind even as he heard them, bits and pieces of a dream he had never dreamed. Almost before the item had finished, he was reaching for the phone.

Neither Harry nor Clarise Phelan had been listening to the radio at all; the first they heard of the existence of the tape was when a newspaper reporter arrived in the dining room of their hotel, where they were having breakfast, and asked for their reaction to what had happened.

'You give us a lift to the police station, pal,' Harry said, already on his feet, putting on his coat, 'and I'll tell you on the way.'

'Charlie . . .'

Skelton pushed his way into Resnick's office without knocking, no gesture of recognition towards Millington, who was sitting this side of the desk.

'Field the girl's parents for me, will you? They're downstairs kicking up a stink and I've got to finish this statement for the press and okay it at headquarters.'

'I thought that was none of my concern any more? Inspector Siddons, isn't she liaising with the Phelans? Or did I get that wrong?' There was an edge to Resnick's voice that took the superintendent by surprise. Resnick, too.

'Christ, Charlie . . .'

It was the first time in memory Resnick had seen Skelton with his shirt in less than good order, his tie at half-mast. He knew he should be feeling more sorry for him than he was, but he was in the middle of a bad day, too. Not so long before he'd had Robin Hidden on the phone in tears, sobbing out every word; best part of fifteen minutes it had taken him to calm the lad down, agree to talk to him if he came in. Resnick glanced at his watch: that'd be any time now.

'Charlie, if I had the slightest idea where she was, I'd get her on to it. Truth is, so far this morning she hasn't showed.'

With a mumbled word and a nod, Graham Millington slipped away to his own desk; he could see all too well which way this particular conversation was going and the last thing he wanted to find himself doing was trying to appease a distraught father with a build like a good light-heavyweight.

'Graham,' Resnick said.

Oh, shit! Millington thought, not quite through the door.

'Why not see if Lynn's still around? Have a word

289

with the Phelans together. If Inspector Siddons arrives, she can take over.'

'If I'm going to deal with it,' Millington said, 'I'd sooner it was from start to finish.'

Resnick gave Skelton a quick glance and the superintendent nodded. 'Fine.'

'What if they want to listen to the tape? The one with their daughter's voice?'

'Yes,' Skelton agreed, hanging his head. 'Let them hear it all. They should have heard it in the first place. I was wrong.' He looked at Resnick for several seconds, then left the room.

Helen Siddons had not been wasting her time. She had acquired the original tapes and their packaging from the radio stations and had them sent off for forensic analysis, though by then so many hands would have touched them as to render that next to useless. But it was a process that had to be gone through. In case. She had listened to the second recording and compared it to the first, taken both to two experts and sat with them, listening through headphones, each nuance, again and again.

These things they were agreed upon: the northern accent identified on the first tape, less obvious on the second, was almost certainly not a primary accent. Certain elements in the phrasing, the softness of some of the vowel sounds, suggested Southern Ireland. Not Dublin, perhaps. More rural. A childhood spent there and then a move to England, the north-west, not Liverpool, but harsher – Manchester, possibly, Bury, Leigh, one of those faded cotton towns.

And the note sent in the Susan Rogel case, Helen Siddons wanted to know, was there any way of telling whether it was written by the same person?

There could be, in certain instances it might be possible, but she had to understand, written and spoken registers were so different. The furthest either of them was prepared to go, it could not be discounted the source was the same man.

For Helen that was enough. All of the suspects in the Rogel case, everyone the police had interviewed, seventeen in all, transcripts of their interviews would have to be double-checked, some would have to be contacted again if necessary. She was quite convinced now, the perpetrator in both instances was the same: and, more likely than not, he was already known.

Forty-two

All day, Lynn had been aware of this uneasy sense of expectation. Through the usual raft of paperwork, the follow-up interviews on the Park burglaries, a session with Maureen Madden about an alleged rape victim who had, twice now, recanted on her evidence and who they thought was being threatened, all through the haze of sexual badinage with which Divine and his cronies clouded every day, the constant ringing of telephones, the unthinking cups of tea, she could never shake off the feeling of waiting for something to happen.

Distracted, Resnick had paused at her desk in the late afternoon, asking for news of her father, automatically passing good wishes.

'Pint?' Kevin Naylor called, putting on his coat by the door.

Lynn looked at her watch. 'I'll see.'

When finally she went down the stairs, out past the custody sergeant's office, the entrance to the police cells, she knew it was Michael she was looking for – exchanging words with the constable at reception, kicking his heels on the street outside. He was nowhere.

Knowing that she'd regret it, promising herself she wouldn't stay too long, Lynn headed across the street to the pub.

'You ask me,' Divine's voice rose above the noise,

'she's been dead since a couple of hours after she was lifted.'

Lynn wasn't about to waste her breath telling him that nobody had.

'What about this ransom business?' Kevin Naylor asked.

'Load of bollocks, isn't it? Some clever-clogs tossing us a-bloody-round. You know yourself, it's happened before.'

'Come on, Mark,' Lynn couldn't keep sitting there saying nothing, 'her voice was on the tape.'

'So? What's to stop him forcing that out of her first?'

'All in two hours?'

Divine raised his eyes towards the smoky ceiling. Why were some women always so literal, jumping on every word you said as if it were gospel? 'Okay, maybe it was a bit longer. Two hours, four, six, what's it matter?'

'To Nancy Phelan or to us?'

Divine emptied his glass and pushed it along the table towards Kevin Naylor, his shout this time. 'All that matters, what we should be looking for is a body. Never mind all this undercover crap out there in the sticks.'

'Wasn't what you said at the time,' Naylor reminded him. 'Not with another Early Starter on your plate.'

'You can talk! Here, you should've seen our Kev and this Gloria, tongue'd dropped any further from his mouth he'd been hoovering up the floor with it.'

Oh, God, Lynn thought, here we go again. 'I'm off,' she said, getting to her feet.

'Not now, look, I'm just getting these in. Pint or a half?'

Lynn thought of what was waiting for her at home,

half a frozen pizza, a bundle of ironing, her mother's call. 'All right,' sitting back down, 'but make it a half.'

A light rain had started to fall, not enough to persuade Lynn to use her umbrella as she took the cut-through beside Paul Smith's shop and came out by the Cross Keys, opposite the Fletcher Gate car park. Later the temperature was due to drop and most likely it would freeze. Last night, on the by-pass out near Retford, a Fiesta had skidded on black ice and collided with a lorry loaded high with scrap; a family of five, mother, dad, two lads, a baby of sixteen months, all but wiped out. Only the baby had survived. She thought about her own good fortune, the car that had some so close to clipping her when she had swung, blinded, wide from her lane.

As she turned through the archway and began to cross the courtyard, the keys were in her hand.

Midway across, she hesitated, looked around. Muted by curtains or lace, lights showed from windows here and there about the square. Soft, the sounds of television sets, radios overlapping. A cat, ginger and white, padding its way along the balcony to the right.

Michael was on the landing, half way up the stairs, sitting with his back against the wall, legs outstretched, breath on the air, a newspaper folded open in his hands.

'You know,' he said, drawing in his legs, 'I can read this thing from cover to cover, front to back, every word, and if you asked me five minutes later a single thing about it, I wouldn't have a clue.'

Lynn had still to move.

'Here,' he offered the paper towards her, 'test me. Name the prime minister of Bosnia-Herzegovina. The Father of the House of Lords. Define once and for all the obligations of the Treaty of Maastricht. I couldn't do any of it.'

'How long have you been here?' Lynn asked.

'Oh, you know, I haven't exactly been counting, but possibly one or two hours.'

She turned away, past the chalked graffiti, to look at the light falling in a spiral at the foot of the stairs. Rain drawn across it like a veil.

'You're not angry?'

'For what?'

'Me being here.'

Angry? Was that what she should be? Looking at him sitting there, Lynn's shoulders rose and fell and she tried to avoid the smile sidling into his eyes: how long had it been since anyone had waited for her five or ten minutes? 'No, I'm not angry.'

He was on his feet in a trice. 'Shall we go, then?'

'Where?'

Disappointment shadowed his face. Doubt. 'You didn't get my message?'

'No. What message?'

'About dinner.'

The iron of the railing was cold against her hand. 'There wasn't any message.'

'I left it where you work.'

'You don't know where I'm stationed.'

'I phoned personnel.'

'And they told you?'

He had the grace to look a little sheepish. 'I told them I was your cousin, from New Zealand.'

'Somebody believed you?'

A laugh, self-deprecating. 'I've always been quite good at accents, ever since I was a child.'

Lynn nodded, moved one step higher, two. 'Where was that? That you were a child?'

'What do you think?' he said. 'Is it too late for dinner or what?'

He had booked a table at the San Pietro. Red tablecloths and candles and fishermen's nets draped from the walls. Crooners murmured through the loudspeakers in Italian, more often than not to the accompaniment of seagulls and a mandolin.

'I've no idea what this place is like,' Michael said, pulling out her chair. 'I thought we could give it a try.'

The waiter appeared with the wine list and a couple of menus.

'Red or white?' Michael said.

'Nothing for me, I've had enough already.'

'Are you sure? You . . .'

'Michael, I'm positive.'

He ordered a small carafe of house red for himself, a large bottle of mineral water for them both. For a first course, he had prosciutto ham and melon, Lynn a mozzarella and tomato salad. They were well into their main dishes – fusilli with gorganzola and cream sauce, escalope of veal with spinach and sauté potatoes – when Michael asked his first question about her day.

'I suppose I shouldn't have been surprised you were late, this terrible business, it must be driving you mad.'

Lynn set down the fork she had half-raised to her mouth. 'Which business is that?'

'That poor missing girl.'

'What makes you think I'm working on that?'

'Are you not? I suppose I thought you all would be, trying to find her, you know, twenty-four hours a day.'

'Well, I'm not, not directly.'

'But you must know all about it. I mean, what's going on.'

She lifted up her fork again; the veal was tender,

sweet to the taste, the breadcrumbs surrounding it not too crisp.

'This latest business, this ransom that was never collected and everything, isn't that all very weird? Didn't I read that setting that trap for him cost so many thousand pounds?'

'You seem to know as much about it as I do.'

'Ah, well, it's only what I read in the papers, you know.'

'I thought,' Lynn said, 'you forgot all that the minute you'd taken it in.'

Michael smiled back at her and summoned the waiter, ordered himself another carafe of wine.

'You're sure you won't?'

'Quite sure.'

For the remainder of the meal, he asked her about the damage to her car, her father's health, talked about plans for setting up on his own again once the recession had really started to turn around. Distribution, that's the thing, wholesale; anything but stationery, deadly stuff, try as you might, never get it to really move. And he'd glanced up at her, grinning, to see if she'd got the joke.

They were back in the courtyard, the cold biting round them; Lynn with her scarf wound twice around the space between her upturned collar and her hair, Michael's hands deep in his pockets all the way back from the restaurant, but now . . .

'You know,' Lynn said, 'I don't think I'm ready for this.'

'What would that be now?'

'Whatever it is you're wanting.'

His hand was on her arm, inches above her wrist. 'To be friends, is there anything wrong with that?'

'No. Except that's not all you want.'

He was close enough to have kissed her with scarcely a dip of his head, not a tall man, not really, three or so inches more than she was herself. 'Am I so transparent, then?' he smiled.

Something happened to his face, Lynn thought, when he smiled. He came to life from inside.

'And am I not going to get my kiss, then? My little peck on the cheek?'

'No,' Lynn said. 'Not this time.'

When she glanced down from the balcony, he was still standing perfectly still, looking back up at her; before she could change her mind, she let herself quickly in, bolted and relocked the door.

Michael only then starting to walk away, whistling softly. Not this time, he was thinking. Well, doesn't that mean there'll be another?

The bath as hot as she could take it, Lynn lowered herself through the rising steam. How clearly had he known she had wanted him to kiss her, standing there with little more than their breath between them? His mouth pressed against her, no matter what. So long since a man had thought of her that way, made love with his eyes. Despite everything, she shivered, imagining his touch.

Forty-three

Alice Skelton was in her bathrobe, towel wrapped around her hair, cigarette between her lips. It was twenty past six in the morning. She had heard his daughter – that was the way she tried to think of Kate now, it made things easier – returning home closer to three than two. Not bothering to be quiet about it any more, no more guarded whispers as she gave some youth a last wet kiss and reached down to slip off her shoes. These days – these nights – it was a slamming of doors and a shout of thanks, and whoever had driven her home turning back up the volume of the car stereo before the end of the drive. Alice had lain awake, said nothing, waited for the raid on the fridge, the toilet flush, the bedroom door. Christ, girl, she thought, what would I have done with my young life if I'd enjoyed your freedom? Would I have screwed it up any less or more?

Beside her, rolled as far towards the edge of the mattress as was possible, Jack Skelton slept on, his body twitching every now and then as if cattle-prodded by his dreams.

At four, Alice had given up all pretence and gone downstairs. Sweet biscuits. Ice cream. Coffee with a little gin. Cigarettes. Finally, just gin. She ran an early bath and lay back in it, her head resting against a plastic cushion, listening to the World Service: *Londres Matin*, the early morning news in French.

Out and dried, she had been considering going back upstairs and getting dressed when the phone rang.

'Hello? Mrs Skelton? This is Helen Siddons.'

'It's also practically the middle of the night.'

'I'm sorry, I wouldn't have called at this hour if . . .'

'If it wasn't important.'

'That's right. Is your husband there?'

If he's not with you, Alice thought, I suppose he must be. 'I expect he's still sleeping, don't you? He tires easily these days.'

'Could you get him for me? It is . . .'

'Important, I know.' She let the receiver fall from her hand and it banged against the wall, bouncing and bobbing at the end of its twisted flex. 'Jack,' Alice called up the stairs, 'someone for you. I think it's the massage service.'

Helen had been backtracking through the Rogel interviews, never quite certain what she was looking for but trusting it would leap out at her when she found it. Motive, opportunity, some connection that somehow they had missed. Something which they had failed to find important then, but now . . .

Those who had been brought in for questioning fell into three broad categories: anyone who might have had a grudge against the three principals involved, known villains with a penchant for extortion, and finally a more haphazard collection of people who had been in the area at the time, possibly acting in a manner that aroused suspicion. In the case of primary suspects, their backgrounds were well-documented, profiles fairly full; other individuals, notably those from the last group, had been lingered over less lovingly. At the time, that hadn't been seen to have mattered.

But when those people were brought into the limelight, the gaps in knowledge were prodigious.

Helen wondered how assiduously some of these stories had been checked – the first alibi but not the second or third? And what was known about them once they had been eliminated from the enquiry? She guessed, very little. In some cases, nothing. How easy, then, for one of them to lie low a short spell, up tracks and move away. Start over again somewhere else.

'Take someone with you,' Skelton said. 'Another detective, someone who can do some leg work if it's needed. Divine, for instance. He could drive you.'

Mark Divine was less than happy, playing chauffeur to a sodding woman! Still, at least he was getting a decent motor; top a hundred in the fast lane with no trouble.

'Divine,' Helen Siddons said. She was wearing a dark suit with a mid-length skirt, her hair pulled back and severe. Divine had in mind she'd not have been out of place in that video he'd rented last night: *Death Daughters From Hell*. He could just picture her wielding a whip.

'Yes, Ma'am.' Divine coming to mock-attention, giving her as much of a come-on as he dared with his eyes. Never knew, if they got a result, might not be above letting her hair down on the way back.

'One word out of turn from you, Divine, and I'll have your balls cut off and dried and strung up for auction at the next divisional dinner-dance. Understood?'

Lynn had sifted through the mass of material on and around her desk, checked the CID room notice board, the message log; during the course of the morning, she contacted the officers who had rotated duty on the desk, got through to the switchboard and asked them to go through all incoming calls. Finally, it seemed incontrovertible – no personal message had been left for her inside the past thirty-six hours. For whatever reason, Michael had lied.

'Problem?' Resnick stopped by her desk on his way back to his own office. A bulging brown bag from the deli was leaking gently into his hand.

Lynn shook her head. 'Not really.'

'Worrying about your dad?'

'Sort of, I suppose.'

'Any news when he's going in for the operation?'

'Not yet.'

Resnick nodded; what else was there he could say? He had promised to call the Phelans this afternoon with a progress report, not that any progress had been made. Whoever had sent the ransom tape, they were in his hands. Every other trail, such as it had been, had long gone cold. Behind his desk, he opened the bag and stemmed a rivulet of oil and mayonnaise with his finger, then brought it to his mouth. Only a few drops fell over the Home Office report on responses to private policing. How long was it since he had spoken to Dana? He should ring her, make sure she was all right. If she suggested meeting for a drink, well, what was wrong with that? But the number snagged in his brain like a wedge of ill-digested food stuck in his throat.

Lynn spent the afternoon with several copies of Yellow Pages and the other business directories. On her eleventh call, the receptionist said, 'Mr Best? He's often out on call, but if you'll hold on I'll see if he's available.'

'Excuse me,' Lynn said quickly. 'But that is Mr Michael Best?'

302

'That's right, yes. Can you tell me what it's pertaining to? If he's not here, perhaps someone else can help.'

'Look, it's okay,' Lynn said. 'Don't bother now. I'll catch up with him some other time.'

That evening she turned down all offers of a drink, left pretty much to time, skin beginning to tingle as she neared home. But there was nobody stretched out across the stairway reading the newspaper, no note slipped beneath her door. So many times she went to the window and looked down over the courtyard, always expecting him to be there. At about quarter past nine, she realised that she'd dozed off in the chair. By ten she was in bed and asleep again, surprisingly unconcerned.

Forty-four

As if it weren't enough of a liability being born black, her parents had to christen her Sharon. One of the few names in current English instantly recognised as a term of abuse. 'Don't want to waste your time with her, right little Sharon!' In addition to all the innuendo and insinuation she'd grown up with from childhood, to say nothing of the outright bigotry, the head-on insults – 'Black scrubber! Black cow! Black bastard!' – for the past five years she had been the butt of Essex girl jokes too numerous to mention. The fact that there was no resemblance whatsoever to this mythical blonde in a shell suit with breasts where her brains should be, seemed to make little difference. It was all in the name. It could have been worse, she sometimes consoled herself, she could have been Tracey.

Sharon Garnett was thirty-six and had been a police officer for seven years. She had trained as an actress, two years at the Poor School, worked with theatre companies, mostly black, doing community work on a succession of shoe-string grants; two small parts in TV soaps, the obligatory black face with a heart of gold. A friend had made a thirty-minute video for Channel 4 with Sharon in the lead and for five or ten minutes it had looked as if her career might be about to take off. Six months later she was back in a transit van, touring a piece about women's rights from an abandoned hospital in Holloway to a youth centre in Cowdenbeath. And she was pregnant.

It was a long story: she lost that baby, sat at home in her parents' Hackney flat, day after day, not speaking to anyone, staring at the walls. One afternoon, between three and four, the sun shining and even Hackney looking like a place you might want to live – she remembered it well, right down to the smallest detail – Sharon went into her local nick and asked for an application form.

'Open arms where you're concerned,' the sergeant had said, 'racial minorities, you're actual flavour of the month.'

Despite the occasional remark, the groups that grew silent and closed circle as she entered the room, the excrement-filled envelope with 'Eat Me' stencilled on the front found one day in her locker, Sharon's training passed pretty much without incident.

Surprise, surprise, her first posting was Brixton, policing the front line. Out on the streets with her black woman's face and shiny uniform, she exemplified the ways in which the Met was changing; black men called her whore and her sisters spat at her feet as she passed.

Three applications for detective were turned down; finally, back to Hackney with the domestic violence unit, but that wasn't what she wanted. She had done her share of caring and consciousness raising already; if she'd wanted to be a social worker, Sharon told her inspector, she would never have applied to join the police.

Fine: back on the beat.

Eighteen months on, a relationship splintering around her, she left London, joined the Lincoln CID; nice, quiet cathedral city, Sharon as out of place as papaya in a Trust House Forté fruit salad. Oh, there was burglary and plenty of it – the recession bit deep here, too – drug-dealing in a minor kind of way, anything and everything you could imagine to do with cars as long as they were other people's. The most excitement Sharon had was when a small-scale row about shoplifting on a pre-war council estate suddenly flared into a riot: youths throwing petrol bombs and insults, ten-year-olds hurling stones as the police retreated, outnumbered, behind their shields. It had taken reinforcements from outside the area and the arrival of a specialist support unit to regain control.

Since then she'd been seconded to King's Lynn. Even quieter.

It was quiet now, thirty minutes shy of sunrise, frost heavy across the hawthorn and the oak, the dark ridges of ploughed fields. Sharon was hunkered down behind an ancient Massey-Ferguson tractor, with two of the other officers, passing back and forth a thermos of coffee unofficially laced with Famous Grouse. The coffee was hot and their breath, dove-grey in the clearing air, testified to the cold. She drank sparingly and passed it on; last thing she wanted to do, crawl off somewhere and squat down for a pee, difficult enough without wearing tights over her tights the way she was that morning.

'They'll never bloody show,' one of her colleagues said. 'Not at this rate.'

Sharon shook her head. 'They'll show.'

She had been working this investigation for five months now, ever since the first incident had been reported, seven pigs slaughtered on a farm this side of Louth, dragged off and butchered in the waiting van. Market stalls the length and breadth of Kesteven had flourished special offers of pork belly, legs, chump chops.

'Times like these,' Sharon's governor said, 'people do what they can.'

She supposed it was true: reports of sheep rustling on Dartmoor and in the Lakes had tripled in the past two years.

'Look! There!'

Her heart began to pump. Headlights, dull in the slow-gathering light, steered between the intervening trees. Sharon spoke into the radio clipped to the shoulder of her padded jacket, instructions that were concise and clear.

'Good luck,' somebody said as he moved swiftly past her.

The breath inside Sharon's body threatened to stop.

The lights were clearer now, funnelling closer, the van shifting out of silhouette against the slowly lightening sky. Resting on one knee, the other leg braced and ready, Sharon's mouth ran dry. Over by the sheds, a few of the animals moved around morosely, rooting at what remained of the straw that had been thrown on to the frozen ground.

The skin beneath her hair tingled as the van slowed and slowed again. Before it had come to a halt, three men jumped out, dark anoraks, black jeans, something bright in one of their hands catching what little light there was.

'Wait for it,' Sharon breathed. 'For fuck's sake, wait!'

Two of the men launched themselves at the nearest pig, one seeking to club it hard behind the head. The animal squealed, terrified, and slithered as the club came down again. Running to join them, the driver of the van lost his footing and went sprawling, long-bladed knife jarred free from his hand.

'Go!' Sharon called, sprinting forward. 'Go! Go! Go!'

'Police!' the shouts sang out around them. 'Police! Police!'

Sharon jumped at the man who had already gone down, heel of her trainer driving into his back and flattened him again into the ground. Satisfied, she carried on running, leaving whoever was in her wake to wield the handcuffs, drag the man away. The hardwood stave that had been used as a club lay in her path and, without stopping, she scooped it up.

Angry voices tore around her, curses and the sharpening clamour of the pigs. One of the thieves broke free and took off in a run towards the van. Sharon watched as two of her colleagues set off in pursuit, feet catching in the ruts that rose like frozen waves from the ground. Two of the others were involved in scuffles, while a third was already on his knees, head yanked backwards with a choke-hold tight about his neck.

The runner had managed to start the van and now it lurched towards them, one of the officers hanging from the side, an arm through the window, grabbing at the wheel. Sharon jumped back as the vehicle slewed round and stuck, the driver's foot on the accelerator serving only to dig deep into the ground, showering black earth high into the air. A fist landed on his temple and a cuff secured him to the wheel as the ignition cut off.

'Sharon!'

A warning turned her fast, pulling back her head to evade the butcher's cleaver swinging for her face.

'Nasty,' Sharon said, and struck out with the club, catching her attacker's elbow as the arm came back, hard enough to break the bone.

Only when their prisoners had been properly cautioned, farmed out into different vehicles for the drive back to Lincoln, the sun showing at last, faint through the horizon of sparse trees, did Sharon wander back across the churned-up ground to where the pigs were rooting eagerly. It took no time at all for her to realise what was at the centre of their attention was a human hand.

Forty-five

The pig farm had been made secure: diversion signs were in place on all approach roads; attached to four-foot metal stakes, yellow police tape, lifting intermittently in the northerly wind, marked off the area where the body had been found. Men and women in navy blue overalls were moving out in a widening circle from the spot, carefully raking over the ground. Others were examining the track, preparing to take casts of tyre tracks, boot marks. Nancy Phelan's body, freed from its shallow grave, lay in the ambulance covered by a sheet. In a maroon BMW, smeared with mud, the Home Office pathologist was writing his preliminary report. Harry Phelan, driven through the morning traffic by a grim-faced Graham Millington, had walked off across the farm track and into the adjacent field as soon as he had identified the body. Now he stood, stock still, hands in pockets and head bowed, while, back inside the car, his wife, Clarise, wept and wanted to walk out and hug him but did not dare.

It was still well shy of noon.

Resnick stood in topcoat and scarf talking to Sharon Garnett, his face pale in the winter sun. Close to five nine and bulked out by the duck-down jacket she was wearing, Sharon was in no way dwarfed beside him. She had known about the disappearance from the television and posters which had been circulated with Nancy Phelan's picture – not so many women missing, thankfully, that the connection didn't spark fast in her mind. Well before her pork butchers had been driven away, she had made her suspicions known, found herself talking to Resnick within minutes.

'How long,' she asked, 'do you think she's been in the ground?'

'Difficult to tell. But my guess, not too long. The pigs would have found her otherwise, even in temperatures like these.'

'Does it help?' Sharon asked. 'Finding her here?'

'To pinpoint the killer?'

She nodded.

'It might narrow down the field. It all depends.'

'But there'd have to be a reason, wouldn't there?'

'Go on.'

'I mean, why here? On the face of it, it doesn't make a lot of sense.'

Resnick looked around at the flat landscape of broad fields. 'It's out of the way, you'd have to say that for it.'

Sharon smiled a little at the corners of her mouth. 'Everywhere round here is.'

'It takes time to bury a body,' Resnick said. 'Even if it's only a few feet deep. And if anyone threatened to disturb you, you'd see them from a long way off.'

'He'd have to know it, though, wouldn't he?' Sharon said. 'Know of its existence, that for long periods of the day there was nobody around. Stuff like that. I mean, you wouldn't just drive along with a body in the back, see somewhere, think, oh, that looks a likely place.'

'You could.'

'Yes, but is that what you think?'

Resnick shook his head. 'No, I think whoever it was knows this area well, this farm, this track. My guess would be he already had the idea in his head, possibly even before he kidnapped the girl. Bury the body here.'

Sharon thought about her first sight of the hand, the rooting pigs. 'But then he must have known, sooner or later, the body would be found?'

'Yes,' Resnick said, 'I think that's part of the point.'

'What point's that?'

'I'm not yet sure.'

The pathologist was on his way towards them, trousers tucked down in green wellingtons. 'I'll have to do the proper tests of course, but I'd say she's been dead, oh, possibly three days, four. My guess is she was killed first, the body kept somewhere, then brought here. Signs of deterioration are remarkably few.'

'Cause of death?' Resnick said.

'Oh, you saw the bruising round the neck. Strangled, almost certainly.'

'How?' Sharon asked.

The pathologist glanced at her over the rim of his spectacles, as if recognising for the first time that she was there. He made no attempt to reply to her question.

'How was she strangled?' Resnick asked.

The response was immediate. 'Not with the hands. A ligature of some kind. Possibly a piece of rope, though that might have torn more of the skin. A narrow belt?'

'How soon,' Resnick asked, 'before we can have a full report?'

'Twenty-four hours.'

'And before that?'

'I'll get something to you as soon as I can. Early afternoon?'

Through this exchange, Sharon had been doing her best to rein in her anger. 'You have any women in your team?' she asked Resnick, as the pathologist traipsed away from them, back towards his car.

'One, why?'

'You always back her up as well as you just did me?' Any thought that she might have been paying him a compliment was dashed by the look in her eyes.

Harry Phelan was standing in the same position, a scarecrow in the centre of a ploughed field, nothing growing there to protect. Clarise had started towards him, ventured as far as the gate and no further. Resnick put an arm round her shoulders and at his touch she began to cry again, her head resting sideways against the broad front of his coat.

'It's Harry I'm fretful for,' she said, sniffling into bits and pieces of damp tissue. 'All of the energy he's got, he's put into willing Nancy still alive. Even on the way out here, he kept saying, she's all right, you see, whoever this is, it'll not be her. Not Nancy, it'll not be her.'

Resnick left her to trudge into the field, Harry turning his head once to see who it was, but moving no further. They said nothing for some little time, two men at either end of middle age. Not for the first time, Resnick felt useless, hopelessly inadequate to the task. How do you begin to comfort a man who has just identified the murdered body of what was once – in his heart still remained – his child? If he and Elaine had ever had children themselves, would he have known any better? Would circumstances, one day, ever have enabled him to understand?

'If the ranson had been paid this would never have happened.' There was no anger in Harry Phelan's voice now, no passion. He was a man whose life had been sucked out.

'We don't know that,' Resnick said.

313

'If it had gone all right, not got messed up, with the money . . .'

'It's possible she may have been killed before.'

Harry looked at him, too numb properly to comprehend. Lapwings rose up as one from the further end of the field, flew a half circle and landed back down between where they stood and the side hedge. Vehicles were starting up back at the farm, revving their engines purposefully; Resnick knew that he should go but he kept standing there.

'Shall you catch him, d'you think?'

Resnick took his time about answering. 'Yes,' he finally said, thinking on balance that he meant it.

'Nothing will happen to him, will it? Even if you do. Some crackpot with a bunch of letters after his name'll stand up in court and spout something and they'll shut him away in some hospital for ten years and then let him back out.'

Resnick didn't reply.

'If you do set hands on him,' Harry Phelan said, voice flat as before, 'for pity's sake keep me clear of him. Because if you don't I'll not be responsible for what happens.'

After a few more minutes, Resnick turned side on and looked at Harry, waiting till the other man returned his gaze; then, together, the two of them set off back across the field.

Sharon Garnett was waiting for him back at the car, slightly tense, legs a little apart, her face set with determination. Resnick thought it likely he was about to get another lecture. 'I was wondering,' she said, 'you ever have vacancies in your team?'

Resnick took a moment to collect his thoughts, not what he had been expecting. 'From time to time,' he said, 'people get promoted, transferred.' He didn't tell her that not so very long back one of his men had been stabbed to death when he sought to break up a scuffle between youths in the city centre.

'What happened here,' Sharon was saying, glancing back across her shoulder to where the body had been found, 'I did all right, didn't I?'

Resnick nodded. 'I should think so, yes.'

'So if I were to apply,' the slow smile starting up again near the edges of her mouth, 'I could rely on you for a recommendation.'

'After what you said before, I'm surprised you'd even think about working with me.'

She stepped back and gave him a slow once-over, amused. 'Basically, sir, I'd say you were okay. You just need somebody around to give you a bit of a nudge.'

Resnick held out his hand. 'Thanks for the help. Maybe I'll see you again.'

'Right,' said Sharon, 'maybe you will.' And she turned to get back to her own business, too much to do to stand there and watch him drive away.

Forty-six

They were heading east, back through Newark towards the city and not a decent passing space in sight. Frustrated behind the wheel, Millington chewed instead mint after extra-strong mint, never letting them remain in his mouth long before crunching them between his teeth.

'Drop a plumb-line down from the first ransom drop to the second,' Resnick said, 'what do you get?'

Millington flicked on the indicator, changed down ready to overtake. 'Long as it had a kink in it, where we've just come from.'

Resnick sighed and shook his head. Out through the nearside window, a farmer was forking feed from the back of a tractor, cattle making their way towards it, waveringly across cold land.

'I wonder what it's like,' Resnick said. 'To be in Harry Phelan's position. Something you must have half-known all along, there in the back of your mind, and then . . . Jesus, Graham! Dug up in a ploughed field. How the hell d'you begin to live with that?'

Millington didn't know. Tight on the wheel, his hands were smeared with just a little sweat. How could either of them really know? Two middle-aged men, neither of whom had ever fathered a child.

Resnick got through to the station on the car phone and asked for Lynn Kellogg. Briefly, he filled her in on what they'd found. 'Get yourself over to Robin Hidden soon as you can,' he said. 'Take Kevin along if he's free. Best if Hidden hears it from you if you can get to him in time. He's going to have the media crawling all over him any time.'

'Right,' Lynn said. 'I'll do what I can.'

'And, Lynn. That friend of his, up in Lancaster or wherever, suggest he goes up there for a bit, keeps his head down.'

'Right.'

Millington cursed quietly, forced to pull in behind a high-sided lorry which the single carriageway left him no room to overtake. Fingering another mint from the packet, he offered one to Resnick, who shook his head.

The phone sounded and it was Lynn calling Resnick back. 'Just to be clear, when I talk to Hidden. We're no longer looking at him as a suspect here?'

'No,' Resnick said. 'Just another victim.'

When Millington dropped him off at the London Road roundabout it was so gloomy the floodlights at the County ground, some quarter of a mile up the road, could scarcely be seen.

'Tell Skelton I'll be there in half an hour.'

'He's going to love that,' Millington said.

Resnick didn't care; this was something he had to do himself. Climbing the slight hill towards the Lace Market and turning left on to Hollowstone and up towards St. Mary's Church, he stepped into the full force of the wind. There was a hole in the stone wall a third of the way up the hill, giving way to a space large enough for a short man to stand up in. Two figures were huddled inside, newspaper and cardboard around their legs and feet; Resnick guessed another three or four had slept there that night.

When he turned right in front of the church, there

317

was Andrew Clarke's red Toyota illegally parked outside the architects' office, Clarke's name, the senior partner, in tasteful lower case on the glass beside the door.

Yvonne Warden was chatting to the receptionist at the desk, fresh cup of coffee in her hand, green plants luxuriating quietly to either side. Framed photographs of office blocks and hotels the firm had designed hung from the wall, alongside copies of the original plans.

'If you want to see Andrew,' she began, 'I think he's still in a meeting . . .'

'It's all right,' Resnick said. 'That's not why I'm here.'

Dana was at her desk in the library, looking through a box viewer at a slide of one of Philip Johnson's Houston buildings, a high-rise version of one of those gabled houses she'd fallen in love with by the canals in Amsterdam. A shame, she was thinking, Johnson never got to follow through on his design for a Kuwaiti Investment Office opposite the Tower of London that was a replica of the Houses of Parliament, twice life-size. At least the man had a sense of fun.

She looked around at the soft click of the door and when she saw it was Resnick she said hi and smiled, but half way out of her chair the smile died.

'It's Nancy, isn't it?'

He nodded and held out both hands, but she turned aside and walked towards the window; stood, resting her head against it, eyes closed, holding on. The glass was cold against her face.

Resnick didn't know any other way to do this. 'Her body was found early this morning. She'd been buried in a field. She'd been strangled.'

Dana jolted, as if a current had passed through her, and her forehead banged against the window hard. Carefully, Resnick eased her back against him, until she was leaning against his chest, her hair soft on his face. Her breathing was like rags.

'Do her parents know?'

'Yes.'

'Oh, God!' Slowly this time, Resnick still holding her, the top of her body arched forward until the crown of her head was once again against the glass. Someone came into the room and, on a look from Resnick, went quickly away again. 'She was so ... beautiful,' Dana said.

'Yes, she was.'

Dana turned, shaking, into his arms and Resnick held her, trying not to think about the time. By now Skelton would be taking counsel, issuing orders, readying himself for a press conference. As the senior officer present when Nancy Phelan's body had been lifted from the ground, Resnick himself would have to go before the television cameras before the day was out. From the square, faint, came the sound of the bell on the Council House ringing the hour.

'You'd better be going,' Dana said, releasing herself and moving past him to where she kept the tissues at her desk. 'God, I must look a mess.'

'You look fine.'

Dana sniffed and summoned up something of a smile. 'Only fine?'

'Terrific.'

'Did you know I've got another job?'

He shook his head.

'Yes, in Exeter. Starting next month.' She laughed. 'Andrew gave me such a wonderful reference, they could hardly understand why he'd agree to let me go.'

'Are you sure you'll be all right?' Resnick said.

'In Exeter?'

'Now.'

Dana sighed. 'Oh, yes. I'll be . . . I'll be fine. Just like you said. Fine.'

Resnick squeezed both of her hands, kissed her softly on the mouth. 'Phone me, if things get bad.'

Michelle had sat down early with the baby, thinking it had to be almost time for *Neighbours*; what she got was the last third of the news. Some black woman standing in front of some farm buildings, answering questions to the camera. Michelle thought it was something about – what was it? – Salmonella or mad cow disease until the photograph of Nancy Phelan appeared top left of the screen. Quickly, she shushed Natalie down and leaned forward to turn up the sound. Almost immediately, the picture switched and there was this man, round-faced, sad-looking, Michelle thought, speaking about the same thing. Detective Inspector Charles Resnick, read the caption bisecting his tie. 'Deep regret,' he said, and 'renewed effort', and when the interviewer, out of sight, asked whether he thought Nancy Phelan's death had come about as a direct and unfortunate result of police incompetence the inspector's mouth tightened, his eyes narrowed and he said: 'There's no way of knowing if that's the case. Any attempt to suggest otherwise would be pure speculation.'

Not that that was going to stop it happening.

Back across the Trent, Robin Hidden had disconnected his phone but could do nothing about the steady stream of local newsteams and reporters who beat a path to his door. Finally, he clambered over three sets of gardens, sneaking between rose bushes and around artificial ponds, until he found a path back on to the street.

He bought a paper at the newsagents to get change

320

and rang Mark's number from memory. His friend had been replacing some tiles in his bathroom and had heard what had happened on *The World at One*. 'Why don't you come up?' Mark said, without waiting to be asked. 'I've still got some time off. We could have another go at Helvellyn. Three thousand feet up in the snow.'

'Are you sure?'

'Course I'm sure.'

'I'm not exactly going to be good company.'

'Robin, for heaven's sake! What else are friends for?'

There were tears already in the corners of Robin's eyes. Across the paper, the headline read MISSING GIRL'S BODY FOUND and underneath, POLICE PLAN FAILS. *Just after dawn today,* the report began, *the body of Nancy Phelan, missing since Christmas Eve, was discovered, naked and apparently strangled, buried in the mire of . . .*

Numb, Robin walked on till he came to the footbridge over the river, turned down past the Memorial Gardens and continued on until the roundabout by the old Wilford Bridge. Shoulders slumped, he leaned on the masonry to catch his breath. Through the sour grey of the day, all he could see was the image of Nancy, that last time together, getting out of the car and walking away. The air stuck in his lungs like a fist.

Going by on a bike, rod resting across the handlebars, a fisherman turned his head and stared at him curiously.

Robin pushed himself on, without any real aim down through the close streets of the Meadows until he came out near to the railway station. Although he had only the clothes he stood up in, he knew he wasn't going back to the flat. Mark could lend him an anorak, his spare pair of boots, he'd done it before. The ticket and anything else he needed, he could pay for with the credit card in his wallet.

Forty-five minutes to wait for a train, Robin bought an orange juice from the buffet and carried it along to the end of the platform, collar buttoned up against the curl of the wind. The train that would carry him across country was one of those little Sprinters, two carriages at most, but if he stood where he was, before long one of those expresses would come hurtling in. He looked through blurred eyes at the dull shine of the rails, heard Nancy's name falling softly from his lips.

Forty-seven

The briefing room was cramped and airless, too small for the number of officers clustered inside. Pinned along one wall, stretching away from a colour photograph of Nancy Phelan, smiling and alive, were grainy black and white 10 × 8s of her in death. Other photographs showed the location where her body had been buried, strips of coloured tape pinned to them, marking spots where tyre tracks had been found, so far unaccounted for, a boot mark, incomplete and etched into a hardened ridge of soil. A map of Lincolnshire and East Anglia showed the two roadside restaurants where the ransom money had been left, the locations north and south of a line that swung gently eastwards as it traced, inland, the curve of the coast around the Wash. Almost directly between, circled in red, was the spot where the pig farm was situated and where Nancy's body had been found.

'Stinks of stale farts in here,' Cossall said, moving towards the rear of the room.

Divine looked offended. 'Only just let that one go.'

Along the corridor in the computer room, extra civilian staff were in place, entering and accessing the information obtained so far, including what Helen Siddons had retrieved from the investigation into Susan Rogel's earlier disappearance. All this would be checked against the national Holmes computer. Once connections were established, it was from here that fresh action would be generated.

'More sodding paper,' as Cossall liked to put it, 'than you'd need if you had four hands, two arses and a bad case of diarrhoea.'

Jack Skelton had recently returned from a press conference where he'd come within an inch of losing his temper. To listen to the most prevalent line of questioning, you'd imagine that Nancy Phelan had been abducted and murdered by a combination of the city's police force and the Conservative government through the good offices of the Home Secretary.

Wearing a black suit, hair pinned back, shoes with a slight heel, Helen Siddons was leaning slightly towards him, talking earnestly.

Resnick sat with eyes closed, arms folded across his lap, trying to ignore the way his stomach was rumbling while he marshalled his thoughts.

Skelton nodded to Helen, who stepped smartly away, got to his feet and signalled for silence. 'Charlie, what have we got so far?'

Notepad in hand, Resnick got to his feet, moving towards a more central position. 'Right, preliminary pathologist's report states death by asphyxiation; bruising consistent with the use of a leather belt or similar, no more than a centimetre and a half across. Marks under the hair, towards the back of the skull, left side, consistent with a fierce blow to the head. Whichever weapon was used, it may have been padded or covered in some way, as, although the bruising's severe, there are only minimal cuts to the skin. Other bruising, particularly to the arms, legs and back suggest Nancy struggled with her attacker, possibly in the immediate time before she was strangled.'

'Good for her,' said a voice from one side.

'Much sodding good it did her. Poor cow!' said another.

'Probable scenario, then,' Resnick went on, 'for whatever reason, either he's coming for her or she's trying to make her escape, the two of them struggle, he subdues her with a blow to the head, strangles her while she's unconscious.' There were other permutations, worse still.

'As far as can be ascertained,' he continued, 'there was no sexual attack, no evidence of semen inside or outside the body. There's no recent evidence of sexual intercourse.'

'Bloody waste,' Divine said quietly.

'Thought you were one of those,' Cossall said, overhearing him, 'didn't give a toss if they were alive or dead.'

'The fact that she was buried where she was,' Resnick was saying, 'makes examination of the body difficult. There were some samples of skin tissue found under her nails, however, and here and there particles of fertiliser-enriched soil which don't seem appropriate to the ground she was buried in. Tests are continuing on all of these.'

'Time of death, Charlie,' Skelton prompted.

'Again, not easy, due in the main to unusually low temperatures. But the best guess as of now is that she'd been dead for four or five days, with the body only being transferred to the point where it was found as little as six hours or less beforehand.' Resnick looked around. 'I don't need to spell out for you what this means: she was almost certainly already dead when the attempt to follow the ransom instructions were carried out.'

Muted cheers and more than a few prayers

answered. At least they didn't have to take the blame for that.

'Not a lot else from here,' Resnick said, flipping over another page of his notebook. 'As you know, there's a partial print of a boot, composite rubber, wellington or similar, size eight or nine. Tyre marks are marginally more interesting, weight and spread suggests a medium to large saloon, but I think we're being a bit hopeful going that far.'

'Hopeful isn't sodding in it,' intoned an anonymous voice, miserably.

'What we still lack is anything positive to link whoever killed Nancy Phelan with the person who returned her clothes to the flat. Analysis of the skin tissue found under her nails might give us that, if we can find a match in our records.'

'And pigs might do the proverbial,' Cossall remarked sourly.

'Something to add, Reg?' asked Skelton.

Cossall smirked and shook his head. Resnick stood his ground. 'What we might have, however, is a better suspect than any of us thought. Someone a few of us have actually seen.'

In the hubbub that followed, Resnick moved back towards his seat and now it was Helen Siddons' turn. The level of conversation rose again as she stepped forward and she was careful to wait, eyes surveying the room, until it had died down and she was sure of everyone's attention.

'Most of you will know something about the Susan Rogel investigation and will be aware there are certain basic similarities with this one. Woman disappears without trace, after a brief period a ransom demand is made and when an attempt is made to make payment, the money is ignored. So far so good. Here, though we have a body, in Susan Rogel's case we've turned up nothing and it's not outside the realms of possibility that she engineered her own disappearance. Except . . . listen to this.

'Thirty minutes after the time appointed for the ransom to be collected, a car pulled in at the pub where the money had been left near the outside toilet; the driver went inside and ordered a half of bitter and a ham roll, left ten minutes later, still finishing off the roll and went to the Gents'.'

'Must've pissed with his left hand,' Divine said.

'When he drove off, he was followed and detained. At first, he got a big shirty, thinking it was a random breath test, but as soon as he realised it was something else, he was as co-operative as you like. Ended up asking almost as many questions as we did. Claimed he'd started studying once for a law degree, but for some reason had dropped out. Still thought about going to university, reading criminology.

'He said he was currently working as a sales rep for a firm called Oliver and Chard, based in Gloucester. Specialised in work clothes, farms and factories, you know the kind of thing, overalls, protective clothing, reinforced boots. He was on his way to a dairy farm in Cheddar and after that had a call to make in Shepton Mallet. Car he was driving had been hired from Hertz that morning; normally he used his own, but he'd been experiencing difficulties getting it to start.'

Helen Siddons looked right to left around the room; not too many people were staring at their shoes.

'His name was Barrie McCain. Of course we checked him out with his employers, appointments log, car hire, everything. It all tallied. There was never any follow-up; there didn't seem to be any reason. Not until

Patrick Reverdy turned up at the Little Chef and fished the duffel bag of money out from the toilet.'

'This McCain,' Reg Cossall said, 'I presume we wouldn't be going through all this if he was still working for the same firm.'

'Gave in his notice,' Helen Siddons said, 'the week after the non-collection of the ransom. Some story about his mother being ill Manchester way, Wilmslow, the personnel manager thinks she remembers. He'd been a good salesman, friendly, they'd been sad to let him go.'

'Photograph,' Cossall said, 'too much to hope for.'

'Company policy is to keep one on file. McCain kept forgetting to bring one in. After a while, they got fed up asking. Figures were so far up in his area, they didn't want to get the wrong side of him. However,' continuing among the moans and groans, 'D.C. Divine described the man he saw close to in the Little Chef, the one calling himself Reverdy. According to the personnel manager, in outline it fitted him to a T. Similar height, five eight or nine, medium to slight build, sometimes she said he used to let his moustache grow a little but before it became established normally he shaved it off. McCain was seen at close quarters by two other officers – getting a photo-fit together is a priority, I think, as soon as this is through.'

'Thanks, Helen,' Skelton said. 'Charlie. All right, the rest of you. Without shutting off other avenues, there's a lot to work on here. I want every element of this Reverdy's story checked forwards, backwards, then checked again. McCain, too. If we can clear connections between them, anything that's more than circumstantial, for the first time we might be ahead of the game.'

Forty-eight

Lynn was in the bath, lying back, listening to GEM-AM. She had been in there long enough for the condensation that had steamed over the glass front of the wall cabinet to begin clearing, the pine-scented bubbles to all but disappear; the water was starting to feel cold. She considered running some more hot, finally decided long as she'd been there, it wasn't time enough for the tank to have properly heated through. Another few minutes and she would have to get out. On the radio, a commercial for quick-fit exhausts came to an end and back came the music. They seemed to have been playing Everly Brothers' songs, off and on, all evening. Another one now: 'Till I Kissed You'. Her mum used to love their stuff, sing it around the kitchen when Lynn was young. Days when she still had something to sing about. She'd even been to see them once, the Everlies, her mum. Yarmouth, it would have been. Phil and Don. Hadn't there been something about one of them being ill? Not being able to appear. Drink or drugs. Don or Phil.

Lynn pushed herself up in the bath and the water splashed, chill, around her waist. Maybe it was some kind of Everlies anniversary. Perhaps one of them had died and what she was listening to was a tribute. She hoped not, one thing her mum didn't need, another reason to be sad. For long enough for the picture to form, Lynn closed her eyes and saw Robin Hidden's face.

That morning, when she'd told him about Nancy's body, he had turned grey listening to the words. Right there as Lynn stood watching. Robin, face crumpling in like a balloon losing air, the life being sucked out of him. 'Why don't you sit down?' The words stale even as she said them, stale and inadequate. 'Would you like me to make some tea?' But he had, and Lynn had negotiated her way between the unwashed pots and empty packets and found the PG Tips.

'You haven't got any milk.'

'I know. I'm sorry, I . . .' He had looked back at her, helplessly. He still hadn't found the way to cry.

'You stay there,' Lynn had said. 'I'll nip down to the corner shop and get some.'

By the time she had come back, the tears had been there, clear in his eyes. They sat in the airless room, drinking tea, while he told her about the first time he had met Nancy, the time he got cramp during his run; the first time and the last.

'I should have g-gone after her,' he said. 'Instead of letting her walk off the way she did.' Panic and guilt jostled in his voice. 'If I'd r-run after her it wouldn't have happened.'

'You weren't to know that.'

'But if I had.'

'Look, it was her choice. She didn't want to be with you. Not any longer. If you'd gone haring after her, she wouldn't have thanked you.'

Tears tumbled down Robin Hidden's face. 'N-now she would.'

When he sobbed, she'd gone and stood beside him, patting his shoulder, telling him it was okay to cry, feeling genuinely sorry for him at the same time as she sneaked glances at her watch.

'Don't you think,' Lynn had said later, pieces of tissue wadded and damp on the floor, 'it would be a good idea if you got out of here? Went away somewhere. You've got family.'

He hung his head. 'I don't want to go there.'

'Friends, then. Isn't there this friend . . .?'

'Mark.'

'Yes, Mark. Couldn't you go and stay with him? Give him a ring.'

'I suppose . . . Yes, I suppose I sh-should.'

'I would. If I were you. Climbing, isn't that what you do?'

'Yes.'

Lynn had looked back once from behind the wheel of her borrowed car, half expecting to see him looking down, but between the half-drawn curtains the window had been bare. 'How am I ever going to get used to it?' Robin Hidden had said. 'The fact that I'll never s-see her again. Not ever.'

Lynn realised, as she released the plug and climbed out of the bath, that she had been thinking of her father all that time; then and now. When it came to it, how would she get used to never seeing him again? At least, not alive. 'Dream, dream, dream,' sang the Everly Brothers. Reaching out, Lynn switched off the radio. She was still drying herself, one foot on the side of the bath, when the doorbell rang.

Michael was standing outside, a bottle of wine wrapped in green tissue paper balancing in the palm of one hand. 'I thought you'd have had a busy day. Time to relax, maybe, wind down.'

Lynn had pulled on her terry-cloth dressing gown,

belted tight. She could see his eyes, quick to where it hung open a little at her breasts. That look.

'If it's not convenient, I'll just leave this and go, why don't I? Early as it is, you could be ready for your bed.'

She stepped back and let him inside. 'Wait a sec while I get dressed.'

Michael smiled.

'There's a corkscrew in the kitchen,' she said over her shoulder, moving to the bedroom. 'Drawer to the left of the sink.'

She put on blue jeans, a cream sweater over a cotton roll-neck, sports shoes on her feet. Michael was sitting on the two-seater settee, leafing through that evening's *Post*; two glasses of red wine stood on the low table before him. 'Amazes me,' he said, 'the way people open themselves up like this.' The front page held a picture of a weeping Clarise Phelan being led towards a waiting car by her husband. *MY AGONY by murdered girl's mother.* 'I mean, wouldn't you want to keep those feelings private?'

Lynn took her glass over to the easy chair angled towards the small, rented TV.

'I expect, though, you've seen some progress now, what with the poor girl's body and all.'

'Oh, yes,' Lynn said, 'as a matter of fact, we have. Quite a few new leads just today.'

'And you,' Michael tasting his wine, 'you're more at the centre of things?'

'In a way, yes, I suppose I am.'

He put down his glass and crossed the room, not hurrying, smiling all the time with his eyes. As he leaned down towards her, Lynn instinctively braced herself, a vestige of fear. His mouth was strangely soft and his lips as they slid over hers were pleasantly warm and curranty from the wine. His tongue pushed gently and she let it in.

'I've been thinking about that for the longest time,' he said. He was sitting on the arm of the chair, leaning across her, face pressed close against her neck. 'Really, the longest time.'

'A few days, that's not so long.'

'Oh, no. Longer than that.'

She shifted her head away till she could see his face.

'You didn't recognise me, did you?' Michael said.

Not taking her eyes from him, Lynn shook her head.

'And you don't now?'

'No.'

His hand was stroking her arm, fingers beneath the sleeve of her sweater. 'It was the monkey suit . . .'

'The what?'

'Dinner jacket, evening dress, black tie. I've noticed it before, the way it changes a man.' He smiled again and she noticed for the first time a chip of green in the grey-blue of one eye. 'Moss Bros, cheaper than a trip to your local neighbourhood plastic surgeon.' The smile widened. ' "Let me get those." Remember?' He took a twenty-pound note from his top pocket and passed it in front of her nose. 'You were wearing a blue dress. Such beautiful shoulders. And your hair, your hair was pushed up at the back like this . . .'

She caught hold of his wrist and held it fast; his pulse she could feel beating against her ear.

'You do remember now, don't you? Or did I make that poor an impression?'

What she remembered was the black suit, smart, one face amongst others, ranged along an overcrowded bar. The voice, pursuing her away, offering to buy her a drink later, but surely the voice was not the same?

'That policeman you were with then, wasn't that him

I saw being interviewed this evening on tele? The one talking about the body?'

Lynn nodded. 'My inspector. Resnick.'

'Good, is he? At his job. What would you say, a good copper?'

'Yes, that's what I'd say.'

Michael made to move his hand from her hair and she let it go. He brought down his face to kiss her again and just before he did she said, 'Meeting me on the road that evening, when I almost crashed the car – was that a coincidence or what?'

His mouth brushed against her lips. 'Oh, I don't think there's any such thing as blind coincidence, do you? I prefer to think it's all pre-ordained, part of some wider plan. Whatever . . .' Kissing her again, ' . . . will be, will be.' More strongly, she kissed him back. 'No songs,' Michael sighed, 'like the old songs.'

'I think I'd better go.'

They had slid to the floor between the chair and the settee, Lynn's sweater was bunched up by her neck, the belt loosened at the top of her jeans. Michael lay with one leg between hers, not looking at her, tips of his fingers making small circles on her skin.

'You're sure?' Lynn said.

'I think so.' Still not looking at her, strange for a man who usually did nothing but. 'Early start tomorrow, busy day.'

Lifting his leg, Lynn rolled away from him; sitting up, she smoothed her sweater into place. 'Me, too,' she said.

'Catching up with your man.'

'Could be.' On her feet, she tightened her belt. 'We can always hope.'

'Yes,' Michael said. 'Can't we?'

334

Lynn leaned forward to kiss him, but he slid his face away. She picked up the wine glasses, one from the table, one from the floor.

'Here,' Michael said, 'let me take those. I need a drink of water. Trouble with red wine, leaves you with such a thirst.'

While he was in the kitchen, Lynn slipped into the bathroom and looked at herself in the mirror, ran a comb through her hair. She was more than ordinarily flushed.

'Till I see you again, then,' said Michael, over by the door.

Lynn turned the handle to let him out. 'Phone me, next time. I don't always want surprises. Phone me first.'

He kissed her deftly on the cheek and stepped outside. 'You best get back in quickly, you don't want to be letting in the cold.'

She could hear his footsteps echoing down the stairs as she locked and bolted the front door. Resnick picked up his phone on the seventh ring; faintly, in the background, Lynn could hear music playing. 'Hello,' she said. 'It's me, Lynn.'

'It's not your dad,' Resnick said. 'Nothing's happened?'

'No. It's the investigation.'

'Nancy Phelan?'

'Mmm.'

'What about it?'

'I could explain easier if we met somewhere. It's not too late for a drink.'

'The Partridge?'

Lynn glanced at her watch. 'Twenty minutes.'

'Done.'

She set the phone back down and it was some sixth

sense, a split second before she heard the sound, that swung her round.

When Michael had gone into the kitchen for a glass of water, he had slipped the catch on the window that led on to the walkway. 'Now I wonder,' he said, 'exactly what you and your colleague were going to talk about. Over your friendly pint.' He had an old-fashioned tyre jack in his hand, wrapped around with rubber and cloth; if he could avoid it, he didn't want to damage her face. Not unless he had to: not yet.

'Michael . . .' she began.

'No,' he said, smiling even as he made that slow shake of the head. 'Don't waste the words.'

She made a lunge past him but his arm was fast and the jack struck her twice, the first time high on the shoulder, hard enough against the bone to make her scream; the second blow was to the back of her head as she fell, face first, unconscious, to the floor.

'Well, now, Mr Resnick,' Michael said towards the telephone, 'let's see how good a good copper you really are.'

Forty-nine

Resnick had not been in long when Lynn rang, back from a couple of hours at Marian Witczak's house in Mapperley, listening to her account of New Year's Eve at the Polish Club. She had dropped a note through his door earlier, inviting him, and Resnick, partly through guilt at having let her down, partly to avoid another evening frustratedly anticipating the glories of his Billie Holiday box set, had accepted. In Marian's drawing room, comfortable in armchairs guarded by ornate antimacassars, the ghost of Chopin hovering around the grand piano, Resnick had sipped plum brandy and listened to what he had missed – the politics, the polkas, the member who had drunk his way through fifteen flavours of vodka before clambering on to one of the tables and re-enacting the Polish cavalry's defence of Kraków down to the last despairing fall.

He had walked home with lengthening strides, head clearing rapidly in the cold air. Time enough to find a little supper for an insistent Dizzy, grind and brew coffee, before answering the telephone and hearing Lynn's voice. Going back out again, especially for another drink, was close to the last thing he wanted, but he knew she wouldn't be suggesting a meeting unless it were important. Resnick dialled the DG taxi number from memory and lifted his topcoat from where it hung in the hall.

Both bars of the Partridge were fairly full and

Resnick checked them carefully, right and left, before settling for a half of Guinness and a seat between an elderly man whom Resnick knew by sight, nursing his last pint of mild for the night, and a group of four who were still arguing their way through last Saturday's match, ball by ball. When his own glass was more or less empty and there was still no sign of Lynn, Resnick went to the phone and dialled her number. No reply. He checked with the station to see if, for whatever reason, she had gone there. No one had seen her since early evening. Resnick finished his drink and picked up another cab, across the street by the clock from the old Victoria station.

No lights showed through the windows of Lynn's flat, no response to knock or bell. When he peered into the glass and saw his own face reflected there, he saw a fear that so far he could only feel, not understand. The door had not been double-locked and he considered gaining access with the credit card that otherwise he rarely used, but noticed, when he looked again, the catch on the kitchen window was unfastened. No difficulty hauling himself up and through the space, flicking on the light.

'Lynn?'

Two glasses stood on the metal drainer, freshly rinsed. A corkscrew, cork still attached, lay beside a sheet of crumpled tissue. Resnick found the bottle in the main room, unfinished, on its side; a little wine had spilled out on to the carpet and made a stain, still damp. The coffee table had been shunted aside, the chair pushed at an odd angle against the wall. There was a second cluster of stains, darker and less sweet; Resnick touched the tip of his finger against the carpet and lifted to his nostrils the unmistakable taint of blood.

Graham Millington was at the head of the stairs, talking with two of the uniformed men they'd pulled in from routine duties. One of those nights when club brawls would either peter out of their own account or end in more than tears. Millington had been asleep in front of the television when the call had woken him, his wife tucked up already with a cup of Horlicks and a biography of Henry Moore. 'What d'you call that?' he'd asked, looking over her shoulder at a photograph of one of Moore's sculptures. 'Hole in heart patient?' 'Isn't there football on, Graham?' she'd asked, long-suffering. She had been right: Wolverhampton Wanderers and Southend United. Millington had felt his eyes going before the first yellow card.

'They don't appreciate being dragged away from their shut-eye,' the first constable was saying.

'I don't give a bugger what they appreciate,' said Millington, 'not till we've something more than nothing.'

It was Divine, not a happy man himself, called out just three short moves away from manoeuvring last year's Miss Ilkeston past checkmate, who came up with the first witness. His knock brought Corin Thomas to the door of his flat, smelling more than slightly of beer, overcoat on, chip pan in his hand. 'Soddin' central heating's packed up again,' Thomas said. 'Too much to hope you've come to fix it?'

Divine told him it was. 'You're dripping oil,' he pointed out, 'all over the lino.'

'Better come in, then.' Once the chips were starting to sizzle, Thomas told him what he had seen, a man and a woman, pretty much clinging to one another, going down the stairs past him and staggering over towards a parked car.

'Didn't occur to you to report it?' Divine asked.

'Love it, wouldn't you, if, I jumped on the old phone every time someone round here got half-pissed.'

'Is that what you thought they were?'

'She was, no mistake. Hardly keep her feet at all, if he hadn't been half-carrying her. All but went over, the pair of them, more than once.'

'The woman,' Divine asked, 'you recognise her?'

'Oh, yes. That one from lower down. Kellogg. One of your lot, isn't she? What all the hoo-ha's about, I suppose.'

'What about the man?' Divine asked. 'Ever seen him before?'

Corin Thomas shook his head.

'Sure?'

'Yes. It was dark, but, yes, there's lights enough down there. Good enough to make out someone you know.'

'You could describe him, though?'

Thomas shrugged. 'I don't know. I mean, I didn't exactly stare. Minding me own business, like. But, yes, the bloke, he'd be closer my height than yours. Five seven, eight. Far as I remember, darkish hair. Forties, maybe. Didn't get that good a look at his face.'

'Recognise it if you saw it again?'

Thomas thought about it as the chip fat bubbled. 'I might. Couldn't say for sure.'

'Shame,' Divine said, 'but you're going to have to have your chip butty another time.' Reaching across, he turned off the gas. 'I know you'll want to help; do whatever you can.'

Resnick and Skelton were leaning on the balcony outside Lynn's flat, while Scene of Crime operated the proverbial fine tooth comb. Most of the windows were lit up around the courtyard. Men and women, uniformed and in plain clothes, moved with purpose from

340

door to door, up and down stairs. Breaths of both men blurred white on the air.

'No good, Charlie,' Skelton was saying. 'No way we can be even close to sure. She rings you, wants to talk about Nancy Phelan. Sometime in the next – what? – forty-five minutes, she's disappeared.'

'And you don't think there's a connection?' Resnick was experiencing difficulty keeping his voice under control.

'We don't *know* there was any connection. Whatever happened, could have been sheer coincidence . . .'

'We don't have to know there's a connection, we can work it out for ourselves. Making those kind of connections, that's what we *do*. Or have you forgotten we're supposed to be bloody detectives?'

Skelton fidgeted his wedding ring round his finger. 'Charlie, you're not in danger of letting your feelings get the better of you here?'

Resnick gazed, amazed, around the room. His breathing was ragged and loud. 'We're not supposed to think, now we're not supposed to feel, what the hell are we supposed to do? Other than keep fit and wear a clean sodding tie!'

'Charlie.' Skelton laid a hand on Resnick's arm, lowered his voice. 'Charlie, I know what you're feeling. Think a lot of her, I understand that. All I'm saying, what we mustn't do, go off at half cock. Wasted time, wasted effort, she'd not thank us for that.'

Resnick hung his head. 'Yes, I know. I'm sorry. Forget what I said.'

'Most likely has to be,' Skelton said, 'either she had someone round for the evening, few drinks, got nasty, out of hand. Either that, or someone broke in, there was a struggle . . .'

'I can't buy that. Why wouldn't he just take off soon

341

as he got the chance?' Resnick looked Skelton in the eye. 'The first, maybe, yes, possible.'

'But you still think it's more?'

'Yes.'

'You think it was him. Whoever did for the Phelan girl.'

'Yes.'

'But, how, Charlie? How, for God's sake? Somehow, some fluke, she got to know him? Found out who he was? Goes some way to stretching the imagination.'

'Suppose,' Resnick said, 'it worked the other way. Suppose he was the one who got to know her?'

Get Corin Thomas talking and it was difficult getting him to stop; all the way back to the Canning Circus station, he kept Divine and the driver less than enthralled with accounts of where he'd been earlier that evening (a desultory trip round the city centre pubs, looking for women), where he'd been the previous year on holiday (a fortnight of days eyeing up the talent on the beaches, all the while becoming red as a Forest shirt, followed by a desultory trip round the night clubs, looking for women) and what it was like driving a single-decker for Barton Buses. Poor bastard, Divine thought, no wonder he hated being dragged away from his chip supper, highlight of his tossing week.

Inside the station, they shut Thomas up long enough to sit him down in a corner of the CID room, tell him what he had to do. Divine and Naylor had spent a good couple of hours with the appropriate officer, trying to get the photo-fit to do precisely that. Problem was, part of the problem, once you got past the colour of the hair and the shape of the mouth – small, both of them were agreed, turning down a little at the edges – there wasn't a lot about the individual calling himself

342

Reverdy that was remarkable. Except, that is, for the eyes. And the one thing Divine and Naylor could not agree on was the colour of the eyes.

Not that eye colour seemed to phase Corin Thomas over much. 'You realise I never got much of a look? I mean, you do realise that?'

They understood.

'And the light out there ...?'

They understood about the light.

'Well, in that case – and I wouldn't want you to hold me to this, not in court, like, not something I'd want to swear about on a Bible – but, yes, I'd say, what I'd say, the bloke I saw going across the courtyard with that mate of yours, I'd say, yes, it could be him.'

'Boss,' Divine stood beaming at Resnick's door, 'the bloke from the Little Chef, him and the one who's got Lynn – looks like they might be one and the same.'

'Right.' Resnick was on his feet, on the move. 'Just got confirmation from Manchester CID. The car he was driving belonged to Reverdy right enough. Stolen some time in the last ten days. Owner was away. Holiday. Insurance documents in the glove compartment.'

'Think he pulled the same stroke again?' Divine asked. 'Lifted something to pull this?'

'Likely. Let's check the lists. See if you can tickle the witness's memory about the car. We might have one or two more by now, corroboration.'

'Right, boss.'

'Kevin,' Resnick called.

'Sir?'

'Copies of that photo-fit, priority. Big a distribution as we can.'

'Straight away.'

As Naylor set off, Resnick pulled a copy of Reverdy's statement; the Cheadle address wasn't an invention, like a lot of practised liars, this was a man who'd found it paid to stick close as possible to the truth. Resnick was reading through the pages as he walked back to his office, wondering which elements might lead them where they had to go before it was too late.

Fifty

Lynn had woken with a dull pain somewhere in her head and a taste like cleaning fluid in her mouth. At least, the way she imagined it tasted. Probably, it was the smell. As soon as she had had the thought, her neck and shoulders spasmed forward and she threw up. Christ! Wet, on the inside of her leg. Looking down, Lynn saw her leg was bare. The pain in her head was sharp now and more precise, high at the back of her skull. Her eyes watered and stung and a rope of spittle and saliva hung from her mouth. She began the move that would allow her to wipe it away but of course her hands were tied. Clasped. When she shook her arms, which were stretched behind her back, she recognised the clink and touch of handcuffs.

Oh, Christ!

Lynn blinked her eyes into focus. She was inside a caravan, secured to one corner, something – a chain, she guessed, twist her head as she might, she couldn't see – attached to the handcuffs prevented her from moving more than inches either way. She had been stripped down to her cotton top and blue knickers and there were goose bumps all the way along her legs. That and the pale trail of her own vomit, as if snails had slithered their slow way across her thighs. At least, she thought, I followed my mother's advice about accidents and underwear. You never know ... She knew, this was no accident. *Oh, I don't think there's any such thing as blind coincidence, do you*? Suddenly, she was shaking, startled by tears.

'You're awake, then?' Michael was standing in the doorway, a tray balanced on the fingers of one upturned hand. 'Considering the time of year, it's a beautiful day.'

Behind the sleeve of his brown sweater, Lynn glimpsed the pale blue of open sky, smudge of darker green. Reaching behind him, Michael swung the door to.

The interior of the caravan was unremarkable: a small formica table and skimpy chairs, a narrow bunk along one wall, a calor gas cooker, some cupboards, a sink. Near the centre a gas heater burned low. Opposite her, fly-specked, a calendar showing the month of January below a colour photograph of tulip fields, two years out of date.

'Here, I thought you'd be ready for this.' On the tray he set near her on the floor were a mug of what appeared to be tea, the steam still rising softly from it, a slice of bread dabbed here and there with butter, some kind of cereal mushed up with milk. 'You must be hungry. You slept a long time.'

His eyes were never still. Lynn listened for the sound of traffic, other people; only the slow thrum from some kind of motor could be heard – besides their breathing, his and hers.

'You will eat?'

She didn't answer; looked at him, wanting his attention. Needing it.

'Wouldn't it be awful, when they found you, if you had just faded away?' He scraped the underside of the spoon against the edge of the dish before bringing it towards her mouth. 'One thing I wouldn't want them

346

to say, you were neglected. Not looked after. I wouldn't want them to be thinking that.'

The tip of the spoon passed between her lips and tapped against her teeth and Lynn was reminded of his kiss. She opened wide enough to let it in. The cereal was lukewarm and tasted both of sugar and of bran.

'Good?' Michael enquired pleasantly. 'Is that good? Should you like some more or is it a drink of tea?'

The tea was more difficult, she had to tilt back her head and still some of it escaped and ran down on to her neck.

'Here,' he said, opening a tissue from his trouser pocket then folding it again into a pad, 'let me do something about that.'

Unwillingly, Lynn flinched from his hand.

Michael just smiled and tried a second time. He noticed then the damp residue drying on her thigh. 'A little accident,' he said. 'Is that what this is?' Carefully, he refolded the tissue before gently releasing spittle on to it, a gesture Lynn had seen her mother make a hundred times. 'There now,' Michael said, dabbing at her leg, 'that's better now.'

Damn you, Lynn thought, I am not going to cry again.

Smiling, Michael lifted another spoonful of cereal to her mouth and gratefully she swallowed it down.

Robin and Mark had made an early start; there was still some mist hanging quite low and when that finally cleared they knew there would be snow on the tops. But the local forecast was good and besides they were well equipped, compasses and extra clothes and food, regulation survival kit in their rucksacks. Robin had scarcely spoken of Nancy since he had arrived and Mark had been content to leave it that way, thought it

347

best. What Robin needed most of all, Mark reckoned, was something to take him out of it, not long, cloistered conversations centred on nostalgia and regret. Not that, if it came to it, he would be anything less than sympathetic.

They had been walking now, steadily gaining altitude, for a little over an hour. Mark had set off in the lead and after a while they had changed places, Robin pushing on ahead, lifting the pace. Even though they were still at the lower levels, the effort was enough to test their breath and, of necessity, conversation was kept to a minimum.

'Look. There.'

Mark stopped and followed the direction of Robin's arm, eastwards to where the sun had finally broken clear above the peaks.

'Didn't I tell you?' Mark said. 'Didn't I tell you this was going to be a great day?'

Robin smiled before turning back and continuing to climb.

Lynn had asked for the rest of her clothes back, complaining of the cold. For reply, he had turned the heater up a notch and laughed. An eerily musical sound. She thought now she had heard him earlier, moving around outside, singing. No way of knowing if that were true. Somebody else? A dream? 'I thought you were meant to be looking after me,' she'd said.

He had left the caravan instantly, returned with an old piece of sacking and thrown it down across her legs. 'There.'

When the door had opened for him to leave, she had heard it more clearly, the same insistent sound. Possibly a generator, the report on the tape's background noise had said. If she twisted her head a little she could make out the lettering, faded into the weave of the material: *Bone Fertiliser – Saddleworth & Sons*.

Michael came back half an hour later, whistling quietly. Lynn watched as he drew round one of the folding chairs and sat there, one leg crossed over the other, relaxed. 'I'm sorry,' he said, 'that I lost my temper.' He smiled. 'That's unusual for me. I don't like it, never have. The way it affects you when that happens. Out of control. That's not what I want for us. I'd rather we continued to be friends.'

'We could have been, Michael. You know that. That's why this is such a shame.'

'And we're not now? Is that what you're saying?'

'Not exactly, Michael. Not any more.'

Disappointment passed across his eyes. 'But why ever not?'

'After this? After what you've done?'

'To you? What have I . . .?'

'Not only to me.'

'I've been good to you. I like you.'

'Really?'

He moved off the chair and sat close beside her on the floor.

'You've got a strange way of showing it, that's all I can say.'

'But I do, you know I do.' She could feel his breath against her thigh.

'How much, Michael?'

He looked at her, questioning.

'Enough to let me go?'

'Maybe.' His hand was resting on her thigh, a little above the knee, the thumb tracing small circles on her skin. 'I'll have to think about it. I don't know.'

'What will it take, Michael? What will I have to do?'

'What?'

'For you to do that? Let me go?'

He looked at his hand as if it belonged to someone else, before pulling it away. 'It isn't like that.'

'It isn't?'

'Threats. Promises. We don't have to do that.'

'We don't?'

'I could have you ...'

'Could you?'

'I could have had you ...'

'Michael, it's true.'

'What ...?'

'That night at my flat. You could have had me. Whatever you wanted.'

He was looking away, shoulders hunched, head down. 'You think I didn't know. The way you were lying there ...'

'Then why didn't you? What stopped you?'

'Nothing stopped me. I stopped myself. I ...'

'No good like that, is it? Straightforward. Normal. Normal sex. Two people. Me and you, Michael. Me and you.'

'Stop it.'

'Is that what it is, Michael? Is that the problem?'

'Stop.'

'Part of the problem?'

'Stop it!' He kicked the chair away and it smashed against the wall. His hands were clamped over his ears. He was shaking.

'Michael,' Lynn said, 'I could help you. Really. But you have to trust me. You have to.'

She had no idea if he had heard her or not. Without another glance, he walked from the caravan and locked the door behind him. Oh, Christ, Lynn thought, all of the energy suddenly sapped out of her, I hope to God I haven't just pushed him too far.

He didn't come back for well over an hour and when he did he came in humming softly to himself, a small tape recorder in his hand. 'I thought you'd be wanting to send a message to your friends. That inspector now – Resnick, wasn't that his name?'

Robin and Mark had continued their climb, the conditions causing them to detour once or twice from the marked path, but now they were back on track and moving towards Striding Edge. Both left and right, whichever way they looked, lower peaks were topped with snow. Grey and white, the mountain rose up before them.

They had stopped once, drinking from their flasks, eating chocolate, Mark breaking off a piece of Kendal Mint Cake.

From nowhere, Robin said, 'Perhaps she's better off in a way, Nancy, where she is.'

Not knowing how to respond, Mark had said nothing, but nodded, waiting for Robin to go on. But there was nothing more. Ten minutes later, everything was stowed away again and they were on the move.

The Edge was a narrow traverse, broad enough only for climbers moving in single file, the drop close to sheer on either side and deep. Robin and Mark had been across it many times.

'Want me to go first?' Mark asked.

'N-no, it's okay. I'm fine.'

The sun caught his shadow as he went carefully forward, flattening it against the rock floor. Watchful of his footing on the icy surface, taking his time, Robin continued to the midpoint and his face, when he turned, was lost in a blaze of light. He stood there, stock still, for perhaps five seconds, looking back at

Mark from the centre of that golden haze and then, without a word, stepped sideways into space.

Fifty-one

Michelle woke to the sound of rain sweeping against the windows, the blip-blip-blip as it dripped through the gap in the roof into the plastic bucket below. Beside her, Gary's breathing was steady and when she turned towards him, twisting her leg beneath his, she could smell cigarette smoke in his hair. Out drinking again last night. Herself, too. She couldn't remember when they'd spent so much time at the pub. Not feeling so good about leaving the kids alone, not even for half an hour, but they'd been fast off by then and once they were sleeping they almost never woke. Besides, Gary, he'd only have got into a mood if she'd said no. Just one drink, she'd said when she'd arrived, but Brian, flash bugger, had been flush again, laughing and making a fuss of her, insisting she and Josie have Bacardi and Coke, rubbing his hand up her leg too, the moment she sat down. Gary, thank God, he'd been too far gone to notice.

Michelle was more certain than ever Brian was into something dicey. Brian and Gary both, the way they kept up the clever looks and nudges, going off into corners and getting their heads down, whispering. Not that Gary seemed to have got so much out of it, whatever it was. Some things, she thought sadly, never changed.

She looked down at Gary now, his features softened by the half-light; one of those blokes, no matter how old they got, who never really looked any different to when they were kids. The ones who were always looking the wrong way, stuck standing at the end of the wrong line. He stirred and, suddenly tender towards him, Michelle bent her head and kissed him and smiled as he flapped a hand towards his face as if at a fly. Downstairs, the baby was waking, the day's first cry.

Michelle rolled away from Gary towards the edge of the bed.

Resnick had been unable to sleep at all. Twice he had tried, forcing himself to lay down at one and half-past three, both times getting back up after thirty minutes of flailing around, unable to clear thoughts of Lynn from his mind. Awake, he had paced distractedly from room to room, phoned, periodically, the station to see if there had been any developments, any news; in the kitchen, he had toasted bread, eaten it with cheese, strong Gorgonzola that had tasted of nothing. He had been so certain the trawl through the Open University lists would yield something. McCain and Reverdy, neither of them usual names. But blind alleys were all it had brought them, blind alleys and false trails. Wasted time.

Resnick remembered Harry Phelan's face, distorted by anger: *Forty-eight hours, that's what they reckon, isn't it? Forty-eight hours. If you don't find them in that, likely they're sodding dead!* Harry Phelan, standing in an open field, while behind him, inside the waiting ambulance, his daughter's body lay covered by a plastic sheet. Resnick willed himself not to look at the clock.

Maureen Madden, Kevin Naylor, anyone and everyone Lynn might have talked to, Resnick had quizzed them, anything she had mentioned about seeing somebody, a new boyfriend, a man. She had said something to Naylor about her car breaking down on the way back from her parents', someone stopping to lend a hand, offering her a lift. Nothing more than that.

Resnick stood in the top room of the house, one of the cats in his arms, staring out into the rain.

Michelle had just got to the bucket in time, the water only an inch from the top. Emptying it quickly into the bath, she had replaced it before hurrying downstairs and mopping up at the back where the rain had driven in through the gaps at the edge of the door Gary had failed to fix. The cup of tea she had made herself was little better than lukewarm.

In her cot, Natalie lay on her back gurgling away happily now she had been changed and fed.

'Oh, Karl, just look at you!'

Left in the kitchen to his own devices, he had managed to get more Rice Krispies on the floor than in his bowl. The last of the fresh milk was dribbling from its carton into the sink.

'Karl, for heaven's sake!' The boy backed away, blinking, wearing Gary's old County shirt, long past his knees. 'Come on, mind out of the way. Let me get this cleared up before your dad comes down.'

Karl trundled into the doorway and bumped into Gary, still prising the sleep from his eyes.

'Bloody heck, Karl! Look where you're going, why don't you?'

'Hang on a minute,' Michelle said. 'You'll be treading all that into the floor.'

'What the hell's it doing there in the first place?'

'Karl had an accident.'

'Karl *was* a sodding accident.'

'Gary, that's not fair!'

'Not fair, it's sodding true, though, i'n' it?'

355

'Gary, don't. Look, he can hear.'

'So what's that matter? Doesn't know what we're on about, hasn't a clue, have you, pal?'

'Asthdent,' Karl said just inside the door. 'Asthdent.'

Michelle shook her head, pushed Gary aside while she swept the remaining Rice Krispies into the dustpan.

'Make him come back here and eat it, that's what you should do. Teach him a bloody lesson fast enough.'

Michelle shot him a look and tipped the cereal into the bin. 'There's tea in the pot. Likely cold. If you want fresh, you can make it yourself.' And she shooed Karl into the other room and closed the door behind them: let him take his rotten temper out on himself.

The cats had decided it was time Resnick saw to their welfare. Dizzy had attracted his attention, weaving in and out of his legs, nudging his head against Resnick's ankles.

Downstairs in the kitchen, radio tuned to the World Service, Resnick had forked Whiskas into their bowls, ground the first coffee beans of the day and looked to see what else there was for breakfast other than toast.

Near the back of the fridge he found a section of smoked sausage, which, when he held it close to his nose, failed to give off any warning signs. Using a sharp knife he sliced the sausage into rings and pushed them to one side of the board, lifted a pan on to the stove and poured in some olive oil, set the gas to low. A few cloves of garlic he peeled with his hands, making much use of his nails. An onion and then he'd be there.

Bud made his familiar pathetic wail and without looking Resnick used his foot to shift Dizzy from the smallest cat's bowl.

The onion he sliced into half and half again, knife

cutting down, smaller and smaller each time. By the time he had finished, he could scarcely see what he was doing for the tears. Resnick sniffed and fumbled for a handkerchief; finding none, he reached for the tea towel instead. When his eyes were clear he saw at last something he should have recognised before.

Two of the cats' bowls were overturned as he ran to the door, Pepper leaping for safety to the refuge of the largest pan. Only with his coat on, car keys in his hand, did he remember the gas, and dash back to the kitchen to switch it off. Hearing him coming, Miles and Bud cowered in corners, Dizzy stood his ground and arched his back.

'Where's Karl gone now?'

'I thought he was with you.'

Gary was up some steps he'd borrowed from the neighbours across the street, trying to do something about the hole in the roof. Already there'd been a stream of shouts and swearing and, from experience, Michelle knew he was about to explode. But when Michelle had come back in with the baby, Karl, who she'd thought was stretched out on his stomach watching cartoons, was nowhere to be seen.

'Gary where . . .?'

'I told you, I haven't fucking seen him!'

From their bedroom, the answer came in a scream. Karl was alongside the wardrobe when Michelle got there, continuing to scream, staring at his hands. The knife lay on the floor before him, smeared with blood.

'Oh, Jesus!'

When she ran to him, Karl turned away and threw himself against the wall.

'Karl, Karl, it's all right. Let me see. Let me see, now, sweetheart, let me see.'

Gary stood just inside the doorway, saw the knife. 'What the fuck you been doing, you stupid little bastard? What the fuck you doing, sticking your nose where it's got no business? Eh? Eh?'

'Gary. Shut up and leave him alone.'

'I'll leave him alone.'

'Gary!'

He grabbed Michelle by the arm and half-pulled, half-pushed her out of the way. Karl saw the blow coming and threw up his hands, but the force of the punch knocked them aside and the fist struck the boy smack on the side of the head.

Karl let out a cry and toppled into the corner, weeping.

'Gary, you bastard! You pathetic, cowardly bastard!' Michelle had snatched the knife from the floor and set herself between father and son, handle grasped in both hands, blade pointing towards Gary's chest. 'You dare touch him again. You dare!'

Gary stared back at her, breath uneven, hands falling slowly back to his sides. What the hell did the stupid bitch reckon she was doing, turning the bloody knife on him? But when he tried moving half a pace forward, it was clear she was not about to budge. With a curl of his lip, Gary turned away. Until she had heard him lurch heavy-footed down the stairs, the slam of the front door, Michelle wouldn't move. Only then did she drop the knife on to the bed and pick the terrified child up into her arms.

Resnick hadn't been the only one for whom sleep had been more or less impossible. Kevin Naylor had finally given up at around three and taken the spare duvet into the front room so as not to disturb Debbie, settled down in the armchair and watched a discussion between an American academic who seemed to have written a book about bondage and a fiercely unfunny female comedian, the pair of them arguing about the effects the increase in oestrogen in the water was having on the male sperm count. Fifteen minutes of that and he quickly showered, changed, wrote a note for Debbie and set off for the station.

There had to be something, something they'd over-looked. In the CID room, he began to go through Lynn's desk, drawer by drawer, file by file, paper by paper. Almost an hour later, increasingly agitated, frustrated, he came close to missing it. The Yellow Pages scarred with the rings of numerous coffee mugs, he had gone through pretty thoroughly, but all that was marked were pizza deliveries, Indian takeaways, taxi firms. Kevin picked up the Thomson Directory that had been underneath it and gave it a quick flick through. The first time he noticed nothing, only on the second, carrying the directory across the room to add it to the general pile, did he spot the biroed asterisk, name printed at an angle in the column beside it.

SCHOTNESS STATIONERY LTD. Wholesale Supplies.

The address was a factory estate near the Clifton flyover.

The name written beside it was *Michael Best.*

Naylor's fingers fumbled the numbers twice and when he did get through, the phone rang and rang.

'Shit!'

'Something a problem, Kevin?'

When he saw Resnick in the doorway, Naylor could have given him a hug. Almost. 'Look,' he said, grabbing the directory from Lynn's desk. 'Look here.'

Taking the book from him, Resnick set it back down again to read it. 'Good lad,' he said. 'Well done.'

Naylor was too excited to blush.

Resnick checked his watch. 'Too early to expect anyone there to set us straight. Meantime, what you can do is this. Names we took of everyone who was at that Christmas Eve do at the hotel where Nancy Phelan disappeared, that's all on file?'

'On the computer, yes.'

'Right. Get it up on screen. I wouldn't mind betting Michael Best was one of the guests.'

Across the room, Resnick picked up one of the photofit posters awaiting distribution. Not a perfect likeness, which was maybe why he'd not seen it immediately, but now he didn't think there could be any mistake. *'Later, then. Let me buy you a drink later.'* A dark-haired man in a dress suit, his eyes pursuing Lynn down the bar.

'Sir. Take a look at this.'

Schotness Stationery were one of two small firms who had shared their celebrations on the third floor of the hotel and M. Best was listed among their guests.

Resnick was reaching for the nearest phone when it rang. It was Sharon Garnett, calling from King's Lynn. 'Just had something delivered for forwarding, addressed to you, personally. It's a tape.'

Fifty-two

Lynn woke to the sound of Michael masturbating close by where she lay. Without moving her head, she could see the outline of his body, rocking forwards and back in the almost dark. Closing her eyes again, she could only listen as he gasped towards his climax, hear the final sigh and shudder as he came.

Lynn waited, held her breath. She had talked him into letting her have back her jeans, complaining of the excessive cold. He had loosened the chain that held her cuffs a little at nightfall, sufficient for her to be able to draw her arms up against her back. Nevertheless, she was stiff, sore; the side on which she had mostly lain was numb.

She heard Michael moving and realised he was looking down at her to see if she were awake. Tense, when his finger touched her cheek she managed not to react. For several minutes he stood there, bending forward, stroking her face. When she thought she could endure it no longer, he went away.

The caravan door clicked shut and she heard the key turning in the lock. Nothing now that she could do but wait. Continue waiting. Any attempt she had made the previous evening to engage Michael in conversation had come to nothing. Just, now and then, that recognisable smile – you think I'm going to fall for that? Think I don't know what you're doing?

Somewhere, Lynn knew, they would be looking for

her. Resnick and others – officers that she had never met and would never know – using everything at their disposal, searching, following every clue. But what were they? What were the clues? She had come so close that last evening to telling Resnick Michael's name. Instead, she had put down the phone. Put off the moment. Why? As long as she lived, she might never know. Not that that need be so very long a time.

Resnick was in King's Lynn within the hour, motorcycle escort all the way, headlights and sirens. Sharon Garnett's sergeant greeted him with a strong handshake, a quiet, 'Anything we can do to help you land the bastard,' as Resnick walked past. They sat in a small low-ceilinged room with a view out over wet cobbled streets. Quite close, a church bell was insistently ringing. 'I wish they'd give over with that bastard thing,' the sergeant remarked. Sharon looked towards Resnick, waiting for a signal to play the tape.

Though he was expecting it, Lynn's voice made him start and he missed the first few words.

... I have to tell you that I'm all right. I mean, I've been given something to eat and drink and so far nothing bad has happened to me. I'm being well looked after, I suppose. I'm not in any pain. The reason ... She hesitated. *... the reason I'm here is that ...* Another hesitation, longer. Some movement of the microphone. Crackling. ... *the reason ...* Without a break, the man's voice, close to anger, interrupting. *She's here because she thought she could outsmart me, that's the way of it. Outwit me. Use me, that too. Get inside my defences. And she's got to learn, you've got to learn, like I told you, that's one thing you can't none of you do.* Another pause, short,

and then, *And that includes you, Mr Resnick, that includes you.*

'That's it?' Resnick said. 'That's all?'

Sharon nodded. 'We played it right through, both sides.'

'Nothing about a ransom, then,' the sergeant said. 'Not like last time.'

'That was a game,' Resnick said.

'Nasty bloody sort of a game.'

'His kind. But it's gone beyond that now. He knows that.'

Sharon Garnett looked at him. 'You know who he is, don't you?'

'We've got a good idea.'

'How come?'

'Staring us in the face,' Resnick said. 'More or less.'

A fresh-faced PC knocked on the door and waited for the word to come in. 'Inspector Resnick? Call for you. Shall I put it through here?'

It was a short journey from the stationery warehouse to where Michael Best lived in a rented house on the outskirts of Ruddington, south of the city. A short street of anonymous, flat-fronted buildings that stopped abruptly at the entrance to a field. Curtains twitched as the two cars slowed to a halt outside number five; the front door opposite opened and a man and woman came out to stand on their path and gawp. A word or two from Kevin Naylor sent them, reluctantly, back inside.

Millington was in no mood for niceties. He gave the nod to Divine, who grinned and sent the sledge-hammer crashing against the front door, through wood and glass, and with a second swing they were inside.

The upper part of the house seemed hardly to have been used, a few boxes, mainly empty, a broken stiff-backed chair which someone had made an unsuccessful attempt to mend. Balls of dust fluffed around their feet where they walked. The bathroom was downstairs at the back, a converted scullery with black spots of damp high on the walls; toothbrush, toothpaste, shaving things were missing. In the kitchen the cupboards contained mostly tinned food – Baxter's pea and ham soup, HP baked beans, seven tins of sardines. A nub end of bread at the back of a chipped enamel breadbin, going green.

In the small front room a framed photograph of Michael Best and an older woman, enough like him to be his mother, hung above the tiled mantelpiece. She with her head half-turned towards him, Michael looking slightly bashful, self-conscious, the woman's pride clear in her eyes.

Shelved in the alcove behind the one armchair, Michael Best's library of books on running a small-holding, horticulture, tips for the independent businessman, the commercial growing and marketing of flowers. There were a pocket guide to Byzantine Art, a selected poems of Andrew Marvel, two paperbacks by Thomas Clancy. Beside a handy guide to hyacinths and gladioli was a copy of *Killing for Company*, the story of Dennis Nilsen.

'So what?' Millington said when Divine flourished it with something close to triumph. 'I've got a copy of that at home myself.'

Divine redeemed himself by finding the letters, hand written, either copies or unsent.

Dear Patrick,

*It was good to hear from you and to know that
you are well. Things have moved on a little here and
it looks as though my plans for setting up on my own
should see fruition by this summer, autumn at the
latest. I have been looking in the area around King's
Lynn, which as you know is where my mother originally comes from, and think I may have found
something . . .*

Dear Mother,

*I'm so glad the flowers arrived safely, and the card,
and that you say they made a nice display. I only
wish I could have been with you, but as you know,
I'm virtually holding down two jobs, what with all
the travelling and trying to make sure I don't lose the
chance to . . .*

Dear Mr Charteris,

*I am writing to you with considerable regret con-
cerning your decision not to grant in full the loan we
recently discussed. I had hoped that during our meeting I had been able to convince you . . .*

Dear Lynn,

*I hope this letter from someone who is as yet a
complete stranger . . .*

At the bottom drawer, underneath the letters, there
was an application form for the Open University
Science Foundation course, filled in but never sent.
There were OS maps of Norfolk and Lincolnshire, with
locations marked in blue-black biro, some of them
circled in red; creased and well-used, a Little Chef
motorists' map for 1993. In an envelope there were

colour photographs of a woman taken indoors using flash, bright spots reflecting back from the centre of bewildered eyes.

'Any ideas?' Divine said, holding them up.

'Susan Rogel, I wouldn't mind betting,' Millington said. 'Let's get Siddons down here to be sure. Meantime, get through to the boss, arrange for copies of these maps to be faxed across. I hope to Christ we find the right place and in time.'

Lynn could hear a dog barking, quite far off; the same note, almost, it seemed, without interruption. She had heard Michael singing earlier, close by, the sound of hammering, ten minutes at most and then it had stopped. Her bladder was starting to burn. What she prayed for was the sound of approaching cars. A key turned in the lock and Michael came in.

He was wearing a white shirt, old corduroy trousers, boots on his feet. 'Let me just get these off now. No sense getting mud over everything.' He set down the bucket he was carrying and pulled off first one boot and then the other, placing them outside the door.

'Rain's given over,' Michael said. 'Going to be a nice day.' He approached her with the bucket, fished from his pocket a small key. 'If I trust you to help yourself with this, you're not going to be doing anything stupid?'

Lynn looked back at him but didn't answer.

Michael moved round behind her and knelt down on one knee. 'Don't want me to be doing everything for you, not like a baby.' He unlocked one of the cuffs and it swung against the back of her leg. 'Get those jeans off, why don't you, and I'll move this bucket underneath you.'

'Do I have to do this while you watch?'

'Why not? It's only natural.'

Lynn shook her secured hand in sudden anger, rattling the chain. 'Natural? Like this? What the hell's natural about this?'

'Temper,' Michael smiled, on his feet above her, 'temper. You know what I think about temper.'

'All right,' Lynn said, head down. 'All right.'

With her free hand she eased her pants down along towards her knees; the instant she sat down, as she'd known it would, the urine streamed from her, splashing back against the underside of her thighs.

'Now then,' he said, moments later, lifting the bucket away, 'what have we got here?' Folded in his pocket, several sheets of toilet paper. 'Will you or shall I?'

Staring at him all the while, she dabbed herself dry and dropped the damp tissue in the bucket when he held it out.

'I suppose now,' he said, locking the cuff back around her wrist, 'you'll be expecting something to drink?'

With her free hand, she took hold of his hand but immediately he pulled away. She waited until he was almost at the door. 'I was watching you,' she said, 'this morning. The way you were just watching me.'

He stopped in his tracks and she thought he was going to turn around, angry, even strike her, but instead he carried on, out through the door, and soon she heard him again, moving around outside the caravan, alternately whistling and singing a snatch of a song she had only ever heard him sing.

Fifty-three

By the time Michelle came away from casualty, Natalie grizzling in her arms, it was mid morning. Karl's hand had taken nine stitches and was securely bandaged. Lucky, the doctor had said, none of the tendons were touched. The staff nurse, checking Karl's name against the records, had noted this was his second visit within a short space of time. 'I explained all of that when the social worker had me bring him in,' Michelle told her. 'He had an accident, ran into the door.' And this time, the nurse thought, he just happened to pick up a knife someone had left lying around. Wrigglesworth, the social worker's name was on the card; the nurse made a note to call his office as soon as she got a spare moment. The local police would be informed as a matter of course.

LOCAL CLIMBER KILLED IN FALL read the placard outside the corner shop.

'Fish fingers, Karl? Is that what you'd like?'

'Ish fingus,' Karl beamed, jumping up and down, hand forgotten. 'Ish fingus.'

When she unlocked the front door and called Gary's name, she was relieved there was no reply.

'What do you think?' Lynn said.

He had brought her tomato soup from a can, heated up for lunch; sliced bread, buttered then folded in half. Freed one hand so she could eat. Michael sitting on

368

one of those insubstantial chairs, chattering away quite happily, not eating himself save for what remained of a chocolate bar, all the while watching her. Concerned.

'Is that all right? The soup, I mean. Precious little choice in the village and, besides, I'm never sure which kind is best. Heinz, I think, that's what they say. I like to buy that Scottish one, but they never have that. The bread was all they had left. I shall have to go earlier tomorrow.'

'Michael, why won't you answer me?'

'What?' he said. 'Sorry, what did you say?'

'I asked, what do you imagine's going to happen?'

He seemed to give it some thought. 'Oh, I suppose we'll stay here for a while. Quite cosy now since I got this thing, don't you think? Throws out quite a good heat.'

'Michael . . .'

'What I've got to do this afternoon though – well, I suppose tomorrow would do – see about hiring some kind of rotavator. That soil out there, I'm not turning it enough by hand.'

'Michael, you're not listening.'

He blinked. 'Aren't I? I thought . . .'

'I mean me.'

'What about you?'

'What d'you think's going to happen about me? About this . . . situation?'

He looked at her for a long time before answering. 'Oh, we're not getting on too badly now, are we?'

Five years ago, on an application to open an account at the Halifax Building Society, Michael Stuart Best had given his place of birth as Dublin; as a guarantor he had cited his father, Matthew John Best, an address in Germany, serving with the British army overseas.

Applying for a small business loan two years later, he had stated that he was born in Greater Manchester and that his father was deceased.

'He talked about it just the once,' the sales manager at Schotness Stationery had told Graham Millington that morning, 'the accident which took his parents off, like. Both of 'em. Aye. Lucky to get out himself, strapped in the back, see. On their way to visit relatives, Norfolk way. Terrible. Something you never get over, a thing like that. Good salesman, though, say that for him. When he was in the mood, talk the birds down out of the trees.'

A quiet chap, the general verdict had been, Divine and Naylor going round the neighbours in Ruddington, knocking on doors. Kept himself to himself; friendly enough, though, not standoffish. Nice, the way he used to buy flowers, drive out to take them to his mum in the nursing home every Sunday.

They had made a room available in the local station; Skelton was there now, something of a sparkle back in his eye. 'She was right,' just about the first thing he'd said to Resnick when he arrived. 'About the Rogel case. Helen. The connection.'

Resnick didn't give a shit about Helen. The person he cared for here was being held prisoner, her captor a man who had killed one woman already, probably two.

They were steadily narrowing the marked locations down and Resnick continued to pace from desk to wall and wall to desk again, willing the phone to ring.

'Tactical unit's ready to move, Charlie. Helicopter on stand by if we want it. Two ARVs on their way, one from the city, one from Leeds.'

Resnick's thoughts had jumped back several years to the unexceptional living room of an unexceptional house save that, cold in the small garden, Lynn Kellogg had just come upon her first dead body, a woman with blood drawn like ribbons dark through her hair. 'How are you feeling?' Resnick had asked, and Lynn had fallen, fingers of one hand hooked inside his mouth, face pressed against his chest.

'Charlie?'

Before he could answer, the phone startled to life and Resnick fumbled it into his hand. Listening, his forefinger traced lines along the surface of the map before them. 'You're sure?' he asked. 'No room for doubt?'

'No,' Sharon Garnett said. 'None at all.'

Before turning to Skelton, Resnick withdrew two of the remaining pins from the map and set them aside, leaving just the one in place. 'Got him,' he said, his voice now strangely calm.

'On your way,' Skelton said. 'I'll call up the troops.'

*

Michelle had been mixing Natalie's food when Josic came to the door, short of breath from running almost the length of the street on high-heeled shoes.

'The law, they've nicked Brian. Gary's done a runner.'

Michelle stared back at her, open-mouthed. 'What's Gary ... Brian ... I don't understand.'

'Christ, girl, where the fuck've you been? Brian's been dealing since before Christmas, I thought you knew.'

'But Gary, he'd never ...'

'Oh, Gary. You know what your Gary's like. Wanted to feel big, go along for the ride. Anyway, look, what it is, I've got to go see Brian's brief. Okay if I bring the kids down, dump 'em with you?'

Michelle nodded, arms tight across her chest. 'Josie, what'm I going to do?'

'My advice. Pray they lift Gary before he gets back here. Once he's inside, change the locks, move. Anything. Gary's a loser, always will be. Whatever happens, you'll be better off on your own.'

Michael was sitting at the far end of the caravan, thumbing through a catalogue, making notes in the margins, occasionally copying prices down on to a sheet of paper. From time to time he would purse his lips and whistle. 'These now,' he remarked from time to time, 'they'll look something special, you'll see.' In some part of his mind, Lynn thought, the two of them, Michael and herself, were living together on this piece of land, working happily side by side. The perfect couple. 'Your father,' Michael said once, looking up suddenly. 'Maybe there's a way you could phone him, find out how he is. Set your mind at rest.' But that had been close to half an hour ago and he'd mentioned no more about it. Lynn wondered if Skelton had asked for a news blackout or whether her mother, pottering in the kitchen, had been startled by her name. Tears pricked her eyes at the thought and for the first time she was close to breaking down.

'Nancy,' she said with a sniff, needing to say something, needing to talk. 'Did you know her too? Beforehand?'

Michael seemed surprised, his mind full of calculations, seedlings, yields. 'That was nothing,' he said eventually. 'Casual. Not like this.'

The main buildings were several hundred yards from the caravan and the ramshackle shed nearby, with its buckling walls and rusting corrugated roof. 'It's more than I can ever manage myself,' the farmer said, 'since I had this trouble with my leg. When he come along last year looking to rent that parcel out, seemed like a fair blessing.'

Resnick nodded and passed through to the back of the house. Sharon Garnett handed him the binoculars, pointed in the direction of the cream caravan standing on blocks in the corner of the far field.

There were marksmen in place on three sides, the nearest flat on his belly only ninety yards away, elbows braced in the ridged earth. Just moments before he had had a partial sighting of the target through the caravan window, moving left to right across his vision. He swore softly when he failed to get the order to fire.

'I'm going to try,' Resnick said, 'to get to the shed.'

'Michael,' Lynn had said, 'why don't you leave all that for now? Come and talk to me.'

In response, he had laughed. 'I'm not stupid, you know. You won't catch me falling for some old trick.'

Lynn had rattled her handcuffs against the chain. 'What can I do?'

So he came over and sat beside her, wary, as if maybe expecting for the first time that it would all come springing back at him. What had attracted her in his eyes had disappeared and been replaced by the uncertainties of a child.

'You were going to tell me about Nancy,' Lynn said.

Michael moved closer, his leg almost touching hers. 'She wasn't like you. Screaming and swearing and kicking out at me every chance she could get. The rest of the time pretending to be nice, nice as could be. Making all those promises, things she would do for me if only I'd let her go.' He laughed.

'What happened to her, it was her own fault. There was nothing else I could do.'

'You kidnapped her. You killed her. How can that be her fault?'

'Don't!' The chair spun back, knocked from beneath him. 'Don't talk to me like that. As if you had any right. Who d'you think you are? I'm in control here, me. And you'll just do well to remember that. You hear?'

'I'm sorry.'

'Oh, so you say. Got you frightened now, have I? Well, maybe that's not before time.'

'I mean it, I'm sorry.'

'Yes? You expect me to believe that? What you always say, all of you, when it's too late.'

'All of who, Michael?' Lynn asked. 'All of who?'

But by then it was too late; he had heard the sounds of the helicopter, distant, coming nearer.

Not quite in position at the shed, still some twenty yards away, Resnick heard it too and swore repeatedly as he began to run, heavy-footed, cursing whoever had given the order too soon.

The caravan door burst open and Lynn emerged first, pushed out, Michael close behind her, one arm tight about her neck, the knife held unsteadily in front of her chest.

'Police,' Resnick called, stumbling, running, stumbling again as the helicopter circled above them. 'Armed police,' came the distorted warning. 'Stand still. Stand still where you are.'

They ran. Lynn's ankle twisted beneath her and she fell sharply sideways, Michael grabbing at her arm and dropping the knife as he did so, grasping for her hair and catching nothing, Lynn rolling fast as soon as she touched the ground.

For a moment, Michael gazed about him and saw Resnick running, arms flailing, towards him; he felt the currents of air from the helicopter tugging at his clothes and hair. He turned and began to run again, back towards the caravan; the marksman in the field was up on one knee now, the back of Michael's head smack in his sights.

'Michael!'

Lynn called his name, yelled with all her might, and he faltered in his step and turned towards the sound of her voice. Resnick's dive struck him half way up the body, head into his midriff, elbow sharp against his chest. Winded, Michael toppled backwards, kicking wildly, as Resnick, breath rasping, clung on so hard it took three officers to prise him free. They cuffed Michael Best and read him his rights before dragging him away.

Only then did Resnick turn to where Lynn had sunk back to her knees and begin to walk towards her, walk then run. No holding the tears now, no stopping till finally he lifted her into his arms and held her, sobbing, safe, the daughter he had never had, the lover she would never be.